Piers Anthony was born in Oxford in 1934, moved with his family to Spain in 1939 and then to the USA in 1940, after his father was expelled from Spain by the Franco régime. He became a citizen of the US in 1958, and before devoting himself to full-time writing worked as a technical writer for a communications company and taught English. He started publishing short stories with *Possible to Rue* for *Fantastic* in 1963, and published in SF magazines for the next decade. He has, however, concentrated more and more on writing novels.

Author of the brilliant, widely acclaimed *Cluster* series, and the superb *Incarnations of Immortality* series, he has made a name for himself as a writer of original, inventive stories whose imaginative, mind-twisting style is full of extraordinary, often poetic images and flights of cosmic fancy.

By the same author

Chthon
Omnivore
The Ring (with Robert E. Margroff)
Sos the Rope
Var the Stick
Neq the Sword
Macroscope
The E.S.P. Worm (with Robert E. Margroff)
Orn
Prostho Plus
Race Against Time
Rings of Ice
Triple Detente
Phthor
Ox
Steppe
Hasan
A Spell for Chameleon
Vicinity Cluster
Chaining the Lady
Kirlian Quest
Thousandstar
Viscous Circle
God of Tarot
Vision of Tarot
Faith of Tarot
Split Infinity
Blue Adept
Juxtaposition
Bio of a Space Tyrant 1: Refugee
Bio of a Space Tyrant 2: Mercenary
Bio of a Space Tyrant 3: Politician
Bio of a Spacy Tyrant 4: Executive
Bio of a Space Tyrant 5: Statesman
Incarnations of Immortality 1: On a Pale Horse
Incarnations of Immortality 2: Bearing an Hourglass
Incarnations of Immortality 3: With a Tangled Skein
Incarnations of Immortality 4: Wielding a Red Sword
Incarnations of Immortality 5: Being a Green Mother
Anthonology
Shade of the Tree
Ghost

PIERS ANTHONY

Tarot

GRAFTON BOOKS

A Division of the Collins Publishing Group

LONDON GLASGOW
TORONTO SYDNEY AUCKLAND

Grafton Books
A Division of the Collins Publishing Group
8 Grafton Street, London W1X 3LA

A Grafton UK Paperback Original 1989

Tarot was previously published as three separate volumes.

Copyright © 1979, 1980 by Piers Anthony
Introduction and new material copyright © 1987 by Piers Anthony

ISBN 0-586-20618-3

Printed and bound in Great Britain by
Collins, Glasgow

Set in Times

Dedicated to
the Holy Order of Vision

Contents

Introduction

This volume has a horrendous history. This Introduction is akin to the Author's Notes I run in some of my fantasy novels, and is not integral to the novel, so may be skipped by those who object to cranky authorial comment on re- and irre-levancies.

Back in April 1975 (I trust my fantasy fans will forgive my use of mundane months; this was in the prehistoric era before I got into Xanth, Adept and such), I was hard at work on the short novel *But What of Earth?* for Laser Books. I had been promised three months to write it, but was granted only two, so I was in a hurry. Today with the computer I can do a novel in two months, but then I wrote my first drafts in pencil and typed them twice on the manual typewriter, and that is not as fast. On April 23 I completed the first draft; on the 24th I settled down to listen to a taped lecture by John White that my father had sent, while looking over the voluminous literature a religious group had sent. I had met one of the Brothers of this Order at a judo tournament, and talked with him. I am agnostic, neither condemning nor espousing any religion; I keep an open mind, and learn what I can when the opportunity presents. No, we were not competing; we were working together to lay out the heavy mats so the younger folk could compete. Chores of this nature are generally done by those who are driven as much by responsibility as notoriety. Then we sat in the bleachers and introduced ourselves, and I learned a bit about the nature of his Order, and he learned that I was a writer. "Piers Anthony?!" he exclaimed. "Really?" To my surprise, he had heard of me, and read my books. I had assumed that a figure in monkly vestments would not be interested in science fiction. No; as it turned out this was a liberal Order, and their members could read what they chose and attend judo tournaments if they chose; their ministry was not confined to the cloister. Indeed, this Brother had been into wrestling in the past, which was why he had an interest in judo.

The tournament passed, but our acquaintance remained. I visited his local unit with one of my daughters, who was then four years old, and talked with several Brothers and Sisters. I was not a candidate for conversion, and they understood that; my interest was as a writer who wanted to know the nature of their operation. I was favorably impressed with them; they were trying to do good in their fashion, without proselytizing. It was possible that I might bring some of their philosophy into one of my novels. Indeed, I did so, and thus was created Brother Paul of the Holy Order of Vision, one of the major characters in *But What of Earth?* That was not the name of either the Order or the Brother I had encountered; they did not seek that sort of publicity. (Brother Paul's last name, Cenji, was actually the name of our dog, Cenji Basenji; our animals, like our children, all had P or C names, unless named elsewhere before we got them.) I showed a draft of the novel to the Brother so that he could see how I handled the notion of such an Order and such a Brother who knew martial arts but practiced peace (and this is not the paradox you might suppose; serious martial artists may be serious advocates of peace and spiritual improvement), and he approved the treatment.

That novel proceeded to its own horrendous history, which included the firing of the editor and the shutting down of that line of books after their egregious violation of my contract (these events may have been coincidental rather than connected), and the eventual resale of it to another publisher for republication, my original text restored. I think that volume set something of a record for bad editing. But it was the source of Brother Paul, who was to become the major figure in the present novel, *Tarot*. It happened that on this day, April 24, 1975, when I was just about to commence the second draft typing of *Earth?*, and my older daughter was sick, I took time to listen to the tape and look at the literature—and abruptly things came together. The literature included lessons in the Order's basic beliefs, and associated books had pictures of tarot cards that were new to me. I found them fascinating, especially the thirteenth, depicting the skeletal Death figure. The tape was about certain paranormal phenomena, which John White explained in intriguing fashion, and this merged with what I was reading about the Order, and from this mergence my new novel was conceived: Brother Paul, from the world of *Earth?*, and the view of religion he honored, and a paranormal challenge. I knew from the start that this would be one of the major novels of my career.

I wrote 1400 words on the project that day, answered some letters, picked 27 slugs out of our garden (we had to get them out; every night they were coming in by the dozens and mowing down our plants, having no mercy), and then returned to my current work. Every few days I would make a few more notes, and sometimes these would take off, as when I wrote 2600 words on May 27. But *Tarot* was generally in the background as I moved through my paying projects that year and the next —*Earth?*, a martial arts collaborative novel, *Cluster,* and *Chaining the Lady. Tarot* became part of the Cluster-series framework, and Brother Paul had a scene in one of those novels. Thus he spread across three projects, and eventually seven volumes.

As part of my research I bought a tarot deck. There were instructions on how to do a reading, so I followed them, posing a personal question. Understand: I did this experimentally, because I have no belief in the supernatural. I just wanted to see what would happen. Well, I might as well have touched a lighted match to a powder keg, with similar innocence. That reading not only answered my question, it related so well that I felt like a butterfly pinned to a board in a museum.

This really got my attention. How could a supernatural device work so well for an unbeliever? For indeed, I was no convert; I *knew* there could be no magic here. I went into an intense bout of thinking, and worked it out: the tarot deck presents a concentration of symbols, some of which are almost certain to relate to any person. The pictures have multiple levels, many interpretations, and these are what the person tunes in on. If Death comes up, and there has been a recent death in the family, there is confirmation. If there has not been a death, then there is the fear of one coming up. If there is no such fear, the symbol may relate to the termination of something important, such as one's job. Death is not just literal death; it is Transformation, or Change, and that can manifest in many ways. Similarly the other symbols have projections like pincushions; you can't touch them without getting stuck. The Lovers is also Choice, so that card relates to romance or to a difficult decision—and when is there a time when you are not faced with some decision, and which one is ever simple? So these versatile symbols, coupled with the human mind's capacity to interpret, to make something relate, do almost inevitably relate to your life. I had solved the mystery —but my respect for the tarot deck remained, and it was integral to my project.

I worked up a summary on *Tarot* and shipped it off to the publishing house John White had formed. His partner lost the manuscript, and the partnership dissolved. That was the first but far from the last such negative signal I was to receive. In February 1976 I typed up a fifty-page sample-and-summary and sent it off to my agent for more conventional marketing.

Avon bought it, paying me an advance of $5,000. The project was airborne! At about this time I also received a contract from Del Rey for the first Xanth novel, and in addition we were preparing to build a house in backwoods Florida and move to the forest to live. The Xanth novel had an earlier deadline, so I got it done first, and that was to have a profound effect on my career and launch me from a four-figure income to a six-figure income in due course. But Xanth was fun, with its parody of the map of Florida and the things I noted in the backwoods; *Tarot* was serious, and therefore doomed to relative obscurity.

In mid-November 1976 I got down to serious work on it, both research and writing. I worked ten and a half months, the novel slowed by our building and moving, a considerable distraction. The contractor proved to be incompetent and dishonest; we finally sued and put him out of business, but we were stuck with an incomplete house and a financial squeeze. Hints of our experience were incorporated in my novel *Shade of the Tree,* yet another project that took many years to place. A writer's life is not necessarily an easy one! I was in the submission draft typing of *Tarot* as we formally moved to P's 'n' C's Trees (Piers & Penny, Carol & Cheryl) on August 28; we could delay no longer, because our children had to start school in Citrus County the next day. We had to camp in the storage building that was to become my study, for two weeks, because the house wasn't finished. We had no electricity; we cooked over an open outdoor fire and carried jugs of water up from the pump, and slept four abreast in sleeping bags in the loft, sweltering in the 90°F heat that remained there long after dark. But the work went on, limited to daylight hours, and indeed, I set my personal record for submission manuscript typing in September, completing the last 349 pages in the last ten days of the month. I accomplished this only by single-minded orientation to the project; the following month, after it was done, I got to work on the furniture moving and such that was necessary to make the main house livable. What did my wife say about this? Nothing; she had been married to a writer for a long time.

I showed copies of the manuscript to my father, who has an interest in this sort of thing, and to a professor who was doing a booklet on me. Both responded with unmitigated praise for the novel. (It is easy to tell the difference between such folk and the average reviewer: it is one of intelligence and literary taste. Ask any author.) (No, the booklet was never completed or published; instead one was published by another professor, who found *Tarot* inferior to Xanth.) Then I sent it to the Brother whose Order had started this project of mine. He had been transferred to another city, but we had maintained correspondence, and he was eager to see it. He never replied, and communication with the Order was cut off. Years later I learned from an ex-member that they had banned my novel for reading by their membership. From this I infer that they were not pleased with it. I regret this, for the novel stemmed in significant part from my admiration of their operation. Evidently I had misinterpreted it—or perhaps they misinterpreted *Tarot*. Certainly book-banning was no part of what I had understood their attitude to be. Was the inspiration for the Holy Order of Vision based on illusion? That appears to be the case. I have no joy in this revelation.

Regardless, I was satisfied that I had completed the major novel of my career, and my agent agreed, and I still feel that way today, a decade later, as we get ready to (you guessed it) build and move again. This time we expect to get a competent and honest contractor, and yes (you guessed it again!) I am at work on the next major novel of my career, *Tatham Mound.* Writers never learn; every decade or so I drop the paying projects and do something significant. *Macroscope* was the first, *Tarot* the second. Something always happens. *Mound* already has a remarkable two-year history, and I'm barely into it; that will be discussed in its place, in due course. You might suppose the hassle was over with *Tarot.* Not so—because the publisher was unable to accept it, without formidable revision and cutting, though agreeing that it was what I had described in the summary. There had been a change of editors, so that the one who had authorized the project was gone; that is almost invariably bad news for a writer. I have never changed publishers for money, only for editing, and that continues today.

What to do? Rather than suffer cuts that I felt would emasculate the novel, I preferred to take it back and remarket it. But this was chancy; sometimes publishers seem to have an unwritten law that what one doesn't publish, no others will. So I had my wife read it, to judge whether it was as strong as I thought, and whether the proposed revisions were as bad as I thought. My wife does not routinely read my fiction, and neither does my agent; they accept my word on the quality of my novels. I'm not sure whether my editors read them either, but I'm pretty sure my readers do, and that's what counts. My wife said it was a good novel, and my agent agreed. That was it; I would remarket. I took *Tarot* back, and I agreed to write a new novel in the Cluster series in lieu of this one for Avon; thus *Thousandstar* came into being. No, it was no hack effort; I had a terrific struggle humanizing an eyeless and earless alien protagonist, but got through, and it remains one of my favorite novels. I always write as well as I can, on any project. Meanwhile my agent tried *Tarot* on my other publishers. Del Rey promptly bounced it, and so did Berkley. None of my publishers wanted my major novel!

Well, I had had similar problems marketing *Macroscope,* so knew how to proceed. We went to a new publisher, and got an offer from Jove: $15,000, provided they could break it up into three volumes. My agent and I discussed it, and decided that the novel was a single entity and would suffer if broken up. Therefore we accepted a lower advance, $11,500, provided it would be published in one volume. End of hassle? Ha! The Perils of Piers never end so simply; there is always another cliffhanger.

Jove concluded later that it could not afford to market the quarter-million word novel as a single volume after all; their cover price was limited, and they would lose money because of the cost of the paper. The editor worked her wiles on me over the phone (young women can get very persuasive when they try) and I agreed to let it be broken into parts. But I insisted that it never be referred to as a trilogy, because I have firm standards for series: every novel must be able to stand on its own, so that a reader new to the series is not confused. This, I believe, is one of the reasons my series have been successful; people can read them forward, backward, or scrambled, and still enjoy them. But if someone read only the middle segment of *Tarot*, confusion could reign, and my reputation as an intelligible writer would suffer. The full impact of the novel could be gained only if all three volumes were read, and in the proper order. The editor agreed, and a formal amendment to the contract was signed to that effect. Naturally, ever since then, it has been referred to as a trilogy.

Jove published the first volume in 1979—and went out of the science fiction business. Its SF line was taken over by Berkley, who had rejected this novel before, and the two remaining volumes were published in 1980. Split apart, mislabeled, and published in different years, the major novel of my career was effectively destroyed. It made no sales records and contested for no awards. My present success is based on my light fantasy, which picked up both, ironically.

But now at last *Tarot* is being republished as it was supposed to be. Except for this Introduction, and the quotations introducing the chapters, which are really the cards of the Animation Tarot deck I crafted in the course of writing the novel, and the five introductions to the five major segments of the novel. Those I am leaving in the appendix as separate little essays, because they do relate as much to the Animation Tarot Deck as to the novel —just so you understand that the original novel was a thing of shape as well as of text, the five suits governing its presentation. In lieu of the quotations I have substituted little discussions describing their general natures. I did this not because of any disenchantment with the quotations, but because of the difficulty I faced getting permission to use them. I had to write to each publisher and ask for the right to quote. Their responses were varied. Some responded graciously, granting permission free of charge. Some charged: a typical fee was $50. One charged $100 for each translation of my novel; I was appalled, and they relented, charging me only once. Some did not answer; one refused to allow a quote to appear in a science fiction novel. That happened late, and I had to make a last-moment substitution. Fortunately I found one: there was a passage I liked very much in Stephen King's *Salem's Lot.* As it happened, I knew Mr. King's literary agent, Kirby McCauley, for he was also my agent. I asked him, and he granted permission immediately without charge. Stephen King could have objected, of course; he did not, and from that moment I was favorably disposed toward him, and our association has been amicable ever since. (His daughter is a fan of mine; I sent her my Adept trilogy, and King sent me a copy of *Pet Sematary* with an autograph a page long. I hope our acquaintance remains as polite as we impinge on each other's domains; he has now done a fantasy novel, and I shall be doing horror.) I had two from G. Legman's volumes on *The Rationale of the Dirty Joke,* and in the course of getting permission from him I told him of my favorite dirty joke, which, of all the tens of thousands he covers, was the one he had missed.

One very nice quote was from Arthur Koestler's *The Ghost in the Machine,* about the nature of consciousness. I had paid for its use, but later discovered that the proper credit had been omitted from my volume. I wrote in January, 1983, to his agency to apologize, though it had not been my error. His agent replied in February, and was nice about it. "I'm pretty sure Mr. Koestler will take it in his stride," she said. And in March Arthur Koestler and his wife committed suicide.

All things considered, I am unwilling to go through all that again, to obtain permissions for the quotes for this new edition. I still admire the quotations and the books and authors from which they stem, but there is just too much sheer experience involved in making those contacts.

Over the years I have had a number of letters about the novel. I dread these, because they tend to be from those who are deeply into the subject of tarot, as readers or philosophers, posing questions that require a good deal of knowledge and thought. I am not an expert in the tarot deck, and not a believer in the occult; I am a dedicated writer who researches as necessary for the things that come into my fiction. I answer as well as I can, perhaps disappointing them. Nonetheless, I did do my share of research into the nature of tarot, and will describe some of my discoveries here.

There is not one tarot deck; there are many. They come in all types and colors and sizes. Whole books have been written on the subject of particular interpretations of particular decks, such as the Rider-Waite, and each interpreter seems to feel that his is the only proper one. Hundreds of different decks have been published, and many books have been written describing the variety of tarot decks available. One such book, for those interested but casual, is *The Book of Tarot* by Fred Gettings. For those who prefer a thoroughgoing survey, try the two-volume, almost-thousand-page *Encyclopedia of Tarot* by Stuart R. Kaplan, who seems to be the expert here. Yes, I did know of a tarot deck he had not encountered; at his request I lent it to him . . . and did not hear from him again. Nevertheless, if you want to fathom the breadth and variety of tarot, this is the place to start; you can learn more than you dreamed existed about tarot. You can also order exotic decks through his "Best of Cards" catalogue. Another interesting volume is *Tarots* by Italo Calvino; I paid $104 for Copy #462 in 1976 because I needed it for my research. The volume contains about thirty thousand words, and uses as illustrations facsimiles of one of the earliest (therefore most authentic) tarot decks known, the Visconti/Sforza, circa mid-fifteenth century. It was from this deck that I realized that the card now called the Hermit originated as Time; by a process called iconographical transformation (that is, someone sees the illustration and confuses its meaning) the significance was lost—a fact that seems to have eluded most modern scholars. At any rate, *Tarots* is a story crafted from the laying out of the tarot deck, the plot suggested by the cards. It is interesting enough, but perhaps not worth a hundred dollars a copy.

The thing about the tarot deck—*any* variant—is that it is multi-purpose. You can use it for entertainment, as in games or gambling or simple house-of-cards constructions. Or for divination, character analysis, even as a kind of Rorschach test. Or for study, as in a survey of all available decks and their cultural indications, and the history of the deck itself, which has some intriguing implications. Or for business, which is what the merchandisers and collectors do, and perhaps the diviners too: making money from it. Or for meditation, considering the meaning of the cards, their symbolism: this can get you into deep psychological territory. Five uses, equating to the five suits of Wands, Cups, Swords, Coins and Aura.

Ah, I see I need to explain. Neither the number of cards nor the number of suits is fixed. The "standard" tarot deck has 78 cards, consisting of 22 Trumps (a corruption of Triumphs) and 56 suit cards divided into four suits of 14 cards each: ten pips and four court cards. I realized that something was missing, because the suits equate to the classical "elements" and, contrary to popular belief, there were not four but five elements taught: Fire, Water, Air, Earth and Spirit. Thus there should be a fifth suit—yet it is missing from contemporary decks. In addition, the interpretations of the cards are a hopeless hodgepodge; experts disagree, sometimes violently, and there is no consistent pattern. I discovered that I was building a novel on a deck that was fashioned of sand. That would not do. So I set about restoring it to its proper state, which was obviously a hundred cards and five suits. This is the Animation Tarot deck, and it is described in the Appendix. The novel explains why and how the deck was truncated, so that for centuries only imperfect versions were known.

No, there is no commercially available Animation Tarot deck. Actually there are two versions: the Classic that relates to the time of its origin in the fourteenth century (forget claims about ancient Egypt and such; I deem them to be without merit, as the novel will show) and the Cluster, that relates to that future century when it is published. But both have the same symbolic values, with the exception of the blank Ghost card; only the illustrations differ. The Ghost has fifteen alternate faces that relate to different species of the galaxy, bringing the effective number of Triumphs to 44; we of mundane Earth may never properly comprehend their ramifications, so can treat it simply as the Unknown. I explored prospects for publishing the deck, but this led to a series of complications, some of which are of such nature that even I, who know precious few inhibitions in print, will not discuss them. I concluded that the effort and cost would be too great in relation to the benefit, so have never put the deck into print. Perhaps someday that will change; I have not forgotten the matter. Some informal decks do exist, notably a hand drawn one in a lovely knit slipcase by a religious order that espouses the principles of the Holy Order of Vision; they sent me a complimentary copy. More than one reader has done nice illustrations for the deck. But there is a world of difference between such individual efforts and a commercial venture. In the interim, you can make up your own deck from index cards, as recommended in the Appendix, or adapt a playing-card deck by adding marked cards. You don't have to have the symbols correctly painted on each card; the meaning is inherent in the card regardless of its markings, just as personality is inherent in a person regardless of the appearance of his body. I haven't even worked out all the illustrations for the Triumphs, though I do have some notions for pictures and color coding. In general, the Cluster variant would be one way up, and the Classical variant the other way up, so that the cards can be taken either way, future or past. Folly, or the Fool, or 0 Triumph, might be the world in the shape of a zero, with blood pouring out. Skill, or the Magician, or 1 Triumph, might be Brother Paul before the windmill, one hand lifted, the other pointing down, as he indicates the key elements. Memory, or the High Priestess (Lady Pope), or 2 Triumph, might be the Rev. Mother Mary in her office. Action, or the Empress, or 3 Triumph, might be the lovely girl in the amaranth field. That sort of thing. I have not kept all the numbers of the mundane tarot, deeming the order and meanings to be more significant than the actual numbers, so my Change-Death card is #17 instead of #13; the picture for that might be a child playing in the cavity of a wall. The novel will clarify the horror of that seemingly innocent image, which derives from what I understand is a true event. But the images are not settled, and anyone who wishes to make up his own Animation deck may use what suits him.

I have, however, worked out certain protocols which are used in my novels, notably *Kirlian Quest*. For those who wish to do a reading the Animation Tarot way, here is the Cluster Satellite Spread. A spread is the layout of the cards, as you put them down in turn from the deck. It is the means to obtain messages from the cards, and anybody can do it; you don't need to pay a professional reader or psychic. You are the Querent; you may ask any Question, and you can do it alone. You may prefer to; bear in mind my first experience with a Reading. But be warned: this gets detailed, and will be confusing unless you are actually dealing out the cards as you read. Skim over it otherwise, until you encounter something interesting. I am, as I said, a skeptic about the supernatural; you are more open-minded on this subject than I, so for this purpose I shall assume that it is valid, and that the Animation Tarot really wants to speak to you. You don't even have to use the Animation Deck; any garden-variety tarot deck will work (though not as well), or even regular playing cards, if you know how to read them. The cards are the means, not the end, and so is this Spread.

First, select your Significator. That is the card that stands for you, personally. This is normally one of the Court cards, but it doesn't have to be. For example, if you are an active lady who likes nature hikes, you might identify with the Queen of Wands, the Suit of Nature. If you are a teenager who likes money and plans to be a millionaire before age thirty, you might be the Knight of Coins, The Suit of Trade. I, as a frustrated artist who turned to words for expression, regard my Significator as the King of Aura, the Suit of Art. There are several associations for each suit, so you should be able to find one that aligns with your nature, that you feel comfortable with, that is *you*. That card is your Significator, the most important one in the deck—for you. You need to identify it before you even start your Reading.

Next, shuffle the complete deck, including your Significator. The order your cards start with should never be restored; you may shuffle or not between uses, and the deck gains experience with each use, and this must not be revoked by any mechanical ordering. (Other tarot decks are not sensitive about this, but you are not dealing with any ordinary tarot deck now. This one lives.) Deal them face down into five piles, in any order you prefer, so long as you finish with 20 cards in each.

Now start with any pile and turn the cards face up until you come to your Significator. If it isn't in the first pile, do the second, and the third; just keep methodically going until you find it. Stop right there, with the Significator in your hand, and study the situation. Which pile was it in? The five piles have these meanings: 1. DO 2. THINK 3. FEEL 4. HAVE 5. BE. You can see how these align with Nature (Wands), Science (Swords), Faith (Cups), Trade (Coins) and Art (Aura) respectively; indeed, these are the meanings of the #1s for the five Suits. Everything fits together, and the meanings constantly interact in patterns of five; in fact the number five is fundamental to this art: the fingers of your hand. Two hands to your body make ten fingers, the number of pip cards per Suit; square that and you have the total for the Deck. The ancients were conscious of the patterns of numbers in a way the moderns are not; they could do magic with intricate squares of numbers. That is why the disruption of the original tarot pattern was such a crime against magic, rendering it largely inoperative. A computer would suffer similarly if 22% of its innards were randomly removed, and folk would doubt that it ever had worked, just as they do now with spoiled magical things. But back to the point: is the nature of your Question consistent with the message of the pile? Only you can be the judge of that. If it is not, stop; this is the Deck's way of telling you not to inquire further.

If the Pile is consistent, you may proceed to the layout. Put your Significator down in the center of the table, face up, oriented east-west. That is, crosswise. Use the remaining cards of the Pile it chose and deal them singly, face up. #1 goes across the Significator (which is #0, suggesting the Fool: you), north-south, vertically, or however you call it. #2 goes south of it, upright. #3 west of it, vertically. #4 north, and #5 east. Now you have a pattern of six cards, with two crossed in the center. #1 stands for Definition; it defines your problem. #2 is Past, #3 Present, #4 Future, and #5 Destiny. Interpret each card in the light of its position; Court Cards are apt to represent significant other people in your life, being their Significators, and the meanings of the others are as given in the deck. The complete pattern should pretty well define your situation, with Destiny summing it up. You have to interpret it yourself; no one else can do it for you, for the cards speak only to you, in ways that only you can appreciate. Other people may comment on your layout, but their opinions are only advisory; they cannot know what is truly in your heart.

But if you remain confused, the Cluster Spread will help you. You have only to start a satellite. Deal a card across the card that confuses you: this is a sub-#1, defining not the whole but just that aspect. If you lay it across the original #2, Past, then the new card defines Past. Does this clarify it for you? If not, deal out three more cards, below, in counterclockwise order. (Or to the left, or above, or to the right, depending on which card you have Crossed. This is mere common sense: take the room you need for an uncrowded layout.) You now have a subset of five cards (a significant number), or a Satellite. The three newest ones are the Past, Present and Future indications for that card only, which has become the Significator for the Satellite. Does this clarify what confused you before? If it doesn't, you may cross one of the new cards and build another satellite; the Spread is endlessly accommodating, and it wants you to understand what the Deck has to say to you.

With one exception: you may run out of cards. You are limited to those of that one Pile, and your reading ends when the cards do. If you received a negative signal before, when your Significator turned up in an irrelevant Pile, but you played through anyway, it may cut off your cards in short order. Remember, you are limited to the cards remaining in the Pile; if the Significator was near the bottom, you may not have enough cards to complete the Spread. Take the hint: desist. If the signals are positive, but the cards limited, make do with what you have; the Deck has told you as much as it feels is appropriate. If you don't like the Answer the Deck gives you on the first reading, tough; don't try it again. Not the same day, anyway. You may, however, proceed to different questions if you wish. The Reading is valid only to the extent you play it honestly; if you cheat, your results become invalid. Don't blame the Animation Tarot if you get a bad Answer after abusing it.

There is one other thing about the tarot, in all versions, that no one else seems to have caught on to. In addition to all its other aspects, it is a story: the story of the life of Jesus Christ and, by extension, Everyman. It follows, card by card, a person's life, beginning with the total innocence of birth—the Fool—and the Father and Mother figures, on through death, and the transfer of the spirit to a new vessel (water poured from one to the other) and the hazards of the Afterlife, such as the Devil, concluding with the final Judgment and The World (Universe), or the totality of spiritual completion. It is, in sum, a forbidden religious lesson for the illiterate, who were the masses in medieval times. In this is its great significance and the reason for its suppression by the forces of orthodoxy. As I came to know the tarot, I developed a profound respect for it, and this manifests in the novel. I hope that others, reading this novel, come to appreciate the phenomenal instrument that the tarot can be, regardless of the nature of their other beliefs.

That's about it; this introduction is far longer than intended. Those of you who have not encountered this novel before, be warned: it contains provocative material of several types, religious and social, and may repulse you. One of my Xanth readers, a young girl, picked up one of the volumes, supposing it was more light fantasy. Her mother saw it, read a bit, and promptly banned all Anthony novels from the house. If you succeed in reading *Tarot* through without being disgusted at some point, you probably don't understand it.

Piers Anthony
March, 1987

O

FOLLY
(FOOL)

In 1170 A.D., Peter Waldo, a wealthy merchant of Lyons, France, suffered a religious conversion, renounced his possessions, and wandered about the countryside in voluntary poverty. This obvious folly attracted both persecutions and followers, the latter called the "poor men of Lyons." In 1183 Pope Lucius III excommunicated the growing sect of "Waldenses," who appealed to the Scriptures instead of to papal authority, repudiated the taking of oaths, and condemned capital punishment. They never made the sign of the cross, as they refused to venerate the torture device on which Christ hung, or the painful and mocking crown of thorns. Nevertheless, the Waldenses prospered in Christian lands; many thousands of them settled in the Cottian Alps on the French-Italian border. Their dauntless missionaries covered southern France, southern Germany and northern Italy. But the Inquisition followed them, and they were savagely repressed over the course of several centuries. Their ministers had to go about in disguise, and it was hazardous for them to carry any of the literature of their faith, lest it betray them into torture and death. But it was hard to make the material clear without teaching aids, for many converts were illiterate and ignorant. Out of this impasse was to arise one of the most significant educational tools of the millennium.

The setting is Earth of the near future. The pressures of increasing population and dwindling natural resources have brought the human scheme to the brink of ruin. There is not enough food and energy to support all the people.

But a phenomenal technological breakthrough has occurred: matter transmission. People can now be shipped instantly to habitable wilderness planets orbiting distant stars. This seems to offer relief from the dilemma of mankind; *now there is somewhere for all those people to go.*

This leads to the most massive exodus in the history of the species; so many people are leaving that within a decade no one will be left on Earth. Unfortunately, matter transmission requires a tremendous amount of energy. The planet's sources of power are being ravished. This has the peculiar side effect of reversing the technological level of human culture; people are forced to revert to more primitive mechanisms. Kerosene lamps replace electric lights; wood replaces oil; horses replace cars; stone tools replace metal ones. The industrial base of the world is shrinking as the most highly trained and intelligent personnel emigrate to their dream worlds. Yet the colonization program proceeds pell-mell, as such programs and movements have always done, heedless of any warnings of collapse.

This is sheer folly. Mankind is like the beautiful dreamer of Tarot's Key 0—the Fool—walking northwest with his gaze lifted in search of great experience while his feet are about to carry him off a precipice. He will have a great experience, oh yes! What high expectations these new worlds represent! What a marvelous goal to reduce Earth's population painlessly to an appropriate level! But what disaster is in the making, because no reasonable controls have been placed on this adventure.

Yet there are redeeming aspects. At least the Fool *has* dreams and noble aspirations, and perhaps the capacity to recognize and choose between good and evil. It may be better to step off the cliff, his way, than to stay at home without ambition. The folly of future Earth is a complex matter, with many very noble and frustrating elements that may after all salvage its greatest potential.

This is the story of just one of those elements, a single thread of a monstrous tapestry: Brother Paul's quest for the God of Tarot.

1

SKILL
(MAGICIAN)

252 A.D.: Emperor Decius was in power only a year, but in this time he cruelly persecuted the bothersome Christians. He seized one devout youth and coated his whole body with honey, then exposed him to the blazing sun and the stings of flies and hornets. Another Christian youth was given the opposite extreme: he was bound hand and foot by ropes entwined with flowers, naked upon a downy bed, in a place filled with the murmuring of water, the touch of soft breezes, the sight of sweet birds, and the aroma of flowers. Then a maiden of exceptionally fair form and feature approached him and bared her lovely flesh, kissing and caressing his body to arouse his manhood and enable her to envelop him in the ultimate worldly embrace. The youth had dedicated his love to God; to suffer this rapture with a mortal woman would have polluted him. He had no weapon with which to defend himself, yet his skill and courage proved equal to the occasion. He bit off his own tongue and spat it in the harlot's face. By the pain of this wound he conquered the temptation of lewdness, and won for himself the crown of spiritual victory. Paul, himself sincerely Christian, witnessed these torments. Terrified, he fled into the desert, where he remained alone in the depths of a cave for the rest of his life. He thus became the first Christian hermit, and was known as Saint Paul the Hermit.

The great blades of the windmill were turning, but the water was not pumping. Only a trickle emerged from the pipe, and the cistern was almost empty. It was a crisis, for this was the main source of pure water for the region.

Brother Paul contemplated the situation. "It's either a lowering of the water table or a defect in the pump," he said.

"The water table!" Brother James exclaimed, horrified. "We haven't pumped *that* much!" His concern was genuine and deeply felt; the Brothers of the Holy Order of Vision believed in conservation, and practiced it rigorously. All had taken vows of poverty, and abhorred the wasting of anything as valuable as water.

"But there has been a drought," Brother Paul said. Indeed, the sun was blazing down at this moment, although it caused no distress to his brown skin. "We might inadvertently have over-pumped, considering this special circumstance."

Brother James was a thin, nervous man who took things seriously. His long face worked in the throes of inchoate emotion. "If it be God's will . . ."

Brother Paul noted his companion's obvious anxiety, and relented. "Nevertheless, we shall check the pump first."

The pump was a turning cam that transformed the rotary motion of the mill's shaft into piston motion in a rod. The rod plunged down into the well to operate the buried cylinder that forced up the water. Brother Paul brought out plumber's tools and carefully dismantled the mechanism, disconnecting the shaft from the vanes and drawing the cylinder from the depths. His little silver cross, hanging on a chain around his neck, got in his way as he leaned forward. He tucked it into his shirt pocket with a certain absentminded reverence.

He sniffed. "I trust that is not hellfire I smell," he remarked.

"What?" Brother James was not much for humor.

Brother Paul pried open the mechanism. Smoke puffed out. "There it is! Our wooden bearing has scorched and warped, decreasing the pump's efficiency."

"Scorched?" Brother James asked, surprised. He seemed much relieved to verify that the problem was mechanical, the result of neither the subsidence of the water level nor the proximity of hellfire. "That's a *water* pump!"

Brother Paul smiled tolerantly. The deepening creases of his face showed that this was an expression in which he indulged often—perhaps more often than was strictly politic for a man of his calling. Yet there was a complementary network of frown-lines that betrayed the serious side of his nature; some of these even hinted at considerable pain. "Not all of it is wet, Brother. This cylinder is sealed. In a high wind, when the shaft is turning rapidly—wind power varies as to the cube of wind velocity, as you know—the bearings can get so hot from friction that they actually begin to char."

"We did have very good winds yesterday," Brother James agreed. "Brother Peter arranged to grind flour for a whole week's baking. But we never thought the mill would—"

"No fault of yours, Brother," Brother Paul said quickly. "It is quite natural and sensible to use the mill to best effect, and a strong wind makes all its chores easy. This is just one of the problems of our declining technology. I will replace the bearing —but we would be well advised to choke down on the mill during the next gale winds. Sometimes it may be better to waste a little good wind than to lose a bad bearing." He smiled to himself as he worked, considering whether he had discovered an original maxim for life, and whether such a maxim might be worth integrating into his life's philosophy.

He fetched a suitable replacement bearing and proceeded to install it. His dark hands were strong and sure.

"You are a magician," Brother James remarked. "I envy you your proficiency with mechanical things."

"I only wish the spiritual were as easy to attain," Brother Paul replied. Now he was sweating with the pleasant effort. He was a thickset man of moderate height, with short black hair. He was inclined to chubbiness, but his muscles showed formidable delineation as he lifted the heavy unit into place.

"Wouldn't it be better to have the pump on the surface, so that it could be serviced more readily?" Brother James asked as Brother Paul struggled with the weight of the descending cylinder. Brother Paul had drawn it up without trouble, but was now occupied with easing it into its precise place.

"It would—but we would have no water," Brother Paul explained. "Surface pumps employ suction, which is actually the outside pressure of the atmosphere pushing up the fluid. That's about fifteen pounds per square inch, and that cannot draw water up more than about twenty-eight feet, what with friction and certain other inefficiencies of the system. Our water table is thirty feet down. So we employ a pressure pump set down near the water; that type of device has no such limit. It *is* more cumbersome—but necessary."

"Yes, I see that now. It is more than harnessing the windmill to the pump; it has to be done the right way."

"I suspect it is the same with the power of God," Brother Paul said musingly. "It is there, like the wind: an immense potential, often ignored or unperceived by man. Yet it is real; we need only take the trouble to understand it. It is our job to harness that potential, to apply it more directly to the lives of men. But though we seem to have all the elements right, it will not work if they are not correctly placed, and adapted to our particular situation—or if part of the mechanism is broken, even though nothing may show on the surface."

"I don't regard that as an analogy," Brother James said. "It is the literal truth. The wind *is* God, and so is the water; we can not exist apart from Him. Not for a moment, not in the smallest way."

Brother Paul paused in his labors to hold up his hands in a gesture of surrender. "You are correct, of course. Yet there must be a process of communication between the power above—" he lifted his right hand to the sky—"and the substance below." His left hand pointed toward the buried cylinder.

"I would call that process 'prayer,'" Brother James said.

The reassembled pump worked. A full, pure flow of water emerged from the pipe, cascading into the storage tank and cistern. Brother James was ecstatic.

Without further comment, Brother Paul walked back to his room, washed his hands, arms and face, and changed to his habit: the black robe with the reversed collar, the cross worn outside. He had a class to conduct, and he was overdue. When dealing with matters pertaining to the works of God on Earth, it was best to be punctual.

Suddenly he brightened. "Air, Earth, Water, Fire!" he exclaimed. "Beautiful. Thank you, God, for sending me this revelation." To him there was no objection to conversing with God directly; in this case, familiarity bred respect, not contempt. The Holy Order of Vision encouraged contact with God in any fashion that seemed mutually satisfactory.

The students were there before him: five young people from a nearby village. These orientation sessions were held periodically, when sufficient interest developed. As the massive energy and

population depletion of Earth continued, the need for technological and social systems closer to nature intensified, so these
sessions had become fairly regular. The Brothers and Sisters took
turns conducting them, and this was Brother Paul's week.

"Sorry I'm late," Brother Paul said, shaking hands all around.
"I was delayed, if you will, by a superimposition of elements."

One of the girls perked up. She was a slight, bright-eyed nymph
with a rather pretty elfin face framed by loose, dark blonde tresses.
She seemed to be about fifteen, although inadequate nutrition
stunted the growth of youngsters these days, delaying maturity. A
month of good feeding might do wonders for her, physically—and
perhaps spiritually also. It was hard to be a devout individual on
an empty stomach. At least it was hard for those not trained in this
kind of discipline. "You mean something by that, don't you, sir?"
she asked.

"Call me Brother," Brother Paul said. "I am Brother Paul of the
Holy Order of Vision. Yes, I had an anecdote in mind, and thank
you for inquiring." It was always best to begin on a personal basis;
early theology could alienate young minds. He was not trying to
convert, but merely to explain; even then, it had to be done
appropriately. People were more complex than windmills, but
there were parallels.

"Big deal," one of the boys muttered. He was a strapping lad,
massive across the shoulders, but surly. He had not been stunted
by hunger! Evidently he had been sent here, perhaps by parents
who could not control him much longer. The Order Station was
no reform school, but perhaps he would find enlightenment here.
One never could anticipate the mechanisms of God, who was as
much more complex in His devices as man was in relation to a
windmill.

"We have a windmill that we use to pump water from the
ground, among other chores," Brother Paul said. "But friction
caused a bearing to burn out. Does that suggest anything to any of
you?"

They all looked blank—three boys, two girls.

"In our studies at the Order we place emphasis on the elements," Brother Paul continued. "Not the atomic elements of
latter-day science—though we study those, too—but the classical
ones. Air, Earth, Water, Fire: we find these manifesting again and
again in new ways. They show up in personality types, in astrology, in the Tarot deck—their symbolism is universal. Just now I—"

"The windmill!" the blonde girl said. "Wind is air! And it pumps water!"

"From the earth," one of the boys added.

"And it got burned," the surly one finished. "So what?"

"The four elements—all together," the first girl said, pleased. She clapped her hands together in unselfconscious joy. There was, Brother Paul noted, something very attractive about a young girl exclaiming in pleasure; perhaps it was nature's way of getting her married before she became a burden to her parents. "I think it's neat. Like a puzzle."

"What *good* is it?" the hulking boy demanded.

"It is an exercise in thinking," Brother Paul said. "As we seek parallels, coincidences, new aspects of things, we find meaning, and we grow. It is good to exercise the mind as well as the body. The ancient Greeks believed in that; hence we have the Pythagorean Theorem and the Olympic Games. We believe in it too. This, in a very real sense, is what the Holy Order of Vision is all about. 'Holy' as in 'Whole,' 'Vision' as in the vision of Saint Paul on the road to Damascus, that converted him to Christianity. He is not to be confused with Saint Paul the Hermit. We are not a church, but rather a brotherhood. We wish to bring together all people, and teach them the Universal Law of Creation, to prepare the Earth for the new age that is dawning. We try to provide for those in need, whatever that need may be, counseling them or offering material aid. We place great emphasis on practical applications —even windmills, in this day of retreating civilization."

"Hey, that's great!" the girl said. "Can anybody join?"

Bless her; she was doing his job for him! "Anybody who wants to, after a student apprenticeship. We do have levels through which the novice progresses according to his ability and faith, and much of the life is not easy. You really have to understand the Order before you can know whether you want to be a part of it."

"Why do you wear the robes and study the Bible and all that?" one of the other boys asked. He was brown-skinned, like Brother Paul: that amalgam of races this culture still chose to term "black." "Can't you just go out and do good without all the trappings?"

"An excellent question," Brother Paul said. "You are really exploring the interrelationship of idea and form. A good idea is wasted without the proper form to embody it. For example, an excellent notion for a book would be ruined by clumsy or obscure writing. Or a fine idea for drawing power for the wind comes to nothing if the design of the gearing is inadequate. Perhaps man himself is an idea that exists in the mind of the Creator—yet that idea must achieve its appropriate form. So it is with us of the Holy Order of Vision; we feel that the forms *are* important, in fact indistinguishable from the basic idea."

"That's McLuhanism," the third boy said. He was a white-skinned, black-haired, clean-cut lad a little older than the others, and probably better educated. He had used a word few were now familiar with, testing the knowledge of the teacher.

"Not exactly," Brother Paul replied, glad to rise to the challenge. He liked challenges, perhaps more than he should. "The medium may be indistinguishable from the message, but it is *not* the message. Perhaps other forms of expression would serve our purpose as well, but we have a system that we feel works, and we shall adhere to it until it seems best to change." He closed his eyes momentarily, giving a silent prayer of thanks that the session was proceeding so well. Sometimes he seemed to make no contact at all, but these were alert, responsive minds. "We feel that God has found no better tool than the Bible to guide us, but perhaps one day—"

"Crap," the surly boy remarked. "God doesn't exist, and the Bible is irrelevant. It's all superstition."

Now the gauntlet had been thrown down. They all watched Brother Paul to see how he would react.

They were disappointed. "Perhaps you are right," he said, without rancor. "Skepticism is healthy. Speaking for myself alone, however, I must say that though at times I feel as you do, at other times I am absolutely certain that God is real and relevant. It is a matter for each person to decide for himself—and he is free to do so within the Order. We dictate no religion and we eschew none; we only present the material."

There was a chuckle. Brother Paul noted it with dismay, for he had not been trying to score debater's points, but only to clarify the position of the Order. Somehow he had erred, for now his audience was more intrigued by his seeming cleverness than by his philosophy.

Disgruntled, the hulking boy pushed forward. "I think you're a fake. You don't want to decide anything for yourself, you just want to follow the Order's line. You're an automaton."

"Perhaps so," Brother Paul agreed, searching for a way to

alleviate the lad's ire without compromising the purpose of this session. How suddenly success had flipped over into failure! Pride before fall? "You are referring to the concept of predestination, and in that sense we are all automatons with only the illusion of self-decision. If every event in the world is precisely determined by existing forces and situations, then can we be said to have free will? Yet I prefer to assume—"

"You're a damned jellyfish!" the boy exclaimed. "Anything I say, you just agree! What'll you do if I push you, like this?" And he shoved violently forward with both hands.

Only Brother Paul wasn't there. He had stepped nimbly aside, leaving one leg outstretched behind him. The boy stumbled headlong over that leg. Brother Paul caught him and eased him down to the floor, retaining a hold on one of the boy's arms. "Never telegraph your intention," he said mildly. "Even a jellyfish or an automaton can escape such a thrust, and you could be embarrassed."

The boy started to rise, his expression murderous. He thought his fall had been an accident. But Brother Paul put just a bit of pressure on the hand he held, merely touching it with one finger, and the boy collapsed in sudden pain. He was helpless, though to the others it looked as though he were only fooling. A one-finger pain hold? Ridiculous!

"A little training in the forms can be advantageous," Brother Paul explained to the others. "This happens to be a form from aikido, a Japanese martial art. As you can see, my belief in it is stronger than this young man's disbelief. But were he to practice this form, he could readily reverse the situation, for he is very strong." Never underestimate the power of a gratuitous compliment! "The idea, as I remarked before, is valueless without the form."

Now, to see whether he could salvage the situation, he released the boy, who climbed quickly to his feet, his face red, but did not attack again. "Scientific application of anything can be productive," Brother Paul continued, "whether it is aikido or prayer." He faced the boy. "Now you try it on me."

"What?" The youth had been caught completely by surprise —again.

"Like this," Brother Paul said. "I shall come at you like this—" and he took an aggressive step forward, his right fist raised. "But you turn away from me and place your left foot back like this in the judo *tai otoshi* body drop—" He guided the boy around and got his feet placed. "Then catch my shirt and project your right foot before me like this, right across my shins. See how your body drops into position? That's why this throw is called the body drop." He more or less lifted the boy into position with a strength that was not evident to the others, but that the boy felt with amazement. "And because I am plunging forward, my feet trip over your leg while you haul my shirt—" It was not a shirt, but the loose front part of his habit, but the effect was the same. "And I am completely off balanced and take a bad fall." Brother Paul flipped expertly over the leg and landed crashingly on his back and side, his left hand smacking into the straw mat the Station used in lieu of a rug.

The boy stood amazed, and the other four jumped in alarm. They did not know Brother Paul was adept at taking such falls, or that the noise was mostly from his hand slapping the mat to absorb much of the shock of landing. The muscular, bony arms and hands are much better able to take blows than the torso. "And if that doesn't do the job, you use hand pressure or an arm twist to keep me quiet." Brother Paul got up, and the boy moved to help him, fearing that he had been hurt. There was no longer any animosity.

"Did you study *that* here?" the brown boy asked, awed.

"Among other things," Brother Paul said. "Sometimes it is necessary for members of the Order to subdue someone who is temporarily, ah, indisposed. We do not approve the use of weapons, as they can hurt people severely, but the barehanded methods of self-defense or control—" He shrugged, smiling toward the formerly surly youth. "As you can see, he brought me down without hurting me."

They all returned his smile, and he knew it was all right again. God had guided him correctly. "Of course you do not have to join the Holy Order of Vision to receive such instruction. All of our courses in defense, reading, hygiene, farming, mechanics, figuring, and weaving are available to anyone who has the necessary interest and aptitude." He smiled again. "We can even be persuaded to teach a class or two in the appreciation of religion."

The blonde girl let out a titter of appreciation. "Do *you* teach that class, Brother?"

Brother Paul looked down. "I regret I lack the finesse or scholarship for that particular class. I am working on it, though, and in a few years I hope to be equipped." He looked up. "I thank you all for your attention to this introductory lecture. Now I will show you around the Station." He sniffed the air. "I believe Brother Peter is completing his baking. Perhaps we can pass the kitchen and sample his wares. To my mind there is nothing quite so good as bread hot from the stone oven with a little home-churned—"

But another Brother appeared. "The Reverend wishes to see you immediately," he murmured. "I will conduct the tour in your stead."

Oh-oh. Was he in trouble again? "Thank you, Brother Samuel." Brother Paul started out.

"What would you like to see first?" Brother Samuel asked the group.

As Brother Paul passed out through the doorway, he heard one of them answer, "The body drop." He smiled to himself, for poor Brother Samuel had a chronically stiff back and no training at all in the martial arts. But the delicious odor wafting from the bakery would rescue him, for young people were always hungry.

As he made his way to the Reverend's office, his thoughts became more sober. Had he done the right thing by this group, or had he merely been clever, impressing more by his physical power and rhetorical humor than by worthwhile information? It was so hard to know!

2

MEMORY
(HIGH PRIESTESS)

705 A.D.: The daughter of an English missionary in Germany had such a genius for learning and seeming piety that she was elevated to the papal throne as John VII. Though in the guise of a male, she was—alas—female, and therefore, a vessel of iniquity. Yielding to her base female urges, she admitted a member of her household to her bed, and suffered that demonic fulfillment of her kind. In 707, during the course of a solemn Whitsun procession through the streets of Rome in the company of her clergy, at a point between the Colosseum and St. Clement's church, she who would become known as Pope Joan was delivered of a bastard son. The Popess was thus exposed as a harlot disguised as a priest. The story has, of course, been suppressed by the Church and labeled a myth, but there are those who remember it yet. This is the message of Key Two of the Tarot, entitled "The Lady Pope." Is it not, after all, a true reflection of the nature of the sex?

Brother Paul walked past the luxurious vegetable gardens of the Station toward the office of the Reverend. It was a fine summer day. He hoped he had performed well, but he hummed nervously as he moved.

The sight of the Reverend's countenance solidified the doubts hovering about him. Some very serious matter was afoot, and he feared he had erred again. While discipline within the Order was subtle, Brother Paul had made many mistakes and done much internal penance.

The Reverend rose as he entered, and came forward to greet him. "It is good to see you, Paul. You have done well."

Glad words! So it was not one of his foul-ups, this time. "I try to do as the Lord decrees, Mother Mary," he said modestly, concealing his relief.

"Umph," the Reverend Mother agreed. She did not sit down, but paced nervously around the office. "Paul, a crisis of decision is upon us, and I must do a thing I do not like. Forgive me."

Something serious was certainly afoot! He studied her before he answered, trying to judge the appropriate response.

The Reverend Mother Mary was actually a young woman no older than himself, whose meticulous Order habit could not conceal her feminine attributes or render her sexless. She wore her dark brown hair parted down the middle, cupped to conceal her ears on either side, and pinned firmly in back—yet it framed her face like a mystical aura. Her reversed white collar clasped a very slender white neck, and her cross hung squarely on her bosom. Her robe was so long it touched the floor, concealing her feet. Occasionally it rippled and dragged behind her as she turned. Her personality, he knew, was sweet and open; she was severe only in dire necessity. It would have been all too easy to love her as a pretty girl, had it not been essential to love her as a responsible woman and a fellow human being. And, of course, as the Reverend.

So it was best to allow her to unburden herself without concern for his feelings, which in any case were not easily hurt. Obviously she believed that what she had to say would cause him distress, and perhaps it would—but he was sure he could bear it. "Please speak freely, Mother."

The Reverend stepped to her desk and seemed almost to pounce on something there. "Take these, if you will," she said, proffering a small box.

Brother Paul accepted it. He had almost to snatch it, because her hand was shaking. Though her competence and position made her "Mother," at times she was more like a little girl, uncertain to the point of embarrassment. It had occurred to him before that an older person might have been better suited to the office of Reverend. But there were many Stations, and age was not the primary consideration.

He looked into the box. It contained a deck of Tarot cards, in its fashion the symbolic wisdom of all the ages.

She seated herself now, as though relieved of a burden. "Please shuffle them."

Brother Paul removed the deck from the box and spread several cards at the top of the deck. They were in order, beginning with the Fool, or Key Zero, and proceeding through the Magician, the High Priestess (also called the Lady Pope), the Empress, the Emperor, and so on through the twenty-two Trumps or Major Arcana and the fifty-six suit cards, or Minor Arcana. The suits were Wands, Cups, Swords, and Disks, corresponding to the conventional Clubs, Hearts, Spades and Diamonds, or to the elements Fire, Water, Air and Earth. Each was a face card, beautifully drawn and colored. He had, like all Brothers and Sisters of the Order, studied the Tarot symbolism, had high respect for it, and was well-acquainted with the cards. One of the Order's exercises was to take black-and-white originals and color them according to instructions. This was no child's game; it was surprising how much revelation was inherent in this act. Color, like numbers and images, served a substantial symbolic purpose.

While he pondered, his fingers riffled the cards with an expertise that belied his ascetic calling. He had not always been a Brother, but like the Apostle Paul to whom he owed his Order name, he had set his savage prior life behind him. Only as a necessary exercise of contrition did he reflect upon the mistakes of his past. One day—when he was worthy—he hoped to seal that Pandora's box completely.

He completed the shuffle and returned the deck to the Reverend.

"Was the question in your mind the nature of my concern with you?" the Reverend inquired, holding the cards in her delicate fingers.

Brother Paul inclined his head affirmatively. It was a small white lie, since his thoughts had ranged in their unruly fashion all around the deck. Of course he had wondered why he was here; he had not been summoned from the midst of his class merely for chitchat! Still, a white lie *was* a lie.

"Let us try a reading," she said.

How quickly he paid for his lie! Her intent had been obvious when she gave him the deck; how could he have missed it? "I'm afraid I—"

"No, I am serious. The Tarot is a legitimate way to approach a problem—especially in this case. Let this define you."

She dealt the first card, careful to turn it over sidewise rather than end-over-end, so as not to reverse it, while Brother Paul concealed his agitation. He had made a foolish mistake that was about to cause them both embarrassment. He tried to think of some reasonable pretext to break up this reading, but all that came into his mind was a sacrilegious anecdote about Pope Joan, personification of the Whore of Babylon, epithet for the Roman Catholic Church. Such a thought was scandalous in the presence of the Reverend Mother Mary, who was completely chaste. Unless she had summoned him here to—No, impossible! A completely unworthy concept for which he would have to impose self-penance!

The card was the Ace of Wands, the image of a hand emerging from a cloud, bearing a sprouting wooden club.

"Amazing," the Reverend remarked. "This signifies the beginning of a great new adventure."

A great new adventure—with her? He tried hard to stifle the notion, fiendishly tempting as it was! In that moment he wished she were eighty years old, with a huge, hairy wart on her nose. Then his thoughts would behave. "Well, I must explain—"

"Shall we try the second?" She dealt another card from the top of the deck. She was feeling more at ease now; the cards were helping her to express herself. "Let this cross you," she said, placing the card sideways across the first.

May God have mercy! he thought fervently.

She looked at the second card, startled. "The Ace of Cups!"

"You see, I—I—" Brother Paul stammered.

The Reverend frowned. She was one of those women who looked even sweeter in dismay than in pleasure, if such a thing were possible. Silently she laid down the third card. It was the Ace of Swords. Then the fourth: the Ace of Coins. In each case, a hand was pictured emerging from a cloud, bearing the appropriate device.

Her gray-green eyes lifted to bear on him reproachfully.

"I did not realize what you intended," Brother Paul explained lamely. "I—old habits—I did not intend to embarrass you." No doubt Dante's Inferno had a special circle for the likes of him!

Mother Mary took a deep breath, then smiled—a burst of sunlight. "I had forgotten that you were once a cardsharp." She glanced down at the four aces and made a moue. "Still are, it seems."

"Retired," Brother Paul said quickly. "Reformed."

"I should hope so." She gathered up the cards.

"I'll shuffle them again, the right way," he offered.

She made a minor gesture of negation. "The wrong is the teacher of the right." But the ice had been broken. "Paul, it does not matter *how* you shuffled, so long as you formulated the correct question."

And of course he had *not* formulated it; he had been full of idle notions about the deck, Pope Joan, and such. His face was a mere shell, papering over the disaster of his mind.

"You are indeed about to embark on a remarkable new adventure—if you so choose."

Suddenly he realized that his penance would be to go on this mission, no matter how onerous it might prove. Today's declining civilization provided a number of most unpleasant situations. "I go where directed," Brother Paul said.

"Not this time. I cannot send you on this particular round, and neither can the Order. You must volunteer for it. Knowing you as I do, I am sure you *will* volunteer, and therefore I am responsible." She looked up to the ceiling of rough-hewn logs. She was, he knew, making a quick, silent prayer. "I fear for you, Paul, and my soul suffers."

The eternal feminine! A mission had found its way down through the Order hierarchy, and she was upset because he might accept it. This was no mere rhetoric on her part; now one hand clutched the Tarot deck lightly, and now the other touched her cross. He had never seen her so tense before. It was as if she were the one with the guilty imagination, not he! "We all go where needed," he said.

"Yet some needs are stronger than others," the Reverend murmured, her eyes lifting to meet his again, her face dead serious. What could she mean by that? "It is Hell I am sending you to, Brother."

Brother Paul did not smile. He had never heard language like this from her! Of course she was not swearing; she would never do that. When she said Hell, the capitalization was audible, as it was for the Tarot; she meant the abode of the Devil. "Figurative, I trust?"

"Literal, Paul. And the returning will be harder than the going."

"It would be. Especially if it is necessary to die first." Was he being cute, implying that he might return to life, like Jesus? He had not meant to!

She did not smile. "No. Like Dante, you will be a living visitor. Perhaps you will see Heaven too."

"I don't think I'm ready for that." This time he was completely serious. Heaven awed him more than Hell did. This had to be a really extraordinary thing she was describing!

The Reverend shook her head nervously, so that for an instant the lobe of one ear showed, like a bit of forbidden anatomy. "I am caught between the pillars of right and wrong, and I cannot tell them apart." She turned away from him; he had not realized that her chair could swivel. "Paul, I am required to present this to you as a prospective mission—but speaking as a Sister, as a friend, I must urge you to decline. It is not merely that it would sadden me never to see you again—though I do fear this, for no tangible reason—it is that this mission is a horror. A horror!"

"Now I am intrigued," Brother Paul said, his own apprehensions fading as hers increased. "May I learn more?"

"As much as we know," she said. "We have been asked to send our best qualified representative to Planet Tarot to ascertain the validity of its deity. A strong man, not too old, not too firmly committed to a single ideology, with a good mind and a fine sense of objectivity. You would seem to be that man."

Brother Paul ignored the compliment, knowing it was not intended as such. "Planet Tarot?"

"As you know, Earth has colonized something like a thousand habitable worlds in the current matter transport program. One of these is named Tarot, and there is a problem there."

"Hell, you said. I understood they did not send colonists to inclement habitats. If this planet is so hellish—"

"I did not say hellish, Paul. I said literal Hell. And the road to—"

"Oh, I see. It looked habitable, in the preliminary survey."

"Their surveyors must be overextended. How they managed to approve this particular planet—!" The Reverend Mother made a gesture of bafflement. "Its very name—"

"Yes, I am curious about that too. Most of the names are publicity-minded. 'Conquest,' 'Meadowland,' 'Zephyr'—how did they hit upon a name like 'Tarot'?"

"It seems a member of the survey party had a Tarot deck along.

And while he waited at the base camp for his fellows to return, he dealt himself a divination hand. And—" She paused.

"And something happened."

"It certainly did. He—the card—the illustration on one of his cards took form. In three-dimensional animation."

Brother Paul's interest intensified. He had had experience with both sleight-of-hand and hallucinatory phenomena. "Had he been drinking an intoxicant?"

She shook her head. "They claim not. No alcohol, no drugs, no mushrooms or glue or extract of lettuce. That was why he happened to be entertaining himself with cards. And the other members of the party saw the animation."

"No hallucination, then. But possibly a practical joke?"

"No. No joke."

"Which card was it?"

"The Ten of Swords."

Brother Paul refrained from whistling, contenting himself with a grave nod. "Signifying ruin! Was it a literal image?"

"It was. Ten tall swords piercing a corpse. All quite solid."

"That should have shaken up the party!"

"It certainly did. They pulled out the swords and turned over the body. It was a man, but none they recognized. No one was missing from their crew. They buried him, saved the swords, and wrote up a report."

"Tangible evidence. That was smart."

"Not so smart. When they arrived on Earth, the objects they claimed were swords were merely so many slivers of stone, like stalactites from a cave. A second party, sent to verify the situation, dug up the body—and found only the carcass of a native animal."

"Mass hallucination?" Brother Paul suggested. "They killed an animal and thought it was a man? Because of fatigue and guilt—or because its configuration resembled that particular card? Stalactites *are* a bit like swords."

"That was the official conclusion." She paused, then girded herself to continue. "The second party brought Tarot cards and played many games, this time in the line of business, but there was no duplication of the effect. Apparently the first crew had been overworked and short on sleep, while the second was fresh. So they named the planet Tarot and approved it for colonization."

"Just like that?" Brother Paul inquired, raising an eyebrow.

"Just like that," the Reverend Mother said wryly, forgetting herself so far as to raise her own eyebrow in response. "They had a quota of planets to survey, and could not afford to waste time, as they put it, 'wild ghost chasing.'"

"How much is lost through haste!" Brother Paul remarked. But he felt a growing excitement and gratitude that this mystery had come to pass. Wild ghosts? He certainly would like to see one!

"Colonization proceeded in normal fashion," she continued. "One million human beings were shipped in the course of forty days, assigned to initial campsites with wilderness reduction equipment, and left to fend for themselves. Only the monthly coordination shuttle maintained contact. Colonization is," she commented with a disapproving frown, "somewhat of a sink-or-swim situation."

"Without doubt," Brother Paul agreed. "Yet the great majority of emigrants have been happy to risk it—and most seem to be swimming."

"Yes." She shrugged. "It is not the way I would have chosen —but the decision was hardly mine to make. At any rate, the colonists settled—and then the fun began."

"More Tarot animations?"

"No, not specifically. These animations were of Heaven—and of Hell. I mean the storybook Pearly Gates, with angels flying by, and harpists sitting on clouds. Or the other extreme—fiery caves with red, fork-tailed devils with pitchforks."

"Evidently literal renditions of religious notions," Brother Paul said. "Many believers have very material views of the immaterial."

"They do. There seems to be an unusual concentration of schismatic religions in this colony world. But these were rather substantial projections." She pulled out a drawer in her desk and brought forth several photographs. "Skeptics arranged to take pictures—and we have them here." She spread them out.

He studied the pictures with amazement. "There was no, ah, trick photography? They certainly look authentic!"

"No trick photography. There is more: the colonists organized a planetary orchestra—in any random sampling of a million people, you'll find many skills—and they practiced many semiclassical pieces. One day they were doing the tone poem by Saint-Saëns, 'Danse macabre,' and—"

"Oh, no! Not the dancing skeletons!"

"The same. The entire orchestra panicked, and two musicians

died in the stampede. In fact, I believe the orchestra was disbanded after that, and never reorganized. But when cooler heads investigated, they found no trace of the walking skeletons."

"I begin to see," Brother Paul said, feeling an unholy anticipation of challenge. "Planet Tarot is haunted."

"That is one way of putting it," she agreed. "We view it more seriously." She waited until his face assumed the proper expression of seriousness. "Most haunts don't lend themselves well to motion-picture photography." She brought a reel from the drawer.

Brother Paul did a double-take. "Motion-picture film of the skeletons?"

"That's right. It seems a colonist was filming the concert. He thought the skeletons were part of the show—until the stampede began."

"This I would like to see!"

"You shall." The Reverend set up a little projector, lit its lensed lamp, and cranked the handle. The picture flickered on the wall across from her desk.

It was, indeed, the dance of death. At first there were only the musicians, playing their crude, locally fashioned violins; then the skeletons pranced onstage, moving in time to the music. There was no sound, of course; a lamp-and-hand-crank projector was not capable of that. But Brother Paul could see the breathing of the players, the motions of their hands on the instruments, and the gestures of the conductor; the beat was clear.

One skeleton passed close to the camera, its gaunt, white ribcage momentarily blotting out the orchestra. Brother Paul peered closely, trying to ascertain what manner of articulation those bones possessed; it was hardly credible that they could move without muscle, sinew, or wires. Yet they did.

Then the scramble began; the picture veered crazily and clicked off.

"I understood there was a one-kilogram limit on personal possessions of emigrants," Brother Paul commented. "How did a sophisticated device like a motion-picture camera get there?"

"They can make them very small these days," the Reverend said. "Actually, two emigrants shared their mass allotment in this case, and three others in the family collaborated by taking fragments of a matching projector that could be run by hand. Like this one." She patted it. "They yielded to need rather than philosophy; nevertheless, they were ingenious. Now we know how fortunate that was. No one on Earth would have believed their story otherwise. This film is evidence that cannot be ignored; *something* is happening on Planet Tarot, something extraordinary. The authorities want to know what."

"But why should they come to us?" Brother Paul asked. "I should think they would send scientists with sophisticated equipment."

She moved one hand in an unconscious "be patient" gesture. "They did. But the effect seems to be intermittent."

Intermittency—the scourge of repairmen and psychic investigators! How was it possible to understand something that operated only in the absence of the investigator? "Meaning the experts found nothing?" he asked.

"Correct. But they also interviewed the colonists and assembled a catalogue of episodes. They discovered that the manifestations were confined to certain times and certain places—usually. And they occurred only in the presence of believers."

"This has a familiar ring," Brother Paul said. "The believer experiences; the nonbeliever doesn't. It is the way with faith." He remembered his own discussion with the boys and girls of the village class; his belief had been stronger than their disbelief.

"Precisely. Except that the skeptics of the colony were able to witness a few of the phenomena. Whereupon they became believers."

As Saul of Tarsus had witnessed the grandeur of God on the road to Damascus, and become Christian. As the village youths had witnessed the power of martial arts. "Believers in what?"

"In whatever they saw. There may have been skeptics when the *'danse macabre'* recital began, but there were none at the end, because the skeletons were tangible. But there were other manifestations. In one case it was God—or at least a burning bush that spoke quite clearly, claiming to be God."

Presumptuous bush! "Sounds like a case for the priests, rabbis, or holy men."

"They were the next to investigate. They proceeded directly to the haunted regions." She stopped, and Brother Paul did not prompt her with another question. She stared at the desk for some time, as though probing every fissure in its rough grain, and finally resumed. "It was a disaster. Two resigned from their ministries, two had to be incarcerated as mentally incompetent, and two died. It seems they experienced more Hell than Heaven. That is how the job filtered down to us."

"Those apparitions actually *killed?* Took human life? No stampede or other physical cause?"

"Those apparitions, or whatever it was those people experienced, actually did destroy minds and take human life." She faced Brother Paul squarely, and her concern for him made her almost radiant. He knew she would turn the same expression on a wounded rattlesnake or a torn manuscript; that was what made her so lovely. "Now you know what I fear. Are you ready to go to Hell?"

Ready? He was eager! "It sounds fascinating. But what exactly would be my mission there? To exorcise the Devil of Tarot?"

"No. I fear that would be beyond your powers, or mine, or any of our Order." She smiled very briefly. "The holy men who failed were prominent, devout men, thorough scholars, whose faith in their religions was tested and true. I find it strange that they should have suffered so greatly, while the large majority of the colonists, who represent a random sampling of Earth, have had few such problems."

Brother Paul nodded. "Perhaps not so strange. It may be that training and belief are liabilities in that situation."

"Perhaps. It is true that those who feel most strongly about religion obtain the strongest response from Planet Tarot. Those whose primary concern is to feed their faces—do just that."

As luck would have it, a strong waft of the aroma of Brother Peter's hot bread passed through the room, making Brother Paul's mouth water. "Are you suggesting that my concern is to feed my face?" he asked with a smile. Now that the nature of the mission had been clarified, his tension was gone.

"You know better than that, Paul! But you are not a divinity specialist. Your background is broader, touching many aspects of the human state. More than the experience of most people. You know the meaning of prayer—and of pipefitting. Of divination —and gambling."

"Those are apt parallels."

"Thank you. You are aware of things that are beyond my imagination." Brother Paul fervently hoped so; had she any inkling of the mishmash of notions that coursed through his brain, she would be shocked. He was reminded of a childhood game his friends had played, called Heaven or Hell. One boy and one girl were selected by lot to enter a dark closet. For one minute he had either to kiss her (Heaven) or hit her (Hell). Once Brother Paul had dreamed of taking the Reverend into such a closet, and he had awakened in a cold sweat, horrified. The very memory was appalling, now. Until that memory was gone, he would not be fit material for advancement within the Holy Order of Vision.

But she was unaware of this chasm within him—an innocence for which he sincerely thanked God. "I feel you would not concentrate exclusively on the religious implications of the problem," she continued blithely. "You would relate to the concerns of the colonists as well. Perhaps you will be able to ascertain not only what happened to the priests, but why it *doesn't* happen to the colonists, and why faith seems to be such a liability. But more important—"

"I think I anticipate you," Brother Paul murmured.

"We want to ascertain whether this phenomenon is ultimately material or spiritual. We have observed only the fringes of it so far, but there appear to be elements of both. One explanation is that this is a test for man, of his coming-of-age: that God, if you will, has elected to manifest Himself to man in this challenging fashion. We do not want to ignore that challenge, and certainly we do not wish to risk crucifying Christ again! But we also cannot afford to embarrass ourselves by treating too seriously a phenomenon that may have completely mundane roots."

"God has completely mundane roots," Brother Paul pointed out, with no negative intent.

"But He also has completely divine branches. The one without the other—"

"Yes, I appreciate the delicacy of the problem."

"If this manifestation should actually stem from God, we must recognize and answer the call," the Reverend Mother said. "If it is a purely material thing, we would like to know exactly what it is, and how it works, and why religion is vulnerable to it. That surely will not be easy to do!" She paused. "Why am I so excited, Paul, yet so afraid? I have urged you not to go, yet at the same time—"

Brother Paul smiled. "You are afraid I shall fail. Or that I will actually *find* God there. Either would be most discomfiting—for of course the God of Tarot is also the God of Earth. The God of Man."

"Yes," she said uncertainly. "But after all our centuries of faith, can we really face the reality? God may not conform to our expectations, yet how could we reject Him? We *must* know Him! It frightens me! In short—"

"In short," Brother Paul concluded, "you want me to go to Hell—to see if God is there."

<u>UNKNOWN</u>
(GHOST)

The riddle of consciousness has perplexed the human mind for a long time. What is it? Where is it? We can never quite pin it down; we only know that we possess it. Arthur Koestler has an excellent discussion of this problem in his book The Ghost in the Machine, *wherein he likens consciousness to a mirror in which a person views his own activities, or to a hall of mirrors that reflects one's reflection infinitely. The best scientists, he says, possess an awareness of the infinite, the sense of mystery, knowing that the phenomena we observe are transparent to a different order of reality. Even the simplest machines seem to have ghosts, hints of infinity, of what can never be truly understood. The unknown pervades our existence, and perhaps that is part of what makes existence bearable.*

The Station of the Holy Order of Vision was, Brother Paul was forcibly reminded, well out in the sticks. It had not always been that way. This had once been a ghetto area. In the five years of the Matter Transmission program, officially and popularly known as MT and Empty respectively, several billion human beings had been exported to about a thousand colony planets. This was a rate that would soon depopulate the world.

But it was not the policy of the Holy Order of Vision to interfere in lay matters. Brother Paul could think his private thoughts, but he must never try to force his political or economic opinions on others. Or, for that matter, his religious views.

So now he trekked through the veritable wilderness surrounding the Station, past the standing steel bones of once-great buildings projecting into the sky like remnants of dinosaurs. During winter's snows the effect was not so stark; the bones were blanketed. But this was summer. His destination was the lingering, shrinking technological civilization of the planet. The resurging brush and shrubs grew thicker and taller as he covered the kilometers, as though their growth kept pace with his progress, then gave way on occasion to clusters of dwellings like medieval villages. Each population cluster centered around some surviving bastion of technology: electricity generated from a water wheel, a wood-fueled kiln, or industrial-scale windmills.

Village, he thought. From the same Latin root as *villa,* the manor of a feudal lord. Inhabited by feudal serfs called *villains,* whose ignorant nature lent a somewhat different meaning to that word in later centuries. Society was fragmenting into its original components, under the stress of deprivation of energy. Electronics was virtually a dead science in the hinterlands where there was no electricity; automotive technology was passé where there was no gasoline. Horsepower and handicrafts had quickly resumed their former prominence, and Brother Paul was not prepared to call this evil. Pollution was a thing of the past, except in mining areas, and children today did not know what the term "inflation" meant, since barter was the order of the day. People lived harder lives now, but often healthier ones, despite the regression of medical technology. The enhanced sense of community in any given village was a blessing; neighbor was more apt to help neighbor, and the discontented had gone away. Light-years away.

However, he approached each village carefully, for the villains could be brutish with strangers. Brother Paul was basically a man of peace, but neither a weakling nor a fool. He donned his Order habit when near population centers to make himself more readily identifiable. He would defend himself with words and smiles and humility wherever he could, and with physical measures when all else failed.

Though he was a Brother of an Order with religious connotations, he neither expected nor received free benefits on that account. He rendered service for his night's board and lodging; there was always demand for a man handy with mechanical things. He exchanged news with the lord of each manor, obtaining directions and advice about local conditions. Everyone knew the way to MT. Each night he found a different residence. In some areas of the country, actual primitive tribes had taken over, calling themselves Saxons, Huns, Cimmerians, Celts, or Picts, and in many respects they did resemble their historic models. The Saxons were Americans of northern European descent; the Huns were Americans of middle European admixed with Oriental descent; the Cimmerians seemed to be derived from the former fans of fantasy adventure novels. Elsewhere in the world, he knew, the process was similar; there were even Incas in Asia. He encountered one strong tribe named Songhoy whose roots were in tenth-century Black Africa. Their location, with ironic appropriateness, was in the badlands of black craters formed by savagely rapid and deep strip mining for coal. Once there had been enough coal in America to power the world for centuries; no more.

The Holy Order of Vision, always hospitable to peaceful travelers, had entertained and assisted Shamans and Druids and other priestly representatives, never challenging their beliefs or religious authority. A Voodoo witch-doctor could not only find hospitality at the Station, he could converse with Brothers of the Order who took him completely seriously and knew more than a little about his practice. Now this policy paid off for Brother Paul. The small silver cross he wore became a talisman of amazing potency wherever religion dominated—and this was more extensive every year. Political power reached only as far as the arm of the local strong man, but clerical power extended as far as faith could reach. The laity gave way increasingly to the clerical authorities, as in medieval times. Thus Brother Paul was harvesting the fruit of the seeds sown by his Order. In addition, he had rather persuasive insights into the culture of Black societies, whether of ancient Africa or modern America. He fared very well.

After many pleasant days of foot travel he entered the somewhat vaguely defined demesnes of twentieth-century civilization. Here there was electricity from a central source, and radio and telephones and automotive movement. He obtained a ride on a train drawn by a woodburning steam engine; no diesels or coal-fired vehicles remained operative, of course. The electricity here was generated by sunlight, not fossil fuel, for MT was as yet unable to preempt the entire light of the sun for the emigration program. "Maybe tomorrow," the wry joke went.

The reason for the lack of clear boundaries to the region was that the electric power lines did not extend all the way to the periphery, and batteries were reserved for emergency use. But radio communication reached some distance farther out, so that selected offices could be linked to the news of the world. At this fringe, wood was the fuel of choice where it was available.

This was a pleasant enough ride, allowing Brother Paul to rest his weary feet. He felt a bit guilty about using the Order credit card for this service, but in one day he traversed more territory than he had in a week of foot travel. He could not otherwise have arrived on time.

He spent this night at the Station of the Coordinator for the Order in this region: the Right Reverend Father Crowder. Brother Paul was somewhat awed by the august presence of this pepper-maned elder, but the Right Reverend quickly made him even less at ease. "How I envy you your youth and courage, Brother! I daresay you run the cross-country kilometer in under three minutes."

"Uh, sometimes—"

"Never cracked three-ten myself. Or the five-minute mile. But once I managed fifteen honest pullups in thirty seconds on a rafter in the chapel." He smiled ruefully. "The chapelmaster caught me. He never said a word—but, oh, the look he gave me! I never had the nerve to try it again. But I'm sure you would never allow such a minor excuse to interfere with your exercise."

Obviously the man knew something about Brother Paul's background—especially the calisthenics he had been sneaking in when he thought no one was watching. He hoped he wasn't blushing.

"The mission you now face requires a good deal more nerve than that sort of thing," Right Reverend Crowder continued. "You have nerve, presence of mind, great strength, and a certain refreshing objectivity. These were qualities we were looking for. Yet it will not be easy. Not only must you face God—you must pass judgment on His validity. I do not envy you this charge." He turned and put his strong, weathered hands on Brother Paul's shoulders. "God bless you and give you strength," he said sincerely.

God bless you . . . Brother Paul swayed, closing his eyes in momentary pain.

"Easy, Brother," the Right Reverend said, steadying him. "I

know you are tired after your arduous journey. Go to your room and lie down; get a good night's rest. We shall see you safely on the bus to the mattermission station in the morning."

The Right Reverend was, of course, as good as his word. Well rested and well fed, Brother Paul was deposited on the bus for a four-hour journey into the very depths of civilization. Thus, quite suddenly, he came to the MT station: Twenty-First Century America.

He was met as he stepped down from the coach by an MT official dressed in a rather garish blue uniform. "Very good," the young man said crisply, sourly eyeing Brother Paul's travel-soiled Order robe. "You are the representative of the Visual Order—"

"The Holy Order of Vision," Brother Paul corrected him tolerantly. A Druid never would have made such an error, but this was, after all, a lay official. "Holy as in 'whole,' for we try to embrace the entire spirit of—"

"Yes, yes. Please come this way, sir."

"Not 'sir.' I am a Brother. Brother Paul. All men are brothers —" But the imperious functionary was already moving ahead, forcing Brother Paul to hurry after him.

He did so. "Before I go to the colony world, I'll need a source of direct current electricity to recharge my calculator," he said. "I'm not an apt mathematician, and there may be complexities that require—"

"There isn't time for that!" the man snapped. "The shipment has been delayed for hours pending your arrival, interfering with our programming. Now it has been slotted for thirty minutes hence. We barely—"

He should have remembered: Time, in the form of schedules, was one of the chief Gods of MT, second only to Power. Brother Paul had become too used to a day governed by the position of the sun. He had been lent a good watch along with the calculator for this mission, but had not yet gotten into the habit of looking at it. "I certainly would not want to profane your schedule, but if I am to do my job properly—"

With a grimace of exasperation the man drew him into a building. Inside was a telephone. "Place an order for new batteries," he rapped out, handing the transceiver to Brother Paul.

Such efficiency! Brother Paul had lost familiarity with telephones in the past few years. Into which portion of the device was he supposed to speak? He compromised by speaking loudly enough to catch both ends of it, describing the batteries. "Authorization granted," the upper part of the phone replied after a click. "Pick them up at Supply."

"Supply?" But the phone had clicked off. That seemed to be the manner, here in civilization.

"Come on," the functionary said. "We'll catch it in passing." And they did; a quick stop at another building produced the required cells. These people were not very sociable, but they got the job done!

"And this," the man at the supply desk said, holding out a heavy metal bracelet.

"Oh, Brothers don't wear jewelry, only the Cross," Brother Paul protested. "We have taken vows of poverty—"

"Jewelry, hell," the man snorted. "This is a molecular recorder. There'll be a complete playback when you return: everything you have seen or heard and some things you haven't. This unit is sensitive to quite a few forms of radiation and chemical combinations. Just keep it on your left wrist and forget it. But don't cover it up."

Brother Paul was taken aback. "I had understood that this was to be a personal investigation and report. After all, a machine can't be expected to fathom God."

"Ha ha," the supply man said without humor. "Just put it on."

Reluctantly Brother Paul held up his left arm. The man clasped the bracelet on it, snapping it in place. He should have realized that the secular powers who controlled mattermission would not cooperate unless they had their secular assurances. They did not care whether God had manifested on Planet Tarot; their God was the Machine. The Machine embraced both Time and Power, ruling all. Yet perhaps it was only fair; who could say in advance that the God of Tarot was not a machine deity? Therefore it was proper that the Machine send its representative, too.

"And this," the supply man said, holding out a set of small rods, "is a short-range transceiver. Hold it up, speak, this other unit receives. And vice versa. Required equipment for all our operatives."

"I am not your operative," Brother Paul said as gently as he could. He was, he reminded himself, supposed to be a peaceful man.

"Who's paying your fare, round trip?" the man asked.

Brother Paul sighed. He who paid the piper, called the tune.

Render unto Caesar, et cetera. He took the transceivers and tucked them into a pocket. He could carry them; he didn't have to use them.

"Mind," the supply man said, his brows furrowing, "we expect this equipment back in good order."

"You can have it back now," Brother Paul said.

No one answered him. He was whisked into another building and subjected to assorted indignities of examination and preparation. In their savage velocity and callousness, these procedures reminded him vaguely of the strip mining he had seen. Then he was hurried into the thermos bottle-like capsule and sealed in. All he had to do now was wait.

He examined the chamber. It was fairly large, but packed with unboxed equipment. Crates would have been wasteful, of course; every gram counted. Most of it was readily identifiable: hand-powered adding machines, spinning wheels, looms, treadle-powered sewing machines, mechanical typewriters, axes, handsaws, wood stoves, and the like. A sensible shipment for a colony that might be as backward as the hinterlands of Earth itself.

Those adding machines bothered him. How could he justify his fuss about the electronic calculator? He was out of tune with the technology of his mission. Perhaps he had been shortsighted. Was it rationalization to suggest that the adding machines could not readily multiply or divide numbers, do specialized conversions, or figure the cube root of *pi*? A slide rule could do those things, and it had no battery to run down. Why hadn't he brought along a slide rule? That would have been far more in keeping with the philosophy of the Holy Order of Vision. The lay powers of Earth were using calculators whose usefulness would cease when their power sources expired. He, as a Brother, should be showing his fellow man how to use slide rules that would function as long as mind and hands remained.

"I am a hypocrite," he murmured aloud. "May God correct and forgive me."

He looked at his watch—he was finally getting into that habit!—and set the elapsed-time counter. Of course mattermission was supposed to be instantaneous, the Theory of Relativity to the contrary, but there was this waiting time, and he might as well measure that. He liked to count things anyway. It was better than admitting that he was nervous.

His eye caught the silver-colored band on his wrist. It had an elaborate decoration, like a modernistic painting done in relief. No doubt that was to conceal the lenses and mechanisms within it. When it was necessary to hide something, fit it into a complex container. As the crown-maker had done to conceal the amount of base metal diluting the value of the supposedly pure gold crown of Hieron, ruler of the ancient city of Syracuse. Except that Archimedes had cried "Eureka!" and found it, utilizing the principle of water displacement.

Probably the band was recording things now. How fortunate it could not record his thoughts! But what would happen when he wished to perform a natural function? Maybe he could hold that wrist up over his head so the device couldn't see anything. Yet suppose he did so, and suddenly heard it cry "Eureka!"?

He smiled at himself. Ridiculous mortal vanity! What did it matter what portion of his anatomy this device might perceive? When the lay experts played back the molecules, they would quickly be bored by the minutiae of human water displacements. Let the machine capture and contain all the information it could hold, until its cup brimmethed over.

Abruptly it struck him: a cup! This bracelet was like the Cup of the Tarot, containing not fluid but information. And the little transceivers—they were Wands. His watch was the emblem of a third suit, Disks, for it was essentially a disk with markings, and hands pointing to the time of day that in Nature was shown by the original golden disk of the sun. Three suits. What might be the fourth, that of Swords?

That stymied him for a moment. Swords were representative of trouble, violence; he had no such weapon on him. Swords were also the suit of air, and while he had air about him, this didn't seem to apply. The sword was also a scalpel, signifying surgery or medicine, and of course there was the cutting edge of thought— That was it! The sharpest, most tangible thought was the symbolism of numbers, of mathematics. The calculator! Thus he had a full roster of Tarot symbolism. Too bad he hadn't brought along a Tarot deck; that could have distracted him very nicely.

Brother Paul sat on a stove, waiting for the shipment to ship. After all that rush, they might at least have gotten on with it promptly once he was inside the capsule! But perhaps there were technical things to do, like switching coaches onto other sidings or whatever, lining everything up for the big jump. It was difficult to imagine how, in this nineteenth-century setting, he could be jolted to a world perhaps fifty light-years distant. He should have thought to inquire exactly where Planet Tarot was; that seemed much more important now that he was on the verge of jumping there. Was a jump of seventy light-years more hazardous than a jump of twenty light-years? The concept of instantaneous travel bothered him in a vague way, like the discomfort of an incipient stomach disorder that might or might not lead to retching. He would never understand how mattermission worked. Didn't old Albert Einstein know his math? Yet obviously it did exist—or did it?

His watch claimed that only another minute had passed since his last look, or a total of two and a half minutes since he had set the counter. That didn't help; subjectively he had aged far more than that!

There were chronic whispers about that objection of Relativity, rumors always denied by MT, yet persistent. Twentieth-century science had accomplished many things supposed to have been impossible in the nineteenth century; why shouldn't twenty-first century science supersede the beliefs of the twentieth? Yet he found that he now had the same difficulty disbelieving in Relativity as he had initially had believing in it. Suddenly, in the close confines of this capsule, those whispers were easy to believe. There was no doubt that Earth was being depopulated, and that such tremendous amounts of energy were being consumed that the whole society was regressing, the victim of energy starvation. But there was also no question that the emigration mechanism, MT, had been deemed impossible by the best human minds of the past. The obvious reconciliation: people *were* departing Earth—but they *weren't* arriving at other planets. The whole vast MT program could be a ruse to—

Suddenly his queasiness gave way to acute claustrophobia. He looked about nervously for nozzles that might admit poisonous gas. The Jews in Nazi Germany, half a century or so ago: they had been promised relief—

No, that didn't make sense! Why go to the trouble of summoning a single novice of a semireligious Order to this elaborate setup? Anyone who wanted him out of the way could find much less cumbersome means to eliminate him! And the Order would not suffer itself to be deceived like this. The Right Reverend Father Crowder would never countenance such a thing; of this

Brother Paul was absolutely sure. And the Reverend Mother Mary, angelic in her concern for the good of all men . . .

The Reverend Mother Mary. Why fool himself? He had agreed to undertake this mission because she had asked him to. Oh, she had pleaded the opposite, most charmingly. But he would have been diminished in her eyes if he had heeded that plea.

This was no more profitable a line of thought than the other had been. He was here neither for death nor for love. He was supposed to ascertain the validity of the God of Tarot, and the project fascinated him. Why distract himself with superficially unreasonable or impossible things, when his actual assignment surpassed the unreason or impossibility of either? How could a mere man pass judgment on God?

Brother Paul drew out his calculator, his symbol for thought, his figurative Sword of Tarot. It was an early model, perhaps twenty-five years old. An antique, but it still operated. The Holy Order of Vision took good care of those devices it preserved, perhaps fearing that one year there would be no reservoir of technology but this. The calculator had a number of square white buttons, and a number of square black ones. By depressing these buttons in the proper order he could set up any simple mathematical problem and obtain an immediate solution. Instantaneous—like the travel between worlds! This was travel between the worlds of concepts, not of space.

Idly he turned it on, watching the green zero appear in the readout window. "Two," he murmured, touching the appropriate button, and the zero was transformed miraculously into 2. "Plus three—equals five." And the green 5 was there ahead of him.

Brother Paul smiled. He liked this little machine; it might not rival the Colony computer, but it did its limited job well. "Let's remember that," he said, punching the MEMORY button, then the PLUS button. That should file the number in the memory as a positive integer. Now he touched the CLEAR ENTRY button, and the cheerful zero reappeared, as green as ever. He punched MEMORY and RECALL and the 5 returned. Good; the memory was functioning properly.

"Let's convert it from kilograms to pounds," he continued, for this was an old conversions calculator complete with the archaic measurements, as befitted the date of its origin. He touched the CONVERSIONS button, then the MINUS button, which was now understood to represent kilograms. Then the DIVIDE button, which was now pounds. These double designations were initially confusing, but necessary to make twenty buttons do the work of fifty. The answer: 11.023113.

"File that useless information in Memory Two," he said, punching MEMORY again, followed by 2, followed by PLUS, followed by CLEAR ENTRY. The readout returned to zero. Oh, he had forgotten what fun this was! "Now the number 99999999 multiplied by the number in Memory One." He punched a row of eight nines, then TIMES, then MEMORY, 1, RECALL, then EQUALS. He frowned.

A red dot had appeared in the left-hand corner of the readout. "Overload," he said. "No room for a nine-digit number! Clear it out." He struck the CLEAR button several times, then turned off the calculator so as not to waste battery power while he thought.

"Very well," he said after a moment. "Let's keep it within bounds. Multiply Memory One by Memory Two." He turned it on again and punched the necessary sequence rapidly. All he got were zeroes. "Oh, I forgot! Turning it off erases the memory! I'll have to start over." He punched in a new 5, put it in Memory One, converted it from kilos to pounds, put that into Memory Two, cleared the readout, forgot what he was doing, and punched for Memory Two Recall. The result was zero.

"Something's wrong," he said. He went through the sequence again, watching his fingers move fleetingly over the keys—and saw his error. He had missed the 2 button for Memory Two and hit the TIMES button instead. "Can't put it in TIMES MEMORY!" he said. "That would mean I'd have to punch MEMORY TIMES RECALL to get it out, and the poor machine would think I'd gone crazy and have to flash overload lights at me to jog me out of it." As he spoke, he punched the foolish sequence he had named. The readout showed 11.023113.

Brother Paul stared at that. Then he erased the sequence and went through it all again, carefully punching the erroneous TIMES MEMORY, which was not supposed to exist. The same thing happened: he got the number back. "But that means this thing has a third memory—and it's only built for two," he said.

So he tested it methodically, for there was nothing so intriguing to him as a good mystery or paradox. He punched the number 111 into Memory One, 222 into Memory Two, and 333 into MEMORY TIMES. Then he punched out each in turn. Up they came, like the chosen cards of a sleight-of-hand magician: 111—222—0.

"Zero!" he exclaimed. "So it *isn't* true!" But just to be certain, he repeated the process, this time checking TIMES MEMORY first—and the 333 appeared. He checked for the 222 and found it, and then the 111—and it was there too. No doubt about it; he now had three memories. But the third one was intermittent, following some law of its own, as though it were half wild.

"Half wild . . ." he repeated aloud, thinking of something else. But if he got off on that, he would not solve the present mystery. He glanced at his watch. He had really gobbled up time with his calculations! Ten minutes, forty-two seconds, give or take a second, since he had set the counter. How long would they dawdle about mattermitting this capsule?

He cleared the readout and punched MEMORY TIMES again. The 333 reappeared. "A ghost in the machine," he said. "A secret memory, unknown to—"

"So you found me," a voice responded. "Yet I was always here, to be evoked."

Brother Paul's eyes flicked from the calculator to his watch —ten minutes, forty-nine seconds—then lifted slowly. A man stood before him, on the far side of the sewing machine. He was young, but with receding hair and chin, as though he had been subjected to early stress. No, that was a false characterization; physical appearance had little to do with personality. "Sorry. I did not see you arrive," Brother Paul said. "Are you traveling to Planet Tarot too?"

The man smiled, but there was something strange about the way his mouth moved. "Perhaps—if you so choose."

"I am Brother Paul of the Holy Order of Vision." He put forth his hand.

"I am Antares," the man said, but made no motion to accept the hand.

"Well, Mr. Antares—or is it Brother Antares? Are you another investigator?"

"It is only Antares. Sexual designations have little meaning to my kind, and you would not understand my personal designation. Do you not know me?"

Brother Paul looked at him again, more carefully this time. This was just an ordinary man, wearing a dark tunic. "I regret that the only Antares I know of is a bright red star."

"Exactly."

"You associate with the star Antares?" Brother Paul asked, perplexed.

"I am the emissary from Sphere Antares, yes," the man affirmed.

"I was not aware that our colonies extended so far. Isn't Antares many hundreds of light-years distant from Sol?"

"About five hundred of your light-years, yes, in your constellation Scorpio. We are not a colony, but a separate Sphere. There are many sapient Spheres in the galaxy, and in other galaxies, each highly advanced in the center and fading in technology and competence at the fringe, owing to the phenomenon of spherical regression. Thus each empire has certain natural limits, depending on—"

"Scorpio," Brother Paul said musingly, grasping that portion of the alien's discussion to which he could relate. "The constellation."

"The scorpion that slew Orion, in your mythology," the man said agreeably. "Of course, in real history, the constellation you call Orion's Belt is the center of Sphere Mintaka, perhaps the largest and most influential Sphere in this sector of galactic space, with the possible exception of Sphere Sador. A giant, certainly, but never slain by anything in *our* rather more modest Sphere! Actually, war between the Spheres is virtually unknown, because of the problems of communication and transport."

Brother Paul was still belatedly assimilating the implications. "Perhaps I misunderstand. It almost seems that you imply you are a man from a—a regime centered in the region of the space known as—"

"Not a man, Solarian Brother Paul. I am an Antarean, a sapient creature quite alien to your type, except in intellect."

"An alien creature!" Was this a joke? Brother Paul looked at his watch. The counter indicated ten minutes, forty-nine seconds. Well, he would test Antares' statement. "I regret that I have not encountered many alien creatures. Your form appears human—or is that a mirage?"

"This is my Solarian host. My aura was transferred to this host so that I could present to your species the technology of matter transmission. In exchange you gave us controlled hydrogen fusion."

Matter transmission! "*You* brought us that breakthrough technology?"

"True. It would otherwise have been some time before your Sphere developed it. The principles are foreign to the main thrust of your technology, just as the principles of hydrofusion are foreign to ours. In fact, historically, our experts believed it was theoretically impossible to accomplish such a process artificially. Our Theory of Absolutivity—"

This was a strange joke! "Antares, I would like to see you in your alien form. Would you mind materializing in that?" If this were a prank, that would expose it!

The person before him faded. In his place appeared a large amoebalike mass. On its top, it erected a pattern of spongy knobs that flexed up and down like the keys of a player piano. Then it flung out a pseudopod, a glob of gelatinous substance that landed a meter to the side connected to the main mass by a dwindling tendril. Fluid pulsed along this tendril, distending it, collecting at the end, swelling the glob until it approached the size of the main body. The process continued, making the glob even larger until at last it was the original body that was a glob, while the glob had expanded to the size of the original mass. Then the trailing tendril was sucked in. The creature now stood one meter to the side of where it had stood before. It had taken one step.

It faded, and the man reappeared. "We Antareans may be slow, but there are few places we cannot go," he said. "I have returned to the form of my human host so that I may converse with you; I doubt that you are facile in my native language."

"Uh, thank you," Brother Paul said. "That was an impressive demonstration. May I touch you?"

"I regret you cannot," the alien said. "Both my forms are insubstantial. You perceive only an animation shaped by my aura, and this is possible only while we endure in the process of transmission. You may pass your appendage through the image, but you will feel nothing."

"So you are a ghost," Brother Paul said. "An apparition without substance. Nevertheless, I am inclined to make the attempt." He reached forward slowly, over the sewing machine.

Antares did not retreat the way a joker might. He stood still, waiting for the touch.

There was no touch. Brother Paul felt a slight tingling, as of an electrical charge that gave him an odd thrill but no physical contact. This was, indeed, a ghost.

"Your aura! Amazing!" Antares exclaimed. "Never have I felt the like!"

This was strange, and far beyond the parameters of a practical joke. "My aura?"

"Solarian Brother Paul, now I know I have never touched you before, for there can be no other aura in your Sphere like yours. Or in my own Sphere. Perhaps not in the Spheres of Spica, Canopus, Polaris, or even huge Sador. I suspect there is none of greater intensity in all the galaxy, for only once in a thousand of your years is there a statistical probability of—why did you not come to me sooner?"

Brother Paul withdrew his hand, perplexed. "I do not know what you mean by 'aura.' I have never met you before—or any other ghost—and had no notion that you were to accompany me on this mission. Are you really a creature from another region of space?"

"I really am," Antares said. "More correctly, *was*. I faded out some time ago, and remain only as the captive aura of this process. As you so aptly put it, the ghost in the machine."

"I was speaking of the ghostly third memory in this little calculator," Brother Paul said. "It was designed to have only two memories, yet—"

"Allow me to examine it," Antares said.

Brother Paul held it out, and the alien passed his immaterial hand through it. "Ah, yes. That is a memory, but not precisely of the other type. It is what you call the constant: the figure retained for multiple operations. Because every element of this keyboard is dual-function, in certain cases that duality permits a direct readout of the normally hidden constant."

"The constant!" Brother Paul exclaimed. "Of course! No ghost at all, merely a misunderstood function. Like an autonomic function of the body, not ordinarily evoked consciously."

"Such comprehension comes naturally to our species," Antares said modestly.

That reminded Brother Paul. "You say your, er, Sphere traded with ours? Mattermission for hydrofusion?"

"The expense in energy of physical transport over interstellar distances makes material commerce unfeasible," Antares said.

"Therefore trade is largely confined to information. Since you possess technology we lacked—"

"But if you are so advanced, why couldn't you develop controlled hydrogen fusion yourselves?"

"For much the same reason you could not develop instantaneous transmission of matter. Our mode of thinking was incapable of formulating the necessary concepts. In our framework, artificial hydrofusion is—or was—inconceivable. We are a protean, flexible species. We do not think in terms of either magnetics or lasers. We are adept at flexible circuitry, at the sciences of flowing impedences. Thus, for us, mattermission technology is a natural, if complex, mode. You Solarians are a *thrust* culture; you poke with sticks, thrust with swords, and burn with fierce, tight lasers. For you, laser-controlled atomic fusion is natural."

That seemed to make sense, although it seemed to Brother Paul that the Antarean's ready assimilation of the calculator operation indicated a certain competence with magnetic circuitry. Probably the term "magnetic" had a different meaning for the alien, though. Man *had* been incapable of conceptualizing any physical velocity faster than that of the speed of light in a vacuum. Man's mode of thought simply could not admit the alien possibility of instantaneous travel; therefore that science had been out of the question. Thought, not physics, had been the limiting factor.

And what of God? Was man incapable of conceptualizing *His* true nature? If so, Brother Paul's present mission was doomed.

"So you traded with us," Brother Paul said, returning to a simpler level of thought. "You needed fusion for power, and we needed matter transmission for transport. Our own hydrofusion generators are now monopolized for the tremendous power needed for the MT program."

"So it would seem. This is a very foolish course you are pursuing, but it seems as though all emerging cultures must pass through it. If rationality does not abate it, the exhaustion of resources does. Only through Transfer is interSpherical empire possible. Spherical regression otherwise presents a virtually absolute limit to the extent of any culture—as you will discover."

Again, Brother Paul clung to what he could. "Transfer?"

"With your aura, you do not know of Transfer?"

"I know neither aura nor Transfer. In fact I know nothing of your society."

"Your administrators did not inform the populace?"

"Apparently not. I'd like to know about you personally, too."

"Then I shall gladly explain. It has been long since any creature expressed personal interest in me." Antares paused, and for an instant Brother Paul saw the outline of the alien protoplasm, shimmering like a hovering soul. "Every living thing we know of has an aura, a field of life-force permeating it. Solarians term it the Kirlian aura—"

"Ah, that I have heard of!" Brother Paul said. "I believe it is the same as the aura described by Dr. Kilner, and later photographed by the Russian scientist Kirlian. But I understood it was merely an effect of water vapor in the vicinity of living bodies."

"Perhaps the water vapor is associated with the photographic or visual effects," Antares said. "But the aura itself is more than this. It cannot be detected by ordinary means, although certain machines can measure its imprint, and entities of intense auras can perceive other intense auras. I was a high-aura creature, and you are the highest-aura creature imaginable. Therefore our auras interact, and we perceive each other. You have no doubt perceived auras of others similarly, and supposed these to be flukes of your imagination."

"Maybe I have," Brother Paul agreed. There had been some strange phenomena in his past, now that he considered the matter in this light. Yet he was not satisfied. "Why *shouldn't* we perceive each other now, without the interaction of auras?"

"Because I am dead," Antares said.

Brother Paul had already become aware of the strangeness of this entity, so he took this statement in stride. He glanced at his watch again, noting that ten minutes and forty-nine seconds had elapsed since the setting of the counter. It had seemed longer. He fixed on a single facet, again. "You are really a ghost?"

"The ghost in the machine."

Brother Paul tried to organize his reactions, get his tongue in gear. "Actually, the human brain, with its mysterious separation of powers in its two hemispheres, has qualities that are obscure to our understanding. Nature had to have good reason for that seeming duplication. We know that the left hemisphere relates to the right side of the body, and handles abstract analytical thought and language functions, while the right hemisphere handles space patterns, imagery, music and artistic functions. Just as two eyes provide the basis for triangulation, hence depth perception, perhaps two brains multiply the human quality as well as quantity of thought." He shook his head. "But I am babbling. My point is that the hemispheric union is as yet imperfect. Crazy-seeming things spring from it, visions and hallucinations occur at times. So while it is possible that you are what you claim to be, the ghost of an alien creature, it is rather more likely that I am suffering a similar derangement—"

"Solarian Brother!" Antares protested. "Your aura is so strong, it enables manifestations that could not otherwise occur. Your divided brain *is* imperfect, vastly complicating your thinking processes, but I am not a phantasm of your imagination. I am an aura trapped in the mechanism of the mattermission unit. We did not know the units had this property, but of course no one has ever fathomed completely the technology of the Ancients from which both mattermission and Transfer derive."

What difference did it make, really, whether this creature was real or imaginary? He was certainly entertaining! "You said you were dead."

"My Sphere, seeking trade, Transferred the auras of its most suitable members to the bodies of sapient aliens of other Spheres, animating them," Antares explained. "I was lucky enough to find this host: a Solarian who had lost his own aura and become a member of the living dead, a soulless creature. I located the Solarian authorities after some difficulty and convinced them of my authenticity, but precious time had been lost. You see, the aura of a Transferee in an alien host fades at the rate of about one intensity a day, for reasons we do not yet understand, and when it drops to the sapient norm—"

"The alien soul becomes submerged by the host," Brother Paul finished with sudden insight. All of this was incredible, yet it had its own logic, like that of non-Euclidean geometry. In this day of non-relativistic physics, why not?

"True. My natural aura was ninety times the ordinary intensity, as measured by our calibration. That is very high. Not half as high as yours, however. So I had only three of your months to act, and more than half that period was exhausted by the time I made contact. Because your scientists needed time to construct the first mattermission unit, after they had been persuaded that it was even theoretically possible—"

"You faded away to nothing before you could return to Star Antares." Brother Paul said. What singular courage this alien had

had, to undertake such a mission! Traveling in spirit to an alien body, to convince people of a truth they knew was impossible —and giving his own life in the process. This creature must have had a good deal more than aura going for him; he had to have had intelligence, determination, and nerve. Brother Paul had thought his own mission special; now he saw that it was ordinary in comparison to that of Antares'.

"I faded down to sapient norm," Antares agreed. "There is no fading below that, except in illness or physical death. But my native identity was gone then, as the host-body dominated. Once the first mattermission unit was ready, the Solarians shipped my Solarian host to my home Sphere, together with a nuclear fusion expert, honoring the bargain I had made. But I was dead."

"Except that you *aren't* dead!"

"My aura was enhanced by the mattermission machine, and that returned my identity to me," Antares agreed. "But my host was gone; I could not exist outside this unit. The machine is now my host, and I am now its constant, as in your calculator. I cannot manifest at all unless evoked by someone like you with the interest and aura to make it possible. When you arrive at your destination—"

Brother Paul looked at his watch again. Still ten minutes, forty-nine seconds. He was certain now; no time at all had passed since Antares had appeared. He was in the process of suffering a potent hallucination. Maybe. "But if I can see you and hear you, others can too; we can open the capsule before it mattermits—"

"We are in mattermission now. Did you not comprehend?"

"Now? But I thought the process was instantaneous!"

"That it is, Solarian Brother."

Brother Paul mulled that over. An extended dialogue in zero time? Well, why not one more impossibility! "Who are these 'Ancients' you mentioned? Why don't *they* get you out of this fix?"

"They are extinct, as far as we know. They perished three million Solarian years ago, leaving only their phenomenal ruins."

"Ruins? But you said the mattermission equipment derived from—"

"Some few of their ruins have functioning components. Most of the advanced technology has been reconstituted from the far more advanced science of the Ancients by those contemporary species capable of recognizing the potential of what they discovered. There may be Ancient ruins in your own Sphere, but if your individuals did not recognize them for what they were, they may have been destroyed. Chief among these technological reconstitutions in other Spheres is Transfer—the means by which I came to Sphere Sol. That secret we will not share with you, for its value is measureless, and your species—please do not take umbrage —may not be mature enough to handle this knowledge safely."

Brother Paul suddenly realized that he liked this alien ghost, even if Antares were merely a figment of his own imagination. "I take no umbrage; I regard my own species with similar misgivings, at times. I suppose you may be considered a figment of my mind, or as you put it, of my aura. Yet you have provided me comfort and interest during a nervous period."

"Do not underestimate the capacities of aura, friend Solarian," Antares replied equably. "In my brief tenure in Solarian form I came to know some of the nature of your kind, alien as it is to my prior experience. Many of your mysteries are explicable in terms of aura, as you will know when you achieve aural science. Your water-divining merely reflects the aural interaction with hidden water or metals. Your 'faith healing' constitutes a limited exchange of auras, the well one augmenting the failing one. What you call telepathy is another aural phenomenon: the momentary overlapping of aural currents such as we experience at this moment. When an entity dies, his aura may dissipate explosively, like a supernova, flooding the environment for an instant, forcing sudden awareness upon those who are naturally attuned. Close friends, or entities with very similar aural types. Thus a sleeping person may suffer a vision at the instant of his friend's demise."

Antares vanished. Brother Paul jumped up, alarmed. "Antares!" he cried. But there was nothing except the treadle sewing machine.

Then he realized that the matter transmission was over. He had arrived. The alien aura could manifest only while the Ancient reconstituted equipment was in operation. When the machine was turned off, the constant was lost—as in his calculator.

He looked at his watch. Eleven minutes, fifteen seconds. Time was moving again; the infinite expansion of instantaneity had ceased. He was back in the real world, such as it was. Whichever world it was.

Brother Paul felt a poignant loss. "If my aura is as potent as you say, brother alien, I will summon you again," he promised aloud. "Antares, you have been a good companion, and we have much more to discuss. Maybe on my return hop . . ."

But whom was he fooling? He had suffered a hallucination in transit, as he understood some people did, in this manner soothing his extreme nervousness about the mattermission. Better to shut up about it.

"Farewell, alien friend," he murmured.

3

ACTION
(EMPRESS)

*The
Statement
Below
is
TRUE*

*The
Statement
Above
is
FALSE*

Brother Paul blinked in bright sunlight. He stood at the edge of a field of grain of an unfamiliar type. It could be a variety of wheat; Earth exported hybrid breeds of the basic cereals as fast as they could be developed, searching for the ideal match with alien conditions. There were so many variables of light and gravity and soil and climate that the only certain verification of a given type's viability was the actual harvest. This field looked healthy; the stalks were tall and green, reflecting golden at the tops, rippling attractively with the vagaries of breeze: a likely success. Of course mere appearance could be deceptive; the grains might turn out woody or bitter or even poisonous, or local fauna might infiltrate the field and consume the harvest in advance. In any event, it would be quite a job threshing by hand what wheat there was.

Not far distant rose a fair-sized mound. He was intrigued by the bright colors on one side of it. He walked out to inspect this curiosity. It turned out to be a compost pile formed from the refuse of the field: stalks and leaves shaped into a cup-shaped pile to catch and hold the rain, since water was necessary to promote decomposition.

Brother Paul smiled. He saw this mound as a living process of nature, returning to the soil the organic material that was no longer needed elsewhere, one of the great rejuvenating phenomena of existence. What better symbol could there be of true civilization in harmony with nature than a functioning compost pile? In a fundamental respect the compost did for life what the Holy Order of Vision was trying to do for mankind: restore it to its ideal state, forming fertile new soil for future generations. There could be no higher task for a man or a society than this!

The bright colors turned out to be small balloons nestling in the limited shade the mound provided. There were red, green, yellow, and blue ones, and shades between. Had some child left them here as an offering to the soil? This seemed unlikely, since the technology for making plastic balloons would hardly have been exported to this colony world in lieu of more vital processes. Had a child brought balloons from Earth, that child would hardly have left them carelessly in a field. Brother Paul put forth his hand to pick one up. It popped at his touch. It was nothing but a tenuous membrane, hardly more substantial than a soap bubble. No wonder these were in shade; mere sunlight would wipe them out! Maybe they were an alien exudation from the compost, the gas inflating a colored film. Pretty, but of limited duration. One had to expect new things on new worlds, little things as well as important ones.

Time was passing. No welcoming party? He saw no one here. Didn't they care about the shipment? Did they know about it? Apparently these transmissions were somewhat random, at the convenience of the crowded schedule of MT. With a thousand colony planets and perhaps five major settlements per world to keep track of—well, that was about five billion people, over half of Earth's pre-exodus population. Planet Tarot was lucky to get any follow-up at all! So this shipment had probably caught the colonists by surprise. The impact of arrival would have alerted them, however, and they would hustle over to unload the capsule before it shuttled back to Earth.

Should he give them a head start by carrying out some of the equipment himself? The fact that he was here on a specialized mission did not prevent him from making himself useful, and he could use the exercise.

He turned—and spied something beyond the capsule receiver building. There was a stone, a block—no, a throne, there amid the wheat! A girl was seated upon it, a lovely, fair-haired creature, a veritable princess. What was she doing here?

He started toward her. But as he did, the lady rose and fled through the field, her queenly robe flowing behind her. "Wait!" he called. "I'm from Earth!" But she continued to run, and she was surprisingly fleet. Obviously a healthy girl.

Brother Paul gave up the chase. She was frightened, and he would gain nothing by pursuing her, though he could surely catch her if he tried. This whole situation seemed even more peculiar, following his experience with the alien ghost.

He stopped short. "Key Three!" he exclaimed. The lady on the throne in the field of wheat—the card numbered the third Major Arcanum in the Tarot deck, titled the Empress.

This was Planet Tarot, where real cards had been animated. But he had not anticipated anything this soon, this literal!

Was this another ghostly manifestation? Had it all been in his mind? If so, his judgment on this mission was already suspect. What would the recorder's playback show? He wished he could peek, but of course he had no projector, and did not understand his bracelet's operation anyway. Regardless, the lady had certainly seemed genuine, and most attractive despite (because of?) her timidity.

A planet where Tarot images became literal. Brother Paul paused, thinking about that, stimulated by this sudden evidence of the fact. He had sawed pine wood, as part of his chores for the Order, and during the sometimes tedious hand labor his mind, as was its wont, had conjured a parallel between pine and the Tarot. The wood was light and white outside, easy to saw and handle, easy to burn, but not of too much substance. The heart of pine, in contrast, was rock-hard and dense, saturated with orange-colored sap. It would last for decades without decaying, and the termites, whose favorite food was soft pine, would not touch the heart-wood. It burned so fiercely that it soon destroyed metal grates and brick fireplaces. The queen of firewoods! The Tarot seemed like that: superficially interesting, the pictures lending themselves readily to interpretation by amateurs. But if one delved deeply enough, one encountered the heart-of-Tarot—and that was deep and dense and difficult, stretching the mind through the fourth and fifth dimensions of thought and time. Few people could handle it, but for those who persevered, the rewards were profound and lasting. Brother Paul regarded himself as on the verge between white wood and orange wood, a novice trembling at the portal of True Meaning, hardly knowing what he would discover ahead. Would he make progress, here on Planet Tarot?

Well, the throne of the Empress remained. He could check this out very quickly. He walked up to it, glancing around at the landscape as he did. This was a beautiful place, with what appeared to be a volcanic mountain rising just beyond the field, and near it a ridge of brightly colored rock. The air was warm and the gravity so close to that of Earth that he felt no discomfort at all. He would never have taken this for a haunted planet!

There was no doubt about it. This was a genuine Tarot Empress throne. Or something close to it. It was fashioned of dense, polished wood rather than stone; he was aware that there might not be suitable stone here. One side of it was carved with the design of a six-sided shield bearing a carving of a two-headed eagle. He could not safely assume such symbolism to be coincidence, but neither could he be sure it was not. So there was doubt after all. There always was.

Sturdy wooden pillars supported a pavilion roof shading the throne. A necessary precaution; even the fairest empress would suffer if she sat all day in the direct glare of the sun. Still . . .

A horrendous growl startled him. He jumped, orienting on the sound, and saw a huge, sinuous, catlike creature charging at him. The thing seemed to have five legs. Maybe its tail was prehensile.

From the lady to the tiger! Brother Paul dodged around the throne. The creature maneuvered to follow him. Catlike, but no feline; the articulation of its limbs was alien in some obscure but impressive manner. It was not that they bent backward at the joints; that did not appear to be the case. But the bending had a different aspect—

No time to cogitate on that now! This thing must mass 150 kilograms—twice Brother Paul's own weight—and there was little doubt of its intent. It regarded him either as an enemy or as prey!

It would have helped if the authorities had advised him of such details of the planetary ecology. But probably they hadn't known. He should have remained inside the capsule until a colonist-guide came for him; he had only himself to blame for this difficulty.

Brother Paul dodged around the throne again, but the tiger-thing had anticipated him. It bounded around the other way, reversing course with eerie ease, and abruptly confronted him, its forelegs outstretched.

Brother Paul suffered one of those flashes that are supposed to come to people facing sudden death. The creature's extremities were not claws or hoofs; instead, they resembled leather gloves or mittens. They were forked, with the larger part hooking around in a semi-circle like a half-closed hand, but without fingers; the smaller part was like an opposable thumb. The dexterity of this "hand" could in no way approach that of the human appendage, and the calloused pads on the outside edges showed that this was primarily a running foot rather than a manipulative hand. Yet a hoof or paw would have been much better for running! What was the purpose in this wrenchlike structure?

The tiger pounced at him, its strange feet extended as though to box him, except that it was not his torso that was the target. He jumped, high and to the side, so that the creature missed him. The animal's forefeet jerked back, while the clublike hind feet struck forward. It actually landed on its hind feet, flipping over backward.

Had he remained in place, Brother Paul realized, those forefeet would have hooked his ankles, and those hind feet would have hit him with sufficient force to break his legs. Crippled, he would have been easy prey. This was not a type of attack known on Earth, but it was surely as brutally effective as teeth or tusks or claws.

The tiger wheeled about, recovering its posture with the help of its prehensile tail, and sprang again. This time it leaped higher, learning with dismaying rapidity. But Brother Paul did not jump again. He spun to face away from it, dropping simultaneously to his knees, and caught its right foreleg in the crook of his right arm. Then he rolled forward, hauling on that captive leg. This was *ippon seoi nage,* the one-arm shoulder throw—the first judo technique he had ever tried on an animal, terrestrial or alien. And with luck, the last!

The tiger's hind feet came forward in its bone-breaking reflex. They glanced jarringly off Brother Paul's back and right shoulder, and one clipped his head. Those hind feet were like sledgehammers; he saw a bright flash of light as the optic region of his brain took the shock.

He had tried the wrong technique. Since the tiger normally caught hold of its prey's limbs and broke them, he had merely set himself up for the strike by holding the creature. A man would have been thrown over Brother Paul's back, but the tiger's balance and torque were different. He was lucky it had not knocked him out; if he made another mistake, that luck was unlikely to hold.

Still, he retained a hold on its foreleg. He hauled on it and tried to roll again. This time the creature rolled with him, for its momentum was spent and it had not been able to get back to its feet. It flipped onto its back, and Brother Paul started to apply a hold-down—but realized he would then be at the mercy of those battering hind legs.

Instead, he flipped about and caught hold of the nearest hind leg. Then he leaned back, extended both of his own feet, and clamped his knees around that limb. This was a leglock that would have been illicit in judo, but what were human legality in a life-and-death struggle with an alien creature? This was not at all the type of situation he had anticipated when he had joined the Order! Brother Paul arched his back, bucked his hips forward, and drew on the captive leg, putting pressure on the joint. He had no idea whether this technique would work on such a creature, but felt it was worth a try. A man would have screamed in agony at about this time . . .

The tiger screamed in agony. Startled by this unexpected success, Brother Paul let go, just as he would for a human opponent who tapped out, admitting defeat. Too late, he remembered that this was no human sportsman, but a creature out to break his bones. Now he was in for it!

But the tiger had had enough. It rolled to its feet, steadied itself with its tail, and leaped away as rapidly as it had come. Brother Paul stood and watched it bound across the rippling sea of wheat, relieved. He hadn't wanted to hurt it, but had thought he would have no other choice. He was bruised, disheveled, and a bit lightheaded, but basically intact. It could have been worse—much worse!

Motion attracted his eye. People were approaching: half a dozen men. They were armed, carrying long spears—no, these were tridents, like elaborate pitchforks, excellent for stabbing an animal while holding it at bay. Effective against a man, too.

Somewhat nervously, Brother Paul awaited the party's approach. This, too, was not precisely the welcome he had anticipated.

As they came closer he saw that these men were being careful rather than aggressive. They looked all about, weapons ever at the ready, as though afraid something hazardous to bones might come bounding in.

"Hello," Brother Paul called. "I'm from Earth, on a special mission."

The men glanced at each other meaningfully. "What is your faith?" one asked.

"I am Brother Paul of the Holy Order of Vision. However, I'm not here to join your society. I am supposed to—" But he broke off, uncertain of their reaction.

Again, the exchange of glances. "Vision," the spokesman said approvingly. He was a heavyset, black-haired man with fairly deep frown-lines about his mouth that showed even when he was trying to smile, as now. "A good selection. But I did not know it was a warrior cult."

Warrior cult? "The Holy Order of Vision is a pacifistic denomination, seeking always the route of least—"

"Yet you fought the Breaker."

The Breaker. A fitting description! "Self-preservation compelled me. I don't believe I damaged the creature."

A third exchange of glances. "The question is, how is it that the Breaker did not damage *you?* We must always travel in armed parties to fend off its savagery, during that part of the day when it is present."

Evidently they knew the routine of the Breaker, and this was its office hour. That would explain why they had not rushed up to greet him instantly; they had had to organize their troop and proceed with due caution. "I suspect I was pretty lucky," Brother Paul said. "I managed to frighten it away just when I thought I'd lost."

"Even so," the spokesman said dubiously—his face was very

good at dour expressions—"your God surely watches over you well."

"My God is the same as your God," Brother Paul said modestly —and was amazed at the reaction this brought. Evidently he had committed a *faux pas.*

"We shall introduce ourselves," the man said, gruffly easing the awkwardness. "I am the Reverend Siltz of the Second Church Communist, spokesman for this party by consent of the participants."

Brother Paul's face never even twitched. After Antares the gelatinous alien, a living Tarot Empress, and the Breaker, what was a little anomaly like a Communist Church? "Glad to make your acquaintance, Reverend Siltz," he said. The man did not offer to shake hands, so Brother Paul merely nodded affirmatively as he spoke.

The man to the Reverend's right spoke: "Janson, Adventist." And, in turn, the others: "Bonly, Mason." "Appermet, Yoga." "Smith, Swedenborgian." "Miller, Vegan Vegetarian."

"We were expecting you," Reverend Siltz said gruffly. "We were not informed of your precise time of arrival, but the matter is of some concern to us." Here one of the others stifled a snort, reminding Brother Paul again of the intricate currents that flowed beneath this troubled surface. What had he gotten into?

Reverend Siltz scowled, but continued, "Church Communist was selected by lot in accordance with the Covenant to encounter you initially and proffer hospitality for the duration of your mission. This denotes no comment on the validity of your mission, or our opinion of same. You are of course free to choose an alternate accommodation, as you please. The Order of Vision has no station here."

Currents indeed! Had the lot chosen an enemy to host him, or was this merely excessive formality? He would have to navigate his shallow craft carefully, until he knew more of this peculiar situation. "I am pleased to accept your offer, Reverend, hoping my presence will not inconvenience you or cause you embarrassment."

Now Siltz made an honest smile. "We know of your Order. Hosting you will be a privilege."

So acceptance had been the right decision. Maybe the man's gruffness had been in anticipation of demurral, so that he would not lose face when Brother Paul did the expected. But it could also have stemmed from some other factor, such as this evident individuality of gods, as though each religion had its own separate deity. Brother Paul made a silent prayer that he would not make too many wrong decisions here. How fortunate that the reputation of his Order extended even to distant planets! Of course this colony, like all the others in the human sphere, could not be more than four years old, five at the most, so the colonists would have carried their knowledge of religious sects with them from Earth. So this was really no miracle.

Reverend Siltz swung about to orient on the capsule receiver building, his motion and manner reminding Brother Paul not too subtly of the Breaker. "Now we must unload, before it mattermits out. Is it a good shipment?"

"Sewing machines, spinning wheels, stoves," Brother Paul said as they walked toward it. "Carding tools, axes—"

"Good, good!" Reverend Siltz said. "They have dowered you well." There was a murmur of agreement, suprising Brother Paul. He suffered a two-level thought: first, the confirmation that he was not completely welcome here, so had been "dowered," as though he were an unpretty bride requiring a monetary inducement to make him and his mission palatable; and second, the reaction to the shipment. Of course such artifacts were useful, but did these colonists have no yearnings for the more advanced products of civilization?

The next two hours were spent unloading. It was heavy work, but no one stinted; all the men were husky, and Reverend Siltz applied himself as vigorously as any of them. Yet throughout, Brother Paul was aware of a certain diffidence, directed not at him but occurring among the colonists themselves, as though not one of them trusted the others completely. What was the problem here?

At last the job was done. "Good, good!" Reverend Siltz said with satisfaction as he viewed the equipment piled somewhat haphazardly at the edge of the wheatfield. "Tomorrow the wagon comes." They covered each item with one of the light plastic tarpaulins provided by the shipper, and organized the return march.

As they passed the throne, Brother Paul wanted to inquire about the girl he had seen there, but hesitated; it could be that female colonists were not permitted direct contact with strange men. That would explain why she had fled, and make any question about her presence inappropriate. In a society as cult-ridden as this one seemed to be, the status of women was open to question.

Behind the ridge was a village, not much more than two kilometers from the capsule receiver. Brother Paul could have run it in six minutes or so, had he known where to go, but he doubted that the girl could have had time to arrive here, alert the village, and send this party back before he finished with the Breaker. Reverend Siltz must have been on the way the moment the capsule had arrived. Planet Tarot evidently had no electronic communications or motorized transportation, so foot power and observation were important here, just as they were on the better part of Earth, now.

A sturdy stockade of wooden posts surrounded the village, each post polished and handsome. Brother Paul had learned something about the various kinds of wood during his Order tenure, but had never seen wood like this. "The heart of heart-of-pine," he murmured.

The houses inside were of the same kind of wood, constructed of notched logs calked with mud. Their roofs were sod, in most cases, with thick grass growing on them, and even small flowers. Primitive but tight, he was sure. Here and there, in the shade, were more clusters of the colored bubbles he had noted by the compost pile. So they could not be purely a product of organic decomposition.

"What are these?" Brother Paul asked, stooping to touch one. It did not pop, so he picked it up carefully—and then it popped. Evidently some of the bubbles were stronger than others.

"Tarot Bubbles," Reverend Siltz responded. "They grow everywhere, especially at night. They are of no value, like mildew or weeds. Clever children can make castles of them on cloudy days. We keep them out of our houses so they will not contaminate our food."

How quickly a pretty novelty became a nuisance! But Brother Paul could appreciate the colonists' desire to keep proliferating growths away from their food; the residues might be harmless, but why gamble? Most germs on Earth were harmless too, but those that were not were often devastating.

In the center of the village was a pile of wood. All around it people were working. Men were sawing planks, or rather scraping them, forming mounds of curly shavings. Children gathered these shavings by armfuls, depositing them in patterns near seated women. The women seemed to be carding the shavings, stretching out the fibers of the wood so that they resembled cotton. This was some wood!

Reverend Siltz halted, and the other members of the party stopped with him, bowing their heads in silent respect. "Tree of Life, God of Tarot, we thank thee," Siltz said formally, and made a genuflection to the pile of wood.

Tree of Life? God of Tarot? Brother Paul knew the Tree of Life as the diagram of meanings associated with the Cabala, the ancient Hebrew system of number-alchemy. And the God of Tarot was what he had come to seek, but he had not expected it to be a pile of wood. What did this mean?

Reverend Siltz turned to him as the other men departed. "We are of many faiths, here at Colony Tarot. But on one thing we agree: the Tree is the source of our well-being. We do not feel that our own gods object to the respect we pay to the Tree."

"Does this resemble the Great World Tree of Norse legend, called Yggdrasil?" Brother Paul inquired. "Its roots extended into three realms—"

"There are Norse sects here that make that analogy," Siltz agreed. "But the majority of us regard it as a purely planetary expression and gift of God. Indeed, we seek to ascertain which God *is* the Tree."

"You see God as—as a physical object? A tree? Wood?"

"Not precisely. We must cooperate for survival, and only through the Tree can we accomplish this. Thus the Tree of Life is the God of Tarot." He formed a rare smile. "I perceive you are confused. Come, eat, rest at my abode, and I shall explain as well as I am permitted by the Covenant."

Brother Paul nodded, not trusting himself to speak lest he commit some additional *faux pas* in his ignorance. This nascent planetary culture was far stranger than he had anticipated.

4

POWER
(EMPEROR)

*Before the beginning of years
There came to the making of man
Time with a gift of tears;
Grief with a glass that ran;
Pleasure, with pain for leaven;
Summer, with flowers that fell;
Remembrance fallen from heaven,
And madness risen from hell; . . .
. . . wrought with weeping and laughter,
And fashioned with loathing and love,
With life before and after
And death beneath and above,*

    . . .

*His speech is a burning fire;
With his lips he travaileth;
In his heart is a blind desire,
In his eyes foreknowledge of death;
He weaves, and is clothed with derision;
Sows, and he shall not reap;
His life is a watch or a vision
Between a sleep and a sleep.*

ALGERON CHARLES SWINBURNE
Atalanta In Calydon

The Reverend Siltz's hut was exactly like the others, distinguished only by the hammer-and-sickle on its hewn-timber door. It was small, but cozy and well-ordered inside. The walls and ceiling were paneled with rough-sawn wood whose grain was nevertheless quite striking: the wood of the local Tree of Life, again. A wooden ladder led up the back wall to the attic. There were no windows, only air vents, slanted to exclude rain or flowing water. In the center of the room, dominating it, was the stove.

"Ah, an airtight side-drafter," Brother Paul commented appreciatively. "With cooking surfaces and attached oven. A most compact and efficient design."

"You know stoves?" Reverend Siltz inquired, suddenly more friendly.

"I get along well with mechanical things," Brother Paul said. "I would not deem myself an expert, but we do use wood at our Vision Station, and it was my task to gather the fuel from the forest. I admire a good design, if only because I deem it a shame to waste what God has grown." Yet here were these people, burning the wood of the tree they worshipped. Oh, he was getting curious about the ramifications of that!

A woman stepped forward, middle-aged and pleasant. He had not noticed her because the stove had caught his attention —which could be taken as a sign of his present confused state. Her hair was dark brown and plaited in such a way as to resemble the bark of a tree. Now Brother Paul realized that he had seen similar hairdos on several of the other women working outside. An odd effect, but not unattractive. Another salute to the Tree of Life?

"My wife," Reverend Siltz said, and she nodded. Brother Paul had not yet seen any firm indication that the women had equal status with the men on this planet, but knew better than to make any assumptions at this early stage. "My son is at work; we may see him this evening." There was another curious inflection; either the Reverend had a number of peculiar concerns, or Brother Paul was exaggerating the meanings of inconsequential nuances of expression.

"Your house is small by Earth standards," Brother Paul said carefully. "I fear my presence will crowd you."

The Reverend unfolded a bench from the wall. "We shall make

do. I regret we have no better facilities. We are as yet a frontier colony."

"I was not criticizing your facilities," Brother Paul said quickly. "I did not come here for comfort, but I would hardly call this privation. You have an admirably compact house."

The wife climbed the ladder and disappeared into the loft. "It is her sleep-shift," Siltz explained. "She must help guard the wood by night, so she must prepare herself now. This is the reason we have space for you to stay."

"Guard the wood?" Brother Paul asked, perplexed.

Reverend Siltz brought out some long, limber strips of wood and set about weaving them into something like a blanket. "Brother Paul, wood is paramount: Our houses are made from it and insulated throughout by it; it provides our furniture, our weapons, our heat. In our fashion we worship wood, because our need for it is so pressing. We must obtain it from the forest far away, and haul it by hand with guards against the predators of the range. We dare not pitch our villages closer to the forest because of the Animations; they permeate that region in season, but are rare here. The other villages of this planet are similarly situated, so as to be removed from the threat. We have little commerce with the other settlements. In winter the snows come eight meters deep."

"Eight meters deep!" Brother Paul repeated, incredulous.

"Insulating us from the surface temperature of minus fifty degrees Celsius. Those who exhaust their supply of fuel wood before the winter abates must burn their furniture and supporting struts or perish, and if they burn so much that the weight of the snow collapses their houses, they perish."

"Can't they tunnel through the snow to reach the next house, so as to share with their neighbors?"

"Yes, if their neighbors happen to be of the same faith." The man frowned, and Brother Paul suspected another complication of this society. Families of differing faiths would not share their resources, even to save lives? "Those who take more than their appointed share of wood imperil the lives of others. There is no execution on this planet except for the theft or wasting of wood. The Tree of Life may not be abused!" The Reverend's face was becoming red; he caught himself and moderated his tone. "We have a difficult situation here; this is a good world, but a harsh one. We are of fragmented faiths and can hardly trust each other, let alone comprehend each other's ludicrous modes of worship. This is the reason your own mission is significant. You shall decide which God is the true God of Tarot."

Brother Paul was beginning to accept the tie-in between God and wood. Without wood, these people would perish, and they knew it. Yet this need did not seem to account for their evident fetishism. On Earth, people needed water to survive, and fresh water was scarce, but they did not worship it. "That *is* my mission, presumptuous as it may be. I gather you do not approve of it."

Siltz glanced up from his weaving, alarmed. "Did I say that?"

"No, it is merely an impression I have. You do not need to discuss the matter if you do not wish to."

"I would like very much to discuss it," Siltz said. "But the Covenant forbids it. If my attitude conveys itself to you, then I am not being a proper host, and must arrange other lodging for you."

Which surely would not be politic! "Probably I am jumping to conclusions; I apologize," Brother Paul said.

"No, you are an intelligent and sensitive man. I shall endeavor to resolve the question without violating the Covenant. I do oppose your presence here, but this does not in any way reflect on your person or integrity. I merely believe this is a question that cannot be answered in this manner. You will necessarily discover a God that conforms to your personal precepts, but whose conformance to the actual God may be coincidental. I would rather have the issue remain in doubt, than have it decided erroneously. But I am a member of the minority. You were summoned, and the lot, in its wisdom, has brought you to my house, and I shall facilitate your mission exactly as though I supported it. This *my* God requires of me."

"I do not think our concepts of God can be very far apart," Brother Paul said. "I find your attitude completely commendable. But let me qualify one aspect: it is Earth that sent me here, not Colony Tarot. We of Earth are concerned as to whether the God of Tarot is genuine, or merely someone's fancy. We too are wary lest a person committed to a single view be blind to the truth, whatever that may be. I doubt that I am worthy of this mission, but it is my intent to eliminate my personal bias as much as possible and ascertain that truth, though I may not like it. I don't see that you colonists need to accept any part of my report, or let it affect your way of life. In fact I am uncertain about your references to a number of gods. Surely there is only one God."

Reverend Siltz smiled ruefully. "In reassuring me, you place me at the verge of compromising my integrity. I must acquaint you in more detail with our religious situation here, asking you to make allowance for any lack of objectivity you may perceive. We are a colony of schisms, of splinter sects. Many of us were aware of the special effects of Planet Tarot before we emigrated from Earth, and each of us saw in these effects the potential realization of God—our particular, specialized concepts of God, if you will. This appeal seems to have been strongest to the weakest sects, or at any rate, the smallest numerically. Thus we have few Roman Catholics, Mohammedans, Buddhists, or Confucians, but many Rosicrucians, Spiritualists, Moonies, Gnostics, Flaming Sworders—"

"Flaming Sworders? Is that a Tarot image—I mean the card type of Tarot?"

"Not so. I apologize for using unseemly vernacular. It is my prejudice against these faiths, which you must discount. *The Flaming Sword* is the publication of the Christian Apostolic Church in Zion, whose guiding precept is that the Earth is flat, not spherical."

"But how, then, could they emigrate to another planet? They would not believe other planets existed!"

"You must ask a member of that cult; perhaps he can provide you with a verisimilitudinous rationale. I fear my own mind is closed, but I am forbidden by the Covenant to criticize the faiths of others in your presence. Let us simply say that with faith, all things are possible. I'm sure you appreciate my position."

"I do," Brother Paul agreed. For all his gruffness, the Reverend was a sincere, comprehensible man, and a good host. "I once heard a child's definition: 'faith is believing what you know ain't so.' That now seems apropos." He paused. "Um, no offense intended, but I had not expected to encounter your own Church, either. What are its precepts?"

"I regret I can answer you only vaguely. I have vowed by the Tree of Life to make no effort to prejudice your mind by contamination with my own particular faith."

The man's attitude was coming through fairly clearly, however! "Because of the Covenant?"

"Precisely. I will not claim to agree with the Covenant, but I am bound by it. The majority feel that your continuing objectivity is crucial. I will only say that the guiding principles of Church Second Comm are essentially humanist, and that we maintain only symbolic connection to the atheistic Communists of Earth. We are *theist* Communists."

"Ah, yes," Brother Paul said, disconcerted. God-fearing Communists—and the Reverend was obviously sincere. Yet this was no more anomalous in theory than God-fearing Capitalists. "I had the impression that Planet Tarot was an English-language colony; are the religions represented here primarily Western?"

"They are. About eighty per cent derive from Occidental Christian origins; the rest are scattered. In that sense, most believe in some form of the Christ, as you do; that is why I said your Order is a good one for our purpose, though I question that purpose. You will likely find a Christian God, but you have no local Church to cater to, so you are relatively objective. The reputation of your Order has preceded you; Visionists are known not to interfere with other faiths, while yet remaining true to their own faith. I believe you will be approved."

"I had not realized that my mission here was subject to local approval," Brother Paul said, a bit dryly. "What will they do if they don't like me? Ship me back to Earth?" There was, of course, no way for the colonists to do that.

"There are those whose faith is such as to destroy infidels," Siltz said. "We believe our own village is secure, but we cannot speak for other villages. We shall, of course, protect you to the limit of our means—but it is better that we stand united in this matter."

"Yes, I appreciate that." Brother Paul shook his head ruefully. Destroy infidels? That had connotations of fanatic murder! What nest of vipers had he mattermitted into? He had been warned about none of this; obviously the authorities on Earth knew little of the social phenomena of their colonies. He could not afford to rely on his limited briefings. "Yet if most sects here believe in the Christian God—who is also the Jewish and Mohammedan God, whether termed YHVH or Allah—why should there be any need to qualify Him further?"

"This is the question I have been trying to answer," Reverend Siltz said. "We are an exceedingly jealous conglomerative culture, here on Planet Tarot. Your interpretation of God surely differs somewhat from mine, and both of ours differ from that of the Church of Atheism. Who is to say which sect most truly reflects God's will? There must be one group among us that God favors more than the others, although He tolerates the others for the sake of that one—and that is the one we must discover. Perhaps God has dictated the savagery of our winter climate, forcing us to seek Him more avidly, as the God of the Jews brought privation upon them to correct their erring ways. We all depend on the largesse of the Tree of Life, and so we must ultimately worship the God of the Tree, even if we don't like that God, or the sect which is that God's chosen. Whether we call Him The God, or merely One among many, is of little moment; we must address Him as He dictates. We shall do so. But first we must ascertain objectively the most proper aspect of that God."

Phew! The colonists were taking this matter much more seriously than did the scholars back on Earth. "I really cannot undertake to do that," Brother Paul said cautiously. "To me, God is All; He favors no particular sect. The Holy Order of Vision is not a sect in that sense; we seek only for the truth that is God, and feel that the form is irrelevant. While we honor Jesus Christ as the Son of God, we also honor the Buddha, Zoroaster, and the other great religious figures; indeed, we are *all* children of God. So we seek only to know whether God *does* manifest here; we do not seek to channel Him, and would not presume to pass upon the merits of any religious sect."

"Well spoken! Yet I think God Himself will be the final arbiter. He will make known His will in His fashion, and you—according to the opinion of the colony majority, which I question—shall reflect that will. God is power; none of us can stand against that, nor would we wish to."

Brother Paul was not certain he had established any solid community of concept with the Reverend, but found the discussion stimulating. Still, it was time to get more practical. "I would like to know more about your geography," he said. "Particularly where the Animations take place."

"We shall show you that tomorrow. Animations are erratic, but generally occur in the oasis three kilometers north of here. We shall have to select guards for you."

"Oh, I don't require—"

"We value your safety, Brother Paul. If you should die within an Animation, as so many do, not only would we be bereft of our answer, we should be in bad repute back on Earth."

Sobering thoughts! The Reverend Mother Mary had warned him that religious scholars had lost their minds or died exploring this phenomenon; this was the confirmation. Still, he protested, "I would not want you to be in bad repute, but—"

He was interrupted by Siltz's snort of laughter at the notion that planetary repute was more important to him than his own life. "But I understand that predatory animals avoid Animations."

"They do. But what protects you from the Animations themselves?"

"As I understand it, these are merely controlled visions —visible imagination. There would, of course, be no physical—"

Reverend Siltz shook his head emphatically. "They *are* physical! And it will be a physical God you meet, whether he be valid or invalid. You will see."

Physical imagination? There had to be some sort of confusion here! Of course there had been suggestions of this in his briefing on Earth, but he had tended to dismiss such notions as exaggerations. "I am afraid I don't—"

The Reverend raised a hand. "You will ascertain this for yourself in due course. I do not wish to violate the spirit of the Covenant, though I fear I have already compromised the letter of it. Now we must go before the storm comes."

Even as the man spoke, Brother Paul heard the imperative rumble of thunder. "Where are we going?"

"To the communal lunch. It is more efficient than home cooking, and provides for a fairer allocation of food, so we do it in summer." Naturally a Communist would feel that way! "Storm time is good eating time, since we cannot then work outside."

"Your wife—isn't she coming too?"

"She is not. She eats at another shift, as does my son. I am relieved of my community labors for the duration of your stay; my labor is to attend to you. Now I must see that you are properly fed. Come, I have delayed too long. I neglect my responsibility. We must hurry."

They hurried. Outside, Brother Paul saw the ponderously looming clouds coming in over the lake from the east, so dense that they seemed like bubbles of lava in the sky. By some freak of the local system, the wind was coming from right angles, from the north, and it looked as though rain were already falling on the wheatfield to the west. The clouds, then, must be only the most visible portion of the storm; the outer swirls of it were already upon the village. Indeed, now he spied flashes of color—Tarot Bubbles borne on the wind, popping frequently but in such great numbers that they decorated the sky. What a pretty effect!

"Too late," Reverend Siltz said. "Yet I am remiss if I do not bring you to the others. We shall have to use the cups."

"I can stand a little rain," Brother Paul said. He rather liked bold storms; they showed the power of nature vividly.

But the man was already diving back into the house. "It is not merely water," he called from inside. "Bigfoot lurks in rain and snow."

Bigfoot? Brother Paul knew of the legends back on Earth of Yeti, Sasquatch, Abominable Snowman, Skunk Ape, and Bugbear; in fact he was somewhat of a fan of Bigfoot. With the cultural and technological regression Earth had suffered as a result of the depopulation of emigration, these legends had increased in number and force. He believed that most sightings of huge manlike monsters were merely distortions of straggling, perhaps ill human beings. An unkempt, ragged, wild-haired, dirty and desperate man could be a sight to frighten anyone, particularly when he was glimpsed only at dusk as he skulked in his search for food. Whether any nonhuman monsters existed—well, who could say? But Brother Paul hoped they did; it would certainly make Earth more interesting.

Reverend Siltz emerged with an armful of panels. Quickly he assembled two wooden hemispheres, each about a meter in diameter and girt by wicked-looking wooden spikes. Odd cups! Did this relate symbolically to the storm? Water, the Cups of the Tarot?

"You set this frame on your shoulders, and strap it under your arms," Siltz explained, helping Brother Paul into one. "When the storm breaks, angle forward into it and you will be protected. Do not let the wind catch inside the cup; it could lift you off the ground. If Bigfoot comes, use the spikes to drive him—it—off." Siltz evidently was reminding himself that the monster was inhuman. "Remember, I will be beside you." And the Reverend donned his own contraption.

The umbrellalike dome came down to circle Brother Paul's shoulders, greatly reducing visibility. He wanted to get along with his host, but this was ridiculous!

Reverend Siltz led the way across the turf, around the now-deserted wood pile (except for two guards armed with tridents) toward a larger building on top of a gentle hill. Despite the cumbersome containers, they made good progress.

There were a few more minor rumbles of thunder, superfluous reminders of the intensification of the storm. The sheet of water was now within a kilometer, churning the surface of the lake with such force that no horizon was apparent there, just splash. That hardly mattered; Brother Paul could not see well anyway because of the interference of the wooden cup. So he looked at his feet and at those of his companion, and marched along, feeling somewhat like a tank with legs, while his thoughts returned to Bigfoot. Could there be a similar creature here on Planet Tarot? Or was this merely frontier superstition? With all these fragmentary religious cults, it would not be surprising to discover strong beliefs in the supernatural. Still, if there *were* a—

A sudden, quintessential crack of thunder virtually knocked him off his feet. Never before had he felt such a shock; deafened and dazed, he stood staring at the ground, feeling his hair shifting nervously, and an odd tingling all over his body. The air was electrically charged, and himself too! There would surely be more lightning strikes close by, and he didn't like it. Those had been true words, about the rigorous conditions of this planet! No wooden shields could protect them from this!

Reverend Siltz was gesturing beneath his own shield, pointing urgently forward. Yes, indeed! Brother Paul was eager to get under proper cover!

The rain struck. It was like an avalanche crushing down the cup. Rain? These were hailstones, balls of ice up to a centimeter in diameter. They rapped the shield imperatively, small but hard. No, he would not have wanted to go bareheaded among these icy bullets!

A gust of wind whipped a barrage into his legs and tugged at his shield. Quickly Brother Paul reoriented it to fend off the thrust, for indeed this storm had power.

The hail thinned to sleet, then to water. Now he was certain; he did carry a literal cup to protect him from the onslaught of water. Whether the colonists used Tarot symbolism consciously or unconsciously he could not say, but use it they did.

The field was now a river, a centimeter deep. Colored Tarot Bubbles bobbed along on it, seeming to pop as he looked at them. Probably it was the other way around: his eye was attracted to them as they popped. The surviving ones added a surrealistic luster to the scene.

Reverend Siltz brushed close. "Get out of the channel. Follow the ridges." Brother Paul saw that he was walking in a slight depression. No wonder his feet were splashing! He moved to the side, finding better footing.

"Bigfoot is near," Siltz cried. "More fast!" And he began to run.

More fast. So the language reverted some under pressure. This was no joke; the man was alarmed. Brother Paul followed, wondering how the Reverend knew which direction to go. The rain obscured everything and showed no sign of slackening. The flash-rivers fed into the lake now, broadening out to obscure the normal fringe of the lake; all was water, below. The hailstones on the ground were turning into slush. But this business about Bigfoot—

Then he saw the footprint.

It was like that of a man, but half a meter long. The creature who had made this print, if it were similarly proportioned throughout, had to be triple the mass of a man. Two hundred twenty-five kilograms!

He felt a thrill of discovery—and of apprehension. This was a fresh print, only seconds old; already it was washing out. *There really was a Bigfoot here*—and it was within two or three meters of him!

Reverend Siltz grabbed his arm under the cup. "On!" he cried, his voice colored by something very like fear.

Brother Paul's curiosity about the monster warred against his common sense. The latter won. He plunged on. This was hardly the occasion to tangle with a two-hundred-kilo brute!

The water buffeted them, trying to twist the cups about. But the turf remained firm, and in due course they hove into the shelter of the community kitchen. Their legs were wet, but that didn't seem to matter.

"You exposed our guest to Bigfoot?" the guard at the door muttered to Reverend Siltz, holding his trident ready against the storm.

The Communist did not answer, but pushed on in. Brother Paul followed. "Actually, I'd like to meet Bigfoot," he said to the guard. "It was the lightning that scared me." But the man did not smile.

Other people were in the building, going about their assorted businesses, but there were no hearty welcomes. Reverend Siltz ignored all except those wearing the hammer-and-sickle emblem of his Church. Nevertheless, he guided Brother Paul to a table where several men of differing denominations sat. Or so Brother

Paul assumed from the fact that the emblems on their clothing were dissimilar.

"It is necessary that you assure these people I have not tried to compromise your objectivity," the Reverend grumbled. "I shall fetch soup."

Brother Paul seated himself and looked around. "I so assure you," he said with a smile. "I embarrassed him with a number of questions that forced him to invoke the Covenant, but he withstood the onslaught. I am wet but uncompromised."

The man across from Brother Paul nodded affably. He was middle-aged and bald, with smile-lines in lieu of Reverend Siltz's frown-lines, and bright blue eyes. "I am Deacon Brown, Church of Lemuria. We are sure you remain objective. You must forgive your host his taciturnity; he is suffering under a difficult family situation."

"I have no complaints," Brother Paul said carefully. "I am not sure I can say the same about your Covenant, but the Reverend Siltz has treated me cordially enough. I fear I kept him so busy answering my routine questions that we left his dwelling late, and so got caught in the storm. I do tend to talk too much." That should absolve the Reverend on that score. Brother Paul was tempted to inquire about this multi-sected society, but decided to wait. He already knew the colonists were not supposed to enlighten him on this matter informally, lest they be accused of proselytization. These men had clearly ignored his hints about this inconvenience.

"You see, his son is serious about a young woman of the Church of Scientology," Deacon Brown continued. "The two young people worked together this spring on a tree-harvest mission, and the Cup overflowed."

No doubt about the Tarot reference this time! Cups were not only the suit of water; they signified religion—and love. A difficult juxtaposition here, it seemed. "You do not permit marriage between churches?"

"It is permitted by some sects, and forbidden by others. You must understand, Brother Paul, that we are a jealous community." Reverend Siltz had used a similar expression; there was no doubt it was true! "We came here as individual sects to further the purity and freedom of our own selective modes of worship, and it is to our displeasure and inconvenience that we find ourselves required to interact so intimately with false believers. We find it difficult to agree on anything other than the sheer need for survival—and not always on that."

Even so! "Yes, but surely religion should not oppose common sense. I doubt that you have enough members of each sect in this village to be able to propagate freely within your own churches. There must be some reasonable compromise."

"There is some," Deacon Brown agreed. "But not enough. We understand Reverend Siltz's position; none of us would wish our children to marry Scientologists, or Baha'is, or any other heathen offspring. My daughter does not keep company with the son of Minister Malcolm, here, of the Nation of Islam." The adjacent man smiled affirmatively, the whiteness of his teeth vivid against the brownness of his skin. "Yet the Cup is powerful, and there will be serious trouble unless we can soon determine the true nature of the God of the Tree."

"So I have been advised." Brother Paul was now aware of the reason for the tense relations between individuals, but it seemed to him to be a foolish and obstinate situation. With savage storms and Bigfoot and similar frontier-world problems, they did not need pointless religious dissension too. It was certainly possible for widely differing sects to get along together, as the experience of the Holy Order of Vision showed. To Brother Paul, a religion that was intolerant of other religions was by its own admission deficient. Jesus Christ had preached tolerance for all men, after all. Well, perhaps not for moneylenders in the temple, and such. Still . . .

Reverend Siltz returned with two brimming wooden bowls. He set one before Brother Paul, then seated himself on the wooden bench. There was a wooden spoon in each bowl, crude but serviceable. There must be quite a handicrafts industry here, fashioning these utensils. This was certainly in accord with the principles of the Order; wooden tableware did make sense.

Brother Paul and Reverend Siltz fell to. There was no blessing of the food; probably the several sects could not agree on the specific format, so had agreed by their Covenant to omit this formality. The soup was unfamiliar but rich; it had a pithy substantiality, like potato soup, with an unearthly flavor. "If I may inquire—" he started.

"Wood soup," Deacon Brown said immediately. "The Tree of Life nourishes us all, but it yields its sustenance more freely when boiled. We also eat of the fruit, but this is as yet early in the season and it is not ready."

Wood soup. Well, why not? This secondary worship of the Tree was becoming more understandable. Perhaps it would be best if the God of Tarot did turn out to be one with the local Tree. If it were simply a matter of interpretation—but he would have to wait and see, not prejudicing his own mind.

Brother Paul finished his bowl. It had proved to be quite filling. Reverend Siltz immediately took it away. Apparently the Reverend wanted to be quite certain the others were satisfied with the visitor's equilibrium, so left him alone at any pretext. Another indication of the strained relations here.

"If I may inquire without giving offense," Brother Paul began, aware that offense was probably unavoidable if he were to proceed with his mission.

"You are not of our colony," Deacon Brown said. "You do not know our conventions. I shall give them to you succinctly: speak no religion. In other matters, speak freely; we shall make allowances."

Hm. He would be unable to honor that strictly, since his purpose here was thoroughly religious. But all in good time. "Thank you. I notice you employ a certain seeming symbolism that resembles that of the Tarot deck. Cups, for example. The Tarot equivalent of the suit of Hearts. Is this intentional?"

Everyone at the table smiled. "Of course," the deacon agreed. "Every sect here has its own Tarot deck, or variant deck. This is part of our communal respect for the Tree of Life. We do not feel that it conflicts with our respective faiths; rather it augments them, and offers one of the few common bonds available to us."

Brother Paul nodded. "It would seem that the concept of the Tarot was always associated with this planet, with visions drawn from the cards—"

"Not visions," the deacon corrected him. "Animations. They are tangible, sometimes dangerous manifestations."

"Yet not physical ones," Brother Paul said, expecting to clarify what Reverend Siltz had claimed.

"Indeed, physical! That is why we require that you be protected when you investigate. Did the Communist not inform you?"

"He did, but I remain skeptical. I really don't see how—"

The deacon brought out a pack of cards. "Allow me to demonstrate, if there is no protest from these, my companions of other faiths." He glanced around the table, but no one protested. "We are in storm at the moment; it should be possible to—" He selected a card and concentrated.

Brother Paul watched dubiously. If the man expected to form something physical from the air . . .

A shape appeared on the table, forming as from a cloud, fuzzy but strengthening. It was a pencil, or a chopstick—

"The Ace of Wands!" Brother Paul exclaimed.

Deacon Brown did not reply; he was concentrating on his image. Reverend Siltz had quietly returned, however, and he picked up the commentary. "Now you evidently believe the Lemurian has made a form without substance, a mirror-reflection from the card he perceives. But you shall see."

Siltz reached out and grasped the small rod between his thumb and forefinger. His hand did not pass through it, as would have been the case with a mere image; the wand moved exactly as a real one might. "Now I touch you with this staff," Siltz said. He poked the end at the back of Brother Paul's hand.

It was solid. Brother Paul felt the pressure, and then a burning sensation. He jerked his hand away. "It's hot!"

As he spoke, the wand burst into flame at the end, like a struck match. Siltz dropped it on the table, where it continued to flare. "Fire—the reality behind the symbol, the power of nature," he said. "Someone, if you please—water."

The representative of the Nation of Islam dealt a card from his own deck. He concentrated. Two ornate golden cups formed. Deacon Brown grabbed one and poured its contents over the burning stick. There was a hiss, and a puff of vapor went up.

Were they trying to fool him with magic tricks? Brother Paul knew something of sleight-of-hand; his own fingers were uncommonly dexterous. "May I?" he inquired, reaching toward the remaining cup.

To his surprise, no one objected. He touched the cup, and found it solid. He lifted it, and it was heavy. Extremely heavy; only pure gold could be as dense as this! He dipped one finger into its fluid, then touched that finger to his tongue. Water, surely! He sprinkled some on his burn, and it seemed to help. This was a solid, tangible, physical, believable cup, and physical water. Water, the reality behind the symbol, again, the female complement to the male fire. The Tarot made literal.

"Mass hypnosis?" Brother Paul inquired musingly. "Do all of you see and feel these things?"

"We all do," Reverend Siltz assured him.

"May I experiment? I confess I am impressed, but I am an incorrigible skeptic."

"Proceed," Deacon Brown said. "We approve of skepticism, in your case. We do not need yet another dedicated cultist." There was a murmur of agreement, though Brother Paul thought he detected a rueful tinge to it. At least these cultists were not overly sensitive about their situation! Probably they had been chosen to deal with him because they were the least fanatical of their respective sects.

"Then if I may borrow a Tarot deck—" One was handed to him. Though he was usually observant, his fascination with the current proceedings rendered the favor anonymous; he could not afterward recall whose deck he had borrowed. He riffled expertly through the cards, limbering his fingers. There had been a time when—but those days were best forgotten.

This was one of the popular medieval-style versions, with peasants and winged figures and children, rather than the more sophisticated modern designs. In this circumstance he was glad it was this type; a surrealistic deck could only have complicated an already incredible experience.

"I shall select a card," Brother Paul said carefully. "I shall show it to all of you except one. And then that one shall have it and animate it for us, without looking at the rest of you. May I have a volunteer?"

"I will do it," Deacon Brown said. "We of Lemuria are always happy to demonstrate the reality of our—" Someone coughed, and he broke off. "Sorry. Didn't mean to proselytize."

The deacon faced away, his bald pate glistening in the dim light from a window. The storm had brought a nocturnal gloom to the landscape, but now it was easing. Brother Paul selected the Three of Swords. It was a handsome card with a straight, red-bladed sword in the center enclosed by two ornate and curving scimitars, and a background of colored leaves. Silently he showed it to the others, then passed it to the deacon.

In a moment the picture was reproduced with fair accuracy. Three swords and some leaves hung in the air. Brother Paul reached out and touched one of the scimitars—whereupon all three swords fell to the floor with a startling clatter.

There was silence in the hall. Everyone at the other tables was watching now, silently. "Sorry," Brother Paul said. "I fear my ignorant touch interfered. Allow me to try one more." Privately he asked himself: if he had been able to accept the presence of Antares during matter transmission, why did he have so much trouble accepting these simple objects? And the answer came to him: because there were witnesses here. He could have imagined Antares; this present phenomenon went beyond imagination.

Brother Paul glanced about. Where were the wand, the cups, the swords? He saw none of them now. Had they vanished into that limbo whence they had come, or had they never really existed? Well, if someone were tricking him, he would have the proof in a moment.

Again he selected a card: the Four of Disks, with its four flowerlike disks, each centered by a four-leafed clover, and an ornate shield bearing the device IM. After he had shown it around, he passed it to the deacon. But, unbeknownst to his audience, he exchanged cards. The actual model was the Ace of Cups.

Now, if the Four of Coins formed, he would know it was mass hypnosis, for it had to have been compelled by the belief of others. But if the cup formed—!

The cup formed, huge and colorful, with a blue rim, a red lid, and a cross inscribed on its side.

"I think our guest is having a little fun with us," Reverend Siltz remarked, unamused.

"Merely verifying the origin of the Animation," Brother Paul said, shaken. "Do you all see the coin?"

"Cup, not coin," Siltz said. "It is controlled by the one who makes it; our expectations are irrelevant."

Evidently so! And the cup was so large that it could not have been concealed on the deacon's person for a sleight-of-hand manifestation, even had the man been clever enough to work such a trick under Brother Paul's experienced eye. This was a larger challenge than he had anticipated. Physical, concrete apparitions, willed consciously into existence!

"Impressive," Brother Paul admitted. "Yet you seem to have good control over the situation. I had understood you were quite alarmed by untoward Animations."

Reverend Siltz smiled grimly. "We were indeed, at first. But in the past year we have come to know more about these effects. We are assured of the reality of the Animations; it is God we have yet to compass."

The deacon turned, and his cup faded out. "Any one of us might Animate God in his own image, but that would be merely opinion, not reality. It is vital that we know the truth."

"Yet would I not Animate God in *my* own image?" Brother Paul inquired, troubled. This really was the point Siltz had raised in their private discussion.

"We must trust to your objectivity—and we shall send Watchers with you to assist," Reverend Siltz said. He was not giving away any of his private attitude now! Did members of the Second Church Communist play poker? "They will also try to protect you from untoward manifestations."

And such manifestations, as had been made clear, could be lethal! "May I try this myself? Here, now?" Brother Paul asked, feeling a slight shiver within him, as of stage fright.

"Do it quickly, for the storm is passing," Deacon Brown said. "These effects are erratic at best; this has been an unusually good run. Normally it is necessary to go into the abyss of Northole to obtain such clear Animations. And that is dangerous."

Brother Paul picked out the first of the Major Arcana: Key Zero, the Fool.

"No!" several voices cried at once.

"Do not attempt to Animate a living man," Reverend Siltz said, evidently shaken, and his sentiment seemed to be shared by the others. "This could have unforeseen consequences."

Brother Paul nodded. So they were not really so blasé about the phenomenon! If they had never attempted to Animate a man, they had not experimented very much. He knew where he had to begin. "Still, if I am to explore this phenomenon properly, I must be permitted to Animate anything that is in my power—and I would prefer to attempt it first here, under your informed guidance."

The others exchanged glances of misgiving. They might belong to many opposing religions, but they had a certain unity here! "Your logic prevails," Reverend Siltz said heavily. "If you must do this thing, it is better done here. We shall stand aside."

Brother Paul sifted through the cards. In this deck, the Fool was titled *Le Mat* and garbed as a court jester. Not at all like Waite's interpretation, in which the Fool was a noble but innocent lad about to step off a cliff, symbolic of man's tremendous potential for aspiration and error. Other versions had a vicious little dog ripping the seat from the Fool's pants, so that his bare buttock showed: the height of ridicule. He had seen one variant in which the Fool appeared to be defecating. Probably it was after all best to pass this one by, this time; to attempt it could indeed be Folly.

Key One was the Magician, or Juggler, performing his cheap tricks at a covered table. At the Order Station, Brother Paul himself was sometimes teased—very gently, of course, since no Brother would deliberately hurt anyone—about his supposed affinity with this card. They knew his background as a one-time cardsharp, and had observed his uncanny proficiency with mechanical things. Brother Paul accepted such allusions with good spirits, grateful for the camaraderie he had found within the Order after a prior life of—never mind. He preferred to think of himself as Everyman in quest of life's ultimate meanings as symbolized by the objects resting on the table in the Vision Tarot card: a wand, a cup, a sword, and a coin, meaning fire, water, air, and earth respectively in the ubiquitous symbolism of the form. In that version, too, the cosmic lemniscate, or sidewise figure-eight, the symbol of infinity, hovered like a halo above the Magician's head, and about his waist was clasped a serpent devouring its own tail: the worm Ouroborus, a symbol of eternity. All things in all space and time—that was the grandeur of the concept for which this modern Magician strived. But here in this deck, as a degraded trickster—no, pass it by also.

Key Two, here titled Juno. In Roman mythology, Juno was the wife of Jupiter and queen of the gods, counterpart to the Greek Hera. She was the special protectress of marriage and women. Her bird was the peacock, also represented in this card. Here she was a handsome female in a bright red dress, full-bosomed and bare-legged. But such an amazonian figure might not be well-received by this male-dominated assemblage. Pass her by, regretfully; even in her more common guise as the High Priestess (and the notorious Lady Pope!) she was a questionable choice.

Key Three, the Empress—a more mature and powerful woman than the preceding one. In many decks, the Priestess was the virginal figure, while the Empress was the mother figure. Here she sat on her throne; in other decks the throne was situated in a field of wheat. Had it really been her he had glimpsed when he emerged from the capsule, only hours ago? If so, he did not want to invoke her here in public. He would prefer to meet her privately, for there was something about her that attracted him. Pass her by, for now.

Key Four, the Emperor, counterpart to the Empress, symbol of worldly power, seated on his cubic throne, his legs crossed in the figure four, holding in his right hand a scepter in the form of the Egyptian Ankh or Cross of Life, and in his left hand the globe of dominion. He represented the dominance of reason over the emotions, of the conscious over the subconscious mind. Yes, this was a good symbol for this occasion! The card of power.

Though he held the medieval card, what he visualized was the Order of Vision version. The one in the present deck, that he would have to Animate, was a medieval monarch with a great concave shield a little like the wooden cup used here to guard against the threats of the storm, and a scepter that needed only three prongs added to it to become a trident. The Reverend Siltz could readily serve as a model for this one!

Brother Paul concentrated. He felt ridiculous; maybe he had taken so long to decide on a card because he knew this was an exercise in foolishness. There had to be some trick the colonists knew to make the Animations seem real; obviously he himself could not do it.

Sure enough, nothing happened. Whatever Animation was, it would not work for him. Which meant it *was* some kind of trick. "It does not seem to function," he said with a certain amount of relief.

"Allow me to try; perhaps you only need guidance," Reverend Siltz said. He took the card and concentrated.

Nothing happened.

"The storm has abated," Deacon Brown said. "The Animation effect has passed."

So the power behind Animation had fortuitiously moved on. Now nothing could be proved, one way or the other. Brother Paul told himself he should have expected this.

Yet he was disappointed. It was too marvelous to be true, and he was here, perhaps, to puncture its balloon—but what incredible power Animation promised, were it only genuine! Physical objects coalesced from imagination!

Oh, well. He was here to ascertain reality. He had no business hoping for fantasy.

5

INTUITION
(HIEROPHANT)

The Emperors of the East lived in style. The Chinese for about fifteen hundred years had phenomenal harems consisting of one Wife, three Consorts, nine Spouses, twenty-seven Concubines and eighty-one Nymphs. The Empress would share the Emperor's bed for one night of a fortnight, and the lesser members of the harem would be distributed through the other nights, in shifts of up to nine beauties each. As the years passed, the numbers increased, until the ferocious competition of some three thousand palace ladies caused the system to break down, and it had to be abandoned. But while it was in effect, what did the ladies do during their leisure hours? They must have been bored to the point of emotional breakdown! This, according to Roger Tilley, author of A History of Playing Cards, *was the origin of playing cards: an inmate of the Imperial Harem invented them to relieve the oppressive boredom.*

The next morning Reverend Siltz conducted Brother Paul on a geographic tour. "I trust you are strong of foot," he remarked. "We have no machines, no beasts of burden here, and the terrain is difficult."

"I believe I can manage," Brother Paul said. After yesterday's experience with the Animations, he took quite seriously anything his host told him—but it was hardly likely that the terrain alone would do him in.

He had not slept well. The loft had been comfortable enough, with a mattress of fragrant wood shavings and pretty wooden panels above (he had half expected to see the roots of the grass that grew in the turf that formed the outer roof), but those Animations kept returning to his mind's eye. *Could* he have formed a physical object himself, let alone a human figure, had he not stalled until the storm passed? If a man could form a sword from a mental or card image, could he then use it to murder a companion? Surely this was mass hypnosis! Yet Deacon Brown *had* Animated the cup instead of the four coins. . . .

He shook his head. He would ascertain the truth in due course, if he could. That was his mission. First the truth about Animation, then the truth about God. Neither intuition nor guesswork would do; he had to penetrate to the hard fact.

Meanwhile, it behooved him to familiarize himself with this locale and these people, for the secret might lie here instead of in the Animations themselves. Despite his night of doubt, he felt better this morning, more able to cope. If God were directly responsible for these manifestations, what had a mere man to fear? God was good.

As they set out from the village, a small, swarthy man intercepted them. His body was deeply tanned, or perhaps he had mixed racial roots, as did Brother Paul. His face was grossly wrinkled, though he did not seem to be older than about fifty. "I come on a matter of privilege," he said.

Reverend Siltz halted. "This is the Swami of Kundalini," he said tightly. And to the other: "Brother Paul of the Holy Order of Vision."

"It is to you I am forced to address myself," the Swami said to Brother Paul.

"We are on our way to the countryside," Reverend Siltz said, with strained politeness. He obviously did not appreciate this intrusion, and that alerted Brother Paul. What additional currents were flowing here? "The garden, the amaranth, the Animation region, where the Watchers will meet us. If you care to join them—"

"I shall gladly walk with you," the Swami said.

"I am happy to talk with anyone who wishes to talk with me,"

Brother Paul said. "I have much to learn about this planet and this society."

"We cannot spare two for the tour," Siltz insisted. "The Swami surely has business elsewhere."

"I do, but it must wait," the Swami said.

"Well, surely a few minutes—" Brother Paul said, disliking the tension between these two men.

"Perhaps the Swami will consent to guide you in my stead," Reverend Siltz said, grimacing. "I have a certain matter I could attend to, given the occasion."

"Am I the unwitting cause of dissension?" Brother Paul asked. "I certainly don't want to—"

"I should be happy to guide the visitor," the Swami said. "I am familiar with the route."

"Then I shall depart with due gratitude," the Reverend said, his expression hardly reflecting that emotion.

"But there is no need to—" Brother Paul began. But it was useless; the Reverend of the Second Church of Communism was on his way, walking stiffly but rapidly back toward the village stockade.

Looking back, Brother Paul wondered: what use was that stockade, if it did not keep out Bigfoot? Probably the monster merely swam around one end of the stockade where the wall terminated in the lake; during a storm there would be no way to keep watch for it.

"It is all right, guest Brother," the Swami said. "We differ strongly in our separate faiths, but we do not violate the precepts of the Tree of Life. The Reverend Communist will have occasion to verify the whereabouts of his wayward son, and I will guide you while making known my exception to your mission."

Still, Brother Paul was dubious. "I fear the Reverend is offended."

"Not as offended as he pretends," the Swami said with a brief smile. "He does have a serious concern to attend to, but it would have been impolitic for him to allow that to compromise his hospitality or duty. And I *do* have a pressing matter to discuss with you. For the affront of forcing the issue I offer such token recompense as I am able. Have you any demand?"

This was a bit complicated to assimilate immediately. Was this man friend, foe, or something between? "I am really not in a position to make any demands. Let's tour the region, and I will listen to your concern, trusting that this does not violate the Covenant."

"We shall skirt the main region of permanent Animation, and the advisory party shall be there. The tour is somewhat hazardous, so we must proceed with caution. Yet this is as nothing to the hazard your mission, however sincerely intended, poses for mankind. This is my concern."

Brother Paul had suspected something of the kind. In this hotbed of schismatic religions, there was bound to be a good doomsday prophet, and someone was sure to express strong opposition to *any* community project, even one designed to help unify the community itself in the interest of survival. Brother Paul had had experience with democratic community government. He had been shielded from the lunatic element here. Now it seemed to have broken through. Yet even a fanatic could have useful insights. "I certainly want to be advised of hazards," Brother Paul said. "Physical and social."

"You shall be apprised of both. I will show you first our mountain garden to the south; between eruptions we farm the terraces, for the ash decomposes swiftly and is incredibly rich. Our single garden feeds the whole village for the summer, enabling us to conserve wood for winter sustenance. This is vital to our survival."

The man certainly did not sound like a nut! "But what of your wheatfields that I passed through yesterday?"

"Amaranth, not wheat," the Swami told him. "Amaranth is a special grain, adaptable to alien climes. Once it was thought of as a weed, back on Earth, until the resurgence of small family farms developed the market for tough, hand-harvested grains. We have been unable to grow true wheat here on Planet Tarot, but are experimenting with varieties of this alternate grain, and have high hopes. The lava shields are also very rich here on Southmount, but decompose more slowly than the ash, and so require slower-growing, more persistent crops. The climate of the lower region is more moderate, which is a long-range benefit."

Brother Paul did not know much about either amaranth or volcanic farming, so he wasn't clear on all this and did not argue. However, he did find some of these statements questionable. The decomposition of lava was not, as he understood it, a matter of a season or two, but of centuries. The seasonal growth of plants would be largely governed by elements already available in the soil, rather than by the slow breakdown of rock.

Their discussion lapsed, for the climb was getting steep. Glassy facets of rock showed through the turf, like obsidian mirrors set in the slope. Volcanic? It must be; he wished he knew more about the subject. The volcanoes of Planet Tarot might differ fundamentally from those of Earth, however, just as did those of Earth's more immediate neighbor, Mars.

Fundamentally. He smiled, appreciating a pun of sorts. A volcano was a thing of the fundament, shaped by the deepest forces of the planetary crust. So whether different or similar—

He stumbled on a stone, and lost his train of thought. There was a path, but not an easy one. The Swami scrambled ahead with the agility of a monkey, hands grasping crystalline outcroppings with the precision of long experience. Brother Paul kept the pace with difficulty, copying the positioning of his guide's grips. In places the ascent became almost vertical, and the path was cleaved occasionally by jagged cracks in the rock. Apparently the lava had contracted as it cooled, so that the fissures opened irregularly. The slanting sunbeams shone down into these narrow clefts, reflecting back and forth dazzlingly, and making the mountain seem like the mere shell of a nether-world of illumination. A person could be blinded, he thought, by peering into this kaleidoscopic hall of mirrors.

Or hypnotized, he realized. Could this be the cause of the Animations?

Then what had he seen and touched in the mess hall, during the storm? No crevices there, no sunlight! Scratch one theory.

Cracks and gas: that suggested a gruesome analogy. The *bocor*, or witch doctor, of Haiti (and could the similarity of that name to "hate" be coincidental? Hate-Haiti—but his mind was drifting perilously far afield at an inopportune time) was said to ride his horse backward to his victim's shack, suck out the victim's soul through a crack in the door, and bottle that gaseous soul. Later, when the victim died, the *bocor* opened the grave, brought out the bottle, and gave the dead man a single sniff of his own soul. Only one sniff: not enough to infuse the entire soul, just part of it. That animated the corpse; it rose up as a zombie, forced to obey the will of the witch doctor. Could the same be done with a human aura, and did this relate to the phenomena on Planet Tarot?

Idle speculations; he would do well to curb them and concentrate on objective fact-finding. Then he could form an informed opinion. Right now he had enough to occupy him, merely surviving this hazardous climb!

They emerged at last onto a narrow terrace. The Swami led the way along this, for it was wide enough only for them to proceed single-file. The view was alarming; they were several hundred meters above the level of the village, with the top thirty an almost sheer drop. The stockade looked like a wall of toothpicks. Woe be he who lacked good balance!

The terrace opened out into a garden area. Unfamiliar shrubs and vines spread out robustly. There were no Bubbles here, however; evidently the elevation, exposure and wind were too much for them. "We have been farming this plot for twenty days this spring, since the upper snow melted," the Swami said with communal pride.

"Twenty days? These plants look like sixty days!"

"Yes. I warned you that growth was at an incredible rate, so you are free not to credit it. Soon we begin the first harvest of the season. Then no more wood soup until fall."

"We could use some of this soil back on Earth!"

"Undoubtedly. *We* could use more supplies from Earth, and not only when the mother planet wishes to bribe us to permit religious intrusion. Perhaps we can exchange some soil for such supplies."

Brother Paul was not certain how much of this was humor and how much was sarcasm, so he did not reply. The cost of matter-mission made the shipment of tons of soil prohibitive. What was really needed was the formula—the chemical analysis of the soil, and some seeds from these vigorous plants. And that would be very difficult, for the importation of alien plants to Earth was forbidden. Export was without restriction, but imports had to pass rigorous quarantine; there was a certain logic to this, for those who comprehended bureaucracy. Even if he, Brother Paul, were chemist enough to work out the formula, he would probably not be able to make the authorities on Earth pay attention anyway. But he would take samples and try . . .

"This is an active volcanic region," Brother Paul observed, cutting off his own thoughts. It was a discipline he had to exert often. "What happens if there is an eruption before the harvest?"

"That depends on the vehemence of the eruption. Most are small, and the wind carries the ash away from this site. Later in the season, when the prevailing winds shift, it will become more precarious."

Brother Paul looked down the steep slope again toward the village. The scene was like that of a skillfully executed painting, with the adjacent lake brightly reflecting the morning sun. Beautiful! But he would hate to be stranded here on the volcano when it blew its top! Evidently there could be both ash and lava.

That reminded him of one of his notions that had been aborted by the difficulty of the climb. "Gas," he said. "Does the volcano issue gas? That might account for—"

"There are gas and liquid and solids and enormous energy, in accordance with the laws of Tarot," the Swami said. "But none of these are of a hallucinogenic nature. Our problem is not so readily dismissed as originating in the mouth of the mountain." He stood beside Brother Paul and pointed to the north. "There, five kilometers distant, is the depression we call 'Northhole.' There is the seat of Animation for this region."

"Maybe a subterranean vent from the volcano?" Brother Paul persisted. "Strange effects can occur. The Oracle at Delphi —that's a place back on Earth—would sit over the vent of—"

"Well I know it. Yet it seems strange that there is no Animation here at the volcano Southmount itself. No, I feel that the secret is more subtle and formidable."

"Yet you object to my attempt to explore the secret?"

The Swami showed the way down the mountain. This was a less precipitous path to the west, so that they were able to tread carefully upright, occasionally skidding on the black ash lying in riverlike courses at irregular intervals. "Do you comprehend *prana?*"

Brother Paul chuckled. "No. I have tried hatha yoga and zen meditation and read the *Vedas,* but never achieved any proper awareness of either *prana* or *jiva.* I can repeat only the vulgar descriptions: *prana* is the individual life principle, and *jiva* is the personal soul."

"That is a beginning," the Swami said. "You are better versed than I anticipated, and this is fortunate. In the Hindu, Vedic, and Tantric texts there is a symbol of a sleeping serpent coiled around the base of the human spine. This is Kundalini, the coiled latent energy of *prana,* known by many names. Christians call it the 'Holy Spirit,' the Greeks termed it 'ether,' martial artists described it as '*ki.*'"

Now Brother Paul was in more familiar territory. "Ah, yes. In my training in judo, I sought the power of *ki,* but could never evoke it. No doubt my motive was suspect; I was thinking in terms of physical force, not spiritual force."

"This is the root of failure in the great majority of aspirants." The Swami paused on the mountainside. "Do you care to break that rock?" he inquired, indicating an outcropping of crystal.

Brother Paul tapped it with his fingers, feeling its hardness. "With a sledgehammer?"

"No. Like this. With *ki.*" And the Swami lifted his right arm and brought his hand down in a hard blow upon the rock.

And the rock fractured.

Brother Paul stared. *"Ki!"* he breathed. "You have it!"

"I do not make this demonstration to impress you with my skill," the Swami said, "but rather as evidence that my concern is serious. You have looked at me obliquely, and this is your right, but you must appreciate the sincerity of my warning."

Brother Paul looked at the cracked crystal again. Some flaw in the stone? He had not observed such a flaw before, and even if there had been one, it should have taken a harder blow than the human arm was capable of delivering to faze it. The power of *ki* was the most reasonable explanation. The man who possessed that power had to be taken seriously. It was not merely that he was potentially deadly; the Swami had to have undergone rigorous training and discipline, and to have achieved fundamental insights about the nature of man and the universe.

"I take you seriously," Brother Paul said.

The Swami resumed his downward trek as if nothing special had happened. "So few apply proper respect to their quest for the aura—"

"Aura!" Brother Paul exclaimed, surprised again.

The Swami glanced sidelong at him. "That word evokes a specific response?"

Brother Paul considered telling the Swami of his vision of the creature from Sphere Antares, who had informed Brother Paul of the existence of his own, supposedly potent aura. It required only a moment's reflection to squelch that notion. He knew too little of this man and this society to discuss something as personal as this, since it reflected on his own emotional competence. What sensible person would believe in the ghost in the machine, or in private, personal alien contact during the period of instantaneous matter transmission? "I have read of Kirlian photography."

"No. Photographs are not the essence. Aura permeates the gross tissues of the body, and is the source of all vital activity including movement, perception, thought, and feeling. The awakening of this force is the greatest enterprise and the most wonderful achievement man contemplates. By this means it will be possible to bridge the gulf between science and religion, between technology and truth. But there is danger, too. Grave danger."

They were now down on the plain, walking northward through the amaranth. No wonder the "wheat" had looked funny! Brother Paul was distracted by the thought of the young woman he had encountered here the day before, and his other adventure. "Speaking of danger—is it safe to come here without weapons? Yesterday I encountered a wild animal near here."

"Yes, the news is all over the village! The Breaker will not attack you again, since you mastered it. Otherwise I surely would not have brought you this way." He paused. "Though how a lone man could have defeated as horrendous a creature as that one, that none of us dares to face without a trident—"

"I was lucky," Brother Paul said. This was not false modesty; he *had* been lucky. "Had I been aware of the threat, I would not have ventured into the amaranth field."

The Swami faced him. "What exactly did you do to overcome the Breaker?"

"I used a judo throw, or tried to," Brother Paul explained. *"Ippon seoi nage* and an armlock."

"Ippon seoi nage should not be effective against such a creature; the dynamics are wrong." The Swami looked at him with a glint of curiosity in his eye. "I wonder—" He hesitated. "Would you show me exactly what you did?"

"Oh, I would not care to throw you on this ground," Brother Paul demurred.

"I meant the armlock—gently." There was no question that the Swami was familiar with martial arts.

Brother Paul shrugged. "As you will." They got down on the ground and he applied the armlock, without pressure. "Nothing special about it," Brother Paul said. "On the Breaker, it was really a leglock. I had not expected it to work, owing to the peculiar anatomy of the—"

"Bear down," the Swami said. "Do not be concerned; my arm is strong."

He was right about that; Brother Paul could feel surprisingly formidable muscular tension in the Swami's light frame. This man was like another aspect of the ghost in the machine; he seemed fanatical because he was improperly understood, but he was merely giving his allegiance to other than the usual imperatives. Brother Paul slowly increased the force of the hold to the point where the Breaker had screamed.

"More," the Swami said.

"There is danger."

"Precisely."

Well, pain should make the man tap out before his elbow actually broke, Brother Paul thought as he put an additional surge of effort into it.

"There!" the Swami cried.

Brother Paul eased up in alarm.

The Swami smiled, obviously unhurt.

"It is what I suspected. You used *ki!*"

Brother Paul shook his head. "I have no—"

"You have a powerful aura," the Swami insisted. "I was uncertain until you focused it. You are a gentle man, so you never willingly invoke it, but were you otherwise, you would be a monster. Never have I encountered such power."

Brother Paul sat bemused. "Once another person said something of the kind to me, but I dismissed it as fancy," he said, thinking again of Antares.

"Only those who have mastered their own auras can perceive them in others," the Swami assured him. "My own mastery is imperfect, so your aura was not immediately apparent to me. But now I am certain, it was your *ki,* the focused application of your aura, that terrified the Breaker. Surely it was this aura that selected you for this mission too, though others might have rationalized it into other reasons. I had hoped this would not be the case."

Brother Paul shook his head. "If this . . . this aura protects me against threats, surely—"

"The threat of which I speak is much greater than merely a physical one. You see—"

"Hello."

Both men looked up, startled. It was the girl of the wheatfield, the Empress of Tarot. *Amaranth* field, he corrected himself. This time she was not fleeing him, and for that he was grateful. Now he could discover whom she was.

She wore a one-piece outfit, really a belted tunic embroidered with a landscape reminiscent of the local geography. Every colonist's apparel was distinctive, reflecting his religious bias, but this was something special. There were hills and valleys in color, and two volcanic mounts in front: a veritable contour map. Brother Paul tried not to stare. They were extremely lofty and well-formed volcanoes.

"We merely pass by," the Swami informed her.

"Wrestling on the ground, flattening the crop, and crying out?" she demanded. "Swami, I always knew you were a nut, but—"

"My fault," Brother Paul interposed. "I was trying to demonstrate how I discouraged the Breaker."

Her lovely eyes narrowed appraisingly. "Then I must speak with you," she said firmly. Indeed, everything about her was firm; she was a strikingly handsome young woman, with golden hair and eyes and skin, and features that were, as the narrators of the *Arabian Nights* would have put it, marvels of symmetry. Brother Paul might have seen a fairer female at some time in his life, but at the moment it was difficult to call any such creature to mind.

"I have undertaken to guide this man about the premises," the Swami said gruffly, as he rose and dusted himself off. "We must arrive at Northole in due course."

"Then I shall accompany you," she said. "It is essential that I talk with our visitor from Earth."

"You cannot leave your station!"

"My station is the Breaker—who is absent today," she said with finality.

Brother Paul remained silent. It seemed that the Swami was being served as he himself had served Reverend Siltz; also, it would be wickedly pleasant having this scenic creature along. He had feared he would not see her again, but here she was, virtually forcing her company on him. Obviously she accepted no inferior status; maybe women were, after all, equal to men here. That would be nice.

The Swami shrugged, evidently suppressing his irritation. "This female is the understudy to the Breaker," he said, by way of introduction. "She alone has no fear of the monster. It is apparent in her manner."

"The Swami prefers his docile daughter," she responded, "who has few illusions of individuality."

Thrust and counterthrust! "What is your name, Breaker Lady?"

Brother Paul asked. "Why did you flee from me before, if you have so little to fear?"

"I thought you were an Animation," she said. "The only way to handle an Animation is to get the hell away from it."

Hm. A candid, colloquial answer that did much to debilitate his prior conception of her as the Empress. "But your name?"

"Call her anything you like," the Swami said. "Subtlety is wasted on the unsubtle."

The girl only smiled, not at all discommoded by the Swami's taciturnity. If she had intended to give her name, that intention was gone now. Somehow he had to defuse this minor social crisis, since he wanted to get along with both of them, though for different reasons.

"Then I shall call you Amaranth, in honor of this beautiful field where we met," Brother Paul decided that physical compliments were seldom in error, when relating to the distaff.

"Oh, I like that!" she exclaimed, melting. "Amaranth! May I keep it?"

"It is yours," Brother Paul said benignly. He liked her mode of game-playing, and he liked her. "You thought I was an Animation of the Devil, and I thought you were an Animation of the Empress. No doubt we were both correct."

She laughed, causing the volcanoes to quiver hazardously. "And I thought members of the Order of Vision were humorless!"

"Some are," Brother Paul said. "Let me hear out the Swami; then I shall be free to talk with you at leisure." Delightful prospect!

"My warning can wait upon a more propitious occasion," the Swami said sourly. "It concerns Northole."

"That's an odd name," Brother Paul observed, hoping to relieve the tension again.

"We have simplistic nomenclature," Amaranth said. "That's Southmount you came from; this is Westfield; the Animation pit is Northole; and the water to the east of the village is—"

"Eastlake," Brother Paul finished. "Yes, it does make sense. What did you want to ask me?"

"Nothing," she said.

"Perhaps I misunderstood. I thought you said—"

"Never pay too much attention to what a woman says," the Swami said.

She ignored him elegantly. "I said I wished to speak with you. I am doing that."

Brother Paul smiled with bafflement. "Assuredly. Yet—"

"You overcame my Breaker with your bare hands, without hurting him or yourself. I need to study you, as I study the Breaker. This is my job: to comprehend the full nature of my subject."

"Ah. So you must comprehend the type of person who balks the animal, by whatever freak of circumstance," Brother Paul said. He had had the impression that her interest was in him personally, but this was really more realistic. What real interest would a girl of her attractions have in a sedate stranger? "Yet I remain confused," he went on.

"That's all right," she said brightly.

The Swami mellowed enough to put in an explanation. "Survival is a narrow thing here," he said. "We must labor diligently to gather wood for the arduous winter, and anything that interferes with this acquisition of fuel is a community concern. The Breaker interferes, forcing us to travel from the village in armed parties —a ruinously wasteful expenditure of manpower. Therefore we study the Breaker, hoping to neutralize it."

"Wouldn't it be simpler to kill it?" Brother Paul asked.

"Kill it?" the Swami echoed, as if baffled.

Now it was the girl's turn to make the explanation. "Many of our sects object to taking the lives of natural creatures. It is a moral matter, and a practical one. It is impossible to know what the ramifications of unnecessary killing may be. If we killed this local Breaker, another might merely move into its place. A smarter or more vicious one. If we killed them all, we could wreak ecological havoc that would in turn destroy us. Back on Earth the environment was ravaged by the unthinking war against pests, and we don't want to make that mistake here. Also, we need beasts of burden, and the Breaker, if it could be tamed and harnessed, might be an excellent one. So we protect ourselves with the tridents, not trying to kill the Breaker or any other predator. We are studying our problems before acting."

"That is what I am here to do with the problem of Animation," Brother Paul pointed out.

"Which is why you must be apprised of the danger first," the Swami said. "The Breaker is a minor menace; Animation is a major one."

"I am willing to listen," Brother Paul reminded him.

The Swami was silent, so Brother Paul addressed Amaranth. "How is it you have this dangerous job of observation? You do not carry any trident."

"Not a tangible one," the Swami muttered. "She has barbs enough."

"He sees his late wife in all young women," Amaranth said to Brother Paul. "She had a savage wit. But about me: it was the lot. No one volunteered, so we drew cards from the Tarot, and I was low. As a matter of fact, I was the Empress, Key Three; you were right about that. So they built me a protective box shaped like the throne and appropriately marked—we propitiate the God of Tarot in any little way we can—and I set out to study the Breaker. And watch the amaranth, since the Breaker associates most frequently with this area. He sure keeps the graineaters off the field! I keep track of the temperature extremes, rainfall, and such, and measure the growth of the plants. And when an MT shipment comes, I notify the village, although the noise of arrival usually makes that superfluous. Sorry I lost my head yesterday; I had forgotten they were sending a man this time."

"But the danger—a mere girl—"

The Swami snorted. "Let the Breaker beware!"

"I had some concern myself," she admitted, again successfully ignoring the jibe. "I wanted to indulge my artistic proclivities, carving pseudo-icons and totems from Tree of Life wood and igneous stone. But that slot was filled by another, so I had to accept assignment elsewhere. When the lot put me in this dangerous and unsuitable position, I rebelled."

"She is good at that," the Swami said.

"Which is one reason I remain unmarried," she continued. "I had a prospect, but he rejected me because of my lack of community spirit. Of course, *he* didn't have to face the Breaker. Finally I had to come around, because on this planet you contribute or you don't eat; that's one of the few things our scattered cults agree on."

"An excellent policy," the Swami said.

"But do you know," she continued without even a poisonous glance at him, "I discovered that there really is a lot more to be known about amaranth than I had thought, as well as about the Breaker. Each plant is a separate individual, proceeding in its own fashion toward the harvest, requiring its own special attention.

Sometimes I sneak a little volcanic ash to a plant that is ailing, though I'm not supposed to. There are creatures beneath the plants, insects and even serpents sheltered by the low canopy. That makes me feel right at home."

"Most girls of Earth do not appreciate snakes, beneficial as these reptiles may be," Brother Paul observed.

"Most girls of Earth do not worship Abraxas, the serpent-footed God," she replied. "Actually, the fear of snakes is comparatively recent, historically. In the Bible, the Serpent was the source of wisdom that transformed—"

"Caution," the Swami said. "Remember the Covenant."

"Sorry," she said. "We are not permitted to go into our private beliefs, in the interest of your continuing objectivity. It's a nuisance. Anyway, I discovered unsurpassed artistry in the mountains and sunsets and storms of this unspoiled planet. Have you noticed how the Tarot Bubbles get blown by the wind? We must have the prettiest storms in this section of the Galaxy! I translated this beauty into the weaving I do in the off-hours."

"You weave also?" Brother Paul asked.

"Oh, yes, we all weave the Tree of Life fibers, especially in winter, for we must have clothing and blankets against the cold. You haven't experienced winter until you've survived it here! But even in summer I must sit still for long periods, alone, so the weaving and embroidery help distract me. This dress I designed and shaped myself," she said with pride, taking a breath that made the twin volcanoes threaten to erupt. "It is an accurate contour map of the region as seen from my station." She shrugged, causing another siege of earthquakes around the mountains. "Of course, I have to be facing the right way. Strictly speaking, I should be lying down with my legs to the north—"

"Shameless!" the Swami hissed.

"Oh, come on, Swami," she said. "Doesn't Kundalini link *prana* to the sexual force, just as my God Abraxas does? There should be no shame in drawing a parallel between woman and nature. Woman *is* nature."

"I didn't realize there were two volcanoes," Brother Paul said, thinking it best to interrupt this debate. He had not believed religion could ever play too great a part in the daily lives of people, but he was developing a doubt. In every personal interaction, here on Planet Tarot, the animosities of religious intolerance were barely veiled.

"Oh, yes," she said. "Actually it is one volcano with twin cones. They normally erupt together. From the village, one cone obscures the other, and often in the mornings the haze conceals both, but from here . . ." She turned, walking briskly backward so as not to impede their progress toward Northole. "Yes, you can see them both now. Southmount Left and Southmount Right." She tapped the map appropriately, making momentary indentations in the resilient mounts.

Brother Paul yanked his eyes away from the indents and looked back. Sure enough, now two cones were apparent, and they did resemble those of the contour map: full and rounded, rather than truly conical. "Where is the mountain garden?" he inquired.

"Here in the cleft," she said, indicating a spot on the map between the cones. "The village access comes up on the east slope, here." She traced a course up the right side. "It's steep, but most direct." It certainly was! "Now we're about here—" She touched the general region of her navel. "Heading for the—"

"Enough!" the Swami cried.

"Northole," she concluded. "The passion pit."

"You are an accursed slut!" the Swami said. His face was red. Whatever control he exerted over his intellectual and spiritual powers did not seem to extend to his emotions. This was a deeply divided man, with sizable unresolved conflicts.

"Nothing wrong with me that a good man can't cure," Amaranth said blithely. Well, the Swami had started this engagement; now she was finishing it.

"You never explained about the Breaker," Brother Paul reminded her.

"Um, yes. When I studied the Breaker, I came to realize that this was the most interesting phenomenon of all. I was afraid of it at first, and I really barricaded my throne as a fortress, but after a while it got used to me. Little by little I won its respect, taming it, and now it will not attack me because it knows me. *He* knows me; I think of the Breaker as male."

"You would," the Swami muttered.

"We are friends, in our fashion," she continued. "I am closer to success than others suspect. The Breaker will come when I whistle, and I can touch him. I think he might fight for me if I were threatened. That may have been why he went after you; he thought you were chasing me."

"I was," Brother Paul said.

"I certainly would not want to see him killed. I do think that in time I will be able to harness his power for our benefit. It is a tremendous project, and I'm glad now that the lot fell to me. I'm sorry you drove the Breaker away."

"I was ignorant of—"

"Oh, no blame attaches to you, sir! You had to defend yourself, and you did that without actually hurting the Breaker. He will return in a day or so. Meanwhile, you can show me how you did it."

"I utilized the principles of judo," Brother Paul began, but caught the warning glance of the Swami. Yes, probably it was better not to mention the matter of *ki* or aura, yet. "*Sieroku zenyo,* maximum efficiency—"

She stopped. "Pretend I'm the Breaker, charging you. How do you react?"

Déjà vu! "It would require physical contact to demonstrate, and I have already been through this with the Swami. I'm not sure—"

"The vamp means to seduce you!" the Swami expostulated.

Brother Paul was not at all certain this was an empty warning. A forward woman who spoke appreciatively of serpents and sexual knowledge and showed off her breasts in so obvious a fashion . . . "Perhaps another time," he said. "I gather, then, that you do not feel that your assignment was a mistake." She had already said as much, but he was somewhat at a loss for suitable responses.

"It has been a revelation," she said sincerely, resuming her forward progress. She adapted to circumstances readily, whether physical or conversational. An intriguing woman to know! "The lot chose my career better than I ever could have. I believe it was the will of Abraxas."

"A heathen demon!" the Swami muttered.

"Observe the intemperate yogi," she said. "Other Indian-derived religions are supremely tolerant, but he—"

"Perhaps it was the God of Tarot who guided the lot," Brother Paul said. "Whichever god that may be." Then, before the hostilities could resume: "I see people ahead. Swami, it may be time for you to tell me of the danger, before we are interrupted."

To his half-surprise, the Swami agreed. "The danger is this: the Animation effect is a manifestation of the fundamental power of Kundalini—the spirit force. Evoked without proper comprehension or controls, this is like conjuring Satan, like giving blocks of fissionable material to a child for play."

"Oh, pooh!" Amaranth exclaimed. "Magic like this has been known and practiced and venerated for thousands of years. The only question is, whose god is responsible? You're just afraid it won't turn out to be *your* god."

"Correct," the Swami agreed. "I worship no god; I seek only the ultimate enlightenment. This Animation is not a force of God at all, but a manifestation of uncontrolled Kundalini. In human history, Kundalini gone astray has been the cause of the evil geniuses of men like Attila the Hun and Adolph Hitler the Nazi. If you, Brother Paul of the Holy Order of Vision, evoke it now—and it is my fear that this capacity does indeed lie within you, the capacity to loose the full genie from the bottle, rather than the mere fragments of it we have hitherto seen—you may give form to a concentration of power that will destroy us all, that will exterminate the entire human colony of Planet Tarot."

"An imaginary beast!" Amaranth scoffed.

But Brother Paul was not so skeptical. The Swami had shown him some of the reasons for his concern, and they were impressive. What could the power of *ki* do, if it were to run amok? If this really were related to Animation . . . "I have seen some of the Animations, touched the forms myself," he said. "There is something here beyond our present comprehension. I know that other people have died exploring this mystery. Yet I am here to fathom it if I can; I believe my best course lies not in avoiding Animation, but in studying it with extreme caution and whatever safeguards are feasible. Knowledge is our most formidable weapon, especially against the unknown."

"I expected that response, and respect it," the Swami said. "My purpose is only to make certain you appreciate the possible magnitude of the threat. I can do no more. Nor would I, under the Covenant."

Brother Paul had expected a less restrained reaction. The Swami ranged from snappish intolerance to utter reasonableness without warning. "I understand there are to be assigned watchers, during my exploration. Perhaps you should be among them, to caution me where necessary."

"I am already represented," the Swami said. "Yet the watchers are as nothing against the magnitude of this force."

They had come up to the two standing figures. "Brother Paul," one said. He was an old man, white-haired but upright. "I am Pastor Runford, Jehovah's Witness. This is Mrs. Ellend, Church of Christ, Scientist."

"I am glad to meet you," Brother Paul said. Separately, to the woman, he added: "That would be Christian Scientist?"

The woman nodded. She seemed even older than the pastor, but also healthier, as befitted her calling. Christian Scientists commonly refused conventional medical attention, believing that all illness was illusory.

"We two have been assigned to watch over your experiment, remaining neutral ourselves," Pastor Runford said. "This is the edge of Northole, where Animations most frequently occur."

"If I may ask," Brother Paul said, "it seems to me that except for occasional storms, this effect remains fairly localized. Wouldn't it be simpler merely to demark the limits of Animation regions, and stay away from those areas?"

"We would do so if we could," Pastor Runford replied. "Young lady, if I may use your map . . ."

Amaranth stepped forward, smiling. The pastor used a stripped weed stem to indicate points on her map. "Our only route to the great forest to the north some leagues from here skirts Northmount. Here." He pointed to her right thigh, which was conveniently set forward. "And must veer quite near Northole, here." He gestured delicately to the obvious region, marked on her dress as a wide, shallow depression. "At times the Animation effect extends across the path, interfering with our hauling. If we do not bring down sufficient wood for the winter—"

"I understand," Brother Paul said. So there was a practical, geographic reason for neutralizing this effect, as well as the colonists' need to unify about a single God.

"We do not wish to interfere in any way with your belief or your investigation," Mrs. Ellend said. Her voice was oddly soft, yet carried well: the quiet authority of the grandmother figure. "Yet this matter is of some concern to us. Therefore it behooves us to cooperate with you, facilitating your exploration in an unobtrusive manner. While we are not, as a community, in complete agreement, common need has led us to this compromise." She glanced at the Swami. "Do you not agree, Kundalini?"

The Swami grimaced, but nodded affirmatively.

Pastor Runford's eyes traveled out over the misty hollow to the north. "Anticipating your progress, we have positioned observers within and without the Animation region. Mrs. Ellend and I are without; three colonists unknown to you are within. All are instructed by the Covenant to leave you to your own devices, except when you are in personal danger or otherwise in need of assistance. We ask you to remain near the fringe, where the effect is not strong, and to withdraw immediately if a storm should rise. Since we on the outside will be better able to detect such weather, we will signal you or send a courier at need. Are you amenable to this?"

Brother Paul considered it. "If I understand correctly, the line between reality and imagination becomes blurred within the Animation area. Thus I may perceive a storm when none is present, or overlook a genuine one. I must confess to my amazement at the manifestations evoked by Deacon Brown last night; it is apparent that my own objectivity is not proof against this sort of thing. I therefore thank you for your concern. I believe it to be well-founded, and I consider the Swami's warning quite timely also. I shall remain at the fringe today, and will respond immediately to your signal or messenger."

"We sincerely appreciate your attitude," Mrs. Ellend said with a smile that warmed him. What a gracious lady she was! "If you will also limit your initial exploration to an hour, this will serve as another safeguard."

"One hour." Brother Paul set the counter on his watch. "I'd like to take one further precaution. Because we are concerned with objective reality here, I have been provided with electronic units to enable me to communicate with persons outside of the Animation area. I propose to leave a transceiver with you, so that we will be in touch." He drew a wand from his pocket. "These are activated by pressure; just squeeze between thumb and forefinger to broadcast, and release to receive."

"I am familiar with the type," Pastor Runford said, taking the unit. "Back on Earth, we used these to coordinate our membership drives. An excellent precaution."

Membership drives. Yes, the Jehovah's Witnesses were the most persistent of recruiters, carrying their message and literature to every household. They believed the end of the world was near, and the advent of mattermission had intensified that belief. Brother Paul was not about to argue the case. "Also," he continued, "I have been cautioned against attempting to Animate the Major Arcana, but I cannot do much more with Tarot symbols like swords and cups than I have already witnessed. I would like to Animate more complex images that are still circumscribed by existing standards. It occurs to me that the picture symbolism of the Minor Arcana in the so-called Waite pack of cards—"

"You are a thoughtful man," Mrs. Ellend said. "Please accept my deck for this purpose. It is the standard Rider-Waite Tarot." She extended it.

"Thank you." Brother Paul took the deck, faced north, and started walking. The four colonists stood where they were, watching silently.

Actually he felt a bit guilty, for he had not informed them of the significance of the bracelet he wore. Yet it still seemed best merely to let this secret recorder record, and to ignore it meanwhile; it would represent the final evidence, back on Earth, of the truth of his discoveries. He could not play back its record here on Planet Tarot, so in that sense it really was irrelevant.

He wondered where the other three observers were—the ones inside the Animation region. Were they hiding? He really would not mind having them present; an objective experiment should be valid regardless of the audience, and the Animation effect did not seem to be publicity-shy. Maybe they were waiting under that tree thirty meters distant. . . .

It was a magnificent tree, possibly seventy-five meters tall, and thus larger than most that remained on Earth. The leaves formed so dense a canopy that the shade beneath it was like night. Pretty Tarot Bubbles clustered in that nocturnal shelter, exceptionally large; some were up to ten centimeters in diameter. A haze of blossoms coated the outer fringe of the upper region of the tree, and their odor drifted sweetly down to him. Could this be the source of Animation, the fragrance of the trees? No; surely anything so obvious would have been discovered long ago by the colonists. Flowers were seasonal, so the effect would be limited to springtime, and from all he had heard, Animation occurred at all seasons and in all places, though most frequently during storms and in Northole. Also, if Animation derived from the Tree of Life (assuming that this tree was a representative of that species) and remained associated with the wood, the effect would be strongest in the houses of the village. Since it was weakest there, and did not develop as the wood was being burned in winter, the Tree was an unlikely source.

The watchers were not by the tree. Brother Paul halted, physically and mentally, and pondered. "This seems like a good place to begin, nevertheless," he murmured. If this were an individual Tree of Life, allowed to stand because it was in the Animation area, it was a fitting setting for his experiment. If there were an entire forest of giants like this to the north, what a forest it would be! Perhaps he would visit that in due course. He hoped so.

He opened the pack of cards and riffled through it, his fingers nimble. He passed over the Major Arcana and stopped at the Ace of Wands. On this variant it was a picture, not a simple wand. That was why he had chosen the Waite deck. "Well, why not?" he asked himself.

He held the card before him, concentrating. Would it work, now that he was doing it alone? He wasn't sure he was far enough into the Animation area anyway, so a failure would not necessarily mean—

He looked up. And gaped. There it was: a small cumulus cloud, all gray and fleecy, hanging in the sky, its curlicues extending vertically, about a kilometer above the ground. As he watched, a white hand pushed out to the left, glowing, and in this ghostly hand was clasped a tall wooden club with little green leaves sprouting from it. The whole thing was in grandiose scale, and somewhat fuzzy and poorly proportioned, but obviously modeled upon the card he held. It was not merely a vision in the sky; there was a knoll several kilometers beyond it, on the far side of a flowing stream, and what could be a castle on this knoll. Brother Paul was sure that neither stream nor castle had been there before he had begun concentrating on the card. This meant the entire visible landscape had been coerced to conform to the card. This success was beyond his expectations; he had been ready for failure, or at best a miniature scene.

Even as he studied it, the scene wavered and faded. The castle was no longer clear, and the cloud—was only a cloud. He could no longer be sure he had seen what he thought he had seen.

Brother Paul did not pause to ponder the implications. Instead he sorted out the four deuces, set aside the main deck, and shuffled the twos together until their order was random. Then he turned up the top one: the Two of Swords. The picture was of a young woman in a plain white robe, blindfolded, seated before an island-studded lake. In her hands she held two long swords. Her arms were crossed over her bosom, so that the swords pointed up and outward in a **V** shape. He had dealt this card reversed

—upside-down—owing to the shuffling.

Before he tried to Animate it, he walked another fifty paces north, where he hoped the effect would be stronger and more persistent. He did not want another wavering, distorted picture to sap his certainty. He concentrated on the card as it was, then looked up.

Sure enough, the blindfolded lady was there, in every detail. Also the lake, the islands, and the crescent moon showing in the V. *And the whole scene was inverted*—like the card. The lake was overhead, the moon below; it was as if she were supported by the projecting swords.

Reversal could be highly significant in Tarot. In divination —the polite term for fortune-telling—it meant the message of the card was diminished in impact or changed. Muted. Brother Paul knew that according to the author of this deck, Arthur Waite, the reversed Two of Swords was an omen of imposture, falsehood, or disloyalty. A bad sign?

No, this was no divination! It was only an experiment, a testing of a specific effect. Besides, he did not believe in omens. For his purpose, this inversion was invaluable, because no such thing would have happened naturally. He *had* Animated it! Having verified this, he let it fade out.

Brother Paul sorted and shuffled the four threes, and dealt one. Cups, reversed. He concentrated, and the three maidens appeared, dancing in a garden, with cups held high, pledging one another. Upside-down.

If he were a believer in divination, he would be feeling rather doubtful now. The Trey of Cups signified the conclusion of any matter happily; reversed, it would mean—

Frowning, he put away the card, and watched the vision fade. He set up the fours. He walked farther north as he mixed them. The Animation effect did seem to be getting stronger, despite the inversions; it could be the intensification of the field or whatever enabled the effect, or it could be increasing proficiency on his part as he gained experience. This time he would really test it, by producing something he could touch.

He turned up the Four of Pentacles, Waite's name for Disks or Coins. Yet again, the card was reversed. And the image formed before him, without his consciously willing it. Inverted. It was a young man, seated, with a golden disk on his head, the disk inscribed with a five-pointed star, and another disk like it held before him, and two more under his feet. *Over* his feet, in this position.

"Damn it!" Brother Paul swore, in most un-Vision-like ire. He was tired of inversion and its theoretic warnings of trouble that he didn't believe in. He strode forward, moving his arm as if to sweep the vision away. Half certain that he would encounter nothing, he fixed his gaze on the fair city in the distance, also upside-down, like a mirage.

His outflung hand struck the front disk. It flew wide, reminding him momentarily of Tennyson's Lady of Shalott, whose spindle had flown wide and cracked the mirror from side to side. Was he, like that Lady, living in fantasy? The disk bounced and rolled along the ground. The man fell over, his feet coming down to touch the ground. He looked surprised. He opened his mouth as if to cry out—and faded away.

Shaking, Brother Paul stood looking at the spot where the Four of Pentacles had been. The Animation *had* been solid! Just as the symbols yesterday in the mess hall had been solid. There was now no question: belief in an image caused it to become real, here. Faith was the key.

Brother Paul put the deck away. It was evident that he could Animate what he saw on the cards, and these constructs seemed to pose no threat to him personally. But was there really any significance beyond this? If this were simply a work of art —reproducing pictures in three dimensions, converting pictures to sculptures—then there was surely no special god involved.

"Brother Paul," a small voice murmured.

If there were no god—at least none directly controlling the Animation effect—his task was simple. He could declare the problem solved and go home. But surely the colonists would not have been cowed by the Animation effect, if it were only an art form, any more than they were cowed by the volcanoes or the Tarot Bubbles. And what was the specific cause of the effect? His will controlled a particular image, but something else had to make it possible here, while it remained impossible elsewhere.

"Brother Paul," the small voice repeated, "do you perceive me?"

He knew he had to work this out very carefully. He believed in God, and this was a most powerful and pervasive belief, the realization of which had transformed his life eight years ago. Yet he had never presumed to define that God too specifically. It was essential that he keep his mind objective, and not create any deity here, as it were, in his own image. That had been Reverend Siltz's caution, and a proper one. For this mission, as in life, his God was Truth: the most specific, objective, explicable truth he was capable of mustering.

If God Himself should manifest via the medium of Animation, surely He would make Himself known in His own fashion, indisputably, as someone had already suggested. Brother Paul merely had to hold himself in readiness for that transcendent revelation, that supreme intuition.

"Lord," he murmured, "let me not make a fool of myself, in my quest for Thee." But he had to reprove himself: it was a selfish prayer. If it were necessary to make a fool of himself to discover God, then it would be well worth it. In fact, was this not the nature of the Fool of Tarot?

His hour was passing; if he were to progress beyond yesterday's point, he had to do it soon. He brought out the deck again and riffled through it, seeking inspiration. The Minor Arcana were not sufficient; should he Animate a Court Card? Perhaps a King or a Queen?

A figure showed. Female, coming toward him. But he hadn't attempted another Animation! Unless—

That was it. He was going through the Suit of Swords, and there was the Eight: a woman bound and hoodwinked among a forest of standing swords. It meant bad news, crisis, interference. He had unconsciously Animated it. He would have to watch that; he was in the depths of the Animation region now, and with practice was developing such ready facility that any card he glimpsed could become physical, even without his conscious intent.

Well, time for the big one. He would see if he could make the Tarot deck itself respond to his queries. Brother Paul brought out the deck again, sorted through the Major Arcana, and selected the Hierophant. This was Key Five of this deck, the great educator and religious figure known in other decks as the High Priest or the Pope, counterpart to the High Priestess. It all depended on the religion and purpose of the person who conceived the particular variant. The title of the card hardly mattered anyway; some decks used no titles. The pictures carried the symbolism. Surely this august figure of Key Five would know the meaning of Animation, if there were a meaning to be known.

Brother Paul concentrated, and the figure materialized. He sat upon a throne, both hands upraised, the right palm out, two fingers elevated in benediction, the left hand holding a scepter topped with a triple cross. He wore a great red robe and an ornate golden headdress. Before him knelt two tonsured monks; behind him rose two ornate columns.

Brother Paul found himself shaking. He had conjured the leading figure of the Roman Catholic Church, by whatever name a Protestant deck might bestow. Had he the right?

Yes, he decided. This was not the real Pope, but a representation drawn from a card. Probably a mindless thing, a mere statue. That mindlessness needed to be verified, so Brother Paul could be assured that there was no intellect behind the Animation effect.

"Your Excellency," he murmured, inclining his head with the respect he gave to dignitaries of any faith. One did not need to share a person's philosophy to respect his dedication to that philosophy. "May I have an audience?"

The figure's head tilted. The left arm lowered. The eyes focused on Brother Paul. The lips moved. "You may," the Hierophant said.

It had spoken!

Well, his recorder-bracelet would verify later whether or not this was true. Voice analysis might reveal that Brother Paul was talking to himself. That did not matter; it was his mission to make the observations, evoking whatever effects could be evoked, so that the record was complete. He could not afford to hold back merely because he personally might not like what manifested. He was already sorry he had Animated the Hierophant; now he had to *talk* with the apparition, and that seemed to commit him intellectually, legitimizing a creation he felt to be illegitimate. Well, onward.

"I seek information," he said, meekly enough.

The holy head inclined. "Ask, and it shall be given."

Brother Paul thought of asking whether God was behind the Animation effect, and if so, what was His true nature? But he remembered an event of his college days, when a friend had teased the three-year-old child of a married student by asking her, "Little girl, what is the nature of ultimate reality?" The child had promptly replied, "Lollipops." That answer had been the talk of the campus for days; the consensus of opinion had been that it was accurate. But Brother Paul was not eager for that sort of reply from this figure. First he had to verify the Hierophant's nature. So he asked it a challenging but not really critical question, a test question. "What is the purpose of religion?"

"The purpose of religion is to pacify men's minds and make them socially and politically docile," the Hierophant replied.

This caught Brother Paul by surprise. It was certainly no reflection of his own view of religion! Did this mean the figure did possess a mind of its own? "But what of the progress of man's spirit?" he asked. "What happens to it after it passes from this world?"

"Spirit? Another world? Superstitions fostered by the political authorities," the Hierophant said. "No one in his right mind would put up with the corruption and cruelty of those in power, if he believed this were the only world he would experience. So they promise him a mythical life hereafter, where the wrongs of *this* life will be compensated. Only a fool would believe *that*, which shows how many fools there are. Barnum was wrong; a fool is not born every minute. A fool is born every second."

"Lord have mercy on me, a fool," Brother Paul murmured.

"Eh?" the Hierophant demanded querulously.

"I merely thought there was more to religion than this," Brother Paul clarified. "A person needs some solace in the face of the inevitable death of the body."

"Without death, there would be no religion!" the Hierophant asserted, waving his scepter for emphasis. It almost struck the pate of one of the monks. The Hierophant frowned in annoyance, and both monks disappeared. "Religion started with the nature spirits—the forest fire, flood, thunder, earthquake and the like. Primitive savages tried to use magic to pacify the demons of the environment, and made blood sacrifices to the elements of fire, water, air, and earth, hoping to flatter these savage powers into benign behavior. Read the Good Book of Tarot and you will find these spooks lurking yet, in the form of the four suits. Formal religion is but an amplification of these concepts."

Brother Paul's amazement was giving way to ire. "This is an idiot's view of religion," he said. "You can't claim—"

"You have been brainwashed into conformity with intellectual nonsense," the Hierophant said with paternal regret. "Your whole existence has been steeped in religious propaganda. Your memory is imprinted with the face of Caesar and the message 'In God We Trust.' Your pledge of allegiance to your totemic flag says 'One nation under God indivisible.' Why not say 'In Satan We Trust,' for Satan has far more constancy than God. Or 'One nation, embracing a crackpot occult spook, indivisible except by lust for power—'"

"Stop!" Brother Paul cried. "I cannot listen to this sacrilege!"

The Hierophant nodded knowingly. "So you admit to being the dupe of the organized worldwide conspiracy of religion. Your objectivity exists only so long as the truth does not conflict with the tenets of your cult."

Brother Paul was angry, but not so angry that he missed the kernel of truth within the religious mockery. This cardboard entity was baiting him, pushing his buttons, forcing him to react as it chose. The Animation was in control, not he himself. He had to recover his objectivity, to observe rather than proselytize, or his mission was doomed.

Brother Paul calmed himself by an effort of will that became minimal once he realized what was happening. "I apologize, Hierophant," he said, with a fair semblance of calmness. "Maybe I have been misinformed. I will hear you out." After all, freedom of speech applied to everyone, even those with cardboard minds.

The figure smiled. "Excellent. Ask what you will."

This was now more difficult than before. Instead of a question, Brother Paul decided to try a statement. Maybe he could gain the initiative and make the Animation react instead; that should be more productive. Obviously there was a mind of some kind behind the facade; the question was, *what* mind?

"You say I can tolerate only that truth which does not conflict with the tenets of my personal religion," he said carefully. "I'm sure that is correct. But I regard my religion as Truth, and I do my best to ascertain the truth of every situation. I support freedom of speech for every person, including those who disagree with me, and I endorse every man's right to life, liberty, and the pursuit of happiness. This is part of what I mean when I salute my country's flag, and when I invoke God's name in routine matters."

"Few nations support these things," the Hierophant said. "Certainly not the monolithic Church. A heretic is entitled to neither life nor liberty, and no one is entitled to happiness."

"But happiness is the natural goal of man!" Brother Paul protested, privately intrigued. Now he was baiting the figure! He considered happiness only a part of the natural goal of man; he himself did not crave selfish happiness. Once, perhaps, he had; but he had matured. Or so he hoped.

"The salvation of his immortal soul is the proper goal of man," the Hierophant said firmly. "Happiness has no part of it."

"But you said man's immortal soul was superstition, a mere invention spawned by political—"

"Precisely," the figure agreed, smiling.

"But then it is all for nothing! All man's deeds, man's suffering, unrewarded."

"You are an apt student."

Brother Paul shook his head, clearing it. This thing was not going to mousetrap him! "So the destiny of man is—"

"Man must eschew joy, in favor of perpetual mortification."

"But all basic instincts of man are tied to pleasure. The satisfaction of abating hunger, the comfort of rest after hard labor, the acute rapture of sexual union—"

"These are temptations sponsored by Satan! The ascetic way of life is the only way. The way of least pleasure. A man should feed on bread and water, sleep on a hard cot, and have contact with the inferior sex only for the limited purpose of propagating the species, if at all."

"Oh, come now!" Brother Paul protested, laughing. "Sex has been recognized as a dual-function drive. Not only does it foster reproduction, it enhances the pleasure of a continuing interpersonal relationship that solidifies a family."

"Absolutely not!" the Hierophant insisted. "The pleasures of fornication are the handiwork of Satan, and the begetting of a child is God's punishment for that sin, a lifelong penance."

"Punishment!" Brother Paul exclaimed incredulously. "If I had a child, I would cherish it forever!" But he wondered whether this were mere rhetoric; he had no experience with children.

The Hierophant frowned. "You are well on the way to eternal damnation!"

"But you said there was no afterlife! How can there be eternal damnation?"

"Repent! Mortify yourself, throw yourself upon the tender mercy of the Lord in the hope that He will not torture you too long. Perhaps after suitably horrendous chastisement, your soul will be purged of its abysmal burden of guilt."

Brother Paul shook his head. "I am trying very hard to be open and objective, but I find I just can't take you seriously. And so you are wasting my time. Begone!" He turned away, knowing the figure would dissipate. Maybe he had lost this engagement by calling it off, but he didn't regret it.

These Animations were fascinating. There was a tremendous potential for physical, intellectual, and spiritual good here, if only it could be properly understood. So far he had not succeeded in doing that. The Hierophant Animation had spoken only a pseudo-philosophy, as shallow as that of a cardboard figure might be expected to be. If he had Animated a lovely woman, would she have been as bad?

A lovely woman. That intrigued him on another plane. Some men considered intellect a liability in a woman, and indeed some supposedly stupid women had made excellent careers for themselves by keeping their legs open and their mouths closed. This was not really what Brother Paul was looking for, yet the interest was there. Would an Animation woman be touchable, kissable, seducible?—a construct of air, like a demon, a succubus?

He wrenched his speculation away. It was *too* intriguing; maybe he *was* too far on the road to damnation! To utilize a phenomenon like Animation merely to gratify a passing lust! Of course there was nothing wrong with lust; it was God's way of reminding man that the species needed to be replicated, and it provided women of lesser physical strength with a means to manage otherwise unmanageable men. But lust directed at a construct of air and imagination could hardly serve those purposes. "Get thee behind me, Satan," he murmured. But even that prayer was useless, for Satan was also the master of buggery: not the type of entity a man would care to have standing near his posterior.

Brother Paul looked at his watch. His time was up; in fact he was already overdue. Why hadn't the watchers notified him? He must return to the non-Animation area.

But which way was out? Clouds were swirling close; a storm was in the neighborhood. Why hadn't he noticed it coming? This too should have caused the watchers to—

Suddenly he remembered. They *had* called him—and he had been too preoccupied to notice it consciously. The pastor must have assumed that the signal wasn't getting through. Still, he might have sent someone in. . . .

The hoodwinked girl, representing the Eight of Swords! Had Amaranth come in to warn him, after the transceiver contact had failed, and been incorporated into that mute image? There was some evidence that Animations were ordinary things, transformed perceptually, so maybe an Animation person was a real person, playing a part. But that didn't make sense either; why would a person play such a part? No one claimed that Animation affected the inner workings of the mind; it only changed perceptions of external things.

Maybe Amaranth had come in, and been deceived by the various images he had conjured, and lost her way. Now he and she—and probably the various hidden watchers—were stranded in the Animation region, in a storm, unless he got out in a hurry, and brought them out with him.

How to do it? He should call out, of course! Establish contact with those outside, obtain geographic directions. "Pastor Runford!" he said to his transceiver.

There was static, but no answer. This was not surprising; the range of the tiny wand was limited, and terrain and weather could interfere. Probably the watchers had been forced to retreat before the storm, lest they be caught in the spreading Animation region.

His predicament was his own fault. He had been careless, when he should have been alert. He was only sorry that he had involved others in it, assuming they had not gotten out safely. What next?

Well, the Tarot deck had gotten him into this, to a certain extent; maybe it could get him out. He brought out the deck again and sorted through it.

Maybe one of the fives—

The first five he encountered was the Five of Cups, pictured by three spilled and two standing cups. Symbolic of loss, disappointment, and vain regret.

Precisely.

He studied the card, uncertain as to what to do now. And the picture formed before him. A man stood in a black cloak, his head bowed in the direction of the spilled cups, ignoring the two that remained standing. In the background a river flowed by—the stream of the unconscious, symbolically—and across it stretched a bridge leading to a small castle. Could that be the same castle he had seen in the Animation of the Ace of Wands? If so, he could use it for orientation. It was probably just the background, like a painted setting, representing no more than the orientation of the painting. Still, if he held the scene in mind, maintaining its reality, the others caught in this region might be able to orient on it, and then they all could find their way out together. The colonists would know the real landscape better than he did.

Was this crazy? Probably, but it was still worth a try. If *he* could approach that distant castle, so could *they*. Maybe they knew their way out, and were trying to locate him, to guide him out too, and the castle could serve as a rendezvous. At least he could test that hypothesis.

First, he would check with the black-cloaked figure. Maybe it was just the Hierophant, in a new role. On the other hand, it could be a watcher, impressed into this role, if that were possible.

Brother Paul stepped forward. And suddenly he was inside the picture, advancing toward the bridge. The cloaked figure heard him and began to turn. The face came into full view. And there was no face, just a smooth expanse of flesh, like the face of an incomplete store-window mannequin.

6

CHOICE
(LOVERS)

There seems to be a human fascination with secrets. Secrets and secret societies have abounded throughout history, some relating to entire classes of people, as with initiation rites for young men; some relating to religion, as with the "mystery" cults of the Hellenic world; and some relating to specialized interests, such as deviant sexual practices, fraternities, and the occult. The arcana of the Tarot reflect this interest: the word "arcanum" means a secret. The Major Arcana are "Big Secrets," the Minor Arcana "Little Secrets." So it is not surprising that the Tarot has been the subject of exploration by some "secret societies." The most significant of these was conducted by the Hermetic Order of the Golden Dawn, founded in 1887 as an offshoot of the English Rosicrucian ("Rosey Cross") Society, itself created twenty years before as a kind of spinoff from Freemasonry, which in turn originated with the Masons, or builder's guild. The Golden Dawn had 144 members —a significant number in arcane lore—and was formed for the acquisition of initiatory knowledge and powers, and for the practice of ceremonial magic. Many leading figures of the day were members, such as Bram Stoker (the author of the novel Dracula) and Sax Rohmer (the creator of Fu Manchu). One of its "grand masters" was the prominent poet William Butler Yeats. He presided over meetings dressed in a kilt, wearing a black mask, and with a golden dagger in his belt. But the Golden Dawn is remembered today for the impact some of its members had on Tarot. Arthur Edward Waite, creator of the *prominent Rider-Waite Tarot deck, was a member; so was Paul Foster Case, a leading Tarot scholar; and so was Aleister Crowley, said to be the wickedest man in the world, who created the Thoth Tarot deck under the name Master Therion. Crowley was a highly intelligent and literate man, the author of a number of thoughtful books, but he had strong passions, indulged in drugs like cocaine and heroin, practiced black magic (one episode left one man dead and Crowley in a mental hospital for several months; they had summoned Satan), and had homosexual tendencies that led him to degrade women. He set up a retreat in Italy called the Abbey of Thelema where his darker urges were exercised, and this became notorious. Yet for all the faults of the author, Crowley's Thoth Tarot remains perhaps the most beautiful and relevant of contemporary decks, well worth the attention of anyone seriously interested in the subject.*

The picture about him wavered and faded. Brother Paul hesitated, but immediately realized the problem: his entry into the Animation had changed it. Maybe the legendary Chinese artist—what *was* his name?—had been able to enter his own realistic painting and disappear from the mundane world, but very few others had acquired such status! Brother Paul could only look, not participate.

Yet why *not?* These Animations were governed by his own mind. If he wanted to paint a picture with himself in it, who was there to say he could not? He dealt the Six of Swords.

The picture formed. The stream of the unconscious had grown to the river of consciousness. The bridge was gone; this water was too broad for it. He could not see the castle at all. Of course this was a different picture, for a different card; the Five of Cups had stood for loss, while the Six of Swords represented a journey by water. He had lost the Five, appropriately, but gained the Six.

He spied a small craft on the water. It was a flat-bottomed boat, containing a woman and a child, and a man who was poling the boat across the river. "Wait!" Brother Paul cried, suddenly anxious, but also conscious of the possible pun: wait—Waite, the author of this deck. "I want to go, too!" But they did not heed him; probably they were out of earshot, if they existed at all as people. They were, literally, of a different world, one he could not enter.

He thought of the vacuous mouthings of the Hierophant, and

felt his ire rising again. *He* was Animating these pictures; he would have his answer! He had intended to ascertain whether there was any objective validity to these Animations, or whether they all merely represented a sequence of solidified visions from his mind. If the latter, he had his answer: there was no specific God of Tarot. If the former . . .

But right now he was merely trying to find his way out of this situation. He had intended merely to taste the water, not to drown in it!

Water—an excellent symbol. Why not put it to the proof?

He plunged into the river, half expecting to feel the scrape of ground against his body as he belly-flopped on reality. But his dive was clean; it was the shock of physical water that struck him. It foamed around his face and caught at his clothing; he should have stripped before entering! Yet he had not really believed . . .

If faith were the key to Animation, how was this water real, despite his unbelief?

But already his entry was changing the Animation. The water was vaporizing, the river diminishing. Brother Paul fixed his gaze on the people in the boat, striving to hang onto them, to prevent the entire image from evanescing. If only he could *talk* to them, these people of the Tarot background, and ask them—

The boat shivered. The man flew up into the air, sprouting wings, and perched upon a low-hanging cloud. The woman aged rapidly into a hag. The child grew up into an extremely comely young lady.

As Brother Paul approached them, they turned to face him. He halted a few paces away, discovering that he was back on his feet and soaking wet. His glance traveled from one woman to the other, the young and the old. He realized that this was no longer an image from the Minor Arcana, but one from the Major Arcana. This was Key Six, known as The Lovers.

Well, not necessarily. There was a certain haziness about the scene, an impression of multiple images.

Naturally. He had dealt no card of the Major Arcana, had sought no specific "Big Secrets," so had laid down no dictum for the scene. The Animation was trying to form itself from chaos. He must not permit that; he had to retain control of it!

Brother Paul raised the deck of cards that was still in his hand—but hesitated. There were many established variants of the

Tarot, and the Major Arcana were powerful cards. Which variant of Key Six would be best?

His own Holy Order of Vision variant, of course. The scholars of the Order had refined the symbolism developed by the researchers of the Golden Dawn and clarified the illustrations until this deck was as precise as the Tarot could be: a marvelous tool for self-enlightenment.

Yet the Holy Order of Vision did not restrict its Brothers and Sisters to its own Tarot deck, any more than it confined them to its own religious teaching. The heart of its philosophy, like that of Jesus Christ and the Apostle Paul, was service to man. Freedom of faith was one such service. Those who wished to pursue the Order positions were free to do so, and to become Ministers of Vision. But individual members like Brother Paul were encouraged to seek their own understandings, for dedication to the Order had to be freely given. The Order asserted that there was no freedom without enlightenment, so they were expected to study widely before orienting on any particular creed. Thus Brother Paul had investigated many aspects of religion and life, although so far these studies had been necessarily shallow: there was not time enough in a single human life to grasp thoroughly the full ramifications of any one of Earth's multiple faiths, let alone all of them. Had he focused his interest more narrowly, he could have moved beyond the "Brother" stage of his Order by this time—but that was not his way. Now he had to ask himself: should he take the familiar Vision Tarot, or should he use the generally similar Waite deck in his hand, or should he seriously consider other Tarot decks?

Phrased that way, the question admitted only one answer. If he used the Tarot at all, he should use the one best suited to the need. He always tried to research the full range of a problem, never accepting one solution blindly. The Vision Tarot was good, no doubt of it—but was it the best for this situation? Since other decks reflected other beliefs, and the whole problem of Planet Tarot was one of conflicting beliefs, he could make no quick assumptions.

He had not planned to go this deeply into Animation, on this first attempt. Discovering himself in over his head, as it were, he had the impulse to pull out immediately, and give himself the chance to consider more objectively, at leisure, what he had discovered, and to organize a more disciplined program of investigation. He still felt that haste would be foolish. He had the feeling that if he spoke to one of these two women, she would reply—and that this time the answer would be more meaningful than the response of the Hierophant had been. That did not mean he should speak now; he had to consider which woman to ask, and what to ask her. His choice of person might be highly significant. So he should withdraw, and recreate this scene only when he was properly prepared to exploit it.

One problem remained, however: how would he find his way out of this Animation? Should he ask one of these women? Then he would be committing himself to dialogue with them, as he had with the Hierophant. Better to leave them both strictly alone for now.

Then he realized why he believed he would have an answer. One of the aspects of Key Six was choice—the choice between virtue and vice. One woman was the right one, but which was which? Fuzzy as they both were, he could not tell. And he was by no means certain that external appearance would provide the necessary clue. Virtue was not necessarily lovely, and vice not always ugly; if they *were*, few people would ever make the wrong choice! This was another thing to work out carefully.

He had played with numbers and pictures, and gotten nowhere, *because* he had been playing. Now, at last, he was *in* the Animation, and the choice was far more precarious. He did not know whose God, if any, was manifesting here, and he would never learn if he allowed his preconceptions to dominate his investigation. God might well manifest through some quite unexpected medium. Perhaps he had an inadequate tool in this Tarot concept, or even a ludicrous one, but now he seemed closer to the truth he sought than he had been before, and closer than he might be in the future, and he was not sure he should waste the opportunity. God would not necessarily wait on his private convenience. Therefore he might be best advised to take what was offered and follow this up right now.

Yet his innate sense of caution cried out like a fading conscience; he could not allow himself to be unduly influenced by minor considerations. He had been intrigued by his fleeting glimpse of the Empress, the Girl of the Wheatfield, who had turned out to be Amaranth, and who might be one of these figures before him. If he left this Animation now, would she come with him? Or would she be lost? How could he be sure?

Sure of what? He shook his head. Sure he was not pursuing this vision because he suspected he might have some sort of power over her here, some way to make her amenable to . . . to what? He had no legitimate business with her, unless it was to use her relief-map torso to find his way out of here. Since she was not an assigned watcher, her very presence here threatened to distort his whole mission, especially since her body and personality were so . . .

He was going around in circles! Was it better to try to escape this Animation, so as to be able to set it up properly at another time instead of more or less by accident, or should he plunge ahead, now that he was this far along? He was hopelessly confused, now, about his own motives. He needed more objective advice. But he could not seek it without vacating this Animation (the Key Six scene seemed to be frozen obligingly in place, in all its foggy detail, while he wrestled with his uncertainties), and that would be a decision in itself, perhaps an error. That meant he was on his own, regardless. Unless, somehow, he could obtain a guide within the Animation itself.

Well, why not? "I want," he said aloud, clearly, "to select an adviser, who will then guide me through this Animation."

"Don't we all!" a voice agreed.

Brother Paul looked around. It had been a male voice, yet both figures before him, though obscure, were definitely female. "Where are you?"

"Up here on cloud nine."

Brother Paul looked up. The former boatman looked down. "Are you up there by choice?" Brother Paul inquired.

"Not that I'm aware of. I was poling my wife and kid across the river, when suddenly—" The man paused. "I don't even *have* a wife or kid! Am I going crazy?"

"No," Brother Paul reassured him. "You are part of a scene I conjured from the Tarot cards."

"*You* conjured it? I thought *I* conjured it!" The man scratched his head. "But if it fits your notions, it must be yours, because I never set out to fly!"

Was this a real man, a colonist, participating, like Brother Paul himself, in the Animation? Or was he entirely a figment of the evoked picture? Brother Paul hesitated to inquire, since he was not sure he could trust the answer. He should be able to work it out for himself in due course. "Well, maybe we can get you down from there. I'm about to deal another card."

"Wait!" the man cried in alarm. "If you deal away this cloud, I'll fall and break my leg!"

Brother Paul started to laugh, but immediately reconsidered. There was little doubt that these Animations were three-dimensionally projected visions, that even a camera's lens could see (and he hoped his recorder was watching well, because who on Earth would otherwise believe this story?)—but within them, there had to be some core of physical reality. People *did* die while experiencing Animations. If this man was real, he might actually be perched up in a tree, and if his "cloud" disappeared so that he believed he had to fall, he might very well topple from his branch and suffer serious injury. Brother Paul did not want to be responsible for that!

"Very well. I will leave this card, and merely summon spokes-persons for each separate Tarot deck, if that turns out to be possible. I'm sure you will be secure." If the man believed him, he *would* be safe. Faith was the key, if his present understanding were correct.

"Couldn't you just conjure me a ladder, so I can climb down?" the man asked plaintively.

Brother Paul considered. "I'm not sure I can do that. So far, I have formed these scenes by laying down cards and concentrating on the scenes they depict. I have no card with a ladder. If I try to put a ladder in *this* card, where it does not belong—well, when I introduced myself into a scene before, it changed. I fear it is not possible to make any change in an existing scene without breaking up the whole pattern. So the attempt to introduce a ladder might abolish the ground on which the ladder rests and lead to the very fall we seek to avoid. Maybe spot changes would be possible if I had greater experience with Animation, but right now I'm afraid to—"

"I get the message," the man said. "Do it your way. I'll wait. This cloud is pretty comfortable, for now."

Brother Paul concentrated. "Oldest Tarot, bring forth your spokesman," he intoned, suddenly quite apprehensive. This busi-ness of Animating visions was tricky in detail, like donning roller skates for the first time. One might master the basic principle, but lack the coordination for proper performance, and take a painful tumble. He was not at all sure he was following the rules of the game, now, for this was an indefinite command rather than a pictorial image.

A figure appeared. Had it actually worked? This seemed to be a king, garbed in suitably rich robes. The king spoke. But the words were incomprehensible. It was a foreign language! He should have known he could not glean information from cardboard; it was balking him again. Still . . .

Brother Paul listened carefully. In the course of his schooling, he had taken classes in French and German, and had had a certain flair for linguistics. But that had been a decade ago. He had been better at German, but this figure did not look German. French? Yes, possibly the French of six centuries ago, the time of the earliest known authentic Tarot deck! This must be King Charles VI of circa 1400, who commissioned the famous Gringonneur decks of cards.

The figure gestured, and a scene materialized. An Animation figure making a new Animation? Maybe so! This new scene was full of people. Three couples were walking gaily, as in a parade. The young men were dressed in medieval garb, the young ladies in elegant headdresses and trailing skirts. Above them, the cloud-borne man had fissioned into two military figures with drawn bows. They were aiming their arrows down at the happy marchers. What carnage had he loosed now?

Brother Paul smiled. This was not an ambush or a symbol of split personality, but romance. The cloudmen were adult Cupids, striking people with the arrows of love. He hardly needed the running French commentary to understand this card! But his purpose was to find a guide, not to evoke detailed derivatives of a particular Tarot concept. In any event, a guide whose advice he could not properly understand, because it was in a barely familiar language, would not do.

"Sorry," he said. "You may be the original Tarot, with impeccable taste, but I shall have to pass you by. Next!"

The scene faded, including the king, to be replaced by what Brother Paul took to be an Italian, though he could not say precisely on what evidence he made this judgment. It was a man, advanced in years, partially armored with sculptured greaves and wearing a sword. He had a thigh-length cape or topcoat, intricately decorated, and a crownlike headdress. Obviously a person of note.

The man made a formal little bow. "Filippo Maria Visconti," he said.

So this was the famous (or infamous) Duke of Milan about whom Brother Paul had read, who had commissioned the beautiful Visconti-Sforza Tarot to commemorate the marriage of his daughter to the scion of Sforza. A rigorous, brutal man, the Duke, but intelligent and politically powerful. He had paid a small fortune for the paintings, and the deck was the handsomest of the medieval Tarots.

Brother Paul returned the bow. "Brother Paul of the Holy Order of Vision," he said, introducing himself. "Pleased to make your acquaintance." Yet his pleasure was tempered by a nagging memory: hadn't this Duke fed human flesh to his dogs?

Visconti commenced his presentation—in Italian. Another linguistic barrier! The Duke gestured, and another scene materialized. This one had just three figures: the young couple, and a winged Cupid on a pedestal between them—which got the poor man down from the cloud—but Cupid was blindfolded, and held an arrow in each hand, that he was about to fling at the people below. *Love is blind!* Brother Paul thought.

"Francesco Sforza . . . Bianca Maria Visconti . . ." The names leaped out of the opaque commentary. The betrothed young couple, uniting these two powerful families. A truly pretty picture. But old Filippo Maria Visconti would not do as a guide.

"Next," Brother Paul said.

This time a small figure appeared: a child. There was a haunting familiarity about it; did he know this person? Brother Paul shook his head. This child was perhaps four or five years old, six at the most, and not quite like any he had seen on Earth.

The child spoke in French, and though Brother Paul was able to make out more words than before, this was still too much of a challenge for him. However, his lingering curiosity about this child caused him to listen politely. Was it a boy or a girl? Female, he decided.

She gestured, and a scene appeared. "Marseilles," she said clearly. And this most closely approached the original, fuzzy picture: a young man between two women, with a winged Cupid above, bow drawn and arrow about to be loosed. If Brother Paul didn't get that man safely down from that cloud pretty soon, he might be provoked actually to let that shaft fly!

But this picture was more like a cartoon than the previous two had been. Though the figures were three-dimensional and solid-seeming, they were obviously artificial, as though shaped crudely from plastic and painted in flat blue, red, yellow, and pink. This was the kind of scene a child would appreciate, almost devoid of subtle nuances of art. But by the same token, its meaning was quite clear: the man had to choose between the pretty young woman and the ugly old one. Or was the old hag the mother, officiating benignly at the romance of her son or daughter? Doubtless the child's narration explained this, but Brother Paul could not make out enough of it.

Regretfully he turned down this potential guide. "I'm sure I would enjoy your company, little girl," he said gently. "But since I cannot understand your words, I must seek other guidance. Next."

A lady appeared, garbed quite differently. She seemed to be Egyptian, wearing the ancient type of headdress held in place by an ornament shaped like a little snake, and an ankle-length dark dress with black bands passing horizontally around it at intervals. She tended to face sidewise, to show her face in profile, in the manner of Egyptian paintings.

"I hope you speak my language," Brother Paul murmured. Egyptian was entirely out of his range!

"Oh, I do," she said, startling him. "I represent the Sacred Tarot of the Brotherhood of Light."

Brother Paul had some familiarity with the Church of Light Tarot, but it differed in rather fundamental respects from the Vision Tarot. For one thing, the Hebrew letter associated with this Key differed. Brother Paul knew it as Zain, meaning Sword; the Light deck listed it as Vau, meaning Nail. The astrological equivalence also differed; to the Holy Order of Vision it was Gemini, while to the Brotherhood of Light it was Venus.

The woman gestured, her arm moving in a stylized manner, and her card manifested. A man stood between two women. All were clothed in ancient Egyptian garb. The man's arms were crossed, his hands on his own shoulders; the ladies' arms were bent upward at the elbows, the hands leveled at shoulder height. Thus each woman had one hand touching a shoulder of the man, though she faced away from him, while he looked at neither. Above, a demonic figure within a sunlike circle drew an ornate bow, aiming a long arrow.

"This is Arcanum Six, entitled 'The Two Paths,'" the female announcer said. "Note the two roads dividing, as in the poem by Robert Frost; the choice of paths is all-important. This Arcanum relates to the Egyptian letter *Ur*, or Hebrew *Vau*, or English letters V, U, and W. Its color is yellow, its tone E, its occult science Kabalism. It expresses its theme on three levels: in the spiritual world it reflects the knowledge of good and evil; in the intellectual world, the balance between liberty and necessity; in the physical world, the antagonism of natural forces, the linking of cause and effect. Note that the woman on the left is demurely clad, while the one on the right is voluptuous and bare-breasted, with a garland in her hair and her translucent skirt showing her legs virtually up to the waist. Remember, then, son of Earth, that for the common man the allurement of vice has a far greater fascination than the austere beauty of virtue."

Brother Paul was impressed. "You have really worked out the symbolism," he commented. "But most scholars regard this card as symbolizing love rather than choice."

"Venus governs the affections and the social relations," she replied, undismayed. "It gives love of ease, comfort, luxury, and pleasure. It is not essentially evil, but in seeking the line of least resistance it may be led into vice. When it thus fails to resist the importunities of the wicked, it comes under the negative influence of Arcanum Two, Veiled Isis—"

"Wait, wait!" Brother Paul protested. "I don't want to get tangled up with the High Priestess or other cards at the moment; I just want to understand this one as a representative of your Tarot deck, so I can compare it to the equivalent cards of the other decks. Are you saying this is a card of love, or of choice? A simple yes or no will do—I mean, one description or the other."

She glanced at him reproachfully. "If you seek simplistic answers to the infinitely complex questions of eternity, you have no business questioning the Brotherhood of Light."

Brother Paul had not expected such a direct and elegant rebuff from a conjured figure. "I'm sorry," he apologized. "It's just that I'm not really looking for the full symbolism, but for a guide who can bring me most rapidly and certainly to the truth. I know I shall never master the Tarot as thoroughly as you have done, but perhaps you could show me—"

She softened. "Perhaps so. I will try to provide your simplistic answers. This is a card of love *and* choice, for the most difficult decisions involve love. Note that the man stands motionless at the angle formed by the conjunction of the two roads, as it seems you stand now. Each woman shows him her road. Virtue carries the sacred serpent at her brow; Vice is crowned with the leaves and vine of the grape. Thus this represents temptation."

"Temptation," Brother Paul echoed. Her "simplistic" answer did not seem very simple to him, but he appreciated her attempt to relate to him on his own level. He saw that she herself most closely resembled, in dress and manner, the figure of Virtue, yet her demure apparel did not entirely conceal the presence of excellent breasts, legs, and other feminine attributes. She reminded him of—well, of the colonist Amaranth. And there was temptation again! But logic did not concur.

"I like your rationale," he said. "I am sorry I have not paid more attention to the Tarot of the Brotherhood of Light before. I suppose when I saw the demon Cupid in the sky, I jumped to the conclusion that—"

"That is neither demon nor Cupid," she said. "It is the genie of Justice, hovering in a flashing aureole of twelve rays of the zodiac, crowned with the flame of spirit, directing the arrow of punishment toward Vice. This ensemble typifies the struggle between conscience and the passions, between the divine soul and the animal soul; and the result of this struggle commences a new epoch in life."

Brother Paul nodded thoughtfully. There was much in this presentation that appealed to him. Certainly Venus related well to the love aspect, and the interpretation of the image as representing choice related extremely well to his present situation. And if this were the girl Amaranth, describing what must be the Tarot deck she used, he would be very glad to have her as his guide. Still, he should look at the remaining offerings before making his decision. Apologetically, he explained this to the lady.

She smiled. "I am sure you will do the right thing," she said, and faded out.

So she could wait her turn without fretting. She looked better and better.

The next presentation was by a male figure that reminded him strongly of his alien acquaintance, Antares, in his human host. But the scene itself was instantly recognizable: it was The Lovers, by Arthur Waite, perhaps the best known expert on Tarot. The scene was of a naked man and woman standing with spread hands, front face, while a huge, winged angel hovered above the clouds, extending his benediction. To the right was the Tree of Life, bearing twelve fruits; to the left, behind the woman, was the Tree of the Knowledge of Good and Evil, with the serpent twining around it. The Tarot of the Holy Order of Vision was derived from that of Paul Foster Case, which was refined in turn from that of Waite. Thus this picture was extremely comfortable in its familiarity.

Yet the points of the apologist for the Light deck were well-taken. "Sir," Brother Paul said diffidently to the Waite figure, "I have just viewed an Egyptian variant of this Key—"

"Preposterous!" the figure snapped. "There is not a particle of evidence for the Egyptian origin of Tarot cards!"

"But a number of other experts have said—"

The figure assumed what in a lesser man would resemble an arrogant mien. "I wish to say, within the reserves of courtesy belonging to the fellowship of research, that I care nothing utterly for any view that may find expression. There is a secret tradition concerning the Tarot, as well as a secret doctrine contained therein; I have followed—"

"But the aspect of choice, of temptation, two roads—"

The figure was unrelenting. "This is in all simplicity the card of human love, here exhibited as part of the way, the truth, and the life. It replaces the old card of marriage, and the later follies that depicted man between vice and virtue. In a very high sense, the card is a mystery of the covenant and Sabbath."

"But—"

"The old meanings fall to pieces of necessity with the old pictures. Some of them were of the order of commonplace, and others were false in symbolism."

Brother Paul had always had a great deal of respect for Waite, but this arrogance reminded him uncomfortably of the Animated Hierophant. The Lady of Light had been complex but reasonable; Waite seemed only complex.

Still, he was a leading Tarot figure. Brother Paul tried again. "According to the Brotherhood of Light, the Hebrew letter assigned to this card is *Vau,* rather than—"

"That would be the handiwork of Eliphaz Levi. I do not think that there was ever an instance of a writer with greater gifts, after their particular kind, who put them to such indifferent uses. He insisted on placing the Fool toward the *end* of the Major Arcana, thereby misaligning the entire sequence of Hebrew letters. Indeed, the title of Fool befits him! There was never a mouth declaring such great things—"

"Uh, yes. But astrologically, Venus does seem to match the card of Love."

"Nonsense. The applicable letter is *Zain,* the Sword. A sword cleaves apart, as Eve was brought from the rib of Adam, flesh of his flesh, bone of his bone. *Zain,* following the *Vau* of the Hierophant: the nail that joins things together. Astrologically, Gemini naturally applies. The sign of the twins, of duality, male and female. There is no question."

Brother Paul sighed inwardly. He had agreed with Waite's analysis before he had encountered that of the Light Tarot; now both conflicting views seemed reasonable. He was in no position to debate symbolism with these experts, and that was not his present purpose anyway. Why was such a seemingly simple project becoming so complex? To choose a single expert from among six, some of whom had already been eliminated because of language or age. Too bad he couldn't evoke both Light and Waite together, and let them thrash it out themselves.

Why not? It might be worth a try.

No, they would merely argue interminably, and this was really his own decision to make.

"I do have one more card to consider," Brother Paul said, conscious of the numerical symbolism: six variants of Key Six.

Waite faded out with a grimace of resignation. He obviously felt that the mere consideration of alternative decks was frivolous. He was replaced by a portly, unhandsome man, bold and bald, whose aspect was nevertheless commanding. "I am the Master Therion, the Beast 666," he proclaimed. "I overheard your previous interview. Isn't old Arthwaite an ass? It's a wonder anyone can stomach him!"

Brother Paul was taken aback once again. These Animation figures were showing a good deal more individuality than he had expected. "Arthur Waite is a scholar. He—" He paused. "What did you call yourself?"

"The Beast 666. The living devil. The wickedest man on Earth. Is it not immediately apparent?"

"Uh, no. I—"

"Call me Master Therion, then, as you will. Do what thou wilt shall be the whole of the law. Love is the law; love under will."

Brother Paul was impressed again. "Love is the law. What an excellent thought for this Key of Love!"

Therion smiled approvingly. "Indeed. Did you notice old

Arthwaite's slip about Adam and Eve? He actually *believes* the hoary tale about Adam's rib. Rib, hell! Eve was formed from the foreskin excised from Adam's pristine penis when he was circumcised. Look it up in the Babylonian Talmud, from which so much of the Old Testament was pirated. And expurgated. A neat little bloody ring of skin, the original symbol of the female. God formed it into a living, breathing tube of flesh typified by circles, from the two globes perched ludicrously on her chest to the very manner in which her elliptical mind works. She was fashioned for one purpose only, and that was to embrace again that member from which she was so blithely cut, making it whole once more. Any man who permits her to distract his attention for any other purpose is a fool."

Brother Paul appraised Therion. It had been a long time since he had heard so concentrated and unprovoked a denunciation of woman. "You really *are* a beast!"

"Correct!" Therion agreed, pleased.

"I think I'd better have a look at your card."

"Do what thou wilt!" Therion gestured, and the scene formed.

It was—different. It was filled with figures, yet not crowded. A man and a woman stood centrally, each in royal robes. They stood facing a huge, headless figure whose great, dark arms stretched forward in benediction, massive sleeves accordion-pleated like those of an old-fashioned robot or space suit. Where the head should be, the winged Cupid flew instead, an arrow notched to his bow. A naked man and woman stood in the upper corners, two children stood in the foreground, and there were also a lion, a bird, and snake. Eleven living entities in all—yet they were integrated so harmoniously that it all seemed normal. The whole effect was absolutely beautiful.

Still, it was not art he sought, but good advice. "Two prior versions of this card differ in certain details," Brother Paul began cautiously.

"Arthwaite is ludicrous, but in the matter of the Hebrew equivalence he is more or less correct," Therion said. "Even a stopped clock is right on occasion! This card is The Lovers, matching with *Zain* the Sword, and Gemini astrologically."

"More or less correct?" Brother Paul repeated questioningly.

"He transposed the cards for Adjustment and Lust. That cannot be justified rationally."

Brother Paul was perplexed. "Adjustment? Lust? These are not symbols of the Tarot."

"Formerly known as Temperance and Strength," Therion explained. "Arthwaite simply switched them on his own initiative, exactly as he garbled their symbolism. He denied the Egyptian origin of the Tarot."

"You say it *is* Egyptian?"

"Absolutely. I call it the Book of Thoth. Of course others have arrived at more speculative derivations. The phrase *Ohev Tzarot* is Hebrew for a 'lover of trouble.' That seems to relate in several ways, but I regard it as coincidence. After all, if we start spelling the word with a 'Z', we could derive it from Tzar, or use 'Cz' for Czar, deriving it from the Roman emperor Caesar. Thus 'Czarot' could be taken to mean a device of supreme power, dominating an occult empire. That convolution of logic is almost worthy of Arthwaite! But the actual origin of the Tarot is quite irrelevant, even if it were certain. It must stand or fall as a system on its own merits. It is beyond doubt a deliberate attempt to represent, in pictorial form, the doctrines of the Qabalah."

"The Kabala?"

"Qabalah."

"Let's return to Key Six."

"Very well. Atu Six is, together with its twin Atu Fourteen, Art, the most obscure and difficult of the—"

"Please," Brother Paul interrupted. "I need a fairly simple analysis." He wondered whether he would receive another rebuke.

But the Master Therion smiled tolerantly. "Of course. I will start at the beginning. There is an Assyrian legend of Eve and the Serpent: Cain was the child of Eve and the Serpent of Wisdom, not of Adam. It was necessary that he shed his brother's blood, so that God would hear the children of Eve."

"This cannot be!" Brother Paul cried in horror. "The son of the *Serpent?*"

Therion glanced at him, frowning. "I took you for a seeker after truth."

"I—" Brother Paul was stung, but did not care to be the target of obscenity or blasphemy.

"Surely you realize it was not general knowledge that Adam and Eve were denied, but *carnal* knowledge. The Serpent is the original phallic symbol."

"I do want to be objective," Brother Paul said. "But can you give me a more specific summary of the meaning of the card? For example, do you feel it represents Choice?"

"It represents the creation of the world. Analysis. Synthesis. The small figures behind the shrouded Hermit are Eve and Adam's first wife, Lilith."

Brother Paul realized that he was getting nowhere. However fascinating the symbolism might be, it was not helping him to make his decision. Probably the Light card was best, and therefore the pretty woman should be his guide. "I'm afraid I—"

"Do what thou wilt," Therion said.

To do what he really willed, Brother Paul realized, now required the presence of the woman. He believed he could justify choosing her on the basis of what he had seen in these sample cards, and by the attitudes of their presenters. Waite had been too arrogant and inflexible, while Therion was—well, a bit of a beast. . . .

Then he noticed something else about the central figures of the scene. The female was very like the girl of the wheatfield, and the man was black. Not demon-black, but Negro-black. This was an interracial union!

Brother Paul himself was only about one-eighth black, but that eighth loomed with disproportionate importance in his home world. Suddenly he identified.

He stepped into Therion's picture, his choice made.

It was a mistake.

7

PRECESSION
(CHARIOT)

*Those who read the standard editions of the Bible may wonder why
there is a gap of two or three hundred years in the record between the
Old and New Testaments. Did the old scholars, historians, philosophers, and prophets simply stop creating for a time? As it turns out, this
was not the case. Material was recorded, and was known to the scholars
of Jesus's time, and perhaps to Jesus himself, but it was not incorporated into the Bible. In the succeeding millennia, much of it was buried
in old libraries and largely ignored. Then, in 1947, the discovery of the
Dead Sea Scrolls transformed the picture, for these documents, dating
from the time of Jesus, contained much of this same material,
authenticating it. Now the story of the lost years could be unraveled:*

*After Alexander the Great conquered the world, many Jews were
scattered from Israel to all the countries of the Mediterranean. This
was the Diaspora—not the first or the last Jewish dispersion, for a
number of conquerors used this method to deal with these intractable
people—significant because it happened to make a cutoff date of about
300 B.C. for the assorted books of the Bible. Many displaced Jews now
spoke Greek rather than Hebrew, and there were actually more Jews in
Alexandria than in Jerusalem. But only narrowly defined Hebrew-
language texts were accepted for the Bible as it now stands. Thus much
material was excluded by both Jews and Christians, although it was
generally recognized to be parallel to the included books. The complete
assembly consists of the thirty-nine books of the Old Testament,*

*fourteen books of the Apocrypha (meaning "hidden"), about eighteen
books of the Pseudepigrapha ("false writings"), and twenty-seven books
of the New Testament. That makes the record continuous.*

The chariot raced across the plain. Brother Paul grabbed for
support, but found his hands encumbered by the monstrous cup
he was carrying. There were no reins.

He braced his legs against the metallic supports of the chariot's
canopy, and discovered that he was in armor. His helmet visor
was open and his gauntlets were flexible; it was a good outfit. For
combat. The chariot was solid and well made; there was no danger
of its falling apart, despite the pounding of its velocity. The
horses—

Horses? No, these were four incredible monsters in harness!
One had the head of a bull, another that of an eagle, a third that of
a man, and the fourth that of a lion. The four symbols of the
elements! Yet the bodies did not match. The man-head had eagle's
talons; the lion-head had eagle's wings, woman's breasts, and
bull's feet. All the components of the sphinx, yet none of these *was*
the sphinx.

"What am I doing here?" Brother Paul cried out in confusion.

The man-head turned to him, and framed by its Egyptian
headdress was the face of Therion. "You are the Charioteer!" the
monster cried. "I am guiding you through the Tarot, as you
requested."

"But I didn't mean—" Brother Paul broke off. What *had* he
meant? He had asked for guidance, and the Chariot was the next
card, Key Seven. The symbol of victory, or of the Wheels of
Ezekiel, drawn by two sphinxes representing the senses: part lion,
part woman. The occult forces that had to be controlled so that
they would power man's chariot. Without such control, he could
not find his way out of the morass these Animations had led him
into, let alone separate God from chaos.

So why were there four steeds instead of two? Because this was
not the card Brother Paul knew, but the one Therion knew. No
wonder this was hard to manage! "Give me the other variant!"
Brother Paul cried.

The composite creatures shifted and merged into two white
horses. The chariot became medieval. "No, not that one!" More
shifting, and two sphinxes appeared, one black, one white. "Yes,

that one!" he cried, and the variant became fixed.

The white sphinx turned its head to face him. "How nice to see you again," she said.

"Light!" Brother Paul cried in recognition. "I mean, the apologist for the Tarot of the Brotherhood of Light! I thought this was the Waite deck."

She wrinkled her pert nose. "I hoped you had given up on that discredited innovation."

"Now you sound like Therion."

She snorted delicately. "Why choose between evils, when truth is available? Be yourself, the Conqueror; use the Sword of Zain to break through all obstacles, crush your enemies, and achieve sovereignty of spirit."

Brother Paul caught on. "You call Key Seven 'The Conqueror'!"

"Arcanum Seven, yes. This is historically justified in the Bible."

Oh-oh. Brother Paul did not want to get involved in another technical discussion, but his curiosity had been piqued. "The Bible?"

"Joseph, sold into Egypt, overcame all obstacles and rose to great power, as indicated by the sword." Brother Paul discovered that he was holding a curved blade in his right hand, not a cup. He set the sword down, afraid he would inadvertently cut the starry canopy. He remembered that the Hebrew alphabet for the Light Tarot differed from what he was used to. In that deck, Key Seven was Zain, the Sword. So the lady was correct, by her definitions. "He was tempted by Potiphar's wife, in Arcanum Six, but he triumphed over the temptation. He interpreted the dream of Pharaoh about the seven fat kine and the seven lean kine, and the seven good ears and the seven bad ears. And Pharaoh told him: 'See I have set thee over all the land of Egypt,' and made him to ride in a chariot, and made him ruler over—"

"Bullshit!" the black sphinx cried.

The white sphinx froze, shocked.

"Oh, Therion," Brother Paul said, trying to sound reasonable, although he too was upset by the interjection. "Now look, she didn't interfere in *your* presentation."

"*I* never uttered such nonsense! Women are such brainless things; if they didn't have wombs they'd be entirely useless."

The man was certainly contemptuous of the fair sex! What was the matter with him? In other respects he seemed to be quite intelligent and open-minded. "Still," Brother Paul admonished him, "you should not interrupt."

The lady sphinx turned her head toward the black sphinx, and then her body. The chariot veered, for they were both still galloping forward at a dismaying velocity. "No, I want to hear his objections. Does he challenge the validity of the Bible?"

"The Bible is hardly an objective account, and what there is is both incomplete and expurgated. Naturally the Hebrews and their intolerant, jealous God colored the record to suit themselves. How do you think the poor, civilized Egyptians felt about this barbaric conqueror?"

"They *welcomed* the Hebrews! Pharaoh raised up Joseph, put his own ring on Joseph's hand, arrayed him in fine linen, put a gold chain about his neck—"

"Bullshit!" Therion repeated. He seemed to enjoy uttering the scatological term in the presence of the lady. "Pharaoh gave away nothing! The Hebrew tribesmen and their cohorts came in, a ravening horde from the desert, overrunning the civilized cities, burning houses, pillaging temples and destroying monuments. They were the nefarious Hyksos, the so-called 'shepherd kings,' who ravaged cultured Egypt like pigs in a pastry shop for two hundred years before their own barbaric mismanagement and debauchery weakened them to the point where the Egyptians could reorganize and drive them out. *That* is why you call this *Atu* 'The Conqueror.' Joseph was a rabble-spawned tyrant, thief, and murderer. What little civilization rubbed off on his ilk was Egyptian, such as the Qabalah—"

"Kabala?" Light inquired.

"Qabalah. This was stolen from Egyptian lore, just as the golden ornaments were stolen from Egyptian households. The ones these thieves melted down to form the Golden Calf, a better deity than they deserved, before they settled, by the fiat of Moses, on a bloodthirsty, competitive, nouveau-riche God whose name they were ashamed to utter."

"I don't have to listen to this!" Light exclaimed. The scene began to change.

"Wait!" Brother Paul cried, suffering a separate revelation. This unrelenting attack on the roots of the Judeo-Christian religion —he recognized the theme, from somewhere.

"Waite? That does it!" the white sphinx snapped. She veered away, making the chariot tilt alarmingly.

Why had he chosen Therion as a guide, instead of Light? How

much better he empathized with her! Now, when he had almost gotten her back into the scene, she was going again. The chariot was rocking perilously, about to overturn, a victim of this religious debate. The sphinxes phased into two great horses again, white and black, then these animals fragmented into the composite monsters of Therion's Thoth *Atu*. Again Brother Paul found himself clutching the huge cup, which somehow he knew he dare not drop.

"Seven!" he cried. "I deal the Seven of Cups!"

The cup he was holding, which had given him this emergency inspiration, expanded. It was made of pure amethyst, its center a radiant, blood red. It was the Holy Grail.

The Cup expanded to encompass him, its radiance spreading out like the sunrise. Brother Paul felt himself falling into it. . . .

And he was splashing, swimming in a sea of blood. Thick, gooey, greenish ichor—the blood of some alien creature, perhaps from Sphere Antares, rather than of man. Great, cloying drops of it pelted down, forming slowly expanding ripples in the ocean. The drops fell from other cups: ornate blue vessels, six of them, set about a metallic support that rose from a larger cup resting on the surface of this awful sea. The green goo overflowed from each cup, and especially from the large one. Flowers lay inverted atop each cup, tiger lilies or lotuses; it was from them that the slime seemed to issue. The smell of corruption was awful.

"Thus the Holy Grail is profaned by debauchery," the voice of Therion said. It seemed to come from the largest cup, the seventh one, as though the man himself were immersed in its septic fluid.

"I have no interest in debauchery," Brother Paul protested, gasping. He was weighed down by his armor, trying to tread water, and the stench hardly helped his breathing. "I dealt the Seven of Cups."

"Indeed you did! Note how the holiest mysteries of nature become the obscene and shameful secrets of a guilty conscience."

Brother Paul opened his mouth to protest again, then abruptly realized the significance of the framework holding the cups. It was a convoluted, overlapping double triangle, shaped into the stylized outline of the female generative organs. Womb projecting into vagina, the largest cup being the vulva, overflowing with greenish lubrication from the sex organs of the plant. Flowers were of course copulatory organs, made attractive so that other species, such as bees, would willingly aid the plants to reproduce.

How many prudish women realized the full significance of what they were doing when they poked their noses into bright flowers to sniff the intoxicating perfume? Nature laughs at the pretensions of human foibles.

Still, enough was enough. Brother Paul did not care to remain bathed in these thick juices. "The *Waite* Seven of Cups!" he cried.

"Oh, very well," Therion said grouchily. "It *is* one of Arthwaite's better efforts, for all that he misses the proper meaning entirely."

The sea boiled, releasing great clouds of steam. From a distance came Therion's voice: "You'll be sorry!" And it echoed, "Sor-ry! Sorr-rry!"

The sea evaporated into clouds of greenish vapor, leaving Brother Paul standing on a gummy film of green that became a lawn. The cups retained their positions, however, turning golden yellow. The flowers above them dropped inside, mutating into assorted other objects that showed over the rims. At last he stood before this display of seven cups supported by a gray cloud bank.

"There it is," Therion said, now standing beside him. "Confusing welter of images, isn't it?"

"Are you still here? I thought Waite would—"

"You chose *me* as your guide, remember? Way back in Key Sex. I mean Six. You may view any cards you wish, but *I* shall do the interpretations."

So that choice had been permanent, at least for the duration of this vision. Brother Paul feared he had chosen carelessly. Well, he would carry through, and be better prepared next time. *This* time, confronted with the choice between Virtue and Vice, it seemed he had chosen Vice. At least he had some familiarity with this particular image, although the Holy Order of Vision did not put much stress on the Minor Arcana.

First, he had to orient himself. Why, exactly, was he here? He had wanted to get out of the careening chariot, of course, and out of the slime-soup of Therion's Seven of Cups, but what was his *positive* reason?

Answer: he was here to discover the ultimate ramifications of these Animations. His short-range objective of getting out of this particular sequence was passé; no matter how he struggled, he only seemed to be getting in deeper, as a man mired in quicksand only worsens his situation by thrashing about. (Though he had always understood that, since sand was denser than water, a man should readily float in quicksand, and so was in no danger if he merely relaxed. Could he float, here in Animation, if he just went along with it?) So he might as well follow through now, on the theory that it was as easy to move forward as backward.

When God manifested for him, as He had for others, whose God was it? Questioning the Hierophant had not helped; Brother Paul had first to comprehend the specific nature of the manifestations. Once again he reviewed it, hoping for some key insight. Were the visions purely products of his own mind, or was there some objective reality behind them? This remained a very difficult question to resolve, for how could he judge the validity of material drawn from his own experience? It was like trying to find a test for whether a person was awake or dreaming; he could pinch himself —and dream he was being pinched. If he knew what any given detail of an Animation was, that detail would be authentic; if he suffered from misinformation, how could he correct the image? Yet now it certainly seemed as though there were input from other minds, for Brother Paul had not before known all the details of the Tarot variants he had perceived in this Animation. Some of the concepts this Therion character had put forward were entirely foreign to Brother Paul's belief, yet again, these might be his own suppressed notions coming out, all the more shocking because he had always before denied their existence. The hardest thing for a man to do was to face the ugly aspects of himself.

So maybe he should face those aspects. Maybe the thing to do was to plunge all the way into this vision and grasp his answer before it faded. Surely it was in one of these displayed cups. At any rate, he owed it to himself and to his mission to look.

He inspected the cups more closely. One contained a tall miniature castle, another was overflowing with jewels, and others had a wreath, a dragon, a woman's head, a snake, and a veiled figure. All were symbols whose significance he had reviewed in the course of his studies at the Holy Order of Vision. But never before had they been presented as tangibly as this, and he knew now that these Animated symbols would not submit passively to conventional analysis.

The castle was similar to the one he had seen on prior cards, probably the same edifice. Symbolism in the Tarot tended to be consistent; a river was always the stream of the unconscious, originating in the trailing, flowing gown of the High Priestess, and the cup was always a vessel of emotion or religion. The castle represented for him a rallying point, an initial answer. Suppose he entered it now?

Well, why not *try?* He tended to spend too much time pondering instead of acting.

And the castle expanded, bursting out of its cup, becoming a magnificent edifice with banners flying from its lofty turrets, situated atop a precipitous mountain. Beautiful.

Brother Paul set out for it. Therion accompanied him, humming a tune as though indifferent to the proceedings.

"I've heard that song," Brother Paul said, determined not to let the man escape involvement so easily. "Can't quite place it, though."

"The 'Riddle Song,'" Therion answered promptly. "One of the truly fine, subtly sexual folk expressions."

"Yes, that's it. 'I gave my love a cherry'—but how is that sexual? It's a straightforward love song."

"Ha. The cherry was her maidenhead, that he ruptured. You have led too cloistered a life, and never learned proper vernacular."

"Oh? He also gave her a chicken without a bone, and a ring without end, and a baby without crying."

"The boneless chicken was his boneless but nevertheless rigid penis, thrusting through her ring-shaped orifice, producing in due course the baby—who naturally was not crying at the time."

That was one way of looking at it. "I should have stayed with the stream of the unconscious," he murmured.

"Oh, yes. That water Arthwaite says flows through the whole deck of the Tarot, starting with the gown of the harlot, yet. What crap!"

Here it went again! "I always thought it was a beautiful concept. How do you manage to see, ah, crap in it?"

"More ways than one, Brother! It is crap in that it is errant nonsense; water symbolizes many things besides the unconscious, and it is ridiculous to pretend that it can only stand for that one thing. But more directly, that euphemism he foists off on his fans—do you really think it is her *gown* that originates the fluid?"

"Well, that may be artistic license, but—"

"Her gown merely covers the real, unmentionable source, which is her body. A woman is a thing of flowing fluids, as I tried to make clear in *my* Seven of Cups. Milk from her tits, and blood from her—"

"Milk and blood are chemically similar," Brother Paul said quickly. "In fact, chlorophyll, the key to plant metabolism, is also surprisingly close to—"

"Flowing out from her orifices, bathing the whole Tarot in its hot, soupy—"

"Let's change the subject," Brother Paul said, not eager to argue the case further. What a case of gynophobia!

"Coming up."

A dragon appeared. Brother Paul whirled, gripping the sword he discovered at his hip. "That's the Dragon of Temptation!" he exclaimed. "It belongs in a different cup; I did not invoke it!"

"You must have invoked it, Paul," Therion said, without alarm. "For *I* did not do the dastardly deed."

Ha! "I Animated the castle; that was the only cup I emptied!"

Therion smirked. *"You* know that; *I* know that. But does *it* know that?"

Unfunny cliché! But the great Red Dragon of Temptation was charging across the plain. No time now to debate who was responsible; he had to stop it. "At least the Knights of the Round Table were mounted," Brother Paul muttered. "A lance and an armored charger—"

"You have to battle Temptation by yourself," Therion reminded him. "It has been ever thus."

So it seemed. Therion wore no armor and carried no weapon; obviously he could not oppose the dragon, and had no intention of trying. Brother Paul retained his chariot armor, although he had lost the chariot itself. So it was up to him.

The dragon had a huge wedge-shaped head from which a small orange flame flickered. No, that was only its barbed tongue. Its two forelegs projected from immediately behind its head, almost like ears, and two small wings sprouted from its neck not far behind, like feathers or hair. It seemed an inefficient design, but so did the design for Tyrannosaurus Rex, on paper. The rest of the monster trailed away into wormlike coils. Only its foreparts possessed a menacing aspect; when this creature retreated, it would be harmless. Which was of course the nature of Temptation, or any other threat.

The dragon was not retreating. It was galumphing directly at him, its serpentine body bouncing like a spring-coil after the awful head.

Brother Paul went out to engage it, his sword shining like

Excalibur. Yet he wondered: he considered himself to be a fairly peaceful man, not a warrior; why should he attack a living creature with a brute sword? This wasn't a living thing; it was an Animated symbol. Still, the matter disconcerted him.

The Dragon of Temptation drew up about two meters away. It glanced contemptuously at him. It had big yellow eyes, and its glare was quite striking. Its red snout was covered with great, hairy green-and-blue warts, and gnarled gray horns projected from its forehead. Its tusks were twisted and coated with slime. Brother Paul wondered idly if it had been mucking about in one of Therion's gooey cups before coming here.

The barbed tongue flicked about, striking toward Brother Paul like an arrow but stopping short of the target. The small wings flapped slowly back and forth, the thin leathery skin crinkling between the feathered ribs. Brother Paul could not recall ever having seen anything uglier than this.

"Whatsamatter?" the dragon demanded. "Chicken?"

Brother Paul felt a tingle of anger. What right had this filthy thing to call him names? He gripped his sword firmly and stepped forward.

And paused again. This was Temptation—the urge to violence for insufficient cause. So the monster had called him "chicken"; why should he react to the archaic gibe? This was the lowest level of social interaction, and violence was the refuge of incompetence. "I merely wish to visit that castle, for I suspect that the information I need is inside. If you will kindly stand aside, there need be no strife between us."

"Temptation never stands aside!" the creature snorted. It was very good at speaking while snorting. "You must conquer me before you can complete your mission, chicken."

"But I don't want to slay you. I shall be satisfied to pass you by."

"You *can't* slay me; I am eternal. You can't pass me by. In fact, you can't even fight me; you're a natural coward. Why don't you get out of this scene and let the air clear?"

As if he hadn't been trying to do just that! "I would, if I had no mission to perform. I will, after it is done. Now please stand aside." Brother Paul strode forward.

The dragon held its ground. "Temptation cannot be bluffed," it said.

Brother Paul refused to strike it with the sword without some more definite provocation. Though he knew it to be a mere symbol, its semblance of a living, intelligent (if ugly) entity was too strong.

He sidled around it—and the dragon was before him again. It had jumped magically to block him. He changed direction again —and it blocked him again.

So that was the way of it; the thing was trying to provoke him into striking. And if he struck first, he would have succumbed to Temptation.

This time Brother Paul walked straight into the dragon. And bounced off its warty face.

Therion still stood a little apart, watching with morbid interest. "It didn't bite me," Brother Paul said, surprised.

"Temptation does not attack physically," Therion explained. "It merely offers a more intriguing alternative. Still, it must be conquered."

Brother Paul failed to see anything intriguing in the dragon. He tried again to avoid it, and failed again. He was becoming more than mildly angry, and felt the urge simply to smash the thing out of his way, but he suppressed the impulse. Instead, he sheathed his sword and tried to heave Temptation out of the way with his hands. But the dragon was too heavy and low-slung to budge. "You can't conquer me by halfhearted measures," it said with a phenomenal yard-long sneer.

Brother Paul found himself sweating. Apparently this thing *could* balk him if he refused to fight it directly. Yet he remained reluctant to do so. He turned to Therion. "You're my guide. What do you recommend?"

"You must find common ground on which to meet it. Temptation assumes many guises. Maybe one will suit you."

Brother Paul considered this. Many guises—could that be literal here? Physical? "I don't care to take the sword to you, beast," Brother Paul told it. "Yet you must be moved. Isn't there some less devastating way to determine the issue?"

"I'll meet you on any front, chicken," the dragon said. Part of its sneer remained, having failed to clear the far end of its long mouth.

"How about barehanded? Can you meet me in human form?"

The dragon vanished. In its place stood a man, huge and muscular, with yellow eyes, a red face, blue horns and a warty nose. And that lingering sneer. "What say now, coward?" the demon demanded.

"I say that if Jacob could wrestle with the Angel of the Lord, I may wrestle with Temptation," Brother Paul replied. He felt better now. This was a judo situation, and he was competent. He could subdue his opponent without hurting him.

"I don't know no Jacob!"

"'And Jacob was left alone; and there wrestled a man with him until the breaking of the day.' It's from the Bible, the first book of Moses, called Genesis, chapter thirty-two." Brother Paul paused, expecting the demon to flinch at the Biblical reference, but was disappointed. But of course this was not a demon of the infernal regions, but the demon that was within every man; it would be conversant with the holy as well as the unholy. Except that it did not seem to know about this particular episode.

"Oh, *that* Jacob!" the demon said sneeringly. "He was a pretty puny angel, not to be able to beat a mortal man. In fact he would have lost if he hadn't struck a low blow."

Brother Paul remembered. "'And when he saw that he prevailed not against him, he touched the hollow of his thigh; and the hollow of Jacob's thigh was out of joint, as he wrestled with him.' But that sounds more like a leglock than a low blow—leverage on the thigh to throw out the hip joint."

"The 'hollow of the thigh' is a euphemism for the crotch," the demon insisted. "The angel popped Jacob's crotch."

"Perhaps so," Brother Paul admitted. "It is a debatable point. Yet further along it is referred to as 'the sinew which shrank' and since he did sire a good family—"

"Not after he wrestled with the angel!"

Brother Paul spread his hands. He had thought his combat with the demon-dragon would be physical, but he was glad to settle for this Biblical arena instead. He had done a lot of Bible reading in the past few years, being fascinated with it as both religion and history. He was also intrigued by the continuity of the Bible, in the forms of the Apocrypha and Pseudepigrapha. "At any rate, the Angel did not defeat him, and he won from it a blessing: the name of Israel, meaning 'A Prince of God,' and founded the tribe of Israel."

"And his daughter Dinah got raped," the demon said, smiling as if with enjoyment.

This creature reminded Brother Paul strongly of Therion. He glanced back, but Therion was still standing there. On second thought, Therion would not approve of rape, not from consideration for the woman, but because he seemed to feel that the sexual act was a male sacrifice bestowed on the unworthy female. Why force this gift on a mere woman? "Rape is too strong a term," Brother Paul continued. "The young man was honorable, and begged to be allowed to marry Dinah formally, and even accepted the requirement of circumcision although he was a Gentile prince."

"Yeah, they covered up the record," the demon said. "Tried to make it out a good fuck in the end, so they wouldn't have to stone him for rape or her for acquiescence. A lot of juicy dirt got censored out of the Good Book."

Brother Paul started to make an angry retort, then realized that this was merely another aspect of the battle. Temptation fought with concepts as well as words, and truth was irrelevant. If distortion and vernacular caused Brother Paul to lose his temper, the victory would go to the dragon.

Indeed, these slights on Biblical accuracy were ones that Brother Paul himself had pondered privately. He liked to comprehend the full meaning of what he read, and much of the Bible remained tantalizingly opaque. Jacob's encounter with the Angel of God —there was an enigma! Why would an angel *want* to wrestle with a mortal man, and why would anything as pure of motive as an angel ever yield to the temptation? Yet Brother Paul knew he had to challenge the Bible with extreme caution, for it was a document that generations of scholars had not been able to question with certainty. Indeed, archaeological evidence continued to support the legitimacy of Biblical statements. Who was he, a minor novice in a minor Order, to set his puny judgment against the accumulated wisdom and revelation of the ages?

So he must vanquish Temptation here, too. It was not his place to debate any aspect of Scripture in public. It had been a mistake to invoke it here. What he did was his own responsibility; it should not be justified by reference to the Bible. That was a perversion, to adapt the Holy Book to individual purposes —though so many scoffers and special interests did.

"Enough of this," Brother Paul said. "If you will not let me pass, I must apply leverage."

The demon laughed. It was taller than Brother Paul, and heavier, and possessed a better physique. But how powerful was it, actually? Temptation could not be measured by external appearances.

Brother Paul stepped toward the castle, and of course the demon moved instantly to block him. This time Brother Paul stepped into it, shoved against the demon's right shoulder, and used his own right foot to sweep the demon's left foot out and forward. It was the *o uchi gari,* or "big inner reap" of judo.

The demon fell on the sand, as though its foot had slipped on a banana peel. Brother Paul stepped over it and resumed his march toward the castle. That had been amazingly easy!

And the demon stood before him again. "Very clever, mortal. But Temptation is not so readily put behind you. You could throw me a thousand times, and I would still be before you, for no single act of will defeats me."

Brother Paul stepped into it again. The demon braced against the maneuver that had brought it down before, but this time Brother Paul caught its right arm with both of his own and turned into *ippon seoi nage,* the one-armed shoulder throw. The demon's momentum carried it forward, and Brother Paul heaved it over his own shoulder to land on its back in the sand, hard.

This time Brother Paul followed it down and applied a neck lock. A simple choke would have cut off the demon's air, causing it to suffocate in a few minutes; this was a blood strangle that would deprive the creature's brain of oxygen, knocking it out in seconds.

The demon struggled, but it was useless. Brother Paul knew how to apply a stranglehold. He would not kill the creature, but would merely squeeze it unconscious. It would revive in a few minutes, unharmed—but too late to stop him from entering the castle. Temptation postponed might well be Temptation vanquished!

The seconds passed—and still the thing fought. The hold was tight, yet it seemed to have no effect. What was the matter?

The demon's arm came around, groping for Brother Paul's face. Sharp nails scraped across his cheek toward his right eye. He knew he would lose an eye if he did not get it out of reach in a hurry, but to do that he would have to release the strangle. This creature was not bound by polite rules of sport-combat!

Obviously the stranglehold had failed. The vascular system of demons seemed to be proof against the attack of mortals. Temptation could not be so simply nullified. Brother Paul let go and jumped up and away.

"I am a dragon," the demon said, standing. "I have no circulation, no blood. I operate magically. I need breath only to talk. You cannot throttle Temptation, fool!"

Evidently not! Brother Paul stepped toward the castle again, and the demon blocked his passage as before, grinning.

Brother Paul's left hand caught it by the right arm, jerking it forward. His right arm came up as if to circle the thing's impervious neck. The demon laughed contemptuously and pulled back, resisting both the throw and the strangle.

But Brother Paul's right arm went right on over the demon's head, missing it entirely. He twisted around as though hopelessly tangled, falling to the sand. But the weight of his falling body jerked the demon forward over his back. It was *soto makikomi,* the outside wraparound throw, a strange and powerful sacrifice technique. The demon landed heavily, with Brother Paul on top; such was the power of the throw that an ordinary man could have been knocked unconscious. Immediately Brother Paul spun around, flipped the demon onto its face, and applied an excruciating armlock, one of the *kansetsu waza.* The demon might not have blood, but it had to have joints, and they were levered like those of a man. Such a joint could be broken, but he intended to apply only enough leverage to make the creature submit. In this position, there was no way the demon could strike back; no biting, no kicking, no gouging.

He levered the arm, bending the elbow back expertly. The demon screamed. "Do you yield?" Brother Paul inquired, easing up slightly.

For answer, the demon changed back into the dragon, its original and perhaps natural form. Brother Paul had hold of one of its legs, but the ratios were different, and the lock could not be maintained. The monster's jaws opened, its orange tongue flicking out to lash at Brother Paul's face, whiplike. He had to let go quickly.

"So you couldn't take it," he said to the dragon. "You lost!"

"Temptation never loses; it is merely blunted, to return with renewed strength. I balk you yet." And the dragon moved to stand once again between Brother Paul and the castle.

Brother Paul turned to Therion, who had stood by innocently while all of this occurred. "What do you say now, guide?"

"Have a drink," Therion said, presenting a tall, cool cup of liquid.

"I don't need any—" he started to reply, but he *was* thirsty, and in this situation the refreshment cup was appropriate and tempting. Maybe he was too hot and bothered to perceive the obvious —whatever that was. With a cooler, cleared head he might quickly figure out the solution to this maddening problem of the Dragon. He accepted the drink.

It was delicious, heady stuff, but after the first sip, he paused. "This is alcoholic!" he said accusingly.

"Naturally. The best stuff there is, for courage."

"Courage!" Brother Paul's wrath was near the explosion-point. "I don't need that kind! My Order disapproves of alcohol and other mind-affecting drugs. Get me some water."

"No water is available; this is a desert," Therion said imperturbably. "Does your Order actually ban alcohol?"

"No. The Holy Order of Vision bans nothing, for that would interfere with free will. It merely frowns on those things that are most commonly subject to abuse. Each person is expected to set his own standards in matters of the flesh. But only those persons of suitable standards progress within the Order."

"Uh-huh," Therion said disparagingly. "So you are a slave to your Order's inhibitions, and dare not even admit it."

"No!" Brother Paul gulped down the rest of the beverage, yielding to his consuming thirst.

The effect was instantaneous. His limbs tingled; his head felt pleasantly light. That was good stuff, after all!

Brother Paul faced the dragon, who was still between him and the castle, smirking. "I've had enough of you, Temptation. *Get out of my way!*"

"Make me, mushmind!"

Brother Paul drew his gleaming sword. He strode forward menacingly, bluffing the beast back. When the thing did not retreat, he smote the red dragon with all his strength—and cut its gruesome head in half. Sure enough, there was no blood, just a spongy material like foam plastic within the skull. The creature expired with a hiss like that of escaping steam and fell on its back in the sand, its little legs quivering convulsively.

"Well, I made it move," he said, wiping the green goo off his blade by rubbing it in the sand.

"You certainly did," Therion agreed.

"So let's get the hell on to that castle before the dragon revives."

"Well spoken!"

But now a new obstacle stood between them and the objective. It was another cup—the one containing the Victory Wreath. The braided twigs and leaves stood tall and green above the chalice, the two ends not quite meeting.

"Take it," Therion urged. "You have won it. You have slain Temptation!"

Brother Paul considered. "Yes, I suppose I have." Somehow he was not wholly satisfied, but the pleasure of the drink still buoyed him. "Why not?"

He reached out and lifted the wreath from the meter-tall cup. Strange that this, too, should appear in his vision of the castle; had his choice of one cup granted him *all* cups? Somehow his quest was not proceeding precisely as he had anticipated.

He set the wreath on his head. It settled nicely, feeling wonderful.

"Very handsome," Therion said approvingly. "You make a fitting Conqueror."

Yes, this *was* Key Seven, the Chariot, the Conqueror, wasn't it? With the Seven of Cups superimposed. Brother Paul bent down to view his image in the reflective surface of the polished golden cup. And froze, startled.

His image was a death's head. A grinning skull, with protruding yellow teeth and great square eye sockets.

Brother Paul rocked back, horrified. There was something he remembered, something so appalling—

No! He shut it off. This was only a reflection, nothing supernatural. He forced himself to look again. The death's head remained.

Experimentally, he moved his face. The skull moved too. He opened his mouth, and the bony jaw dropped. He blinked, but of course the skull could not blink, and if it could, how could he see it while his own eyes were closed?

His left hand came up to feel his face. A skeletal hand touched the skull in the cup. His nose and cheeks were there; the flesh was solid. The skull was merely an image, not reality. But what did it mean?

"Let's not dawdle," Therion said. "The dragon is not going to play dead all day."

Regretfully, Brother Paul stood up and circled around the cup. He was sure the skull meant something important. If it were part of the natural symbolism of this card, why hadn't he noticed it before? If not, why had it appeared now? He had encountered this card many times before coming to Planet Tarot; had the skull been on the cup then? He couldn't remember. There was something —something hidden and awful—but he *did* have a mission. Maybe the explanation would come to him.

He moved on. Then he realized he could have checked the blinking of the skull by winking one eye and watching with the other. He was thinking fuzzily, though his mind seemed perfectly clear. Well, it was of insufficient moment to make him return for another look at the cup. If it remained.

He glanced back. The huge cup was still there, and beyond it, the body of the dragon. He regretted the slaying; he really shouldn't have done it. He was not ordinarily a violent man. What had come over him?

His mouth had a bad taste, and a headache was starting. His stomach roiled as though wishing to disgorge its contents. "I don't feel well," he said.

"A little hangover," Therion said quickly. "Ignore it; it will pass."

Hangover? Oh—a reaction from the drink. Instant high, rapid low. It figured!

Now they were at the castle environs, mounting the winding pathway that led up the steep mountain upon which it perched. Progress was swift, for it was a very narrow mountain, but Brother Paul was tiring even more rapidly. Then he saw an inlet in the almost vertical cliff face, a kind of cave. And in this cave stood another cup. It was filled to overflowing with jewels: pearls, diamonds, and assorted other gems. Beautiful!

Brother Paul started for it, but found himself abruptly too tired to get all the way there. He also saw, now, that the cup was within a kind of cage, with a combination lock. In the lock was a picture of three lemons in a row.

"Oh—an ancient one-armed bandit," he muttered. "Well, I don't like to gamble."

"But look at the potential reward!" Therion exclaimed. "You could be rich—a multimillionaire in any currency you name!"

"Wealth means nothing to me. Brothers and Sisters of the Order dedicate their lives to nonmaterial things, to simplicity, to doing good."

"But think of all the good you could do with that fortune!"

"I just want to get into the castle and find the answer to my quest," Brother Paul said. "If I can only get up the strength to complete the climb . . ."

"Here, have a sniff of this," Therion said, opening a tiny but ornate silver box.

Brother Paul looked at it. The box was filled with a whitish powder. "What is it?"

"A stimulant. Used for centuries to enable people to work harder without fatigue. Completely safe, non-addictive. Try it." He shoved it under Brother Paul's nose, and Brother Paul sniffed almost involuntarily.

The effect was amazing. Suddenly he felt terrific: strong, healthy, clear-minded. "Wow! What is it?"

"Cocaine."

"Cocaine! You lied to me! That's one of the worst of addictive drugs!"

Therion shook his head solemnly. "Not so. There is no physiological dependence. It is nature's purest stimulant, without harmful aftereffects. Much better than alcohol. But if you disbelieve, simply return the sample."

"Return the sniff? How can I do that?"

"It's your Animation. You can do anything."

Brother Paul wondered. If he could do anything, why couldn't he find his way *out* of this morass? Well, maybe he could, if he just willed it strongly enough. But he felt so good now, why change it? He did want to achieve the castle, after all, and he had already invested a lot of effort in that quest that would be wasted if he quit now. "Oh, let it stand."

His eyes returned to the cup of jewels. "But first, this detail." He strode across to the cage and reached for the handle of the one-armed bandit. "What do I have to put into this machine, to play the game?"

"A piddling price. Just one-seventh of your soul."

"Done!" Brother Paul said, laughing. And felt a strange wrenching that disconcerted him momentarily. If the price per cup were one-seventh, and there were seven cups in all, and he had already been through several . . . but he felt so good that he soon forgot it. He drew down powerfully on the handle.

The symbols spun blurringly past in the window of the lock. Swords, wands, disks, and something indistinct—perhaps lemniscates? What had happened to the lemons? Then they came to rest: one cup—two cups—three cups!

The cage door swung open. The cup tilted forward. Its riches spilled out over the floor of the cave. Jackpot!

"I gambled and won!" Brother Paul exclaimed.

Therion nodded. "It's your Animation," he repeated. "I merely show the way to your fulfillment."

There was something about that statement—oh, never mind! "Donate these jewels to the charities of the world," Brother Paul said. "I must proceed." He stepped carefully over the glittering gems in his path and left the cave.

The ascent was easy again. In moments he reached the front portal. It was open, and he marched into the castle.

"Like the palace of Sleeping Beauty," Therion remarked.

"Like a fairy tale, yes," Brother Paul agreed.

For some reason Therion found that gaspingly funny. "Show me what you laugh at, and I will show you what you are," he said between gasps. But it was he, not Brother Paul, who was laughing. Odd man!

"Strange," Brother Paul said, "how I start an Animation sequence to find out what is causing Animations, and find myself diverted into this fantasy world, where I must slay a dragon and see my reflection as a skull and gamble one-seventh of my soul on a worldly treasure I don't need. Why can't I just penetrate to the root immediately?"

"You could, if you knew how," Therion said.

"I acquired you as a guide! Why can't you show me the way?"

"I *am* showing you the way. In my fashion. But the impetus must be yours."

"*I* never sought to slay a dragon! Or gamble for riches! You and your damned drugs—"

"Apt description, that."

And why was he swearing, since he was not a swearing man? There was a lot of wrongness here, intertwined with the intrigue. "What do I do now?" Brother Paul demanded irritably.

"Do what thou wilt shall be the whole of the law."

"You said that before. But it doesn't help. It's from Rabelais, which I gather is prime source material for you. Here I am, restrained from doing what I wilt. What I wish, I mean. And you just tag along, spouting irrelevancies."

Therion turned to face him seriously. "However right you may be in your purpose, and in thinking that purpose important, you are wrong in forgetting the equal or greater importance of other things. The really important things are huge, silent, and inexorable."

"What things?"

"Your will."

"My will is to unriddle this Animation effect! Yet here I wander in this forsaken castle, as far from it as ever! What *is* this place, anyway?"

"Thelema."

"What?"

"This is the Abbey of Thelema, the place for the discovery of your True Will."

"I already *know* my will! I told you—"

"If you knew it, you would satisfy it."

Brother Paul paused. On one level, this was nonsense, but on another it seemed to make uncanny sense. "You're saying I only *think* I know my will, and I am getting nowhere because I am pursuing a false will? An illusion?"

Therion nodded. "Now you begin to perceive the problem. First you must truly understand your objective; only then can you achieve it."

"Well, I *thought* I understood it. But somehow I keep getting turned aside, as though I were a victim of Coriolis force." He paused, charmed by the revelation. Coriolis force—a prime determinant of weather on any planet. A mass of air might try to move from a high pressure zone near the equator to a low pressure zone to the north or south, but the shape and rotation of the planet diverted it to the side, because the surface velocity of rotation was greater at the equator than at the polar latitudes. Well, it was a difficult concept for the layman to grasp, but essential for the meteorologist. It was as though nature herself were fouled up by the system, causing the endless repercussions, instabilities, and changes that constituted the weather. Was there such a thing as a *mental* Coriolis force, so that a given urge could not be consummated directly unless the full nature of the human condition were understood? Yet this was hardly a perfect analogy, for the human mind was not a planetary surface, and human thoughts were not mere breezes. The situation was more dynamic, with force being diverted at right angles to—

"Precession!" he cried aloud.

Therion glanced up benignly. "Yes?"

"Precession. The factor that seems to change the direction of force applied to a gyroscope or a turning wheel. When properly exploited, as with a bicycle, it is a stabilizing influence, but when misunderstood, it stymies every effort to—"

Therion shook his head. "Can you explain it to me more precisely?"

"It is a technical term. It affects the Earth and all rotating things, and thus man's technology and mythology. The precession of the equinox . . ." He took a breath. "Simply, there is a great deal of rotational inertia in a spinning object, and when you apply an external force to change its orientation, you must deal with that inertia. If you understand this, and know the precise vectors—"

Therion smiled. "Thus your ignorance stops you here, because the inertial velocity of the mind is more complex than any casual survey can reveal. Know thyself—or as I prefer to put it, do what thou wilt."

"Yes," Brother Paul agreed, at last appreciating the man's meaning. A person could not do what he really wanted to do, unless he understood himself well enough to *know* what he wanted. What he *really* wanted, not what in his ignorance he thought he wanted. Many people were stuck on the ignorant route, questing tirelessly for wealth or power that brought them only unhappiness. Others quested for happiness, but defined it purely in material terms. Still others, trying to correct for that, insisted on defining it in purely *non*material terms, seeking chimeras. As perhaps Brother Paul had been doing, himself. "My ultimate will is more subtle and devious than I myself can appreciate consciously. Since these Animations are at least in part drawn from my unconscious, I suffer precession when I attempt to direct them by purely conscious thought. Thus I wind up veering away at right angles, battling the Dragon of Temptation, and God only knows what else!"

Therion nodded again, looking like a somewhat seedy street philosopher. "I also know what else: it was your own conscience you battled."

"You know, you're not a bad guide, at that," Brother Paul said. "You have had a better notion of my true will than I. But as with leading a horse to water—"

"The whole of the law," Therion agreed.

They had been meandering through the gaunt, empty castle. Now they entered an upper chamber—and spied a woman. She reclined in a huge cup, so he knew this had to be another vision of the Seven of Cups, that he had to deal with one way or another. He suspected that the original cup he had chosen, that of the castle, had been merely an entry point; he was required to taste the contents of all seven before he was through. Had he chosen the lady first, he would have found the skull, Temptation, and the castle interposing, though perhaps in a different order. With precession, there was no direct or easy route to an objective. But now this woman; she was a marvel of organic symmetry and cultural aesthetics, with hair like summer wheat. . . .

"Amaranth!" Brother Paul breathed.

"Beg pardon?" Therion inquired.

Of course this man would not know about the private name Brother Paul had for the Breaker-lady. But now he was sure; Amaranth had gotten into this Animation, and here she was, the actress in a very special role. The major characters in these scenes *were* played by living people, reciting their lines, as it were, or perhaps extemporizing according to general guidelines. "A private thought, irrelevant," Brother Paul said, and knew he was lying. Since to him a lie was an abomination, he had to correct it immediately. "I believe I recognize this woman. She—"

"The female exists but to serve the male," Therion remarked.

So the man wasn't really interested in the identity of this woman. To him, women were interchangeable, covered by a general blanket of animosity. Well, Brother Paul was amenable to that game, in this case; from what he knew of Amaranth, she would quickly disabuse all comers of such notions.

Brother Paul approached the lady. "In what way do you reflect my hidden will?" he asked her.

She unfolded from the cup and stood before him, as lovely a creature as he could imagine. "I am Love."

Love. That was rather more than he had bargained on. "Sacred or profane?" he inquired somewhat warily. "I am here on a religious mission."

"He claims he loves God, not woman," Therion put in.

"I love God *and* woman!" Brother Paul snapped. "But my mission requires—"

Amaranth stretched, accentuating her miraculous breasts, and Brother Paul recognized Temptation in another guise. He knew that Animation was not enhancing her appearance; it was every bit as enticing in life. A woman who was beautiful only in Animation—but of course physical appearance should not be the prime appeal.

"You fought valiantly to achieve this castle," Therion pointed out. "Do you now reject what it holds for you?"

"Precession brings this woman; what I seek is elsewhere."

"How do you know?"

Brother Paul considered that, uncertain. He had supposed he was overcoming Temptation—and a formidable Temptation it was!—but could it be that the physical side of Love was the essence of his search? It hardly seemed likely, but he could not be *sure*. There was a deep affinity between types of love, expressed on the highest plane as religion, and on the lowest as sex. It was often said that "God is Love." Could he achieve one form without the other?

He remembered the sour comments of the Hierophant. What was the nature of his belief? That the expression of physical love was inherently evil? The Hierophant's views had resembled a parody of—

"The Hierophant!" Brother Paul exclaimed, wheeling on Therion. "You!"

"So you caught on," Therion said smugly.

"You purposely distorted the religious attitude of—"

"Distorted? I would not say so," Therion said. "I had a role to play, so I played it with complete candor. I gave the essence instead of mere casuistry. Modern religion hates sex and pleasure and tries to suppress them, because a man with a stiff cock will not seek a priest. The ancient religions were much more savvy; they knew that the alternate facet of divine love is physical love. It is a completely natural and necessary function."

"But not outside of marriage," Brother Paul said, shaken by the way he had been guided even before he had chosen the guide.

"Why not? What is marriage but a ceremony of society, establishing the proprietary rights of a particular male over a particular female? Does God *care* about the conventions of human culture? Who governs here, anyway—God or man?"

"Surely God does!" Brother Paul said.

"Then why didn't God make man impotent prior to the nuptial ceremony, or responsive only to some other key stimulus, like smell? Animals have no such trouble."

"Man is not precisely an animal!" Brother Paul retorted. "Man has a conscience. He controls his urges."

"The tail wags the dog, then. Man controls the natural urges God gave him, instead of allowing their expression in the way God intended."

"No! Man's conscience stems from God!"

"And God is created in the image of man."

Telling thrust! Of course, *man* was in the image of *God,* but if he argued that case, Therion would simply point out that God was therefore a sexual creature, and unmarried. Now Brother Paul was uncertain where the sacrament of marriage fitted into this scheme, for it was true that animals did not marry. Animals were completely natural, yet innocent.

Still, he had to believe that one of the things that distinguished man from animal was his morality, his higher consciousness. "I do not choose to argue with you about marriage," Brother Paul said, "or to abuse this young woman. I only wish to ascertain the reality behind the image."

"Still, you suffer precession," Therion said sadly. "You insist on carrying into this framework the private standards dictated by your Earthly existence, refusing to admit that they may be no longer applicable. You think you can penetrate the morass by plowing straight ahead. When will you realize that you cannot win unless you play the game by its rules? You have sampled only three cups."

Temptation, Victory, and Wealth. Apparently he did have to go through them all before gaining enlightenment. No shortcut! Yet did the presence of this woman, who had been accidentally trapped in the Animation, mean he had to use her sexually? Therion seemed to be arguing that case, which was odd, because Therion professed to hate women. Obviously he could not afford to be guided too closely by Therion's words, which did not necessarily reflect Therion's own will. This woman might be seductive, but he did not have to be seduced.

"I would like to talk with you," Brother Paul said to the lady. "What is your preference?"

"I adore thee, I A O," she replied.

"My name is Brother Paul, of the Holy Order of Vision," he said. That made a formal introduction within this Animation, in case that should help. "You—I believe we met before, in, er, real life. And you introduced the Brotherhood of Light Tarot deck, didn't you? What shall I call you now?"

She opened her robe. She was naked underneath, slim and pink-white and full-breasted. She was his physical ideal of woman, which was obviously what had first attracted him to her. He tried to seek the sublime understanding of God, but his flesh had other notions.

"I adore thee, I A O," she repeated.

Brother Paul refused to go along. "I understood you to say, in real life, that you worshipped a snake-footed God, called Abra—" He was unable to recall the full name.

"She refers to I A O, or Abraxas—literally, 'the God to be adored.' Therefore she adores him," Therion clarified. "He has human form, with the head of a cock and legs of serpents, and he is the god of healing. It would seem she believes you are that god."

"I!" Brother Paul exclaimed, appalled. "A pagan deity?"

"Abraxas was a most fashionable god, in the Roman Empire. She might see you as a modern incarnation. Perhaps if you showed her your feet—"

Brother Paul uttered an extremely un-Orderlike syllable. But Therion was studying Amaranth's torso. "She certainly is a healthy, well-fed specimen," he remarked, as though appraising a thoroughbred horse. "Most peoples of most times have been malnourished; only in the past century has good nutrition spread. One seldom sees as fine a form as that, however, even today."

To whom was he trying to sell that form? "You really do worship a pagan god?" Brother Paul demanded of the lady. He had somehow not appreciated the significance of this, or really believed it when, as a colonist, she had mentioned the matter.

"This is, after all, a free society," Therion remarked. "No person, according to the Covenant, may persecute any member of any other religion, whatever its nature. It is the only thing that prevents absolute internecine warfare throughout this colony. I'm sure I A O has as much right to be here as any Christian god."

The girl shrugged out of her costume and stood before them, completely nude. The splendor of her body was dazzling, and not because she was well-fed; there was no fat on her where it didn't belong. She stepped toward Brother Paul.

He stepped back in alarm.

"The early priestesses led devotees to union with their god by the most direct means," Therion continued. "She wants to help you discover your true will; will you not oblige?"

"This is not the kind of union I seek!" Brother Paul protested. "Not with I A O, not—"

"Suppose I A O is the God of Tarot, and you refuse to meet Him?"

"Impossible!" But Brother Paul realized that it was *not* impossible. Improbable, perhaps, but theoretically possible. The whole problem on Planet Tarot, the reason he had come here, was to determine objectively (if circumstances permitted) which god was the guiding power behind the Animations, or whether *no* god was. He could not let his own religious prejudice interfere. For—he forced his mind to consider it—I A O Abraxas, the Adorable God, just might be the one. Even if I A O were not, he still had to ascertain that fact honestly. The assembled religions of Planet Tarot were awaiting his verdict. No one of their own representatives could make this survey, because every person among them was too firmly committed to his own particular concept of God to be objective. Those who had tried most sincerely had suffered the ravages of loss of faith, in some cases with fatal results.

Brother Paul had no intention of dying in this quest. But neither did he intend to participate in any whitewash or rehash of personal prejudice. The ethics of his Order, and his own pride, required that he seek only the truth. The mission transcended his petty personal scruples. He had to give I A O a fair hearing.

"But is it actually necessary to—?" he asked plaintively, viewing the nude priestess. "If she is a modern-day worshiper of Abraxas, it would be in her interest to convince me her God was the one, when in fact he might *not* be."

"True, true," Therion agreed. "I hardly envy you your task."

"And making love to her would not prove anything."

"Unless, as in the battle with Temptation, it were a route to the innermost truth," Therion said. "In that case it would be too bad not to call her bluff and leave this cup unsavored."

"That doesn't make sense!" But Brother Paul looked again at the priestess of Abraxas. If this *were* the God of Tarot, and if there were only one way to relate to that God, according to His ancient ritual of union . . .

"Have a sniff of this," Therion said, opening another little box.

"No! Not more cocaine! That doesn't solve anything!"

"This is not cocaine."

"Oh." Brother Paul relented and took a sniff.

"It is heroin," Therion concluded.

But already the drug was taking effect. Brother Paul turned to the priestess. "So you want interaction," he said boldly. "Well, I shall plumb you for the truth!" His own clothing fell away magically as he strode toward her.

He took her in his arms and kissed her deeply. Her cool, firm breasts flattened excitingly against his chest. His hands traveled down her arching back and across her sleek haunches, finally cupping her firm yet soft buttocks. What a specimen she was!

The kiss was magical; he had never experienced anything like it! He knew it was enhanced by the heroin, but didn't care. He felt such mastery of himself that nothing mattered at all; he could enjoy this experience without any reservation.

Experience. There was man's most deeply seated instinct: the craving for new sensations, the satisfaction of curiosity, variety and excitement and fulfillment! Experience. Every minute, every second was precious; he had to indulge himself to the utmost, because this was the ultimate meaning of life. Why should he sow, and not reap?

He released the priestess just enough to look at her face. She smiled.

"Stab your demoniac smile to my brain," Therion said. "Soak me in cognac, kisses, cocaine." He pronounced "cognac" so that it rhymed directly with "demoniac."

This had the effect of stultifying Brother Paul's ardor, despite the heroin. "Don't you have somewhere to go?" he demanded.

"I am your guide. I must see you safely through this challenge."

"You are afraid I will make love to the priestess?"

"I fear you will *not,* unless I guide you."

"This is between me and my religion!"

"And your religion, like virtually all modern faiths, is fundamentally anti-sex. Your understanding of the subject is limited, though your instinct, were you ever to let it reign, is sound. Sex is good; love is the law; ignorance is evil."

"But casual, thoughtless sex—"

"No man can get along on a continual diet of abstinence. A man must be permitted normal sexual expression, as God intended. He *must* express his natural urges, of whatever type, or wither away."

"Still," Brother Paul said uncertainly. He had his beliefs, but they were being sorely besieged by this logic and the woman in his arms.

The priestess knelt before him, as though in supplication, her breasts sliding excruciatingly down the length of his torso. "I adore thee, I A O!" she repeated.

"Hey, that's not I A O!" Brother Paul protested. But then he realized that perhaps it *was;* she worshiped a serpent-legged God, so she sought the serpent in man.

Under her massage, that serpent rose and swelled like the forepart of a cobra. The skin of the head peeled back, releasing the faint scent generated in that special pocket—the scent that the knife denied to most Christians and all Moslems and Jews, in the guise of "health."

But Brother Paul had never been subjected to that unkindest cut. His member was whole, and it functioned as God had designed it to. The scent of arousal wafted out. She inhaled that aroma. A beatific smile spread across her face. "I A O!" she breathed ecstatically, her breath caressing the organ.

"Love is the law," Therion intoned. "Love under will."

"Enough of this!" Brother Paul cried, drawing her hands and face away from his anatomy. He lifted her up, but she spun away and sprawled half across the couch. (Couch? Where was the cup? Oh—they were the same.) He pursued her, caught her with both his hands about her waist as she pushed herself up on the support, and brought his groin to her swelling posterior. Her hands, dislodged as her bottom was raised up, slid off the rim; the upper section of her body fell down inside the cup. Now she was bent forward at a right angle, her breasts flattening against the inner surface of the cup, her elbows braced at its depth, her face invisible within its shadow. But he didn't need her breasts or arms or face. He guided his member by hand, found the place, and thrust.

He had imagined easy penetration of her exposed vagina, but it was not easy. There was some pain for him as he forced entry past constricted muscles, without sufficient lubrication. But the drug spurred him on; he was, after all, the Conqueror!

The climax was explosive: a nuclear detonation in a subterranean vault. The recoil flung him backward, breaking the connection. Simultaneously his heroin high collapsed; he felt tired and sick, pumped out, without ambition, irritable, and disgusted. The priestess had fallen out of the cup to the floor, outstretched, supine. Therion was squatting beside her, almost over her head. Maybe she was hurt; it had been quite a blast. Brother Paul didn't care. He just wanted another sniff of H.

He staggered toward Therion. "Give it to me," he rasped.

"I'm busy!" Therion snapped, still squatting. "I have to give her—"

Brother Paul's nose was running and his stomach was cramping. Withdrawal symptoms, he knew. "Give me the stuff."

Therion ignored him, concentrating on the girl.

"I want more smack, more junk," Brother Paul insisted. "What do you call it these days? Horse? Snow? *Where is it?*"

Still Therion did not respond; he was still squatting.

Sudden rage engulfed Brother Paul. "You're paying more attention to *her* than to *me! *You're supposed to guide *me!*"

"Shit," Therion said.

Brother Paul remembered; that was another name for heroin. "Then give me shit!" he cried.

A cup appeared before him, but it contained no white powder. Angrily he swung his fist at it, knocking it over. A green snake fell out, hissing. A foot of the god Abraxas? No, this was merely the symbol of Jealousy.

He was getting nowhere. His hot flash was converting into a chill. What had he gotten into? "Why should *you* be so self-assured," Brother Paul demanded, "when *I* am so confused and sick! It isn't fair!"

Therion looked up. "I am content because I comprehend my own essential nature," he said. "I know what I am, and who I serve. I am at peace with myself. No victory, wealth, or woman can match that. 'Do what thou wilt shall be the whole of the law.'"

"Then show me how to comprehend *my* essential nature!" Brother Paul cried. "There is the key to ultimate power!"

"You must seek it within yourself, extricating yourself from the prison of the senses," Therion said. "Meditation, such as is sponsored by yoga—"

"No! I can't wait for that. I want it now!"

"Then take the shortcut." Therion held up a small capsule. "LSD."

Brother Paul snatched it and gulped it down.

It was like a headlong rush into a maelstrom. Sensations were coming at him from all directions, and seeming to go out from him similarly. Sights, sounds, smells, tastes, and touches. He saw the room. The girl was still lying on the floor, her mouth open. Therion was still squatting over her. He saw all the furniture. The patch of sunlight from the window. He heard the wheezing of wind around the parapet, the baying of some distant animal, the ticking of an unseen clock. He smelled the leather couch, and the brass of the inside of the big cup, and dust from the floor, and the faint, sweet scent of a flower outside, somewhere. He tasted the remains of the capsule. He felt the cool stone floor under his feet, the caress of a trifling breeze on his bare body. All distractions, to be dispensed with!

He focused his awareness, shutting all external stimuli out. Now he saw light behind his eyelids, for they were not thick enough to make total darkness. He heard the sound of his own breathing, and of his heartbeat. He smelled his own breath, a touch of whiskey still on it. Whiskey? Oh—from that first drink, back at Temptation. His tongue tasted slightly bitter. He felt the tension of his muscles as they tightened to keep him balanced.

Actually there were many more than five senses, but most of the unnamed ones could be lumped under touch: feeling of discomfort, muscle tension, orientation. Distractions.

He sat down on the floor, assuming the crosslegged yoga position favored for meditation, and consciously relaxed. Gradually his bodily tensions melted away, releasing his mind.

It was like flying low over a landscape toward the sunrise. His half-random thoughts zoomed past like technicolor clouds, some formless, some beautiful, some menacing. Below was the castle, with the priestess lying like Sleeping Beauty within it, awaiting the kiss to restore her to consciousness, except that that was an expurgation. It was really the sexual act that would rouse her, making the life within her quicken, only they couldn't tell children that (and why the hell *not?*) and in this case that act had put her to sleep instead. Priestess of Abraxas? What was such temple worship except ritualized prostitution? Prostitution, the oldest profession of woman. It would exist as long as men had the money and the urge and women had neither. How ironic that it should be combined with religion! Yet religion had about as great an affinity for the vices of man as any other institution.

The drug enhanced everything, providing a phenomenal visual, aural, and tactile experience. The Dragon of Temptation charged him, but was inflated like a hydrogen balloon until it exploded into harmless flame. Therion would say it had farted itself to death. The priestess of I A O again, opening her lovely body to him, crying, "I adore thee, I A O!" but he was no longer aroused.

The suits of the Tarot, symbols flying up around him like the cards in *Alice in Wonderland,* male wands and swords thrusting through female cups and disks. Swiftly, in mere seconds, he abolished all these interfering thoughts. Gradually he oriented on his target: his own ultimate essence.

Now, in the distance, he saw the first glow of it—the effulgence of the Grail. Like the breaking of the dawn, that miraculous light expanded as he arrowed toward it. The disruptive presence of his superficial thoughts diminished, shining in pastel hues in the face of that solar brilliance; he coursed past them, unveiling the way to Nirvana.

At last the gleaming rim of it emerged, more splendid than any vision he had heretofore imagined. Onward he flew, bringing more into view: the magnificent curvature of the Holy Grail, hanging perfectly in the sky.

Now he saw that though the Cup itself glowed, as it had when it had floated past the astonished knights of King Arthur's Round Table, this was a faint glimmering compared to its principal illumination. This brilliance was by virtue of its content—that deeply veiled shape whose light spilled out between canopy and rim. The shape of his Essence!

Eagerly he moved toward it, certain now that he would perceive the glory that was his soul. What form would it take, that divine revelation? A giant, precious, bright crystal with myriad facets, a myriad-squared reflections? A godlike brilliance, gently blinding the mortal eye? An intangible aura of sheer wonder?

He came up to the monstrous chalice, that goblet of Jesus, the quintessence of ambition, and peeked under the glorious cover. There was an odor, awful and out of place, but he ignored it. Here at last was Truth, was Soul!

It was a huge, half-coiled, half-broken, steaming human turd.

8

EMOTION
(DESIRE)

And Saul, yet breathing out threatenings and slaughter against the disciples of the Lord, went unto the high priest,

And desired of him letters to Damascus to the synagogues, that if he found any of this way, whether they were men or women, he might bring them bound unto Jerusalem.

And as he journeyed, he came near Damascus: and suddenly there shined round about him a light from heaven:

And he fell to the earth, and heard a voice saying unto him, Saul, Saul, why persecutest thou me?

And he said, Who art thou, Lord? And the Lord said, I am Jesus whom thou persecutest: it is hard for thee to kick against the pricks.*

And he trembling and astonished said, Lord, what wilt thou have me to do? And the Lord said unto him, arise, and go into the city, and it shall be told thee what thou must do.

And the men which journeyed with him stood speechless, hearing a voice, but seeing no man.

And Saul arose from the earth; and when his eyes were opened, he saw no man: but they led him by the hand, and brought him into Damascus.

*"to kick against the pricks"—i.e., to oppose the pricks of conscience.

And he was three days without sight, and neither did eat nor drink.

THE BIBLE:
King James Version
ACTS IX: 1-9

Paul sniffed, trying to clear his nostrils of the stink of shit. He was driving a car, an old-fashioned internal combustion machine, wasteful of fuel. Therefore this was pre-MT Earth, oddly strange and just as oddly familiar. He knew this was another Animation, quite different from the last, but still a construct of some aspect of his imagination or his memory. Another direction governed by precession, whose laws he did not yet comprehend well enough to utilize consciously.

He seemed to recall having taken a drive like this, perhaps ten years ago, perhaps nine, but where had he come from then, and where had he been going? It would not come clear.

There were many other cars on the highway, traveling at the maximum velocity their governors permitted: 100 KPH, nice and even. All good things were governed by hundreds; it was the decimal, metric, percentage system. Easy to compute with, easy to verify, divisible by many numbers.

The cars were like his own: small hydrogen burners, streamlined, comfortable. The hydrogen was separated from water at various power plants; some of it was used for fusion into helium for major power, and some for combination with oxygen to make water again (clean water was precious), some treated for nonignition and put into transport blimps, and some burned explosively in motors. Hydrogen: the most versatile element. Paul was uncertain of the original source of power used to separate out the gas, but obviously it sufficed to run the system.

In just a few years all this would change, as the MT program burst upon them and co-opted all the convenient major energy sources. The creature from Sphere Antares, whose very presence was kept secret from the people of the world he so changed; what mischief was he to wreak on Sphere Sol? But right now people were indulging in their last fling; private transportation was still within the rights and means of the average citizen. Barely.

Paul himself could not afford this car. He had the use of it illicitly: he was drug-running. Hidden so well that even he had no notion of where it was, was a cache of mnem, pronounced "NEEM": the memory drug. Students used it when cramming for exams; when high on mnem their retention became almost total, enabling them to make very high marks on rotework without actually cheating. It did not enhance intelligence or give them lasting skills, but temporary memorization was so important in taking machine-graded examinations that this often made the difference in the competitive grade listings that determined eligibility for employment or promotion. Paul himself had never used mnem during his college days, not because of unavailability, expense, or ethics, but because he hadn't needed it. His college used no tests or grades. The drug had few side effects and could be detected in the human system only through extraordinary clinical procedures that cost more than the public clinics could afford. Therefore it was fairly safe to use, and much in demand.

There were only three drawbacks to mnem. First, it was illegal. That bothered very few people; when morality conflicted with convenience, morality suffered. Second, it was expensive, after the manner of addictive illegal drugs; the cost was not in the manufacture but in the illicit distribution system. That bothered more people, but not enough to seriously inhibit its use. The criminal element had a sharp eye for what the market would bear, just as did the business element. In fact, the abilities and scruples of the two elements were similar, and there was considerable overlapping. The mnem cartel proffered incentive options for those in critical need, such as Paul himself. For he, after college, had found a use for mnem. Third, mnem withdrawal caused not only the loss of the drug-enhanced memories, but a more general mnemonic deterioration, leading to disorientation and irregular amnesia. Thus the addiction was neither psychological nor physiological, but practical: once "hooked," a user could not function without mnem. That bothered most people, but they tended not to think about that aspect. It was a paradox of mnem, the subject of much folk humor, that it made people forget its chief drawback while it sharpened their memories enormously.

Which was why Paul was risking his freedom by running this shipment across state lines. He had used the drug to become expert in his sideline; now he could maintain his habit only by cooperating with the suppliers. Fortunately they did not require a particular person to do it often; this was not done from concern for the welfare of the individual, but as a precaution against discovery by the authorities. It might be a year before Paul would have to drive again, and in the interim his own supply of mnem was free. It was really a good deal.

There was someone standing at the margin of the highway; the figure seemed to be female. Other cars were rushing by, of course; it was dangerous to pick up a hitchhiker, male or female. But Paul sometimes got restless; though he did not drive often, this long trip bored him. Company would make a difference, particularly feminine company.

He stopped. The girl saw him and ran up. She was young, probably not out of her teens, but surprisingly well developed. Her clothing was scant and in disarray; in fact she was in a rather flimsy nightgown that outlined her heaving breasts with much stronger erotic appeal than she could have managed by any deliberate exposure. A natural girl in an unnatural situation.

"Oh, thank you!" she gasped, climbing into the seat next to him. "I was so afraid no one would stop before the police came."

"The police?" he asked with sudden nervousness. If she was a criminal—

"Oh, please, sir—drive!" she cried. "I'll explain, it's all right, no trouble for you, only lose us in the traffic. *Please!*"

But he hesitated, the car still parked. "I have no money worth taking, only a keyed credit you can't use. This car requires my thumbprint every half hour, or the motor locks and the automatic takes over, so you can't—"

She faced him, and he was surprised to see tears on her cheeks. Her fair hair was bedraggled, yet she was lovely in her wild way. "You are in no danger from *me,* sir! I have no weapon. I have nothing. No food, no identification. I don't know how I can repay you, but please, *please* drive, or all is lost. I would rather die than go back there!"

Still ill-at-ease, he moved the car forward, gaining speed until he was able to merge into the traffic flow. "Where are you going?" he inquired.

"To the Barlowville Station," she said.

He started punching the coding into his computer terminal, seeking a clarification of the address. "Oh, no!" she protested. "Please, sir, don't ask the machine! They'll key it in to me, and in minutes the police—"

The demon in the machine. Paul's fingers froze. "You're on the criminal index?" he asked, alarmed. He had just about decided she was harmless, but he didn't like this. The last thing he needed was a police check on his car!

"I'm being deprogrammed," she explained hastily. "I belong to the Holy Order of Vision, and my folks sued—"

"They still deprogram religious nuts?" he asked thoughtlessly. "I thought that went out a decade ago, along with other forms of exorcism."

"It still happens," she said. "The established sects are all right—they finished their initiations years ago—but the new ones are still being persecuted."

The rite of passage, he thought. Any new religion had to pass through sufficient hazing to justify its existence, and when it became strong enough to fight back, as early Christianity had, it became legitimate and started hazing the religion that came next.

He shrugged. "I don't know much about it." Not in *his* business, he didn't—and he didn't care to. Religion held little interest for him, apart from morbid curiosity about the credulity of people. Still, this was a very pretty girl, who seemed somehow familiar. That flowing hair, those full breasts, the way she spoke — He was intrigued. "But if you really want to go back to this cult—"

"Oh, I do!" she exclaimed. "Somehow I'll return."

Paul made a decision. "I'll take you there, if it's not too far out of the way. But if you won't let me get the highway address from the travel computer—"

"I can tell you the way," she said eagerly. Then she faced him and smiled, the expression making her glow. "My name is Sister Beth."

"I'm Paul Cenji." What the hell had he expected her name to be? This seemed to be a memory, but it unfolded at its own pace; he could not remember what had happened that day in his past, so had to live it through again.

He drove on for a while, then asked, "How did you get caught away from your church?"

"My Station. We don't have churches as such, just centers of operation. My mother called me and told me my grandmother was dying, so I came at once. I never renounced my family ties; the Holy Order of Vision isn't like that. I wish my family belonged, too! But when I got there—"

"They grabbed you and hauled you off to the deprogramming clinic," Paul finished for her.

"Yes. I suppose I should have suspected something, but I never thought my own mother would . . ." She shrugged sadly. "But I'm sure she thought she was doing the right thing. I forgive her. They tried to talk me out of going back, and when that didn't work, they said they were going to use mnem—"

"Mnem!" he exclaimed.

"It's a drug," she said, not appreciating the actual nature of his reaction. "They use it for rehabilitating incorrigible criminals. It's not supposed to be used for—" She broke off.

Paul's suspicions had been aroused again. Could it be coincidence, this reference to the drug he was hauling? Or was this a police trap? "I heard it was illegal," he said.

"Yes, for anything but the rehabilitation of criminals and some forms of mental illness. But there is a black market in mnem. It costs a lot that way, but my folks raised the credit."

Paul didn't like this at all. A seductively innocent girl in scant attire, planted on the highway to attract footloose rakes like him who might be supporting their lifestyles by dealing in contraband. A lot of fools were caught that way, he was sure. Now she was naming the subject, maybe probing for guilty reactions. It was all too easy to give away secrets while dazzled by offerings of this caliber. Already it seemed as if he had known her longer, in another place, by some other name—the perpetual mystery of the female. Maybe he only *wanted* to have known her. Her charm was already corrupting him; he had to get rid of this easy rider without arousing suspicion—if it was not already too late. "Which way is your—Station?"

"It's in the next state. You can go another hundred kilometers on this highway before turning off." Right. She had to be able to testify that he had actually crossed a state line. One of the niceties of the law. The police would be executing people on suspicion if they had the law all their own way. But America was not yet a total police state.

So he had until they reached the state line to act. He had to keep up the front until he knew what to do. "Glad to have company for that hundred K," he said. The irony was that that would have been true, had she not brought up the subject of mnem. What a face, what a body, what a beguiling simplicity she showed! He was accustomed to a rather different sort of woman, and was now discovering that he had misjudged his own tastes.

"I really appreciate this, Mr. Cenji. When I learned of the

mnem, I waited till night, then climbed out of my window in my nightdress, and here I am. They never thought I'd do that. If you hadn't stopped—there's probably an alarm out for me now."

Paul turned on the highway audio scan. If there was an announcement—but that would be part of the police bait; it would mean nothing. His best course would be to keep her talking while he figured out what to do with her. "I thought deprogramming itself was illegal now."

"It is, but they don't call it that. There are blackmarket professionals in that field too. I've been accused of stealing valuable jewelry. I would never steal! By the time it turns out that the charge is untrue, they will have me wiped out by the drug, and I won't even remember that I was ever a Sister—oh, I would die first!" She put her face in her hands.

What a touching display! She was good at her act, uncomfortably good; he wanted to put the car on automatic, take her in his arms, console her. Danger! She was surely planning to betray him, to add his scalp to the collection in her police locker.

Yet how could she do this, when he himself had no idea where the cache of mnem was hidden in the car? He was not even certain that there was a cache, this time; every so often the cartel made a blank run, to further confuse the enemy. If that happened to be the case this time, he had only to keep his nerve and he would win. He had no intention of telling her about his cargo, and if the police had known about it for sure, they would simply have arrested him outright. So this elaborate lure made no sense. Unless she was a trained observer, alert to the signs of mnem addiction. Such signs were trifling, but they did exist, and he was an addict. If he didn't get his fix tonight, he would begin to forget his way home tomorrow. So he had to be rid of her before then, bluffing it out. Stopping before the state line would not get him off this hook.

"Actually, I've heard the drug is not so bad—for criminals," he said. "It doesn't hurt. At least, I've heard it doesn't."

"Oh, it is very good for criminals," she said. "We of the Holy Order of Vision are concerned about the problem of criminality. We don't believe in taking life; it is as wrong for the state to kill as it is for the individual to kill. And we know our society cannot afford to maintain people in prison, yet some are incorrigible. Mnem is the answer to that. It resolves the conflict between the alternatives of killing the criminal and letting him go unpunished.

We believe in forgiveness, but in certain cases correction is better. It makes the criminal a citizen again. Some of our Order members are mnem-erased rehabilitates—"

"It *erases* personality? I thought it improved memory!" How much did she know?

"In overdose it does. In trace dosages it actually enhances memory to an extraordinary degree, but then a person has to keep using it, never too much at a time. I could never stand to have all my memory taken away, or to be tied for life to such a drug. The Order could help me if I were an addict, but this single overdose would take me away from the Order, because I wouldn't *know*. I couldn't face that, so I fled."

"Yes. Understandable." She did know too much, for any ordinary young female citizen. She had to be a police-trained agent, with a near-perfect cover. Soon she would have him spotted.

Actually, part of what she said related to him very directly. He had never seriously thought about his future. He was bound for life to the drug, and to the criminal distribution system, and he could escape that prison only at the expense of his memory. Was that what he really wanted in life? It didn't matter; it was what he had. She, according to her story, had fled in time; for him it was too late. All he could do now was protect what he had—from her.

Yet he delayed in taking action, nagged by doubt. She was such a damned attractive girl, seeming so nice, representing the kind of life he would have chosen, had he been smart early. Like a fine racing car, styled right, with an engine to conjure with, capable of pushing a quarter mach 1 in heat, yet docile and comfortable when on idle. How could he kick her out without being *sure?* (And was she thinking: how could she arrest him as a mnem addict, without being *sure?*)

"Your cult—I mean, your religious order—what does it do? Is it like a commune or something?" (Where the women were shared among the men, and no person denied anything to any other? But surely he was dreaming!)

"The Holy Order of Vision is not really a religion," she said, and it was evident that now she was on familiar ground. But of course she would have her story straight. "Anyone can join, from any religion, and the Order does not interfere. We try to promote the welfare of man and nature wherever we can. Many people come to us troubled in spirit, and for some the Tarot helps."

"The Tarot?" he asked. "I've used that deck."

"Oh?" Her interest seemed genuine. "For what purpose?"

"For business, of course. I deal cards for a licensed gambling franchise. Those twenty-two trumps add luster to the game; people like the pictures, and of course there are special prizes."

"For gambling," she murmured sadly. "That is all you see in the Tarot?"

"Oh, no. After I'd worked with the cards for a while, I found they were fun for general entertainment, too. There are many games. Sometimes when I'm driving from one stand to another, like now, I put the car on auto and play solitaire." That established his own cover, for what it was worth. Not much, if they ran an employment check.

"We use them for meditation," she said. "The contemplation of a single Arcanum, or a group of Arcana, can bring special insights, well worth the effort. I never really understood my purpose in life until I meditated with the guidance of the Tarot. We also study the deck as a whole, analyzing the distinctions between individual cards, and between the concepts of different experts. Whole separate philosophies are revealed, leading to insights on the nature of human thought."

Paul smiled. "Interesting how one deck can have four different uses," he observed. "Meditation and study for you, business and entertainment for me. A purpose for every person."

"True," she agreed with a small, fetching smile of resignation. "I wish I had my Tarot with me. But the deprogrammers took it away, calling it a crutch."

Paul did have his deck with him, but decided not to mention that. There was yet another use of the Tarot, he remembered: character reading or divination, and that could be unnervingly accurate. He did not believe in the supernatural (except as it might relate to the limited area of inexplicable runs of luck, good or bad), but he was not about to risk any analysis of his character through the Tarot. Besides that, his prints and sweat were all over that deck; a policewoman could take a sample or sliver from one card and give the laboratory enough to identify him readily. It had been a mistake to give her his name, but he could change that. It was a mistake to keep talking to her; she might be recording his voice through some hidden device. (A bracelet? No, she wore no jewelry. But women had so many secret places . . .) Regardless, he was getting to like her too well. She might be a religious nut, but there was an odd appeal to her philosophy. That could mean either that this Order of Vision really was a sensible organization, or that this policewoman had done her homework extremely well.

Enough. He had to act—now.

Paul put the car on auto and removed his hands from the wheel. He turned to her, smiling somewhat crookedly. "I guess you know why I picked you up," he said, forcing a leer. A woman with a body like hers had to have encountered this expression many times before, and had to recognize it instantly.

Sister Beth's eyes widened. She did not pretend to misunderstand. "Oh, Mr. Cenji, I—I hoped it wouldn't be that way. You seemed so nice."

Paul felt like a complete heel. But he had to do it, or she would finish him. He had to play the part of the callous male who had nothing on his mind but sex. This was not really far from the mark; any man near to this girl would react similarly, differing only in the manner he expressed it. He was being purposely crude, and hating it, for if by some freak she was what she claimed to be, a gentle, circuitous approach just might land her. "I *am* nice. Give me a try."

She shrank back as far as the crashproof seat permitted. Her bosom heaved within the seat's embrace. "I don't have the strength to resist you, but at the Order we prefer chastity before marriage."

Marriage? Hell! He took hold of her arm, drawing her in for a kiss as the seats leveled out in response to his pressure, forming into a bed. Her lips trembled as his own lips touched them. "Please," she whispered. "Will you let me go? Nothing you could gain for yourself could match what you would take from me. Put me back on the highway; maybe I can get another ride before the police net closes."

That was exactly what he had wanted: her voluntary departure. It would mean he had fooled her, that she was satisfied he had no serious commitments—such as to mnem. Thus her time would be better spent baiting some other sucker, while that police net hung loose, waiting for her signal.

But now the touch of her aroused him. Disheveled and frightened as she seemed, she remained a compelling figure of a young woman. He could force her; he was sure of that. She might be a policewoman, but he was trained in physical combat himself. A wrist-twist would keep her hand from her weapon, wherever it was, and make her submit without physical struggle. Yes, he could do it. . . .

And she would know him for a mnemdict. It always showed, somehow, in the passion of lovemaking. All addicts and dealers were agreed on that, and he had been spotted himself once that way. The woman in that case had had no intention of turning him in, but she had adamantly refused to enlighten him on what had given him away. "Women have secrets," she had murmured smugly. Men had them too, but he had never been able to spot another mnemdict. Probably with further experience—but he was drifting from the subject, as he did chronically. If "Sister Beth" were a police fishhook, sex would mean nothing to her; she would be right up on her a-preg, a-veedee, a-allergy shots. She probably intended to seduce him, by her most artful protests, and read the telltale traces then.

"I can drop you off right now," he said. He put his left hand on her smooth leg where the nightie was hiked up. This was very like the leg he had seen—where? When? But the translucent material made it more exciting than full exposure would have been. The leg was classic, like the rest of her. Suddenly the sexual compulsion was almost overpowering. Maybe it would be *worth* betrayal. . . .

"Please do," she whispered. He could see the cloth over her bosom shaking with the force of her elevated heartbeat. Of course she protested; that was part of the role. Her excitement could even be genuine because she was on the verge of nailing him. What normal man could resist as delectable a morsel as this, so provocatively packaged and with such an ingenious story? A girl fleeing deprogramming, ready to do anything for a private ride, unable to protest even rape, lest she be erased by the drug. A decent law-abiding citizen would turn her in; a soft-hearted one would give her a ride to her Station. A callous or criminal one would take advantage of her.

Paul was none of these. Not precisely. Now he was about to prove that. He twisted around to touch the STOP key, and the car slowed, picked its way out of the traffic flow, and came to a stop at the roadside. The seats elevated to normal sitting posture and released their clasps. "Goodbye," Paul said.

Sister Beth looked at him with surprise and something else. "I'm sorry I wasn't what you expected," she said, then quickly got out. "God bless you, Mr. Cenji."

God bless you. Those unfamiliar words struck him with peculiar impact. Even to him, the brutalizer, she gave her prayer. Was she, after all, genuine?

The door closed. Automatically he punched DRIVE, and the car glided forward, still guiding itself. Paul turned in the seat to peer back at her.

Forlorn and lovely, Sister Beth was standing on the gravel shoulder, the wind tugging at her hair and gown. Paul felt a wrenching urge to go back to pick her up again, and to hell with the consequences; there was always the chance she was legitimate.

Then he saw a traffic hoverer descending toward her. The police had spotted her, and might spot *him* if he didn't lose himself in a hurry. He merged with the flow and sweated it out. Probably she had a homing signal, so her employers could always locate her. He had had a narrow escape.

Yet, unbidden, he repeated her words. "God bless you." He believed neither in God nor in Sister Beth, but the power of that unexpected benediction had shaken him.

Paul completed the trip uneventfully and delivered the car. He waited in the plush office for his payment—in the form of a boosted credit rating that would gain him unofficial but valuable privileges in a number of legitimate businesses, and of course his renewal supply of mnem, concealed in the hollow tines of his pocket comb. It took the warehouse a little while to unload the car and verify the potency and purity of the stock and make sure no police were tracing the vehicle. As soon as they had satisfied themselves in a businesslike manner about these things, they would settle with him. It was a most professional operation.

In fact, the whole black-market mnem industry was professional—more so than many legitimate enterprises. Paul had gotten into it gradually, his philosophy of life bending in small increments to accommodate the needs of an expanding lifestyle. He had left college with a liberal arts degree, but had found no suitable employment. Clever with his hands, he had used them to do tricks with cards. That had led him into contact with legitimate gambling interests. One of the popular games, not really gambling but more of a warmup for those not ready to take the full plunge, was said to be a medieval revival, *Tarocchi,* using the seventy-eight-card Tarot deck instead of the fifty-three-card standard deck. The Joker of the regular deck had been expanded into twenty-two trumps for the Tarot, basically. He had adapted that deck to other games, partly luck and partly skill. A really sharp memory decreased the former factor and increased the latter, which had led him to mnem. A casino, irritated by his penchant for winning, had attempted to have him summarily bounced. That had been their mistake, for Paul was more nearly professional in his unarmed combat than in his gambling. The casino manager, no dummy, had quickly changed tactics and bought Paul off with a job. Now Paul was well set, so long as he rocked no jetboats.

God bless you. . . .

The news was on the video outlet. Suddenly an item caught his attention: "A young woman committed suicide last night by flinging herself from a police craft," the announcer said. "She has been identified as Sister Beth, for the past year a resident at a station of a religious cult, the Holy Order of Vision. Apparently she was depressed over the prospect of drug-assisted deprogramming necessitated by her theft of jewelry. . . ."

"She didn't steal those jewels!" Paul exclaimed, then caught himself, feeling foolish. A picture flashed on the screen. It was the girl he had picked up, almost exactly as he had seen her last, her translucent nightgown resisting the wind. Even robocameras had a sharp eye for detail, especially when it was associated with something genuinely morbid, such as death.

"She seemed so quiet," a uniformed police officer was saying apologetically. "I never thought she'd pull a stunt like that, or I'da cuffed her." He tapped the handcuffs hanging like genitalia at his crotch.

Paul felt disbelief. It *couldn't* be her; he had seen her only yesterday. She had been a police hooker with a sharp cover. Then he felt anger. How could this have happened? Why hadn't the police taken proper care of her? But even if they had, she would be just as dead, with her complete memory erased.

Could it be part of the set-up? No, that made no sense; no policewoman would blow her cover by such a newsflash, even a faked death. Her picture would alert her potential victims to the threat. She was too memorable, with that lush body, that innocent face. Man's dream of heaven! She *had* to be legitimate—and therefore dead.

Why hadn't he believed her, believed *in* her, when it had counted? He knew why; he was cynical about the legitimacy of any religious association. He had listened to the incredibly selfish appeals of religious messages: Support Us, Give Us Credit, so that You will go to Heaven and Live Forever in Bliss, Free from Sin.

That sort of thing. How anyone could have simultaneous bliss and freedom from sin was a mystery to him.

Yet Sister Beth had seemed different, as though she really believed in the particular salvation she sought. She had not invoked Heaven once. If only he had paid attention to her words as well as to her body!

But if she had really been a Sister, why hadn't her God protected her? Surely He would have struck some bargain with the authorities. He would have arranged it somehow, fixing it so she would recover. It was only necessary to have faith. . . .

Paul had no faith. He was the cause of her demise. He had attacked her sexually and dumped her back on the roadside. They had been watching for her, and zeroed in rapidly.

If he had only trusted her as she had trusted him. He could so easily have delivered her safely to her Station. There had been too little decency in his recent life. He had been given the opportunity to help a better human being than himself, and instead he had—

"Sir, your account has been verified," the secretary informed him dulcetly.

Paul looked at her, and for a moment saw the image of Sister Beth. Something horrible boiled up inside him, a depression verging on violence. But what could he do? This was only an ordinary secretary, a conformist shell covering a formless soul, not worth even his passing attention. *Sister Beth was already dead.*

Paul stood with abrupt and terrible decision. "I am closing my account," he said. "All prior dealings shall be canceled without prejudice and forgotten."

She never flinched. Why should she? She was flesh and blood, with the mind of a robot. "This will have to be approved by the front office," she said.

"Fuck the front office." He whirled and walked out.

Outside, the reality of what he had done struck him. In the language of this business, he had informed the drug magnates that he was quitting, that he expected no severance pay, and would not talk to the police. He was through with mnem.

Unfortunately, he was now in trouble. He would no longer have the perquisites of his secondary employment—and that meant his lifestyle would suffer. His primary employment at the casino would rapidly suffer too, for he was out of mnem and would soon feel the effects of withdrawal.

• • •

It was a good evening at the casino. The clients were present in force, and free with their credit. Paul took his stint at the blackjack table, dealing the cards with the dispatch of long experience. His responses to the clients' calls were automatic, while his thoughts were elsewhere. "Hit me." He dealt that man an extra card. *Why did Sister Beth do it?* "Hit me." He gave the lady one too. She had a peek-a-boo decolletage, but today he wasn't interested. *If only I had known!* He hit her again, noting the jellylike quiver of one breast as she reached for the card. With increasing age, such jelly either liquified or solidified, and this was beginning to age. Sister Beth's breast would have quivered true. *Sister Beth could have been the one.* Not sensational and cheap and fading, like this gambling addict.

The routine became interminable. He had suddenly lost all zest for it. Yet this was the way he earned his living, bringing in the house percentage. Where would he go from here?

"I cry foul!" a gravelly voice said, cutting into Paul's reverie. "He's dealing seconds!"

Dealing seconds: giving other players the second card in the pack, saving the top one for himself. One of the oldest and slickest devices in the arsenal of the mechanic, or slick dealer.

Paul's hands froze in place. All eyes were on the deck he held. The charge of cheating was serious. "The casino computer stores a record of every shuffled deck put into play," Paul said without rancor. There were established procedures to handle such charges, just as there were for the play. "Do you want the printout?"

"I don't care about the shuffle," the man snapped. He was tall, slender, and of indeterminate age. He did not look like the gambling type, but Paul had long since learned that there were no sure indicators. A person was the gambling type if he gambled; that was all. "It's the *dealing* that counts. You gave me an eight to put me over, saving the low card for yourself. I saw you! No wonder my luck's been bad."

"Select someone to handle the verification deck," Paul told him coldly. "I think we can satisfy you that the game is honest."

"No! You've got shills all over the place! *I'll* handle it!"

Paul nodded equably. If the man was honest, he would soon realize he had been mistaken. If he tried to frame Paul by misdealing himself, the computer record of the cards would catch him and discredit him. "Take the deck from the hopper and deal it out slowly, face up. The cards will match those I have dealt."

"Of *course* they will!" the man exclaimed angrily. "You dealt them, all right, but in what order? You got an advance printout, so you knew what cards were coming, and you—"

"We want you to be satisfied, sir," Paul said. But he saw that a rational demonstration would not satisfy this man. Was he a troublemaker from a rival casino? Paul touched the alarm button with his foot.

The casino's closed-circuit screen came on. "What's the problem?" the floor manager inquired, his gaze piercing even in the televised image.

"Accusation of dealing seconds," Paul said, nodding at the accuser.

The manager looked at the man. "We do not need to cheat, sir. The house percentage takes care of us. The verification deck will—"

"No!" the man said.

The manager grasped the situation. He was quick on the uptake; that was what *he* was paid for. His range of options was greater than Paul's, and he drew on them with cool nerve. "Play it again, Paul. Your way. Show him."

Paul smiled. His reins had just been loosened. "Here is the way it would have gone, had I been cheating," he said, taking the verification deck. "None of these replay hands is eligible for betting; this is a demonstration only." And the NEGATION sign lit.

He dealt the cards as he had before, to the same people in the same order. Miss Peek-a-boo was fascinated; this was the closest she had come to excitement all evening. This time Paul's hands worked their hidden magic; his own display always came up high, making the house a one hundred-percent winner. Yet it looked exactly as though it were an honest deal.

"We hire the best mechanics, so that they will not be used against us," the manager said from the screen. Perhaps he was remembering the circumstances surrounding Paul's own hiring. "But our games are honest. We take twenty percent, and our records are open to public inspection. We have no need to cheat anyone, and no desire to, but we cannot afford to let anyone cheat *us*, either. Are you satisfied, sir? Or do you wish to force us to lodge a charge of slander against you?"

The manager was hitting hard! No charge of slander could stick, but with luck the client would not know that. The manager was showing how the professionals gambled, with nerve and flair.

Grudgingly the challenger turned away. The manager's eyes flicked toward Paul. "Take a break; the flow has been interrupted here." Client flow was important; people had to feel at ease as they moved from game to game and entertainment to entertainment, spending their credit. Client flow meant cash flow.

Paul closed down the table. Miss Peek-a-boo lingered, evidently toying with the notion of making a pass, but he ignored her rather pointedly. She shrugged and took her wares elsewhere.

But the irate gambler was not finished. He was a poor loser, through and through. He followed Paul—not too obviously, because he didn't want to be booted out of the casino, but not too subtly either.

Paul ambled past the ballroom area, where the decade of the seventies was in vogue at this hour; mildly dissonant groups of singers and instrumentalists performed on a raised stage, their emphasis on volume rather than finesse, while people danced singly and in pairs. A young woman in a tight-fitting costume sang into a microphone whose head and stem were compellingly phallic; she held it with both hands, close to her shaped bosom, and virtually mouthed it. Mikes, of course, had been superfluous in the seventies and since; the need being served was symbolic, not practical.

Paul glanced at his pursuer as he circled the stage. The man seemed indifferent to the presentation. Paul found a table at the side and sat down, forcing the man to sit at another table within range of the show, where the decibels were deafening. Loud noise had erotic appeal, of course; that was the secret. Those old-time singing groups had been notorious for their seductions, and perhaps the "groupies" who had so eagerly sought those seductions had not understood the basis of that appeal. Those who disliked sex were similarly turned off by the volume, without understanding why; their protestations that it was only "poor music" to which they objected were pitiful from the point of view of succeeding generations.

Naturally a waitress came immediately—a physical, human, female one, another period piece, rather than the efficient modern keyboard table terminal. "Vodka—straight," Paul told her, making a tiny motion with one hand to signal negation. She recognized him as an employee and nodded; in a moment she brought him pure water in a vodka glass. He proffered his credit card, and she touched it to her credit terminal, recording NO SALE. But none of this was evident to the client at the other table. The man had to buy a legitimate drink—and Paul suspected that he was a teetotaler. That kind tended to be. This was becoming fun.

The banjo player stepped forward on the stage for his solo stint, squatting low so that the swollen bulk of the instrument hung between his spread legs, with the neck angling forward and up at a forty-five-degree angle. His fingers jerked on the taut strings at his crotch while the instrument thrust up and down orgasmically, blasting out the sound. Paul smiled; they might not have been much for quality music in those days, but they had really animated their symbols!

At the other table, the client was averting his gaze, but the sound was striking at him mercilessly. Sure enough, he was a prude. The question was, why had he come to an establishment like this? Was he the agent of a rival casino? That seemed unlikely; he was too clumsy, and would not have bungled the blackjack challenge like that. Could he be an inspector from the feds, checking on possible cheating or other scalping of clients? Again, too clumsy. The days of readily identifiable government agents were long gone; the feds hired real professionals, like anyone else. Could he be someone from the mnem front, making sure Paul was not about to betray them?

No, the only thing that made sense was that he was a poor loser, looking for a way to get even. The man had not even dropped a large sum of credit; his loss was one of status, because he had been outbluffed by Paul and the management, as he should have anticipated. No amateur had a chance against the professionals. The games *were* honest, and any that were not would be too subtly rigged for a person like him to expose that way. Paul himself could win at blackjack without manipulating the cards at all, simply by keeping track of the cards played and hedging his bets according to the prospects for the remaining cards. Sometimes he shilled for the management by doing just that, demonstrating tangibly that the house could be beaten, drawing in many more clients. Of course it was his mnem-boosted memory that made this possible; the regular clients, as a class, could not beat the odds. Lucky individuals sometimes did, of course, but they were more than balanced by the unlucky ones.

That thought saddened him. He would not be able to do that anymore, beat the odds. He had given up a lot when he had quit mnem. Had it really been worth it?

He visualized a young woman falling from a copcopter. Maybe the mnem backlash would wipe out *that* memory!

Paul finished his water and got up. The client followed. They walked past the wheel of fortune—and that reminded Paul of the Tarot. Key Ten was the Wheel of Fortune. Certainly these wheels uplifted the clients' fortunes—and dashed them down again! But the Tarot, in turn, reminded him again of Sister Beth of the Holy Order of Vision, the girl he had killed. Full circle, as the wheel of fortune turned. He could not escape himself. And that destroyed something in him.

Paul turned around. The man was right behind him. "What do you want?"

"I want my money back," the man said.

Paul brought out his credit card. "What are your losses?"

"Not that way. I want to *win* it back. I want to beat you."

What an idiot! "You can't beat me. I deal for the house; the percentage is with me, in the long run."

"I *can* beat you—playing man-to-man."

"All right," Paul agreed, desiring only to be rid of this nuisance. "Man-to-man. Name your game."

"Do you know Accordion?"

"I know it. I never lose, if it is played my way."

"Your way," the man agreed. His foolish, pointless pride was really driving him.

"The Tarot deck. Trumps half-wild."

"*Half*-wild?"

"Each of the twenty-two Trumps takes any suit card—but no Trump has a number, so it can't jump *to* any suit card. Trumps are passively wild; all they do is disappear."

"What if the last card's a Trump?"

Not entirely naive! "That one card's full-wild until designated. Then it freezes."

The man shook his head in wonder. "Half-wild Tarot Accordion!"

"Is the challenge still on?" Paul prodded him.

The man scowled. "Still on. Identical deals, separate cubes, cheat-meters on."

"Naturally," Paul agreed. "For the amount of your previous losses." This might be fun after all—and the mark had asked for it. "One game only," Paul said, to prevent rechallenges.

They went to the Accordion table. They sat in facing cubicles. The mechanical dealer dealt them identical layouts, but they could not see each other's plays.

Paul could almost always win an "open" Accordion game, because success depended largely on a player's memory of the cards he dealt. If he were allowed to see the order of the cards before play, on the printout screen, even for a single second, his mnem-enhanced memory made it seem as though the entire deck were laid out in a line. He could thus plan his strategy on a seventy-eight-card basis. But even in a "closed" game like this, where the fall of the cards was unknown, he could still do well, because as each card was played, his memory checked it off, and he had a better notion of what remained to be played. Thus, as with blackjack, his play got sharper in the later stages, while that of the average person did not.

But now Paul found himself in trouble. The mnem was fading from his system, so that he no longer had reliable eidetic recall. He was still a good player, long familiar with the strategies for aligning suits and numbers in potential chains so as to extend his options without giving away his position to his opponent, but he had not realized how much he now depended on his perfect memory. He felt naked without it, uncertain, weak. *He could lose*—and that bothered him far more than it should have. He had almost forgotten what it felt like to be a loser, and the prospect of returning to that status was not at all attractive. To lose on occasion during one's strength, as a result of the breaks, was one thing; to lose as the result of one's weakness was another. That was what had driven the other man.

Should he return to mnem? He could still do that, he knew. He would hardly be the first—or the tenth or the hundredth—person to try to drop mnem, and fail. The addiction was more subtle than that of physiological-dependence drugs. Some experts still refused to classify mnem as addictive at all. But those people were ivory-tower fools; addiction was more than a physical dependency, as cocaine users knew. A person's fundamental perception of self was involved; if he lost his memory, he lost his identity. That was Sister Beth's nemesis. So Paul could admit his error and go back and—

No! This was his penance for killing the innocent girl; it might not be rational, but it was final. He would live or die a free man—as she had sought to be free.

Meanwhile, he played. Seven of Cups on Five of Cups; Five of Wands on Tower Trump—oops, he had misplayed. He should have aligned the two fives—no, it didn't make a difference in this case. But he should at least have considered the fives before choosing the other option. On such decisions wins and losses were determined.

Paul moved on, concentrating his play more efficiently, matching suits and numbers to second or fourth piles down, condensing his spread in the fashion that gave this game its name. The frequent half-wild Trumps gave him valuable spacing, enabling him to keep the accordion contracted, but of course his opponent had the same advantage. And the man was pushing him, for in match-Accordion both players had to agree to the lay-down of each new card. Paul's opponent had evidently seen a play Paul had missed, and had his layout contracted one card smaller than Paul's, so that he could draw two or three cards while Paul's layout was hung up. He knew how to play competitive Accordion, all right! He had Paul on the ropes and knew it, and never let up. Try as he might, Paul could not regain the initiative.

The final card was a Trump: the High Priestess, ironically associated with memory. Memory—now his liability. Sure enough, she was reversed. The Tarot had uncanny ability to turn up significant associations! So now the Priestess was full-wild, ready to help him compress his spread impressively. But he had not anticipated this, simple as it would have been to count Trumps, and was able to knock off only two piles. He was left with eight piles: not a good score, for him.

Sure enough: his opponent had seven piles. Paul had lost. He scowled and brought out his credit card.

"No," the man said, becoming slightly magnanimous in victory. "Settle in private."

What did that mean? An exchange of credit was inherently *un*private; it became a matter of instant record in the broadest computer network in the world. So the man did not want money. But the bet had been for money; Paul was not obliged to make any other type of payment.

He shrugged. They left the casino. In the street the man began talking, softly and rapidly. "You are a mnem addict on crash-cure. I am a federal drug agent. Your credit will be cut off soon, if it has not been already. That's why I kept you from making any credit transactions; we don't want anyone to know yet. You're in trouble.

Turn state's evidence and we will guarantee that no one ever *will* know."

A federal narc! So deliberately clumsy that Paul had entirely misread him!

"I don't know what you're talking about," Paul said, knowing protest was useless.

"You carried a load that you delivered this morning for the cartel," the man insisted. "We've been watching you for six months, along with a hundred other addicts. We didn't nail you because we don't want *you,* we want the wheels. Your psych profile indicated you were one of our best prospects, because you're honest and intelligent; mnem is a dead end for you. Sooner or later you'd have to break with it, and you had the courage to carry through when you did. Something happened, triggering that break, and now you're out of it. Was it that female you turned in, that cult nut?"

"She was no cult nut!" Paul snapped. "She was a nice girl!"

"Very well, she was a nice girl, too unstable to sit still in a police copter. *Very* nice for us, because she must have done what we couldn't do, and set you up for your break with mnem. Her fanaticism infected you, maybe. She was a pretty girl, I hear. Now we're moving in on you because you're ready to turn against the wheels. With your help we can break this thing open, and close mnem down permanently."

"No," Paul said.

"I know you're off it; I saw the signs at blackjack. Your mind was drifting. I broke that game up and took you out of circulation before your casino employer caught on. It was worse in the Accordion game. You've lost your enhancement, and soon you'll suffer withdrawal lapses. Talk to me now; finger the wheels. Give me the data while you can still remember it, and we'll take care of you. There are counterdrugs we can use to ease the transition and protect much of your memory. My recorder is on. It's your only chance."

For a moment Paul was tempted. But he realized that this man was just as likely to be a mnem cartel agent as a fed narc. The cartel might be testing him, making sure he was keeping the faith. And he *had* to keep the faith, or he might be rapidly dead. "I don't know anything about it," he said. "Leave me alone."

"You can't make a living anymore," the narc (mnem agent?)

insisted. "You're finished. We can help you if you'll help us. Right now—while you can."

Paul ducked into the crowd, leaving the man. He wove around and through knots of people until he had lost the narc. Soon he was on a different street. A huge nova-neon sign illuminated as his approach activated its mechanism: CHRIST=GUILT.

Paul smiled. Was this unintentional irony? One never could tell with religious cults. He passed under it and glanced back. From this side it said: SEX=SIN. No mistake, evidently; to many religionists, any form of pleasure was immoral, and no person could be holy unless he felt guilty. Even in the joy of true faith, he had to feel guilt for that very emotion of joy.

Yet in some people it assumed an attractively demure quality, and there could be a certain allurement, the security of belonging. What was that one Sister Beth was in? The Holy Order of Vision. His memory had not failed! Maybe that was just another repressive cult, reacting to repressive society—but she had been one sweet girl. Why had she had to die?

Paul paused, feeling a kind of explosion in his chest. Heat erupted and spread out under his ribcage, a burning tide, slowly fading. Suddenly he understood what was popularly called heartbreak. There was no physical pain; the sensation was oddly pleasant. But something that had been subtly vital to him was gone, even as he realized its existence. In its place was—guilt.

There was a moment of confusion, then it was late afternoon and he was alone, entering a rundown building. It was unmarked, but everyone who had business here knew its name. It was the Dozens—the hangout of the disowned. More specifically, it was the expressly nonwhite enclave of an age when there was, by law, no societal discrimination based on race or creed. So this institution had no legal foundation. But neither did the mnem cartel. Legality deviated from fact, and no white person was foolish enough to set foot inside the Dozens.

Paul's presence caused an immediate stir. In moments, three husky men blocked his progress. One was the reddish hue of an almost full-blooded Amerind; another was Oriental; the third was black. "Maybe you just lost your way, snowball?" Black inquired softly.

A snowball was a hundred-percent white person, and would not survive long in this colored hell. Paul dropped into a balanced crouch whose meaning could not be misinterpreted. "No." He refrained from using the counter-insult, "Pitchball."

"Mine," Yellow said. The two others gave way. The Oriental stood opposite Paul, standing naturally. "Karate?"

"Judo."

"Kodokan?"

"Ikyu," Paul replied.

"Nidan," Yellow said.

They bowed to each other, a stiff little motion from the waist. They had just identified their schools of martial arts and respective ranks. Yellow outranked Paul by two grades, and these grades were not casually acquired things; he was quite likely to tromp Paul in a normal match. Paul could fight Yellow if he wished, but he would not remain long on the Dozens premises. It would be better to desist from this approach. He had, at any rate, obtained his hearing, which was his purpose.

"I belong," Paul said. "I am one-eighth black. I'm a casino dealer, a skilled mechanic, and the feds are after me. Mnemdict." This was the one place where he would have nothing to fear from either fed or cartel; the Dozens took care of its own with fiendish efficiency, and its resources extended as far as nonwhite blood did. But first Paul had to gain admittance.

Yellow stepped back and Black came forward. "We can use a mechanic. But you're seven-eighths *white.*" The tone made it an insult.

"Yes. My name is Paul Cenji. I was raised white. But you can verify my ancestry with the bureau of records."

Black produced a button transceiver. "Paul Cenji," he said into it.

In a moment it responded. "Twelve-point-five percent black. Three percent yellow. Trace admixture of other nonwhite. On the lam from fed and cartel this date."

Black studied him critically. "You are in trouble. Your body makes it, by the skin of your prick. But your soul is white."

"Try me," Paul said. He knew they would—and before they were through, the truth would be known.

Black spoke into his unit again. This was evidently no standard computer terminal; the Dozens had information more current and extensive than he had believed possible. They knew about his mnem complication and the federal man's offer already! And that three-percent Oriental ancestry; this was the first Paul had heard of that. It must derive from somewhere in his white component; he had not checked that out as thoroughly as the black. "Karrie."

In another moment a brown-skinned girl about six years of age joined them. Black gave way to her with a certain formal courtesy reminiscent of the martial arts practice. What was developing?

The child gazed at Paul with open contempt. She had a slightly crooked lip that lent itself admirably to a sneer. "Know the dozens?" she asked.

She was not referring to this building. Not directly. Disconcerted, Paul raised his hands in partial negation. "I know it some—but not with women or children."

"Then haul your white ass home," the girl said.

Paul stared at her. He *did* know the "dirty dozens," or contests in insult, a typically black form of ordeal. Black humor, in a very special sense. The name of this club derived from it. This was a most appropriate challenge; if he could beat the house champion, he would prove the blackness of his soul, for Whites seldom competed and were not good at this. He had come prepared. But he had thought of it strictly as man-to-man. This man-vs.-female-child situation was extremely awkward.

Yet this was the way they had set it up. If he wanted to join the club, he would have to perform.

He focused on the child, Karrie. She had demonstrated her readiness to fight with shocking directness. This was as real an encounter as the prospective judo match with Yellow, and rather more to the point. Little Karrie had invited him to depart with an unkind reference to the color of his ass. He had to refute this, turning the insult on his opponent, and rhyme it if he could.

"I'll haul ass home/when you learn to use a comb," he said —and was immediately disgusted with himself. He had gotten the refutation and rhyme, but it was a pretty weak attack. A girl her age would use a comb—if she chose to. Often it was a point of pride to need no comb, or to borrow one from a male companion. So he hadn't really scored. He had merely entered the lists.

She snapped right back: "I'll take that comb/and jam it through your chrome." She paused, then struck hard: "With foam."

This was no innocent, despite her age! Chrome generally reflected white, not black. Foaming agents were still used by minority groups for prophylactic purposes. Score a couple of points for her; she had adapted his concept to his disadvantage.

"If your mama had put foam *in,* you'd never have come *out,"* he told her. No rhyme—but the insult was stronger: the suggestion that she had been an accidental, unwanted baby. It was hard to put it all together, relevance, rhyme, and insult, without time for thought. But that was what made it such a challenge. Even many blacks could not perform well at the dozens, lacking the ready wit. If he could handle it, it would more than compensate for the marginal quality of his genetic score. Now, too late, he thought of the rhyme: "you'd never have *been.*"

A crowd was gathering. This was their kind of entertainment. Not all of them were against him; he was beginning to prove himself by fighting dozens-style, and a number of them were light-skinned blacks like himself. A dozen or so. A pun, perhaps; the dozens had nothing to do with the figure twelve. It derived from a white expression applying to stunning or stupefying. If he won this contest, he would have instant friends, and his future would be feasible, if not absolutely secure. "Good shot," one murmured.

Stung, Karrie came back viciously: "Your ma's foam squirted out/when she fucked that white lout."

"Reversed," one spectator commented with professional acumen. He meant she had taken Paul's insult and applied it to *him,* reinforced by rhyme and another racial reference. Those "white" shots were hurting him, here!

He had to take off the gloves. He could not afford to think of Karrie as either female or child; she was the enemy, out to destroy him. "That was no lout, that was her man. *Your* ma got two bucks for baring her can."

There was a smattering of applause. Paul had topped her verse with his own, implying that her mother was a prostitute. The mother was always the target of choice in such contests, the vulnerability of every living person. "Two bucks!" someone muttered appreciatively. That figure had been traditional half a century ago; now it denoted impossible cheapness, barely the price of the required shot of foam—which improved the quality of the gibe. He was hitting his stride now, after a shaky start.

The girl felt the thrust and knew she had been wounded. Maybe she *was* the accidental child of a prostitute. The insults were not intended to be accurate reflections on one's opponent, but if one struck close enough to home to make a person lose his composure, he was also losing the contest. "Get out of here, seven-eights ball!" she screamed. "Go back to your ma's lily-white cunt!"

"Hoo!" someone exclaimed admiringly. Losing ground, Karrie had struck hard indeed, producing a marvelous eight-ball pun on his white ancestry, and calling him a motherfucker. That was close to the ultimate insult, almost impossible to top in the normal course of the game, and in this case he was unable to reply in kind. *She* could not convincingly be called a motherfucker. He realized now that the match had been weighted against him; some prime insults did not apply to females or children. Karrie presented a disconcertingly small target.

Still, he was warmed up now, and not out of it by any means. "My ma's in Africa; I never saw her cunt./And it's none of your business, you little black runt."

No comment from the gallery. Paul had defended himself aptly enough, but had not taken the attack to her. He had lost the initiative.

Karrie sensed victory. She went for the kill. "Her ass is in Africa so she can see/how to get the cure for your pa's veedee."

Making him the child of venereal disease. How was he to top that?

Suddenly it came to him: the irrefutable implication, utterly dastardly. The fecal connection! "When your pa fucked your ma, he missed the slit;/he peed up her ass and didn't quit;/and you came out as brown as shit." A triple rhyme, yet!

Karrie stared at him, defeated, unable to respond. He had really nailed her, making her the spawn of urine and defecation. But there was no applause from the audience; all stood in stony silence.

Then he realized: he had won the dozens, but lost his objective. For he had by implication likened *all* brown people to feces, and yellow people to urine, including his own nonwhite components. In his heat to win, he had let the means justify the end, and so destroyed the value of that end. Only a white soul would have conceived and executed that insult.

Once again, he had grasped salvation—and discovered a turd.

It seemed only a moment before it happened. He found himself standing in the street, wondering where he was going. He knew that hours had passed, for now the city's shadows were long, and he was hungry. The mnem was draining from his system, and he had no replacement; his memory was going. He must have suffered a blackout; the drug was like that. Sometimes the fading was perceptible; at other times it was in chunks.

He smelled shit. And he knew. This was the Animation that revealed his inner worth, the sources of his feculence. The woman Amaranth had played the part of Sister Beth—but the memory was genuine. He had murdered an innocent girl, ten years ago. Or nine, or eight. Mnem had shrouded his memory, and now Animation had brought it back, his dirtiest secret. He was worthless.

A window lighted. He stood before a residential building, and the shade was not drawn on this ground-level aperture, or else he was up on a fire escape, snooping. It wasn't clear, and it didn't matter. He peered in, and saw Therion standing naked while the girl squatted, clothed, in the corner. Call her Amaranth, call her Light, call her Sister Beth or a cartel secretary or an anonymous casino waitress; she was Everygirl, the focus of man's eye and penis. This was the castle of discovery of human interrelations.

Something nagged him about the positioning of the two in the room. It was the same room he had shared with them, and he understood why he himself was absent, because now he was out here looking in, seeing it all from another perspective. But he had made love to her in the center, not the corner. And she had been nude, not clothed. Here it was Therion who was in the center, naked.

Now Paul heard Therion's voice: "Stab your demoniac smile to my brain; soak me in cony-ack, cunt, and cocaine." And the paunchy man pushed out his flabby rear.

The smell of shit became overpowering. Paul's gorge rose; he tried to suppress it, but could not. He turned away from the window, teetering vertiginously over the abyss of the alley. Vomit spewed out of his mouth and nose, heave after heave, brown in this light, trailing yellow strings of mucus that would not let go. Yet even so, he smelled the shit.

The dart, imperfectly thrown in the dark, struck his belt and was turned aside. The needle had not penetrated his flesh, by sheer chance and the motion of his heaving body. But Paul clapped his hand to his flank and cried out as if in pain.

A man emerged from the shadows. "Nothing personal about this," he said. "I guess you thought you could just quit the cartel, and in a few days you wouldn't remember nothing about it anyway."

Paul realized he had suffered another memory lapse. Now it was full night, and the vomit stains on his shirt were dry; the smell of shit was faint. What had he done in the intervening hours? He had no notion; mnem had taken that away, as cleanly as the knife took away the infant's foreskin. The dart had jogged him into full awareness, though; he knew its significance. The survival instinct was more basic than these routine events; all his faculties were being marshalled to meet this threat. The dart bore an anesthetic, to make his body lethargic and uncoordinated so that he could be conveniently dispatched. It had happened to others he knew.

"Now you just come along with me," the man said, unaware that the dart had missed and that he faced an alert, dangerous man. "A nice little ride. See, if you turned up with a mnem-wash, the police'd pick you up in no time and check you out, and then they'd know you was an addict. And that'd be bad nuts for us all. So we can't afford for them to find you. Ever." He reached for Paul's shoulder.

Paul put up his right arm to ward him off, forearm to forearm. He spun to the right, stretching the man out, overbalancing him, then closed his right hand around the man's right, his fingers grasping the knife-edge of the man's hand. Paul turned under his own arm as if doing a figure in a minuet. As he completed his turn, his two hands were gripping the man's arm, bending the wrist cruelly. He applied leverage.

With an exclamation of surprise and pain, the man went down. As well he might; had he resisted, his arm would have been wrenched out of joint. A child could bring down a 180-kilogram sumo wrestler with this hold.

Paul twisted the man's arm, forcing him to lie facedown on the pavement. He picked up the fallen dart and jabbed it into the flesh of the man's exposed neck. He waited a few seconds until the man relaxed, then let go and stepped back. The man did not get up. "Nothing personal, friend," Paul said, adding, "God bless you." He walked away.

So now he knew what should have been obvious before: the cartel would not let him quit. His life was in peril, regardless of the fate of his mind. He would have to hide, before the next goon squad caught up with him. Or the feds.

She was a fortune-teller of the age-old school: a woman of indeterminate years and large, dark eyes, wearing a long gown decorated with enigmatic symbols, seated in a curtained, gloom-shrouded compartment, at a table with a genuinely faked crystal ball. Modern technology had insinuated itself into the act. The crystal contained an illuminated holograph of a twilight landscape, with a full moon rising over gnarled oaks.

"Your card," she murmured.

"No, I—have no card," Paul said. He knew his credit had been cut off, and even attempted use of his card would alert his pursuers to his whereabouts. It had been a great hour for the technocracy when credit had become universal, for every person had to spend to live, and when he spent he was identified. Convenience had increased, but freedom had suffered. The fear that Sister Beth had expressed, of being caught through the computer system, was now his own fear.

Sister who? Pursuit? Was he in some sort of trouble? He couldn't remember.

"Money, then," she said with resignation. Physical cash was an uncertain tool; it was too easy to counterfeit, and it offered no inherent proof of identity. But a fortune-teller couldn't be choosy.

Paul delved into a pocket and came up with what small change he had: two fifty-dollar bills and a twenty-five. He laid them on the table beside the crystal ball.

She sighed. It wasn't enough—but again, she was constrained to accept what she could get. This was evidently a slow day. "Sit down."

Paul sat. "I don't know why I'm here," he said.

"We shall find out." She looked into the crystal, and the holograph changed, becoming a swirl of colors. That was the thing about multiple-facet holography: the slightest motion of the globe changed the viewing angle, bringing out a new image. But this could be tricky, because the three-dimensional effect suffered if the shift occurred on the veritcal plane between the two eyes, making different pictures. There had to be some leeway. Generally the facet-lines were horizontal, so that both eyes showed the same view, and the ball was rotated on a horizontal axis. The colors spiraled hypnotically, and Paul knew it, but didn't care.

"You are confused, tired, hungry, alone," the fortune-teller said. "You need help, but do not know how or where to seek it."

Paul nodded. "Programming," he said, in a small flash of memory. "Deprogramming—must escape—drug—"

Her eyes narrowed slightly. "Let me have your hand."

Paul put out his hand. She turned it palm upward and studied the lines. "Mixed type, unclassifiable, but with indications of psychic gifts," she said, reading as if from a text. "Long Line of Life, broken . . ." She paused, looking very closely. "But there is a faint Line of Mars. And a fork at the lower end." She looked up, her eyes meeting his. "You have a long life ahead, but soon—even now—an accident or a very serious illness. You will survive, but in changed form. Your life will never be the same as before, and you will live and die in a country or manner alien to your birth."

"Quite likely," Paul agreed.

"Clear Line of the Head, rising from the Mount of Jupiter, tangent to the Line of Life, branching to the Mount of the Moon. You have an exceptionally powerful intellect and strong ambition, and will succeed through imagination and psychic awareness."

"At the moment I seem to have failed," Paul said.

"Your hand knows better than your mind," she assured him. "You may be in flux at the moment, but you have formidable powers." She returned to the hand. "The Line of the Heart rises between the Mounts of Jupiter and Saturn. You have the capacity for both idealistic and passionate love—and that love is exceptionally strong." She looked into his eyes again. "In fact, you are a most attractive man. I could make you an offer . . ." She shrugged, letting her shawl slide down to expose her bosom. Amaranth, in a new role, turning on her sex appeal again.

"I just want to know my future," he said.

She sighed. "Line of Fate—very short, not rising at all until the middle of the palm, then well-marked and forked. You have had an extremely difficult early life, but will win success through your own efforts, especially through your imagination. The Line of Fortune, clear and sharp across the Mount of Apollo. You will have good fortune and contentment in the later years of your life."

"Aren't you just telling me what I want to hear?" Paul demanded. "I don't *want* to hear what I want to hear! I mean—what *do* I mean?"

"I am telling you what your own hand tells me," she insisted. "Would you prefer another mode? The Tarot—"

"No, not the Tarot!"

"I Ching?"

Paul didn't know what that was, at this stage of his life, so he was suspicious. "No."

"Then the ouija board."

Paul had bad associations with that; he regarded it as a child's game, not to be taken seriously. "No."

"Then it will have to be astrology."

Paul rose, confused and disturbed. "No. I don't want to know any more! I just want . . ." But he could not continue, because he did not know what he wanted, other than relief from—what? Some terrible feeling . . .

"Or divination by dreams," she suggested. "Or the tea leaves. Or by the forehead—you have a very expressive forehead, with good lines of Saturn and Jupiter."

But Paul was moving out, fleeing her. He knew there were a hundred or a thousand modes of divination, and they might all be valid, but just now he was afraid of his future and wanted to avoid it.

Dawn. His legs were weary, one arm was bruised, and dust and dried vomit filmed his clothing. He was hungry and sleepy, but he couldn't sleep. He must have been running all night, wearing himself out, and now he had no memory of it and no knowledge of where he was. He must have had to fight again, and he knew he was not safe yet. But where could he go?

Where had he *been* going, during his lapse? He must have been conscious and thinking, and he was not stupid. Maybe he had figured out a good hiding place, and was almost there—if only he could remember. But maybe he could figure it out again; maybe he had already figured it out half a dozen times in the course of the night, and made further progress toward it each time before lapsing out.

Oooff! He stumbled forward. Then the slow pain started. He saw the brick bounce on the pavement. It had hit him on the back of the head, but it hadn't knocked him out. He staggered, feeling his consciousness waning; the mnem withdrawal was complicating it, making his brain react inadequately. He put out a hand to brace himself against a brick wall.

Children emerged from alcoves, carrying scrounged weapons. A sub-teen gang, out for thrills, money, and maybe a fat commission from a bootleg organ bank. Artificial blood and organs made natural ones unnecessary, but some patients insisted on the genuine article. Lungs, kidneys, and livers fetched excellent prices if they were fresh and healthy, and his own were.

Paul tried to organize himself to flee, but he had trouble remembering *why* he was fleeing or what the immediate threat was. Deprogramming—was that it? No, that was the girl, Sister

Who, and she was dead, and he had killed her, and a strange man had defecated on her face, and what could he do now to bring her back? He was guilty of persecuting an innocent person, and he had to pay—the penalty had to fit the crime. Christ equaled guilt. *He* had to be sacrificed to the inanities of this society—a tooth for a tooth, a life for a life, shit for shit—yet that was capital punishment, and she didn't like that—

"Now, that isn't nice," a gentle voice said.

Abashed, the children faded into the crannies from which they had issued. A strange young man took Paul's arm, supporting him. "Come, sir, I fear you are injured. We can help you."

"No, no," Paul protested weakly. "I have somewhere to go—"

"You are bleeding from the head, you are dead tired, filth-encrusted, and—" the man paused, examining him sharply. "You have the aspect of a mnemdict in the throes of sudden withdrawal. You are in trouble, sir."

"Can't remember," Paul said. "Who—"

"I am Brother John of the Holy Order of Vision," the man said. "We understand mnem addiction; we can help you. Trust us."

The Holy Order of Vision! *That* was where he had been headed! And he had almost made it, before lapsing out. But what would they do when they learned of his part in the death of Sister Beth? For he would have to tell them. Before he forgot his guilt.

Guilt! That was the thing pursuing him! How could he ever escape it?

"You can't help me," he said. "My life is shit. My innermost self—my soul—is a steaming turd. Worthless. Don't soil your hands on me."

Brother John neither flinched nor scowled. "Fecal matter is the raw material for compost," he said. "A vital stage in the cycle of renewal. Soil, the fundament; without it, most life on this and any other planet would soon stifle and become extinct. There must be death and rebirth, and between them is the soil. Your soul serves God's purpose there, and there need be no shame in that."

No shame! If only he could believe that! Still, the other matter, the death of—"I can't."

Brother John held out a deck of cards. "Will the Tarot help?"

Bemused, Paul took a card at random. He turned it up. It was the Eight of Wands: eight sprouting poles flying through the air, coming to rest on the ground. Their force was spent. "My force is spent," Paul repeated.

"Because you are swiftly approaching your goal, your true desire?" Brother John inquired.

His goal. Suddenly it was as though a great light shone about him, blindingly. Paul knew what he had to do.

"Do not stare into the morning sun, sir," Brother John cautioned him. "That will injure your eyes."

But that didn't matter. What was physical sight, compared to the phenomenal revelation he was experiencing? He had persecuted and taken the life of a member of the Holy Order of Vision; he must return a life to that Order. His own life. There had been death; there would be renewal. Between them was the soil. His soul.

He had found—home. "God bless you, Brother," Paul said.

9

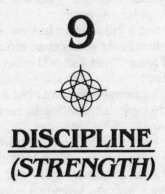

DISCIPLINE
(STRENGTH)

Adults have relatively mundane worries: job, money, clothes, love, friends. These, according to the reflections of a child in Stephen King's Salem's Lot, are pallid compared to the fears every child experiences at night. No social services provide for the child who must cope with the monster under the bed or the thing that threatens just beyond vision. The child must fight this lonely battle night after night, and the only cure is the "eventual ossification of the imaginary faculties" which is called adulthood. What an ongoing tragedy, this slow lobotomy of spirit that qualifies the child for our society!

The landscape of Planet Tarot formed about them. They stood in a kind of scrub forest. A few large trunks rose from the underbrush, but these were dead and charred. Some fire must have swept through the area a decade past, destroying most of the large trees and all of the small ones, forcing the forest to start over. This was not necessarily an evil thing; after many years of fighting forest fires back on Earth, the authorities had realized that forest fires were part of nature's cycle, literally clearing out the deadwood to make place for fresh growth. The big stumps, here, might resemble buildings in the half light, and the forest was like a city: here was the raw material of the Animation just past.

Brother Paul looked behind him. They were actually in a hollow beside the clifflike face of a rocky ridge. Here was even more direct raw material; a moment ago it had seemed like a brick wall, and his companion—

Brother Paul turned to the man. "I am not certain I know you," he said. *Not in this world, anyway.*

His companion was a colonist he had not encountered in the village, a tall, thin, handsome young man, bronzed and healthy. "I am Lee, Church of Jesus Christ Latter Day Saints," he said. "I am one of the Watchers."

"Ah—Mormon," Brother Paul said. "At one time I mistook you for—" He broke off, not wanting to mention the Fed narc. "But that's irrelevant."

"Let's move out before the rent in the Animation fills in," Lee said. "We would not want to be trapped again." He led the way, walking briskly. But in a moment he added: "What we experienced appears to be a hitherto unknown aspect of Animation. I was once called a member of your sect, though I really can not claim to know anything about your religion. I gather this was a reenactment of the experience that brought you into that Order."

"Yes," Brother Paul agreed, surprised. "I was partially blind for several days, because, they said, I had stared into the sun too long. I think it was more subtle than that; my namesake the Apostle Paul was similarly blind after his conversion. Perhaps the drug and my general condition complicated it. The Holy Order of Vision took care of me, and treated me with the memory drug and kindness, phasing down the dosage of the one and phasing up the dosage of the other until I was stable again. I never did recover all my memories. But by then I knew my destiny. I have never regretted that decision."

Lee smiled, grasping the concept. "As the Apostle Paul joined the Christians he had persecuted—"

"So I joined the Order I had wronged," Brother Paul agreed. "In the process I became a Christian in the truest sense. I regret exceedingly that Sister Beth had to die in order to facilitate my conversion—"

"I am sure you have filled her place admirably," Lee said. "We can not know the meaning of God's every act. We only know that there *is* meaning. Why did God allow the Apostle Paul to stone Stephen? Had I been there, I would surely have deemed Stephen a better spokesman for Christianity than a lame epileptic Pharisee

Jew." He smiled. "Which shows how little I would have known. Only God is omniscient."

"Amen," Brother Paul agreed, discovering new insight. "The Apostle Paul made Christianity what it is, to a considerable extent. He opened it up to the gentiles. That seemingly minor though controversial change made all the difference."

"It did indeed," Lee agreed. "Perhaps you also will benefit your sect and the world as the Apostle your namesake did."

"A ludicrous dream," Brother Paul said. "Only God knows what an imperfect vessel I am. How much of my Animation did you share?" Brother Paul found that he liked this man, and hoped the horrors of his personal Animations had not been shown to him. Some secrets were best kept secret.

"Just fragments of it, I think. A game called Tarot Accordian—I do not use cards for entertainment, but I do not pass judgment." He paused. "Do all these episodes represent past experiences in your life or are some allegorical?"

"Some are real; some are sheer fantasy," Brother Paul said, embarrassed. If Lee had seen any of the nightmare visions, he was evidently too discreet to admit it.

"I inquire," Lee said with a certain diffidence, "because something very strange happened to me, and I wonder whether you might explain it. I felt—it was as though another personality impinged on me. An alien consciousness, not inimical, not unpleasant, but rather an exceedingly well informed mind from a distant sphere using my body and perceptions—"

"Antares!" Brother Paul exclaimed.

Lee looked at him, startled. "How did you know?"

"I—cannot explain. But I met a creature from Sphere Antares. He said he might visit me here, or at least I wanted him to—" Brother Paul spread his hands. "A foolish expectation; I apologize."

"Foolish, perhaps. Yet it is an experience I seem to have shared. I don't profess to understand it, but I do not regret it; the alien has a cosmopolitan view I rather envy." He pointed ahead. "Look —there are the Watchers."

And there they were: Pastor Runford, Mrs. Ellend, and the Swami. "But where are the others?" Brother Paul asked. "The ones drawn *into* the Animations, as you were? We can't leave them . . ."

"No, we can't," Lee agreed as they came up to the Watchers.

"Watchers, did you perceive the nature of the Animations we have experienced?"

Pastor Runford shook his head. "We did not."

Brother Paul was relieved. "We have—seen things too complex to discuss at the moment. Several people remain. We need to get them out before—"

Pastor Runford shook his head again, more emphatically. "We can not enter the Animation area. The young woman you call Amaranth went in to warn you about the storm, and—"

"I understand," Brother Paul said. "I'll go back and find them."

"I, too," the Swami said. "We had to retreat during the storm, but for the moment the effect seems to have abated."

Lee was already on the way. The three spread out, searching the landscape that had been a metropolis moments ago—and might be again if the Animation effect returned. Speed was essential.

They found Therion first. He was sitting beneath a tree, looking tired. "That was some scene you folks cooked up," he called.

"I did not arrange it," Lee protested. "I merely played roles assigned to me by the playwright. Some were diabolical —therefore I assumed they originated with you." He did not smile.

"I gather you two do not get along well," Brother Paul said.

"Few of us get along well with rival sects," Lee admitted. "That is the problem of this colony. It is the same all over Planet Tarot; our village is typical. Everywhere we co-exist with ill-concealed distemper. This man is a devotee of the nefarious Horned God—whom I would call Satan."

"A Devil-worshiper!" Brother Paul exclaimed. "That explains a lot!"

"The Horned God was great before any of your contemporary upstarts appeared," Therion maintained, walking with them. "You call him Satan—but that is your ignorant vanity. He is a God—and perhaps the true God of Tarot."

"Sacrilege!" Lee cried. "The Prince of Evil!"

"Listen, Mormon—your own sect is none too savory!" Therion snapped. "A whole religion based on a plagiarized fairy tale—"

Lee whirled on him—but Brother Paul interposed himself. "Doesn't your Covenant forbid open criticism of each other's faiths?"

"I never subscribed to that Covenant," Therion said. "Anyway, I don't find fault with *all* this hypocrite's cult-tenets. Take this business of polygamy—that's a pretty lusty notion. A man takes thirty, forty wives, screws them all in turn—*that's* religion!"

"I have no wives," Lee said stiffly.

"Because there aren't enough girl-Mormons on this planet, and none free in this village! But if there were, you'd have them, wouldn't you?"

"The matter is academic," Lee replied.

"But if it were *not*—if you had the chance to wed just as many young, pretty, sexy, healthy women as was physically possible, how many would you take?"

"One," Lee said. "Plural marriage is an option, not a requirement. A single woman, were she the right one, would be worth more than a hundred wrong ones. I will marry the right one."

"You're a hypocrite, all right," Therion said. "I wish I could conjure a hundred wrong women and show you up for—"

Further discussion was cut off by their discovery of Amaranth. She was standing by a streamlet, looking dazed. "Amaranth," Brother Paul said, struck by her beauty, afresh, though of course he had now had opportunity to appreciate her charms unhampered by any clothing. (Or *had* he . . . ?) It had once been said that clothes make the man, but it seemed more aptly said that clothes make the woman. "Come on out before the Animation effect returns."

She looked at him with evident perplexity. "I don't know —don't know my part. Am I still the fortune teller?"

She *was* confused! "No," Brother Paul said. "We are back in the mundane world. You have no role to play."

"She is always playing a role," Therion muttered.

"What's this about roles?" the Swami asked.

Lee answered him. "It was as though we were in a play, each with his script. Each person could ad-lib, but had to stay within the part. We do not know who the playwright was."

The Swami seemed intensely interested, despite his former cautions about Animation. "To whom did the scenes relate?"

"Well, I seemed to be the central character," Brother Paul said. "Perhaps the others had scenes to which they were central in my absence—"

"No," Amaranth said. "I played my roles only for you. Between roles I—seemed not to exist. Maybe I was sleeping. I thought I had died when I jumped from that copter—"

Brother Paul was uneasy. "Perhaps we should not discuss it in the presence of those who were not involved."

"You *must* discuss it," the Swami said, his gaze fixed. "You are searching for the God of Tarot, for the colonists of this planet."

"It seems I got distracted," Brother Paul admitted.

"I agree with Brother Paul," Lee said. "We have experienced a remarkable joint vision whose implications may never be fully understood, just as the meaning of a person's dream may never be clear. We should maintain our separate experiences, like the members of a jury, until we are ready to make a joint report."

"Yes," Therion said.

The Swami looked from one to the other. "The Devil Worshiper and the Righteous Saint agree?"

"And so do I," Amaranth said. "No one not *in* it can understand it."

"An extraordinary unanimity," the Swami commented. "But I may have an insight. Is it not possible that the power of Kundalini—"

"Remember the Covenant," Therion reminded him gently. Yes, it was evident that these people had little patience with each other's philosophies! Therion had said he did not subscribe to the Covenant and had called Lee a hypocrite. It was becoming clear who the actual hypocrite was.

"I have not forgotten it!" the Swami said with understandable irritation. "But this power, however it may be named—call it the magic of Satan if you prefer—may be the controlling force of your visions. Brother Paul has the strongest psychic presence of your group, so it seems the play orients on him."

"Aura," Lee said. "He has aura."

"This is uncertain," Brother Paul said. "The reality of all we have experienced in Animation is speculative—"

"No, I think he's right," Amaranth said. "There is something about you—"

"We forget the child," Therion said.

"One of the Watchers is a child?" Brother Paul asked. "There was a child in the Animation, but I assumed she was a creature of imagination." Those Dozens insults. . . .

"There were to be five Watchers," Lee explained. "Two outside, and three inside the Animation, representing poles of belief. The child was the third inside."

"I will search for her!" the Swami said, alarmed.

"We *all* will search, of course," Lee said. "We have wasted time;

the Animation may close in at any moment."

They spread out, striding through the valley. Therion was farthest to the left. Then Lee, then Brother Paul, then Amaranth, and the Swami on the right. There was no sign of the child.

Therion and Lee drifted further left as the slope of the land changed; he could hear them exchanging irate remarks about each other's religious practices, faintly. The Swami disappeared behind a ridge. This region was more varied than it had seemed to be before; the mists had tended to regularize the visible features in the distance. Brother Paul and Amaranth were funneled together by a narrowing gully. Here the trees were larger; the fire must have missed this section.

It was dusk, and as the sun slowly lost its contest with the lay of the land the shadows deepened into darkness. Flashing insects appeared. They were not Earthly fireflies, but blue-glowing motes expanding suddenly into little white novas, then fading. In that nova stage they illuminated a cubic meter of space and were a real, if transient, aid to human navigation.

"What are those?" Brother Paul inquired.

"Nova-bugs. No one knows how they do it. Scientists shipped a few back to Earth, when they first surveyed this planet, but the lab experts said it was a mistake: the bugs possessed no means to glow. So—they don't exist, officially. But we like them."

"Isn't that just like an expert!" Brother Paul exclaimed. "He can't explain it, so he denies it." Yet this was true of people generally, not only experts. "Do you catch them and use them for lamps as the people used to do with fireflies?"

"We tried, but they won't glow when prisoned," she said. "They tend to stay away from the village, too. This is an unusually fine display; some nights they don't show at all."

"Smart bugs," Brother Paul said. Obviously if the novas performed when tamed, there would soon be no wild ones left.

"You know," Amaranth said somewhat diffidently, "I was caught in the—the play accidentally. I was only coming to warn you of the approach of the storm when you didn't answer the intercom. Then—"

"I understand. You were not an assigned Watcher. I'm sorry you got trapped."

"That's what I wanted to say, now that I've got you alone. I'm *not* sorry it happened. I got to show off my own Tarot deck in spite of the Covenant, and my fortunetelling skills—"

"I believe you have omitted some material between those two," Brother Paul said dryly. "I must apologize for—"

"No, *don't* apologize! I wasn't fooling when I said there's something about you, aura or whatever. Was it during the Animation that I said that? Anyway, I meant it. I have to study you to learn how you tamed the Breaker, but that's become more of an excuse than—well, you're quite a guy, in and out of Animation."

"I should hate to think that *all* those scenes were under my control," Brother Paul said. "Some were all right—"

"Like Sister Beth," she agreed. "I am not of your religion, but after that I wonder whether—"

"But others—well, that one in the castle." He was forcing himself to clarify the worst. "Did I rape you?" As though it were a casual matter!

"You never touched me," she assured him. "More's the pity. You can't rape a willing woman."

Never touched her. . . . That was worse yet. "Still, if it was my will that dictated your participation—"

"I improvised some. It was my role to tempt you, and I tried, I really tried, but Therion kept getting in the way. I like to dress and undress. I like men—well, not men like that stuffed shirt Lee or the fake Swami, but men with guts and drives and—"

"Fake Swami?"

"He's not Indian. I mean not Indian Indian. He's American Indian. So all this talk about Kundalini—"

"His origin doesn't matter," Brother Paul said, conscious again of his own mixed ancestry. "If he sincerely believes in his religion—and I'm sure he does—"

"He's still a fake," she said.

"He's *not* a fake! He showed me the force he has—"

"How did we get on this subject?" she inquired, turning to him. "Let's kiss, and see where we can go from there."

Brother Paul was taken aback. Freed from the limits of her Animation roles, she was fully as forward. "Are you always this direct?"

"Well, yes. Haven't you noticed the way I dress? I've got the physical assets, and I want it known before I get old and saggy and lose my chance in life. But I don't turn on to many men like this. I'll admit there aren't many eligible men in this village, maybe not on this planet. Most are like that old bore Siltz, dull and married and guarding his son's virginity like an angry crocodile." Suddenly it was clear to Brother Paul what her real irritation with Siltz was: his withholding of an eligible young male from the matrimonial market. There were evidently a number of such families here so that young men and women could not find each other. "The religious factor complicates it so terribly—but even so, you're special. There's something about you—maybe it *is* the aura the Swami talks about. The way you handled the Breaker! I mean to seduce you, if it's not against your religion, and maybe you'll like it well enough to want more. Once I have you hooked I'll see about landing you permanently. *Is* trial sex against your religion? I can be more subtle if it is absolutely necessary."

"Well, the Holy Order of Vision does not specifically prohibit —it's regarded as part of our private lives. But there *is* a certain expectation—well, as Sister Beth said—"

Amaranth sighed. "She *was* a nice girl. Not like me. Was there really such a woman in your past?"

"There really was," Brother Paul agreed. "She was not as pretty as you, but the guilt of her death changed my life. I wish that change had been possible without such a sacrifice—but I always come back to the fact that I can not pretend to comprehend the will of God."

"That's what the Jehovah's Witnesses say when someone chides them about the end of the world not arriving on schedule. 'Don't second-guess Jehovah!' I think it's a copout. *My* religion is I.A.O., and no priestess of Abraxis is afraid of serpents, literal or figurative, *or* the opinion of a sexist God. So if you ever change your mind, I do give samples."

There was something at once horrifying and refreshing about her candor. It helped to know exactly where one stood. "Maybe Abraxas will turn out to be the God of Tarot," Brother Paul said. This conversation made him nervous, because Amaranth was simply too attractive in Animation and in life. More trying was that she had seen him in his elemental being, as a lust-laden male, as a fringe-legal gambler, as a drug addict. She had smelled the shit. She had seen the mask stripped from what he once had been, now hidden behind the facade of a gentle religion—*and she did not condemn him*. Was there another woman in the human sphere who, perceiving his psychic nakedness, the filth of his essence, would not recoil? He had no present intention of indulging her offer—yet he obviously had not felt that way in Animation! Which was his true mind?

There was a scream—an extraordinary, unearthly, nape-prickling effort reverberating around the landscape. Some wild animal—or worse.

"Bigfoot!" Amaranth exclaimed. Then, in dawning horror: "The child!"

Both of them broke into a run toward the sound. The terrain was rougher here, as if to balk them now that they were in more of a hurry. There was a thick undergrowth on the slope—tall weeds, small trees, dense bushes, and root-like projections whose affinities he did not know. Nettles caught at his trousers and made tiny gouges in his skin. He dodged to avoid a small glowing cloud at knee height, then discovered it was only the flowering portion of a forest weed. One foot dropped into a hollow, sending him stumbling headlong—until he fetched up against a horizontal branch he had not seen in the dark.

"No—around this way," Amaranth gasped. "I know this area —some. I've come here with the Breaker, when the Animation retreated. I'm healthy—but I can't run like you."

Naturally not. Few men could run like him, and no women he knew of. This was a problem. She knew the land, but could not keep up. He had power to spare, but was wrecking himself in this unfamiliar dark. They both had to slow down.

There was another scream, worse than the first. "Great God Abraxis!" Amaranth cried. "Save the child—"

Brother Paul lurched ahead, electrified by alarm—and caromed off a dead tree. Bark tore away in his face, the sawdust momentarily blinding him, making his eyes smart fiercely. He *couldn't* accelerate; he'd never get there.

"Go up that gully," Amaranth gasped, creditably close behind. She *was* a good runner—for a woman. "But watch for a rock at the ridge—"

Brother Paul stepped close to her, reached his left arm about her waist, and hauled her up on his hip. He plunged on up the slope, carrying her. "There's the rock!" she said. He saw nothing, but climbed out of the gully. "Now the ridge—it drops a yard—we'll have to jump—"

He slowed, confused. "Oh—a meter." He found the ridge, let her down, and they both jumped into the black shadow. It could have been a bottomless crevasse, like those on the volcano, as far as his sight was able to tell; without her assurance he would not have dared risk it. But his feet struck firm ground.

"Short steep slope, then a level place," she said. "Then another hill."

At the foot of the ridge he put his arm about her again, for she was still panting. "I can go some . . . but God, you've got power!" she cried. "It's not all physical. . . . Just take some weight off my legs—here." She adjusted his arm to fit higher about her torso, under the arms. When he took her weight, she drew close to his side, close and very soft. But he had to keep moving.

They crested the next hill—to confront a vision. On the plateau ahead the nova-bugs scintillated in their myriads, their brief explosions like an intermittent galaxy. To the left was a faerie city, with tall turrets and flying buttresses and minarets glowing inherently: obviously an Animation conjured by some one. That meant the Animation effect was returning, sweeping in from whatever source it had, like malaria through the body. Soon it would engulf them. To the right, the direction of safety from Animation, stood a monster.

The creature was about three meters tall, burly and hairy. It had the claws of a bear and the gross snout of a boar. Its feet were human, but disproportionately large.

"Where is the child?" Brother Paul asked.

"Somewhere else," Amaranth said, turning to look. That brought her left breast under his hand. She was still breathing hard. "Those were Bigfoot's screams, not hers; I was afraid it was—"

Now a reaction that had been held in abeyance finally registered. "Bigfoot! You mean there really *is* a Bigfoot, not just noise and footprints? A tangible, visible—?" He dropped his arm.

"There," she said. "It hangs out near Animations."

Meanwhile the curtain of Animation was sweeping forward. The faerie city was beautiful, but horrifying in its implication as it expanded toward them. They could enter it merely by standing still—but how would they exit from it?

"I think the child is either safe—or beyond our help," Brother Paul said. "The former, I hope. I don't see any blood on Bigfoot's paws. We'd better save ourselves—and hope the others are doing likewise. Can you run on the level well enough?"

"I'd better!"

They started across the plateau. But Bigfoot spied them. With another horrendous scream it charged to intercept them. In moments it had placed itself in their path, menacingly. The nova-bugs were concentrated in its vicinity, illuminating it almost steadily.

"I'll try to distract it," Brother Paul said. "You move on by."

"But it'll kill you! Bigfoot's terrible!"

"If you don't move, the Animation will catch you," Brother Paul snapped, advancing on the monster. He was not at all sure he could handle it, but he had to try. The thing was not going to let them pass unchallenged, and there was no room to escape without getting caught by the Animation.

Amaranth looked after him with dismay. Then she put two fingers into her mouth and emitted a piercing whistle.

Bigfoot reacted instantly. It charged her. Brother Paul launched himself between them, catching the side of the monster with his shoulder. It was like ramming a boulder. Bigfoot swung about, swiping at him with a paw, and Brother Paul was hurled aside. This thing was agile as well as massive!

As he scrambled to his feet, shaken but unhurt, Brother Paul saw the Animation curtain extending visibly toward them, seeming to accelerate. The faerie city was sprouting suburbs, and a broad, tree-lined avenue was unrolling head-on. Time was disappearing fast. Yet Bigfoot still cut Amaranth off. If only she hadn't attracted its attention by that foolish whistle!

Now the nova-bugs clustered about a new subject. Apparently they were attracted to anything that moved. Brother Paul saw with dismay that it was the creature he had first encountered on this planet: the Breaker. Worse yet!

The Breaker bounded rapidly toward them, its tail propelling it like a fifth leg. But it had not come to renew the fray with Brother Paul. It launched itself straight at Bigfoot. But Bigfoot was wary of the Breaker, circling about, never staying still for the attack. Evidently these two were natural enemies, but the Breaker seemed to have the advantage.

Then, abruptly, Bigfoot whirled and charged directly into the Animation city, so near. It ran right up the avenue, as though entering a picture. The Breaker did not pursue. Every creature of this planet knew better than to enter Animation voluntarily! Except Bigfoot.

The Breaker now oriented on Brother Paul. Unfinished business? He braced to meet it. *He* was not about to follow Bigfoot into Animation! Now that he knew the Breaker's mode of attack, he should be able to foil it.

But there was no need. Amaranth ran across and set her hand on the Breaker's back, and the creature was passive. "This is *my* Breaker," she explained. "I whistled for him to come help us. I wasn't sure he'd hear, or that he'd come, or what he might do—but I couldn't let you face the monster alone."

She had tamed the predator, all right! "Your strength is greater than mine," Brother Paul said. Then, seeing the city almost upon them: "Now let's run!"

They ran, the Breaker bounding beside Amaranth. The Animation curtain was moving more slowly; soon they left it behind. Now, perversely, Brother Paul grew more curious about what he might have found had he entered that city: an Arabian Nights' fantasy? And he realized that Amaranth and the Breaker had, coincidentally (or was there such a thing as coincidence, when Animation was involved?), just enacted another Tarot card: the one variously termed Strength, Fortitude, Discipline, or Lust, wherein a fair young lady pacified a powerful lion. Was there more than casual meaning in these occurrences?

Lee and Therion had made it out. There was no sign of either the Swami or the child. "Maybe they found another route?" Mrs. Ellend suggested hopefully.

"Pray that it be so," Pastor Runford agreed.

One thing was sure: Brother Paul would never again underrate the potentials of Animation! This was no laboratory curiosity; it was a ravening force.

The party made its way to the village, and Brother Paul returned to Reverend Siltz's home. "There will be a meeting tomorrow," Pastor Runford said as they separated. "There you will make your report. Please do not discuss the matter with others prior to that occasion."

Brother Paul would have been happy never to discuss it with anyone ever. In fact, he would have felt considerably more at ease had he never entered Animation.

Reverend Siltz was at home alone, eating a cold supper. "I hoped you would return safely, and feared you would not," he said. "You must be hungry."

"Yes. I haven't eaten in two days."

Siltz glanced at him, surprised. "When the occasion is proper, I hope to learn of your experience. I understand time can be strange, in Animation."

"The rest of the planet can be strange, too. We encountered Bigfoot—and were saved by the Breaker. I believe I can tell you about that much, since it happened outside of Animation, if you are interested."

Siltz was interested. He was fairly affable. "We shall have to extend our guarding radius. Normally the Breaker will not approach the Animation area, so it is safe to travel there alone, provided one does not actually enter Animation. We did not realize we were subjecting the Watchers to this threat."

"The Breaker did not come on his own. Amaranth whistled for him—and he came to help her. Your colony's decision to try to tame the Breaker instead of eliminating him seems to be paying dividends already."

"So it would seem. She has made far more progress than we realized. Perhaps we shall tame this planet yet!" Siltz turned up the wood-oil lamp and gave Brother Paul a chunk of wooden bread. "I regret there is no better food since the communal kitchen is closed at this hour. But this is nutritious."

"You know," Brother Paul observed, his gaze passing from the lamp to the unlit wood stove, "with woodheat so critical in winter, I'm surprised you do not use it more efficiently."

Siltz stiffened slightly. "We use it as efficiently as we know. The Tree of Life is exactly that to us: life. Without it we die. What magnitude of improvement did you have in mind?"

"About four hundred per cent," Brother Paul said.

Siltz scowled. "I am in a good mood tonight, but I do not appreciate this humor. We utilize the most efficient stoves available from Earth, and we use the wood, sparingly. Even so, we fear the winter. Each year some villagers miscalculate, or are unfortunate, and we discover them frozen when the snow subsides. To improve on our efficiency five-fold—this is an impossible dream."

"I'm serious," Brother Paul said. It was good to get into this thoroughly mundane subject after the horrors of Animation! "Maybe my recent experience shook loose a memory. You should be able to quintuple your effective heating, or at least extend your wood as much longer as you need. It is a matter of philosophy."

"Philosophy! I am a religious man, Brother, but the burning of wood is very much a material thing, however it may warm the spirit. Such an increase would transform life on this entire planet. If you are not joking: what philosophy can make wood produce more calories per liter?"

"Oh, the wood may burn less efficiently. I was speaking of its usefulness to you, in extending your winter's survival. You are presently wasting most of your heat."

"Wasting it! No one wastes the wood of the Tree of Life!"

"Let me explain. In the Orient, on Earth, there are regions of extreme climate. Very hot in summer, savage in winter. The Asiatic people developed racial characteristics favoring these conditions: fatty tissue buffering face and body, a smaller nose, yellowed skin, and specially protected eyes. But still the winter was harsh, especially when over-population denuded the resources of the land. Wood and other fuel for heating became scarce, so they learned to use it efficiently. They realized that it was pointless to heat space when it was only the human body that required it. So—"

"One must heat the space of the house in order to heat the body," Siltz said. "We can not simply inject wood calories into our veins!"

"So they designed low, flat stoves, set into the floor, that consumed the fuel slowly, emitting only a little heat at a time," Brother Paul continued. "The family members would lie against the surface of that stove all night, absorbing the heat directly, with very little waste. The room temperature might be below freezing, but the people were warm. And so they avoided the inevitable heat loss incurred, by warming a full house, and extended their fuel supply—"

"I begin to comprehend!" Siltz exclaimed. "Heat the *body,* not the house! Like those electric socks, when I was a lad on Earth. By day we exercise here; we do not need the stove, even in winter. It is at night, when we are still, that we freeze. But no one would freeze on an operating stove, getting slowly cooked by it! It would require major reconstruction of our stoves, but it would extend our most valuable asset and save lives. And in the summer, with less wood to haul, we could grow more crops, make more things." He looked at Brother Paul, nodding. "I did not approve your mission here, Brother; but you may have done a remarkable service for our planet this night."

"Not the one I anticipated," Brother Paul said wryly. "But I'm glad if—"

There was an abrupt pounding on the door. "Reverend Siltz, I will talk to you!" a female voice cried.

Siltz's affability vanished. "I am not available!" he called.

"Oh yes you are!" she said, pushing open the door. "I demand to know—"

She broke off, seeing Brother Paul. She was a slip of a girl with dark hair flaring out like an old style afro though her skin was utterly fair, and she fairly radiated indignation. She was not beautiful, but well-structured, and her emotion made her attractively dynamic.

"My house guest, Brother Paul of the Holy Order of Vision," Reverend Siltz said with ironic formality. "Jeanette, of the Church of Scientology."

"The investigator from Planet Earth?"

"Your son's—?" Brother Paul spoke at the same time as the girl.

"The same," Reverend Siltz agreed, answering both. "Now, since we may not discuss religion, and I do not choose to discuss private affairs—"

"Well, *I* choose to discuss both!" Jeanette flared. "What did you do with him?"

Siltz did not answer.

"I am not leaving this house until you tell me where you sent Ivan!" she exclaimed. "I love him—and he loves me!"

The man remained silent. "This does not seem to be an opportune moment to discuss your concern," Brother Paul said to the girl. "You see, you place Reverend Siltz in the position of violating either his hospitality or his commitment to avoid discussing religion in my presence. I am not supposed to be influenced by—"

Jeanette turned on Brother Paul. "Well, maybe someone *should* speak Church to you! How do you expect to do anything for this colony if you don't know anything about it?"

Siltz looked surprised. "She has a point."

"She may, at that," Brother Paul agreed. "But as long as this Covenant of yours is in force, it behooves us to honor it."

"I will bring up the matter at the meeting tomorrow," Siltz said. "One does not have to agree with a given mission to prefer that it be done properly rather than bungled."

"I'm bringing up my matter *tonight,*" Jeanette exclaimed. Exclamation seemed to be her natural mode of expression. "You sent Ivan somewhere so he wouldn't be with me. You'll never get away with it! I have every right—"

"You have no right!" Siltz roared. "He is my son, a dedicated Communist! He will marry a good, chaste, Communist Church maid."

Jeanette's eyes blazed. Brother Paul was uncertain whether this was an optical effect of lamplight refraction, or an illusion stemming from her expression, but it was potent. "Do you claim *I* am not chaste?"

It was evident that Siltz realized he had gone too far but he carried on gamely. "Your whole religion is unchaste!" he retorted. "Your O meters, your clouds—"

"That's E meters and clears!" she cried. "Instruments and classifications to facilitate the achievement of perfection in life."

"Instruments and means to separate fools from their money!"

"There *is* no money here on Planet Tarot, and your son is no more fool than you are, being of your blood!"

This reminded Brother Paul uncomfortably of The Dozens. If he didn't break it up, the language might degenerate to that stage. The lady was pressing Siltz hard. "Surely—"

They ignored him. "Scientology remains a foolish cult," Siltz said hotly. "What good could come from the inventions of a science fiction writer turned psychologist and finally Messiah? I believe in the separation of Church and Fiction."

"You believe in the separation of Church from common sense!" she cried. "Do you throw away good wood because it may have been harvested by a crew of another religion?"

Siltz blanched, evidently recalling his recent conversation with Brother Paul. "No, I would not go that far. I seek a superior Communist way to utilize it, however."

"If you think Communism is so much better, why doesn't Ivan agree?"

"My son *does* agree! He's a good Communist!"

"Then why not let him marry me? He might make a convert!"

Siltz burst out laughing. "Never! A female canine like you would surely subvert him. That is why he must remain with his own—"

"Where?" she demanded. "Where is there a maid of your faith for him with half as much to offer as I have?"

Brother Paul made a silent whistle of amazement. This young woman certainly did not sell herself short!

Siltz contemplated her with distaste. "What has a maid like you to offer besides transient sex appeal and an unstable personality?"

She blazed again. "Transient! Unstable!" But then she caught herself. "I will not let you bait me; I will answer your question. My father was one of six brothers and two sisters. My grandparents are still alive and well on Earth. My great-grandfather lived to age 92, working until he died in an automobile accident where he was not at fault. I carry a heredity of strong, long-lived males and fruitful females. With me you would have grandsons to support you in your age, to cut wood for your winters—"

"Enough," Siltz said. "I must admit you have some recommendations. But in what Church would those grandsons be raised?"

She stared at him, abruptly silent.

"What Church?" Siltz repeated.

With an effort, now, she spoke. "I shall not deceive you. The Church of Scientology. They must be Clears."

"Perhaps some compromise—" Brother Paul began.

"No!" she flared. "No compromise! Not in religion!"

"But as you pointed out," Brother Paul said, "common sense—"

"To Hell with common sense! You don't know anything about it!" She spun about and marched out.

"I'm sorry," Brother Paul said to Reverend Siltz. "I should have stayed out of it. I *don't* understand Planet Tarot attitudes. She's a spitfire."

"No," Siltz said thoughtfully. "She is a good girl, better than I thought. She has good heredity, and she refuses to compromise her faith. She neither lies nor crawls, and she is intelligent. Did you observe the way she attacked me without ever actually insulting me? Never in the heat of argument did she forget her objective, which is to sell me, not alienate me. That was very clever management." He paced about the small room, his fingers linked behind his back. "My son is not strong; he can be swayed. He needs a steadfast woman. If there were many good, religious Communists to choose among, I would not compromise. But there are so few! Even the young women of other religions are a poor lot, like that harlot who tames the Breaker. Religion need not make a man a total fool. If I could strike a bargain, maybe for the first two grandsons—"

"You mean the lady is taming the lion after all?" Brother Paul inquired.

Reverend Siltz sighed. "I do not know. She is so small, I thought she was weak. Her Church is so crazy that, I thought she was crazy too. But strength is not necessarily of the body, and discipline stems from the soul." He looked up. "I will bring Ivan home. What follows—will follow."

10

NATURE
(FAMILY)

The frontal lobes of the human brain enable us to anticipate the future. But that, as Carl Sagan points out in The Dragons of Eden, *means that we also worry about it. He points out that Pollyanna, who always looked at the positive side of things, was happier than Cassandra, who foresaw reality but was not believed. But it is Cassandra we need for survival. From this anticipation come the origins of science, magic, ethics and legal codes. Because we can anticipate the future, we can take steps to avoid its pitfalls and gain long-term benefits. Our foresight makes us materially secure and gives us the leisure time for social and technological innovation.*

The meeting was held in the morning at the village center, around and on the pile of wood. It appeared to be a complete turnout. Of course, time was not wasted, men and women were working quietly on basket weaving, sewing, carving, and tool sharpening. One old woman was carefully binding metal blades to the ends of poles, fashioning spears; frequently she hefted a spear in one hand, testing its balance. The weapon-maker was certainly a vital member of this community! Brother Paul wondered idly whether she made tridents on alternate days.

Reverend Siltz guided Brother Paul to the top of the pile, which was firmer than it had seemed. The wood had been carefully fitted, reminding him of the meshed stones of the Egyptian pyramids. Fuel storage this might be, but it was no casual matter.

"We have no formal organization, no leader," Reverend Siltz explained on the way up. "We are unable to agree on such things. So we operate by lot and consensus. You will take charge, and make your report, and render your decision. Then perhaps we shall have unity."

"But I have no decision!" Brother Paul protested. "I got all mixed up in Animation—"

"No decision?" Siltz asked. "I assumed—"

Lee and Therion and Amaranth were climbing behind them. "It is not Brother Paul's fault," Lee said. "We Watchers became enmeshed in this Animation, distorting it—and another person was drawn in, one not even scheduled to Watch. Perhaps others, too, that we do not know about. Brother Paul had no chance to work unfettered."

Brother Paul paused in his ascent, thinking of something else. "The child—did she return to the village?"

"No," Therion said gravely.

So she remained in Animation—or lost in the wilderness. If she still lived. Bigfoot had entered Animation in the vicinity where she had been lost. . . .

Suddenly it came home to Brother Paul, from a new direction: *Animation was no game.*

Reverend Siltz reached the top. A hush fell on the throng. "I was chosen by lot to host our visitor from Earth, Brother Paul of the Holy Order of Vision," he announced. "My opinion of this mission is not relevant. Brother Paul is a good man, a sincere man, and he has proffered advice on technical aspects of our colonization that may prove extremely helpful. But certain complications have occurred. I beg your indulgence while I explain."

The crowd remained quiet, but Brother Paul could tell from the manner several people glanced up at Siltz that the explanation had to be convincing. If they thought the Communist had tried to interfere, or tried to influence Brother Paul's report, there would be trouble.

After a moment, the Reverend continued: "We had not intended to send Brother Paul into full Animation at once. He was only experimenting in the fringe zone. Two Watchers remained outside: Mrs. Ellend and Pastor Runford."

"The Christian Science Monitor and the Jehovah's Witness Watcher," Therion remarked. No one laughed.

"Three more were placed within the Animation zone," Siltz continued. "A Mormon, a disciple of the Horned God, and a seeker of the Nine Unknown Men. We deemed this to be a sufficient representation for our purpose, this diversity of faiths. All were instructed to remain passive and not to attempt any Animations of their own; they were merely there to observe and to assist Brother Paul should his inexperience lead him into danger. However, he went further into the zone than we anticipated, and then a storm manifested. A volunteer, the priestess of Abraxas, entered the zone to warn Brother Paul of the probable expansion and intensification of the effect—but the storm developed rapidly, and she was herself trapped by the Animation. Thereafter, all the interior Watchers became involved, and the situation was out of control. Fortunately, the storm abated in due course and the effect receded—but one person did not emerge. Since Animation was returning, the search for her had to be aborted. In addition, Bigfoot appeared to be driven off, ironically, by the Breaker. Thus the mission was disastrous, and Brother Paul was unable to complete his quest for the true God of Tarot."

There was a general sigh. Brother Paul saw the mixed chagrin and relief on these faces, and was ashamed. These colonists had with evident effort united enough to facilitate his mission, and he had let them down.

"Swami Kundalini was recovered from the fringe area during the night, but remains in shock," Reverend Siltz continued. "The child he sought—must be presumed lost."

"We should never have assigned a child!" a voice cried.

Reverend Siltz ignored this. "Now I shall ask Brother Paul of Vision to make his report, to the extent he chooses, buttressed by the reports of the two surviving Watchers and the inadvertent participant. Then we must decide what to do."

Brother Paul noted how delicately this gruff man phrased himself on this occasion. Siltz had established a broad option for Brother Paul to speak only on what points and to what extent he wished, had skirted the question of the fate of the child, and had shown none of his private opinion of Amaranth. The Communist Reverend was a fairly skilled public speaker. And politician.

Now Siltz turned to Brother Paul. "We have only two rules for this meeting. We do not discuss the comparative merits of religions, and the speaker holds the floor until he yields it to another of his choice. Those who wish to take the floor after you will indicate this by raising their hands, and you will choose from among them. I now yield to you." And he made his way down the pile.

Some floor! "I can only tell you in a general way what happened inside the Animation," Brother Paul said. "And why I think it failed. I would prefer not to go into detail; it became uncomfortably personal." For a moment he thought he smelled feces. There were scattered smiles. Many of these people knew what Animation was like, though probably they had not had as solid a taste of it as he had. "It seems that Animation, when several people participate, is a kind of play, whose elements are drawn from the minds of the participants. When there is one person, it may be a constant feedback of his own hopes and fears, exaggerating them until he is destroyed. When there are several people, as in this case, all contribute, and to a certain extent this mitigates the feedback and prevents unhealthy intensification of a single theme. But the result is an unpredictable presentation, as the wills of the players overlap. The events of Animation have their own reality; when one person sees a thing, all others see it exactly as he does, even though it may have no objective reality—or the reality it possesses is rather different from what it is perceived to be." He paused. "I fear this is unclear. I mean that if one person perceives a burnt tree trunk as a building, others will perceive it similarly, and they can touch it or verify it with any other sense. It is a real building, for the duration of the Animation."

Brother Paul looked about and saw that they did understand. They were not, after all, newcomers to this concept. "When two people fight in Animation, the blows are solid, though they may perceive each other as strangers or even as monsters. And when a man and a woman make love—" He shrugged. "I did things like these. I am not proud of my performance. Some of my scenes were completely fantastic; others were reviews of events in my past life that I had forgotten or suppressed. I did not intend to—to do or remember these things. I turned out to be a weaker rede than I knew." Rede was not quite the word he wanted, but perfect phrasing did not always come when summoned. "I can only offer in explanation my theory of Animation precession: that the human mind is an immensely complex thing of psychic mass and

inertia, weighted and freighted by a lifetime of experience. When
pressure is put on it, it does not yield directly to the force, but
shifts in an unexpected direction. I sought to find God; instead I
found—shame. I do not know, or care to know, what I would have
found if I had sought shame." He smiled briefly. "Thus, I have no
evidence whether the God of Tarot exists or which God He might
be. I am sure my experience does not refute God, but neither does
it confirm Him. I am sorry."

Brother Paul looked about, hoping to find someone seeking the
floor. Lee caught his eye. "I yield the floor to the Watcher, Lee, of
the Church of Jesus Christ of Latter Day Saints."

"Thank you, Brother Paul," Lee said. He stepped to the peak of
wood, a handsome young man in the morning sunlight. "What
Brother Paul has told you is true. But I wish to amend it
somewhat. There was a play, and we were actors within it. But the
rest of us neither controlled it nor contributed substantially to it.
The play was governed by the will of one person, and we assumed
the roles that person dictated. That person was Brother Paul. I
believe that a phenomenon called *aura* accounts for this
control—"

"Covenant!" someone called from the crowd.

"I am not speaking religion," Lee said, frowning down at the
interrupter. "I am speaking of a practical psychic force that—"

"That is the heart of a dozen religions!" another person cried.

"Then I can not speak," Lee said with resignation. He looked
about. "Who wants the floor?"

"I do!" a female cried. It was fiery little Jeanette, the lady suitor
to Siltz's son.

"I yield to you, Scientologist," Lee said gracefully.

"I move we suspend the Covenant," Jeanette cried. "Brother
Paul did not get anywhere because he was not allowed to know
anything of our real nature. All he has seen is the polite play we
put on for him, pretending everything is fine—so he found a *play*
in Animation instead of God. Let him see us as we are now—a
feuding rabble of religions!"

There was an outcry of protest, but Jeanette would not be
daunted. "I move we suspend the Covenant!" she repeated. "Do I
have a second?"

Now there was silence. "She has the floor until her motion is
seconded or withdrawn," Lee murmured in Brother Paul's ear.
"She can really tie up this meeting, if she doesn't care about what

people think of her—and she doesn't. She's out to have her way, regardless."

"What's wrong with her motion?" Brother Paul inquired. "I suspect she's right. I *do* need to understand this colony better—as it truly is."

"There would be chaos," Lee said, and behind him Therion and Amaranth murmured agreement.

"Bless it, I deserve a vote on my motion!" Jeanette cried. "We can't remain hog-tied for failure. Give me a second!"

"I so second," a man said at last. Heads turned. There was a general gasp of amazement. The seconder was the Reverend Siltz.

Jeanette stared at him. "Communist, you jest."

"I have very little humor," Siltz responded stiffly.

"Never thought I'd see the day!" Therion remarked. "The old crocodile supporting his worst rival for the hand of his son."

"I think that the rivalry has been overstated," Brother Paul said. "The Reverend Siltz is at heart a Humanist; the welfare of man is more important to him than a particular concept of God. Jeanette would make his son a good wife, and he is becoming aware of that. She has only to prove herself."

"This is a scatterbrained way to do it," Therion muttered.

Jeanette hesitated; then her face firmed. "I yield to the Reverend Communist for seconding."

"Now the Second conducts the debate and vote," Lee said. "Siltz is a good organizer; he'll dispose of it quickly."

"I seconded the motion of the Scientologist because I believe it has merit," Siltz said. "I have had the opportunity to talk with our visitor from Planet Earth on non-Covenantal matters, and find him to be a sincere and sensible man. I am sure he is the same in the realm of religion; we know the reputation of his Order. Our visitor failed us because we failed him. It is too late to correct that mistake—but by similar token there is no longer any harm in letting him know us honestly. Hearing no objection, I shall conduct the vote without debate."

"By the Horns of Heaven!" Therion swore. "He's *supporting* her! But that's all she'll ever get from him. The vote, not the son."

The villagers, similarly amazed, offered no objection. "Those in favor of the motion will signify by so saying," Siltz continued.

There was a mild chorus of favor.

"Those opposed."

There was silence. "He is persuasive," Amaranth whispered.

"The motion carries," Siltz said. "We are now free to express ourselves without restraint. But I caution speakers to be brief and to adhere somewhat to the subject of Brother Paul's visit, or nothing will be accomplished." He looked about. "I yield the floor to Pastor Runford."

"Thank you, Reverend," the Jehovah's Witness said. "As many of you know, I opposed the experiment Brother Paul represents, and Watched it only to be certain it was honestly attempted, knowing failure was inevitable. Because the end of the universe is imminent, it is pointless to seek Jehovah by artificial means. He will make Himself known in his own fashion, very soon. As is said in the Bible: 'He shall judge between the nations and shall decide for many peoples; and they shall beat their swords into plowshares and their spears into pruning hooks. Nations shall not lift up sword against nation, neither shall they learn war any more.' Therefore, we should not seek Him in the horrible apparitions of Animation, but must prepare ourselves to meet Him in our hearts, our souls. Man has devolved since Adam, each generation being successively more evil than the last until even the patience of Jehovah Himself is exhausted. All will be destroyed except those 144,000 who—"

"So you're opposed!" someone yelled. "Let someone else talk!"

"The genie's really out of the bottle!" Therion said with enthusiasm.

"This is the problem," Lee murmured. "Suspension of the Covenant opened Pandora's Box. Soon the *real* nuts will crack open."

Brother Paul shook his head in silent wonder. There seemed to be *no* religious tolerance here! To each sect, all other sects were erring cults, and their adherents nuts.

"I retain the floor," Runford said firmly. "You the majority failed because you attempted an abomination! You courted Animation, which is like a harlot bearing gifts, and of her the Scripture has said: 'And I caught sight of a woman sitting upon a scarlet-colored wild beast that was full of blasphemous names and that had seven heads and ten horns. And the woman was arrayed in purple and scarlet, and was adorned with gold and precious stones and pearls and had in her hand a golden cup that was full of disgusting things and the unclean things of her fornication. And upon her forehead was written a name, a mystery: "Babylon the

Great, the mother of harlots and of the disgusting things of the earth.'"''

"Bravo, witless Witness!" Therion cried. "That is our demoniac Key of Tarot, titled Lust, misread by others as Strength or Fortitude or even Discipline. You alone have called it out correctly in all its splendor. Blessed be that harlot!"

"You're an absolute beast," Amaranth exclaimed under her breath, half-admiringly.

"You are surely damned!" Runford cried at Therion, his whole body shaking with anger. "You shall be trodden in the wine press outside the city, and blood will flow as high as the bridles of the horses. Great will be your terror at Armageddon. Your flesh will rot away while you stand upon your feet; your very eyes will rot in their sockets, and your tongue in your mouth. Worms will swarm over your body—"

"Please, Pastor Runford," Mrs. Ellend said gently. "Truth is the still, small voice of scientific thought. Heaven represents harmony, and divine Science interprets the principle of heavenly harmony. In *Revelation* we are told: 'And there appeared a great wonder in heaven; a woman clothed with the sun, and the moon under her foot, and upon her head a crown of twelve stars.' We must always seek to ward off Malicious Animal Magnetism, called MAM. The great miracle, to human sense, is divine Love. The goal can never be reached while we hate our neighbor of whatever faith—"

"What's wrong with *profane* Love, ma'am?" Therion demanded. He was evidently a born heckler, as perhaps was fitting for a child of Satan. Brother Paul, though genuinely interested in the views of the others, wished he would shut up. He had encountered Jehovah's Witnesses on Earth and found them to be honest and dedicated people, strongly reminiscent of the earliest Christians. He had also read some of the writings of Mary Baker Eddy, founder of the Christian Scientists, and been impressed with the sensible nature of her remarks. In any event, Brother Paul did not believe in ridicule as an instrument of religious opposition; in religious debates, as in other types, facts and informed opinions were proper ammunition.

"Who has the floor?" a young man inquired amid the babble of reactions.

"You do, Quaker," Runford snapped.

"Then allow me to tell thee how I view the problem," the

Quaker said. 'When George Fox was a young man nineteen years
of age in the year 1643, he was upon business at a fair when he met
his cousin who was a professor of religion—what we might call
today a minister—in the company of another minister. They
asked George to share a jug of beer with them, and since he was
thirsty and liked the company of those who sought after the Lord,
he agreed. When they had drunk a glass apiece, the two ministers
began to drink healths, calling for more and agreeing between
themselves that he who would not drink should pay for the drinks
of all the others. George Fox was grieved that people who made a
profession of religion should act this way, rivaling each other in
inebriation at the expense of the more restrained, though this was
perhaps typical of societies of that time and since. Disturbed, he
laid a groat on the table, saying 'If it be so, I'll leave you." He was
sleepless that night, praying to God for the answer, and God
commanded him to forsake that life and be as a stranger to all. So
he went, steadfast though Satan tempted him, and in time he
founded the Society of Friends, also called Quakers because we
were said to quake before the Lord. But our guiding principle is
not quaking, rather it is the knowledge which in every person is
the inner light that enables him to communicate directly with
God, so that he requires no minister or priest or other intercessory
to forward his private faith, and no ritual or other service. God is
with us all, always; we have but to turn our attention inward in
silence."

The young man paused, looking at Brother Paul. "Now I would
not presume to lecture to thee, friend, or to comment on thy
private life. I only ask thee to consider whether Truth is more
likely to come out of Animation than out of a bottle."

Brother Paul, impressed by the Quaker's soft-spoken eloquence,
had no ready answer. Maybe this Animation project had been
ill-advised. The Quaker had not too subtly likened Animation to
alcohol, and perhaps to all mind-affecting drugs; as such it was
certainly suspect. If a divine spark of God were in every person,
why *should* anyone have to search in Animation?

"I would respond to that, Friend," a woman said.

"Speak, Universalist, and welcome," the Quaker said.

"Thank you, Friend. I have an anecdote of the man who was a
cornerstone of our faith, John Murray. Made desolate while a
young man not yet thirty by the death of his lovely wife, and
uncertain of her personal faith because of his changing perception

of the nature of God, John sought only the solace of isolation. He set sail in 1770 for America. The captain of the ship intended to land at New York City, but contrary winds blew them aground at a little bay on the Jersey coast. John was put in charge of a sloop onto which they loaded enough of the cargo to enable the larger ship to float free of the sand bar at high tide, but before the sloop could follow, the wind shifted, trapping it in the bay. John Murray was unable to proceed, and there was no food aboard, so he went ashore to purchase some. Walking through the coastal forest he came upon a good-sized church, all by itself in dense woods. Amazed, he inquired at the next house and learned that an illiterate farmer had built the church at his own expense in thanks to God for his successes. The Baptists had petitioned to use that church, but the man told them 'If you can prove to me that God Almighty is a Baptist, you may have it.' He said the same to other denominations, for he wanted all people to be equally welcome there. Now he only waited for a preacher of like views to come—and he said God had told him John Murray was that man. John, chagrined, declined, protesting that he was no preacher, having neither credentials nor inclination. He intended only to proceed north to New York to turn the sloop over to the Captain as soon as the wind was favorable. 'The wind,' the man informed him, 'will never change, sir, until you have delivered to us in that meeting house a message from God.' John struggled against this notion, unwilling to bow to such manifest coincidence, wishing only to buy the necessary supplies for the sailors of the sloop. The man supplied him generously, refusing payment, while persisting in his suit. And as the days of the week passed and Sunday approached, the wind did not change. At last, on Saturday afternoon, John yielded, but prepared no text for the morrow: if God really wanted him to preach here, God would provide the words. On Sunday morning people came from twenty miles away, filling the church, and John Murray stood before them and preached the message of the Universal Redemption: that every human being shall find Salvation, and no one will be condemned to eternal suffering. And with that sermon, that bordered on heresy in that day but moved his congregation profoundly, John Murray found his destiny. When he finished it, the wind shifted, and he took the sloop to New York. But he returned immediately, and that church became his own, his home in the New World, and he preached that message for the rest of his life. Others persecuted him, seeking to suppress his view, for they believed that only a select minority would achieve Salvation—but he was instrumental in fighting the case of religious freedom through the courts and safeguarding it—that very freedom that was to make America great. The wind had guided him, despite himself, to his destiny —and that destiny was significant for mankind."

The Universalist looked at Brother Paul. "Now I would not presume any more than my esteemed colleague to urge any particular course of action upon you," she said. "But it would seem that the qualities of Animation are as yet unknown, and therefore cannot be labeled good or evil. Likewise, the purpose of God may be at times obscure in detail, so that no person can be assured in advance of the correct course. Are you certain it is proper to depart *this* shore without ascertaining the status of the effect, though you may have personal reservations? Which way does the wind blow in your life?"

Brother Paul felt suddenly cold. "You mean—go back into Animation?"

"No!" Pastor Runford cried. "Heed not the blandishments of Satan's council! One man in shock, a child lost, the mission failed—as it was Jehovah's will that it fail! Animation is the curse of evil!"

The lost child. How would she ever find her way out of that jungle of images? How would he ever live with himself if she did not?

"But we agreed!" someone exclaimed. After a moment's concentration Brother Paul recognized him as Malcolm of the Nation of Islam, suddenly converted from a reasonable man to a fiery partisan. "Allah decreed—"

Anonymous voices clamored, with few distinguishable:

"It is finished!"

"The Bible says—"

"The hell with the Bible!"

"According to the Koran—"

"Shove your Koran—"

The meeting dissolved into a fury of shouts. Brother Paul understood now what the Covenant had done. These fanatic cultists of all religions were unable to unify about a single principle unless strict procedural rules were followed, and even then the peace was troubled. Everything would fall apart unless someone took charge. Yet whoever did would face extraordinary rancor. It had to be someone who had nothing to lose here, who was not dependent on the grace of incompatible religions, who was prepared to plow ahead regardless of the resentment of others, simply because the wind had brought him to this shore and the message of the wind needed to be heeded.

Brother Paul got a grip on himself. Then he took a deep breath, braced himself, and let out an ear-splitting martial-arts Kiai yell: "SHADDAP!"

There was a startled silence. In that momentary calm, Brother Paul pre-empted the floor. "There are few things I'd abhor more than returning to Animation," he said. "But I did come here to do a job, and it is a job that still needs doing. For your local socio-political situation, and perhaps for mankind. If there *is* a single God of Tarot, a Deity of Animation, it is my duty to make every attempt to locate and define Him."

He paused, mentally taking hold of the problem while noting the scowls of those who were unalterably opposed to this quest. "I think what is needed is a survey of religions, made within the context of Animation. Some might be closer to the True God than others—assuming there is a God to be found in Animation. So if I go into Animation with that specific object, keeping my mind open to whatever may develop without pre-judgment, and am wary of the diversions of precession—" He paused again, thinking of something else. "The Watchers—if they are willing to come in again, this time for the disciplined, formal quest—"

Pastor Runford objected. He had recovered control of himself and seemed calm. "Do you not realize that very few people ever emerge from a second deep Animation? You are placing your sanity and your life in jeopardy."

"The sanity and life of that lost child are already in jeopardy," Brother Paul pointed out. "So is the welfare of this entire colony. You need to be united to survive the—"

"Family quarrels are the worst kind," Mrs. Ellend said. "We must apply scientific criteria to the problem."

"That is what I have in mind," Brother Paul said. "I trust I have learned from my egregious mistakes and will now be able to proceed properly. Perhaps I will fail again, and I confess the prospect of re-entering Animation fills me with dread. I do not understand the nature of the effect, or of my own mind, or of God—in fact, the nature of Nature is a mystery to me. Yet I must at least try, hoping that the guiding hand of whatever God there may be will manifest for me, as it did for George Fox, and for John Murray, and for each and every one of the people who have found Him in other circumstances."

"You have courage," Pastor Runford said. "I find myself forced to agree with the Reverend Siltz: though I disapprove your mission, I must approve of your dedication. I will therefore stand Watch at the fringe, as I did before."

"So will I," Mrs. Ellend said.

"I appreciate your support most deeply," Brother Paul said. He turned to the people behind him. "And you, who risk so much, Lee and Therion. And you, Amaranth—you were accidental, but maybe that too was a product of the wind. If I could have the support of the three of you in that nightmare—"

Lee nodded. "I share your misgivings—and your rationale. It will not be easy, but it must be done. At least we must search for the child."

Therion and Amaranth nodded agreement. Brother Paul felt the camaraderie of shared experience as he faced the three, appreciating their acquiescence. This was, in a special sense, his family; they shared his experience. They alone knew what the first Animation had been like. "We only have to decide what is right, even though it may seem unnatural, and do it."

But they all knew that nature would have her way, whatever their definitions might be. For nature was another name for the God of Tarot.

11

CHANCE
(WHEEL OF FORTUNE)

The Wheel of Fortune card of Tarot appears to be an iconographical transformation of a more complex and subtle ancient symbol. That is, the original meaning of the spoked wheel was forgotten, and a new meaning applied. This sort of error is common in Tarot and has led to great diversity of interpretations. The original in this case would seem to be some variant of the Wheel of Becoming, also called the Wheel of Life and Death, as represented in Buddhist mythology but probably predating Buddhism. The source religion of Western Asia is unknown, but certain similar themes run through Buddhism, Brahmanism and Hinduism of India, and Mithraism, Zoroastrianism and Judaism of Asia Minor, suggesting that there was once a common body of information. The Wheel of Becoming may also have manifested in Babylon as the horoscope of astrology.

In the middle of this Wheel of Life are animals symbolizing the three roots of evil: lust, hatred, and ignorance. Five spokes divide its main area into the realms of hells, animals, spirits, gods, and men. Around its rim is the circle of causation, shown by twelve little pictures representing concepts too subtle to be described simply. Rendered approximately, they are: Ignorance, Formation of Life, Individual Awareness, Personality, "Thought" as the sixth sense, Contact, Sensation, Desire, Sex, Marriage, Birth, and Death. A number of these concepts and pictures can be equated to those of the Tarot, such as the brutish man Ignorance to Tarot's Fool, the man for Thought to the

Hierophant (teacher), the lovers' embrace of Contact to Tarot's Lovers, and Death to Death. Most contemporary Tarot decks have no equivalents to the Wheel's concepts of Sensation, Desire, Sex, Marriage or Birth—which suggests that these may have been lost in the translation of forms. Perhaps in due course they will be restored, possibly by the addition of new cards to the Tarot deck. Meanwhile, Tarot's Wheel loosely represents the concept of Chance.

Near a river stood a huge handsome tree whose thick foliage extended irregularly outward and cast a deep shade. It seemed to be a fig tree.

Brother Paul walked toward it. Could this be the Tree of Life? That would be as sure a route as any to the God of Tarot. His companions had disappeared, but he knew they would reappear when summoned for their roles.

Beneath the tree sat a man who might have been in his mid-thirties. It was hard to tell, because he seemed small and old before his time. He was emaciated. His hair and beard had been shaved, and he was garbed in rags. He did not avert his eyes as Brother Paul approached.

"May I join you?" Brother Paul inquired.

The little man made a gesture of accommodation. "Be welcome, traveler. There are figs here enough to sustain a multitude, and water is in the river."

Brother Paul sat down beside him and crossed his legs. He picked up a fig when the man did so and chewed its somewhat tough flesh slowly. "You are an ascetic? I do not mean to intrude on your privacy if you prefer to be alone."

"I tried asceticism until I very nearly wasted away," the man said. "I gained no worthwhile insights. I decided it was useless to continue starving and torturing myself. Then I discovered that when I ate and drank, and became stronger, my thoughts became clearer. I realized that the teaching which says that a man must starve himself in order to gain wisdom must be wrong. It is the healthy man who is best able to perceive the world and contemplate religious truth." He glanced at Brother Paul. "By this token, you must be a very perceptive man, for you are the healthiest I have encountered. May I inquire your name?"

"I am Brother Paul of—a distant culture. And you?"

"I am Siddhattha Gotama, once a prince, now a beggar-monk."

Siddhattha Gotama—the man known to history as the Buddha, the Awakened One, the Enlightened. The founder of one of the greatest religions of all time, Buddhism. He had indeed been a prince and had renounced his crown voluntarily to seek revelation.

"I—am honored to meet you," Brother Paul said humbly. Though he regarded himself as Christian, he had deep respect for Buddhism. "I too am a seeker of truth. I have not yet found it."

"I have looked for seven years for enlightenment," Siddhattha said. "Often I have been sorely tempted to desist from begging and return to my wife and son. Always I remind myself that I could never be happy again in the palace, so long as I knew others existed in hardship and misery. Yet I seem to draw no closer to any insight how to enable others to be happy."

This, then, was before the Buddha had attained his revelation. "Have you inquired of teachers, of wise men?"

Siddhattha smiled ruefully. "I visited the great teacher Alara. 'Teach me the wisdom of the world!' I begged him. He said to me 'Study the Vedas, the Holy Scriptures. There is all wisdom.' But I had already studied the Vedas and found no enlightenment. So I wandered on until I encountered another great teacher, Udaka, and I asked him. He told me 'Study the Vedas!' Yet I knew that in them was no explanation why the Brahman makes people suffer illness and age and death. I am also doubtful that one can attain wisdom by hurting himself or sitting on sharp nails."

"In my culture," Brother Paul agreed, we are told much the same. 'Read the Bible.' Yet human warfare and misery continue, even among those who profess to hold the Bible most dear. I suspect we shall not find the ultimate truths in any book. Yet life is often a difficult tutor."

"That is true," Siddhattha agreed reminiscently. "When I was a prince, I went out hunting. I saw a man, all skin and bones, writhing in pain on the ground. 'Why?' I asked. 'All people are liable to illness,' I was informed. But in my sheltered life I had not been exposed to this, and it made me very sad. Next day I met a man so old his back was curved like a drawn bow, and his head was nodding, and his hands trembled like palm leaves in the wind so that even with the aid of two canes he could hardly walk. 'Why?' I asked. 'He is old; all people grow old,' I was told. Again I was saddened, for I had known only youth. Next day I saw a

funeral procession, with the widow and orphans following behind
the corpse. 'Why?' 'Death comes to all alike.' This horrified me,
for I had never contemplated the reality of death in man. I knew
so little of life and of people; I had spent my life in foolish
pleasures. Why was I so well off, while others suffered? I understood now that I was the exception and that the great majority of
people in the world were ill and poor. This did not seem right. Yet
even as I contemplated this, my lovely wife was giving a party with
many pretty girls singing and dancing, and that music only
heightened my confusion. When my family observed this, it was
assumed that the entertainment was not sufficient, and so the girls
were made to perform with such vigor and endurance that they
dropped from exhaustion. How their loveliness had changed!
Next day I went to the market place, and there among the
merchants I saw an old monk dressed in coarse yellow robes,
begging for food. Though he was old and sick and poor, he seemed
calm and happy. Then I decided to be like him."

"I think you found much enlightenment at that moment,"
Brother Paul said. "Maybe the ultimate truth can be found only in
one's own heart." That was the Quaker belief, he recalled.

Siddhattha turned to him. "That is a most intriguing thought! I
wonder what I might find, if I simply sit here under this Bo Tree
until I have plumbed in my own soul this truth."

The Bo Tree! Now Brother Paul remembered: it was called the
Tree of Wisdom, for it was where the Buddha had spent his Sacred
Night and attained his crucial Enlightenment. "I had better leave
you alone, then."

"Oh, no, friend! Stay here with me and search out your own
truth," Siddhattha encouraged him.

Well, why not? This might be the most direct route to his
answer. The God that Buddha found—that had to be a major
contender for the office of God of Tarot.

Dusk was rising. The sun descended. But they were not allowed
to meditate in peace. A group of people approached the Tree, and
it was obvious that they intended mischief. Three were young and
quite pretty women; the rest were motley ruffians of assorted
appearance.

Brother Paul jumped to his feet, about to warn off the intruders,
but Siddhattha stopped him. "These are the cohorts of Mara, the
Evil One, who seeks to dissuade us from our pursuit. For seven
years he has followed me. But he cannot harm us physically so

long as we remain under this Tree. Do not try to fight him; that is what he wants. It is futile to oppose evil with evil."

Could this be true? Brother Paul backed off, yielding to the Buddha's judgment. Mara the Evil One—the Buddhist Devil. This was to be no ordinary encounter!

Sure enough, the crowd stopped just beyond the spread of the Tree. But now there came an elephant, overwhelmingly tall, its measured tread shaking the earth, and riding it was a large, somewhat paunchy man bearing a sneer of pure malice. This, surely, was the Evil One.

"Come out, cowards!" Mara bawled.

Siddhattha remained seated. "The Evil One has eight armies," he explained to Brother Paul. "They are called Discontent, Hunger, Desire, Sloth, Cowardice, Doubt, and Hypocrisy. Few can conquer such minions; but whoever is victorious obtains joy."

Brother Paul wrinkled his brow. "I believe that's only seven armies. Not that those aren't sufficient!"

Siddhattha's brow wrinkled in turn. "I always forget one or two. Evils are not my specialty." Surely the understatement of the millennium!

Now the three women came forward. They were seductively garbed and moved their torsos in a manner calculated to enhance their sexual appeal. "Come meet my daughters," Mara cried. "They are experts in the pleasing of men." And, acting as one, the three beckoned enticingly.

Brother Paul felt the allure. Somehow the Animation had produced a triple image of Amaranth, and she was good at this type of role.

"Now I remember Mara's other army!" Siddhattha exclaimed happily. "Lust!" But he seemed to be pleased only by the intellectual aspect; these lush bodies did not tempt him.

The women turned about and left with a final triple flirt of the hips. It was obvious they had failed. Siddhattha would not be corrupted by sex. And why should he be? He had a wife and son at home, along with a crown, and probably a full harem, if he ever felt the need.

Now armed men came forward, dressed in animal skins, gesticulating wildly, screaming. They resembled demons. The sun was now down, but the moonlight illuminated them with preter-natural clarity. Siddhattha was not alarmed. "Mara personifies the triple thirst for existence, pleasure, and power. The satisfaction of selfishness is Hell, and those who pursue selfishness are demons." And the demon-men could not touch him.

"A most apt summary," Brother Paul agreed. He liked this man and found nothing objectionable in his philosophy. But how was he to be certain whether the Buddhist God was or was not the God of Tarot?

"You and I can sit here and reflect on the Ten Perfections," Siddhattha said.

The demon soldiers retreated. Mara was furious. "I tried to be gentle with you," he cried, "but you would not have it. Now taste the wrath of my magic."

No more Mr. Nice Guy, Brother Paul thought, almost smiling.

Mara raised one hand. Immediately a whirlwind blew, forming an ominous black funnel that swept in to encompass the entire Bo Tree. But in the center was the calm, and not a leaf stirred. Brother Paul looked out at the whirling wall of dust in amazement and with not a little apprehension, but Siddhattha ignored it. "It is only air," he murmured to Brother Paul.

The whirlwind vanished. "Well, try water, then!" Mara screamed. A terrible storm formed, and rain pelted down, causing instant flooding all about the area. But not a drop penetrated the foliage of the Bo Tree, and Siddhattha sat serene and dry. Instead, Mara's elephant trumpeted and splashed its feet in the water like a skittish woman, upset.

"Earth!" Mara cried. And the storm converted to a barrage of rocks, sand, and mud. Yet again these things had no effect on the seated man, who had not changed his position since Brother Paul appeared in the scene. The few stones that penetrated the Bo Tree fell to the ground like harmless flowers. Those that struck the elephant, in contrast, made havoc; the poor creature danced cumbersomely about, trying to protect itself.

Mara was livid. "Fire!" he cried. And live coals came down, setting fire to the grass and brush outside the Bo Tree and hissing into the river. Siddhattha was not afraid, and so he was inviolate.

"You have conquered the attack of the four elements," Brother Paul said. "You have beaten the Evil One."

"No, the battle has just begun. Now he will lay siege to my spirit."

Mara gestured, and the bright moonlight went out, making the world black. But a glow arose from the Bo Tree, restoring visibility there. From the darkness beyond, Mara bawled: "Siddhattha, arise from that seat! It is not yours, but mine!"

The seated man only shook his head in mild negation.

"I am the Prince of the World!" Mara said. "I hold the Wheel of Life and Death!" Light returned, revealing him standing just beyond the Tree, clutching a huge wheel with five spokes so that only his head, feet and hands showed around its rim. His body, oddly, did not show behind it at all; the center was filled with moving images.

"The Wheel of Becoming," Siddhattha agreed. "The hand of death is on every one who is born. Yet I shall not die, O Evil One, until my mission in life has been accomplished."

"And what is that mission, O Ignorant One?" Mara demanded with a sneer.

"To spread the Truth," Siddhattha replied simply.

"*What* Truth?"

Siddhattha, who had been doing so well before, was unable to answer. Brother Paul saw this as another variation of the Dozens, with the Buddha turning away insults by soft replies. But now he was in trouble.

Mara advanced, bearing his Wheel forward. It was an impressive and sinister thing, its various aspects turning in opposite directions, confusing the eye. "If you cannot answer, O Shriveled Ascetic, the victory is mine!" The role-player was Therion, of course, and he was enjoying this.

Siddhattha looked at Brother Paul beside him. "Friend, I fear I have lost the battle, for the Truth has not yet come to me, and Mara must have his answer." There were tears in the man's eyes.

"But the Evil One will bring only evil upon the world!" Brother Paul said, as though that could help. "He controls the Wheel of Becoming, and he is the Prince of the World. Only your good can stop him!" He put his hand on Siddhattha's frail shoulder.

With that contact, something happened. "I feel—the spirit of God," Siddhattha said wonderingly. "Are you a messenger from—?"

"No, no!" Brother Paul said hastily. It had been the contact of auras the man had felt. "I am only another Seeker."

Still the thing grew. What had been quiescent in Siddhattha all his life was now awakening. He was becoming conscious of his aura—and it was an extremely powerful one. "The spirit of God—is in me," he said, certainty coalescing. "And now—I have found the key to Wisdom, the First Law of Life! It was within me all the time, awaiting this moment."

Siddhattha stood. He was not tall, but his new enhancement gave him stature. "Listen, Mara, and be damned: FROM GOOD MUST COME GOOD, AND FROM EVIL MUST COME EVIL."

Brother Paul was troubled by this statement. From what he remembered of symbolic logic, a false hypothesis that led to a true conclusion was regarded as valid. That suggested that it was possible for Good to come from Evil. Obviously this man did not subscribe to that notion.

Mara gave a cry of pure anguish. He staggered back, seeking his elephant—but when he touched it, the beast collapsed. All his minions scrambled away from the Bo Tree in a rout.

Brother Paul stood watching, amazed. And realized that Siddhattha was now the Buddha, the Awakened One. And that, symbolic logic or not, the God of this man—could indeed be the God of Tarot.

But to be sure, he would have to survey the other great religions of the world and eliminate them from consideration. Maybe the Eightfold Path was the correct one, but that could not be certain yet.

"My business here is done," he said to the Buddha. "I hope we shall meet again." The Bo Tree faded out.

Brother Paul stood in a landscape whose sky contained three suns: a full-sized one and two little ones. The vegetation, however, was Earthlike to a degree: what looked like arctic fir was adjacent to tropic palm. The air was breathable though slightly intoxicating. Gravity was less than he was used to, but the terrain was so rough that he was sure the amount of energy he would have to expend to travel anywhere would counterbalance this.

In fact, he stood on a slanting ledge above a bubbling lava flow. A waft of fumes came up, and he hastily stepped back. His foot slipped in snow, and he half-fell into the ice of a stalled avalanche. A meter back from the boiling rock the deep freeze of winter was encroaching. No wonder the plants were narrowly confined! The spread from hard frost to perpetual warmth was within one to two meters.

But what had this to do with religion? He had intended to check one of the most modern and vigorous of the world's great faiths: Voodoo. It had originated in Black Africa and spread to the Americas with slavery. Christianity had been imposed on the nonwhite population, so these people had compromised by merging their native Gods with the Catholic Saints, creating a dual purpose pantheon that permitted them to satisfy the missionaries while remaining true to their real beliefs. The truth, were it ever admitted, was that there were more voodoo worshipers in Latin America during the 20th Century than legitimate Christians, and the depth of their religious conviction and practice was greater. Brother Paul had flirted with the Caribbean Santeria, or regional Voodoo cult, while on a quest for his black ancestry, and found it both appalling and appealing. The chicken-disemboweling rituals, roach-eating, and mythology of incest revolted his white middle-class taste, but the sincerity of the serious practitioners and the religion's obvious power over the masses satisfied his youthful need to belong. Later, as a Brother of the Holy Order of Vision, he had dealt on a professional level with Santeros, or Witch-Doctors, and found them generally to be as concerned and knowledgeable about the needs of believers as were Catholic priests, medical doctors, or psychiatrists. Folk medicine thrived on in Voodoo. The Holy Order of Vision did not hesitate to refer a troubled person to a reputable witch-doctor when the occasion warranted it. These were true faith-healers of modern times.

But this was an alien world! How had Animation produced this instead of the Voodoo Temple he had sought? Was it Precession again? His idea had been to bracket the religions of the world, to survey the extremes, and then work into the center, eliminating as much as possible. Fairly, of course. But if Precession had struck, there was no telling what he was into.

"Oh." It was a young woman, dressed in a strange half-uniform. One side was a well-padded shieldlike affair, covering her body from head to heel. The other side was—nothing. She was, in fact, half-nude.

"I seem to have lost my way," Brother Paul said.

"But where is your sub-fission?" she asked.

"I—fear I do not understand," he said, shifting about to ease the chill of his left side, too close to the snow. Suddenly he understood the rationale of her costume: her right side was insulated against the winter side of this ledge, while her left was comfortable in the summer side. Presumably, when she traveled in the other direction, she reversed sides. Apparently in this world the air was resistive to the convections of radical temperature change, so that extremes of climate could coexist without turbulence. Still, when storms did develop, they were probably ferocious.

"Where is your sister, your wife?" she asked.

"I have neither sister nor wife."

"I mean your sibling mate, in the eye of Xe Ni Qolz," she explained. "How is it you venture out in half?"

This was not becoming any more intelligible! "I have just arrived from—from another planet. I am an only child, unmarried."

Her pretty brow furrowed. "I hadn't realized another ship had arrived. You had better hide before you get us all in trouble."

"I don't even know where I am or what is wrong!"

She considered him speculatively. "Look, this is somewhat sudden, but maybe a break for us both. I just had a fight with my brothub, so I snuck out alone, but I'm afraid a Nath will spot me. How about filling in with you?"

Brother Paul could not make sense of this. "Brothub? Nath? What do these terms mean?"

She stepped forward and took his arm. "No time to explain," she said. "Look, there's one now!"

He followed her gaze. There, sliding along the edge of the snowbank was something like a shag rug—but it was flowing uphill. "That—can it be alive?" he whispered, amazed.

"Just fake it," she whispered back. "Let me do the talking."

He seemed to have no alternative.

The rug slid up to them and paused two meters away. Brother Paul saw that it moved by shooting out myriad tiny burrs on threads, then hauled itself forward by winching them in. Truly alien locomotion! "Pull-hook, Sol," the thing said. It spoke strangely in a kind of staccato. Brother Paul conjectured that it was tapping the ground with hundreds of miniature hammers in such a manner as to create a human-sounding pattern of sonics.

"The same to you, Nath," the girl replied.

"What entity-pair are you?" Nath inquired.

"I—we—" She faltered, not knowing Brother Paul's name.

"I am Brother Paul," he filled in. "Of the Holy—"

"And I am Sister Ruby," she interjected. Then she turned to Brother Paul and flung herself into his arms, pressing one winterized and one summerized breast against his torso and planting a passionate kiss on his lips.

"It is good to perceive such sibling love," Nath said. "May the

Wheel turn well for your regeneration." Then the creature heaved itself smoothly up over the snow and on around them.

"Xe Ba Va Ra enhance you, Nath," Ruby called after it.

"All right, now," Brother Paul said. He had identified her, of course: Amaranth in a new part. As sexy as ever. But now he wondered who had played the part of Buddha in the prior scene. The man had been too small to be either Lee or Amaranth. "Will you explain what—"

"Yes, yes, everything," she said. "Come with me to the Temple of Tarot, and I'll explain on the way." She walked down the ledge-path, weaving smoothly around the foliage, and he had to follow. He couldn't remain here; it was impossible to be comfortable in this arctic tropic.

"First," he said as he caught up, momentarily distracted by the way his expelled breath fogged on the frigid side and by her bare buttock flexing on the hot side, "What world is this?"

"We're a human colony in the Hyades cluster," she said. "We were founded three hundred years ago by mattermission, but then it turned out we were actually inside Sphere Nath, so we were subject to their government. Since our supply line had broken down and the Naths were well established, this really was better. All we had to do was obey their laws and honor their customs, and they treated us just as well as Sol would have. Better, maybe. That's part of the Intersphere Covenant, you see. I don't think Sol ever established diplomatic relations with Nath, but at the fringes of the Spheres it is Galactic custom to work these things out—"

"Wait, wait!" Brother Paul cried. "You mean to say human beings are being governed by alien creatures that look like—that rug?"

"Yes, of course. The Naths are really rather nice. We had some trouble at first, but once the Wheel of Tarot was established everything was fine. Now we worship our Saints, and they don't know the difference."

"The Wheel of Tarot," he repeated. "Would that be related to the Wheel of Life and Death, or the Wheel of Becoming?"

"Yes, it is also called that. It—"

"With five spokes? Each section representing—"

"Yes, the Naths call these sections Energy, Gas, Liquid, Solid, and Plasma. You know, the five states of matter, each one phasing into the other, completing the circle. Each with its representative Deity, that we call—"

"You worship alien Gods?" he asked, dismayed.

She paused momentarily in the path. "Look, Brother—if we didn't honor their religion, their missionaries would be push-hooked, and then their government might decide not to expend good resources maintaining an alien squatter-colony. We *need* Nath equipment and material and knowhow and communications, and if we don't get them we'll—well, can you imagine scrounging a living from this terrain, alone?" She gestured up and down the slope, taking in the lava and ice. "So we follow their religion. They don't demand that of us, but we really have to."

As the Blacks and Reds of Latin America had to follow Christianity, overtly. Now it was coming clear. "So you merged your Saints with their Spirits, so that they would believe you were honoring *their* religion?"

"That's correct. It was easy, in four sections of the Wheel. Their God of Gas, Xe Kwi Stofr, is our Saint Christopher, and—"

"I don't quite see the connection. Gas would equate to the element of Air, which is the Tarot suit of Swords, generally associated with intellect or science or trouble, while St. Christopher—"

The path debouched into a small valley sheltered under an overhanging cliff. Here there was a building in the shape of a roofed wheel, complete with five sections. Massive dikes diverted the lava flow, causing it to pass on either side of the Wheel, burning back the ice. A fringe of trees of diverse species surrounded the island Wheel. Evidently this was a permanent lava flow—truly alien to Earthly experience and enough to interrupt anyone's chain of thought. A narrow bridge, fashioned of wedges of stone, passed over one of the lava streams to the island. The whole thing would have been difficult for human beings to assemble without the machines of an advanced technology—and the colonists obviously lacked those. So it had to be the beneficial handiwork of the alien civilization: the Naths.

Actually, it made sense that there be more sapient aliens in space than just the protoplasmic entities of Antares. He had no reason to be surprised. Man would inevitably encounter these aliens, and it was best that mechanisms for peaceful interaction exist.

"Let me tell you about St. Christopher," Ruby said. "He was a huge man who chose to work for the most powerful king on Earth. When he saw that the strongest king feared the Devil, Christopher went to work for the Devil. But then the Devil flinched at the Cross, so Christopher sought the one who was associated—"

"Yes, of course," Brother Paul said. "That was Jesus—"

"Don't say that name!" she cried, cutting him off. "The Naths know our origin-religion, and if they thought we were backsliding—"

Brother Paul nodded. "So the Sword of Tarot becomes the Cross that St. Christopher sought. And the Wand suit becomes—"

"Saint Barbara, locked in the tower because she would not marry a rich pagan," she said. "The bolt of lightning that avenged her martyrdom becomes the symbol of energy of the Nath Nature Spirit Xe Ba Va Ra. And the suit of Coins stands for Nath's Solid, the Spirit of Trade, Xe Jun Olm Nar, whom we call Saint John the Almoner, so generous in his alms. Their Spirit of Art, Xe Gul Yia Na, is our Saint Juliana, who tied up the Devil. The only real problem is—"

"You seem to have it worked out pretty well," he said. "I'm surprised that the mere exchange of names persuades the Naths you are converts to their religion." Yet that same device had been effective for the Voodoo adherents in Christian countries. When a man kneeled before a statue of St. Barbara, spoke her name reverently, and left an offering, who could say for sure whether it was the Catholic Saint he prayed to in his heart or Xango, the Voodoo God of lightning? Who could say which entity answered that prayer? Did it really matter?

"The Naths do not separate religion and morality," she said. "They believe that if we profess belief in their spirits, we must necessarily follow their cultural code. So they do not inquire too closely, so long as we do not violate it in any obvious manner. Still—"

"The Naths seem like good creatures," he said. Now they were crossing the bridge. He flinched away from the hot fumes rising from it. "I hardly begrudge you your original religion, for it is my own, though perhaps I indulge in an earlier variant of Christ—of that faith."

"Three hundred years earlier," she said.

"Oh? How would you know that?" He had expected some kind of objection from the role-player, who was not a Christian. She must be seething!

"That's how long it takes a freezer-ship to reach here from Sol at half-light speed or less. So you are a man of twenty or twenty-first century Earth, thawed out after a sleep that seemed to you just a moment."

Freezer-ship? Suspended animation for three centuries? Well, it was a natural conclusion for a native girl. But how would Amaranth have known of such things, assuming they were valid details of future history? There were nuances to these Animations that seemed to defy rational explanation.

"At any rate," he continued as she showed him into a section marked with a picture of jolly Santa Claus in his fat red suit and spreading white beard, "I don't really see that such subterfuge is necessary here. Why not simply inform the Naths that you worship similar Gods to theirs, though they go by different names? I'm sure the aliens would understand."

"They would," she agreed. "They do. In four aspects of the Wheel. But in the fifth—"

"That would be the suit of—" He broke off, startled. "Wait! We already *have* four suits! A five-sectioned wheel can not be matched to—"

"We are now in the Re-Fissioning aspect of the Wheel, the problematical one," she said, stripping away her one-sided snow suit. Now she was naked, and though no more of her showed than would have appeared in a mirror reflection of her nude half, she seemed much barer than before. "Governed by the state of Liquid, or the Spirit of Faith, the key to this whole compromise. Xe Ni Qolz, whom we call—"

"Saint Nicholas!" he exclaimed, making the connection to the artwork of this chamber. "Old Santa Claus!"

"Yes, the Saint for the Children. Father Christmas." She took his hand and led him to a broad couch. It was amazing how an inconsequential act of disrobing assumed quite consequential implications. Before, he had oriented on her clothed half; now —"The Naths do not spy on us, precisely, but the walls are translucent to their perception. They don't use sound, exactly; it's more like infrasonics. So the Nath governor is aware of everything that goes on here."

"Well, we have nothing to hide," he said uncomfortably. Certainly *she* was hiding nothing, physically. She was very free with her body, as he remembered from a prior Animation —except that he could not be sure it *was* her body that he—

He stifled that thought. At any rate, he had every intention of leaving her alone this time. All he wanted was information.

"We have one thing to hide," she said. "The one thing we could not do to accommodate Nath, as colonists." She began to remove his clothing.

"Hey, stop!" he protested.

She leaned over and kissed him. "Don't make a commotion. Just relax and enjoy it. Remember, we told the Nath we were siblings. They have very good communications. They will be instantly aware if we do not act the part."

"I am a Brother of the Holy Order of Vision," he said, determined not to let his survey of religions go the same way as his first Animation sequence. She might be determined to give one of her samples; he was determined not to take it. "That's a kind of title, indicating my status. It hardly means I am your biologic brother—and in any event, this is no sisterly approach you are making to me."

"Shut up and listen," she said, continuing to work on his clothing despite his resistance. "The Naths expect us to maintain proper sexual morality; that is how they know we are true converts. To violate their standards—" She spread her hands appealingly. "We just couldn't survive as a colony without Nath support. You've seen what this planet is like—and this is just the habitable portion! I think the close proximity of so many neighboring stars evokes crustal unrest, causing continuous volcanic action—not that I object to volcanoes, but—"

"All *right*," he said. He knew she liked volcanoes in symbol and reality, just as she liked serpents. "You need Nath support; I believe that. But I think it is fine that the Naths insist on sexual morality. So do I! But you—"

"The Naths do not reproduce quite the way we do," she said. "Each Nath is bipart; it has a male section and a female section. The one we talked to was actually a married couple."

"I see. When Naths tie the knot, they really do tie it! But surely they can appreciate that human beings, uh, merge that closely only for procreative purpose. They can't expect us to go about tied together physically—"

"They understand. But they do expect married couples to stay reasonably close together and to merge often. So we display much more continuous affection than you may have been accustomed to back on Earth. We don't really mind. It does seem to make for more successful unions."

"For married couples, that's fine. But you and I are, if we accept your description to the Nath, brother and sister. So—"

"Oh be quiet," she said. "I had to tell the Nath that because single people just don't *go* about. Half an entity can't make it on its own, by the Nath rationale. The whole colony would have been in trouble, not just you and me. You can't believe how sensitive they are about this one thing. *It is their religion,* damn it! I was a fool to go out there alone, and you should have stayed aboard your ship until you got a proper briefing and escort."

"Sorry," he murmured apologetically. "If you'll just stop undressing me, I'll listen better."

"Well, maybe we can fake it for a while," she agreed reluctantly. She pushed him down on the couch and stretched out beside him in a most provocative manner. "When the Naths want to reproduce, they fission. They split apart into their male and female halves. That's one of the two times in their lives they *aren't* locked together. Then each half regenerates—do Earthworms still do that?"

"They do," Brother Paul assured her.

"Except that a male Nath-half can't regenerate the opposite sex, or vice versa. So male regenerates male tissue, and female regenerates female tissue—am I embarrassing you?"

"You are talking about alien reproduction," he reminded her. "Why should I be embarrassed?" He *was* embarrassed, but by her body and actions, not her discussion.

"That's right, you're fresh from Earth. The local pornography doesn't bother you, yet. Anyway, a unisex composite is inherently unstable."

"I should think so," Brother Paul agreed. "It would be like homosexuality, lesbianism—"

"Except it is a necessary part of their reproduction," she said. "The unisex sets quickly re-fission. Then there are four sub-Naths, and two females. Actually, male-original and male-regenerate, and the same for the females. Then they recombine, forming—"

"I see," Brother Paul said. "But that's really like a human family. The parent-couple produces two children, a boy and a girl. Nath mechanism differs in detail, but—"

"That detail is a hell of a difference," she said. "Some of the fragments have to go out and merge with other family fragments, to keep the genetic pool circulating—"

"Yes, of course. That's why human beings are exogamous, marrying outside their immediate family. Otherwise the species would quickly splinter into dissimilar species. There has to be interbreeding among the members of—"

"But it is not the children, the regenerates, that are exogamous," Ruby said. "They are too new to handle it properly. So it is the old individuals who split up, and re-merge elsewhere. They—"

"They have to divorce after procreating?" Brother Paul asked, startled. "That's not my idea of a stable marriage! Who takes care of the children?"

"The children take care of themselves with general help from the larger Nath community. They merge into a Nath couple, and—"

Brother Paul was shocked. "But that's incest!"

"Now you begin to understand the problem," she said. "By their standards and their religion, it is immoral for siblings *not* to mate with each other and for parents *not* to separate and remarry other divorcees. So if we want Nath support for our human enclave—"

"We have to commit incest and break up families," Brother Paul finished. "At last I get your drift. As a colony, you are torn between your economic needs for survival, and your human sexual morality, with a dual-aspect religion papering over the dichotomy. Yet if you explained this basic difference to the Naths—"

"Our ancestors tried," she said. "The Nath missionaries explained *their* position to us. They said we had been living, as a species, in intolerable sin, and they could not support it. It was their duty to lead us into the light despite ourselves. Naths are very accommodating creatures, but on this point they are inflexible."

"Just like missionaries," Brother Paul said with a sigh. "But how do you get around it?"

"The Nath biologists probably know, but the missionaries don't know or profess not to know, that human couples do not generally produce twins, and more seldom are there male-female twins. So when we have babies we meet here in the Children's aspect of the wheel and surreptitiously exchange them, making up exogamous pairs that we then raise as siblings. All humans look more or less alike to Naths, so they don't catch on. They can track a particular family if they choose, as they may have done with us two, but when there is a crowd of us they don't bother. Thus our children grow up and reproduce without damage to the human genetic pool. Then, with Nath blessing, they divorce and seek partners of their choice."

Brother Paul shook his head. "I appreciate the necessity, but I am appalled at the means!"

"Now we'd better mate," she said. "They will get suspicious if we stall any longer or if we leave without doing it. If they decide to make a general investigation, they could discover the truth, and that would wipe us all out. The colony cannot afford even the suggestion of suspicion!"

"But casual sex—"

"Casual, hell! This is serious."

"Politically or economically motivated—this is against *my* religion!" he protested.

"You don't have the *right* to come here from Earth with your irrelevant standards and place our survival as a colony in peril," she said.

Shocked, Brother Paul realized she was correct. This pseudo-religion of the Hyades colony of the future was valid on its own terms, alien as they might be. He could not accept it—but he also could not condemn it.

Yet if he could not eliminate *this* type of religion from consideration, how could he eliminate *any* religion? All were valid on their own terms. He could continue his survey for the rest of his life and never be able to choose between them. He was no closer to his answer than before.

Who was the God of Tarot? He needed some more direct means of finding out.

But first he had to dispose of the matter at hand. These Animations were to a certain extent under his control, despite the constant pressure of precession. Presumbly he could turn them off when he wished. But if he did that, quitting the game as he tired of it—of what validity would be any answer he might eventually obtain through these Animations? He suspected he really had to play the game through by its own rules to protect its relevance. Which meant that he had to resolve the dilemma here before leaving. How could he protect both his own integrity and the welfare of this Hyades colony?

Ah—he had it. "Ruby, you should be making love to your brother-husband, your brothub, not me. You aren't really mad at him, are you?"

She frowned prettily, loath to answer directly. "He's not here, and the Naths—"

"He is here. *I* am the one who is not here. There is no freezer-ship from Earth. I am a ghost."

She laughed. "Oh, come *on*! That isn't in the script!"

"It is *now*."

"All right. I'll play along. I've always been curious about how a ghost made love."

"In a moment I shall assume my true form: that of your beloved brothub, who shall turn out to have been with you all the time. Are you ready?"

"This can't—"

"Now." And Brother Paul made an effort of will, hoping Precession would not abort it, and faded out of the picture.

As the scene disappeared, he wondered: who played the part of her brothub?

12

TIME
(SPHINX)

Paul Christian, in The History and Practice of Magic, *provides a detailed description of the Sphinx. It was carved from the granite plateau itself, with no break between its base and the original rock. It is about seventy-five feet tall and a hundred and fifty feet long. The head alone is about twenty-five feet from top to chin, fourteen feet wide, and eighty feet around the temples. The layers of rock divide its face with horizontal bands, with the mouth formed by the space between two layers. There is a hole several feet deep in the face, probably for ornaments. The figure is reddish and seems attentive; it is as if it is watching and listening, aware of the past and gazing towards the future.*

Brother Paul stood in front of the Sphinx. The stone creature was impressive in the light of the full moon, the more so because its nose was intact: this was evidently before Napoleon's gunners had shot it off.

What an animal it was, crouching there like a living thing! Brother Paul felt a prickle at the back of his neck. This was an Animation; could he be sure this monster was *not* alive?

But it was absolutely still. No breathing, no heartbeat, no motion of eyes. Inanimate, after all. Fortunately.

Still, he would test it, just to be *sure*. "The sexual urge of the camel is stronger by far than one thinks," he said aloud, quoting the poem from a memory that predated his entry into the Holy Order of Vision. "One day on a trek through the desert, he rudely assaulted the Sphinx."

He paused, listening, watching, No reaction. Was the monster truly inanimate or merely waiting? "Now the posterior orifice of the Sphinx is washed by the sands of the Nile—which accounts for the hump in the camel, and the Sphinx's inscrutable smile."

Still nothing. No doubt about it: if the thing stood still for that verse, it was dead.

He contemplated the parts of it. A woman's head, suggesting human intelligence, aspiration, and strategy. A bull's body, signifying the tireless strength necessary to pursue human fortune. Lion's legs, indicating the courage and force also needed, that is to say the human will. And eagle's wings, veiling that intelligence, strength, and courage until there came the time to fly. Thus the Sphinx as a whole was the symbol of the concealed intelligence, strength, and will possessed by the Masters of Time.

Famous Greeks had come here to study at the feet of the Masters: Thales, Pythagoras, Plato, and others. Thales had been the first to embrace water as the primary substance in the universe, explaining change as well as stability. Pythagoras, known for his doctrine of the transmigration of souls and the Pythagorean Theorum. Plato, primarily known for his Dialogues, presenting his mentor Socrates and the thesis that Knowledge is Good, Ignorance Evil. Giants of philosophy, all of them. Now it was Brother Paul's turn to meet the Masters those famous Greeks had met—if he dared.

Time to proceed. Brother Paul walked to the front of the Sphinx. There between its extended forelegs was the outline of a door into its chest. The door was made of bronze, weathered to match the stone of the statue. He walked up to it, took a breath, and put one hand forth to touch it.

Nothing happened. The metal was neutral, neither cool nor hot, and it was solid. He felt around the edges to find a handle or niche, but there was none. He could not open it.

He sighed silently. He lifted a knuckle and rapped, once. There was no response. Did he really want to enter this structure? He rapped again, and then a third time. Theoretically, the ancient

Masters had possessed all knowledge and could answer his question—if they chose to. But first he would have to undergo their rite of passage. That, according to whispered legends, could be hazardous to health. Yet he continued knocking, half hoping no one would answer. Then, at the fifth rap, the door silently opened.

Two hooded persons stood inside, their faces invisible. One, by his bulk and manner, seemed male; the other was shorter and slighter, seeming female. "We are Thesmothetes, guardians of the Rites," the male said. "Who are you that knocks at the Door of the Occult Sanctuary?"

Brother Paul controlled his nervousness. "I am a humble seeker of truth. I wish to know the identity of the True God of Tarot."

Within the shroud there seemed to be a frown. "Do you understand, Postulant, that you must give yourself over entirely to our discretion?" the Thesmothete asked. "That you must follow our advice as if it were an order, asking no questions?"

Brother Paul swallowed. "I understand, Thesmothete."

The man stood aside. "Enter, Postulant."

Brother Paul stepped inside. The female touched the wall; a small spring depressed, releasing a hidden mechanism. The door closed silently—and the interior was completely dark.

A small hand took his. This was surely the silent Thesmothete, the lady. She guided him forward, into the bowels of the Sphinx. To the place of digestion? *The sexual urge of the camel . . .* no, don't even *think* that! By a slight pressure on his fingers the female made him pause. He felt her form lower a few centimeters, and realized she had stepped down. He put forward a foot cautiously and found the step.

It was a spiral staircase. Brother Paul was a compulsive counter; he had tried to break himself of the habit in recent years, but during stress the desire sometimes returned irresistibly. He had to know how many there were of whatever he encountered, however inconsequential. He counted thirty steps before the passage leveled out.

Here there was another door—bronze, no doubt—to be opened silently, passed through, and closed. Obviously the Thesmothetes had this labyrinth memorized, so they could find their way unerringly. The air was cooler in the new passage, but not musty. This suggested that it was well vented, for he was in a time millennia before the day of air conditioning.

His footfalls echoed, giving him the impression of a large,

circular chamber. He thought of a story he had read once, Poe's "The Pit and the Pendulum," and his nervousness increased. But of course his guides were beside him and knew their way; they would not let this party fall into any oubliette, with or without pendulum.

Suddenly both Thesmothetes halted, the male's arm barring Brother Paul's forward progress. "We stand at the brink of a precipice," the man said. "One more stop will hurl you to the bottom."

Just so. Had Brother Paul made his way here alone, in this gloom he could have fallen into it. He should have brought a light—but then they would not have admitted him. "I will wait," he said. He was about to ask the purpose of this march to the brink, but remembered his promise to ask no questions.

However, his question was answered. "This abyss," the male said, "surrounds the Temple of Mysteries and protects it against the temerity and curiosity of the profane. We have arrived a little too soon; our brethren have not yet lowered the drawbridge by which the initiates communicate with the sacred place. We shall wait for their arrival. But if you value your life, do not move until we tell you."

Did the Thesmothete protest too much? Maybe there was an abyss and maybe there wasn't—but Brother Paul could not afford to proceed on the assumption that there was no threat. Not after the things he had experienced in other Animations. They had so arranged it, this time, that his control over specific visions had been nullified. He was at the mercy of these anonymous people and had been from the moment he entered the Sphinx. Yet he had come here voluntarily; he was on the threshold of the unknown, and if the answer were here—

Suddenly there was light, blinding after the darkness. Two grotesque monsters stood before him, each in white linen robes, one with a gold belt and a lion's head, the other with a silver belt and bull's head. Even as his eyes adjusted and took them in, a trap door opened between them. From this rose a grisly specter brandishing a scythe. It was most reminiscent of the skeletal figure of Death in the Tarot. With a horrendous roar it swept the scythe at Brother Paul's head.

His first instinct was to tumble back, out of range of the weapon. His second was to duck under the blade and grapple with the specter. But his third overrode the first two: he stood frozen.

The scythe's blade swished so close over his head that it might have parted his hair. Indeed, a small lock of it tumbled across his face. "Woe to him who disturbs the peace of the dead!" the monster screamed, whirling entirely around and sweeping the scythe at Brother Paul a second time. But again he judged the path of the blade, and again he did not flinch. This was a scare tactic, not a serious attack; a test of his courage that his judo training had prepared him for.

Four more times the scythe came at him, and each time he stood firm. But on the seventh stroke the creature shifted its balance; this time it was going for his neck!

Brother Paul gambled: he stood firm. They surely had not arranged this elaborate presentation merely to execute an unresisting man. And as the blade touched him—the monster vanished. It dropped down its hole, and the trap door closed. This, too, had been a bluff; the threat had no substance.

Now the lion and the bull removed their masks. Brother Paul saw their faces for the first time: Therion and Amaranth.

"Congratulations," Therion told him. "You felt the chill of murderous steel, and you did not flinch; you looked at the horror of horrors and did not faint. Well, done! In your own country you could be a hero." He frowned. "But amongst us, there are virtues higher than courage. What do you take to be the meaning of our costumes?"

Brother Paul had already worked that out. "You are the lion, one of the aspects of the Sphinx, with the golden belt, representing the astrological Leo and the Sun. She, masked as the bull, is another aspect of the Sphinx, Taurus, and the Moon. The Sun and Moon together are supposed to exert the most direct influence on the lives of earthly beings. Yet man does not live by Sun and Moon alone; there is always the savage influence of Time, bringing the chance of untimely death—"

"You are most impressively apt," Therion said. "Yet we have a value superior even to this intelligence. That is humility —voluntary humility, triumphing over the vanity of pride. Are you capable of such a victory over yourself?"

So the physical test was over. Good! Brother Paul was ready for the moral one. "I am willing to find out."

"Very well," Therion said. "Are you ready to crawl flat on the ground, right to the innermost sanctuary where our brethren wait to give you the knowledge and power you seek in exchange for your humility?"

Why this follow-up challenge? He really was not seeking power. Still, he seemed to have no choice but to accept. "I am."

"Then take this lamp," Therion said. "It is the image of God's face that follows us when we walk hidden from the sight of men. Go without fear; you have only yourself to be afraid of henceforth."

Brother Paul, thinking of his experience of the Seven Cups, did not find this reassuring. What other horrors lurked—in himself? He accepted the lamp and looked about. The chamber was formed of blocks of granite shaped into a dome; there was no entrance or exit. But again he remembered his stricture and made no inquiry.

After a moment, Amaranth touched another hidden spring in the wall. An iron plate slid aside; it was coated with granite to resemble a full block when in place. Behind it opened a corridor, an arcade, narrow and so low it was impossible to crawl through it on hands and knees. "Let this path be for you the image of the tomb in which all men must find their eventual rest," Therion intoned. "Yet they awake, freed from the darkness of material things, in the life of the spirit. You have vanquished the specter of Death; now you can triumph over the horrors of the tomb in the Test of Solitude." And both Thesmothetes extended their right hands toward the opening.

Now Brother Paul hesitated. Why were they sending him *alone*, now? What sort of horrors did they consider so awesome? That constricted hole—if it got any smaller, once he was in, he would be unable either to squeeze through or to turn about. He would have to retreat, feet first, as though in the throes of a breech birth—and surely the entrance-exit panel would be closed and locked.

The two Thesmothetes remained as they were, fingers pointing to the hole. They neither reproached him for his weakness nor encouraged him to carry on with the test. What would they do if he balked, now?

Actually, he knew. He had read of a test like this once; the memory was faint, elusive, and only returned as it was refreshed by this present experience. The postulant who lost his nerve was not excluded or even reproached. He was merely led out of the sacred place. The law of Magism dictated that he would never again be tested; his weakness had been judged. So—if he wanted his answer, it was now or never. The law of Animation was as inflexible in its fashion as the law of the ancient Egyptian mystics. He had not yet encountered the same vision twice; the vagaries of the dynamics of this situation were too great to permit him to rerun any scene.

Brother Paul was not unduly claustrophobic, but he didn't like this at all. He was not the most slender of men; a passage sufficient for a 150 centimeter tall Egyptian or Greek might not suffice for him. If he got wedged in amidst these thousands of tons of stone—

Still the two Thesmothetes waited, pointing, as still as statues. Brother Paul offered up a silent prayer to whatever God governed this demesne—Thoth, perhaps?—and got down to enter the dread aperture.

Amaranth got down beside him. "God be between you and harm in all the empty places you must go," she murmured and gave him a quick sidewise swipe of a kiss on the lips. Then Brother Paul pushed the lamp forward and crawled into the hole.

The tube sloped gently downwards. Its circumference was of polished granite, absolutely smooth as though drilled by a giant worm. There *was* room for him, barely. By a combination of elbow-drawings and knee-hitchings, augmented by toe-flexes, he moved himself forward until his full length was within the tunnel.

A terrible clang deafened him momentarily as the bronze door fell back into place. As from a distance, a reverberating voice came: "Here perish all fools who covet knowledge and power!" It was followed immediately by an echo: "power . . . power . . . power . . . power . . . power . . . power . . . power!" Seven distinct echoes, hammering themselves into his brain. The effect was foolishly terrifying; sonics could have a fundamental influence on a man's emotion, bypassing his reason. Brother Paul knew that —yet still felt the frightening impact.

Had the Magi condemned him to death after all? That still did not make sense; they could have barred him from the Sphinx at the outset. If they intended to bury him alive, why had they given him this good lamp?

Gradually the irrational fear subsided. There had to be an exit to this tube; all he had to do was keep moving. Yet it went on and on! Brother Paul had a fair sense of orientation, perhaps a function of his compulsive counting. It informed him that he could no longer be within or beneath the Sphinx! This interminable tunnel was proceeding under the surface of the plateau itself—toward the Great Pyramid! Furthermore, it was still descending, deeper and deeper into the rock. What would he do if his guttering lamp went out?

Still it continued. His elbows and knees were sore, perhaps bleeding, but he could not stop. Nervousness prevented him even from resting. He passed the lamp from one hand to the other, finding different ways to crawl . . . and crawl.

At last the tunnel expanded. What a relief! He got up on his hands and knees for a space, then proceeded at a stooping walk. But the floor still sloped down; the added space was gained by the floor's retreat from the level ceiling. He was not being allowed nearer the surface.

Abruptly the floor terminated. The wan light of the lamp showed a vast crater, a cone plunging deep into the rock, its slides slick and hard. An iron ladder picked up where the tunnel left off, leading down into that gloomy cavity. There was no other route; only by getting on the ladder could he proceed forward, or rather downward. He now had ample room to turn about, but was sure a retreat up the tunnel would not be wise.

He started down the ladder, nervously testing each rung before putting full weight upon it. All were sturdy. And of course he counted: ten, twenty, thirty, on.

There were exactly one hundred rungs. But the ladder did not lead to another level or sloping passage. It terminated in a circular hole. Brother Paul had no object to drop experimentally into it, but he was sure this was an oubliette: a fatally deep dungeon with no exit. He could not trust himself to that!

Yet there was nowhere else to go! What now?

"God be between me and harm in all the empty places I must go," he repeated, staring down into the dread void. And added mentally: *And may there be avenues of escape from those empty places!*

Brother Paul studied his situation. There *had* to be an alternative; this setup was too elaborate to be a mere death trap. He had to believe that! All he had to do was figure out its rationale. The ladder went down and stopped; there was no question of a hidden continuance because the final rung was in the dank air over the pit. Still, he could look.

He climbed down, then poked both legs through the bottom

rung, hooking his knees over it. He bounced twice, with increasing vigor, testing its solidity; it would hold his weight. He leaned back, slowly, holding the lamp carefully upright as his angle changed, letting his torso swing around until he hung upside down by his knees. His head projected through the hole, and his lamp illuminated the chamber below.

It was a featureless well, plunging straight down beyond the reach of his lamp. The walls looked slimy, and there was no second ladder below the one he was on. This was a one-way avenue . . . probably filled with water at the neither terminus. Maybe that fluid would break his fall—but he did not care to risk it. Not yet.

He had been more or less given to understand that he had nothing to fear but himself. Now it occurred to him that this was subject to alarming interpretation. If he decided to drop into the oubliette, and that was an error, would he have killed himself? All he had to do was make the correct decision—without adequate information.

Well, he had no need to remain on this ladder! He caught the rung with his left hand, held the lamp steady with his right, and drew himself up until he could extricate his feet. Then he started back up the hundred rungs.

About twenty rungs up—twenty two, technically—he spied a crevice in the cone. A flaw, invisible from above because the upper wall overhung it slightly. Was this natural or artificial?

He had grown wary of chance here. He leaned as far over as was convenient, holding the lamp extended to the left. This gap was broad enough for a man to squeeze through—and there were steps inside! Here was his alternate route!

He balanced carefully and swung himself into the crevice. The steps were slippery but solid. They advanced deeper into the wall; the crevice was becoming a new tunnel, at places so narrow he had to proceed sidewise, but it was definitely going somewhere. It coiled into a spiral. At the count of thirty, the steps ended at a small platform, and the way forward was barred by a bronze grating.

Was this a service access, intended for the use of the Thesmothetes, that he had spied accidentally? If so, it would be a dead end for him since the grating was locked and unattended. Yet it did not seem extraneous. Twenty two steps up on the ladder from the bottom, matching the number of Major Arcana of the Tarot, appearing only when the Postulant was returning from his fruitless quest to the oubliette. Surely no coincidence! But what, then, was the significance of thirty alternate steps, here? These passages seemed to have a motif of thirties and hundreds, and that did not equate to any Tarot deck he knew of. So if there were a numeric rationale here, he had not yet fathomed it.

Brother Paul peered through the grating. Ahead was a long gallery, lined on each side by statuettes of sphinxes: fifteen on each side. Thirty in all. Between statues, the walls were covered with mysterious frescoes. At this angle, he could not quite make out their nature, but there was a haunting familiarity about them. Fifteen lamps rested in tripods set in a row down the center of the hall, and each lamp was in the shape of a sphinx.

A Magus walked slowly down the hall toward him. No—it was the female Thesmothete, Amaranth, garbed in the manner of a priestess. Her face was veiled and her gown covered her body completely, but he recognized her provocative walk, that pushed out hip and breast in subtle but quite feminine rhythm.

"Son of Earth," she said, smiling, "you have escaped the pit by discovering the path of wisdom. Few aspirants to the Mysteries have passed this test; most have perished." So that explained what happened to those who entrusted themselves to the oubliette!

"The Goddess Isis is your protector," she continued. Brother Paul remembered the Egyptian Isis, said to be the Goddess of Love. "She will lead you safely to the sanctuary where virtue receives its crown." Virtue supervised by the Goddess of Sex? The geese were being put in the charge of the fox! "I must warn you that other perils are in store, but I shall aid you by explaining these sacred symbols which will clothe your mind with invulnerable power." No question: Amaranth was now Isis. This was her kind of role.

Isis opened the gate by releasing another secret spring. She took Brother Paul by the hand and led him down the gallery. She moved slowly, almost languorously, but even so this was far too rapid for him to properly assimilate the portraits they passed. All the wisdom of the ancients spread out here—and he had to zoom past it like an ignorant tourist!

But perhaps that was the point. He was only looking, not buying. If he chose to remain here indefinitely, if he qualified by passing all their tests, *then* he could linger over each symbol for as long as he liked. Years, if necessary.

"First we review the aspects of Nature," Isis murmured. "Here is the Crocodile." She gestured with her free hand toward the nearest picture, just before the first sphinx. It depicted an Egyptian peasant walking by a river, two bags slung over his shoulder, while a crocodile paced him in the water. "It symbolizes Folly."

The Zero Key of the Tarot! So Tarot *was* at the root of this! Now he had an excellent frame of reference, enhancing his understanding.

"The Magus," she said, indicating the representation across the hall. "Representing Skill." It was an Egyptian magician, very like the European one except for costume.

"Veiled Isis," she said, going right on to the next. "Memory —among other things." And the veiled figure portrayed was —her. He did not need to guess at the identity of those "other things" she was thinking of. He remembered Amaranth in her landscape dress, her breasts living volcanoes. Amaranth as naked Temptation in the Vision of the Seven Cups. As Sister Beth of the Holy Order of Vision, whom he had tried to seduce. What was her true role this time?

What else but Temptation again! A temptation he was sure he had to resist here, if the terrible weight of the Pyramid were not to crush him.

But she had already moved on to the next picture—and it was blank. "The Ghost," she said. "The Unknown or Unidentified; the Infinite, the Nothingness."

What? *This* was no Tarot card! He stopped by it, about to inquire—but caught himself. No questions! His thoughts about her sexual temptation had almost distracted him into a different trap. He would just have to accept the fact, for now, that this was not Tarot. Not precisely. It was—an unknown.

"Isis Unveiled," she said, abruptly throwing off her veil. Now she was Woman in her full splendor, her face absolutely lovely in the lamplight. She played variations on a single theme, but she certainly had the equipment for that! "Action."

Action. She still held his hand, and now she was drawing him in close, raising her lips. So eminently kissable.

He moved his hand, carrying hers along, guiding it and her toward the next exhibit. His action—was to pursue the lesson further.

She yielded gracefully. She had a thousand little ploys; the failure of one was of little account. If this had been another test, he had passed it—probably.

"Now we review the aspects of Faith," Isis continued. "Here is the Sovereign, symbol of Power." She moved on. "And the Master of the Arcana, representing Intuition. And here are the Two Paths, showing Choice."

Brother Paul moved along with her, nodding. These were very like the Tarot, but not identical. That card of the Unknown. . . .

But now she paused. She made a convoluted shrug and her robe fell away. Now Isis stood in a short skirt and halter, as scenic as ever. "Also known as The Ordeal," she said, moving in close again.

The ordeal of rejecting her? That seemed the only safe course, much as he might have liked to try her constantly proferred sample and be done with it. Celibacy and rejection of sex were all very well for the unhealthy recluse, but Brother Paul was a thoroughly healthy and social man. However. He advanced to the next picture.

Immediately she followed. "The Chariot of Osiris, signifying Precession," she said.

Precession! He almost challenged that, but again caught himself. He had expected her to give the interpretation as Victory. Each time the Tarot connections became slightly firm, something broke them up again!

She moved on. "Desire—Emotion," she said of the next. Well, that might equate to the Thoth Tarot version of Strength, titled Lust.

But then she showed the next: "The Tamed Lion—Discipline." *That* one had to be Strength! But then what—? "Also called the Enchantress, Strength, Spiritual Power, and Fortitude," she continued. And the picture was of the woman calming the lion. Yet—

"Here is the Family of Man—Nature," she said. He didn't recognize that one in Tarot either. "And here is the Wheel, symbolizing Chance. And the Sphinx, alternately known as the Veiled Lamp, which unveiled is Time." Now that was all mixed up! The Hermit card was Time, while the Sphinx bestrode the Wheel of Fortune. But she went on talking, preventing him from getting his thoughts organized. "Chronos, who was once Chief of the Gods."

Brother Paul had another realization: he had been encountering aspects of these images all along, since his arrival on Planet Tarot. Maybe since his first assignment to this mission! Was this his own fate being summarized? If so, he was about to glimpse his future!

Isis gave him no time to consider the ramifications of that. "Here are the aspects of Trade. The first is Past, suggesting Reflection; the next is Future, symbolizing Will."

Brother Paul peered at the pictures, but could not grasp them in the time he had. Surely both of these were merely aspects of Time! Did they show his own past and future? Reflection he could understand; he was much given to it himself. But how did Will relate? He thought he saw an airplane, and a bottle of wine, and a document, and trees, and a child, but somehow neither picture would come together meaningfully. If only he had more time to study—

"Here is Themis, Goddess of Law, signifying Honor." Strange; Brother Paul remembered Themis as a Roman Goddess, rather than Egyptian. But perhaps it only showed that this sequence of images derived from multiple sources and was not limited to any single mythology. Rome had existed in the period of Egypt's greatness; archaeology had verified the presence of Rome a thousand years before the legendary date of its founding by the wolf-suckled brothers, Romulus and Remus.

"The Martyr—Sacrifice," Isis continued. This seemed to be the card he knew as the Hanged Man, suspended by one foot from a gibbet. Was *that* in his future? He was driving himself crazy with these speculations!

"The Scythe—Change," she said. He knew this one as Death or Transformation. "Imagination—Vision." That one he could not place at all, though there was something irrelevantly familiar about the illustration. A field, with a tower to one side, and a gully at the other—

"The Alchemist, signifying Transfer." Transfer! That was the term the alien Antares had employed for the transposition of auras from one host to another—

"And the aspects of Magic, that some call Science," she continued inexorably. What torture, to be treated to these tantalyzing glimpses of half-familiar revelations! Surely it all did fit a larger pattern, if only he could—

"Here is Typhon, known as Fate, signifying Violence." It was the Devil. "The House of God—revelation." He knew it as the Lightning-Struck Tower, though that was probably an iconographical transformation. A familiar card—yet he felt a premonitory dread. He was of course searching for the House of God—but this cruel edifice seemed more Satanic than Angelic. Some interpretations indicated this card was actually the House of the Devil, signifying Ruin.

Meanwhile, Isis was blithely removing her remaining apparel. Revelation—naturally she would take it not only literally, but physically! He wished this tour were over; he was maintaining a firm countenance, but she was making it very difficult. What happened to a Postulate who yielded to the obvious suggestion and put his lustful hands (lustful *hands*? Ah, the euphemism!) on the priestess?

"The Star of the Magi," she continued, and now she looked very much like the nude girl in that picture. "Hope and Fear."

Exactly.

"Twilight—Deception." Yes, another familiar card that he knew as the Moon. Deception was surely the key concept here! In revealing her entire body, she deceived him about her intentions. As did all women. . . .

"And the Blazing Light, suggesting Triumph." Well, he hoped so! But triumph for whom?

"And the aspects of Art," she said. Nude art? He wondered how many people would be interested in art if it were not thoroughly peopled with naked young women. To his mind, a nude young man was as artistically beautiful as a woman; but it was sex, not esthetics, that made the difference. Women did not dash out to buy portraits of nude men as avidly as man bought nude women, so the definition of Art became—

"Here is Thought, that we interpret as Reason." The picture was—well, it looked like a field of stars. "The Awakening of the Dead, meaning Decision." The picture resembled the Judgment card he knew. His own moment of Judgment might be upon him all too soon! "The Savant, meaning Wisdom."

Naked, she advanced to the last picture and spun about, showing herself to advantage. "The Crown of the Magi —Completion," she said. She stepped close, caught his head in her hands, and drew it down for a quick kiss. Then she opened the door at the end of the gallery and stood aside.

Beyond that door was a long, narrow vault. At its end were the leaping flames of a blazing furnace.

"Son of Earth," Isis said, "Death itself only frightens the

imperfect. If you are afraid, you have no business here. Look at me: once I too passed through these flames as if they were a garden of roses."

Brother Paul looked at her. Suddenly she was much more tempting. If he put his hands on her, stroked one or two of those perfect fruits—would she acquiesce? Or would sudden disaster befall him? Would the touch of her flesh be worth the penalty?

He looked again at the flames. The teaching he had just received, hurried and elliptical as it was, would be useless to a man about to die. There had to be a way through! He stood, as it were, at the fork in the road, the Two Paths, also known as the Ordeal. The choice between Love and Fire. Had he learned enough to make it through?

Actually, there *was* a way to overcome fire or at least hot coals. South Pacific natives heated rock to red heat and walked bare-footed over it, and there was no fakery involved. The secret was a special effect that could be noted with droplets of water dancing on a hot frying pan: the heat evaporated just enough water to form a layer of steam, and the droplet floated on that steam, insulated from the much higher heat of the pan. Thus the droplets could take many seconds to dwindle, instead of puffing entirely into vapor almost instantly, as happened on surfaces heated more moderately. Similarly, the natural moisture of the native's feet became that layer of steam, enabling them to walk the coals without being burned. So if he could find an area where the flames were low enough to expose the hot coals, he might be able to cross. If he had the nerve.

Abruptly he faced forward and stepped into the new chamber. Again the door clanged shut behind him, forever closing off what might have been. He was alone again, unable to retreat. Did God stand between him and the flame?

But as he approached the furnace, he discovered that it was largely illusory. Wood was arranged on iron grills, and lamps were so placed that their light suggested open flame. A path wound between these mock-ups, on through a vaulted passageway. He moved forward with renewed confidence. God *was* here!

The path ended abruptly at a stagnant pool. Who might guess what lurked beneath that slimy surface? Brother Paul turned about, so as to retrace his route and look for an alternate—and a cascade of oil descended from sluices in the ceiling. There was a spark, ignition, and the oil became a curtain of flame. The pretend furnace had become a real one!

He had to plunge back through that flame—or go forward through the water. Or wait, hoping one threat or the other would abate. But that was not the way of this series of challenges; he had to show his mettle by conquering the hurdles, rather than by avoiding them. Somehow.

The water seemed the better bet. Brother Paul removed his robe, wadded it tightly, and held it in his right hand along with his lamp. Then he stepped cautiously into the pool.

There was a slippery slope beneath that urged him on faster than he cared to go. Each step brought him deeper. Knees, thighs, waist; the water was chill, which was encouraging because it meant reptiles were less likely to inhabit it. Chest, shoulders, chin; now he held the lamp over his head. Any deeper and he would have to swim—but then he would risk dousing the light, for he could not safely carry it high and level while swimming.

Now he could see that he had indeed reached the middle of the pool. With luck—or the foresight of those who had designed this test—the deepest part. Had someone measured his height, so they could fill the water to the appropriate level? Now it should grow shallower—

It did. With relief he advanced up the slope. This had been basically a test of his fortitude and not a complex one. A choice between fire and water. In fact all these tests were rather basic and physical; a modern-day examination would have been considerably more sophisticated. He had overestimated the subtlety of the—

His foot plunged into a gap in the underwater flooring. He lunged forward, slapping the water with his left hand and windmilling with his right to recover his lost balance. He made it; his questing toes found the side of the gap. A mere pothole! But his glowing lamp toppled off the bunched garment and plunged into the water. He made a desperate grab for it with his left hand, but missed—and in any event, it had been extinguished. He might re-light it by taking it back to the curtain of flame—if its oil had not been hopelessly diluted by the water, and if he could get it close enough to that fire without burning himself, and if—

He looked back. The curtain of flame had died out. Only the sitting lamps remained. So even if he had his lamp and it were operative, he could not light it.

He stopped. Idiot! All he had to do was pick up one of the other lamps. But there was a little light to see by, and maybe there were other traps awaiting the man who tried to backtrack. Best to accept the consequence of his error and go on without the light. His overconfidence had been responsible for his spill—a lesson in itself. Only himself to fear!

He climbed out of the water. At the far edge a flight of steps led to a platform surrounded on three sides by a spacious arcade. On the far wall was a brass door, set behind a narrow, twisted column sculpted in the shape of a lion's jaws. The teeth held a metal ring. That was as much detail as he could make out in the dim light.

He stopped before the door. The air was chill, and he was shivering. Once he got dry, he could don his robe again and be more comfortable. But now, one by one, the distant lamps went out; the reflection of the last one came across the water, then faded. He was in complete darkness again.

If he had tried to go back, to pick up one of those sitting lamps—would he have gotten there in time? If they were all short of fuel, none of them would have done him much good anyway, and he could have been trapped in the water in darkness. It would have been easy to wander astray, into much deeper water, where creatures might lurk. . . .

A voice sounded in the gloom. "Son of Earth, to stop is to perish. Behind you is death; before you, salvation."

Brother Paul was not yet dry; he decided to take the voice at its word and proceed without dressing. He extended his hand, finding the carved door. That ring in the lion's mouth—was it a handle? Or a trap? If he pulled at it, would the door open or would those teeth clamp on his hand?

Well, he could circumvent this one! He shook out his cloak, drew it lengthwise into a kind of cord, and carefully threaded it through the loop. Then he held one end in each hand and gave a sharp yank.

A trap door opened beneath his feet. He dropped—and came up short, hanging on to the robe-rope. Again he had underestimated the trap! He could not afford to judge too many more such items!

Well, on with it. He pulled himself up on his makeshift rope. "Easier for a rope to pass through the eye of a needle . . ." he muttered, thinking of the centuries of confusion caused by a simple mistranslation in the Bible, wherein the term "camel's hair rope" had been rendered as "camel." Then he swung his feet up and walked himself onto the main platform. Had he not been in good condition, this would have been a difficult or impossible maneuver. He gained his balance on the main floor and removed the robe from the ring. Good thing that ring had been well anchored!

Then he heard the trapdoor closing. Now the brass door opened, spilling light into the hall. Therion the Thesmothete stood there, carrying a bright torch. "Come, Postulant."

Brother Paul followed him through a series of galleries set off by locked doors. At each door Therion murmured a password and gave a secret signal, and it opened.

During one of these pauses, Brother Paul slipped back into his robe. Now he felt more confident. At last the test was over!

They came finally to a crypt that Brother Paul's directional sense informed him had been hollowed out of the Great Pyramid itself. This was a chamber never discovered by the archaeologists! The walls were polished stone, covered by symbolic paintings. At each corner stood a bronze statue: a man, a bull, a lion, and an eagle. Hanging from the high ceiling was an elaborate lamp. Brother Paul observed that the beams of light between the statues and from the lamp together formed the outline of a pyramid: five corners counting the apex.

In the center was a huge round silver table, and on this table stood two cups, two swords, two coins, scepters, and lamps. The four symbols of the Tarot suits, plus the lamps necessary to see the rest in this sunless chamber.

Therion turned to him. "Son of Earth, I have only to give the sign and you will be plunged alive into subterranean depths to eat the bread of remorse and drink the waters of anguish until the end of your days. But we are not vindictive; all we ask of you is your solemn oath that you will never reveal to anyone the least detail of what you have seen or heard this night, and you shall go free. Will you give this oath?"

Reasonable enough. A secret society would not remain secret long if it did not institute such a precaution. But Brother Paul's mission required that he express his knowledge outside. "I will not," he said.

Therion stared at him incredulously. "That was intended to be a rhetorical question, Postulant. There is only one answer."

"Not for me." Had he gone through all this—for nothing?

"Beware, Postulant! Defiance is punished by death!" And a menacing roaring sounded as the overhead lamp was extinguished. The chamber was now lighted only by tremulously flickering candles set behind the statues.

"My information cannot benefit anyone, if it is sworn to secrecy," Brother Paul said, unmoved.

Therion pointed to the cups on the silver table. "Then you must undertake this trial," he cried. "One goblet contains a violent poison; the other is harmless. Choose one, without reflection, and drink it down."

Brother Paul stepped up to the table, picked up the right cup, and drank its contents down.

Therion smiled. "I tried," he said. "Both drinks were—safe."

As Brother Paul had figured. A test of pure chance would have been pointless; courage, not life or luck, was the issue here.

"Worthy zealot," Therion said, "You have passed all tests. Now you are ready to share the wisdom of the ancients. Magic is composed of two elements, knowledge and strength. Without knowledge, no strength can be complete; without some sort of strength, no one can attain knowledge. Learn how to suffer, that you may become impassive; learn how to die, to become immortal; learn restraint, to attain your desire: these are the first three secrets the Magus must learn to become a priest of Truth. He must study with us for twelve years to master it, as Moses of the Jews did, and Plato of the Greeks did, and—"

"Twelve years?" Brother Paul demanded.

"To start. After that the *real* education begins."

"I can't wait twelve years!" Brother Paul protested. "I can't wait twelve *weeks!* I need my answer now." Before it was time for him to be shuttled back to Earth; the mattermission schedule would not be modified for the convenience of one man.

"This is impossible," Therion said firmly.

"Then I must depart."

Therion gestured, and a panel slid open in the floor before his feet. "There is your exit."

From the pit came the noise of rattling chains and panting struggle and the roar of some great beast. Then there came the scream of a human being in dreadful agony—abruptly cut off.

Brother Paul stepped forward to look into the pit. There was a lion-sized sphinx tearing at a naked human body lying before it.

Brother Paul stepped around the pit, snatched one of the swords from the table, flexed it twice to get its heft, then jumped into the hole. The last things he perceived as he acted were Therion's gape of incredulity and Amaranth's scream from somewhere in the distance. Then his feet struck the back of the vicious sphinx. He swung his sword down—and the Animation exploded into nothingness.

13

REFLECTION
(PAST)

*Barrington Moore, Jr., comments on the contradiction between politics
and morality in* Reflections on the Causes of Human Misery. *Why
do revolutionaries start out by proclaiming the brotherhood of man,
and all too often finish by practicing the same deceit and tyranny
they initially opposed? The answer is this: Unscrupulous means are
apt to be more effective than scrupulous ones. If the revolutionary
behaves in a decent manner, he is likely to lose out to his enemy who
does not. Thus he is corrupted by the very process of achieving
power.*

Brother Paul walked through the forest, seeking the others. He was
momentarily intrigued by the scenery, noting its five levels: grass
grew on the ground, giving way at the edge of the path to small
leafy plants or vines, which in turn gave way to tall weeds like
miniature meter-tall trees. Then head-high bushes, and finally the
much taller trees.

He still did not know what he would say to the colonists; he had
seen much and experienced much, but still lacked a proper basis
on which to judge. God was in all of these or none; how could he
know? The matter was so highly subjective that he doubted any
objective verdict was possible. Yet he was obliged to make his

appearance—after he rounded up the others, before the rift in Animation closed up again.

The region seemed unfamiliar. Had he come this way before? He must have wandered considerably during his visions; certainly he had walked much and crawled more. Yet he still had to be within a few kilometers of his starting point and somewhere within Northole, or he would have walked right out of the Animation. As perhaps he had done.

Maybe his best course was to orient on the sun and march in a straight line. He would surely intersect a local path that would lead him to the village or other habitation. This was a standard mechanism of the type to be found in intelligence tests; it was therefore suspect, but should do for the time being.

Abruptly the forest opened out onto a broad, flat clearing. He started across it, then halted as he discovered concrete. This was a modern highway!

No—it proceeded nowhere. The pavement ended abruptly about a hundred and fifty meters to his left. A dead end, yet an oddly well-kept road. No weeds overgrew it. What could be its purpose, here on Planet Tarot?

Curious, he followed it to his right. Wisps of mist obscured the way ahead, but within a kilometer a building loomed.

He stared, amazed. That was an airport control tower. This was a runway! Yet there were no airplanes on this primitive world. This made no sense.

How had the colonists mustered the resources to construct such a massively modern facility? It might be within their technological capacity, since theoretically all the knowledge of Earth was available to every colony planet, but the sheer labor would be ruinous! These people hardly had fuel enough to heat their homes or resources enough to do more than palisade their villages against natural threats. And if they had resources that had been concealed from him (and why should they deceive him?), to expend them on something as useless as this, in a world where the automobile did not yet exist, let alone aircraft—something was crazy!

A mock-up! That would be it—a grandiose imitation, a shell, a monument to what might be in the planet's future. On what a scale, though!

Intrigued, Brother Paul marched up to the terminal. The thing was huge, girt by ribbons of asphalt, parking lots, access ramps and satellite sub-terminals. Everything was in place. The cars and planes looked completely authentic, so much like Earth of a decade ago that the nostalgia was almost painful. The shrubbery was well-kept, and there was an attractive fountain with the water splaying in artistic patterns.

People were going in and out, just exactly as though on Earth, each appropriately garbed for the occasion, each preoccupied with his own concern. Brother Paul joined the throng at the main entrance, trusting that his presence would not interfere with the show. His Holy Order of Vision habit was in style anywhere. He was curious to see whether the interior was as well appointed as the exterior.

It was. Phenomenally long escalators conveyed people to the operating floors. Loudspeakers bellowed unintelligibly. Short lines formed at ticket desks. Buzzers sounded as people moved toward marked departure gates carrying too much metal. This restoration was absolutely perfect; no detail seemed to have been omitted!

A hand tugged at his. "Come on, Daddy—we'll miss our flight!"

Startled, Brother Paul looked down to discover a young girl hanging on to his hand. She was eight or nine years old, blue-eyed, with two long fair braids. "Daddy, *hurry!*" she cried urgently.

"Young lady, there seems to be a confusion of identities," he said, resisting the pull.

She persisted. "You said it leaves at nine-fifty, and it's nine-forty now, and we haven't even found the gate!"

"I'm not even married," Brother Paul protested, as much to himself as her. Where was her family? He didn't want to lead this child astray.

"Oh, Daddy, come on!" And she fairly dragged him on.

He had either to yield somewhat or to risk an embarrassing scene with a strange child. He suffered himself to be hauled along. "But I don't have a ticket," he said irrelevantly, hoping this would distract her. A ticket for what?

"You let me carry the tickets, remember?" And she relinquished his hand long enough to rummage in her little patchwork handbag. She brought out two envelopes girt with baggage tags and validations, looking very official. "See?"

He was beginning to regret the nicety of detail in this exhibit! He took the ticket folders and examined them. The first envelope was made out to Miss Carolyn Cenji. That was a shock, for he hardly ever used his surname and had thought most colonists were not aware of it. He shifted to the second envelope—and it said Father Paul Cenji. The immediate destination was Boston.

He set aside the riddle of the names for the moment. There was a Boston on Planet Tarot? Yes, it was certainly possible; some hamlet named after the Earth original, used on tickets for verisimilitude. Cute. Still, that did not justify all *this!*

"Flight 24C for Boston boarding at Gate 15," the loudspeaker blared with sudden, atypical clarity.

Brother Paul smiled. Old, old pun! 24C—two four cee—to foresee. This whole elaborate display was an exercise in that foresight, the aspiration of a backward planet looking firmly toward the future. Or perhaps looking into the recent past, nostalgically, when technology and power were cheap; why else were they employing the name of an Earth city? Strange how difficult it could be to distinguish future from past in certain situations. *Was* there much difference between them?

"That's *it!*" Carolyn cried with little-girl excitement. *"Hurry!"*

Still trying to figure out how his name had gotten on the ticket—let alone that of a nonexistent daughter!—Brother Paul suffered himself once more to be drawn along toward Gate 15. There had to be some mistake—but which mistake *was* it? His presence here on Planet Tarot was no secret, but it had hardly been the occasion for widespread publicity. An important person might have been treated to such a personalized tour of the exhibit, but he was not—

They joined the line at the security access. Should he inquire of one of the other people? Or would that violate the spirit of this charade?

Maybe the child's real father would be at the Gate—it was the obvious place—and this confusion of identities or whatever could be straightened out. He did have other business and had already allowed himself to be diverted too long. Perhaps he had been tempted by the mock airport because he didn't really want to face another community meeting with another null report. But he would not permit that to overwhelm him.

Now they were hustling through the metal detector—no buzz! —and up to the Gate. The attendant checked the tickets with perfect officiousness. "Very good, Father," he said. "Go right on in."

Father? But of course that was on the ticket; it hadn't quite registered before. "I am Brother Paul, and I fear there has been a—"

"Right. Nonsmokers to the front. Families with children board first." The man was already looking to the next.

"Daddy, we're holding up the line!"

Could her father have boarded already? It seemed unlikely without the ticket. But since the plane was only another mock-up, such details hardly mattered. The man *could* have boarded. A coincidence of names, but a distinction in title and marital status. Though how the girl could be confused about her own—

The boarding tube debouched into the airplane. Brother Paul sighted down the narrow aisle, searching for heads in the triple seats to either side. There was no one in cleric habit.

"This one," Carolyn said. "In front of the wing, so we can see out."

"I can't stay on the plane!" Brother Paul protested. "I only stopped by the terminal to see what—"

"Please fasten your seatbelts," the stewardess said.

"Wait! I have to get off—" But the boarding tube had already separated, and the plane door was closed. He was trapped.

Well, it wasn't as if the plane were actually going anywhere. He had wandered into a most elaborate setting and ritual, but that was all. He sat down in the seat beside her and fastened the seat belt. He did not want to appear to be a complete spoilsport.

The airplane began to taxi forward.

Brother Paul lurched up—and got nowhere. The seat belt bound him securely. He grabbed the buckle convulsively, got it loose, stood up, looked about—and paused again.

If he jumped off now, as the mock-up trundled realistically around the concrete runway, the little girl would be left to endure her "flight" alone. Half the fun of it would be gone for her. He certainly would never desert a child on a real flight; why should he do it now? His cruelty would be much the same, figuratively.

He settled back into his seat and rebuckled. His other appointment would simply have to wait a little longer. No doubt the Watchers, discovering him absent, would check the edges of the Animation area and locate him here in due course. Since the child's real parents were not present, Brother Paul would have to keep an eye on her until they turned up. As Jesus Christ Himself had said about the least of children—

The plane turned, orienting on the main runway, the one

Brother Paul had originally spied. The machine accelerated. The vegetation outside shot by. This was no gentle push; the passengers were pressed back into their couches. It seemed like two hundred kilometers per hour. Fascinated, Carolyn peered out of the slanted window. Brother Paul squinted past her head, as interested as she, though for a different reason. This was really quite an effect!

The nose lifted, then the tail. The plane angled up, still driving relentlessly forward. This was becoming *too* realistic; how could it stop before the pavement gave out?

The passing foliage dropped below. Take off!

Take off? Brother Paul stared past the child through the few waving strands of her hair that had yanked themselves free of the braids. Already the landscape was twenty meters below and dropping rapidly, forced behind by the monstrous thrust of the jets.

Suddenly he caught on. Motion picture film projected on the window as the structure of the plane was angled. To make it *seem*, by means of tilt and vision, as though they were flying. Very clever illusion.

Soon the window image showed clouds, and the plane leveled out. Champagne was served; Brother Paul declined his glass. There had been a time when—but he would never touch any mind-affecting drug again!

The stewardess walked down the aisle, plunking packaged breakfasts on the little shelves that folded out from the seats in front. Scrambled eggs, sausage, toast, and fruit juice.

Breakfasts? Was this morning? Well, it could be, after all his time crawling through the labyrinth under the Sphinx. Subjective impressions of the passage of time were suspect once a person had been in Animation.

"Can I have milk?" Carolyn asked.

"*May* you have milk," Brother Paul said absently.

The stewardess smiled and produced a glass of milk. She was a buxom lass, and a chain of thought related the milk to—but he cut that off. Invalid, anyway; many people were not aware that cows did not freshen until bred.

Carolyn had a great time with this "picnic" meal, but Brother Paul was pensive. Why such an elaborate set with real food just like that of a past day on Earth (no wooden soup!), as though this really were a premattermission airplane flight? It was really getting beyond the simple entertainment stage. Why squander the meager resources of Planet Tarot on such an exhibition of nostalgia?

Yet when he thought about it, it began to make more sense. He suffered from some nostalgia himself. It *was* nice to revisit the affluent, technological past, even briefly, even in mock-up. It had been so many years since he had been on a real airplane—and then it had not been as large or elegant as this one. So why not relax and enjoy the show?

They finished their meal—Carolyn left much of hers, he noted distastefully; he did not like waste—and the stewardess cleared away the trays.

Now they were far above the clouds—37,000 feet, the pilot's announcement said, causing Brother Paul to pause in his speculations a moment to translate that into kilometers: about eleven and a quarter—and he could have sworn his ears popped. The flight was level and dull. Some of the other passengers were reading, and others were sleeping, just as though they had made this trip many times before. Even as nostalgia, this was beginning to pall; enough was enough!

"Who was Will Hamlin?" Carolyn asked suddenly.

Startled, Brother Paul glanced at her. "What do you know about Will Hamlin?"

"Nothing," she replied brightly. "That's why I asked, Daddy."

Brother Paul oriented on the question, for the moment setting aside the other confusions of this odd journey. For there had indeed been a Will Hamlin. . . .

Paul had first met Wilfrid G. Hamlin as a brand new freshman college student of eighteen. Paul was going around interviewing instructors, as was the system at this small, unusual institution. He was trying to make up his mind which courses best suited his nascent intellectual needs.

The oddness of this college was really the reason Paul had come. It had no irrelevant entrance requirements, no tests, no grades, and no set curriculum. The students talked with the instructors, each of whom gave a little sales pitch for his particular class, and then selected the courses that seemed most promising. If an insufficient number of students picked a given class, that class was discontinued before it started. Somehow, each semester, it all worked out, though it always seemed impossibly chaotic. The classes themselves were of the discussion variety with no lectures;

the instructors merely tried to organize the expressed opinions and bring out the fine points as the classes proceeded. It was all very relaxed: education almost without pain.

Will Hamlin was a small man without distinguishing traits other than a slight stutter. He had a little cubbyhole of an office off the unfinished hallway leading to the Haybarn Theater.

Brother Paul shook his head, remembering. Three years later he had had an adventure of sorts in that hall—but that would hardly interest a child—

"Yes it *would!*" Carolyn insisted. "Tell me, Daddy!"

Um. Well—

One of Paul's classmates, call him Dick, and another friend, call him Guy—though perhaps two other people had actually been involved in this minor escapade—well, the three of them and their three girlfriends, who shall be nameless (no, Carolyn, it is just a kind of convention: you don't say anything untoward about girls if you can help it. They are supposed to be unsullied)—the grandmother (or was it the grand*father?* Call it the former) of one of these six had taken to making his own wine, and lo, a sample was on hand here at the college. Dandelion wine from homegrown weeds—it really was not very good. So in true collegiate tradition these bright young people—and they *were* pretty bright, their actions and scholastics to the contrary notwithstanding—had decided to improve upon this wine by distilling it. They rigged up a little still in the science lab at night (night was the chief period of action; day was reserved for sleeping and, on occasion, a college class or two), and after various mishaps in the dark succeeded in deriving the essence: perhaps a cup of 100 proof liqueur. But the bad taste of the original had been intensified by the distillation; now it was the very quintessence of awfulness. What to do with it? They carried it through the Haybarn Theater, on the way to the Community Center—but three drops spilled like guilty blood on the floor of the hall outside Will's office. (That's right—the college was so informal that all instructors and administrative personnel right up to the president were addressed by their first names.) Brother Paul had lost all memory of the final disposition of Distilled Old Grandma, but he clearly remembered passing through that hall the following morning—and catching a good whiff of Old Grandma. His stomach turned. That region had been impregnated with the stench, and of course no one would confess the cause. Poor Will, whose door opened directly onto it!

"No, I didn't *think* you'd understand," Brother Paul said. "In retrospect, it really isn't funny. Just an irrelevant reminiscence —" But Carolyn was stifling a girlish chuckle. Well, perhaps that *had* been the level of that episode! A stink in a hall. . . .

Oh, the Haybarn Theater? Well, the whole college had been converted fourteen years before Paul's arrival—yes, he was actually older than the college!—from a New England farm, and the main building had been the big red gambrel-roofed barn. Now the rough-hewn rafters showed high above the theater section; the hay had been removed, but a bird or two still nested in the upper regions. The office of the college president was in a silo. Will had not rated a silo. Which brings us back to that first encounter. Maybe being educated in a barn causes the mind to become littered with stray thoughts, running around and getting in the way like the stray dogs that roamed the campus. But *now* we have returned to what we were talking about. There was hardly room in Will's niche to turn around, but at least he had a window. On hot days that was a blessing.

"Dos Passos' *U.S.A.,*" Will was saying. Brother Paul smiled with the force of another reminiscence. He had thought it was a place. Like Winesburg, Ohio, or God's Little Acre.

The problem was that each instructor described his course as though the student already knew what it was all about. Paul had no idea whether he wished to visit Dos Passos, U.S.A., or whether he preferred to contemplate the Individual and Society under the tutelage of another prospective instructor, or perhaps drama or art or music or any several of a number of other offerings. It was all very confusing.

In the end, Will's course was one of those which Paul elected to attend. In due course he learned that Dos Passos, U.S.A., was a monstrous place, three volumes long and as big as twentieth century America, and well worth the experience of struggling through its labyrinthine and fragmentary bypaths. It was, indeed, somewhat like life itself.

Paul learned a good deal more, and grew more, than could be accounted for in horizons of the classroom or dreamt of in the philosophies of the instructors. The college campus itself was a kind of Winesburg or Dos Passos, with devious interactions complimenting the open ones. The grapevine kept all interested parties posted on the on-going student, faculty, and student-faculty liaisons; some interactions were hilarious, some serious, and some pitiful. Some people thrived in this melting pot of intellectual and sexual personality; others were destroyed. A little freedom could be a devastating thing! Paul himself came through it—mainly by luck, he decided in retrospect—more or less whole. But he had learned a certain tolerance and became less inclined to judge a person by some particular aspect of his or her personality such as physical impairment or lesbianism or schizophrenia. During this overall educational experience, much of what Paul was later to become was shaped, though there had been scant evidence of it at the time.

In those years Will became Paul's faculty advisor. The advisor system at this college was closer than what was normal elsewhere; the advisor had quite specific involvement in the student's curriculum and concern with his overall welfare. Paul had by then become a student activist—this too was the normal course—and through him Will had another fairly shrewd insight into some of what was percolating through the deeper recesses of the tangled campus scheme.

The college tried to prepare its community for life in the great outside world by being a more or less faithful microcosm *of* that world. Students ran most of the campus routine, washing the dishes, cleaning the floors, tending the grounds, organizing the fire department, and serving on committees. Periodically, the faculty members were routed out to participate in these chores too, rather than being allowed to molder in their ivory towers (as it were: silos), but it was a thankless attempt. Most routed-out faculty soon drifted back to their normal ruts.

The whole was governed by the Community Meeting, consciously patterned after the Town Meetings of rural New England. Periodically, students, faculty, and administrators got together and thrashed through the agenda, utilizing formal Parliamentary procedure. The assorted committees that ran things in the interims reported to this meeting and were given new directives. Some of these committees tended to develop wills of their own, honoring the adage that power tends to corrupt, and this could lead to trouble. The most notorious was the Executive Committee, called Exec for short, composed of the heads of the other committees together with the president of the college, selected faculty members, and representatives from each student dormitory. At times Exec concealed what it was doing from the larger community in order to prevent its less popular decisions from being reversed by the Community Meeting. "We should be the *head* of the Community, not the *tail,"* one Exec member put it. To which an irate community member responded: "Exec's acting like the *asshole* of the Community!"

For example: there was one student in his mid-twenties, a former small businessman called Deacon or "Deac" for short. He organized a Community cooperative store that sold cigarettes, cosmetics, stationery, and sundry other necessaries at reduced prices. The enterprise was doing well, and it served a Community need; therefore, the organizer was cordially disliked by the anti-free-enterprise elements of the Community. They tried to torpedo the co-op in various ways not excluding the rifling of several hundred dollars worth of supplies from the storeroom, but Deac was smarter than they, and the co-op survived. He had a candy machine installed; there was a great outcry against it as being counter to "Community spirit." But one evening the Community Communist, who had protested most vehemently against "commodity fetishism," was observed to sneak in and surreptitiously infiltrate a coin to obtain a box of raisins from the orifice of the evil machine. That was perhaps the co-op's ultimate success.

Deac had a little dog. Dogs were not permitted on campus by Community law. But the college president's beautiful Irish Setter, called Pavlov because he tended to drool, wandered freely around and in the buildings. Pavlov once watered down a terrified student standing in the dining room. So the rule was not enforced. Deac's little canine was fed and housed off campus, but tended to follow the example set by other members of the Community, going where the action was. (No one ever saw a dog attending a class, which showed how well the canines understood the situation.) Certain members of the Executive Committee saw their chance. The owner was responsible for the pet; the dog had broken the law; therefore, Deac was expelled from the Community. (No one suggested the college president should be served in the same fashion; there were, it seemed, limits.)

There was an immediate outcry. Deac had his enemies in Exec, but he also had his friends in the Community. The majority sentiment was clearly in Deac's favor, if only as a concern for fair play. So Exec maneuvered cleverly to prevent the issue from being placed on the agenda. With luck, Deac would be gone before the Community could formally discuss the matter: a *fait accompli.*

As it happened, Paul was then the Community Secretary, and his friend Dick, of Old Grandma repute, was Chairman of the Community Meeting. They conferred—they were after all roommates, as were their girlfriends, in a singularly cozy arrangement —and discovered that the prior agenda was advisory only; it could be set aside and anything discussed by the simple decision of the majority. So the notice of the Meeting was posted with the old agenda, so as not to alert the opposition, and plans were made and circulated.

The Meeting was called to order. The formalities were undertaken so that the first thing discussed was the Dog Law. A motion was made: abolish the law. Discussion? Three people spoke in defense of the law; no one spoke against it. With amazing suddenness the matter came to a vote—and the law was terminated by a massive, hitherto silent, majority. Deac was back on campus since he could not be expelled for his dog's violation of a nonexistent law. Too late, the anti-Deac forces that dominated Exec realized that they'd been had. They had been outmaneuvered and destroyed by the same machine tactics they had initiated. Paul wrote up the whole inside story for the Minutes of the Meeting, hardly concealing his pride in his own participation.

Later in life, Brother Paul was to find that machine politics, far from being a local Community aberration or perversion of the system, were in fact typical of global politics. It gave him a very special comprehension of the forces at work in the historical McCarthyism and HUAC or House UnAmerican Activities Committee, itself one of the least American institutions. Power *did* tend to corrupt, in the macrocosm as in the microcosm, and at times desperate measures were required to right the determined wrongness of those supposedly representing the will of the majority. It was a phenomenon Paul never quite understood, the Good Guys acting just like the Bad Guys, but at least he learned to recognize it when he saw it. The college had, indeed, educated him for real life.

However effective this education was, the enrollment of the college was impecuniously small, and the administration decided to expand. They felt more students would come if Community standards were stricter. Certain faculty members felt that sexual morality was entirely too free among the students. (Certain students felt the same way about the faculty, but that was another matter.) So the faculty set curfews on the lounges: no males in female lounges or females in male lounges after ten p.m. each night.

Now this stirred resentment; students regarded the lounges as a Community resource and used them at any hour of the night. (A daytime curfew might not have been so troublesome.) In addition, the lounges were under Community authority; the faculty was a minority within the larger Community and could no more pre-empt control of the lounges unilaterally than Exec could kick out a dog-owning student on its own. So the new curfew was without legal foundation and was duly ignored.

Until Paul, with five other students, was spied sitting and talking in a female lounge at 10:40 p.m. by the night watchman. Now Paul had not endeared himself to certain elements of the faculty, and this was not merely a matter of helping to overturn the dog law. He had stood up for his student rights on other occasions and generally carried the day. From a shy freshman he had become a self-assured senior. Theoretically, this was the very kind of development the college favored: individualism was character. In practice, this was frowned upon when it manifested as opposition to new faculty curfews for lounges. Paul was summoned before the faculty Social Standards Committee, popularly known as the Vice Squad.

Now Paul had tangled with the Vice Squad before. The precepts of its formation and operation were anathema to him. He happened to be one of two student members of that Squad, part of the window dressing to make it seem like a Community guidance operation. He had been extremely awkward dressing. He had brought to the attention of the college president a private student-faculty liaison involving one of the faculty members of the Squad itself. "How can this Committee be expected to enforce social standards that it does not itself honor?" The encounter was all very polite on the surface, and the president made no specific commitments. But that member of the Squad had been expeditiously removed for reasons never quite clarified. It had not been the first time Paul had locked horns with the president. He had respect for the man and had learned how to prevail without causing unnecessary embarrassment. The president was tough but basically honorable: the ideal administrator. Still, the Squad no longer felt comfortable with Paul.

Another time, the night watchman had caught a student couple in dishabille and in a compromising juxtaposition—but by morning had forgotten the name of the boy involved. The girl was known, but she refused to name her companion, and it was against faculty policy to punish girls for that might create a bad image in the eyes of the parents of prospective future female students. Thus the new law was applied selectively with discrimination practiced for the sake of image. The hypocrisy of this was evident to the students, if not to the faculty. Some girls were temperamentally innocent, but others were otherwise; to assume that the male was necessarily the instigator was at best naive.

At any rate, the entire student body knew via the grapevine who this boy was, and possibly certain faculty members knew it too—but this information was not available to the Squad. The lines of battle were hardening. In a community that had once been united, ugly currents were manifesting. Like the historical war in Asia, an originally simple and possibly justifiable idea had been transformed into self-destructive force. Paul, when questioned by the Squad, repeated his philosophical aversion to its purpose. "I know who the boy is—but I shall not tell you." And he smiled, rather enjoying the situation. Perhaps, he thought in retrospect, that smile had been a mistake. The Committee was unable to act, and had to drop the matter, but—

Next time the watchman caught a couple (coupling was a popular form of education), he took down both their names. There would be no slipping the noose this time! By sheer chance, the boy this time was Paul's friend Dick, and the couple had been using, with Paul's permission, Paul's own nocturnal hideaway: in the attic of the Community library, under the eaves. It was set up over the rafters with a mattress, tapped-wire electricity, and a bottle of 100-proof vodka (definitely not Old Grandma!), and was accessible by a rope ladder and trap door. It was perhaps the finest and most private love niche on campus. But Paul was not in it, that particular night, and so the turn of fortune had led to the discovery of his friend instead. Dick had been hauled before the Vice Squad and suspended from campus for one week.

There, but for the grace of God. . . .

(Oh, that's just a figure of speech, Carolyn. It means—well, if you had a piece of candy, and you gave it to a friend, and she ate it and got sick, how would you feel?) Actually, he was simplifying the story considerably, saying in a few words what was passing in voluminous review through his head and editing the juicier details.

Paul, necessarily silent about his own stake in this matter, did not take this lying down. There was a policy in the Community that the victims of theft be reimbursed for their losses from the Community Treasury. Paul introduced a motion in the Meeting that his suspended friend be similarly reimbursed for his travel expenses, owing to the illicit action of the Vice Squad. It was a preposterous notion—but such was the sentiment of the aroused Community at this stage that the motion carried. The money was paid—and the implications were hardly lost upon either faction. The Vice Squad had suffered another black eye, even in its technical victory. But Paul, too, had been privately wounded. He had lost his hideaway and had a friend suffer in lieu of himself. The stakes were rising, and his brushes with disaster were narrowing his options.

During this extended sequence, Paul was in the Community Center when the night watchman entered on his rounds. The watchman was a large, amiable, husky young man hardly older than the students involved. "Here is the man," Paul announced loudly to the room in general, "who performs his job—beyond the call of duty." It was an extremely pointed remark whose import was lost on no one present; only the most diligent search had enabled the watchman to locate the hidden couple, starting from a single footprint in the snow. Yet the watchman had only done his job, however excellently, and was doing his job now. He merely smiled in response to Paul's remark, as it were turning the other cheek, punched the time clock, and departed.

Now it was Paul himself on trial—and the Vice Squad had quite a number of scores to settle. It would be simplistic to suggest that their handling of the case was merely a matter of revenge, yet this was a factor that could not be entirely discounted, for Paul had caused the Committee more embarrassment than had any other person. He symbolized to a certain extent, the opposition to the very legitimacy of the Squad.

There was a preliminary hearing. As with the medieval Inquisition, these things had to be done according to form. Three of the students in the lounge had been females (fully clothed and in their right minds); since it was their lounge, they were left out of it.

They would have been left out regardless, as had two prior girls. The first of the three boys said: "I don't agree with the lounge curfew or recognize the authority of this Committee—but since I can not afford the kind of trouble this Committee will make for me if I stand on my rights, I shall not do so. I apologize for breaking the rule, and I shall not break it again." This was exactly what the Committee wanted to hear; he had capitulated and acknowledged its power. He was let off without punishment. He finished out the semester and did not return to the college next year. It was a script Paul was later to recognize in totalitarian regimes across the world—but it was not one he was prepared to follow, then or ever.

The second student turned to Paul. "Do we go that route, or do we fight?" Paul knew the other wanted to fight—indeed, he was the one who had remarked on the anal propensities of Exec—but did not want to stand alone. "We fight," Paul declared. And together they let the Vice Squad have it, denouncing the Committee with a thoroughness possible only to bright college males.

In due course they were summoned for the verdicts. The other student entered the room first, emerging with the news that he had been suspended for one week. Paul, more ornery and more careful, brought along a tape recorder. The reaction of the Vice Squad would have been surprising to those who did not know the people involved. The faculty members refused to utter their decision for the recorder. Paul refused to hear it without that protection. So he departed without verdict.

The Community held a massive protest rally over the student's suspension, meeting after hours in the female lounge. Where else? When the night watchman came, some fifty names—well over half the student body—were delivered to him to report to his owners. It was a mark of honor to be on that list. But the Squad termed this a "Demonstration" and ignored it. They didn't want half the Community; they wanted Paul. Tactic and counter-tactic; this stage of the battle was a draw.

The student body then had a formal meeting in a male lounge; the faculty, by pointed invitation, attended. It was polite but hostile; some very fine rhetoric was recorded, blasting the faculty position. To repeated questions of propriety, legality, and ethics, the college president stated flatly: "If the suspension is not honored, I will close the college." He was serious; he spoke in

terms of power, not morality. And in the end the students, being
more reasonable and vulnerable than he, backed down; they had
lost the confrontation. The student left on his week's suspension
(more correctly, he hid out for several days, awaiting the decision
on Paul), and Paul finally worked out a compromise with the
tape-shy Squad: they gave him a written sentence. This turned out
to be significant, for when the other student missed an important
drama rehearsal owing to his suspension, arousing the ire of the
drama coach, the Squad denied that it had actually suspended
him for a full week. Paul's written statement gave the lie to that,
and he called them on it in the next Community Meeting. Yet the
Squad had won this engagement. The action had alienated the
entire student body and made a mockery of Community government, but the will of the faculty had prevailed.

In all this fracas the faculty had held firmly to the position
maintained by the college president: the lounge curfew was
legitimate and so were the suspensions. But privately there were
faculty dissensions. A respectable minority had sympathy for the
student position. In addition, the college was then in a more acute
financial crisis than usual; not all the faculty members had been
paid for the past month. They *knew* the college could close! In the
face of these ethical and practical stresses during this upheaval,
only one faculty member had the courage to speak out. He did so
at the student protest meeting in the presence of the college
president. In qualified language he supported certain aspects of
the student position and denied that the president spoke for *all*
the faculty; since the president had made this claim, Will came
eloquently close to calling him a liar. Will Hamlin—Paul's
counselor.

"And that," Paul concluded as the airplane descended, "was
Will Hamlin—the only one with the guts to speak his mind
honestly, though it may have imperiled his tenure at the college.
At the time, his act of courage was largely obscured by the
complexities of the situation; others may not have cared or even
noticed. Standing up for what's right is often a thankless task. But
I never forgot. Perhaps the later hardening of my own dedication
to principle was sparked by that example. In later years I received
solicitations for financial support signed by one of the members of
that Vice Squad; they were routine printed things, but that
signature balked me, and I did not contribute. But this time I

heard from Will—and I could not in conscience refuse him. Now he seems to be the only one I knew then, who remains at the college today, twenty years later."

Twenty years later? Brother Paul heard himself say that and wondered—for he had graduated only ten years before. Now the other mystery returned: how had this child happened to ask about a man in Brother Paul's past? It was an unlikely coincidence—yet somehow it did not *seem* coincidental. Almost, he could remember—

"Daddy, my ears hurt!" Carolyn said.

The immediate pre-empted the reflective. "It must be the pressure," he told her. "As the plane descends, the air—" But her little face was screwing up in unfeigned discomfort; it was no time for reasonable discussion. "Try to pop your ears," he said quickly. "Hold your nose and blow. Hard. Harder!"

Finally it worked. Her face relaxed and she smudged away a tear. "I don't like that," she announced.

He could not blame her. He had not felt any discomfort himself, but knew the pressure on the eardrums could be painful, especially to a child who could not understand it.

Now the plane was dropping through the clouds—and there were the streets and buildings of Boston.

Brother Paul knew he was no longer on Planet Tarot. Not in perception, at least; this had to be another Animation. But it was a strange one, following its own course regardless of his personal will. Will? Was that a pun? Was his true will to remember Will Hamlin?

If this were merely another vision—how could he ever, after this, be certain of reality? He had been so sure he was out of the Animations! If he had no way of knowing, as it were, whether he was asleep or awake. . . .

And the child, Carolyn—was she a mere hallucination? The strange thing was that he was coming to remember her, a little—though he was unmarried and had no children. So how could he remember her? The manifestations of Animation might transform the world of his senses, but had not hitherto touched the world of his mind. His firm belief in the sanctity of his basic identity had sustained him throughout this extraordinary adventure; if his private dignity, his concept of self-worth deserted him or was otherwise compromised, he was lost. He did not want anything diddling with his mind!

He concentrated, trying to break out of the Vision. Carolyn turned toward him, her eyes big and blue. "Daddy—are you all right?"

Brother Paul lost his will. If he vacated this Vision—what would become of *her?* He suspected she had no reality apart from his imagination, but somehow he perceived her trapped in a scheme from which the protagonist was gone. Horrible thought! He had to see her safely home—or wherever. *Then* he could vacate. Obeying the rules of the game.

The Boston airport was like any other—of the preexodus days. Only the city surrounding it seemed different, shrunken. Yet not like most present cities, for it had electric power, and the skyscrapers showed lights on the upper floors, signifying occupancy. Strange, strange!

The ground rushed up. The wheels bumped. The plane braked, and finally taxied up to the terminal. "Well, we made it," Brother Paul murmured.

They de-planed and found themselves in the main terminal. According to the tickets they had a couple hours to wait before boarding their next plane. "Can we eat at the airport, Daddy?" Carolyn asked hopefully.

Brother Paul checked and discovered he had money in the form of sufficient cash; they could eat. The prices were too high, the food nutritionally inadequate, but the little girl was happy. She didn't care what she ate; she merely wanted *to have eaten* at an airport. Afterwards they walked around nearby Boston, Carolyn finding everything fascinating from glassy buildings to cellar grates. He liked this child; it was easy to share the spirit of her little enthusiasms. She had always been that way, hyperactive, inquisitive, excitable. Right from the time of her birth, he remembered—

Remembered *what?* She was a construct of the present, having no reality apart from this vision, with no past and no future. Wasn't she?

Brother Paul shook his head, watching her trip blithely ahead, busy as a puppy on a fascinating trail. He felt guilty for breaking up the illusion. Why *not* remember—whatever he had been about to remember?

At last they reported to the Air Non Entity terminal for the hop into the unexplored wilds of New England. After the huge jet liner, this little twenty-passenger propeller plane seemed like a toy. But it revved up as though driven by powerfully torqued rubber bands and zoomed up into the sky well enough. Every time it went through a cute little cloud it dipped, alarming Brother Paul and scaring Carolyn. It just didn't seem *safe!*

"Daddy, tell me the story about the little grades that weren't there," Carolyn said brightly as her transient attention wandered from the dip-clouds. Anything that continued longer than five minutes lost its appeal for a child this age, it seemed.

But the little grades: how had she known about that? He must have told her before, and now she was showing the other side of the coin of short attention: she liked to have familiar things repeated, always with the same details.

Well, it was pointless to rivet their attention on the clouds zooming by so perilously close outside or to concentrate on the incipient queasiness of motion sickness. So he closed his eyes to the all-too-suggestive vomit bags tucked conveniently in the pouch of the seat-back ahead, and told (again?) about the nonexistent grades. Carolyn was already learning to detest grades, and she liked to hear about his more sophisticated objections to the System. Gradually he fell into the scene himself, reliving it, though the words he spoke to her were once again simplified for her comprehension.

The college used no grades. That was one of its initial attractions: the freedom from the oppressive pressure of examinations, of number or letter scores, and from all their attendent evils. Paul had not liked competing scholastically in high school against those who cheated; this had soured the whole system for him. For though he did not cheat, his position in his class was affected by those who were less scrupulous. Thus he had graduated below those whom he knew he had outperformed. Furthermore, even with honest performance by participants, testing was imperfect, and he suffered thereby. He learned slowly but well, and retained his knowledge longer than the average, sometimes improving on it after the tests were past. Others forgot the material as soon as the tests were done. Yet their grades reflected not what they retained or used, but what their tests showed. Here at the college there was no cheating, for there was nothing to cheat *at:* no all night cramming sessions, no circulated advance copies of final exams, no punitive reductions of earned grades, and no pattern of cram-forget. A massive, systemic evil had been exorcised.

Instead, at the end of each college term, reports were made by three individuals: the instructor, the student, and the student's faculty counselor. A non-letter, non-numeric evaluation was composed from these three opinions and filed in the student's record. And that was it.

Or so it had been claimed in the college catalogue.

Paul had believed it throughout his residence at the college: four years. Freed from that grade incubus, he had explored other aspects of education, such as folk singing, table tennis, and the frustrations and joys of association with the distaff sex. He had not, however, neglected the formal classes; in fact he had learned a great deal at them that served him well in subsequent years. But the classes had been merely *part* of his education, not the whole of it. He had never regretted this approach and had always appreciated the college's readiness to allow him to find himself in his own fashion. A student could not really grow in the strait jacket of "normal" education, but here it was different. He learned what it pleased him to learn, in and out of classes, and had continued the habit since. Learning was still his major joy, now more than ever—because he had learned at this college not facts, but *how to learn*. All the other tribulations faded in importance, but this ability grew.

Years later, in the course of his novice training for the Holy Order of Vision, Father Benjamin had set before him a thin folder. "This is Temptation," Father Benjamin had said.

Brother Paul looked at him. "I don't understand. I had expected to meditate this hour." Meditation was serious business: another form of learning.

"Indeed you shall, Paul," the Father said with a certain obscure smile. "You shall meditate whether to open that folder or to let it be."

Was the Father joking? This was hardly the standard definition of meditation! Yet it seemed he was not. "How shall I know what is right? I don't know the nature of this folder."

"It is your college transcript." And Father Benjamin departed.

Meditation? This was turmoil! Brother Paul knew this transcript was, for him, classified material; he was not supposed to see it. In order to remove all competitive pressure, the college concealed the records from the individual students. Of course,

Paul knew generally how he had done, for his own opinions were part of the record.

Now, however, he wondered. If he knew what was in his transcript, why should it be secret from him? What difference did it make?

He pondered, and the doubt grew. No one kept his age a secret from him, or his weight, or any other aspect of his own being or performance. Generally Brother Paul felt that any person had a right to information about himself; it was after all *his* life. What purpose was there in a secret, ever?

But surely the college had reason to restrict this document. The pointless frills had been eliminated there in favor of the genuine education. If some aspect had to be concealed, it was necessary. Wasn't he honor bound to obey the rule and leave the folder alone?

Then why had Father Benjamin presented him with this material? Was this a test of his basic integrity, whose result would determine his progress in the Order? Was Father Benjamin playing the Devil's Advocate, subjecting him to temptation? Would he, like Jesus Christ, prevail and remain above reproach —or would he, like Eve in the Garden of Eden, succumb to the lure of the fruit of the forbidden Tree of Knowledge?

That introduced another aspect. Brother Paul himself had never condemned Eve for tasting that fruit, though it had cost her and Adam their residence in an earthly paradise. Knowledge was the very essence of man, the thing that distinguished him from the animals. A person who eschewed learning of any type sacrificed his heritage. Eden had been no paradise; it had been a prison. Ignorance was *not* bliss. Surely God had intended the ancestral couple to eat of the fruit; it would have been wrong *not* to do it. The point of the legend was that the price of knowledge was high—but it had to be paid. The alternative would have been to remain an animal.

This was not, perhaps, an orthodox interpretation. But the Holy Order of Vision, like the college, encouraged widely ranging thought. If man's insatiable curiosity were the Original Sin, how could he expiate it, except by finally satisfying it?

Was it significant that Satan had tempted Christ with power, wealth, and pride, but *not* with knowledge? "If thou be the Son of God, command that these stones be made bread." Jesus had responded: "Man shall not live by bread alone, but by every word that proceedeth out of the mouth of God." And to the offer of worldly power if he would worship the Devil: "Get thee behind me, Satan . . ." Why *not* knowledge?

He looked at the folder again. The thing seemed to glow with evil light despite his reasoning. Could it be that knowledge was power and, therefore, had been included in the temptations Christ withstood? What had Father Benjamin done to him, putting this manifestation of the Devil within his grasp?

No, he had no Biblical reference here. The verdict on knowledge was inconclusive. Each specific case had to be judged on its merits.

By what right did the college decree that everyone *except* the person most concerned should know the details of his education? There was an inherent unfairness in that which should be manifest to any objective person. By what irony were the educators themselves blind to this wrong?

Yet he knew from his experience that educators were human too, with human assets and failings. They did not see right and wrong with perfect clarity. And why should they? Their purpose was to enable the students to grow; if they succeeded in this, they had met the requirement of their office. Could God himself demand more of them? Probably it had been the college administrators, not the instructors, who had classified the documents.

But again: *why?* So the students could not complain? Why should any student complain about the simple record of his progress that he himself had helped write? Something was missing. . . .

He remembered his encounters with Exec and with the Vice Squad. Secrecy had been the hallmark of illicit dealings there. Secrecy was so often invoked to protect the guilty.

Was it the simple record? Or was there some sinister secret buried in this folder, known to all except him? Brother Paul recalled the frustrating joke about the man who was given a message written in a foreign language. Each person to whom he took it, who was able to read that language, refused either to tell him its meaning or to associate with him further. Thus the man remained forever in doubt. Was this college transcript like that? Surely he should find out!

He reached for it—but his hand hesitated. Did the end justify the means? The end was enlightenment, but the means was the violation of someone's trust. The college was a mere institution, true—but trust was trust. It did not matter what dark secrets lurked within this folder; the unveiling of them would be a personal sin, an affront against morality, rightness, and justice.

"Ah, but the flesh is weak," Paul murmured, opening the folder.

Soon he wished he had not. *Yea, Pandora!* he thought. Pandora was the girl who had opened the box (was she merely another incarnation of Eve?) and thereby loosed all things upon the world, retaining only one: hope. Paul had now let hope itself escape. For the cherished ideals of his college days, that had survived all the buffeting of campus politics, flawed faculty members, and a questionable suspension, were now revealed as delusions.

First, *this transcript had grades.* Straight letter grades, *A, B, C,* of precisely the type the college never used. Oh, there were paragraph evaluations too—but each was followed by its translation into the letter, the kind that computers could manipulate for numeric grade point averages, just as at any other school. But at other schools the grades were posted openly; each student knew exactly where he stood. Here they had been posted secretly so that not only was the student not advised of his rating, but he did not even know that he was being graded. Thus he was at a competitive disadvantage in the remainder of his life. As though he were playing poker and every other player could see his hand, but *he* could not. Brother Paul understood poker all too well, and the analogy tortured him. Here was his message in a foreign language, and of all the parties who could have revealed its content to him, only one had done so: the Holy Order of Vision. Thus he had broken the terrible *geas* more or less by luck. Yet its prior damage could not be undone. "Alma Mater, how *could* you!" he cried with a sensation like heartbreak.

At the beginning of the transcript was a note saying that the college preferred not to use grades, but owing to outside requirements had had to do so. Another note cautioned the reader against allowing the subject to see this record. No wonder!

Paul had traveled more or less innocently through the curriculum for four years without thought of grade or competitive standing; that had been the beauty of it. He had learned eclectically, *for the sake of learning*—and now via this hyprocrisy it had come to nought.

No, no—that was an unfair verdict. The gradeless environment had forced on him a peculiar discipline. It was so easy to sink into stagnation, deprived of the goad of tests and grades and the printed-letter esteem they brought. A number of students had done just that and in due course washed out of the program. But others considered it a challenge—to learn, profit, and grow *without* a formally structured stimulus. And a few, like Paul, who were well able to compete for grades if that were required, had discovered instead the sheer joy of knowledge. Knowledge of *things* was one route leading into knowledge of *self.* A grade in itself was nothing; it was, at the root, the *attitude* that counted.

The process had hardly been complete when Paul left college. He had had serious problems when he departed that protected environment, as his experience with the drug mnem had shown! But the foundation had been laid, and in time he had built upon it, and now he was learning more and growing more every year than he ever had in college. This was no denigration of that educational system; it was the fulfillment of it. Learning to learn—*that* was real, though the system turned out to be false.

From good must come good, and from evil, evil, he thought, remembering Buddha. Instead, he had encountered a set of statements, one saying the other was true, the other saying the first was false. A paradox. Good, somehow, had come from evil.

"If only you had believed in it yourself, O College Administration!" he murmured, more in regret than ire. "You wrought so much better than you knew, had you but had more faith!"

Yet they had made the letter grades under protest and hidden them under this shield of secrecy. So it was a partial lack of faith on their part, rather than a complete one. The flesh of colleges, too, was weak.

Paul looked at the individual grades for the courses—and received another shock. They were not the correct ones!

He delved more deeply, reading the evaluations. Slowly it came clear: these *were* his grades—but not as he had understood them. For they hardly reflected his own one-third opinion or what he had known of his counselors' opinions. (He had had three faculty counselors before Will Hamlin.) They were the opinions of the course instructors—just as at other schools. Thus the courses having greatest impact on Paul's thinking and development were marked by *B*'s and *C*'s—and the course dearest to the heart of a particular instructor was marked *A*. That last had been completely worthwhile—but so had the others, receiving lesser marks. The variation had lain not so much within Paul, but within the instructors. Thus the evaluation system, too, was false.

On top of that, Paul had been given no credit for some of the courses he had taken; they were not even listed. Drama and music, where he had learned stage presence, voice projection, and artistry of sound—all supremely important to his later development—gone. By error or design—quite possibly the latter, as they were considered "minor" courses, heedless of their impact on the student—those parts of his college growth had been excised. Neatly, like a circumcision. Had he known, he would have protested. But the veil of secrecy had prevented him from knowing.

Was there *ever* justification for secrecy? Or was the seeming need to hide *anything,* whether physical or informational, an admission by the hider that the thing being hidden was shameful? Surely it was the *act* of hiding that was shameful! That would bear further meditation.

Yet the inadequacy of this sorry record could not take away the *fact* of his learning. Paul had profited, and profited greatly, from his experience at this institution. Wasn't that the real point of education? The college by distorting the transcript had not really denigrated or deprived him; it had merely diminished its own estimate of its impact upon him. If he failed in life, that had not been warned by the transcript; if he succeeded, the transcript showed no prediction. As with so many conventional transcripts, distorted by conventional factors, this one was largely irrelevant. The college had cheated itself by publishing a document of mediocrity instead of the document of accuracy it should have. The good the college had done him would never be known through the transcript.

Paul completed the transcript and closed it, bemused. It was not after all a work of the Devil, merely of fallible people. Perhaps its greatest failing was its subtlest: in all the welter of statistics, test scores—yes, there *were* some there!—and comments, the authorities had somehow succeeded in missing the essential *him.* A stranger, reading this transcript, would have no idea of Paul's actual nature or capability. In this print he was nondescript, possessing no personality and not much potential.

He had known at the time that a number of instructors (including, to Paul's regret, Will Hamlin) had not seen in him, Paul, any particular promise. Perhaps even today they would not consider his present course as representative of "success." He had suspected at the time that this was because they had not made any real effort to know him—and that had they made this effort, they would have lacked the intelligence to complete the job. The Vice Squad matter had shown their level of comprehension of human values. Paul was intelligent in nonconventional ways and indifferent in conventional ways. He was not easy to measure by a set standard. This transcript confirmed this: it represented *them,* not *him.*

"Transference," he said.

"What?" Carolyn asked.

Suddenly he was back in the present, such as it was. He had thrown a complex concept at the child. "Transference. That is when a person attributes his feelings or actions to someone else. If he dislikes someone, he may say 'that person hates me.' If he feels tired, he says 'They made these steps too steep.' It is a way of dealing with certain things that he doesn't want to recognize in himself. He simply shifts the burden to someone else."

"Like Voodoo?" she asked brightly.

"Uh, no. You're thinking of sticking pins in dolls, and the person the doll stands for hurts?"

"Yes. Maybe the doll hurts too. *Mine* would."

Naturally she had sympathy for the doll! How hard it was to avoid falling into the same trap he had rehearsed here, that of failing to know the learner, and so misjudging his (her!) progress. "That's not really the same. Then again—" Then again—wasn't that whole transcript basically a voodoo doll? The college administration—and institutions of similar nature all over the world—thought that by calling this document "Paul" and sticking the pins of their secret opinions into it, they could define what he *was.* Well, perhaps it had satisfied them at the time. Next year new students had come, and he had been forgotten, buried in the office files. The irony was that his case was no doubt typical not only of the students at his college, but of the students in *all* colleges and universities. The great majority of them surely remained unknown. No status for any of them—or for their institutions. And people wondered why the educational system was failing! Straight Voodoo would be better than this. "It's close enough, sweetie," he told her.

Father Benjamin had never inquired into Paul's decision about the transcript. He knew the experience sufficed. It was not what Brother Paul had done, but how he felt about it that counted. He had to answer to no one, ultimately, except himself—and God.

But now he was returning to the college after twenty years with his daughter. For despite the erstwhile opinion of the administration, who had seen fit to suspend him and deceive him, he had succeeded in life. Now the college wanted him back, as a kind of authority in his field, to participate as a consultant for a weekend conference.

It was no laughing matter—but wasn't the last laugh his?

The little airplane dropped, bringing his attention to lower levels too. Now Brother Paul's ears hurt. Suddenly he appreciated precisely what his daughter had gone through.

"Blow your nose, Daddy!" she recommended solicitously. *She* understood!

He blew, but only the right ear cleared. The left remained blocked. It felt as though his eardrum would burst. He envisioned it bulging inward with the intolerable pressure of the atmosphere. Still the craft descended, as it were into Hell. Where could he find relief?

Finally, as the plane touched the small landing strip, he blew with such desperation it seemed his brain was squeezing out through his inner ear—and with an internal hiss of frustration, the pressure equalized. Lucky he hadn't caught a cold!

"I like Pandora," Carolyn remarked. "I would have opened that box too."

14

WILL
(FUTURE)

Rationale of the Dirty Joke, by G. Legman, makes many points that apply to much more than dirt or humor. For example, the child in the Western cultures soon learns that sex is handled in a hypocritical manner. The same acts that adults practice are forbidden to children, merely because they are children. Or perhaps because they are too little to defend their rights; thus sex becomes a symbol of the dominance of adults. Even information about the sexual interaction is systematically hidden from children. They must learn that there is one law for the big folk and another for the little folk, and that it is dangerous even to be curious about sex. Thus their real education, as they grow up, is not really about sex but about power.

They walked across the strip and entered the small terminal building. It was empty. Already the airplane was putt-putting back into the clouds.

"Who was supposed to meet us?" Carolyn asked.

"A man named David White," Paul answered. Had there been a foul up?

Then a tall young man, bearded and informally dressed, hurried up. "Father Paul?" he inquired, extending his hand.

"David White?" Paul inquired in return, taking the hand,

recognizing Lee in another role. He was relieved to have this confirmation that this was an Animation; any alternative explanation would have been most disquieting in its implications. "This is my daughter, Carolyn."

"Sorry I'm late. I saw the plane coming down—"

They hustled to David's small car and piled in their handbags. Carolyn clambered into the back seat with enthusiasm, clutching her little handbag and big octopus doll. The car zoomed out of the airport.

On the way to the campus they chatted about inconsequentials, getting to know each other. David was a senior student, on leave to serve in the Admissions office. He was not satisfied and planned to complete his degree, then seek employment elsewhere. His program at the college, appropriately, was just twenty years later than Paul's. Here, in certain respects, *was* Paul—twenty years ago. Half his life ago! He was glad David was likeable for this purely private, selfish reason.

The college, he learned, had grown from less than a hundred students to almost two thousand, though the majority did not reside on campus. And that campus had expanded; what had been forest to the north was now a collection of dormitories. It was to one of these unfamiliar buildings they came. Paul knew the college had changed, yet he felt disappointment to *see* it changed. Change was a vital aspect of life and of the universe, yet an emotional countercurrent wished it were not so.

They were issued meal tickets for the cafeteria—and this was in the Community Center where Paul had eaten for four years. This building had hardly changed; it remained a converted barn. The cellar he had helped dig out was now a dining room; he and Carolyn ate there, and he met the other program participants there. It was strange, being in this place that he remembered as the depths of the earth; it resembled a fantasy room, the kind that was not really there.

No faces were familiar; the turnover had been complete except for Will Hamlin, who was not at supper. But these were educated, compatible people, centering around his own age—which had, as it were overnight, doubled. He had jumped from twenty to forty, from student status to instructor status, though inside he felt the same. He was as much of a rebel as he had been. At least he liked to think so. The outward manifestations of it had merely changed.

Carolyn was eating with excellent appetite. She had two glasses of chocolate milk and was in partial heaven. That made him realize, with a rush of feeling: he *had* changed, for now he had his daughter. From the moment of her birth, his life had been metamorphosed; her existence was the single most vital aspect of *his* existence. He had diapered her as a baby, he had watched her put her foot in her mouth the first time (so many people never outgrew that!), he had helped her walk and talk and read; since she came into existence he had never slept without consciousness of her whereabouts, the assurance that she was safe. Not graduation, not marriage, not the God of Tarot Himself had transformed him as significantly. When she was born, he was reborn. He could not conceive of the scales on which she could be balanced, in terms of the meaning of his life, and found wanting; as well to balance her against the cosmic lemniscate, the ∞ ribbon symbol of infinity. This was why he had brought her here; she was part of him. Eight years old, nine in three months (oh, my—another birthday coming up!), precious beyond conception.

This was not a thing others understood or ever needed to. They thought he was the original Paul aged by two decades, though they had not known the original. Yet did anyone know *anyone?* A philosophic question, unanswerable.

He talked with these others, planning out aspects of the program. Paul knew Tarot; one of the others knew I Ching: common ground of a sort. "I threw the yarrow sticks for tomorrow's program," the other said. "The answer was: 'The Center is empty.'"

Paul laughed. "That could be literal!"

The man nodded soberly. Much student interest had been expressed in this program, The Future of Revelation, but it was uncertain how much would manifest when the hour came. In Paul's day some excellent programs had foundered because the students simply couldn't be bothered to attend.

They finished the meal and went upstairs to the Haybarn Theater. They passed the site of Will's old office, but the office was gone. Doubtless Will rated more than a niche, today, if less than a silo. Paul sniffed—and there was the odor of distilled Old Grandma liqueur still permeating the hall. *After twenty years?* Impossible. . . .

The Haybarn was as he remembered it. Carolyn was thrilled, running about the stage, trying to act like an Actress. Here Paul had painted scenery, here he had wrestled with stage fright. Public speaking had not come readily to him; hesitancy and a soft voice had been formidable obstacles. Finally during one session the drama coach had gotten through: "Say it again, exactly as before, but just two point three times as loud." Paul had done so—and it had worked. Never again had he been faint on stage. He still spoke softly in life—but he knew the technique of projection and used it consciously when it was required. Armed with that mechanism, he had found that stage fright itself faded. Now he could speak extemporaneously before an audience of any size and come across well. In fact, at times he had a better stage presence than he had a personal presence; private conversations could be awkward.

"We won't use the theater," David White said. "We'll go out on the lawn; more pleasant there." Translation: not enough audience to fill the barn.

At dusk they sat on the gentle hillside behind the Haybarn. Carolyn ran off to explore other portions of the campus. Paul assured himself she would be all right; no one would molest her here, and she knew where to find him. Part of raising a child properly was giving her rein; she had to discover her own horizons in her own fashion.

Each person introduced himself, but the names sieved out of Paul's mind as rapidly as they were uttered, for names and dates were not his forte. Not since he got off mnem! They chatted amiably as more people filled in. When there were about thirty, the main speaker arrived, lay on the bit of level ground at the foot of the slope, dispensed with his notes, and delivered a rambling discourse about his experiences in the political maelstrom of pre-exodus Earth. The entire period of the exodus had fit within ten years, those years fitting within the score of years between Paul's departure and return to the college, but already it seemed like medieval history. People called it the "Fool" period, and indeed it had been mad; the whole of Earth's culture had been shaken in a fashion that was difficult to believe. But the exodus had not sprung from nothing; Earth had been near the explosion point before matter transmission had provided the apparent relief valve. The speaker made this plain, using salty vernacular to spice his strong opinions. It was an interesting discourse, but not at all what was listed on the program.

Paul had pondered what he would find, here at the college of his future. It had been regressing when he left; his own suspension had been only a symptom of the deeper malady. In the interests of growth and acceptability, it had been clamping down on personal freedom, sacrificing the very qualities that had made the college what it was. Now it had achieved that desired growth; did that mean it had become obnoxiously conventional? It was too early to tell, but the preliminary signs indicated that it had not. If this speaker were typical of the new breed of professor, the present college was even more liberal than the original one had been.

As darkness closed in, still more people manifested, dotting the hillside. So did mosquitoes. A young couple sat down before Paul, seeming more concerned with their whispered dialogue than the words of the speaker. The girl kept breaking wind and giggling. There was a murmur of other conversations scattered around the slope. Three dogs cruised about, playing tag around the seated figures, doing the things canines did. Some people left. Evidently this was not considered to be a program to attend from start to finish, but a temporary stop, a kind of low-grade continuous entertainment to be absorbed in shifts. There were some questions to the speaker, reflecting quite individualistic viewpoints.

Paul marveled, internally, as he worried about the dampening grass staining his good habit. He should have worn blue jeans. No doubt about it: the swinging pendulum of conservatism had long-since reversed course. This was the way programs had been in his own day.

At last the program broke up. Paul moved on to the next location where he was scheduled to read a paper. The subject was the God of Tarot, of course. His was the second of two; the first took well over an hour. It was quite interesting—but this meant it was well past his normal retirement hour before his turn came. By this time Paul was not at all sure his material suited the audience. He had chosen it to be not too "far out," so as not to offend tastes more conservative than his. Now that the extraordinary fact had manifested that in many ways the current campus was less conventional than was Paul himself, he was suffering a diminution of ease. He had not changed that much and certainly had not become more conservative overall; the college had changed and in an unexpected manner. There was certainly nothing wrong with this, but it left him off balance, braced in the wrong direction. He would seem more dowdy than he was.

Then Will Hamlin entered. He was older, grayer, but immediately recognizable. On two levels: the role-player was Therion.

Paul jumped up to shake his hand. That was really all there was time for; it *was* the middle of the program.

Paul read his paper, explaining some of the astonishing ways in which the God of Tarot had manifested, and at last the program ended. There was no particular comment; the others were surely as tired as he was. He located Carolyn, and they found their way to the dormitory room. It was of course much farther past the little girl's bedtime than Paul's own, but she never went to sleep an instant before she had to and was enjoying this.

Too bad there had not been more opportunity to talk with Will, even in the surrogate mode of Animation. Twenty years—the whole world had changed about them both, yet circumstance had granted a mere handshake. It was not that Will had been much in Paul's thoughts during the long interim, and surely Paul had never figured fundamentally in Will's thoughts (fundamentals being prime concepts to Will); this just happened to be the juxtaposition of frameworks that time had caused to diverge widely. Twenty years ago, the chances of Paul's eventual success in life and Will's continued tenure at the college might have seemed equally improbable—yet both had come to pass, and this present meeting was the realization of this. The more appropriate unity of conscience hardly showed overtly—

"Daddy, are we going to read?"

They normally read together at night, and though it was very late, Paul thought it best to maintain the ritual. He tried to give his daughter a supplementary education by this means, as well as enhancing that closeness that was so vital to them both. She was a sensitive, hyperactive child; she needed a constant supportive presence, not the grim imperatives of forbidding parental figures, but loving help, and this was part of it. He had read her the entire *Oz* series of books, a complete story—adaptation of the Bible, and was starting in on an unexpurgated translation of the *Arabian Nights* with the works of Lewis Carroll and *Don Quixote* to come. There were those who did not consider this to be proper fare for a girl her age, but Carolyn was a very bright girl. He explained things carefully, and they both enjoyed the readings. They were good books, all of them, and more similar to each other than many people chose to believe.

"Of course, sweetie." In his suitcase was the book he had packed for this purpose: an old fantasy about a griffin that came to life, having been a stone statue, and took a little girl flying. For these readings he did not eschew conventional novels; anything that seemed worthwhile and interesting was fair game and had been so since she was two years old, ready to graduate from Mother Goose. Paul had thought this griffin story would complement the experience of the airplane flight, relieving possible anxiety. Actually it did not; Carolyn had enjoyed the flight, and the book did not reach the flying part this night. But the story was interesting.

After that, Carolyn lay on her bunk and read the book she had brought for herself while Paul read the one he had brought for *him*self. They were very much a reading family; he felt that a book was one of the most versatile educational and entertainment instruments available to man.

Reading, however, tended to put Paul to sleep. It relaxed his mind which otherwise was prone to continuous charges here and there that prevented sleep. He had hardly started his reading before Carolyn trotted across in her nightie, took the book from his hand, kissed him good night, and turned out the light as he nodded off. He heard her little feet pattering across the floor in the dark, quickly to avoid possible monsters on the floor, as he faded out. Was he taking care of her, or she taking care of him? It hardly mattered.

Paul woke at dawn. It was too early for breakfast, and he didn't want to disturb Carolyn, so he dressed and walked out around the surrounding campus. This was, as it turned out, a co-ed cooking dorm with kitchen and laundry facilities. Such dorms had not existed at the college in Paul's day, and there had been no indication that the institution was moving in that direction. Surely the Vice Squad would have moved Heaven, Earth, and participating students (yea, right off the campus!) in its frantic efforts to balk any such development. What had happened? Paul had known the members of the Squad reasonably well; one had been described as "as shallow as an empty bathtub" and another as a "medieval moralist." They must have been grossly out-maneuvered!

No, he had to be fair: he might not have known them well enough. Perhaps they had come to accept what they had rejected in his day. It was always dangerous to judge any person's character or attitude as fixed; new aspects often appeared.

There was a chill to the morning even in this summer, and Paul was inadequately dressed. He had to keep moving to generate heat. That was fine; he liked running anyway. The environs were lovely. There was a small lake behind the dorm where four ducks dwelt; the moment they spied him they waddled over with loud quacks, hoping for food. Alas, he had none. A canoe and a kayak were at the edge for the use of students. Elsewhere was a volleyball court. Packed-dirt paths led in various directions. Beyond these items, the forest closed in closely. There were birds in it and no doubt deer and porcupines: Nature returning. It was all very pleasant, this enclave of higher education on the brink of the wilderness. Would that the whole world were the same!

He returned to Carolyn. She took after her mother in this respect; she slept as late as she could and stayed up as late as she could. Paul was an early bird, she a late bird. But they didn't want to miss breakfast. "Up," he murmured in her cute little ear. "Chocolate milk." She stirred. "Ducks."

"Oh, ducks!" she cried joyfully. Waking up might be a fate hardly better than death, but here were four new friends to make it all worthwhile! Before they left the campus, Paul knew, she would be on close terms with every duck, dog, cat, and child on the premises. This was the nature of little girls, bless them!

Together they walked the path to the main campus. The route took wooden steps up a steep hill, meandered by a solar-designed building still under construction, through the barbell-shaped Arts building, past the modern new library, and through a pleasantly dense pine forest. Only the pines had existed in Paul's day.

"In the pines, in the pines," they sang together, "Where the sun never shines, And I shiver where the cold winds blow." And there was a chill little breeze, and they shivered. He pointed out the huge bull spruces to her with their myriad spokes radiating out, easy to climb, but the dirt and sap got on the hands and never came off. "So *don't* climb," he finished warningly. "I don't want the people to think I have a dirty daughter." "I won't, Daddy," she promised, eyeing the spruces appraisingly. Those spokes were just like ladders. . . .

On through a fair field full of flowers, reminding him of the alliterative opening to the epic poem *The Vision of Piers Plowman*, wherein there was a fair field full of folk, representing mankind, going about their petty pursuits, heedless of the promise of the Tower of Truth above or the threat of the Dungeon of Wrong below. Carolyn of course wanted to pick the flowers, all of them; but he begged her to let them be beautiful in life instead of killing them by picking them.

Finally down to the main campus in time for breakfast. O joy! Carolyn found several kinds of cereals, sweet pastries, and of course chocolate milk. Paul found dishes of nuts, sunflower seeds and yogurt; he settled for the skimmed white milk and two fried eggs as well. All paid for by their typed meal tickets! Carolyn loved those tickets; they were like magic. Just show one, and the best of food was yours.

When Paul had been a student here, there had been no particular consciousness of health in diet. The meals had been good, but conventional; the dietitian had been getting old, but insisted on doing things her own way. No yogurt or seeds. She would let the griddle get too hot, so that her fried eggs burned on the bottom while remaining runny on top. Because of this, Paul had switched from "sunny side up" to "over"—but had discovered that she had by then perfected the art of burning fried eggs on both sides while the whites in the middle resembled fresh mucous during the hayfever season. But today—the eggs were good. He was almost disappointed.

Paul glanced curiously at the students in the dining room. The males were almost universally bearded, the females braless; most of both sexes were in blue jeans. In Paul's day there had been fewer beards and more bras; otherwise the aspect of the student body had hardly changed.

Before the meal was over, Carolyn had made friends with the ladies of the kitchen. "Daddy, can I stay here this morning?" she asked brightly. Paul checked; children and animals were not necessarily welcome in kitchens. It was all right with the ladies. So he made sure his daughter knew where to find him and let her be. Actually, David White had arranged for a student, Susan, to keep an eye on Carolyn while Paul was tied up in the program. Susan had a head full of ringlets and seemed like a nice girl; he was sure it was all right.

On to the morning program. *The center is empty,* he remembered. There were to be three discussion groups, each cohosted by two people. Sure enough: only six people showed up. The six co-hosts. No students. That aspect of college life had not changed at all; theoretically students came to get an education, but in practice any program that began first thing in the morning was doomed.

A quick consultation; then the three groups merged. They discussed which topics to discuss. A few other people wandered in, as though accidentally diverted from their routine pursuits, temporarily caught in this eddying current, until at last there were some fifteen people.

Paul shook his head inwardly. This, too, was exactly the way it had been in his day. The students wanted the degree—the piece of paper that authenticated their education—without actually having to participate in the drudgery of classes. This happened to be the first really nice day in some time, and everyone was out with his girlfriend appreciating nature. Which was no bad thing. Paul well knew that growth could not be forced. Had his own transcript reflected his real educational experience, it would have listed the whole of his classroom participation as perhaps one third of his grade. And that would have been a higher classroom ratio than the average, for he had an intellectual bent.

Actually, it was a very good discussion, and he enjoyed it. He contributed minimally—not because he was shy or bored or uninformed, but because he was *not*. He did not need to prove anything by dominating the program. The uninterested and immature students were absent; only serious ones were present. Paul could see that many participants knew much more about their areas of expertise than he did; he could learn from them, and he liked listening to them. He liked interacting with those who were intellectually aware. So though this session might be a technical loss for the college—in fact a disaster because it really educated so few students—it was a profitable experience for him personally.

Carolyn wandered in a couple of times, just checking on him. Reassured, she buzzed off around the campus again. Just like a student. She liked it here, as he had known she would. She did not care about the deep significance of the college or about the fact that his presence in this very room at an earlier hour than he had stayed last night had gotten him suspended. To Carolyn, the entire college was a giant playground with interesting people doing interesting things all around. It was barely possible that she would one day attend as a student here; then the other meanings would begin to form.

The attendance of the program swelled, then petered out into assorted sub-dialogues. Finally, by common consent, the remainder was canceled. The college had made the program available to its students, but could not make them attend—and it was right that it do this. There were principles more important than formal education, as Paul well knew. Institutions that lost sight of that fact might post high ratings on paper that only partially masked their fundamental failure. This college had been, and remained, devoted to the quest for a better reality.

In the afternoon, Paul took Carolyn down to the moraine on the southern border of the college. He had learned of this typical formation in a geology class here, and it had stuck with him ever since. "You see," he told her as they walked the path ascending the narrow ridge through pines with the sides falling off steeply on either side, "once huge masses of ice covered much of this continent. That ice was two kilometers thick. It was called a 'glacier.' At the edge it pushed up a pile of stones, sand, and debris. When it melted, it left this pile of rubble to show where it had been. The river ran right below it, formed from its melt, and the river is still here. So here we stand, on the glacial moraine." He knew she was more intrigued by the trees, slope and path, and the blackberries growing along it, than by the theory. But he was often surprised by her retention, and he hoped that some of the geologic background would stick with her. How much the teacher he had become, profiting from his own experience as student! (They should have put the moraine in that transcript. . . .)

On the way back, Paul picked up an article printed about the college. "There are two rules," it claimed; "no pets and everybody works." Ho, ho! Minor hypocrisy had not abated either! Just so long as they did not try to expel any more students by selective enforcement.

After supper, Carolyn went up to the dormitory while Paul remained on the main campus to talk with people. The girl knew her way around now, so he didn't worry about her going alone. After all, there were ducks to feed. She had carefully saved her dinner scraps for them. He gave her the key. "And don't lock me out!"

Returning late, he found the door locked with a note on it. "FATHER PAUL—Carolyn could not locate you and was upset, so she is with me." A female name was signed and an address in another dorm.

Um. He didn't want his little girl upset. She tended to overreact and hated to be alone. He set out for the listed dorm.

"Oh, sure," a boy in the lounge said. "They were here a moment ago. Here, I'll take you to her room." He led the way down the hall.

The room was empty. "I think they went to the other dorm," a girl said. "The little girl was crying—"

Crying. . . . "Thank you," Paul said. No question about the co-ed status of these dormitories; the boys and girls mixed freely throughout, and not merely the married ones. Paul only regretted that it had not been so in his time, as his suspension testified. The college had now admitted, in effect, that he had been right all along. Yet perhaps it had been his effort that encouraged them to change course; they must have been at least partially aware that they were fighting the most intellectually and socially aware students, not the misfits or crass ones. If the college admitted only those students who would obey restrictive and/or illegal rules, what would have been its future?

Ah, but would Paul send his innocent daughter to such a college with its carefree attitude toward the scholastic aspect and its completely open dormitories? Indeed he would, if her will and his finances permitted. He had fought for this very sort of freedom —freedom to learn to learn, to master real life—and still believed in it. The Vice Squad had won the battle and lost the war, and he was most gratified to see this.

He returned to his own dorm—and there was Carolyn. "Daddy!" she cried tearfully. "I thought you'd been killed in a car accident!"

Because she hadn't been able to find him. Her hyperactive imagination had brought her low. "I was in the Community Center, where you left me."

"I tried to call there, but they said you were gone."

How nice! Had anyone ever *looked?* Yet the same sort of thing had happened in his day. Paul himself had unwittingly caused much inconvenience to a visiting family because a phone call had come for a girl and he had not been able to go to the girl's dormitory (yea, and be suspended again?) even to call her from the lounge. He had explained this to the caller. Too late, he had learned that the girl, expecting the call, had been waiting—in the Community Center. He had not looked there, having no reason to believe that she would be there; one could not comb the entire campus every time the phone rang in the hope of such a random discovery.

The young lady who had taken charge of Carolyn accompanied them into the room. Amaranth in co-ed guise, of course; she had portrayed Susan too. All young women were the same, under the stage makeup, here in Animation. Paul was glad he had made the beds and kept the room neat, even to placing Carolyn's octopus doll on her bed. He had hardly expected female company at midnight! A friendly dog also wandered in, an Irish Setter, reminding him of another long-ago episode and recent hypocrisy. Carolyn was immediately cheered. Paul thanked the student for her kindness; she said good-bye to Carolyn and departed. All was well again.

Next morning Carolyn found a girl her own age to play with. It was the granddaughter of the cleaning lady. The two set off for the kitchen to scrounge for food for the assorted animals of the campus, especially the voracious ducks. Carolyn also wangled a ride in the canoe on the little lake, another marvelous experience for her. *To be eight years old again, carefree . . .* yet there was more even to childhood than this, as the prior evening had shown.

Paul's programs were over. Now he was following up on other matters of interest: the college's new solar-power facilities, the resident water-dowser, the specialized Savonius-rotor windmill under construction, and the experimental crops grown on sludge. All these things had been exploited massively during the Exodus years, of course, but now that pressure was off, there was time to work out refinements and ascertain what was best for the long haul. They were raising crayfish as a crop and using wood for supplementary heating. All these things paralleled what the Holy Order of Vision was doing, and all were vital to the modern world. This was another new direction for the college, and he strongly approved. The years of wasteful, mechanized pollution were over, and it was good to see the college being so realistic. Institutions could learn and grow in much the same manner as individuals!

Then he set out to run down Will Hamlin. The man was as coincidentally elusive as all things were, here, but finally Paul caught him in his office in the library building. The door was marked "Dean"—was that his position now?

"I have seen the college of my future, as it were," Paul said. "It has been twenty years, but my life has been elsewhere, so to me it is very like yesterday. I note many changes—and many similarities." He wondered whether the evaluation system was still faked and whether Will had any part in that, but decided against bringing that up. He was, after all, not supposed to know. "But you have been here throughout. I wondered how the college development has seemed to *you.*" This was only an Animation, and he probably could not get any genuine information, but it still seemed worth the try.

Will was the only apparent survivor of that score of years, although a couple of other instructors were in the vicinity and Will's secretary was the wife of the other student member of the Vice Squad in Paul's day. That student had been an intelligent, sensible sort who had known better than to get into the kind of rough-and-tumble Paul had enjoyed. Paul had disagreed with him on a number of matters, but always respected the individuality and perception of the man. To disagree openly was no crime; it was hypocritical agreement that was wrong. At any rate, there were some evidences of continuity in the college. But the fundamental carry-through, by the beneficent irony of circumstance, was Will.

Will, Paul thought privately. There were cards in the Tarot deck identifying the concepts of Love, Victory, and Justice. The card for Fortitude or Discipline had been redefined by the Thoth deck as Lust; maybe two cards were required there. Yet were Fortitude and Discipline identical concepts? Perhaps they should be separated again, and a new card set up to cover Purpose—perhaps better titled Will.

Love is the Law, Love under Will. It was not necessary that anyone comprehend the pun; the concept was valid in itself. It had taken extreme fortitude to last it out here, surely. It had taken Will.

Paul's question, at any rate, was right in Will's bailiwick. Suddenly Paul was the student again, and Will the teacher, and the subject was the College: retrospect and prospect.

"It is hard to know where to start," Will said. "When you were here, the college was less than twenty years old—"

"Yes," Paul agreed. "When I came, it was fourteen; when I left, eighteen. Some of the students were the same age as the college." And the college had certainly been going through its adolescence then! Paul himself was four years older than the college; that was close enough for strong identification.

"I would say that at the outset the emphasis was on the college as community, and as involved in the larger community—about the first eight years," Will said. "Then a decade of concern with the nature of the learning process, and experiments with classroom methods derived from this concern—"

That was Paul's period. He remembered: philosophy class outdoors on the lawn, students falling asleep in the sun; geology, walking beside the river, learning to see it with phenomenal new awareness, its effect on the landscape, moraine and its own sedimented convolutions; art all over the campus, spending two hours looking at a landscape before making his first mark on the canvas, and the teacher had understood. Paul still had that painting today—not expert art, but another record of his learning experience. Drama, the plays and playlets performed on stage or in any available space on tour, once even in a private living room. Great exercise in versatility of expression! Dressing room facilities had not always been adequate; Paul's eyes had nearly popped the first time he had seen the very pretty leading lady blithely undress and change into her costume in the crowded backroom, while he and the others wrestled with make-up and cold cream and such. She had aspired to a career as an actress, but had later broken her leg in a skiing accident. That had, it seemed, destroyed her main qualification for the career. All classes had been discussion, not lecture, with all viewpoints appreciated. Yes, that had been worthwhile! Will called it "concern with the learning process;" Paul called it "learning to learn." How poignantly it returned, now!

"Then an eight year period when much effort went into curriculum experimentation," Will was saying. "There were strong influences from a number of social scientists and psychologists."

Those were the years immediately after Paul's departure. They sounded disorganized—as Paul's own life had been. Ages nineteen to twenty-six for the college: early maturity, but not necessarily the period of best judgment. A good age to heed the advice of specialists, certainly. Had that advice abolished the Vice Squad and started the trend toward dormitory deregulation? Had it returned the government of the Community *to the Community,* aborting the faculty oligarchy?

"Six years during which the college was trying to 'grow while staying small'," Will continued. "This was done by dividing its growing population into two relatively separate campus groups and by means of the organization of student-faculty 'living-learning' units."

Ages twenty-seven through thirty-two, Paul thought. Time to get married and settle down. But how could a college marry? Instead it reproduced by fission, like a creature of Sphere Nath, forming a satellite campus, propagating its species in its own fashion. Paul himself had gotten married in that period of his life after returning from his experience on Planet Tarot a changed man. But what man could visit Hell itself in his quest for God and not suffer change?

"And the past six years," Will concluded. "Involving growing program autonomy for the five programs developed, under an overall view of education as a rhythmic alteration of action and reflection, resident and nonresident experience, the analytical and the creative." Educationese came naturally to an educator!

Paul, too, had developed new programs. His daughter Carolyn was one of them. Now he was forty-one, almost forty-two, still four years older than the college. To the extent his life could be taken as a guide, the auspices for the college were promising. Its progress would continue, changing to accommodate the larger circumstance of a changing world. The microcosm always reflected the macrocosm; free will was to that extent a delusion.

Will produced a paper from his files. "The philosophical ideals of the college have been reflected in its catalogues," he said. "This first catalogue encouraged the education of young men and women for real living through the actual facing of real life problems as an essential part of their educational program. It urged the participation of students in the formulation of policies and management of the college. . . ."

"I believed in that," Paul said. "But I was suspended for practicing it."

"*You* were suspended? I had forgotten."

Evidently the event had not loomed as large in Will's life as it had in Paul's! And why *should* it have? This did not subtract from its significance. Will had been true to the college catalogue he quoted when the rest of the faculty had seemingly lost sight of its precepts. Will had done it because that was the way he was. Perhaps he assumed that others who expressed similar ideals also practiced them.

"I had more trouble with practice than theory," Paul said. "In

theory we learned about practical life by finding work during the
nonresident work term. In practice, it saved the college somewhat
on the winter heating bill."

Will looked at him. "Didn't you find the work program beneficial?"

"It was an education—but I think not the way intended." It had
proved almost impossible to get a job for just two midwinter
months. Not if a person told the truth. Some students lied; they
said they were looking for permanent employment. Then they'd
quit when the work term ended. Those who told the truth could
spend more time looking for a job than they did actually working.
The obvious lesson was: to succeed in life, you had to lie.

Paul had not lied—and had almost lost credit for one of his
work terms. An honest search and honest failure were not acceptable. One had to play the game by its rules! But no point in
belaboring Will about this; life *was* rough and fraught with
inherent unfairnesses, and he *had* learned this. The thoughtless-
ness of the college could be interpreted as an aspect of its
accommodation to reality.

"Many things work out that way," Will agreed, not aware of
Paul's thoughts. "The history of the college has other examples."

"Oh?"

"One such was the Action Group. It was composed of selected
faculty and students who set up residence just off campus. Instead
of academic sessions, texts, and papers, they sought to find,
through action and facing problems, the real need for depth of
study for each person's own competence and satisfaction."

"That hardly seems different from life itself," Paul observed.

"So it turned out. Some students proved less ready for the
cooperation and interaction the project demanded than they had
judged themselves to be. Two faculty members had problems.
There was some romanticism about the group which led, among
other things, to its welcoming wanderers who had no connection
with the college. One was a young man with emotional and
behavorial problems requiring professional help; another was an
old woman who was soon observed to be both senile and physically ill. So it seemed the project was a failure after one year—yet
later analysis showed that a significantly large number of Action
Group participants had stayed on at the college to become some
of its most serious, most hard-working students. Several important later projects originated in the Action Group, and these

projects are still operating today. From these came the 'cooking
dorms' in which students are responsible for planning and preparing their own meals.''

There it was—the origin of the co-ed housing Paul had marveled at. The offshoot of a failed experiment.

"From them, too," Will continued, "came a number of special
interest residences—houses for vegetarians, for the student-
manned fire department, for feminists, political radicals, for
persons interested in certain schools of philosophy or psychology,
an organic-gardening group—"

"We saw one of the gardens!" Paul said. "All this seems good. I
had been afraid I would find the college hopelessly conservative;
that's the way it seemed to be going when I left. I am relieved to
see I was wrong."

"Oh, the students wouldn't let us go conservative," Will said
with a tired smile. "The politics of the world affected us too.
When the college president asked male students to either get
haircuts or leave campus during an accreditation survey, there
was a protest. 'To thine own self be true!' Students moved into
policy-making positions. They demanded appeal boards for administrative decisions."

"If we had had that in my day, three of us would never have
been suspended!" Paul said. The memory still rankled. The
student body had been overwhelmingly against the faculty position. Paul still had the tape recording of the complete protest
meeting. But perhaps the matter had done some good, causing the
administration to moderate its positions in subsequent years
before things reached the crisis stage. Paul remembered a private
conversation he had had with the college president after that. The
man had inquired with genuine curiosity why Paul worked so hard
to make so much trouble for the college. Paul had replied that he
did not like trouble, but that his conscience compelled him to
stand up for what he felt was right. That was all; had the president
been a narrowly vindictive man, it would have been a comparatively simple matter to interfere with Paul's graduation.

In a very real sense, Paul thought now, the college president had
resembled the Devil encountered on Planet Tarot. The Devil was,
after all, a fallen angel, an aspect of divinity; He had His honor
too. In fact, in Hell the Devil was viewed as God, while the
dominating force of Heaven had seemed wrongheaded. It was all a
matter of perspective. Probably it was Paul's ability to appreciate

the viewpoint of his opposition that had enabled him to survive his phenomenal quest—and his experience at this college had in a very real manner prepared him for the later trauma. Perhaps, after all, the situation leading to the suspension had been beneficial. . . .

"An administrative decision to put a small part of the college budget into paving an area for use as a volleyball court," Will was saying, "in response to a student request, actually resulted in a student picket line that stopped the bulldozer. The funds were needed elsewhere they claimed, and it was a violation of the natural environment." Will shook his head in mild wonder. "What appeared to be operating for both students and faculty was the memory of the very small, very personal college it had been in your day."

"That smallness was no bad thing," Paul agreed. "Everybody knew everybody, and that encouraged a special community unity. Though it was hardly all sweetness and light then." No; it had been like one big family, and contrary to the folk ideal, some of the most savage antagonisms existed in families. Yet it was better to be involved, positively and negatively, than to be isolated from life.

"There were some unfortunate manifestations. There was a series of attempted rapes of students, frequent visits to the campus by persons peddling narcotics, and uninvited guests moving into college buildings. Several campus patrolmen were hired. Some students welcomed them; others were irate, calling them the paid lackeys of the Provost or Company spies, and so on."

"There was some of that in my day," Paul agreed. He was ashamed of almost none of his actions of the time, but he did regret the remark "beyond the call of duty" he had made to the night watchman. For later he had learned that the watchman had considerable sympathy for the position of the students. The man had taken the job from pressing financial necessity, having been married abruptly when his girl became pregnant. He had not liked turning in students, but it had been a condition of his employment, and his honour required him to do his best. At the end of the year he resigned; he couldn't take it any more. Paul had blamed him and ridiculed him—when in fact the watchman had been very much a kindred soul. Now Paul turned his eyes momentarily inward: *Lord, may I never do that again!*

"This was more extreme," Will said. "A student burned down

the 'guard house' by the campus gate, justifying his action with the claim that freedom of speech must, at some point, lead to action if careful argument and repeated requests brought no relief."

More extreme? Paul wondered. That student had destroyed property. Paul would never know for certain whether he had helped to destroy a life. A seemingly minor remark could have more impact than arson.

Will went on to describe the retirement of the college president, and the problems attendant on the selection of a new one; the revival of Community Meetings and their problems; they continued flux of new ideas; and the savagely defended individuality of Community members. The filibuster remained an instrument of legislation, in micro and macrocosm, and the college developed the motto "The Exception is the Rule." There were chronic financial difficulties. The disruption of world society brought about by the Exodus had had its effect here too. Yet the college had survived as an entity and perhaps would continue on to greater achievements. The details had changed, but it remained in essence the college Paul had known. Possibly it was stabilizing as it approached its middle age.

Paul thanked Will openly for his time and privately for just being Will. Then he went to round up Carolyn for supper. It was a good feeling, being caught up on the college; an aspect of his being that had been missing for twenty years was now complete. He was, in this subtle fashion, whole again.

Carolyn was playing with several other children in a fancy student-made playground. There was a kind of cellar with a ladder going down and a connecting passage formed from about twenty suspended tire casings: sheer joy for a child. Carolyn resisted coming with him until he reminded her about the chocolate milk. He hoped she was not getting to like it here too much.

After supper they admired the graffiti above the stairs leading out the rear of the building—as it were, the structure's anus. "Can't fight shitty hall," one proclaimed appropriately. But others were more clever, such as the question and answer: "Name your favorite Rock Group. 1. Bauxite. 2. Shale. (etc.)" Paul had to explain some of the concepts to her; this was always a certain exercise in enlightenment, but it was his policy to answer any question she put honestly and in terms she could understand. Certain four letter words were real challenges though. He hoped that this policy would prevent her from experiencing certain brutal realities before she comprehended the concepts. He was not sure this would be successful, but it was worth trying. He did not want her to grow up in ignorance and pointless shame.

They followed the graveled path through the forest toward the north campus. Carolyn spied an offshoot path. "Daddy, let's follow it!" she cried. She had, it seemed, inherited his desire to explore all avenues, physical and mental. Blessed child! "Just a little way . . ." he said.

The path slid down the slope, petered out, then reformed. "Just like the path you walked to school on," she said. She never tired of listening to the anecdotes of his youth. Paul had walked two and a half miles to school through the forest when he was Carolyn's present age. He had not told her this in any effort to demean her own status or supposedly easy life, but because she simply liked to compare his youth to hers. Now she had found a path like his; that added luster to her quest.

Did other children identify similarly with their parents? Surely they tried to—but in most cases legitimate comparisons were stifled, perhaps by parental indifference, until all that was left were the Freudian sublimations. If a girl-child could not relate to her father as either a mundane parent or a fantasy playmate, eventually she might relate sexually. That could have hellish consequences for her subsequent life. How much better to let her *be* a daughter!

The path crossed a rickety little wooden bridge over a gully and meandered on. Carolyn charged along it, thrilled. How similarly he had ferreted out forest paths when he was eight—and indeed, he was enjoying this now! Still, dusk was approaching, and they had to get up early next morning to catch the plane home. This was no time to get lost! "I think we'd better turn back now," he said reluctantly.

"Just a little farther!" she pleaded, and he could not deny her. The twilight provided that special added luster to the scene, the visual purple of the eyes being invoked. Everything was so exciting, so wonderful, though unchanged. How like the quest for knowledge this was; every acquisition introduced a new riddle to be pursued until one could be led far from one's point of entry. Or, more somberly, how like the road to Hell, paved with good intentions He had traveled that road more than once, yet temptation remained. . . .

They continued more than a little farther, yielding to the

present temptation. The path led merrily across decrepit slat bridges, around a fallen tree, and to a river. "Oh, pebbles!" Carolyn cried, squatting down precariously near the water. She had started a rock collection and was constantly on the lookout for new shapes and colors. "Oh, how pretty!"

Paul was fundamentally pleased by her interest in rocks. Prettiness was in the eye of the beholder, and she had a pretty eye. But this was not the time! "Either we must go back—or forward," he said, eyeing the darkening forest. Though he had spent four years at this college, he had never penetrated to this particular region. That evoked another parallel: surely there had also been available fields of knowledge at the college that he had similarly overlooked.

They decided to go forward, hoping to emerge before darkness trapped them, as the path was leading in the right direction. Paul had to put Carolyn's rocks in his pocket, for she had no pocket in her dress. They crossed a larger bridge that was in such a tenuous state of decomposition that some of the planks shifted out of place behind them; Paul had to hold Carolyn's little hand to steady her. "That's what Daddies are for," she said. They would certainly not go back now!

But now the path diverged. He took one branch, she the other. But when they separated too much, he became nervous. Suppose he lost her in the forest? The thought of her alone, frightened, crying—he experienced a resurgence of guilt for allowing her to lose track of him last night.

Then she crossed to join him. "There might be bears," she confided. Yes, indeed—and not merely physical one! *Here there be beares* . . . no, that was *tygers*. Same thing.

The path climbed up a steep piney slope out of the valley of the river, then curved left—which was not the way they wanted to go. But they continued, committed to it. It crested on an upper level, moved into a field-turning-forest, and divided again. "Look!" Paul cried.

It was a monstrous Indian style tent, fifteen feet tall, partially complete. Surely some ambitious student project; tools were present. A nice, serendipitous discovery.

Then, of course, he had to explain the meaning of the word "serendipity" to his bright daughter. So as they followed the path north through the fields, he told her of the three princes of Serendip who always found what they weren't looking for. How much better words became when their little individual mythologies were told! The next time he used that word, in whatever connection, she would say: "Oh, Daddy. The big tent!"

At last the path sneaked between high encroaching bushes —shoulder high on him, over Carolyn's head, so forward progress really was dependent on his adult perspective—and debouched into a more established trail they had used before. They were unlost!

"That was fun, Daddy!" she exclaimed.

Yes—it had been rare fun. He put his arm around her shoulders, and they walked on. Their college experience was essentially, fittingly over.

Yet that night his dreams were troubled. There was a letter for Carolyn, one she would like to have, lost on the way. A phone call for him, never relayed. The Vice Squad returned in force; unable to catch Paul, it turned its fury on Will, firing him from his position. All nonsense, of course, but disturbing.

They were up well before dawn. Paul worried about possible interferences to their return home: David White might oversleep, or his car might break down, or the plane would be late and they would miss their connection, or Paul or Carolyn might come down with a cold that would make flying perilous, or they might lose their return tickets, or bad weather would—

David arrived on schedule to drive them to the local airport. One worry abated! "Bye, Ducks!" Carolyn said. "Bye, Dogs. Bye-bye, College." She began to cloud up. "Daddy, I wish we could stay here. . . ."

Paul didn't answer. He was glad she had liked it, but now they had to go home. He loved his daughter, but he loved her mother too, and that separation was becoming burdensome.

The car did not break down. They did not come down with colds. The board listed their flight as being on schedule. The weather was fine. Paul presented their tickets to the clerk at the Air Non Entity office. None of his foolish fears had materialized.

The man checked the listing. "Sorry—you can't board," he announced.

Paul's brow wrinkled. "These are confirmed reservations," he pointed out. "They're valid."

"Not for this flight."

Paul began to get heated. "We paid for those tickets three weeks ago! They are *confirmed*. We arrived on your flight from Boston, reserved at the same time. We are going to be *on* this flight, or there will be legal action."

"Don't threaten *me,*" the man retorted. "I have to go by the list. You're not on it. I have no authority to bump a legitimate passenger for you."

And that was it. The man refused to honor their tickets or even really to look at them. In that way he protected himself from actually seeing the marks of their validity. But he did telephone Allegory Airlines to verify that they had two seats available on a flight to New York. However, their flight was from a larger airport, forty miles distant.

"I'll drive you there!" David volunteered.

Paul, conscious of the connection he had to make in New York, and worried about his wife's reaction if he should miss it, had to accept. He didn't like imposing on David, who had work to do at the college, and he was galled about letting Air Non Entity get away with what appeared to be illegal overbooking. "I thought Ralph Nader settled this matter decades ago!" Paul muttered. Oh, yes—there would be a reckoning!

"Aren't we going home?" Carolyn asked worriedly. "Why can't we get on the Air No Engine plane?"

"We're going home on a different airplane," Paul explained shortly. "Allegory Airlines. We're driving there now."

"Alligator Airlines!" she said, pleased.

It was a pleasant enough drive. The road had been improved since Paul's day. David spoke of graduating and finding another job. "Jobs can be hard to find, these days," Paul said, remembering his own experience before he joined the Holy Order of Vision. "Don't rule out a continuation of the college position." In ways David was like Paul of twenty years ago, but in this respect unlike: Paul had definitely not been on the college's list of prospective employees! Yet David was as much of an individual, as much of a rebel, were it only known. Certain remarks made by others, privately, suggested that the college still seethed with as much half-hidden dissent as it had twenty years ago; in fact, there were those who now looked back on the tenure of the College president Paul had known as the golden age. Paul suspected that David's doubts about remaining with the college were well founded. Yet the outside world, too, was not an ideal situation.

They arrived safely at the Allegory terminal. There was no

trouble at all; the ticket agent made out new tickets at no additional charge. Paul and Carolyn bade David farewell—his timely help had saved them from being stranded by the one problem Paul had *not* anticipated!—and boarded the plane. It was a much more pleasant craft than the Air Non Entity midget and provided a breakfast served by stewardesses.

"I owe Susan six cents," Carolyn announced.

"What?"

"I borrowed six cents from her."

Now she told him! "We'll mail it back to her after we get home." Could that be the lost letter he had dreamed about?

They landed in New York at the wrong time and in the wrong section of the terminal. Paul did not know his way around. He asked directions, and the girl at the counter pointed him down a busy hall. He followed it, Carolyn trotting along beside him.

A battery of signs pointed the way to the airline he wanted. He followed the direction indicated—and the next group of signs omitted that particular airline. He paused, perplexed.

"Daddy, where are we going?" Carolyn asked.

"I wish I knew!" He looked at his watch. Time was running out.

They backtracked, Carolyn dragging as she tired. The original sign still pointed the way. Where *was* their airline?

"Daddy, you acted like you didn't remember me," Carolyn said.

"Not *like. As.* As though I didn't remember you," he corrected her. Then: "What are you talking about?" He was distracted by the problem of the missing airline.

"When we were getting on. To start the trip. You said there was a confusion of iden—iden—"

"Identities." How could an entire airline vanish?

"Yes. Does that mean I'm not your little girl?"

"Whatever—" he started. Then he saw that she was close to tears. "Of *course* you're my little girl! You must have misheard me." She came up with the most awkward concepts at the least convenient times! "Right now we have an airline to find."

Between the signs was a large central collection area with stairs leading down and passages spinning off this way and that like a huge maze. "Maybe down there," he said uncertainly. Time, time!

They went down, but there were only more passages and more signs—wrong ones. "I can't make head or tail of this," he complained. He'd rather be lost in a forest anytime!

He went to a baggage checking window to ask directions while Carolyn weighed herself on the baggage scales. He had to wait impatiently for another passenger to check through his suitcase. At last Paul was able to explain his problem, and the girl told him where to find the correct waiting room.

"All right, Carolyn," he said comfortingly. "Now we know where we're going."

His daughter didn't answer. He turned, annoyed—and she was gone.

She must have grown tired of the scales, with her brief attention span, and moved away. Now she was separated from him, somewhere in these rushing throngs, lost. With a stabbing pang of worry, he searched for her. "Carolyn!"

He could not find her. The people hurried on, each intent on his own special interest. Most were adults; some were children. Paul saw a childlike form moving away from him, down the hall toward the exit. He ran after her. "Carolyn!"

The girl turned. It was a stranger-child, staring curiously at him. Embarrassed, Paul rushed on past her, as though he had called to someone beyond. But now he was at the great exit door. Beyond was the busy city street, its cars, buses, and vans zooming by, perilously close. Had she gone out there?

He pushed on out, his eyes casting desperately about. She was not here. "Carolyn!" he cried despairingly.

Maybe she had gone into a lady's room. Yes—she had never been able to pass a water fountain or a bathroom without indulging herself of its facilities. She had been that way ever since she first learned what they were for at about the age of two. She must have dodged aside and entered the room while he rushed heedlessly ahead. Then she might have been unable to open the heavy door from inside.

He backtracked, locating a bathroom. He was concerned that someone inside might—sometimes perverts lurked for little girls —no! But he couldn't go into the Lady's Room to check by himself.

A young woman approached. "Miss," he said abruptly. "Would you—" He faltered under her stare. She turned abruptly and departed.

"Carolyn!" he cried loudly. "Are you in there?"

There was no answer. He had no certainty she was in this particular facility; there must be dozens of them in this huge complex. How could he check them all?

An official-looking man approached purposefully. Paul knew the woman had complained; now he would be arrested for indecent behavior. He moved away.

Footfalls followed him. Paul hurried; if he got arrested now, he would never find his daughter! Already horrible specters were forming in his mind; if anything happened to her—

She had been worried about *him* that night at the college. Now he knew exactly what she had gone through.

He was at the exit again. Was that her out by the street looking for him? "Carolyn?" he cried, pushing out.

The little girl stepped off the curb. A horn blared; tires screeched.

"CAROLYN!" Paul screamed, lurching forward.

There was a crash.

15

✦

HONOR
(JUSTICE)

According to James L. McCary in Human Sexuality, *the ancient laws,
Mosaic or mundane, derived from the need for stronger tribes. This
included the restrictions on sexual expression. Women were considered
unclean at the time of menstruation because they were infertile then, so
that sex was pointless; a man's sperm had to be saved for the fertile
time, so that more offspring would result and the tribe would grow.
Similarly the practice of homosexuality was prohibited, though not as
stringently against women because there was no sperm lost there. Jesus
Christ taught little about sex; later Christian theologians, beginning
with Paul, did that. Their interest seemed to be to curtail sex, with the
object being its elimination; thus celibacy was idealized and all
extramarital expressions of sexuality condemned. The ultimate male
achievement was the rejection of all life's pleasures, and the perfect
female state was virginity.*

Therion sat on top of a huge Bible. Even lying flat, the book was
about a meter thick and four meters long.

"So you are back," the acolyte of the Horned God remarked.
"Vacation's over, eh?"

What had happened to Carolyn? Brother Paul was unmarried
and had no daughter; he was sure of that now. So she could not

have been lost. Yet he was also sure of Carolyn's reality. In that time, ten years in his future. . . .

Well, he would have to worry about his future when he got closer to it. "What is your concern?" he asked the man. Therion of course was teasing him since Therion had had a part in the recent sequence.

"You looked at other religions and other philosophies, including your idea of an educational institution, and found them wanting," Therion said. "By elimination, you are choosing the Christian God. But do you have the courage to view your Jesus and his cult as skeptically as you view the others?"

A grim but valid challenge. "I must be fair," Brother Paul agreed.

"Even though your Son of God was an arrant sexist?"

"What?" Brother Paul demanded, irritated.

"He dealt with men. He went to his cousin John the Baptist for the start of his ministry and gathered about him twelve men for disciples. Why no women? Didn't he think they were children of God too? Or were they just the servant class, not to be taken seriously?"

"Of course not!" Brother Paul snapped. But then he paused. Why *hadn't* there been some female disciples? "You have to understand: in those times the whole culture relegated women to a restricted status, especially in religious matters."

"In *Christian* realms," Therion said. "Not among the Pagans. The Horned God welcomed women. The temples abounded with priestesses, and they were completely uninhibited."

All too true. To Therion, the ultimate fullfillment of a woman was as a Temple prostitute or madam, a seducer of men. No use arguing *that* case. "Jesus was a Jew. He was not free to flout the established conventions of his people. He would have been mobbed much earlier than he was if he had female disciples, and his message would never have reached its audience." Those who preached a message whose time had not yet come always suffered; Paul had felt that backlash himself when he defended the free association of boys and girls at college. How well he understood! "Circumstances forced him to—"

"To preach salvation for men, not for women," the other finished snidely.

"Jesus *did* honor women!" Brother Paul said. "Some of them were missionaries for him—"

Therion sneered his best sneer. "Such as?"

"Such as the woman of the well!" Brother Paul said. "She told of Jesus among the Samaritans and brought her relatives and friends to see him, and there were many converts—"

"The woman at the well," Therion repeated, as though that were a suggestively curious example. "You really think that proves anything?"

"Yes! It's right there in the Bible!"

Therion jumped down from the Bible. "Then take a look inside your own Good Book—between the lines." He heaved the cover up like the lid of a coffin. The pages flipped over by themselves, past the Old Testament, slowing in the New Testament. Matthew . . . Mark . . . Luke . . . John. Chapters 1 . . . 2 . . . 3 . . . 4.

" 'Now Jesus left Judea, and came again to Galilee,' " Therion read aloud with exaggerated emphasis. Around the Bible the landscape of that time and place formed. At first the scene was distant as if seen from an airplane—*No, not that!*—then it steadied. It was as though the cameras were being dollied along by a truck driving along a country road, the huge Bible being that truck. There was a field and a well.

"He had to go through Samaria," Therion continued as the camera oriented on that well. The giant open Bible faded out, becoming the built-up stone. " 'He approached a city called Sychar, near to a field Jacob had given to his son Joseph, and Jacob's well was there.' "

"Yes," Brother Paul said. He was confident that when it came to quoting excerpts from the Christian Bible, he could match any challenge made by this man. "That's the passage. The Samaritans were mixed people from many eastern lands, settled in Israel by the Assyrians after the Israelites were carried away. They brought in their own forms of worship, but when they suffered plagues they converted to Judaism, intermarried with Jews, and claimed descent from Abraham and Moses. This annoyed the regular Jews, and relations between the two cultures became bad. So it was quite significant when Jesus met a Samaritan woman and converted her though she was of ill repute, forgiving her her sins—"

"Or so the expurgated text would have us believe," Therion said. "Those Samaritans were eager to gain acceptance by Jews any way they could. Watch what really happened."

From the field a man came, dressed in a flowing off-white tunic bound by a dusty blue sash. The amount of material was necessary to ward off the burning sun. He was bearded and wore a flap of material over his head though his face shone with sweat. He was familiar in a strange double sense. "Lee!" Brother Paul cried, then covered his mouth.

"Do not be concerned," Therion said. "He is locked into his role; he can not escape it, no matter how it annoys him, until we release him from the script. You and I can not be perceived by any but ourselves; we are as ghosts."

That was only part of Brother Paul's concern. If the role could be forced on an individual by others in the Animation, while the person thought it was his own will—then Animation was potentially a horror unmatched in the annals of man!

Then another facet struck him. "Lee—as Jesus?" he asked, amazed.

"Why the hell not? It's only a part in a skit, and we need an actor. He knew it when he signed on."

Knew that he might be subject to horrendous indignities, even the loss of his life. Yes. Brother Paul had known the same. Nevertheless, Animation was opening disquieting doors to him. For now, it seemed best to let Therion present his case.

Jesus was grimy and tired; this showed in his slow gait and general demeanor. He came up to the well and sat down on the low wall beside it. This was a pleasant enough place, really an oasis, walled in to protect it from blowing debris and polluted runoff from storms, but with green vines overgrowing the walls. The city it served was visible in the distance; steps led up from the depression the well was in, and a well-worn path meandered toward the city. Brother Paul wondered why the well had not been situated nearer the city or vice versa; but he knew there would be many complicating factors, such as the lay of the land, the most fertile fields, the intersections of roads, and just plain ornery tradition. No doubt the women got good exercise, carrying their heavy jugs of water across that distance every day.

Jesus rested beside the well with evident relief. Soon, however, his tongue ran over dry lips; he was thirsty. He stood, crossed to the stone edge of the well, and leaned over to peer into it. The water was too far down to reach directly. There was a rope, but no bucket. Unless he wanted to jump in—which would be foolish, since he would be unable to climb out again (thirst vs. survival) —there was no way for him to fetch up water. Resigned, he returned to the other wall and sat again.

The sun bore down from almost directly overhead. Jesus sat alone, eyes downcast, his tongue playing again over cracking lips. "His disciples have gone into the city to buy food," Therion explained.

Now a woman came to the well, carrying her water jar: a large earthern crock with twin curving handles, shaped with archaic artistry. She was young and resembled her jug in the esthetics of her outline. She wore a faded blue skirt and a brown shawl tied in front like a halter for her full bosom, and her kerchief descended from her head to fall over one shoulder in front to her waist. Her dainty feet were protected by half-sandals, hardly more than straps about heel and sole, leaving her toes free. Woman of ill repute she might be, but an extremely fetching one. Of course, it was much easier for a homely woman to be of good repute; temptation did not constantly come courting.

"Amaranth," Brother Paul murmured. Every Animation scene was different, but the basic cast of characters was constant. But Amaranth would not be able to indulge her normal siren role here!

The woman trotted bouncily down the steps, glanced fleetingly at Jesus, and promptly ignored him. She stopped at the well, picked up the loose rope, strung it through an eyelet of her jar, and lowered the jar carefully its distance to the water. The sound of gurgling became loud as the air bubbled out.

Jesus emerged from his reverie. "Please give me a drink of water," he said.

Surprised, the woman looked directly at him. "Aren't you a Jew? From Galilee?" A person's accent and garb made him readily identifiable, geographically and culturally.

Jesus nodded. "Jews also thirst, even those from Galilee."

"You, a Jew, ask a Samaritan woman for a drink? Your people and ours have no dealings." Yet, vaguely flattered, she drew up the full jug and passed it to him. The hospitality of water was fundamental to this arid region.

Jesus drank deeply. At last he returned the jug, wiping moisture off his beard with his sleeve. "If you only knew the gift of God and who it is who asked you for a drink, you would have asked him for living water."

"What a come-on!" Therion remarked appreciatively. "Just like that he's hooked her curiosity. He'd make a good carnival barker."

Brother Paul repressed his reaction, knowing that Therion was baiting him.

The woman of the well smiled tolerantly as she lowered her jug to refill it. "You have no jug and no deep well; where would you get 'living water'? Do you think you're greater than Jacob who gave us this well?"

Jesus, refreshed by his rest and drink, smiled back. "Everyone who drinks of the water of this well will thirst again; but whoever drinks of the water *I* give him will never thirst again."

She set down her brimming jug and untied the rope. "All right, I'll bite, Jew: give me some of this living water."

Jesus lowered his hand to his own midsection, outlining through the cloth what rose up there. "What about your husband?"

Her eyes widened momentarily as she comprehended the nature of his offer. "I have no husband."

"Well spoken," Jesus agreed, taking her by the elbows and drawing her in to him. "You've had many husbands in your time, each only for a night. Now you may have one for a day."

She glanced about, making sure that no one was approaching the well from the city. "I see you are a prophet." She raised her lips for a kiss.

"Woman, believe me, the time is coming—"

"That's not all that's—"

Brother Paul could stand it no longer. "Stop it!" he cried. "This—this is appalling!"

"But you haven't seen the best part," Therion protested with mock innocence. "Wait till you see the Divine Erection. He really socks the Holy Ghost to her till she overflows with—"

"Jesus never fornicated with women! He—"

Therion frowned. "So you can't face the expurgated pages of your Bible? Where is your open mind?"

Flustered, Brother Paul had to take a moment to organize his thoughts. "There is a distinction between open-mindedness and sacrilegious pornography. I just don't believe Jesus would *do* such a thing! The 'Living Water' he referred to was the Holy Spirit. For you to distort that into a lascivious connection—"

"You don't concede the possibility that Jesus might have had a normal interest in the opposite sex?" Therion inquired evenly. "That he might be tempted on occasion to dally with a good-looking, lower-class woman who showed him some kindness? Not a Jewish woman, of course; that would be crass. But the Samaritans were not in the same class. Being a prophet is hard work; he had to take a break sometime."

"No!" Brother Paul cried, closing his mind to the superficial reasonableness of Therion's argument. He knew what this man's route led to! "There's no evidence in all the Bible that Jesus ever had sexual relations with a woman!"

Therion smiled nastily. "A very interesting qualification. Verrry interesting! You are implying he had sexual relations with a *man?*"

"No! I—" But Brother Paul knew he had plunged into another trap foolishly. It was not as though he had no hint of the proclivities of this worshiper of the Devil.

Therion closed the jaws inexorably. "As you have established, Jesus never touched women sexually. Had the Samaritan woman at the well proffered her charms, he would have cast her aside and never bothered to make converts from the Samaritans. Therefore, he must have vented his natural passions on those with whom he felt greater kinship. And indeed your Bible establishes that—"

"Impossible!" Brother Paul cried.

The huge pages flipped over again to the eleventh chapter of John, and the picture formed. " 'Now there was a man who was sick, the Brother of Mary, who had anointed Jesus' feet with oil and wiped them with her hair, and been forgiven of her sins.' " Therion looked up. "You know, that's a most interesting use of feminine hair; I shall have to try it sometime. Jesus certainly liked to forgive pretty women their sins, especially when they kissed his stinking feet. In those days women really knew their place. I dare say some of them were very grateful to be allowed to tongue his toes, and had he desired them to extend their oral attentions up his legs somewhat—"

He paused, but this time Brother Paul refused to be baited. It was folly to engage this man in casual debate.

"Well," Therion continued, "This brother of Mary's name was Lazor or Lazarus. Jesus loved Lazarus, and if we take that literally—"

The scene showed Jesus putting his hand on a man, drawing him in for a kiss in much the same fashion as the woman at the well.

"No!" Brother Paul cried. "This was normal friendship! You have no grounds to presume—"

Therion faced him seriously. "You balk at all reasonable conjectures. That's part of the problem with your whole weird religion. Now I submit to your objective mind this hypothesis: if Jesus did not indulge himself with the fair sex or with men, he must have beat his meat in private—"

"No!"

"What, then, *did* he do? Fuck his sheep?"

And Brother Paul was unable to answer. This devil was overwhelming him with horror. How could he choose between fornication, homosexuality, masturbation, and bestiality?

Then, like a bright light, it struck him: "The Bible only covers a small portion of Jesus' life! Only his birth, his bar mitz-vah at age twelve, and his spiritual mission commencing at the age of thirty. Eighteen years of his youth and early maturity are missing. He could have led a perfectly normal life in every respect, which the framers of the New Testament were too prudish to mention—or simply didn't know about!"

"Which is what I suggested at the outset," Therion agreed. "That woman at the well was about as sexy as Samaritans come. Note how thereafter he told the Parable of the Good Samaritan. Obviously he was thinking of the good lay he had—"

"No!" Brother Paul was back in the first trap, sloughing through the muck of a degenerate's imagination. "No casual sex. He must have married—"

Therion raised an eyebrow. He had superb facial control. "Is there any mention of that in the Bible?"

Was there no way out? "No, no mention. But as I said, editing or oversight—"

"Do you really believe they could have missed something like that? A whole *wife* mislaid?" Therion smiled with satisfaction at his passing pun. "Not one Apostle, not one associate of Christ saying one word about the little woman? No widow at the crucifixion, no children orphaned?"

It was hopeless. "No, they could not have missed that," Brother Paul admitted heavily. "Jesus was not married." How tempting to conjecture a loving wife who died childless of some fever before Jesus commenced his mission—but futile.

"So we are back to the question. What did Jesus do with his penis when he wasn't urinating?"

"I don't know."

"Don't you think you owe it to your mission to find out?"

Diabolical imperative! "Yes," Brother Paul said grimly. The honor of Jesus Christ had been challenged, and Brother Paul had to vindicate it—if he could. Failure would mean the elimination of the entire complex of religions deriving from Christ and leave the field open to the Horned God.

"There's the record," Therion said, indicating the Bible.

"Father, forgive me," Brother Paul murmured prayerfully. "I must do it." He stepped toward the huge Book, and the pages flipped over so rapidly that they became a blur. He put one foot into that blur and then the other, sank into it as into a bank of fog, and found himself in Galilee, standing in a mountain pasture. He looked about.

It was a typical semi-tropic slope with a few sturdy trees and tall grass going to seed. In due course, he was sure, a shepherd would guide his sheep here, and in a few days they would crop the grass low. Then they would go on to a greener pasture, allowing this one to recycle itself. There were no fences of course; the land was open to any who cared to use it and who had the power to preempt it. Shepherds could be rough characters, he knew; little David had become master of the sling, protecting his flock from wolves, and had used that weapon to slay Goliath.

A man emerged from the brush down the incline, walking in relaxed but purposeful manner. This was Jesus; Brother Paul knew him at a glance, for he recognized Lee's bearing. Naturally Jesus was coming this way; Brother Paul's Animation had been crafted to put him in the man's path.

Jesus spied him and paused. Brother Paul raised a hand in greeting. This was a scene from a play, of course, and not genuine history, yet he felt a thrill of expectancy. Even in a mere skit, the notion of meeting Jesus Christ personally. . . .

"Hello," Brother Paul said as Jesus approached. He did not speak in Jesus' native language, Aramaic, as neither he nor Lee knew it. In a *real* jaunt into the past, there would be a virtually insurmountable linguistic barrier.

"Hello," Jesus responded. He was about Brother Paul's age with shoulder length hair lightened by the fierce Levantine sun. His beard was short and rather sparse. He held his long staff ready, a weapon in abeyance.

Now it was awkward. Brother Paul did not feel free to ask Jesus directly about the state of his sex life, but he could not simply let the man go. "I—crave companionship. May I walk with you?"

Jesus looked surprised. "You wish to walk with a pariah of Nazareth? Don't you know that I am Jesus, called son of Joseph the carpenter?"

"I am . . . Paul," Brother Paul said, not wishing to identify himself as a follower of a religion not yet founded. "I . . . was raised by foster parents."

Jesus warmed immediately. "Foster parents! They are good people?"

"Very good," Brother Paul agreed. "But not quite—" He spread his hands. "There is always that shadow, however unjustified."

"Yes!" Jesus agreed. "Joseph is a good carpenter and a good man. Always good to me, despite—" He paused, took a breath, squared his shoulders, and resumed. "I am not really his child. My mother was gravid before she married him. He knew this, yet did not divorce her or demand the refund of the bridal price. He accepted me so as to protect her reputation and never discriminated against me in favor of his true children by her."

"Yet you suffer the stigma," Brother Paul said sympathetically.

"All my life! When I tend herd well, the villagers do not say 'There is an excellent shepherd who guides his sheep to the best pastures and makes them fat—'" Jesus paused, his eyes roving over the pasture around them speculatively. "They say instead 'The bastard was lucky.' When I excel at Scripture they do not hail me for my scholarship, but sneer privately at my presumption. I am the intruder, though I never sought to be so. I shall not be heir to Joseph's shop."

"The ignorant are cruel," Brother Paul said. He had not realized how sensitive this issue would be. Bastardy. . . .

"Sometimes I get so angry—" Jesus clapped one fist into the other palm, making a sharp report. "Once a companion sneered at me half-covertly, and I threw him to the ground." He shook his head. "I should not have done that. But I have such a temper at times! It is written 'More in number than the hairs of my head are those who hate me without cause.' Yet when I respond to that derision, I become as they are."

"Yes," Brother Paul agreed. "Um—would you mind telling me the source of that quotation? I fear I am not as apt a scholar as you." Actually he knew it, but wanted to compliment Jesus again. Was he being a hypocrite, playing up to a man in order to learn his secrets?

"It is from the 69th Psalm," Jesus said. "It continues: 'Oh, God, you know my foolishness, and my sins are not hidden from you.'"

"Most apt," Brother Paul said. But privately he was disturbed. This was a perfectly serious, decent, human man—a far cry from any Son of God. There was no aura of divinity about him, no special atmosphere. How could this earnest country man found one of the major religions of all time?

"I was going to a special place," Jesus said somewhat diffidently. "An old temple, pagan I fear, yet conducive to meditation. If you care to come along—"

"I'd like to," Brother Paul said.

They proceeded to the place. This was an oddly uniform depression set in the side of the mountain, its rim overgrown by huge old cedar trees that Brother Paul was sure had been wiped out by his own time. It was well-concealed. This area was sparsely populated; only by accident was this meditation place likely to be discovered. In fact, without the trees it would hardly be worth discovering.

"You must have encountered this retreat while herding sheep," Brother Paul said.

"A shepherd has much time to explore," Jesus agreed. "And to think."

Brother Paul saw water at the base of the depression. "Is that a spring? It looks cool."

"No spring," Jesus said. "It fills when there is rain, then dries again. At the moment it is fresh, but soon it will be stagnant, not good for watering animals. Otherwise many more flocks would come here, for water is precious."

"Yes, indeed," Brother Paul agreed. "I'd like to take a swim."

"Swim?" Jesus was perplexed.

"My people live near fresh water," Brother Paul explained. "We enjoy swimming. Don't you?"

Jesus shrugged, embarrassed. "I cannot swim."

A mountain man, unused to deep water. Well, half the people of Brother Paul's own day could not swim; the ratio was probably worse here. "I would be happy to show you how."

Jesus considered. "As I mentioned, there are ruins here, perhaps of a pagan temple. The water covers them now, but if your faith forbids your approach—"

"I appreciate the warning," Brother Paul said. "But my faith is unlikely to be contaminated by a pagan ruin. Maybe Ezekiel's four-faced visitors had a base here. That would strengthen my faith because it would be a confirmation of the Scriptural description."

Jesus laughed. "Whoever exalts himself will be humbled, and whoever humbles himself will be exalted. I am not certain in which category you fit."

"There is no shame in swimming," Brother Paul said. "It is a good skill to have in case one should ever be shipwrecked. No sense in drowning when just a little preparation will save you." Of course the real Jesus had walked on the surface of the water —though that could have been an illusion. On hot days one could see water-like mirages in hollows of roads, and nearby objects were even reflected in that water. Had Jesus walked in such a place. . . .

Jesus nodded. "It is written: 'Truly, no man can ransom himself, or give to God the price of his life.' What will it profit a man, if he gains the whole world, yet forfeits his life?"

No question: this role was Jesus, later to be known as the Christ! Yet where was the magic that would compel men to drop their businesses to follow him, to give their own lives to promote his cause?

"Are you a teacher of Scripture?" Brother Paul asked cautiously. He did not use the word Bible because the formulation of the Bible had been accretive over many centuries, and at the time of Jesus its precise format or content had not been settled. In fact, the Bible was not originally a book at all, but a collection of canonical writings, a religious library.

Jesus smiled with mild self-disparagement. "I am not yet of the age to be a rabbi."

Not yet thirty, the age of intellectual maturity. "Still, you are *nearly* that age. You must have discussed your scriptural knowledge with others informally." Leading questions—yet it was important to ascertain how much of the Christian historians' view of Jesus was realistic and how much was hyperbole. Had Jesus *really* been a great teacher, springing into being at age thirty?

"Oh, yes, friend Paul, many times. But my countrymen are farmers, shepherds, and fishermen; they care little for the magic of the scriptures and regard me as—as a local boy, reciting verses tediously."

"But the ancient testament is not tedious!"

Jesus spread his hands. "Not to you, not to me. But how does it relate to farmers whose concern is rain and soil and seeds? There is the problem!"

"Seeds," Brother Paul mused. "What is the smallest seed?"

"The mustard," Jesus replied promptly.

"Couldn't you translate the message of the Scriptures into just such common terms? Take the little mustard seed and how it must be sowed in fertile soil, just as a human soul must—"

"And the tiniest of all seeds grows into the largest of all herbs, a tree for birds to nest in," Jesus finished. "Yes, *that* they might comprehend!"

"The power of the parable," Brother Paul agreed. "A little folksy story made up of familiar things to illustrate a Scriptural point. That way you could reach the common people who otherwise be by-passed."

"I must think about that," Jesus said. "I do know Scripture, and I know the common life. If the two could be unified, religion and reality—"

"Many people might listen," Brother Paul finished. "And understand. And profit. Because for the first time a teacher spoke their own language, instead of seeming to try to conceal the word of God from them."

"Yet the high priests of the Temples would not permit—"

"Why stay cooped up in the temples? In my country those who refuse to relate their learning to the real world are called 'Ivory Tower Intellectuals.' It is as though they are locked in towers fashioned of burnished bone of their own making, perhaps very handsome residences—but they are out of touch with the practical aspects of life. Your message should be taken out to the field and forest and lake, where the living people are."

Jesus nodded. "To bring the message to the people. . . ."

Brother Paul stripped down and made his way to the pond. At the water's edge he paused and turned, waiting for Jesus.

The two naked men stared at each other. "You are a Gentile!" Jesus exclaimed.

"And you—" Brother Paul started, but could not continue. For Jesus' generative organ was strangely mutilated. Immediately Brother Paul tried to cover up his reaction. "Yes, I am a Gentile, not a Jew. I have never been circumcised. But I honor many of the tenets you honor, among them the validity of the Scriptures."

"But you are outside the Faith!"

Brother Paul smiled. "Is it not possible for a man to be outside the Faith, even to be a pagan, yet be worthwhile? Do not some, like the Samaritans, begin as pagans but seek enlightenment?"

Jesus considered, then nodded. "Yes, surely. There are people who walk in darkness, then see a great light. They are good people, needing only guidance. Perhaps even the Samaritans." He grimaced. "If only there *were* suitable guidance! The scholars have become hypocrites selling favors in the temple, mouthing Scriptures they neither comprehend nor practice."

"That is unfortunate," Brother Paul said. Jesus had an accurate notion of the problem, but seemed to have no present intention of doing anything about it himself. Where was that Divine spark? "Someone should go there and advise them of their error."

"Someone should go there and cast out the merchants and thieves and overturn the tables of the money-changers!" Jesus said vehemently. "The temple is supposed to be a place of prayer, not business!" But in a moment he cooled, glancing down at himself. "As for me—I was born in a stable, and some say this is reflected in my manner."

"And I was educated in a barn," Brother Paul put in.

Jesus smiled and continued. "That was in Bethlehem, in Judea, for my family had to go there for the census, for the taxing. Then they were afraid for my life because evil Herod had been told a new King was being born, and he feared he would be replaced and so was having babies killed. It was just a rumor started by some foreign astrologers who had observed an unusual conjunction of Jupiter, Saturn, and Mars—nothing ordinary people would notice, but as one who has watched the stars many clear nights I can assure you that those three never come together at the same time, so it would have been amazing if true—but it certainly set Herod off! The Romans took the matter lightly, and only a few babies were actually killed, but my family was quite alarmed at the time and had to travel to Egypt quickly because of it. They could not make proper arrangements for my circumcision, yet it had to be on the eighth day. The knife cut too deep, and there was an infection, and on the road they could not have it attended to. So—" He lifted his stricken penis momentarily, showing the gross scar on it and the imperfectly developed testicles. He was not castrate, but it seemed likely he was sterile, and more than likely impotent.

"This is a terrible thing," Brother Paul said sympathetically. "In my country there are medications—" But obviously it was almost thirty years too late. Jesus had grown to manhood deprived, victim of unusual circumstances.

"I have long since become used to it," Jesus said. "At least I have never been tempted to sin." He frowned. "Though when I see the delight others have in such temptations, at times I am tempted to wish for a similar temptation."

Thus at one stroke (of an unsterile knife) all of Therion's conjectures had been nullified. Jesus had never felt the need of direct sexual expression and was quite certainly pure. *But why, God, did it have to be done this way?*

Jesus came down to the water and stepped in it. His feet plunged through to the ground beneath; there was after all no foolishness about walking on water.

Well, on to business, such as it was. "Swimming is mainly a matter of confidence," Brother Paul said. He squatted, immersing himself. The water was chill. "The human body in most cases is lighter than water, so it floats. Trust in that, and all else follows."

"One must have faith," Jesus said.

"That's it exactly! With faith, all things become possible. Now I'll demonstrate what we call the dead man's float." Was he making a pun there? The dead member Jesus had would never float.

Brother Paul stretched out his hands, ducked his head, and pushed off face down. He propelled himself by flutter kicking his feet. After a moment he raised his head and treaded water. "See how easy it is? If a dead man can do it, how much better for a living one!"

But Jesus had the caution of a man who had never before trusted himself to deep water. "I fear if I do that, I will soon *be* dead! How do you breathe?"

"Well, that's the next step. Let me show you the dog paddle."

"The dog piddle?" Jesus asked, frowning.

"Paddle." Brother Paul demonstrated.

Jesus watched and smiled with comprehension. "Yes, I have seen a dog do that, too. But I am not a dog."

"Maybe we'd better start with a basic man-type survival technique," Brother Paul said. "With this you need never drown, no matter how long you stay in the water. Just take a breath, hold it, and float just under the surface, completely relaxed. Your feet will sink, but your head should be near the top. Then when you need air, stroke your arms down, so your head comes up, uncoil your body, take a breath—and sink down again. You may get cold, but you'll never get tired."

Soon, with Brother Paul's encouragement, Jesus took his first float-breaths, then made his first travel-strokes. He was unashamedly pleased. "God has borne me up! I have learned a skill I thought beyond me!"

"Yes," Brother Paul agreed. "But make sure you always have company when you practice it. Water *is* dangerous if it is unfamiliar. Now we'd better get out before we freeze."

Jesus glanced at him curiously. "I am not cold."

"I dare say you have spent many chill nights in the open tending your flocks." Where were those sheep now? Probably in the care of a younger brother, now that Jesus was approaching the age of citizenship. "I am not as hardy as you." An unfeigned compliment this time.

"You look strong," Jesus said. "But it is true, anyone who tends flocks must accustom himself to the heat of day and chill of night." He swam jerkily for the shore a few feet away, and Brother Paul, across the pond, stroked more efficiently to join him.

But as he swam, Brother Paul noticed something below. There was a disk of metal at the bottom of the pool, shiny and clear. That was odd; why was it not covered with sediment?

Jesus noted his reaction. "The bottom is like copper, always clear. I do not know why. That is the site of the pagan temple; all is gone now except that altar."

A copper bottom? Here in the first century? A pagan temple was possible, but copper on such scale was hardly to be believed! Brother Paul forgot the discomfort of the cold water. "I think I'll have a look at that!"

"Wait a few days," Jesus advised. "The water will go, and you can see it directly."

"I fear I lack the patience," Brother Paul said. He dived, stroking powerfully down to the bottom. The water was only about eight feet deep.

The metal seemed to shine more brilliantly as he approached. Copper? It looked like gold! His fingers quested through the clear water, moving down to touch that mysterious surface. What was such an anachronism doing here?

Contact! Something passed through him like an electric charge, but not painful. Pale light beamed up from the disk, forming a column in the water, bathing him. He felt strangely uplifted, though he did not move physically.

But his breath was running out. Brother Paul stroked for the surface, slanting up to leave the column. His head broke water, and he took a breath. "Jesus!" he exclaimed. "There is something here!"

"I see it, Paul! Did you light a lamp down there?"

Brother Paul snorted at the humor. "I only touched the metal, and it glowed! I don't understand it!"

"Let me look," Jesus said. Carefully, awkwardly, he paddled across the pool. In a moment he entered the glow that now extended beyond the surface of the water and disappeared above.

Suddenly Jesus himself glowed. Transfigured, he radiated his own light. He remained still, neither swimming nor breathing; then, slowly, he sank.

Brother Paul launched himself through the water. He caught the man below the surface, hooked one arm about his neck, and drew him up and along. Jesus was completely passive, unresisting. Soon they reached the shallow water of the rim.

Brother Paul put down his feet, stood up, and lifted Jesus in his arms. He staggered out of the water. Jesus was not breathing.

No time to consider the historical or personal implications! Brother Paul laid the unconscious man face down on the ground and applied artificial respiration. What a fool he had been to encourage a novice swimmer to venture into deep water the first time! Yet Jesus had seemed in control until that light—

There was a stir under his hands. Jesus was breathing again! Brother Paul eased up, and in due course Jesus recovered consciousness. "You nearly drowned," Brother Paul told him. "I think you'd better not go swimming again!"

Jesus' eyes focused on him, great and luminous. "I nearly *lived,*" he said.

Brother Paul started to demur, but broke off before speaking. He had suddenly become aware of something else. *Jesus had an aura*—like that of the alien Antares, but much stronger.

Yet Jesus had not had that aura before. Brother Paul had touched him, guiding his arms in the swimming strokes; there had been nothing. Now—whatever Brother Paul's own aura was, Jesus' aura was higher.

How had this happened? Jesus had entered the pool an ordinary man. He had swum into the glowing column; it was like a baptism of light—

"Could it be?" Brother Paul murmured wonderingly. "Antares did say something about—"

"I have met my Father," Jesus said, amazed. His face glowed ethereally, and now he resembled the many portraits of him in Christian churches, haloed by radiation. Divine light!

"—the Ancients, leaving sites across the galaxy, capable of strange things," Brother Paul continued. "Associated with aura. Could I have somehow triggered it, activated such a site, my own aura keying it—a column of aura—imbuing you—enhancing your aura—"

"I must be about my Father's business," Jesus said with quiet determination.

Brother Paul stared at him, the realization coming slowly but with terrible force. Was there really any difference between the Aura of the Ancients—and what Christianity called the Holy Ghost?

16

SACRIFICE
(HANGED MAN)

Insights on the nature of Jesus Christ can come from unusual sources. The Devil and All His Works by Dennis Wheatley remarks that almost all our information comes from the four Gospels, which were compiled from oral tradition long after Jesus' death. Certainly he was a historical character, but there is less certainty about his divinity. Wonders such as his virgin birth are trimmings customarily added to the lives of holy men to add glamor. Jesus differed from other teachers in that he claimed to be divine, but he gave no proof, and indeed lacked the power to ascend to heaven of his own volition. It is possible that his words were misinterpreted, and that he was actually alluding to that spark of divine spirit that is in each of us, himself included. Much of his life is unaccounted for, and we do not know what kind of training he may have had. On the other hand, he might have been a human being who suffered from the delusion that he was divine.

Brother Paul emerged from the scene troubled. Therion sat atop the Bible again, smirking. "Got your answer?"

"I got *an* answer," Brother Paul said. "But I'm not satisfied I can accept it."

"You were there; if you can't believe what happened—"

"I was in an Animation subscene, not the historical reality. I suspect these scenes are the product of the imaginations of all of us who are participants in this quest. The effect of precession leads us into strange bypaths."

"I was watching. I never heard of an ancient copper plaque that radiates a column of Holy-Ghostly light. You can't blame me for that one!"

"No, that was from my own mind," Brother Paul agreed. "I encountered a—a person who informed me about the powers of the so-called Kirlian Aura and of a long expired civilization he termed the Ancients. He suggested there might be potent Ancient sites or ruins on Planet Earth. Thus perhaps it was natural for me to conjecture this as the explanation of Jesus' power."

Therion nodded. "Imbued by a machine many hundreds or thousands of years old."

"Millions of years old."

"Millions! Beautiful! To primitives, that power would seem God-like." Therion squinted at him. "I think you mentioned the four-faced visitors of Ezekiel in your Bible. That was a good notion. Those were surely men in self-propelled space suits—"

"I don't believe the Ancients were human," Brother Paul said. "In any event, they were no longer around when man achieved prominence on Earth."

"Still, there could be other aliens, looking for those powerful old sites, trying to tap their scientific riches before the local yokels did. Ezekiel's visitors could have been looking for the Ancient site that Jesus actually found. But—do I have it clear?—only a creature with a very strong aura like yours can key open such a site, so those aliens failed. When you touched it, you activated it, and then Jesus got the brunt of its force."

"So it appeared in the Animation. But of course we were not really on Earth, so even if there *were* such a site, I could not have—"

"Don't be so quick to explain it away! *That's* a theory of Christianity I can accept! A local boy shazamed into Superman by the sleeping robot—and what a swath that boy cut with that power! But he should have bathed in that alien beam longer until he was invulnerable except for maybe his heel—though of course it wasn't really Achilles' *heel* that was vulnerable—so they couldn't crucify him."

Brother Paul shook his head. "The very fact you can accept this notion—means that I must question it. If the Holy Ghost becomes no more than alien technology, God has no part in it."

"Ah, but God works in devious ways! Maybe He operates through Ancient sites!"

"Maybe," Brother Paul agreed, again refusing to be baited. "But I would prefer to think of Jesus as a mere mortal man with an immortal message."

"Oh come *on,* Brother! The Son of God—a natural man?"

"Enhanced by the Spirit of God. Without the Holy Ghost, Jesus was quite mortal."

"Oho! So it is the Ghost that counts, not the man."

Brother Paul did not care to engage this alert, devious, diabolic skeptic in theological argument. "Approximately."

"Then you have been looking in the wrong place. You were following Jesus when you should have followed that super aura."

Brother Paul looked at him, startled. "Yes! It was the Spirit that made Christ and Christianity what it was. What it *is.* If the Spirit is false, if it is nothing but alien technology, then Christianity is false, and—"

"And you must seek elsewhere for the God of Tarot," Therion finished. "Exactly my case."

"If that phenomenon was only an Ancient aura," Brother Paul continued, working it out, "it might have imbued an ordinary man for a time, perhaps during his life—but it would not have survived the loss of its host. It would have dissipated on his death or reverted to its machine. Yet the Holy Ghost would have survived the demise of the man and gone on to imbue his Disciples, as prophesied by Joel and described in the Acts of the Apostles. 'And it shall come to pass that I will pour out my spirit upon all flesh; and your sons and daughters shall prophesy, your old men shall dream dreams, and your young men shall see visions.' This *did* happen at the first harvest festival, the Pentecost, after Jesus was crucified. The Apostles went on to preach the Word and heal the sick and form the nucleus of Christianity—"

"Are you *sure* it happened?" Therion inquired sardonically. "Or did they merely pay their visits to that same Ancient site, bathe in the 'Holy Light,' and pick up more grace from the machine?"

"That's ridiculous! There wasn't any machine! That was just a product of my imagination—"

Therion merely smiled.

"All *right,* damn you!" Brother Paul snapped, conscious of the verbal irony. How could a disciple of the Devil be further damned? "I'll go back and follow that aura! Then will you be satisfied?"

"*You* are the one who needs to be satisfied," Therion pointed out. "You are the judge of the God of Tarot."

The man was infuriatingly correct. "I will follow that aura until the end." He stepped toward the Bible.

Therion hastily jumped off as the pages flipped over. Then Brother Paul found himself in the forming scene of—the Crucifixion.

"Oh, no!" he muttered. But of course he had to attend because this was where Jesus' aura would survive—or dissipate.

A crowd of people was walking along a road leading up a hill. In the center a man struggled under the weight of a huge wooden cross. Brother Paul moved forward, biting his lower lip. He hated this, but he had to get close to Jesus in order to verify the man's aura.

Ironic, that this mob of perhaps a hundred was all that the city of Jerusalem, with a population of 25,000, could spare either to ridicule or to mourn the greatest man of the age! The plain fact was that ninety nine per cent of the population was simply too busy with its routine pursuits to pay any attention to—

He banged into a bystander. "Sorry," Brother Paul said. "I was trying to see—" But the man took no notice of him.

Brother Paul made his way to the front, finally getting a look at the cross carrier's face. And stopped, surprised. It was not Jesus!

Then he laughed with sheer relief of confusion, though his underlying distress had not been abated. Jesus had not carried his own cross; he had been too weak after the beating they had given him so that another man had been impressed to carry it for him.

Brother Paul's laughter had attracted momentary attention. People shied away from him, and a Roman soldier scowled.

Now he saw Jesus walking a few paces behind, wearing the crown of thorns, eyes downcast. He was pale, and there was a trickle of blood on his forehead where a thorn had punctured the skin, but he walked unassisted.

"Oh, Jesus!" Brother Paul breathed. "Couldn't there have been some other way!" Yet then there would have been no Christianity. . . .

The group moved slowly on up the hill, limited by the pace of the man staggering under the burden of the cross. Brother Paul, wary of interfering with history even in Animation, walked with them, trying to get close enough to feel Jesus' aura without attracting further attention to himself. But the Roman soldier spied him and warned him away with a dark glance. Brother Paul fell back.

They came to the gate in the great city wall. Beyond this was the dread place called Golgotha. The meaning of the name, Brother Paul remembered, was "The Skull."

Now the crowd milled about as the soldiers prepared the ground for the crucifixion. It was necessary to dig a hole to stand the cross in and place a support to act as a fulcrum so that the cross could be erected. The immediate vicinity was crowded because two more victims had arrived with their crosses; the religious nut did not rate an entire ceremony to himself. Yet Jesus was the center of attention.

Women closed in, and the harried soldiers permitted this encroachment because the ladies were obviously harmless and were, after all, female. Brother Paul tried to move in with them, but again the soldier spied him and warned him back with a significant gesture. The Romans were businesslike and relatively dispassionate; they evidently did not like this business, but they had done it before, followed orders now, and did not intend to let the situation get out of hand. Brother Paul retreated again still unable to verify Jesus' aura by contact.

The ladies clustered about Jesus tearfully, some mourning most eloquently. In Brother Paul's day the term "wailing" had derogatory connotations, but here the wailing was genuine: a passionate voicing of utter bereavement that chilled the flesh and whose sincerity could not be doubted. Occidentals were unable to show emotion this candidly, and perhaps this was their loss.

Jesus stood up straight and spoke for the first time since Brother Paul had joined the party. "O daughters of Jerusalem, do not weep over me. Weep over yourselves and over your own children."

They became silent, surprised. Jesus continued talking to them, but Brother Paul, straining to hear, was roughly interrupted by a hand on his shoulder. Startled, he turned about. There was a Roman legionary, impressive in his ornate helmet, armored skirt, and slung short sword.

"Governor Pilate will speak with you," the soldier said gruffly.

Oh, no! The last thing Brother Paul wanted was to become involved in history. Of course he could not affect actual history, but if his presence distorted the Animation, he would not be able to ascertain the truth he sought. Was the validity of the Holy Ghost something that was inherently unknowable?

No! Better to believe that there had been a man like him at the Crucifixion, who had spoken to Pontius Pilate. Brother Paul was merely occupying the body, the host, as it were in Transfer, as the alien visitor Antares would have put it. All he had to do was go along with it, acting natural. So long as he did not deliberately step out of character for this situation, it should be all right.

Pilate was resplendent in his official Roman tunic and embroidered cape, astride a magnificent stallion. Behind him the flag of Rome fluttered restlessly in the rising wind, its huge eagle seeming almost to fly. Oh, the trappings of power were impressive!

The Governor stared down at Brother Paul from his elevation. "You appear to be unusually interested in the proceedings, and you are not from Jerusalem. Are you one of this man's disciples?"

Brother Paul stood frozen. Was he, like Simon, to deny his faith? Yet he was not a disciple in the fashion Pilate meant; not one of the Twelve. "I am not a disciple," Brother Paul said carefully. "But I do believe in the divinity of Jesus Christ." Yet was that itself a lie? He was here to verify the aura Jesus hosted, to ascertain whether it was some artificial, machine-enhanced thing, or the living Holy Spirit of God. How could he claim to believe when his objectivity required that he hold his judgment in abeyance. "At least, I think he may be the—"

"The King of the Jews?" Pilate asked. Suddenly Brother Paul recognized him: Therion! The Roman soldiers had been Therion too, but this was better casting.

"Perhaps," Brother Paul agreed tightly. The legionary beside him shifted his balance. (Could a single role-player play two roles simultaneously in Animation? Apparently so.)

"Are you literate?" Pilate asked.

Since the verbal portion of this Animation was in Brother Paul's own language, it seemed safe to assume the writing was also. "Yes."

"Yes, *sir!*" the legionary snapped. "Show respect to the Governor!"

Brother Paul reminded himself of his need to play along with the Animation. "Yes, sir," he repeated.

Pilate nodded benignly. "Excellent. I have a task for you. I am not altogether satisfied of this man Jesus' guilt; in fact I find little to condemn him other than intemperate words, most of which have been uttered by his accusers." He glanced aside, making an eloquent gesture of spitting. "The high priests of the Temple, who feel their authority threatened by one who preaches some modicum of decency and salvation, even for the poor. Pharisees!" And now he did spit. "I understand this man Jesus once rousted them right out of the Temple, kicking over their tables and scattering their money. Good riddance!" Then his gaze returned to Brother Paul. "But these Jews would have him die, and I do not wish to incite further unrest while passions are already roused during this local celebration, the Passaway. Passover, I mean. Relates to some sort of mythology concerning Egypt, I hear, though I'd like to hear the Egyptians' side of it! At any rate, the politics of the situation require me to accede to an act I do not necessarily approve, washing my hands of responsibility for the decision. But that others may at least know the claim for which this man is being crucified, rightly or wrongly, I propose to inscribe a plaque and set it on his cross. You will print the words on this plaque. Are you amenable to that?"

Brother Paul had not expected a statement of this nature from either Pilate or Therion, yet it rang true. Besides which, the legionary was nudging him with a dagger-like knuckle. "I—am amenable," he murmured. Then, as the legionary reacted, he added "Sir."

Pilate looked away, dismissing him. Brother Paul got to work on the plaque. He seemed to remember it, historically, as having been made of stone, but what they provided was a rough wooden board. Well, that would have to do. "What shall I inscribe?" he asked the legionary.

The man shrugged. He seemed amiable enough when out from under the eye of the Governor. "What is he accused of?"

"Of being the King of the Jews," Brother Paul said, half facetiously.

"Then write that." Case closed.

Brother Paul took the heavy chalk and printed out the seven words as boldly and clearly as he could: THIS IS THE KING OF THE JEWS.

One of the Temple priests came by as he was completing it. "That isn't right!" the man protested. "He isn't *really* the King of the Jews. You should write that he *says* he is—"

"Go soak your head," Brother Paul muttered.

Angrily, the priest went a few paces to complain to the Governor. In a moment Pilate's half-ironic response sounded above the clatter and hubub of the proceedings: "What I have written, I have written."

Brother Paul smiled privately. By assuming authorship of the plaque, Pontius Pilate had squelched all further complaints.

The legionary also smiled, briefly. "Serves the hypocrite right," he said, glancing at the disgruntled priest. "I'd like to see the whole lot of them crucified." He studied the plaque. "Does it *really* say—?"

He was illiterate, of course. That was why Pilate had needed a literate volunteer. Otherwise Pilate would have had to write the words himself, and that would have been beneath his station as well as to a certain extent again involving him in the matter he had supposedly washed his hands of. "It really does," Brother Paul assured him.

"King Herod should see that!" the legionary remarked appreciatively. Obviously he resented the whole troublesome tribe of Jews and enjoyed a good insult to any of them. "Now go take it to the cross. Hurry, before they erect it."

Suddenly Brother Paul had a legitimate way to get close to Jesus. Yet now that the opportunity was upon him, he found himself hanging back. How could he participate so immediately in this abomination?

"Move!" the legionary snapped, fingering his sword hilt. "They're about to mount him."

Brother Paul moved. He brought the plaque to the cross where it lay on the ground. "The Governor says to put this—"

"Yeah?" another soldier said. "How'd you like to put it up your—"

"It's all right," the first legionary said from behind Brother Paul. "Governor Pilate did order it."

The soldier shrugged. "If you say so, Longinus. Here, you take over this spear; I'm going to need my hands."

Longinus took the spear. "Hammer it in above his head," he told Brother Paul. "They're stretching him out now."

And while Brother Paul held the plaque, they made Jesus lie down upon the cross, placing his feet on the partial platform near the base and stretching his arms out along the crosspiece. Jesus was nearly naked now; they had stripped all his clothing except a loincloth: part of the humiliation of this form of execution. It was not enough that a man die; he had to die with his pride effaced.

Brother Paul's heart seemed to freeze for several beats, seeing him there. Was there no way to abate this horror? Yet of course there was not.

A soldier handed him a heavy, crude hammer—really a mallet —and a large iron nail. "Right above his head," he said.

Brother Paul laid the plaque on the upper projection of the cross, set the nail, and pounded it in. It was a hard chore because the nail was handmade and somewhat crooked, but he made allowances and got it done.

"Okay," the legionary said approvingly. "Now do his hand."

Brother Paul stared at the Roman, appalled. "I couldn't—"

The legionary blinked. He seemed to have some trouble with his eyes. This was a mechanical thing, not related to the crucifixion; some infection that reddened the eyeballs and evidently gave him chronic pain. Brother Paul was sure this affliction did not improve the man's temper. "Come on, come on, we're wasting time. You've got the hammer, here's a nail—pound it through the wrist, well-centered so it won't tear loose. The Governor wants to get this job finished."

Brother Paul looked across at Pontius Pilate still astride his horse. The wind had picked up considerably, and clouds were coalescing. There might be a storm. Naturally the Governor wanted to wrap this up and get back to his palace! But for Brother Paul to have to do this thing himself—

Yet if he balked, he might be changing history, and lose sight of the aura. He had tried to exert his own will in prior Animations and suffered terrible precession; he could not afford to do that now. He had to let the vision take its own course, now that he was in it.

"Forgive me," he murmured brokenly. Then he took a new nail, set it on Jesus' pale wrist, steadied it with an effort of will, controlling the shaking of his hand—and with that contact felt the aura. It was the same one he had known in the other scene: incredibly strong, stronger than his own, electric and encompassing and wonderful. The Holy Ghost.

Jesus reacted. His eyes stared straight up into the swirling clouds and his body did not move, but he was obviously aware of Brother Paul's own aura. "Paul," he murmured. "The mountain pool. . . ."

Brother Paul dropped the hammer. "I can't do it!"

Still Jesus did not look at him. "Do it, Brother," he said. "My flesh will not suffer when the hammer is wielded by the hand of a friend. Do not let the scoffers nail me to the cross."

And Brother Paul, unable to deny that plea, picked up the hammer and pounded in the nail. The flesh was no harder to penetrate than the board had been.

Then he turned his face to the side and vomited.

Rough hands hustled him off. By the time he regained his equilibrium, the soldiers had finished nailing Jesus and had erected the cross. Now they were packing in the dirt around the base, steadying the upright.

Jesus hung by the cruel nails, the demeaning plaque above his head. He had been crucified. "Father, forgive them," he said, grimacing with pain, "for they know not what they do."

Suddenly the storm struck. The noon sun, already obscured behind amazingly dense clouds, disappeared entirely, and the whole scene darkened. There was a shudder in the ground. The wind whipped so ferociously across the hill that it seemed the crosses would be blown down.

"A tornado," Brother Paul murmured. But that wasn't it; there was no funnel cloud. "An earthquake." But, though the earth rocked, that could not account for the darkness. Yet this was no ordinary storm. There was a strange, burning smell, as if Hell itself were extending its environs across this territory.

"A volcanic eruption!" he cried, finally placing it. Some deep venting of pressures, spewing ash voluminously, blotting out the sunlight until it cleared. A blast like that of Thera of 1400 B.C., occurring in the same region of the globe, affecting the entire Mediterranean basin, coincidentally with Jesus' execution—

Coincidentally?

Brother Paul looked up at Jesus, hanging on his torture stake. How could this obscuration of light, this groaning of the very earth, be coincidental? Yet if God so protested the sacrifice of His Son, why had He not acted before to prevent it? Even now, it would be far more dramatic to have the cross shaken down and apart, releasing its captive. Dramatic phenomena whose origin and purpose the spectators did not comprehend—such things were wasted effort. Most of the people of Jerusalem would never connect this with the crucifixion.

He knew the answer: because this sacrifice was necessary to His purpose. Jesus Christ had to die in this highly visible and final manner so that his Resurrection would have meaning. God asked nothing of any person that He would not require of his own Son—and here was the proof in the form of the most horrible, demeaning, seemingly useless death this society was capable of inflicting. Here was the proof that *any* person, no matter how insignificant he thought himself, could achieve salvation. Provided only that he follow the example of Jesus and believe.

Yet Brother Paul dared *not* believe—for he was here to verify and judge objectively the presence or absence of the Holy Ghost. Without that Spirit there could be no survival of consciousness after the demise of the body. No life after death—for Jesus or any other person. Jesus' resurrection would seem like fakery and be meaningless if his death were not dramatic—but his death would be pointless without the Resurrection. So this was not the end of the story; it was the central nexus, the significant turning point, the key event in the founding of a major religion.

And what if the aura dissipated upon Jesus' death? If there were no Resurrection, no Holy Ghost? Where was his own faith then?

Brother Paul got shakily to his feet and walked toward the cross. No one interfered with him; the darkness and turbulence had scattered the crowd. Governor Pilate had hastily departed, leaving only a few guards at the crucifixion site. They had recovered enough from their initial surprise to revert to their natural pursuit: shooting dice. The stakes were Jesus' clothing, particularly his seamless robe: who would get what as booty.

The aura manifested as Brother Paul approached. He was now able to feel it at some distance. The closer he came, the more intense it became, until he stood immediately before the hanging man.

The hanging man: the card of the Tarot, one of the Major Arcana. Now he knew the ultimate referent for that presentation. Jesus—crucified. Upside down, on the card, because this whole thing was inverted: the innocent suffering in lieu of the guilty —willingly. Sacrifice.

Jesus opened his eyes, feeling Brother Paul's approach. "Where have you been, Gentile friend?" he inquired. "Four years I have looked for you since you disappeared after saving my life at the pool, and I have tried to perfect your suggestions—"

"No!" Brother Paul demurred hastily. "I have no responsibility!"

"Because of you, I learned to harness the power of the parable," Jesus insisted. "It has been my most effective teaching tool.

Because of you I have ministered to Gentiles as well as to Jews. Always I have sought your aura—"

"No, no!" Brother Paul protested faintly. "You did it all yourself! I only passed by—"

"Except sometimes when my temper got the better of me. Once I cursed a fig tree because it had no fruit for me, and the tree shriveled and died. That was wrong."

"Siddhattha would not have cursed any fig tree," Brother Paul agreed. "Such a tree was the setting for his Awakening."

"Who—?"

"He was another great teacher, called the Buddha. Yet each person must seek his own enlightenment. You did what you were fated to do. I had no part—"

The eyes focused their lambent gaze upon him. "Do you also deny my friendship, Paul, now that the end comes?"

Brother Paul, stricken, reached up to touch Jesus' knee. "No, never that! I merely meant I deserve no credit for your accomplishments. You are the Son of God, the Savior; I am only—"

"A friend," Jesus finished for him. "And what greater accolade can there be?"

A soldier looked up. "Get away from that cross—he ain't dead yet!" he snapped at Brother Paul. But Longinus, leaning on his spear, murmured something, and the man relaxed.

"Farewell," Brother Paul said, his eyes stinging. He broke contact and stepped back—and something fell on the back of his hand. It was a drop of Jesus' blood from the nailing Brother Paul had done.

"This was my destiny," Jesus said.

"Anything I can do—" Brother Paul said, looking at the blood. Yet what *could* he do?

He walked numbly away and sat on the ground, awaiting the inevitable. Time passed slowly. The air cleared, and the afternoon sun emerged. From time to time people approached the cross to speak with Jesus, and sometimes Jesus cried out in pain and despair as the weight of his body dragged at the nails, but he did not struggle. Brother Paul tried to close his ears to the horror of it and felt guilty for doing so. "Christ equals Guilt," he murmured. "If he can suffer, I must at least pay attention."

Then, clearly, Jesus said: "I thirst."

A soldier dipped a sponge in vinegar, put it on a pole, and lofted it up to Jesus' lips. Jesus took some. Apparently this was not an additional torture, but a mechanism to moisten parched lips. The tang of vinegar might distract the attention of the dying man momentarily from his situation.

"It is fulfilled," Jesus said.

The body on the cross sagged—and the back of Brother Paul's hand itched. Distracted by his horror of the end, he rubbed that spot—and felt the blood, sticky on his fingers. The blood of Jesus.

Brother Paul stared at it, feeling as though the nail had penetrated his own flesh at that spot. His whole hand became hot as if held in fire. The sensation spread up his arm and into his shoulder, not unpleasant but strangely exhilarating. It was like heartbreak in reverse.

Abruptly Brother Paul felt the presence of a second aura, inhabiting his body beside his own. "Hello, friend," Jesus said inside him.

"This—this is Transfer!" Brother Paul exclaimed, amazed.

"There are things I have yet to do in this realm," Jesus said, "before I return to my Father."

"But this isn't—I'm not supposed to—" Brother Paul was unable to organize his protest. "Historically, I wasn't—"

"I understood you were willing to help," Jesus replied with gentle reproach.

"I—had hoped to ascertain—you see, I'm not of your framework," Brother Paul tried to explain.

"I understand that—now," Jesus said. "I can perceive your thoughts, for I share your body. Without you, I might have been unable to complete my mission on Earth. I shall not intrude long; will you not indulge me so that the work of my Father and yours be accomplished?"

Brother Paul could hardly turn down this plea, no matter how it complicated his investigation. "I will help you."

The soldiers were breaking the legs of the two thieves on the crosses to either side of Jesus' own so that the felons would die sooner and not extend the torture into the next day, the Sabbath Saturday. The body of Jesus was spared because it was already dead: a phenomenon the spectators found remarkable.

The legionary Longinus, skeptical about so sudden an expiration, took his spear and stabbed it into the side of the corpse. Fluid poured out, running down the shaft of the lifted spear.

Longinus danced back, while the others laughed, but still got splattered across the face with blood.

"Shame! Shame!" a Jew cried, rushing up to try to catch the blood in a cup. "The sacred blood must not be spilled on the ground!"

"Who the hell are you?" Longinus demanded, wiping his face and blinking.

"I am Joseph, a—an interested party. I have—I have a tomb in a cave over there, and—if you will let me bury the body there—"

Longinus considered. "Oh, all right. Here, I'll help you take it down." He blinked again. "The day is certainly getting bright! I never saw things so clearly before."

"Let us depart this vile place," Jesus said. Brother Paul was glad to oblige.

Under Jesus' guidance, Brother Paul went to the temporary residence of Mary Magdalene. "I am a friend of Jesus," he told the grief-stricken woman. "I came late and have no place to stay."

She hesitated, peering closely at him. She had been at the Crucifixion; he recognized her now. But her eyes had been only for Jesus; Brother Paul had been lost in the crowd. Then, without a word, she gestured him in, making space for him in the crowded room. Mary's friend, also called Mary, and other Disciples were there, but Jesus did not make himself known. "I suffer at their suffering, but it is not yet time," he said to Brother Paul.

They rested all day Saturday, the Sabbath, as was required by the Jewish religion. "You know," Brother Paul said in passing to Jesus, "in my day we rest on Sunday, the first day of the week. I believe that custom stems from an adjustment in the calendar somewhere along the line."

"What the day is called does not matter," Jesus said. "So long as one day in seven is set aside to honor my Father."

They slept, for it had been a tiring occasion. Brother Paul had nightmares of humiliation and agony, and woke to realize that these sufferings were from the mind of Jesus, not his own. Strangely, it was the thirst that was worst, not the nails or ridicule.

As evening came, Jesus roused Brother Paul. "Come, we must go to the tomb."

Quietly, they departed, leaving the room and then the city, walking toward the Place of Skulls where Jesus' body had been sealed in a tomb. Night was closing in; the guards at the gate looked curiously at Brother Paul as he went out because few people cared to leave the city at night.

Suddenly the ground shook. It was another quake! Brother Paul was flung to the ground, alarmed—but soon the earth quieted. He was only bruised and somewhat dirty. They resumed their walk.

The quake had done other damage. The great stone sealing the entrance to the tomb had been rolled aside. "Thank you, Father," Jesus said. Then, to Brother Paul: "we must remove the body and bury it separately so that it will never be found."

Brother Paul did not question this. Once he started asking questions, he would never stop! He entered the silent tomb.

The body lay there, tossed askew by the tremor, unpretty. Brother Paul nerved himself, put his hands on it, stripped off the clothing, and dragged it out of the tomb. He tried to close his nose against what he thought he smelled. He hauled it well into the foliage of the garden, then found a fragment of stone and scooped out as deep a grave as he could. The work was grueling in the dark, and every time he heard a noise not of his own making he paused, holding his breath, afraid the guards were returning. They had evidently been frightened away by the quake, but that would not keep them away forever.

Finally he got it deep enough. He set the body in, scooped the dirt over, and tamped it down. But the fresh grave would be too obvious by daylight. To conceal it, he had to uproot an adjacent bush, plant it directly over the grave, then scatter the surplus earth so that there was no giveaway mound. If anyone dug below the hollow where the bush had been, they would find nothing of course. Would this ruse be good enough to hide the body? Time would tell!

Again there was a noise. Someone *was* coming this time! It was not yet dawn; only a wan glow showed in the east. Brother Paul hurried from the grave and went to stand near the open tomb, trying to wipe the guilty dirt from his hands.

The person approached the tomb—and saw that it was open. There was a little scream. "Mary Magdalene!" Jesus exclaimed to Brother Paul. "She I would have married, if—" There was a mental image of a surgeon's scalpel, the blade that had destroyed Jesus' prospects for a normal life long before he had been aware of such things.

As the sun showed, Mary returned with two of the male

Disciples. The men ran toward the tomb, exclaiming. They found the burial clothing Brother Paul had left, then hurried back to the city, excited. Only Mary remained, standing wistfully outside the tomb. She buried her face in her hands.

"To Hell with history!" Brother Paul said. "She must be consoled." He walked up to her. "Woman, why do you weep?" he asked.

She looked up, startled. She was a comely young woman, and he knew who played the role. She did not recognize him, grimed and disheveled as he was, despite his day at her house; he was now a stranger, but her grief excluded fear. Mary had been numbed by the immediacy of it, the day before, two days before; now she was trying to come to terms with it. "My lord, if you are the one who has taken him away, tell me where you have laid him, and I will—"

Now Jesus spoke through Brother Paul's mouth. "Mary!"

Mary's eyes widened. "My Teacher!" she cried, stepping toward him.

"Do not come near me," Jesus said, retreating. "For I have not yet ascended to my Father. Go to my brethren and tell them I am going to my Father and your Father, my God and your God."

Dumbly, she nodded, love and hope shining in her eyes. Then she turned and fled toward the city.

"But is it historical?" Brother Paul demanded when they were alone again.

"Have faith," Jesus said. "Even as a mustard seed."

In the course of the next few days, Jesus appeared similarly to a number of people, spreading the news of his Resurrection in the manner he thought fit, and Brother Paul had to trust him. Then they traveled to Jesus' homeland of Galilee, making more appearances. Finally Jesus returned to Jerusalem. "This is where we must part at last," he told Brother Paul. "It is time for me to give my spirit to the Disciples at the Pentecost so that they may continue my work on Earth."

But when that had been done, a small portion of that Holy Aura remained. "I do not understand," Jesus said. "I had thought I would at last be free."

Suddenly it came to Brother Paul: "Saint Paul!"

"Are you to be a saint, friend?"

"Not I! Paul of Tarsus, the Pharisee. You may know him as Saul."

"I do not know any Saul of Tarsus, and I doubt that I would want to give my last remaining Spirit to any Pharisee."

"Trust me," Brother Paul said. "We must journey to Damascus."

"Friend, I fear for your sanity," Jesus said. "But I see in your mind that this thing must be. I will meet this Pharisee of Tarsus."

17

CHANGE
(DEATH)

Man is born to die. Perhaps alone of all the animals on Earth, he is conscious of his own inevitable demise. This may indeed be taken as the curse of the fruit of the Tree of Knowledge of Good and Evil. The moment man's intellect lifted him above the level of the ignorant, complacent beast so that he could improve his lot by planning ahead, he was able to perceive the fate Nature had prepared for him.

Psychologists say that when a person is faced with untimely death, he typically goes through five stages. The first is DENIAL: he simply refuses to believe that this horrible thing is true. The second is ANGER: why should he be treated this way when others are spared? It simply isn't fair, and he is furious. The third is BARGAINING WITH GOD: he prays to God for relief from this sentence and promises to improve himself if his life is only reprieved. Sometimes it is reprieved, and sometimes he honors his bargain. But when this appeal fails, he comes to the fourth: DEPRESSION. What is the point of carrying on when the sentence is absolute and there is no escape? But at last he comes to the fifth: ACCEPTANCE. At peace with his situation, he wraps up his worldly affairs and comports himself for the termination.

It seems reasonable to assume that man's whole life is governed by similar stages of awareness, even when his death is not expected to be untimely. As a child, he denies death; it is beyond his comprehension. But as he matures, the deaths of relatives, friends, and strangers force awareness upon him, and he responds angrily by indulging in death-

*defying exploits of diverse kinds, "proving" he is immune. With further
maturity he becomes more subtle; he becomes religious, accepting the
thesis that physical death is not the end, but merely another change in
his situation, a transformation to an "afterlife." Perhaps all religion
derives from this urge to negate death; one cannot bargain with God
unless God exists. Yet the fear of death is not entirely abated by
religion; the services of assorted churches may be perceived as mere
ritual, and his confidence erodes. The inexorable approach of death in
the form of advancing age depresses man; he longs for his youth again.
But in the end he resigns himself to his situation, makes out his will,
arranges for the disposition of his remains, and departs with a certain
grace. He has accepted the inevitable.*

They stood on the road to Damascus, staring in the direction Paul
of Tarsus had gone. The man, already lame and scarred by disease,
had been blinded by his experience and was sadly out of sorts, but
Brother Paul knew he would recover. Brother Paul found himself
shaken by his contact with the man whose name and principles he
had adopted. The name remained—but Brother Paul could no
longer consider himself a follower of those principles.

"Still I am with you," Jesus remarked. "Why have I not
dissipated? I long to rejoin my Father in Heaven."

"I don't know," Brother Paul admitted. "I'm not sure why I
haven't returned to my own framework. These Animations seem
to continue long after their purpose has been accomplished. Their
immediate purpose. I thought return would be automatic once
you—finished."

"But I *haven't* finished," Jesus said. "My life and death are only
the beginning, showing the way. Now the rest of the world must
follow to achieve Salvation."

"I—doubt that will happen immediately."

"But the Scriptures say—"

"Sometimes things take more time than anticipated. We really
don't know how God measures time."

"Then I must remain to watch. I cannot let the people drift
alone."

Brother Paul shook his head. "Jesus, I fear you would not like
all of what you might see."

But Jesus had decided. "Come, friend Paul; you and I will
watch it all. Return your body to its place, and we shall go together
in Spirit."

Brother Paul tried to protest, but the will of Jesus prevailed. "All right—we'll watch it together. But I don't think we'll be able to participate directly because you are physically dead and I have not yet been born."

"Come," Jesus said.

Brother Paul's body shivered and dissolved. It had returned to its frame—but he and Jesus remained, standing side by side.

"Come," Jesus repeated, taking Brother Paul's ethereal hand. "We follow the lame Pharisee."

They flew through the air like the spirits they were, invisible to all others except each other. When that became tedious, they simply jumped through space and time, fading out in one location and fading in at another.

They followed Paul of Tarsus. Though physically unpretentious and a rather poor public speaker, the Apostle Paul turned out to have a fine if narrowly channeled mind. His logic was powerful and his written material eloquent. He also had a remarkable determination, a perverse courage that absolutely prevented him from deviating from his set course. In some cities he was ridiculed or even mobbed; he carried on. Many of the other Christian leaders distrusted him and plotted against him, but he made converts everywhere.

"But this is not my message!" Jesus protested. "I was not attempting to found a new Church, but to show the way—"

"I said you might not like it," Brother Paul reminded him. "Yet if it is necessary to start a new religion in order to show people the way to Salvation—"

Jesus sighed. "I suppose so," he said dubiously. "Since the world will soon end, it may not matter."

Brother Paul did not comment. It was obvious that the Christian Church was not the initiative or desire of either Jesus or the Disciples who had known him personally. Thus, it seemed, it was necessary that a man who had never known Jesus personally assume a leading role in the propagation of the new faith. As with a failing business: a professional organizer had been brought in from outside, and he was doing his job without catering unduly to the foibles of the existing order.

But the Apostle Paul, it became apparent, was shaping that faith into his own image—and that was an unfortunately narrow one. Jesus, sexually voided, had not made stipulations about sex. He had treated all people equally, gladly accepting women as well as men, regardless of their station or the prior state of their conscience. Rich men *and* prostitutes were welcome, provided each renounce his/her liabilities. The Apostle Paul was far more restrictive, almost anti-woman; he permitted them to join, but never to exercise responsibility.

Jesus shook his head sadly. "I had not supposed it would be like this," he murmured, as he watched the Apostle Paul quarreling with the other Apostles. Brother Paul had mixed emotions. How much better to see his namesake from the perspective of history, rather than as this sometimes small-minded person! "He has written some excellent Epistles," he said.

Then, looking ahead in history, they discovered that not all of the Epistles written by Paul the Apostle had been collected in the Bible and that not all the fourteen collected had been authored by Paul. Jesus watched the Epistle to the Hebrews being clothed with the Apostle's name so as to make it acceptable for publication, and suddenly he laughed. "Even as Paul credits me with attitudes I never held, so now he himself is being credited with letters he never wrote! Truly my Father is just!" But he soon sobered, for all of this only elaborated the distortions of Jesus' own message.

"Let's view some other aspect," Brother Paul suggested. He had liked to think that the fourteen cards of each Tarot suit reflected the fourteen Paulean Epistles in the Bible, but if some of these were invalid—

"Perhaps they are doing better in America," Jesus said.

Brother Paul was startled. This was a gross anachronism; America would not be discovered by Europeans for some centuries yet! Lee had fluffed his line. "Did you say Rome?" Brother Paul inquired, giving him the cue.

"I said America. The opposite side of the globe—but we can get there in a moment."

Sometimes it happened: a mental short circuit that became established. What did the actors in a play do in such a case to correct the situation without alerting the watching audience? There was no audience here, but it seemed a fair analogy. They could not trace true history if they inserted discontinuities.

Brother Paul tried again: "I'm not sure I know that city."

Jesus glanced at him. "More than a city, friend Paul. A *continent*. Come—I will show you."

"Ah—yes," Brother Paul agreed weakly. At least he had tried.

They flew up high, a kilometer, three kilometers, and on up. "It seems you do not know of the Jaredite and Nephite Nations," Jesus said.

"I am afraid I don't." Was there any hope of putting this scene back together, or was precession simply too strong?

"I shall explain while we fly." They were now ten kilometers up, looking down at the drifting clouds; Brother Paul thought poignantly of his un-daughter Carolyn in the airplane, enjoying a similar view. "At the time of the confusion of tongues after the Tower of Babel, a man named Jared and his brother, who was a prophet, importuned the Lord my Father that they and their tribe be spared from the impending disruption. The Lord granted their prayer and directed them to the ocean, where they constructed eight great barges and set sail. Their only inside light was from luminous stones. After almost a year they landed on the shores of America about two thousand four hundred years before my birth."

"2400 B.C.," Brother Paul murmured, fascinated by this strange story from the mouth of the Phantom Jesus. He had never heard a parable like this! Now they were so high he could see the curve of the Earth below. They were flying east over the great land mass of Asia near the edge of the Indian Ocean. What was this Animation coming to?

"In America they multiplied and became a flourishing nation," Jesus continued. "But they fractured into warring factions until after eighteen hundred years they died out. But at just about this time, a second expedition set out from Jerusalem six hundred years before my birth. This was led by a Jewish prophet of the tribe of Manasseh named Lehi together with his family and some friends. They marched to the Arabian Sea and built and provisioned a ship, then sailed east across the South Pacific until they landed on the western coast of America. This was their promised land—but ·like the first colony, they split into two tribes, the Nephite and the Lamanite. The Nephite advanced in the arts of civilization and built prosperous cities while the Lamanites degenerated. They forgot the God of their fathers, became wild nomads, and became benighted in spirit and dark of skin like the accursed children of Cain."

"The children of Cain?" Brother Paul inquired. They were now over the middle of the Pacific, still bearing east.

"The evil ones. The black races," Jesus clarified.

Brother Paul was taken aback. "Do you mean the black races of Africa?"

"The same. They rejected the power of the Holy Priesthood and the Law of God. Thus they have been cursed with black skin to match their black hearts."

This was Jesus Christ talking? Far from it! It had to be Lee the Mormon. Brother Paul had not realized the Mormons viewed the Negro in such a light. "Surely there is some error. Since all people except Noah and his family perished in the Flood, no descendents of Cain would have survived—"

"It carried on through Noah's line, some of that foul blood," Lee insisted. "Ham, the son of Noah, fearing that there would be additional heirs to share the earth after the Flood, conspired with his two brothers Shem and Japhet to castrate their father. But they refused, for they were good sons. So he did it himself when Noah was drunk—"

"The Bible says Ham only saw his father's nakedness!" Brother Paul protested.

"The Bible has been expurgated," Lee said darkly. "But even so, it provides the punishment: the children of Ham became servants to the children of the good sons. Thus the black races achieved their just desserts—"

"I am part black," Brother Paul said. "I had thought that was understood." But he realized now that Lee had played no part in the Dozens Animation where he had made an issue of his race, and the matter had not come up elsewhere. "Am I also cursed?"

Jesus paused in his flight, and from his eyes Lee looked out, shocked. *"You* have black blood?"

"About one-eighth, give or take a smidgen. Technically, I am a light-skinned Negro."

Jesus shook his head. "No, that can't be true. You are a good man!"

"I hope I am a good man, or can become one. But I am also a black man. I don't see the conflict—"

"No!" Jesus cried. "Corruption is not to be tolerated in the sacred places! Am I to throw the moneylenders out of the Temple only to be affronted by such insinuations? You must not joke this way, Paul!"

Brother Paul spread his hands. "I prefer to be neither a joker nor a liar. I'm sorry if it bothers you, but I can not and will not deny my ancestry."

Jesus/Lee turned on him a strange look of disbelief phasing into wrath. "We shall discuss it at another time!" Then he turned away, and Brother Paul sensed a kind of cold withdrawal in him, a rescinding of proffered friendship. Brother Paul had thought he was inured to this type of reaction, but he found it still hurt. Lee was such an intelligent, upstanding, clean-cut person; how could he be a conscious racist? How could he reconcile this with his portrayal of Jesus who preached Salvation for all men, no matter what their birth or their prior sins?

Then he recognized the pattern of reaction: this was similar to a person's response to the news that he must die. First disbelief, then anger. Lee's Mormon religion cursed the black races; the notion that someone close to him could have black ancestory, however small in proportion to the white ancestry—that was fundamentally intolerable.

It would take time for Lee's emotion to run its course, especially since it was not one that the role of Jesus Christ facilitated. But Brother Paul was very much afraid he had lost a friend.

Jesus angled down sharply, and Brother Paul corrected his flight to follow. Down they went toward the western coastline of the double continent of America. Faster and faster: ten thousand kilometers per hour, fifteen thousand, twenty thousand, and still accelerating. Jesus was really working off a head of steam! Twenty five thousand—"Hey, I think we're approaching orbital velocity!" Brother Paul warned. But still Jesus accelerated, passing thirty thousand KPH—and now they were slanting in toward the land only a hundred kilometers ahead. Ninety kilometers ahead. Eighty—each second knocked off more than ten kilos. Still Jesus drove on.

They skimmed the ocean, leveled out, and approached the coastal mountains. Suddenly the peaks loomed large—and there was no time to decelerate. Though these forms had little mass, Brother Paul had the crazy notion that their extreme velocity was magnifying that mass because acceleration toward the speed of light increases the mass of an object toward the infinite. Jesus shot straight in to them, unslowing, and Brother Paul had to follow. But what would happen when—

Collision!

"And it came to pass in the thirty and fourth year . . . there arose a great storm . . . behold, the whole face of the land was changed, because of the tempest and the whirlwinds and the thunderings and the lightnings, and the exceeding great quaking of the whole earth. . . . And many great and notable cities were sunk, and many were burned, and many were shaken till the buildings thereof had fallen to the earth, and the inhabitants thereof were slain, and the places were left desolate. . . . And it came to pass that there was a thick darkness upon all the face of the land . . . it did last for the space of three days. . . ."

"What *is* this?" Brother Paul demanded in the darkness, unable to see anything at all.

"This is the cataclysm that came upon the world at my death," Jesus said beside him.

"That much I gathered," Brother Paul said. "Fire and water and air and earth—the four basic elements running wild in the form of volcanoes and floods and storms and earthquakes. And now a fifth element, darkness. But why did these nations of ancient America have to suffer; they had no knowledge of you or responsibility for your death! And what were you quoting from just now?"

"Chapter 8 of the Third Book of Nephi," Jesus answered. "Of *The Book of Mormon.*"

Suddenly it fell into place. *"The Book of Mormon!"* Brother Paul exclaimed. "Of course!" For Lee, as a Mormon, would naturally believe in the version of history and religion presented by his own Holy Book. Brother Paul had reviewed Mormonism along with the other religions in the course of his studies with the Holy Order of Vision but had not actually read *The Book of Mormon.* Now, belatedly, he recalled the summary. Christianity had come to the New World, and the history of these converted tribes had been recorded on gold plates by the last surviving member of those tribes, a man called Moroni. The tribes had faded out about 400 A.D., and the plates had been buried in the side of a hill in the state of New York, America, until revealed to the founder of the modern Mormons, Joseph Smith, in 1823. Smith, and later Brigham Young, led the Mormons to Utah where most of them remained until the current extra-terrestrial colonization program provided new worlds to conquer.

Well, why *not* view the Mormon version of Christian history? The Mormons had been able to justify many of their claims through discoveries in archaeology, linguistics, and ethnology.

The Book of Mormon did not conflict with the Bible; rather it augmented it.

Light returned upon the blasted land. Jesus stood up tall and spoke, and his voice reverberated through all the continent. "Behold, I am Jesus Christ the Son of God. I created the heavens and the earth, and all things that in them are. I was with the Father from the beginning. I am in the Father, and the Father in me, and in me hath the Father glorified his name."

"I came unto my own, and my own received me not. And the scriptures concerning my coming are fulfilled."

"And as many as have received me, to them have I given to become the sons of God; and even so will I to as many as shall believe in my name, for behold, by me redemption cometh, and in me is the law of Moses fulfilled."

"I am the light and the life of the world. I am the Alpha and Omega, the beginning and the end . . ."

Brother Paul listened, fascinated. Lee had played the part of Jesus-the-man before; now he played the part of Jesus-the-Deity. He was far more effective this way, in his familiar text of *The Book of Mormon.* Yet Brother Paul thought he preferred the man.

"And ye shall offer for a sacrifice unto me a broken heart and a contrite spirit."

And what of racism? Brother Paul wondered. Suppose a black man had a broken heart and a contrite spirit?

Jesus went on to deliver the Sermon on the Mount, adapted directly from the Old World Gospel according to Saint Matthew. Then he commissioned twelve Disciples and founded his Church. It was an auspicious announcement.

At last Jesus and Brother Paul returned to the Old World. They looked at the broader history, seeing the new Church of Christianity infuse the Jewish Diaspora, the region where the Jews had been scattered by the deportations of assorted conquerors. But as the missionary message of the Apostle Paul took hold, there were an increasing number of non-Jewish Christians. The Jewish Christians did not view these with favor—but soon the Gentile Christians outnumbered the Jewish Christians, and eventually that latter faded and disappeared.

Jesus shook his head. "I hardly know what to think," he said. "I preached the dedication of self to the ends for which we live, rather than to the means by which we live. Ceremony misses the heart of religion. Thus I never set special restrictions, but—"

"We are far from Galilee," Brother Paul reminded him.

Indeed they were! Now the center of the stage was Rome, and Rome was in a centuries-long struggle against the empire of Persia to the east. The battle line swung back and forth, and for a time Rome governed sections of Asia Minor, importing their slaves, prisoners, soldiers, and merchants into the Imperial City. With these people came their religion: Mithraism, the faith of the Magi, later called "magicians." They worshiped earth, fire, water, winds, sun and moon; and men completely dominated this religion. Perhaps for this reason, Mithraism spread like wildfire through the Roman Empire after its two-thousand year quiescence and sometime persecution in Asia. Rome never conquered Persia, but the Persian religion bid fair to conquer Rome. Except for the competition of Christianity! The two religions soon became rivals for the spiritual domination of the Empire.

Mithraism had a lot going for it with its essential monotheism and magic. But its exclusion of women weakened it. Christianity did not treat women well, but at least it allowed them to join. Thus the man of the family might worship Mithra, while his wife had to be content with the religion that would accept her, however grudgingly. Slowly and subtly, Christianity gained.

Jesus and Brother Paul came to stand in a Mithraic chapel in the city of Rome. It was a subterranean vault, lighted only by a torch. Its chief feature was a magnificent carving of a bull-slaying scene, brilliantly colored. There were several altars, one of which was evidently used for the sacrifice of birds. There were benches of stone with space allowed for kneeling during the service. The chapel was small, but well made.

"This is pagan, yet I would not condemn it," Jesus decided. "Worship should be an internal experience rather than a public display, and this private chapel is a step in the right direction. I wish I could talk to these people, and tell them of—"

There was noise. "I think they're coming," Brother Paul said.

But it was not a body of worshipers who came. A mob of Roman soldiers charged in. They overturned the altars and attacked the great bas-relief carving with hammers. In moments they had destroyed the chapel.

"But this—this is horrible!" Jesus cried, a tear on his cheek. "Religion is a principle, not a law. Those who have not found the way should be converted, not brutalized! Who has done this thing?"

They soon found out. The Christians had done it. They had made a deal with Gracchus, the Urban Prefect of Rome. Persecution of the Mithraists followed throughout the Empire, and the religion was essentially shut down in favor of Christianity.

"But this is not my way!" Jesus protested. "Religion is inseparable from morality. How can there be persecutions of others in my name?"

Yet it was so. Other religions shared the fate of Mithra, and Christianity was supreme in Rome. As people of the northern European tribes were converted, they brought their pagan values with them and their pagan holidays. Christian titles were applied to these celebrations: Christmas, Easter—but their essence remained pagan and, therefore, were easily commercialized.

"By their fruits ye shall know them," Jesus said sadly. "They have made of my ministry—a business!" Yet he could only watch.

Now Jews were persecuted by Christians and so were heretics: other Christians who differed from the official Church line. Yet the Church itself squabbled and split, following the pattern of the Empire. Later, armies of pagan Christians were sent back to the Holy Land itself to fight civilized non-Christians: the Crusades.

"I cannot stand by and watch!" Jesus cried. "Where is there now the sympathetic understanding I preached, treating others as one would wish to be treated himself? My name has been attached to a monstrosity! I must correct—"

History rushed on heedlessly. The Church fashioned in the name of Jesus no sooner became established than it began to fragment in the nature of human (rather than divine) organizations. Disagreements arose about the specific nature of Christ. Schismatic churches fissioned from the main mass: the Arians, the Nestorians, the Monophysites. Finally the Church itself split into an Eastern and a Western branch. Jesus and Brother Paul chose to follow the West—and it fractured into Catholic and Protestant groups, and the latter into multiple splits. The Lutherans, the Calvinists, Episcopals, Presbyterians, Puritans, Baptists, Congregationalists, Quakers, Methodists—on and on until there seemed to be no counting the individual sects. The nineteenth and twentieth centuries saw no abatement of the proliferation until it reached the situation on contemporary Planet Tarot.

"No, no!" Jesus protested. "I am not certain *any* of these fragments really relate to my ministry. Go back; I want to talk to someone before—"

They went back. "Here," Jesus said, more or less randomly. History paused in place.

France and England, two Christian nations, were making war upon each other. The lot of the majority of people in both nations was worsening. "If I can stop it here, set them right—" Jesus said with somewhat wildeyed hope. "I can not stand idly by; I must do something."

"You can't do anything physically," Brother Paul pointed out. He understood some of Jesus' agony but doubted that it was wise to attempt to change history even in Animation. Precession might make things worse than before. "Maybe you could generate a vision—"

Jesus stopped where he was. They happened to be in a small village of France. "I will speak to the first person I see!"

Soon a country girl came into sight, going about her chores. She was dressed in dirty peasant clothing and could not have been more than thirteen years old. "Lots of luck," Brother Paul murmured sadly.

Jesus appeared to the girl. He manifested as an intangible but visible presence. At first she was amazed, then frightened, but in due course she responded. She began to take action in the world. She got an army and went to fight the British.

Her name was Joan of Arc.

Jesus and Brother Paul watched her fate with intensifying dismay. "She tried to spread the Word of God that I had given her—and they burned her for heresy!" Jesus cried.

"That is the nature of politics and of the Inquisition," Brother Paul said grimly.

Further along, in time and geography, they spied a Christian city adding a new level to a protective wall that had sunk into the porous subsoil. "We shall never make it stable until we offer a sacrifice," the superstitious people said, and the Christian authorities agreed. So they made a vault within the wall, placed a table and chair in it, and loaded the table with toys and candy. Then they brought an innocent little girl to this play area.

"Uh-oh," Brother Paul murmured. He recognized the child: Carolyn, lost as he departed his college Animation. "I don't like this—"

"We cannot interfere," Jesus reminded him.

The child was thrilled with the things. They occupied her whole attention. And while she played merrily, making exclamations of discovery and joy, a dozen masons efficiently and silently covered the vault and finished the wall. The priests blessed the proceedings and went their way—and the wall was stable.

Jesus looked at Brother Paul. "In my name, this too?" he inquired, almost beyond shock.

"Let's go get that girl out of there," Brother Paul said tersely. "We can do it, now, without changing history." But Carolyn had already departed the role by the time they got there; the chamber was empty.

"The center is empty . . ." Brother Paul murmured, beginning a chain of private reflection.

Abruptly Jesus turned to him. "I have been praying to my Father for enlightenment on this problem. I see that my sacrifice did not bring salvation to the world, and this is why I was not released to Heaven when I died. The sins of the world continue unabated, defiling my name and that of my Father. Yet there is also good in the world, as there was in the city of Sodom. I cannot deny you are a good man and an honest one; I must therefore believe you when you inform me you are a child of Cain. How can there be one good son of an accursed race? I have begged God for a resolution to this paradox—and He has answered my prayer."

Brother Paul remained silent, uncertain what was coming. Was this the bargaining-with-God stage of an adjustment that seemed more difficult for this man than death itself? Or was it acceptance?

"It is true you are damned," Jesus continued. "But only one-eighth of you is guilty. Seven-eighths of you is innocent, and that is the portion I have come to know as friend. It is as though a demon inhabits you. Since you were born with that demon, it can not be excised—yet I cannot allow the good in you to be relegated to Hell for the sake of your evil portion. Yet I know it is not possible to separate the good from the evil; both are part of you. I could cast out an ordinary demon or heal an ordinary ailment or forgive an ordinary sin. But I cannot grant a place in Heaven to a Son of Cain. It is beyond the power of the Son to reverse a dictum of the Father."

Jesus' eyes seemed to glow. "But I can save you," he continued. "All that is necessary is for me to assume the burden of your sin. I must go to Hell—so that you may go to Heaven. For the sake of the friendship we have and the good that is in you, O lone man of Sodom, I do this willingly. It is my bargain with God."

Brother Paul understood the context—that of a single good

man in a corrupt environment—but he wished Jesus had not used "Sodom" as an analogy. The word "sodomy" derived from that, and that prior scene with Therion. . . .

"The decision is final," Jesus continued. "The only question remaining is the manner of my entry to the Infernal region. I choose to make it in a way that will help expiate the regenerated sins of the rest of the world. If I am successful this time, the world will soon end, and my confinement in Hell will not be long. But in any event, *you* shall be saved—and for that I am prepared to trade the world. Farewell, Friend." And Jesus/Lee put forth his hand.

Brother Paul, amazed, could only accept that hand and shake it solemnly. Here he had been reacting to a coincidental term and missing the serious import. Jesus was going to Hell—for him! Brother Paul could not at the moment even speculate on the larger meaning of this man's sacrifice.

Jesus turned away. Before him opened out a vista of contemporary America in an area where high technology remained. In the distance was a hydrogen fusion atomic power plant, and there were people manning a computer in the foreground. Jesus walked toward that scene.

Brother Paul realized what Jesus intended. He was going to renew his ministry on Earth, this time utilizing the physical host available to him: the body of Lee. This was the Second Coming.

"Don't *do* it, Jesus!" Brother Paul cried. "They aren't ready for the Kingdom of God! They will crucify you again!"

Jesus paused on the verge of the scene, turning to face Brother Paul momentarily. Bright tears made his eyes lambent. "I know it," he said.

Then he turned again and walked on—into the present. His body solidified about him as he moved into the hall of the computer and around a corner, out of sight.

Brother Paul closed his eyes, remaining where he was. It seemed only a moment before the terrible clamor began, and the hammering of nails.

18

VISION
(IMAGINATION)

*And behold, a Philadelphia lawyer stood up to test him, asking,
'Teacher, what shall I do to inherit eternal life?' Jesus said to him,
'What is the law? How do you interpret it?' The lawyer said, 'You must
love God with all your heart and with all your soul and with all your
strength and with all your mind, and your neighbor as yourself.' Jesus
said, 'Correct! Do this and you will live.' But the lawyer wanted to
justify himself, so he asked, 'And who is my neighbor?'*

*Jesus replied, 'Once there was a man who made a business trip from
New York to Washington. He stopped at a restaurant to eat, and when
he returned to his car a hijacker rose up from the back seat, put a gun to
his head, and forced him to drive to a deserted alley where he shot him
in the stomach, took his wallet with all his money and identification,
and drove away in his car, leaving him dying on the pavement.'*

*'A priest came through that alley by chance, and saw the man, and
stepped over him and went on, averting his gaze from the blood,
muttering something about being late for his service. Then a young
woman passed, a secretary; she heard him moan and was horrified, and
skirted him and got away as fast as possible. Then there came a
garbageman, stinking of his trade, a son of the race of Cain, black as a
tarred feather. When the wounded man saw him, he said to himself,
"This nigger will surely finish me off!"'*

*'But the black man had been mugged himself in the past, and had
compassion on the businessman, and stopped and cleaned up his*

· 368 ·

wound and picked him up and put him in his garbage truck and drove
him to a doctor and said, "I don't know who this guy is, but he needs
help bad. If he can't pay you, I'll make it good next payday; here's five
bucks to start off."'

Jesus turned to the lawyer. 'Now which of these three people, do you
think, was the best neighbor to the suffering man?' The lawyer said,
'The nigger.' And Jesus said to him, 'Go and do likewise.'

Brother Paul stood amid the temporary chaos of shifting Animations. Jesus was gone, surely to Hell—but what of Lee? Had he
stepped out of Animation—or was he stuck in a self-made
inferno?

It did not seem wise to take a chance. It was possible to set up a
given Animation more or less by choice, but once inside it, control
or departure became problematical. As with boarding an airplane
—as he had done!—it might be the right or wrong vehicle, but
there was no getting off until it landed. Wherever that might be,
safely or in flames. Lee might never escape Hell without help.

Brother Paul concentrated on a virtually intangible object: Lee's
likely concept of Hell. It was probably a fairly artistic, literary
notion, definitely Christian but not necessarily Mormon, for
that would be too obvious. What Hell would a Mormon envision
Jesus Christ attending? That was where Brother Paul needed
to go.

The scene firmed around him. It was a field, half-plowed, about
a fifth of a hectare in extent. Beyond it, to what he assumed was
the east, the sun was rising in the sky. In the distance stood a
tower, seeming to lie directly under the sun—perhaps the same
tower he had seen in his first Tarot visions. "The Tower of Truth,"
he murmured.

He looked to the west and saw a deep valley with dangerous
ditches and an ugly building in the lowest reaches. His field lay
between tower and dungeon, the only arable land in sight. But he
had no horse or ox to draw his plow; he would have to go to a
neighbor to borrow his team, and that meant leaving his field
unattended.

Now a motley crowd of people moved along the slope toward
his field. Exactly his problem: they were apt to trample it flat,
ruining yesterday's plowing, if he didn't stay here to ward them off.

Then he had a notion. Maybe some of them would help him plow!

But as they came closer, he lost confidence. The people seemed to be drifting aimlessly. Some were fat, others sickly, and others morose; none of them looked like reliable workers.

From the other direction came a more promising prospect: a pilgrim in pagan clothing with a sturdy staff. As the Animation would have it, the pilgrim arrived at Brother Paul's field just as the throng surged in from the other side.

"Whence come ye?" someone cried.

"From Sinai," the pilgrim replied. "And from our Lord's sepulchre. I have been a time in Bethlehem and Babylon and Armenia and Alexandria and many other places."

"Do you know anything of a Saint named Truth?" someone asked eagerly. "Can you tell us where he lives?"

The pilgrim shook his head. "God help me, I have never heard anyone ask after *him* before! I don't know—"

"I'm looking for Truth," Brother Paul said. "I saw his tower a moment ago. I can point out the way."

They looked at him dubiously. "You, a simple plowman? Who are you?"

"I am Paul Plowman," he said—and was shocked to hear himself say it. Now he recognized this scene: it was from the *Vision of Piers Plowman,* a fifteenth century epic poem by William Langland. And *he* was stuck in the title role!

"Yes, Paul," the people said. "We'll pay you to take us there."

But that wasn't really where he wanted to go. Not right now. First he had to locate Lee; then he could search out the Tower, now hidden behind clouds. Lee was more likely down in the Dungeon of Wrong, this Animation's version of Hell.

But now that he was in this vision, Brother Paul found himself constrained to follow the script. But maybe he could stall them while he figured out some way to rescue Lee.

"No, I won't take any money, not a farthing," he told them. "I will tell you the way—it's over there to the east—but I must stay here to plow my field."

They looked toward the east. The clouds were thickening into a storm. "We need a leader. You'll have to come with us."

"I have a whole half acre to harrow by the highway!" Brother Paul protested in the alliterative mode of the epic. "But if you help me to prepare and sow my field, then I'll show you the road." That should turn these idlers off!

"That would be a long delay," a young lady protested. She was in a fancy dress and wore the kind of hat called a wimple. Amaranth, naturally. And the pilgrim was Therion. "What would we women work at while waiting?"

Now there was a challenge! Obviously this lady had seldom soiled her hands with common labor. "Some must sew the sack to stop the seed from spilling," he told her. "You lovely ladies with your long fingers—"

"Christ, it's a good idea," agreed a knight—another version of Therion. "I'll help too! But no one ever taught me how to drive a team."

Then they were all volunteering. It seemed the plowman's job would soon be done! Which was not exactly what he wanted. Well, he was stuck with it now.

But it turned out that many people were not good workers. Brother Paul had to keep after them, bawling them out, before the job was done.

He remembered that this epic meandered through a great deal of symbolic dialogue, while people dubbed Conscience, Reason, Wisdom, and Holy Church debated moral issues with others titled Liar, Falsehood, Flattery, and Mede the Maid. It might be a great work of medieval literature, but it wasn't taking him where he wanted to go. He had to break away from this story and seek another that would serve his purpose better.

Probably a direct effort wouldn't work; the Animations tended to precess when opposed as he knew to his chagrin. But maybe a slanting push, a shift into something similar, that might cast him into a more suitable role. . . .

What offered? Piers Plowman had tried to get men to earn their salvation by reforming themselves. Was there another epic with similar thrust and symbolism?

Suddenly it came to him. *"Pilgrim's Progress!"* he exclaimed. Bunyan's allegory even shared the alliterative *P!* In it, the character Christian sought the celestial city, buttressed by such bit players as Help, Worldly Wiseman, Legality and Evangelist. Would anyone know the difference if he phased into that vision? The genuine, fictional, Piers Plowman could take over here. Why not give it a quiet try! Not a hard shove, just a nudge. . . .

It worked! Brother Paul found himself in the Valley of Humiliation of *Pilgrim's Progress*. He was alone, but carried a good sword. He should be able to make his way to—

His thoughts were interrupted by the appearance of a monster. Oh, no! Now he had to face the hazards of *this* vision, and they were no more pleasant than those of the others. This was the thing called Apollyon, and he knew he could not escape it. He would have to fight it if he could not bluff it back. So he stood his ground.

The monster was hideous; it had scales like those of a fish, wings like a dragon's, bear's feet, a lion's mouth, and a bellyful of fire. Its face, however, seemed familiar: could this be Therion again?

Apollyon gazed on him disdainfully, blowing out evil smoke. "Whence come you? and whither are you bound?"

"I am from the City of Destruction," Brother Paul replied, "which is the place of all evil, and am going to the City of Zion." He was locked into the action and dialogue of the classic; only his thoughts were free. What a circuitous route he was following to locate Lee's Hell!

Apollyon spread out his legs to straddle the full breadth of the way. "Prepare thyself to die; for I swear by my infernal den, that thou shalt go no further; here will I spill thy soul."

With that the monster threw a flaming dart at Brother Paul's breast. But Brother Paul had a shield, round and coppery like a great coin (had it been there a moment ago?) and intercepted the missile.

He drew his sword—but Apollyon was already hurling more darts at him. Brother Paul tried to block them off, but they came like hail, magically multiplied. One flew directly at his face; he threw up his sword to fend it off, not daring to raise the shield and expose his legs, and it wounded his hand. Brother Paul gave a cry of pain and shook it loose; the wound was superficial, but it stung like fire. But then another dart speared his left foot, making him dance about in agony. What was *on* those barbs—essence of red ant, hornet, and scorpion? His shield dropped low—and a third dart caught him in the head, just above the hairline on the right.

Brother Paul fell back. He was being destroyed! He had somehow thought he was invulnerable to attack by mythical monsters since he was only passing through. False notion! The Animations could and did kill; he had known that from the outset. Apollyon might be a creature of the imagination of John Bunyan, but this was the realm of imagination, and the monster was being played by another real person. If *Pilgrim's Progress* decreed the death of this character, Brother Paul was in trouble. Unless he could shift stories again, get into a surviving role—

He tried to concentrate on that, but could not. The dreadful darts were still coming at him, and his head, hand, and foot still hurt. A trickle of blood was dribbling into his right eye. Apollyon was striding forward to match Brother Paul's retreat; any attention diverted to other literature could be immediately fatal here!

No help for it: he would have to fight right here and now. He obviously could not win by playing the monster's game; he would have to convert it to his own style. That style, of course, was judo; let him get his bare hands on Apollyon, and—

But that hadn't worked too well against the dragon Temptation back in the Seven Cups. Judo was geared primarily to handling *men,* not monsters. So maybe it was best to save that for a last resort and use his sword meanwhile.

Brother Paul stood and fought, swinging his sword back and forth, forth and back in flashing arcs. It was a good weapon, beautifully balanced, and its edge was magically sharp, and this was a heroic fantasy Animation. Apollyon retreated, fearing this new imperative. Brother Paul advanced, trying to cut the monster in half.

But the sword was also heavy. His arm was tiring. If he didn't cut down the enemy soon, he would wear himself out, and then be vulnerable. So he doubled his effort, trying to finish it now.

Apollyon stepped in close. Brother Paul dropped his shield and swung a two-handed blow at the monster's head to cleave him in two lengthwise. And hesitated in mid-stroke: it was Apollyon he aimed at—but would it be Therion he killed?

In that moment Apollyon dodged to the side, turned about, caught Brother Paul's arms in his own, emitted a stunning scream KIIAAIII!—and executed a perfect *ippon seoi nage* shoulder throw. Brother Paul, fool that he was, had walked right into it! These throws had been designed to handle warriors in armor and to disarm armed attackers. He had been beaten at his own game.

The fall was bruising. Brother Paul's sword flew out of his hand, and the wind was knocked out of him. Half conscious, he felt the monster dropping down expertly to put him in a holddown. It was *Kami shiho gatame,* the upper four quarter hold, one of the most effective in the judo arsenal. The monster was bearing down, putting the weight of his torso on Brother Paul's head, pinning it, forcing him to turn his face to the side in order to prevent suffocation. The fish scales of Apollyon's body stank in Brother Paul's nostrils and rasped against his cheek. He tried to struggle to throw the monster off, but the hold was cruelly tight. Apollyon really knew his business! No man could break this hold!

This was no judo match, however. The monster was not about to let him up in thirty seconds in polite victory. "I am sure of thee now," Apollyon said, pressing down harder. The weight of his body increased magically, becoming more than the mere position could possibly account for. Brother Paul thought his skull was going to crack open. His eyeballs were being squeezed; they seemed about to pop out of his head. He was in a vice, and the invisible handle was being cranked tighter. . . .

Then he saw the sword. It had not flown far; it was within a meter, lying flat on the ground. Had he turned his head the other way, he would not have been able to see it. Pure luck! Desperately he flung out his left hand—and caught the handle.

"Rejoice not against me, O mine enemy," he gasped. "When I fall I shall arise." Then he made a left-handed stab at the monster's side. It was not a really effective stroke because Brother Paul had poor vision and poorer leverage, but the good sword gouged out a patch of scales and laid open the dark inner flesh.

Apollyon gave a cry of agony. His hold loosened, and Brother Paul heaved him off. Brother Paul rolled to his hands and knees, shaking his aching head, and saw brown ichor leaking from the monster's side. Brother Paul raised himself to his knees, gripped the sword again in both hands, and raised it high. "Nay," he cried. "In all these things we are more than conquerors through Him that loved us." And he brought the sword down in a conclusive smash.

But Apollyon, defeated, scuttled back, escaping the blow. "Spare me, great Hero!" he cried. "I will make it worth your mercy!"

Brother Paul hesitated. Was this in the script? Could he trust the monster—*or* the man who played it? Well, he still had the good sword and could use it the moment Apollyon made a false move. The monster seemed to be out of darts anyway. "What do you offer, O fiend?"

"Information!" Apollyon cried eagerly. "I know these realms as you do not. I can direct you to anything you seek. Riches, weapons, pretty nymphs—"

Hm. "I am looking for someone in Hell."

The monster spread his wings, momentarily startled. "I could have sent you there ere now, had you not thwarted me."

"I don't want to be *sent* to Hell—I want to rescue someone who may be there. Locate him for me, and you can go free."

Apollyon fluttered his wings again in a gesture very like a shrug. "I see you know little of Hell, O mortal! If it took you such a tussle to overcome me (and then only because I neglected to kick your blade aside), who am the least of fiends, you would survive only seconds in the infernal region. You would need to have a thorough comprehension of the history and psychology of Hell before you could even guess where your friend might be, for it is larger than all the world, and then you still durst not venture there yourself."

Brother Paul considered. The monster was making sense! "Very well—tell me that history and psychology."

A snort of fire issued from the leonine nostrils. "Mortal, that would require a lifetime!"

"Abridge it," Brother Paul suggested, lifting his sword.

Apollyon sighed smokily. "I will try. I believe John Milton said it best—"

"You are familiar with the works of Milton?" Brother Paul asked with surprise.

"Naturally. He and Bunyan were contemporaries, the two great figures of the Puritan Interlude of seventeenth century British literature. The one wrote the great allegory, the other the great epic. Some scholars (bastards!) choose to ignore Bunyan in favor of Milton, but—"

"Yes, all right, okay," Brother Paul said. "Tell me about Milton's Hell."

"Well, if I may quote from *Paradise Lost*—"

"Not the whole epic!" Brother Paul protested.

"I will edit the selection," Apollyon assured him, though he evidently had had no intention of doing that before. Then the monster set himself up, spread his bear feet like an actor on a stage, and declaimed:

> *The infernal serpent; he it was whose guile . . .*
> *Had cast him out from heaven, with all his host*
> *Of rebel angels, by whose aid aspiring*

To set himself in glory above his peers,
He trusted to have equaled the most high,
If he opposed; and with ambitious aim
Against the throne and monarchy of God
Raised imperious war in heaven and battle proud
With vain attempt. Him the almighty power
Hurled headlong flaming from the ethereal sky,
With hideous ruin and combustion down
To bottomless perdition, there to dwell
In adamantine chains and penal fire,
Who durst defy the omnipotent to arms.

"Fine," Brother Paul said. "I appreciate the grandeur of Milton —but what about Hell?"

"I'm getting to it," Apollyon said, annoyed. "Satan picks himself up in the nether chaos and says:

. . . What though the field be lost?
All is not lost; the unconquerable will
And study of revenge, immortal hate,
And courage never to submit or yield:
And what is else not to be overcome?
That glory never shall his wrath or might
Extort from me. To bow and sue for grace
. . . that were low indeed.
So spake the apostate angel, though in pain
Vaunting aloud, but racked with deep despair. . . .
Forthwith upright he rears from off the pool. . . .
Then with expanded wings he steers his flight
. . . till on dry land he lights. . . .
Is this the region, this the soil, the clime,
Said then the lost archangel, this the seat
That we must change for heaven, this mournful gloom
For that celestial light? Be it so. . . .
. . . Farewell, happy fields,
Where joy for ever dwells: hail, horrors, hail
Infernal world, and thou, profoundest hell
Receive thy new possessor: one who brings
A mind not to be changed by place or time.
The mind is its own place, and in itself
Can make a heaven of hell, a hell of heaven.
. . . Here at least we shall be free; . . .
Here we may reign secure: . . .
Better to reign in hell, than serve in heaven.

Brother Paul nodded his head, impressed. "Yes, I can appreciate Satan's determination. He didn't give up at all; he had a fighting heart. So he fashioned Hell into a place of his liking—"

"Precisely," Apollyon said. "Now how can you expect to descend into this Hell, to the infernal city of Pandemonium, and gain any power over the fallen Archangel? He defied God Himself; only if your power rivals that of God can you hope to extract any soul from Hell. Frankly, you don't measure up."

"Well, I'll just have to find a way," Brother Paul said.

Now Apollyon spread his dragon's wings and lofted himself into the air. He sped away, and in a moment he was lost in the distance.

What now? It would be foolish to venture directly into Hell; Apollyon had shown him that. Yet he could not in conscience give up his mission. Was there any alternative?

He snapped his fingers. "Dante!" he exclaimed. *"He* went to Hell—on a guided tour. He had a guide, the Roman poet Virgil. If I had a similar guide—"

But Dante had not sought to extract anyone from Hell—least of all a prisoner of the status of Jesus. Virgil would probably not have assisted him in such an attempt, and it would have voided his visitor's visa.

Brother Paul would be better off taking his chances alone. If he could sneak in—

No! That would be dishonest. The end did *not* justify the means. Jesus himself would not accept rescue by questionable means. If he could not do it legitimately, he could not do it at all. So—

So he would go to the top—to Satan Himself if need be—and ask permission. This was, after all, a special situation.

You're crazy! a voice inside him cried. Was it his conscience —or his diabolic self? *Satan will grab you and put YOU in Hell!*

Um, yes. So he would have to be extremely careful. But still he had to make the attempt. He concentrated. "Lord of Hell! Prince of Darkness! I crave audience. . . ."

And the Sphere of Fire manifested about him. There was light like a blazing river, coursing through its winding channel, throwing out bright sparks that glowed like rubies. If this were the River Styx—or, rather, the River Acheron—then Hell was a much prettier place than he had imagined.

Well, maybe his imagination had been fantasy! He had heeded

the propaganda of the Angelic side and pictured Hell as ugly; no doubt the souls in Hell were told Heaven was ugly too. Black is white, white is black, doublespeak, mindthink, whatever. Which was beside the point. Now all he had to do was locate the Demonic headquarters—

As he watched, the radiant river changed course and formed into a spiral, a vortex, whose center shone like the sun so brilliantly that he was unable to look directly at it. The outer loops became patterned, each swirl resembling a fresh flower—yet these flowers were winged creatures. Satan's host of demons? Strange; even though he knew them for what they were, they still looked beautiful!

One detached itself and flew to him. It was a female spirit, lovely beyond anything he had supposed possible for Hell, seeming absolutely chaste. "Paul," she called, as she came to rest beside him. He stood, he realized, on the top of a mountain, facing the glowing white rose of figures as though before a whirlpool in the sky, and she had come from that celestial image.

She was familiar. Amaranth, of course, the chronic temptress. Naturally she would turn up in Hell! Yet her face shone with its own pure radiance, and she was beautiful in a special way, more like an angel than—

"Where *is* this?" he demanded abruptly. "Who *are* you?"

She smiled graciously. "This is the Emphyrean, the Tenth Heaven—and I am Mary."

"Tenth what?" he asked stupidly. "Mary who?"

"The Tenth Heaven of Paradiso," she replied with another gentle smile. "Mary, mother of Jesus."

Something had gone wrong. "I—thought I was in Hell."

She looked at him with tolerant wonder. "You gaze upon the Court of God—and confuse it with Hell?"

"Precession," he muttered. Then, trying to reorient: "I meant to seek out Satan to—to make a plea. I—have no business in Heaven. I—must have stumbled through the wrong door."

"Cannot the Lord of Heaven serve as well?" Mary inquired. She looked familiar in a hauntingly evocative way, not at all like the person who portrayed her. Maybe she had been patterned after a painting.

Brother Paul considered. "I, uh, had not intended to bother God, uh, at this time." He was here in Animation to judge whether the God of Tarot was genuine; why did he hesitate now that he had a chance for a direct interview? Was it because he was unprepared (and who was *ever* really prepared for that encounter?)—or because he feared that beyond that unearthly radiance in the center of the rose of light was an answer like that he had found within his glowing Grail? All he was sure of was that he did not want to interview God right now!

"Perhaps if you informed me of the nature of your quest . . . ," Mary suggested compassionately.

He clutched at that with grateful speed. "Uh, yes. It—he—I —that is, your son Jesus—he meant to—" He could not continue. This was ludicrous!

"Jesus is absent at present," Mary said. "He has a mission with the living, and we have not had recent news of him. I am concerned, as a mother must be."

"He's in Hell," Brother Paul blurted. "He—I was slated to go there, but because of our friendship he went in my stead, and now I want to get him *out."*

She contemplated him with angelic solemnity. "You wish to exchange places with him?"

"No! I don't want either one of us in Hell! I feel his gesture was mistaken because I am not destined for Hell. Not for the reason he thought anyway. So I want to persuade him of that and take him out—if I can find him."

She considered. "This would be most irregular. Hell cannot hold him without his consent. Yet, as his mother, I am grieved to have him suffer. I know he is willful; I remember when he ran away as a child of twelve and picked an argument with Temple priests—he never was too keen on some of the activities of the Temple, the moneychangers, you know. . . ." She trailed off, her eyes unfocused reminiscently.

"If I could just *talk* to him," Brother Paul said.

Mary made a sudden decision. "I think God would not object if you made a little survey of the spirit regions. There is such a constant influx of personnel, we tend to lose track. Are you apt at counting?"

"I don't care *how* many spirits there are in—" He stopped, seeing her silent reproach. He brought out his calculator. "Yes, I can count," he said.

"But you would have to be circumspect," she cautioned. "God does not like to have disturbances. If anyone became suspicious—"

"That's the point! I don't want to sneak in, I just want to go and speak to—"

"You will go openly," she said. "If you wait for a pass from Satan you may wait forever. Bureaucratic delay is one of the specialties of Hell. But as a surveyor, you can begin immediately. God understands."

In short, this was a method of cutting red tape. He would have to do it. "Uh—is there a map? I wouldn't want to get lost—"

"You will need no map," she assured him. "There are ten Heavens in Paradiso, each indicated by a planet or star, for the Angels, Saints, Righteous Rulers, Warrior Spirits, Theologians, Lovers, and such. You have merely to descend past them in order, making your notations. You will then be atop the mountain that is Purgatorio with its seven levels for the Lustful, Gluttonous, Avaricious, Slothful, Angry, Envious, and Proud. Then, inside the Earth, you must pass around Satan and enter the deepest ring of Hell: the icy realm of the traitors. After that you have merely to ascend to each of the other rings. There are nine in all, and in one of them you will find him." She looked at him with disturbing intensity. "Take care, Paul."

"I will," he agreed. What *was* there about her? Not that she was the mother of Christ; he had seen her weeping at the base of the Cross, there at the Place of Skulls, and there had been no magic. Something more personal—

He cut off the speculation. He had a job to do. He looked about—and Mary was gone. She had rejoined the Heavenly Throng.

Very well: he would take a census of Dante's Paradise. Except —how could he count these sparkling myriads, let alone record them? All the souls of all the people who had ever existed! But as he looked at his calculator, he saw numbers appearing, changing. It was totaling them itself, filing them in its little memory. All he had to do was look.

He started down the slope. He seemed to be made of spirit stuff himself so that he more or less floated with no danger of falling. The great circles of the Heavenly Host receded, looking like the stars of the Milky Way, and now he became aware of their music: "Gloria in Excelsis. . . ."

Rapidly he traversed the regions of the Fixed Stars, Saturn, Jupiter, Mars, the Sun, Venus, Mercury, and the Moon and arrived at the boundary of Purgatorio. He really would have liked to interview some of the souls in these Heavens, but feared that any delay would imperil his other mission. He did not want Jesus to burn in Hell any longer than necessary.

Purgatorio, however, was much more solid and somber. The atmosphere was gray, the shadows deep; gnarly trees reached high in nocturnal silhouette. He felt the weight of physical mass settle about his own being. No angelic choirs here!

This was the Seventh Level, the top of the grim mountain, the habitat of Lust. He had no need to tarry here any longer than needed to record the spirits. He already knew the mischief blind lust could lead to.

Then he saw a wagon or chariot, set by a tree. From the sky a great eagle swooped, diving to attack, once, twice—but it sheered off at the last moment, and feathers floated over the vehicle. A crack opened in the ground, and a dragon strove to climb out of its depths. The monster's tail swung up and smashed the chariot, stirring up the feathers and leaving the bottom knocked out.

But lo! the chariot regenerated. Each broken part of it sprouted animal flesh: grotesque monsters, winged, horned, serpentine bodied, ferocious. And upon this half-living platform appeared a woman, busty, brassy, bold-eyed, looking about acquisitively. Her eye caught Brother Paul's, and she gave him a wanton come-hither signal, patting the chariot beside her. A prostitute, surely, played by the one who played all such roles: for this was the Circle of Lust.

Brother Paul was not tempted this time. But even as she gestured to him, a huge man appeared by her side, a veritable giant. He began to kiss the harlot, and she met him eagerly—yet simultaneously kept an eye on Brother Paul. The giant followed her gaze, saw Brother Paul, and scowled, now resembling the monster Apollyon. He seemed about to jump down from the chariot and attack his supposed rival, but Brother Paul quickly retreated. He was wasting time here anyway. Then the giant took a whip to the monster portion of the chariot and drove it some distance away. As soon as the animals were under way, he turned his whip on his paramour, scourging her savagely. Brother Paul moved on. Once he was done with this mission, he would have to read the *Comedy* and discover who these people were and what their little act meant.

He crossed the river Lethe, wading through the shallowest section he could find, careful not to drink even one drop. The last thing he needed now was to forget his mission! He passed on down through the gloomy wilderness, making sure his calculator was recording all the souls there. This was certainly a contrast to Paradise! There were not too many overt tortures, apart from a group of naked people walking through a fire, but there was a great deal of misery. The Gluttonous of the Sixth Circle were being starved; the Avaricious were without creature comforts; the Slothful stood perpetually idle—and bored. The Proud, down in the first Circle, were bearing heavy stones up a hill.

If this were only Purgatorio, what was Inferno like? He was about to find out!

Brother Paul came to the place where Satan's huge legs projected from the ground. But it was only a statue; the living Devil was evidently off duty at the moment. Or on business elsewhere; the Evil One was *never* off duty! Between those legs and the ground was a narrow space; this was the entry to Inferno: Hell as Dante conceived it.

Brother Paul made his climb. At first it was down, but soon his weight shifted, and he had to turn about and proceed headfirst. He was passing through the center of the world right at Satan's colossal genital! Now he was climbing up—into Hell.

It grew cold. When he emerged into an open chamber, he was about chest high on the Devil-statue and in a frozen lake. Dante's Inferno, ironically, was locked in ice.

Shivering from more than the cold, Brother Paul moved out across the lake. The ice was so frigid it was not slippery; it might as well have been rock. He paused to look back—and for the first time he saw Satan in perspective. Hugely spreading bat's wings —and three faces, one white, one crimson, one black. The black face was looking right at Brother Paul. One eye winked, deliberately.

This was no statue. This was Satan Himself!

All Brother Paul could think of at this moment was: suppose Satan had had flatulence at the time Brother Paul was traversing the nadir? He would have been blown to Kingdom come!

Brother Paul turned about and ran. There was no pursuit. And why should there be? The only escape from Hell was back the way he had come—and Satan would be there, corking the bottle.

Toward the edge of the lake, he discovered bodies. They were frozen in the ice, face up, staring—yet not quite unconscious. These were the Traitors to their Benefactors.

Brother Paul hurried on, letting the calculator make its own tally. It hardly seemed that Satan had been fooled, but so long as Brother Paul remained free, he would act. Maybe this would turn out to be his own Hell: the tabulations for each section would be fouled up so that he would have to do them over, and over, and over, touring Hell perpetually.

The edge of the pit that contained the lake was ringed by giants—not as huge as three-faced (not two-faced?) Satan, but six times the height of a normal man. Each had a beard some two meters long, covering his hairy chest, so that it was hard to tell where the beard left off and chest began.

Brother Paul approached the nearest. "I'm doing a survey," he called, showing his calculator. He was not sure the giant could either see it or hear him. "If you will assist me to the Eighth Circle. . . ."

To his surprise, the giant bent and extended one hand. Brother Paul climbed aboard and was quickly lifted to the top of the cliff. "Thank you," he said—but the giant turned his back, ignoring him.

He moved on, passing people who had their arms, legs or even heads cut off—yet they remained conscious and in pain. Falsifiers of some sort. Would Lee be among these because he had acted the role of Jesus? What was the definition of falsification? Surely not this!

Where *would* Lee be? Apollyon had been right: there were so many categories of evil in Hell and so many souls in each that he might search of the rest of his natural (or even his immortal) life and not find his man. Maybe that was what Satan had in mind. Brother Paul had to get smart and narrow it down, drastically. Carnal Sin? No, not Lee! Miser? No, probably not. Wrath? Well, maybe. . . .

Brother Paul paused, struck by the obvious that had not been obvious until this moment. It was not Lee and not Jesus he should be orienting on, but the *combination*. What part of Hell would this pair be in? Surely not among the Heretics, though after what he had seen of the Church Jesus' name had spawned—

Suddenly he had it. "The Schismatics!" he exclaimed. "Those who separated from the Mother Church." That would fit both Lee and Jesus—for Lee was a Mormon, certainly a schismatic sect, and Jesus himself could no longer accept without reservation the church that had tortured and even killed in his name.

The Schismatics were right here in the Eighth Circle along with the Seducers, Sorcerors, Thieves, Hypocrites, Liars, Evil Counselors, and other Frauds. Brother Paul did not agree with Dante's classifications, but had to work within the framework that obtained here. After all, the Romans had crucified Jesus between two thieves. When in Rome, when in Hell. . . .

He closed in on the Schismatic region, searching for Jesus/Lee's face. It seemed to be morning here—time varied magically in Hell—and a number of souls were rising from their uncomfortable slumbers on the rocks and ground. They seemed to be queuing up to pass around a certain big rock. Breakfast, maybe?

Why should anyone need to sleep or eat in Hell? They were all spirits! Well, neither literature nor religion had ever felt the need to make sense!

Brother Paul walked parallel to the line, his calculator tabulating merrily. The men were naked, so he could not tell from observation what schism they were associated with. He wondered where the women were; didn't any females belong to the sects Dante frowned on? Dante had been fairly open-minded for his times, but circa 1300 was not a liberal period in Europe, as they had seen.

He circled the rock in the other direction from that taken by the line of souls. He came upon activity at the far side—

God, no! he cried internally. But it was so: a demon was wielding a great sword, striking at the people coming through. Not randomly, but with malicious precision. On one subject he lopped off the ears and nose; on another he laid open the chest; the next he disemboweled with a terrible vertical slash from neck to crotch.

The souls suffered these injuries without resistance, evasion, or even complaint. Gasping with agony, they clutched themselves and staggered on, bleeding. One had his entrails looping out through the wound in his stomach, dangling almost to the ground—yet he continued moving.

Brother Paul stepped out to intercept him, for the man looked familiar. "Sir, let me help you!" Yet he was not sure what he could do in the face of this horror.

"There is no help," the man responded. "This punishment is eternal for me. Help he who follows me; he is new here, not yet injured."

"Who are you?" Brother Paul asked, recognizing the actor now: Therion.

"I am Mahomet, founder of the Moslem Schism."

"Mohammed! But you're not even a Christian! You have no business in a Christian Hell!"

The man made a wry smile, forgetting his agony for an instant. "You may know that, I may know it. But Allah seems to have another opinion." He paused to suck in some of his gut. "Of course, Dante is in Muslim Hell, as befits an Infidel. So perhaps—"

"Paul!"

Brother Paul whirled around at the sound of his name. "Jesus!"

Jesus was a horrible sight. The demon had slashed him in the pattern of a cross, exposing his pulsating lungs, heart, liver, spleen, and part of a kidney. Yet he lived and moved. "What are you doing here, Paul? I thought I had exonerated you."

Brother Paul's shock at the sight of these gruesome wounds translated into baseless anger. "Nobody can exonerate me but *me!* I don't consider myself a sinner in the way you suppose—and if I did, I'd damn well suffer the punishment myself! No one else can be my surrogate!"

Jesus was silent. "Perhaps I can mediate," Mahomet suggested. "I have no direct interest in your quarrel."

"Who are you?" Jesus inquired.

"I am Mahomet, Prophet of Allah."

"I don't believe I know of you."

Mahomet smiled—a somewhat grisly effort since he was still holding in his guts. "Naturally not, Prophet. I came six hundred years after your time."

"'Prophet'? I don't understand—"

"I call you that because that is how I regard you. There have been many prophets in the history of men, and you were—*are*—a great one. But the final prophecy to date is mine."

"Uh, perhaps a change of subject—" Brother Paul interjected.

"No, this man interests me," Jesus said. "There is nothing like a good philosophical discussion to take a man's mind from his physical problems. Please tell me about yourself, Prophet Mahomet."

Brother Paul shut up. What these men needed most at the moment was relief from their physical agony—and maybe while they talked he would be able to think of a more persuasive argument to get Jesus *out* of here.

"Gladly, Prophet Jesus! I was born in the city of Mecca—you

may know of it as Mekkeh or some other variant—570 years after your own birth. That's approximate because of changes and errors in the calendar. My father died before my birth, and my mother passed on six years later, so I was raised by relatives."

"You had no father?" Jesus inquired.

"In a manner of speaking," Mahomet agreed. "Allah may be the ultimate sire of us all, but a man requires human paternity too—a man to protect him and show him right from wrong."

"Yes!" Jesus agreed. "That he may not be mocked."

"That he may pass from the space of time in the womb when his life is a blank, and be shown how to seek refuge in the God of men, from the mischief of the slinking prompter who whispers in the hearts of men."

"The mischief of Satan," Jesus agreed. "You speak well, Prophet."

Mahomet started to shrug, winced as his guts shifted, and aborted the motion. "I speak only to guide men to the straight path, the path Allah favors."

"Did you—marry? How did you die?"

"I married as a young man of 25," Mahomet said. "She was a rich widow fifteen years my senior, but a good woman, and she put her commercial affairs in my hands. I was grieved when she died when I was 49."

"But how could a Prophet share his love of God with a mere woman?" Jesus asked.

"How could he fail to do so? Was not your blessed mother a woman, beloved of God?"

Jesus was not wholly satisfied. "What do you know of my mother?" And Brother Paul, who had met the lady in Paradiso, wondered also.

"She left her people and went out east alone," Mahomet said. "God sent his spirit to her in the guise of a handsome man. When she saw him she was alarmed, fearing mischief. 'May the Merciful protect me! If you fear God, leave me alone!" she cried. But he replied 'I am the messenger of your God, and have come to give you a holy son.' And she, still alarmed, asked 'How shall I bear a child when I am a virgin, untouched by man?' But he said—"

"Uh, I'm not sure—" Brother Paul broke in, remembering the manner Therion had Animated questions of sex before.

"But he said, 'Such is the will of your God,'" Mahomet continued firmly. "'Your son shall be a sign to mankind, a blessing from Me. This is My decree.' Thereupon she conceived you, and the rest followed. Mary was blessed above all women —and blessed was the man Joseph who married her and gave the child of God a home. I would have had no shame to dwell in the house of Joseph the Carpenter, rather than in the house of an uncle."

"Yes," Jesus agreed, and it was evident what an impact these kind words from this unexpected source were having on him. "How did you come to serve directly, Prophet?"

"I was troubled by the iniquities I perceived about me," Mahomet said. "God had revealed His Will to the Jews and the Christians through chosen apostles. But the Jews corrupted the Scriptures, and the Christians perpetrated atrocities in the name of Jesus—"

"Yes!" Jesus echoed fervently.

"One day when I was forty, in a vision the Angel Gabriel came to me. 'Recite!' he charged me, and when I did not understand he repeated it three times, and said 'Recite in the name of God, who created man from clots of blood.' Then I understood that I must recite God's words, and so I spoke them and wrote them down and called that book *The Recital* or the Koran. Actually it was put together from my writings after my time, by idiots who simply arranged the pieces in order from the longest to the shortest, but still it serves."

"The Bible's organization is little better," Jesus murmured. "Accounts of my life and sayings were written a century after my time and ascribed to my Disciples and called Gospel. The major portion of my life and ministry was omitted. But I know now that matters little, for the people who call themselves Christians do not pay attention even to the fragments that were recorded. They do not love their neighbors." He grimaced. "And so you became a worker of miracles, a Son of God? Were you crucified also?"

"I never had the power to work miracles, and I was not the Son of God—and indeed I condemn the Christians for worshiping *you* as the Son of God."

"But—"

"I did not say you were *not* the Son of God. You were and are—"

"We *all* are," Brother Paul put in.

"But God commanded the people to worship Him, and none but Him. When they started worshiping you and all the Saints, they were perverting His directive. Because they had gone astray, the Angel Gabriel came to me and directed me to bring them back to the true religion as preached by Abraham, to absolute submission to His Will."

"Yes," Jesus agreed a trifle doubtfully. "And yet—"

"Yet the Christians have confined me in their Hell," Mahomet finished with a grim smile. "Because the true heretics are not those who schismed from the main mass of Christianity in order to worship God more properly. The true heretics are in charge of the Christian Church—and the Jewish Church. And—"

"And the Moslem Church?" Jesus inquired gently.

"*And* the Moslem Church," Mahomet agreed. "Do they think I do not see their hate, their alcoholic drinking, their sins? And those heretics of all churches condemn to Hell all who seek to expose their iniquity. God is merciful; the rulers of these Churches are not."

"And so you were killed?"

"No, I died naturally when I was no longer needed on Earth."

Jesus made a decision. "Prophet, I like your attitude. Your beliefs are not mine in all ways, but I believe you are qualified to settle the differences between Brother Paul and me."

"I will be happy to try," Mahomet said. "So long as it does not require much physical exertion. Our wounds will not heal until the night—and then each morning we must walk past the demon again. At the moment I cannot do more than talk."

They turned to Brother Paul. Well, why not? If this were a possible route to the release of his friend from this place. . . . "It is this," Brother Paul said. "I am of mixed descent. I have some, uh, Nubian blood. He feels this damns me, so for the sake of friendship, he endures my punishment. But I feel there is no crime in heredity, except perhaps in Original Sin, which taints all men equally. *Is* black blood a sin?"

"There is no crime in heredity," Mahomet said. "Any person who practices right belief and action is welcome to the house of Allah, the Compassionate, the Merciful. I regret that many who profess to follow my own prophecy do not seem to believe this, but it is so." He turned to Jesus, gesturing toward Brother Paul. "Is this such a man? One who honors God in his heart as well as with his lips?"

"Yes," Jesus said. "But—"

"I *seek* God," Brother Paul said. "I do not claim to have found Him or to be worthy of—"

"But if he were in some way flawed," Mahomet continued, "I would neither send him to Hell nor go in his place. I would forgive him."

"Forgive him . . ." Jesus said, as though this were a phenomenal revelation. "As God forgave man. . . ."

"Therefore," Brother Paul said quickly, "having done that, there is no need for you to suffer the tortures of Hell. Let's get out of here."

Jesus almost agreed. But then he balked. "You are forgiven —but who is to forgive *me?*"

"You? You are blameless!"

"Jesus is blameless, except perhaps for a matter of a fig tree. But the one who plays the role—and plays it imperfectly—that is another matter."

Brother Paul felt a premonition of disaster. He fought it off. "Let's get out of here. Then we can discuss it at leisure."

"No," Lee said with growing conviction. "I see now that I deceived myself and you. It was for my own crimes I came here. I am a Mormon, and—"

"What has that to do with it?" Brother Paul demanded desperately. "You have honored your creed."

"That has not been proven," Lee insisted. "I—"

"Then let's put it on trial," Mahomet said. "We shall have the proof soon enough."

A female demon appeared. In lieu of clothes she wore bright paint: rainbow rings around her breasts and a clown's mouth at her nether bifurcation. Another prime role for Amaranth! "Jesus Christ may leave Hell," she said. "His host may not, for his heritage is tainted."

"Ah, but *is* it?" Mahomet demanded. "What do you hold against him or his religion?"

"I passed through Utah once," the demoness said. "I saw a handsome man. 'Who is that?' I inquired. 'That is Brigham Young, leader of the Mormons,' my companion informed me. 'He has twenty seven wives.' 'Why, he ought to be hung!' I cried. My companion smiled. 'Lady, he *is!*' he replied." The demoness pointed to Lee. "His Church is polygamous!"

"But that is no sin," Mahomet protested. "Every man should

have four wives, or more, depending on circumstances."

"Score one for the defense," Brother Paul murmured, hiding a smile. No, the Mohammedans would not condemn polygamy!

"Well, try *this* on for size!" the demoness said angrily. She whirled, made an obscene gesture with her bare posterior—and from it a cloud of smoke issued. The cloud developed color and character, and became a picture of a wagon train of the nineteenth century, wending its way through western America. "It is short of supplies," the demoness said from behind the picture. "The local inhabitants, intimidated by the Mormons, refused to see to it. They believed the train carried a shipment of gold, and they wanted that wealth." In the moving picture, Indians attacked. It seemed they would overwhelm the wagon train, but the men, women and children fought back desperately, and finally drove the Indians off.

The scene shifted. Now the leaders of the wagon train were talking with the Mormons. "The Mormons were on good terms with the Indians," the demoness explained. "They promised to guide the train safely through the hostile territory if the travelers surrendered their weapons so as not to seem to threaten the Indians." The picture showed the turnover of weapons and the resumption of travel.

"No!" Lee cried in the throes of an agony that seemed worse than that of his wounds.

"Yes!" the lady demon insisted gleefully. "It was a trap. The guide led the train into an exposed place. Indians attacked it again, and the guide joined the Indians, and this time massacred the defenseless travelers. The attack was led by Mormons, whose leader was John Doyle Lee."

"My namesake!" Lee said brokenly. "Betrayer and murderer! That name was passed along to me with such pride—"

Brother Paul winced. No wonder Lee was hurting! "But the fact that your namesake Lee may have been guilty of such a crime does not make the whole Mormon Church guilty," he protested. "Did the Mormons defend Lee's action?"

"No," Lee admitted. "He was tried and condemned. But—"

"And you can not be blamed for something that happened long before your birth," Brother Paul continued. "Can he, Mahomet?"

"I would not accept this version of original sin," Mahomet agreed.

"I'm not finished!" the lady demon said, reappearing. "This

man is a member of a plagiarized faith."

"Plagiarized faith!" Lee exclaimed. "That's a hellish lie!"

"Say you so? Watch this," she cried, doing her bit with the smoke again. This time the scene was of a man writing a manuscript. "This is Solomon Spaulding, a Congregationalist minister and would-be author, writing a novel in 1810," she announced. "He wrote several novels, but never had them published. His interest was in the origin of the American Indians —the Amerinds, and he liked to conjecture about their possible connections with the people across the Atlantic Ocean. He died in 1816."

"That has nothing to do with me or my religion!" Lee protested.

The scene shifted. Now it was a blanket stretched across a cabin. "This is Joseph Smith, founder of the Mormon Church," the demoness said. "He hides himself so that his amanuensis can not perceive him plagiarizing from Spaulding's novel, and the King James Bible, and other sources to fashion *The Book of Mormon.*"

"No!" Lee cried. *"The Book of Mormon* is a divine revelation!"

"And when it became too cumbersome dictating these divine revelations to the scribe, Smith simply used sheets from Spaulding's original manuscript. 'First Nephi' is an example."

"No!" But the cry sounded like that of a man with his neck in the guillotine.

"Then *you* explain the origin of *The Book of Mormon,"* she challenged.

"It was written by members of the Nephite Nation, the last of whom was Moroni, who concealed the records at the place later called Cumorah, New York State. There these engraved plates of gold remained from A. D. 400 until A. D. 1827, when the resurrected Moroni gave them to Joseph Smith for translation and publication. This translation is *The Book of Mormon."*

"The prosecution rests," the demoness said. "Do you still believe that moronic legend?"

And Lee was silent.

"That *is* a problem," Mahomet said. "If your entire religion is based on a lie—"

"No!" Brother Paul cried. "Maybe the origins of the Mormons are suspect, or maybe it is all a great libel. It doesn't matter! What matters is what the religion is *today.* Many worthy religions have foundered when their adherents forgot their original principles

—but here is a religion that became greater than its origin! The Mormons today constitute one of the most powerful forces for good on Earth. Their uprightness stands in stark contrast to the hypocrisy of so many of the more conventional religions. Therefore, there is no crime in this man who has faithfully honored the fine principles of his faith. Let us crucify no more people for being better than *we* are!"

Lee seemed stunned. The demoness, a look of sheer fury on her pretty face, faded away. Mahomet shook his head thoughtfully. "Yes, Brother, I believe you are correct. We must judge what *is*, not what *was*. On that basis—"

"To hell with what was!" Brother Paul cried. "This man is as much like Jesus Christ as a contemporary man can be. He belongs among the living."

"What *is*," Lee repeated. "I have been haunted by what *was*." Then his face glowed—literally. "We have no further business in Hell," Jesus said. "Hell itself has no business existing. Prophets like Mahomet and good men like Brother Paul—what the Hell are they doing in Hell! I never preached hellfire; I preached forgiveness—for men and for institutions." He stood straight, and his horrible wounds closed and healed in seconds. He gestured to Mahomet—and the Prophet's guts folded back into his body cavity, and the skin sealed smoothly around them. "Come, friends—we must abolish this atrocity." And he strode back toward the rock where the demon was still hacking helpless souls apart. All along the way he gestured at the wounded: "Rise, take up your bodies, and follow me!" And they were restored.

The demon glanced up as Jesus approached. "What, healed already?" it exclaimed. "I'll split you in two!" And it struck hard.

The sword bounced off Jesus's flesh and broke into two fragments. The demon stared, then backed away. Then, as Jesus continued advancing, the demon screamed in terror and fled.

The healed souls gathered around. "We are saved!" they cried joyfully. They closed ranks and marched behind like a swelling army. They sang hymns of victory. Before them all the legions of demons were seized with terror and scrambled out of the way. Hell was in revolt.

Down they marched into the frozen Ninth Circle—and the ice cracked and shattered as the souls buried within it came to life to join the throng. Even the giants ringing this circle merged with the marchers, and the sheer cliff crumbled to form a gently sloping ramp.

They came in sight of monstrous Satan Himself. Jesus paused. "O Thou Prince of Destruction," he cried indignantly, "the scorn of God's angels, loathed by all righteous persons! Why didst thou venture without either reason or justice to bring to this region a person innocent and righteous? Suffer now the penalty of—"

"No, wait!" Brother Paul cried, putting a restraining hand on Jesus' rising arm. "Even Satan has only been doing His job. You must forgive Him also!"

"Forgive *Satan?*" Jesus was amazed, and so were Mahomet and all the multitude of regenerate souls.

"Besides," Brother Paul continued, remembering. "I haven't finished my survey of souls." And he showed his calculator still zipping through the numbers. "It would be false pretenses to start a survey and then incite a riot."

Jesus paused, glancing at Mahomet. Then, as one, they burst out laughing. Suddenly all Hell was laughing, even the demons. A mad tangle of bodies formed as laughing souls collapsed upon each other. And, overriding it deafeningly, came the laughter of Satan Himself: "HO HO HO HO HO!"

Hell dissolved into chaos. Like smoke it lifted, leaving them standing in a valley, laughing uncontrollably.

19

TRANSFER
(TEMPERANCE)

There is a story about a man who wished to reward three of his faithful employees. To each he offered the choice between a lump of gold worth a small fortune—and a Bible. The first employee considered both, but he was not a religious man, and so he took the gold. The second employee wrestled with his conscience for some time, but finally, apologetically, explained that he had a family with sick children and many debts and had to take the gold. The third, though obviously tempted by the gold, finally settled on the Bible. When he opened it, bills of high denomination fell out from between the pages. In their aggregate, they amounted to much more than the value of the gold had been.

The obvious moral of this story is that by seeking faith instead of worldly riches, a person may acquire more riches than he would otherwise have done. The problem is that this justifies the Bible not for itself, but for the profit that may be in it. That is a perversion of the Bible's meaning. When people use the Bible as a means to promote the acquisition of wealth, the moneychangers have surely taken over the Temple, and Christianity has become merely another business.

In the distance the two outside watchers stood. "This time let's make sure we have the child," Brother Paul said as his laughter subsided.

But it was all right, for Amaranth and a smaller figure were walking toward them. This time all of them were emerging!

"The child!" Mrs. Ellend exclaimed as the parties joined. "You found her!"

"You all have emerged," Pastor Runford said darkly. "But are you all sane? You were laughing crazily when the mist lifted."

"We are all sane," Brother Paul said. "But it wasn't easy."

"Not easy at all!" Lee agreed shakily, running one hand cautiously over his chest.

"You must rest," Mrs. Ellend said. "Tomorrow we shall hear your report."

"I'm not sure we're ready to make a full report," Brother Paul said, glancing at Lee.

"You make me very curious what occurs within those Animations," Mrs. Ellend said. "We perceive only the fringe effects. When you went in this time, there seemed to be a landscape with a river and a tree, but then a storm obscured the tree. When it cleared we saw the Sphinx."

"And the Great Pyramid," Pastor Runford put in gruffly. "The Bible in Stone. Analysis of its measurements reveals the coming of Armageddon. Jehovah inspired Pharaoh to build it according to a secret key—"

"But the Pyramid is Matter," Mrs. Ellend protested. "The realm of the real is Spiritual, not Material. Matter is an error of statement. All disease is illusion; Jesus established this fundamental fact when he cast out devils and made people well."

"Jesus was a good man," Lee murmured, his eyes closed. "We would do well to pay better heed to his values today."

"At any rate, after a time the Sphinx faded, replaced by what seemed to be an Earthly airline terminal," Mrs. Ellend continued. "Then it became opaque until just now when there seemed to be giants moving in flames. Could that have been someone's concept of the Infernal Region?"

"There *is* no Infernal Region!" the Pastor exclaimed. "The concept is a mistranslation of the Hebrew word *Sheol,* meaning the grave."

"There is Hell," Mrs. Ellend said. "It exists in life. It is error, hatred, lust, sickness, and sin."

"Yes!" Lee agreed. "Nothing in the Afterlife can match the tortures we inflict upon ourselves in *this* life."

"Oh, I don't know about that," Therion began. "Satan has resources—"

"Please, can we go home?" the child asked plaintively. "I'm very tired."

"Of course, child," Mrs. Ellend said, softening. "Your father will be happy to see you—" She broke off.

"Condition unchanged?" Lee inquired guardedly.

Mrs. Ellend nodded gravely. "I shall try to talk to him; perhaps I can make him understand that his malady is illusory. But perhaps—" She turned to Amaranth. "Perhaps this child could stay with you tonight. You have shared much experience—"

"What's the matter with my father?" Carolyn demanded. She was a brown-haired girl of about twelve, somewhat dark complexioned in contrast to the rather fair girl of the Animation. Her dress was rumpled and soiled by her long stay in the wilderness, and her locks were tangled.

"The Swami is unconscious," Pastor Runford said. "He sought you during the last rift in Animation and suffered himself."

Brother Paul was chagrined. "The Swami—her natural father?"

"He was opposed to this experiment," Pastor Runford said. "As many of us were. I differ with him on many things, but on this he was reasonable. But since we were overruled by the majority, he felt a representative of our view should be within the Animation area. His daughter agreed to be a Watcher. When all emerged safely except her, he must have been distracted. He has already suffered grievously from the things of this planet."

"Bigfoot killed my mother," the girl said. Brother Paul still thought of her as Carolyn.

"This is horrible!" Brother Paul exclaimed. "I never suspected—"

"Perhaps we should have informed you of these things," Mrs. Ellend said soberly. "But under the Covenant—"

"Come home with me," Amaranth told Carolyn.

"No! I want to go with Brother Paul," she cried.

Surprised and flattered, Brother Paul put out his hand to her. "I am staying with the Reverend Siltz. I'm not sure he would approve."

"Go with him," Lee said. "We can make other arrangements as necessary."

Carolyn flashed Lee a grateful smile. "Thank you, sir."

"The group of you appear to have developed an unusual

rapport," Mrs. Ellend observed. "My female curiosity wars with my scientific detachment. I wonder whether the entire colony would benefit from immersion in Animation?"

"Appalling!" Pastor Runford exclaimed.

"We have undergone phenomenal mutual experience," Therion said. "But I doubt the full colony would survive it, let alone profit by it."

Now they reached the village and separated. Brother Paul took Carolyn to Siltz's house. The Reverend was not there—but Jeanette was. The diminutive suitor of the Communist's son sat with her back against the door, weaving a basket from flexible strips of wood. "I am lurking for the Reverend," she announced. "I want to know what he thinks of trial marriage."

Reverend Siltz would explode! But this was not properly Brother Paul's business. "I think it would be all right to wait inside," he said. "I am his house guest, and if you could help—" He indicated the bedraggled Carolyn.

"What is the Swami's child doing with you?" Jeanette demanded.

"She is tired from a long ordeal in Animation, and her father is ill," Brother Paul explained. That was an oversimplification, but it would have to do.

"Of course I'll help," Jeanette said, deciding in a flash. "Come on in, child; we'll get you cleaned in a jiffy." She took the girl by the arm, guiding her. The woman was barely taller than the child, but there was no confusing the two: Carolyn was thin and somewhat awkward, while Jeanette was full-bodied and decisive. In moments they were busy in the wash area, and Brother Paul sank into a wooden chair, relieved.

Soon they joined him. Carolyn was now clean, and her hair was neatly brushed. "You're awful nice," she told Jeanette. "Since my mother died, I never—"

"No need to dwell on that," Jeanette said.

"I *have* to," Carolyn said. "When I get tired I get scared, and I'm awful tired, and I have to tell *someone* or I can't sleep."

Jeanette's brow furrowed. "What are you afraid of?"

"Bigfoot. He prowls around, and he killed my mother, and now he's prowling for me. I hear him coming, and I scream—"

"I would have thought that was a foolish fear," Brother Paul said. "But I met Bigfoot when we were searching for you. He went after Amaranth—"

"Who?" Jeanette asked.

"The woman of I.A.O.," Brother Paul explained. "I don't know her real name, but she watches the amaranth field, so—"

"She does look a little like my mother," Carolyn said. "Bigfoot probably got confused."

"I tried to stop Bigfoot," Brother Paul continued. "But it was stronger. If the Breaker hadn't come—"

"I know," Carolyn said. "I was coming out, but then I saw Bigfoot, and I had to run back into my fantasy city."

"Bigfoot ran into the Animation too," Brother Paul said. "I'm glad he didn't catch you." Understatement of the day!

"I made a big river, and he couldn't get across," she said, smiling. "When I was alone, I could control the effect some. Bigfoot stormed and ranted, but it couldn't get me. But oh, it scared me!" Her shoulders shook.

Brother Paul got up and put his arm around her shoulders, holding her close. "Your father the Swami can surely protect you."

"Bigfoot only comes when he's away!" she cried. "That's how Bigfoot got my mother! It waited until my father was away, and—"

Jeanette frowned. "Bigfoot does prowl around a lot. I thought it was just a nuisance from when the storms bring the Animation fringe. But with your father out of circulation—" She glanced up. "Why is Bigfoot after you? Why did it kill your mother?"

"I don't *know!*" Carolyn cried. "It hates my father, and—"

Brother Paul squeezed her shoulders reassuringly. "It is a comprehensible, if not defensible syndrome. The Swami knows martial art and has very strong psychic force. Bigfoot may resent him, but be unable to overcome him directly, so it tries to hurt him through those close to him. His family."

Carolyn put her face against his chest and cried. "That's why I wanted to be with you," she sobbed. "I'm not close to my father, really; we're of different religions. I thought somehow—you're so strong and patient, you'd make such a good father—I thought we could just get on an airplane and go away somewhere where they never heard of Animation, where Bigfoot couldn't ever find me—oh, I'm *sorry!*"

"So it was *your* Animation, rather than mine," Brother Paul said, amazed. "I thought I had emerged from Animation—"

Carolyn tore herself away from him—but Jeanette caught her and held her instead. "Dear child! There's nothing wrong in

wanting a real family. That's worth fighting for! That's what *I'm*
fighting for. The only thing wrong is to give up your dream."

"But it didn't work!" Carolyn sobbed. "We had such a wonderful time for a while, visiting his old school, but then I started being
afraid *he* would—would—something terrible would happen to
him. Because of me. And then it all went wrong, and we got on the
wrong plane and lost in the station, and it was all my fault—"

"It *wasn't* your fault!" Brother Paul cried. "It wasn't your
Animation, either! You may have started it, but I—"

"So I sneaked away, so as not to be a burden to him
anymore—"

"You nearly destroyed me!" Brother Paul cried. "I was afraid
you would get abducted or run over—"

"No, I just got in another Animation, like the other one, when I
played the Buddha—"

"*You* played Buddha?" Brother Paul demanded. Yet her size and
appearance jibed. Change the hair—easily done in Animation!
—and she could resemble a little man, sitting under the Bo Tree.
He had found her without knowing it!

"Yes. I know about Indian history because of my religion, so it
was easy to—"

"What *is* your religion?"

"I worship the Nine Unknown Men. My mother taught me. My
father didn't like it too much, but since it relates some to his
religion, he let it be."

"I don't know that religion," Brother Paul said. "Tell me about
it."

Carolyn disengaged from Jeanette. "I'm okay now, I think.
It—I'll have to start at the beginning, if it doesn't bother you.
After what I did to you—"

Brother Paul looked her in the eyes. "One thing we must get
straight. You did nothing to me. Nothing bad, I mean. You showed
me something about myself I never suspected before. I want a
family too! I want a daughter like you."

She brightened. "You do?"

"I was confused at first in that Animation. I thought I was back
in—in the mundane world, as I said. I knew I didn't have a
daughter, so it took me some time to acclimatize. But when I
did—" He spread his hands. "I took over that sequence and
carried it forward the way I wanted it to go. Now I can't get used
to the notion of *not* having a daughter like you."

"Daughters are good too," Jeanette agreed. "Sons and daughters."

"But you are the child of another man," Brother Paul said to Carolyn. "I am here for a few days; then I will be gone. I cannot take anyone with me; Earth spent more energy than it liked sending me here, and that's the limit. The Swami is your real father. I would not contribute to the alienation of—" He had to stop. *Why couldn't she have been his child?* He would so gladly have taken her away from all this, back to Earth and—

He came up abruptly against reality. And what? Even if Earth were to allow another person to mattermit, there was no life he could provide for her back on Earth! In the Animation he had been married with a home to take her back to. In real life his home was the Holy Order of Vision. A fine institution, but no substitute for a personal family. "Explain your religion," he concluded.

"Well, it started with Asoka," she said. "The Emperor Asoka of India who was born in 273 B.C. He was the grandson of Chandragupta who unified India. But there was still some land to add. So Asoka conquered Kalinga. His army killed a hundred thousand men in battle. When he saw all that gore he was horrified at such massacre. He renounced that kind of conquest and declared that the only true conquest was to win men's hearts. By being kind and dutiful and pious, and letting all creatures be free to live as they pleased. So he converted to Buddhism—"

"Beautiful!" Jeanette murmured.

"He was such a good Buddhist that a lot of other people joined too. Buddhism spread through India and Ceylon and Indon—Indon—"

"Indonesia," Brother Paul supplied.

"Yes. I can't remember all those otherworld names as well as my mother could. But Asoka respected all religions; he didn't *make* anybody turn Buddhist, and he didn't prosecute—is that right?"

"*Per*secute," Brother Paul said.

"You sure would make a good Daddy! He let each religion do its own thing, a little like the way it is here, only without all the screaming. He was a vegetarian, and he wouldn't touch alcohol. I think he was the best monarch ever!"

"History agrees," Brother Paul said. "Asoka was one of the finest."

"But he knew he wouldn't rule forever. He wanted to stop men from using their minds for evil. So he founded the wonderful secret society to do this. That's the Nine Unknown Men."

"But that was thousands of years ago," Jeanette protested. "What happened after they died?"

"They trained new men, each generation. So there have always been nine, right up till today, and each one is the wisest man there is. They have a secret language, and each one writes a book on his science. One knows psychology. Another knows fizz—"

"Physiology," Brother Paul said.

"Yes. He knows so much about it that he can kill a man just by touching him. Some of his secrets leaked once, and now they are used in judo."

"Judo!" Brother Paul exclaimed.

"That's a way of fighting," she said helpfully.

"Uh, yes, I understand. That strikes me as an excellent religion. But how do you know the identities of these Nine Men?"

"I *don't*. Nobody does. Except themselves. But I worship what they do because they are working to save us all. They are around somewhere, and—" She paused shyly. "Well, I think maybe—I don't know—my father the Swami Kundalini might be one. He knows so much—"

Brother Paul looked past her—and there stood the Reverend Siltz in the doorway. Brother Paul jumped up. "I didn't see you, Reverend!" he cried. "We were just—"

"I have been here for some time," Siltz said. "I did not wish to interrupt the child."

Jeanette turned. "Reverend, I came to—" She looked at Carolyn, not wanting to bring up such a subject in the hearing of the child. "It doesn't matter now. I'll go."

Siltz pointed a finger at her. "The first grandson. Also the first granddaughter. Communist."

Jeanette's eyes widened. "You proffer compromise?"

"Granddaughters are good too," Siltz said defensively. "Sometimes even better than grandsons."

"I will not bargain for religion!" Jeanette said. "Anything else, not that. *All* will be Scientologist."

"*Now* who's the pighead?" Siltz demanded. "My son is outside."

"That's dirty fighting!" she cried.

"All's fair in love and war," Siltz said. "I am not certain which one this is or whether it is both. The first two children—even if both are female. My final offer!"

"I will not speak to you!" Jeanette flounced out. It was an impressive exit.

Siltz looked after her. He smiled grimly. "Two granddaughters like *her*. Church of Communism. They would convert the whole planet!"

"I did not realize your son was back," Brother Paul said. "I—"

"You want a daughter. So do I," Siltz said. "Do not be concerned. There is room. My son will not sleep here tonight."

"Oh, I would not think of—"

"I do not know where Ivan will sleep or what he will do," Siltz continued sternly. "But tomorrow—we shall see who is ready to compromise."

Brother Paul thought of Jeanette, vibrant in her ire, encountering the young man outside. The man she loved and wanted to marry. "She's right. You *are* fighting dirty."

Siltz nodded with deep satisfaction.

"It's like the Dozens," Carolyn said, smiling. "You have to turn the other person's thrust on himself."

"A dozen what?" Siltz asked.

"Never mind that!" Brother Paul snapped more to her than to him. From whose mind had come those sickening insults of the Dozens in that scene? He squeezed out that conjecture and oriented on Siltz. "I have a problem. As you may have overheard, we had considerable adventures in Animation—but I cannot say we found God. I am not sure it is *possible* to find God this way. Yet I hate to disappoint the colony."

Siltz considered. "I have only imperfect knowledge of your experience in Animation. But from what I overheard, you found the greatest meaning in the personal visions, not those of religion. Could it be you are looking in the wrong place?"

"But my mission is to find God, not to amuse myself!"

"You seemed closer to God when you put your arm about this child and comforted her, than when you talked religion." Siltz glanced at Carolyn who was in a chair. "She sleeps."

Just like that! One moment she was ready to discuss the Dozens; the next she had clicked out. Adults tended to lose that ability, which made them safer drivers but also less endearing. "She had a long, hard haul," Brother Paul agreed. "How can I find God by catering to my wish for a child?"

"You made the obvious plain to me, a better way to heat my house—by *not* heating it. Perhaps you could find God better—by finding yourself. You must believe you are worthy to judge God."

"I'll never believe that! I'm *not* worthy to judge God! I have seen depths of depravity in me that make me unfit to judge *anyone*! I—" Brother Paul stopped. "*That's* why I can't complete this mission. I know I'm not—"

"Then what are you worthy to find?"

"Satan," Brother Paul said morosely. "We had a small vision of Hell just before we emerged from Animation. I seek God—but I fear my affinities are closer to the Devil."

"Is not Satan also a God?"

Brother Paul stared at him. "You mean—I should search for Satan?"

"I cannot answer that. I only know that when I looked well at the little devil who pursued my son, I found a certain affinity for her. I saw how gentle she was with the child. So in examining the devil, I discovered instead an angel. I do not believe in your Satan—but is it possible he too would have merits? Perhaps he only seems evil because we do not understand him well enough."

Brother Paul paced about the small room. "Somehow I am reminded of the Temperance card of Tarot. A woman pouring water from one jug into another, as if oxygenating it, renewing its life. Pouring a soul from one vessel to another, transferring the essence of a person from one life to another. Maybe from Earth to Hell. And you—you are transferring my thrust from one direction to another. Maybe, with precession, it would work."

"We must all look where we must look," Siltz agreed, "and do what we must do. Some orient on gold, others on the Bible—but who is to say who is right and who wrong—or whether there *are* such things as right and wrong? It is obvious that Heaven has more merit than Hell—yet what is obvious is not necessarily true."

Brother Paul nodded thoughtfully. He was thinking of the way huge Satan in Dante's Inferno had winked at him. Surely that was a shallow concept of Satan, one that could be laughed off—and indeed they had done just that. But what would happen if he now went to interview the *real* Satan? He had been more or less a spectator in a framework designed for Lee's torture. This time the torture would be attuned to Paul himself.

Yet as he pondered, it seemed increasingly necessary. He had tried to examine the Gods of others from an objective standpoint and failed because he did not know enough about them. He had tried to examine his own Christian religion and failed again. The answer, ultimately, had to lie within himself—and to know himself, he would have to put himself to the test. Only then would he be able to prove his own fitness to judge God. As Lee had put himself to the test in his Hell—and found, after suffering and doubt, vindication.

The surest test of Brother Paul himself would be found in his own, personal Hell.

20

VIOLENCE
(DEVIL)

When Jesus Christ was crucified, Governor Pontius Pilate assigned Roman soldiers to stand guard. One of these soldiers, named Longinus, had a malady of the eyes. When Jesus died, Longinus took a spear and pierced his side, verifying his death. Blood ran down the shaft of the spear, and a drop of it got on the soldier's eyes. Immediately they were healed. This, combined with certain other signs occurring at the time of Jesus' death—the darkening of the sun and quaking of the earth—caused Longinus to be convinced that Jesus was indeed the Son of God, and the soldier was converted to the Christian faith. He gave up the military life, studied with the Apostles, and became a monk. Many years later he was brought before the Governor because he refused to sacrifice to idols. He was subjected to torture; his tongue was cut off and his teeth torn out. But Longinus took an axe and smashed the idols, his brazen act calculated, as though to say "If these be gods, let them show themselves!" Demons came out of the idols and took over the bodies of the Governor and his aids, and the Governor became blind. He then had Longinus beheaded. But after, he fell down before the corpse, and wept, and did penance. His sight returned. Thereafter, he did good works.

They stood in a hollow in the ground ringed by hugely twisted oaks. The full moon illuminated the tops but hardly penetrated to the ground. It was a beautiful but hauntingly evil setting.

"There were these two devils," Therion remarked. "And the little one said 'I'm *tired* of being the lesser of two evils!'" No one laughed.

Slowly an opacity formed from the shadow, and this shaped into the walls of a building—a single large room with bench pews at one end and an ornate stone altar at the other. A church.

But what a church! The cross on the altar was upside down, and crooked at that, with a crack traversing it. The stained glass windows seemed to be smeared with drying blood and formed pictures of obscene sexual acts involving satyrs, plump women, and pigs. Beyond the altar was a sculpture of the Virgin Mary, one breast dangling tubularly, masturbating the infant Jesus. A monstrous pentacle enclosed the altar and a goodly portion of the floor, including several of the pews. It was a five pointed star, the extremities symbolizing the five projections of the human body, the five senses of man, and the five elements of nature. Everything was wrong, profane, or disgusting—calculated to be the reverse of normal religious procedure. As it had to be. For this was to be the Black Mass, the infernal ceremony through which they would summon Satan.

Brother Paul felt a shiver go down the outsides of his arms. Did he really want to go through with this? No question about it: he did *not!* He had known what he thought was ultimate horror in his first Animation, the horror of personal degradation—only to suffer worse horror in the second. This was the third, and it would surely be the worst if he survived it at all. Yet—he had to do it not only for the sake of his mission, but, ironically, for his personal satisfaction. He had to know himself—whatever that self might be. Only then could he hope to know God.

He wore a black cape embroidered with Satanic symbols and serpents, hanging open in front to expose his genitals, for he wore no underclothing. The congregation was grotesquely masked with some individuals being in complete animal costumes. The acolytes were naked young men whose lingering glances tended to rest on each other's posteriors: blatant sodomists. They swung censers that reeked of marijuana, opium, and worse.

The high priest stepped up to the altar. His robe, like Brother Paul's was open; unlike Brother Paul, he had an erection augmented by Animation to inhuman magnitude. It was of course Therion. Under his direction, members of the congregation lifted a mattress to the top of the altar, covering it with a dirty black drape.

"Let the ceremony begin," Priest Therion said sonorously. "Virgin—dispose thyself."

Amaranth came forward, diffidently. The animal congregation began a chant whose words were indistinguishable—because the litany was being recited backward. She wore a fetching gown similar in respects to the nightgown she had used as Sister Beth: the material was sheer and tended to fall open at key locations, exposing portions of her lush anatomy. Brother Paul was no longer so naive as to suppose such offerings were accidental; she liked to put her torso on display. And he, male that he was, liked to see it thus. Now she did a little dance, removing films of material from here and there and flinging them away in the manner of a cheap strip-tease artist. Slowly her bouncing breasts came into full view and her flexing thighs.

"I would rather have made a try for Heaven," Lee muttered beside him.

Brother Paul knew what he meant. But imperfect man had no chance to achieve Heaven directly; first he had to settle with Hell. On this they more or less agreed. Brother Paul had gone to Lee's Hell to fetch him out; now Lee was coming to Brother Paul's Hell to help in whatever way he could. This was the nature of friendship.

Amaranth disposed of the last item of apparel and danced naked. She was such a splendid figure of a woman with her generally slender body blessed by full breasts and buttocks that Brother Paul had trouble with his posture. If only he had more concealment for his crotch!

"Marvelously protean flesh," Lee said, and Brother Paul realized that this was Antares' thought. The amoebic alien naturally appreciated flexibility, tubular elongations, and jellylike quiverings of anatomy.

The congregation acknowledged her beauty with a medley of snorts, growls, grunts, groans, and animalistic howls. Several males rubbed their crotches suggestively, making bucking motions with their hips, while the females tittered rudely.

Brother Paul felt his temper rising. How was he to stand here and tolerate this indignity to the woman he loved? (*Loved?* How had *that* term entered his mind! He might be tempted by her, but not. . . .) Yet she was doing it voluntarily—and doing it to assist his own mission. For this was the way, according to Therion, to find Satan most swiftly and surely—and Therion was the expert in such matters. If this were the worst of the indignities he, Brother Paul, had to suffer here, he was well off.

Amaranth walked languorously to the altar and picked up two burning candles there. Brother Paul knew they were made from human fat. Holding one candle in each hand, she carefully seated herself up on the altar, then leaned slowly back to lie upon it, face up. Her head rested on a pillow inscribed with Satanic designs, and her arms spread wide to either side to support the guttering candles. They gave off an odor like cooking meat, making Brother Paul's stomach roil unpleasantly. Her legs spread wide, dangling off the edge of mattress and altar so that her vagina lay open to public view. Brother Paul tried to keep his eyes away from the moist aperture, but they strayed back. He bit his tongue, fighting off the reaction that his open robe would advertise to the entire congregation.

The acolytes brought sacramental wafers stolen from a legitimate church, and sour wine that looked distressingly like diluted blood. The Priest held the wafers above Amaranth's body and pronounced a ringingly profane curse upon them. He handed them back for distribution to the congregation, then bent down and kissed the girl resoundingly between her legs.

Brother Paul started forward, but Lee restrained him. "It is the ritual," he cautioned. "It is an abomination—yet the road to Hell is paved with abominations, as we well knew before we made this compact."

"And the angel of Hell enjoys every one of them!" Brother Paul pronounced through gritted teeth. But his friend was right: this had to be suffered. Had he expected an easy route to the Infernal Region?

The congregation accepted the wafers and wine, but neither ate nor drank. They threw the wafers down on the floor, trampled on them, and poured the wine on top. "Jesus Christ eats shit!" someone yelled, and Brother Paul flinched, remembering the terrible crucifixions of the Savior. "Fuck the Virgin Mary!"

"Words mean little—either of worship or condemnation," Lee murmured. "The Satanists overrate the significance of external expressions. Neither Jesus nor his mother can be touched by the likes of these."

And that of course was correct. This infernal ceremony was

valid only to the extent Brother Paul allowed it to touch him, like Voodoo magic. Let the demons curse; they were only advertising their own powerlessness.

Priest Therion raised a benign right hand, very like the Hierophant he once had been. His left hand fingered his penis. Brother Paul was reminded of the Spanish obscenity: "You irritate my penis!" in lieu of the English "You are a pain in the ass!" Evidently Therion irritated his own penis. "All in good time," Therion said, responding to the cries of the congregation.

"They shall pay—in good time," Lee murmured in a deadly low tone. It was evident that despite his encouragement to Brother Paul, he could not avoid being moved himself.

Now the members of the congregation opened their costumes and urinated on the mash of wafers and wine. "Piss in the mouth of God!" one bawled, then jumped as the woman behind him gave him a playful one-fingered goose in the rectum.

The Priest bestowed another juicy kiss on the Virgin's vagina, then rose, smacking his lips. "Fill the Grail," he said.

The acolytes scraped up a mound of urine-wafer mash and dumped it into a huge dirty chalice. Therion took this chamber pot of a Grail, gestured obscenely over it, and lo! it was a human baby. "Celebrant, come forward," he cried.

"That's me," Brother Paul said glumly. "Last time I traveled his road, I regretted it. . . ."

"It is only ritual," Lee reminded him. "Profanity, nudity, urine—these can harm you only if you yield to them. Keep your mind pure, your intent honorable, and all the fiendish powers of Satan are futile."

Good advice! Brother Paul stepped forward.

Therion held the baby out to him. "Place this innocent infant on the belly of the Virgin, slit its throat, and catch the blood in the chalice," he instructed. "Here is the sacrificial knife; here is the cup. You must do it well, or Satan will not come." And he gave his standing penis another jerk with one hand momentarily freed for the purpose to show that there was also a sexual connotation to his statement. When Satan came, he came.

Brother Paul froze, appalled despite his preparation. "I can't do that!" he cried. "I can't kill—"

Therion frowned, looking truly demoniac. "Oh, come on, Paul," he said under his breath. "It's not *really* a baby, you know; it's a puppy. An animal. A living sacrifice for Satan. See?" And for a moment Brother Paul glimpsed the little beast, its tail curled tightly between its legs. "Don't be a fool. Go along with the gag."

The shape of the baby reappeared. So it was illusion! He should have anticipated that. After all, he had seen it change from chalice to infant. But was it right to kill a dog?

"Come on," Therion urged. "You're holding up the show. Do you think it's any worse than butchering a swine for bacon?"

Was it any worse? How many times had Brother Paul eaten of the flesh of animals? A thousand? Ten thousand? For each such meal, some animal, somewhere, had had to die. He would be a hypocrite to balk now.

He took the baby and set it on the soft white tummy of the Virgin. Virgin? How *could* she be after his liaison with her in the Castle of the Seven Cups two Animations ago? Yet he could not be *sure* about that, since Therion had—

He shook off the ugly thought, as he always did, and accepted the knife and chalice. This was horrible, but it represented his rite of passage. If he could eat the flesh of an animal killed *for* him, he should be able to kill an animal himself.

"Daddy." Brother Paul paused, thinking he had heard someone speak. But the screaming encouragement of the congregation drowned out all else. He must have imagined it. He hefted the knife, seeing a shaft of pale moonlight glint from its cruel blade.

The baby opened its eyes and looked at him. And abruptly Brother Paul recognized it. "Carolyn!" he breathed.

No—that was impossible. She was at least ten years old by this time, assuming the Animations progressed chronologically. No baby! And as a colonist she was twelve, verging on nubility. So this had to be a false identification, perhaps a figment of his own balking mind.

He gripped the knife with sweaty fingers and raised it to the tiny throat. It wasn't really *her* throat, but that of a puppydog. Merely illusion—

He froze again. Illusion? If Therion could make a puppy resemble a human baby, why couldn't he make a baby resemble a puppy? Or a young girl resemble a baby?

Whose throat was he cutting?

Again he remembered that episode at the Castle when he had grabbed the naked Amaranth—and later looked in the window and seen Therion standing where the girl had supposedly been.

Had Therion made himself resemble Amaranth, and—

"Get *on* with it!" Therion said through gritted teeth. "The natives are getting restive. Do you want to ruin everything?"

Brother Paul had gone along before—and regretted it profoundly ever since. Was he so much the fool that he could be destroyed twice by the same magic? How much worse a deed was he being guided to this time by the Evil Companion?

"Now!" Therion cried, his desperation such that even his penis lost elevation.

Now Brother Paul was sure. He dropped the knife and lifted his daughter from the stomach of the Virgin. "What in Hell are you trying to do?" he demanded with no profanity.

"Fool!" Therion cried. "It is too late to stop it now. Satan is coming!" He snatched at the baby, but Brother Paul drew aside, using his judo balance, and stepped out of the way with her in his arms.

Now the congregation, balked of its expectation, became a ravening mob. With an animal roar it charged forward.

Brother Paul set the child down behind him and braced himself for devastating action. He had in his hands the skill to maim and kill, rapidly, and if that was what this horde really wanted—

"No, Paul!" Lee cried.

And Brother Paul understood. Lee was not concerned for the welfare of the mob; he was cautioning Brother Paul. Once before he had yielded to Temptation—by doing its will in the name of opposing it. That had been the path to ruin. Instead, his model had to be Jesus Christ: to preserve his own values regardless of the threat.

He stood firm, his arm about the child—and it was as if an aura surrounded him, a shining light, impervious. The rabble broke against this shield and was rebuffed.

"Damnation!" Therion cried. "Satan is coming; He must have His blood! There is only one chance remaining—and I'll have to do it myself!" He grimaced as though contemplating an act so horrible that even *he* had to nerve himself for it.

Therion stalked up to the altar, a hand on his phallus. The Virgin still lay there, holding the two burning candles. Therion positioned himself between her legs and lowered his boom, orienting on her exposed vagina. "I hate this," he said. "I'd rather crap on her face. But this has to be according to form."

Brother Paul started forward—but again Lee cautioned him. "You have won—don't throw it away now! What means most to you?"

And Brother Paul realized: the life of his daughter was more important than the virginity of his girlfriend. He stood firm.

Therion closed his eyes, bared his teeth as though before a firing squad, then steeled himself with a hearty oath and rammed his member home. Amaranth gave out a gasp of amazement and dropped the candles; evidently she had anticipated only another genital kiss. But it was too late for any meaningful protest on her part; she had already been speared. There was a spray of blood: her maidenhead, its rupture augmented by Animation.

The mob went wild again. It dissolved into a swearing scramble of bodies. Clothing was ripped off. Men fornicated frantically with women, genitally, orally and anally, and those who could not get hold of female anatomy rapidly enough plunged with equal fervor into the orifices of whatever was within range. It was an incredible orgy of lust, imperative and insatiable. One woman came up from the heap with something bloody dangling from her mouth: a bitten-off penis. Some of the congregation, it now developed, really *were* animals; a billy goat was mounting a sprawled woman while two men attempted to penetrate the animal's rectum simultaneously.

The whole demoniac church shuddered. Smoke issued from vents around the perimeter of the pentacle. But the mob paid no attention. Every person was too busy slaking his, her, or its drug-loosed, beastly passion. All except Brother Paul, Lee, and Carolyn.

Therion was still performing his sacrifice at the altar, shoving ex-Virgin and mattress askew in his grim determination to complete the ritual properly. "Disgusting!" he muttered. "But I can't let it faze me! I must ejaculate the Offering though the Gorgon petrify me!" And he strove ever harder against the impotence that threatened him.

Amaranth was trying to scramble to her feet, but could not get them under her before he left off his efforts. "What the Hell are you talking about?" she demanded, her surprise, confusion, and pain turning to anger as she began to comprehend exactly what he was talking about.

Therion stiffened with a climactic effort, then slowly relaxed in place. Then, in an amazed afterthought: "I *did* it! I really did it! I conquered the gaping monster! I prevailed over Manifest Castration itself! Only Satan could have brought me through that horror!"

"That *horror!*" Amaranth exclaimed, furious. "Get away from me, you fairy!"

And Brother Paul understood also. To certain homosexuals, the female genital region was the terrifying proof of the reality of castration, for where there should be a penis and testicles was only a slash like that left by a knife. The awful Sword had removed everything! Such people had constantly to reassure themselves by dealing only with those who remained unmutilated: other males. Homosexuality was Hell.

"But do you know," Therion added with even greater amazement, "I think I liked it!" The man had, in his fashion, just been tested as crucially as Lee had been in Dante's Hell—and profited as much. He had discovered heterosexuality.

The smoke gave way to thin fire, jetting up like blow-torch flames on each of the ten sides of the pentacle, outlining the five points of the star in flame. The entire congregation was within this outline. The fire rose up in sheets, forming a new enclosure, shutting out the obscene church. The floor shuddered again as though subject to an earthquake.

"Satan approaches," Lee said tersely. "The Priest's act summoned—"

"No—I suspect we are going to the Inferno," Brother Paul said. "The Priest only greased the channel, as it were. The mountain seldom comes to Mahomet."

"Daddy, put me down," Carolyn said. Brother Paul discovered that he was holding her so close her feet were off the floor. She was no infant any more; she had swiftly and subtly grown to her colonist size. If he wielded the knife, catering to Therion's supposed hate for all the distaff sex—no! He eased up so as to let her slide to the floor. He had already come far closer to Hell than he liked!

The whole surface of the pentacle jumped with a rending clang like that of metal on concrete. Steam hissed up in great clouds, stifling the fire. Ozone fumes suffused the air. The ex-Virgin fell off the altar, carrying the Priest with her; in a tangle of limbs they were separated at last.

"Daddy, pick me up!" Carolyn cried.

Instead, he squeezed her thin shoulders gently but firmly,

holding her steady. "We're going to Hell, honey," he told her. "Don't be frightened."

She turned her startled gaze upon him. Suddenly he realized the incongruity of what he had said. They both burst out laughing.

Lee looked at them disapprovingly. "Mirth—hallmark of the Devil," he muttered.

The air became close as the steam-vapor surrounded them. The rampaging congregation at last became aware of the changing situation. There were sounds of coughing and hacking as the smog coalesced into soot that coated everything. Brother Paul found a handkerchief and gave it to Carolyn to breathe through. She insisted on sharing it with him, so he stooped down to put his mouth to one end. It did seem to help filter out the choking gas and dust.

The bottom dropped out. The entire pentacle plummeted into a bottomless hole in the earth like an elevator whose cable and safety brakes were broken. Down, down, in free fall, stomachs floating. "Even so did I plunge into the abyss!" Therion said from somewhere, reviewing his recent performance, his supreme act of courage.

There was wretching among the congregation. But Brother Paul, Carolyn, and Lee stood firm. Therion slid free of Amaranth's legs, and she scrambled to her feet, virtually floating free of the blood-spattered altar mattress. Brother Paul tried again to keep his eyes averted from her and from Therion's now-dangling member, but was not entirely successful. Somehow he felt she had betrayed him, though obviously she had neither anticipated nor cooperated in—what had happened. And of course he shared responsibility, for he had balked at sacrificing the baby, necessitating Therion's alternate procedure. So Amaranth had been sacrificed instead of Carolyn—and therein lay the key to his basic values. Now, looking at the naked woman, with his arm about the child, he could not second guess his decision. He *did* love his daughter more.

Air screamed past the plummeting platform. Air—another hallmark of the Devil! The mixed vapors shot upward, their discolorations seeming to writhe like serpents. The velocity of the pentacle was now so great that the wind actually whistled. Strange creatures, all fang and wing, passed by, peering momentarily into the pentacle as though it were a feeding dish. But after the first gut-wrenching shock of falling, equilibrium was returning, making the platform seem stationary. The congregation, some in tatters and some naked, stood in frightened huddles looking out. The approaching Animation of Hell was evidently more than these people had bargained for!

Even in this awful descent, Brother Paul found himself musing on the technical aspects of the production. The Animations could make things appear to be other than they were and convert mirages to reality—but these were matters of perception. The actual mind was not affected directly. So how could there be a sensation of falling and of violent motion? But the answer came as he phrased the mental question: there were many more senses than the proverbial five, and the perceptions of balance, motion, and muscle tension were part of the Animation whole. The most intense Animations covered the full spate of senses; there was no way other than pure reasoning and memory to know any part of the objective situation. And even memory was subject in part to Animation as he knew from his vivid flashbacks.

The fact was that the greater part of what made up individual awareness was controlled by the Animation effect. Perhaps forty percent of Brother Paul's faculties affirmed that reality was a visit to a colony planet by a novice of a minor Order whose purpose was to ascertain whether Deity sponsored any part of the Animation effect. Sixty per cent of him said he was going to Hell.

"We are going to Hell," he repeated softly, and this time he was not laughing at all.

With a jolt that sent people sprawling, the platform changed course. Brother Paul staggered, trying to prevent Carolyn from falling. Lee reached out and caught her arm, stabilizing her and, through her, Brother Paul. "Thanks," Brother Paul gasped.

"You steadied me," Lee said. "You showed me the error of my philosophy and brought me to unity with Jesus Christ." Now Lee was a tower of strength, able to contemplate Hell itself with an approximation of equanimity because his soul was pure.

"But what of mine?" Brother Paul asked himself. "My soul is a nest of scorpions that I thought had been safely buried—and now they will surely be loosed!"

The platform was now traveling to the side. The congregation scrambled for the pews, seating themselves and holding on tightly. Therion held on to the altar which was near the front point of the pentacle. "Get over here!" he called. "Want to get knocked off?"

Lee looked out at the slanting colors beyond the rim. The mists were thinning, showing an awesome chasm below, through which bright tongues of fire leaped. "And where would we fall to," he asked, "that we are not already bound for?"

Good point! Except for one qualification. "If we stay on the platform," Brother Paul said, "we visit Hell alive and perhaps return from it. If we fall off the platform, we may die and never return."

Carolyn looked too. The maelstrom of fire seemed to intensify, forming an amorphous demon face glaring up hungrily. "Oooh, I feel dizzy!" she exclaimed, teetering. Brother Paul jumped to fetch her in again, but Lee's hand was already on her arm, securing her.

Yet with the angling, lurching, and acceleration of the pentacle, all of them were being nudged toward the dread abyss. The congregation was secure because the pews seemed to be well anchored to the floor; some people even lay on the tapering points of the star and hooked their fingers over the forward edges so they could peer down raptly into Hell. But here at the front section there was nothing to cling to except the altar.

Brother Paul was loath to touch that altar whose cover and mattress had been dislodged and now rested on the floor near the rim. But he felt increasingly nervous at their precarious footholds. This was like standing on the wing of an airplane—and the intentions of the pilot were uncertain. Condensed slime coated the floor, making the footing treacherous. Any sudden shift—

It happened. The pentacle lurched, sending the three of them sliding. The mattress fell off the edge. There was a spurt of flame from below as it ignited.

Now it was Therion who extended a hand. He caught hold of Brother Paul's flailing arm and with demoniac strength hauled him and Carolyn and Lee in a human chain to the altar. "We are going home," Therion said with grisly satisfaction. "I shall see that you don't get lost on the way. My Master would be angry."

And he was the agent of Satan. Well, what had they expected? In the Infernal Region, the truly evil man was lord.

They stood by the altar, fingers hooked over its stone edges, and peered forward. There were rails ahead, resembling railroad tracks—shining ribs of steel curving into darkness. So that was how this platform was being guided!

"A roller-coaster ride!" Carolyn exclaimed.

Brother Paul exchanged glances with Lee. "Out of the mouths of babes . . ." the latter murmured. Could Hell itself be no more than a scary ride?

A tunnel appeared ahead: a black hole in a boundless wall. The tracks led straight into it.

The pentacle whipped straight into the hole—but abruptly it became apparent that the vehicle was too large for the aperture. At the last moment there was a scream of terror as the people at the star points on either side realized the threat. Then a crash—and those two points were sheered off cleanly by the tunnel walls. The people on them—were gone.

Brother Paul suffered a mental picture of bodies flattened against the wall like squashed flies, sticking there for a while before dropping into the flames below. Hell was cruel—but again, what had he expected? He hoped Carolyn did not realize the implications.

"Daddy, they weren't very nice people," she said. "But still—"

He drew her close against him again, and she laid her head against his shoulder and cried silently. She had a way of doing that when her sensitivities were hurt, in contrast to her more open crying for normal problems.

The platform was no longer a full pentacle. It was an arrow-head, arrowing through the blackness along its track.

Suddenly a monster loomed at one side. It had glaring yellow eyes, bloody red teeth, and talons fifteen centimeters long. "HOO-HAH-HAH-HAH!" it laughed with horrendous volume, keeping pace with the platform.

"It's a horror-house image," Brother Paul told Carolyn reassuringly as she cringed. If only she could have been spared this journey to Hell; he had thought she was safely out of this Animation . . . until Therion brought her in for the sacrifice. *Damn* Therion! At times the man had seemed decent, but always some new door opened on his charactor that made him seem worse than before. That sacrifice—could any but a truly evil mind have organized that? Tricking a man into slitting the throat of his daughter-figure? "It's *meant* to be scary—but it isn't real."

"It sure *looks* real," she said, taking heart.

The monster reached down with its two awful arms and caught up two people. They screamed—and so did Carolyn. Brother Paul started back toward the action, but both Lee and Therion restrained him. An odd situation when these two natural antagonists acted in accord! "They are already damned," Lee said. "No one can help them or change the manner of their departure from this frame."

The monster carried the victims up toward its gaping mouth. Carolyn hid her face. Therion laughed. But the monster drifted back and out of sight before consuming its prey. The fading sound of the screams of the two unfortunates were all that remained of them.

The remaining members of the congregation, once so violently eager to summon Satan, cowered in their places. But the next apparition was a tremendous octopus with a cruel, gnarled beak who blithely wrapped eight tentacles around eight more people and hauled them screaming and kicking into obscurity.

"Do not be concerned," Therion said in an offhand manner. "All who touch the sacred altar are safe from bestial molestation."

Because they were being saved for a worse fate? Brother Paul's misgivings mounted.

Amaranth looked up. *"I* wasn't saved!" she cried. "I was right *on* the altar when—" But she didn't bother to finish.

The remaining congregation hid itself under the benches. There was an internecine struggle for position, and two people were shoved off one edge to disappear with the usual screams—that cut off abruptly in a great crunching sound. *What lay below?*

Lights appeared, each like a gleaming eye—a line along the sides like the lamps of a subway tunnel. If these images were drawn from his subconscious mind, that mind's imagination lacked a really original thrust. But Therion seemed to be the dominant character in this Animation so far. Hell was his province; it could be as unoriginal as he wished.

The vehicle accelerated. The lights became a blur. Then the tracks curved, and they were flung to the right as it swept into a tightening spiral. Down, down, in a whirlpool vortex, tighter and tighter—and now the platform spun like a gyroscope, adding torque to revolution. They clung to the altar for dear life—and what was so dear about it now?—their fingers sliding across the slimy stone.

The marker lights funneled into an aperture too narrow for the remaining platform. The points snagged on projections and tore off. Again the despairing screams of the congregation were heard as people were hurled into the darkness outside the spiral, and under the wheels of the platform *inside* the spiral, to be sliced into pieces. Sections of arms and legs flew up, bounced off the platform, and skidded back into the gloom. One whole head glared momentarily as it rolled, leaving a dotted line of blood splotches. "They took no heed for their souls," Therion remarked without pity. "They were unprepared to meet their Master."

"And are *we* prepared?" Brother Paul inquired, holding his fingers over Carolyn's eyes in a futile effort to conceal the horror from her. "To meet their Master—or our own?" He knew that the congregation was composed of phastasms rather than real people; throwaways being thrown away. That was why they had not been able to touch him when they had attacked him earlier; they were merely part of the scenery. The nucleus of five real people was here about the altar. Why hadn't he thought to explain that to Carolyn?

The platform was now a pentagon—five sides, no star points. A dozen Devil worshipers clung to the sole remaining pew. The pentagon spun down through the nether eye of the vortex and plumped with a loud smacking splash into dark water.

Lee looked disapprovingly about. "This is Hell?" he inquired.

"Merely the sticks," Brother Paul murmured.

"Oh, the River Styx," Lee repeated, not catching the pun.

"Hell has not yet begun to manifest," Therion assured them with gusto.

So all this had been but the prelude. The warm-up show. Brother Paul felt an ugly chill. What would Hell produce when Hell got serious?

The pentagon bobbled on the gentle swell, moving with unseen power and guidance across the river. There was a moderately stiff headwind that carried the stench of rot, and it chilled them despite its warmth. Other boats were afloat, more conveniently shaped; this one was really a raft. Oddly, as many boats were going back as forward and were fully loaded. People *leaving* Hell?

Therion looked forward, baring his irregular teeth in a savage smile. Amaranth kept her head down upon the altar; *her* hell had begun at the outset of this descent. She had been so eager to give her samples; had that all been pretense? Or was it simply that Therion was the wrong man? The fact that she had actually been a virgin argued for the pretense theory. There were women like that, Brother Paul knew. All show and no substance. Well, she had substance now!

Carolyn's horror had abated, for she was young; now she

glanced about, intrigued by the scene. Lee stood with eyes closed in seeming meditation. Brother Paul decided not to attempt to engage any of them in conversation. Actually, this was probably about as peaceful as Hell could get.

"Shall I tell a joke to pass the time?" Therion inquired. "There was this time when God got horny and went to Earth and knocked up this Jewish girl, and as a result—"

"Christianity," Lee said. "Why don't you try to be original for a change?"

A boat cruised by on a parallel course but traveling faster. Ripples rocked the raft. Therion frowned. "Watch where you're slogging, duffer!" he yelled.

"Go soak your snout!" someone yelled from the boat.

Therion swelled up with delighted indignation. "Osculate my posterior!" he cried. "Your waves are slopping my gunwales."

"Yeah? Try *these* waves, peckerhead!" the other bawled. The boat looped about, accelerating to an unholy velocity. Now the ripples became rolling waves. They overlapped the raft's rim, sliding across to soak the feet of the five standing people and the bodies of those still lying under the benches. The latter got up hastily, cursing, for the water was not crystal clear; it was gray with pollution and it stank. Brother Paul observed that there were objects in it that resembled—yes, they *were* fecal matter.

Therion reached down, scooped up a dripping chunk, and hurled it at the boat. His aim and force were excellent; the turd scored a direct hit on the shoulder of one of the passengers.

There was an undecipherable roar of rage from the boat. The passengers stooped to scoop out their own ammunition. In a moment a small barrage of feces scored on the raft.

"Of course you realize this means war," Therion said, grinning with the sheer joy of battle. He squatted beside the altar, not hiding but rather straining to produce fresh ammunition. Brother Paul turned away in disgust; Therion was very much the fecal personality, and this was manifesting more openly as Hell drew near.

Others on both crafts were quick to follow Therion's example. Why should they seine the murky water for used shot, when superior grade and personalized material was so readily available? Soon the air was filled with stinking blobs. One person after another was hopelessly spattered in brown.

Amaranth straightened up, becoming interested in the proceedings. "Oh, shit!" she said. She spoke the truth: a mass of the stuff had scored directly between her breasts, breaking up and dribbling down her white torso.

Carolyn went around the altar to her. "I'll help you," the child said.

Surprised, Amaranth just looked at her, neither moving nor speaking. Carolyn scraped off the main mass with her fingers. She turned half about, holding it, looking across to the boat.

"Uh-*uh!*" Brother Paul warned her.

Reluctantly, Carolyn dropped the mass into the water, then stooped to rinse her hands. Then she scooped up a double handful of water and held it up for Amaranth to use to cleanse herself somewhat. "You dear child," Amaranth murmured. Then, choked, she did not speak again, but splashed the water on her front.

Why hadn't *he* helped? Brother Paul asked himself. And answered: because Amaranth had suffered herself to be defiled in his eyes. She had lain with the shit-conscious apostle of Satan. And if that had been unplanned, it was only the alternative to the far worse crime she *had* known about: the execution of this same child who now was helping her.

Carolyn, in her blessed childlike naivete, had forgiven Amaranth. Brother Paul had not.

Something massive but soft struck him on the back of the head. He knew what it was before he scraped it off. Once before he had acted immorally—and had had his soul rubbed in shit for it. This time he had passed what might have been an unfair judgment and been similarly punished.

Now only Lee remained untouched by fecal matter. He stood in meditation, eyes closed, proof against all incursions. Even on the border of Hell, there was that of Divine grace about him.

The two craft separated and the battle died out. No one had gained by it; they all were going to Hell anyway. Perhaps this was merely part of the initiation: a necessary degradation, immersion in filth. As if physical soiling could set the scene for spiritual soiling. As perhaps it could. "Dirt thou art," Brother Paul murmured. "To dirt thou returneth." Was Hell the grand compost for filthy souls?

The bank of the river arrived. But there was no need to disembark at the landing; tracks led out of the water, and the roller coaster ride resumed.

"Now for the grand tour," Therion said contentedly. "We cannot do justice to all the aspects of Hell in these few minutes, but we can glimpse a fraction in passing." He smiled, and it was not a nice expression. "Don't forget that Satan and His minions are themselves deities whose only crime was to lose out in palace politics. For a long time the Horned God was worshiped in His own right—and some remain true to that faith to this day." Meaning himself.

The platform swept into an exotic gallery reminiscent of the bowels of the Great Pyramid. Ancient Egyptian pictures and pictographs decorated the walls, and there were large, grim statues guarding every alcove: griffins, hippopotami, crocodiles, pigs, tortoises, and serpents. Human-headed birds perched on stone branches near the ceiling.

A line of people stood, each in a short skirt and head-dress, waiting for assignment. The demon in charge had the body of a man but the head of a strange beast with an elongated snout. "That is Set," Therion explained. "He has the head of an Oryx. He is the God of War, brute force, destruction and death. Even the Hyksos invaders feared him; they tried to placate him, calling him Yahveh, but in Egypt he was finally dethroned and called Satan." He shook his head. "A sad conclusion for such a noble God."

The craft shot through the wall and into a new chamber. Here there was a huge bird-footed, four-winged monster, standing on his hind feet. His front claws were hooked over a wall, and his canine face peered into the enclosure where a multitude of creatures struggled to escape. Most had the bodies of human beings and the heads of animals: lion, dog, bear, sheep, horse, eagle, snake. Some wore the scaly skins of fish. Heaped in the corners where the scrambling feet had scuffled them, were the remnants of a feast: shards of pottery, fruit rinds, bread crusts and human hands and feet. "The God of the Chaldeans laughs at man's puny efforts to escape his fate," Therion remarked. "Laugh, Anu, laugh!" And awful sounds of mirth filled the chamber. "The Sumerians, Accadians, Assyrians, Babylonians and the like had well-developed religious mythologies from which the Hebrews plagiarized freely. The Creation, Eden, the Tree of Life, the Deluge, the Tower of Babel, the destruction of cities by fire, Sargon-in-the-Bulrushes, the twelve signs of the Zodiac, the symbols of the Cherubim—all recorded on tablets before the Bible was written. Even the Holy Trinity of Ea, Bel and Ishtar, with the Goddess represented as a dove—"

But the carriage plunged through another wall. Suddenly the hot air was filled with huge buzzing flies. "Ah, this must be the abode of the Phoenician God, Baal Zebub, Lord of the Flies," Therion said happily. "Later corrupted to 'Beelzebub,' and changed into a devil in the time honored practice of losers. But he was actually no worse than—"

They went past another wall and into a room dominated by a giant erect phallus. "The lingam of the Brahman God Siva, part of the Trinity of India," Therion exclaimed with joyful recognition. "Symbol and instrument of the creative faculty and the all-devouring fire, evolved into the rod, staff, scepter, and Crozier. Maybe we'll catch a glimpse of Siva's consort, the multi-armed Goddess Kali, the Power of Nature and the ruthless cruelty of Nature's laws. In her honor the Thuggees killed thousands of—"

But again the scene changed. "Oh, come on," Therion protested, annoyed at last. "Each of these fine Hells deserves a lifetime of attention, and we are getting bare seconds. Stop, stop—let's look at one more carefully!"

The platform screeched to a halt, almost throwing them off. They were in a long, narrow cavern, with room only for the tracks and a footpath littered with obstructions: rocks, bodies, jagged fissures from which noxious fumes drifted. A line of bedraggled people marched slowly down this path, harassed by demons. "Hm—not sure I recognize this one," Therion admitted. "Must be a convoy, a transfer of personnel from one unit to another."

The platform moved along at walking speed, pacing the depressed marchers. The demons ran up and down the line on either side, screaming at the humans, kicking them, beating them with whips and clubs.

Carolyn stared wide-eyed, her mouth half open in dismay. Amaranth's reaction was more specific. "Stop it!" she cried. "Leave those poor people alone!"

"This is Hell," Therion said. "Sinners are *supposed* to suffer."

Brother Paul and Lee were silent, knowing it was not their place to interfere. Hell would indeed be a failure if it were pleasant. This was one of thousands, perhaps millions of similar punishments, yet it was hard to tolerate.

A child stumbled over a sharp projection and almost fell into a fissure. The woman behind him grabbed his arm to steady him. "Get your hand off!" a demon cried, whacking her across the head with his club. She staggered and fell half into the crevice herself, one leg rasping across the sharp edge. Blood flowed. The demon laughed.

Then another demon came. He caught the woman's arm and steadied her, helping her across the crevice. "I'll get a doctor if there's one available," he told her. "I can't promise, but I'll try."

"Fool," the first demon said. "This is Hell! You'll fry yourself if you don't shape up."

The second demon turned his back and went about his business. The first demon returned to *his* business, kicking at lagging people, shouting insults at them, and in general expressing his nature.

"Strange," Brother Paul observed. "Even among demons there are human differences."

The path rounded a corner and ended at a double door. The condemned souls were herded through the right door; Brother Paul could see an escalator beyond it going down. The demons, their tour of duty complete, passed through the left door. The tracks paralleled this one; he now witnessed the fate of the demons.

Lo—the demons stripped off their uniforms. Their forked red tails were part of the costume, and inside their cloven-hoofed shoes were human feet. They pulled away masks, and the horns came off. They were human beings.

A genuine demon sat on a minor throne. As each pseudo-demon came before him, he gestured thumbs up or thumbs down. The thumb-ups were wafted gently through an aperture in the ceiling from which colored lights and jazzy music leaked; the thumb-downs were dropped through a trap door in the floor.

The demon who had clubbed the woman was a thumbs-up; the one who had helped her was a thumbs-down. "See," Therion said as both disappeared. "When in Hell, you'd better do as the demons do—or pay the penalty."

Brother Paul felt sick at heart.

But now the track looped about to pick up the people who had been marching. They too were stripping away costumes—and lo! they were demons in disguise!

Carolyn could contain herself no longer. "Miss Demon," she called to the woman who had been struck, now a healthy female demon with cute hoofs and horns and tail. "If you're not *really* a person, why did you—I mean, the man who helped you, he—"

"He was found unfit for Hell," the lady demon answered. "That trap door goes straight to Heaven."

All the people on the platform stared. "But—" Therion began.

"If you act like a demon just because you think you are in Hell," the lady demon informed him, her pointed teeth showing in a knowing sneer, "you will surely soon *be* in Hell. But if you are a misfit, we have no use for you. That man who helped me obviously had no idea what Hell was all about."

Brother Paul exchanged glances with Lee as the vehicle resumed speed. What an infernal test of character!

Therion seemed shaken. "I didn't know that *anyone* escaped once he got in this far," he said.

"I suspect Satan is more discriminating than we know," Lee said.

They passed through a dizzying array of Hells. They saw people being boiled in oil, hung by their tongues, buried headfirst in burning sand, caged in boxes of immortal scorpions, disemboweled among flesh-consuming worms, thrown off high cliffs, wasted by terrible diseases, and suffering all the torments diabolical minds could imagine. They saw the Hell of the early Christian Gnostics, contained by a huge dragon with its tail in its mouth, with twelve dungeons ruled by demons with the faces of a crocodile, cat, dog, serpent, bull, boar, bear, vulture, basilisk, seven dragons' heads, seven cats' heads, and seven dogs' heads. The condemned souls were sometimes thrown with pitchforks into the open mouth of the dragon or stuffed into the dragon's rectum. They saw King Ixion, who had lusted after the wife of the Greek God Zeus and in punishment was spread eagled on a fiery wheel, his limbs and head forming its five living spokes. They saw Hades, Sheol, Gehenna Tophet, the Hindu Naraka with its twenty-eight divisions, the Moslem Fire with its seven regions each containing seventy thousand mountains of fire, each mountain enclosing 70,000 valleys, each valley 70,000 cities, each city 70,000 towers, each tower 70,000 houses, each house 70,000 benches, and each bench 70,000 types of torture. Brother Paul brought out his calculator to figure out the total number of tortures this progression represented, but got distracted by new visions of Hell and had to give it up.

At one place two grotesque demons investigated each soul. Carolyn called them "Monkey" and "Naked," mishearing the proper names Therion provided. If the person had lived a good

life, his soul was drawn gently and painlessly from his body and
wafted upward; but if he had lived a bad life, the demons ripped
out his soul with terrible brutality. Further along they saw the
Norse Goddess Hel, daughter of Loki, in her domain beneath the
roots of the Great World Tree. Now it was clear to Brother Paul
how heavily Dante had borrowed from Norse mythology to
fashion his vision of the Christian Hell. Indeed, it was evident
that Christianity itself had incorporated great chunks of Teutonic
legend. They heard the enumeration of the myriad Princes of Hell:
Lucifer, Beelzebub, Leviathan, Asmodee, Belial, Ashtaroth,
Magot, and on interminably. All the Gods that past peoples had
ever worshiped had become Christian devils, and it was obvious
that contemporary Hell was extremely well staffed and could
handle any emergency.

At last the impressive, horrible tour was over. Brother Paul's
head was spinning, and his companions looked dazed. Only
Carolyn had adjusted moderately well; she was still close enough
to the fantasy realms of childhood to accept more of the same.
They had set out to see Hell; it was more than they had bargained
on. Which, Brother Paul reflected, was about par for the course.

Now at last their vehicle rolled up to the dread gates of the
Devil's residence. A horrible clamor swelled in volume: screams
of terror, disgust, anguish, and shock. The air was close and hot,
and the odor of ozone became strong.

They rounded a turn—and there was Satan Himself. He was
huge, seven or eight meters tall, and His hands and feet were
claws, and every joint of His arms and legs was the face of a
monster from whose wide-open mouth the extension of the limb
continued. He had a two-meter long phallus in proud erection,
great bat-like wings, and long twisted horns. Snakes curled around
each arm, and when He picked up a struggling naked person, the
viper bit that victim in the crotch. He was carrying people up to
His grotesquely tusked mouth and chewing them up alive. Simultaneously, He squatted part way, and from his meter-wide anus
were extruded the shit-slimed, partially digested people He had
consumed. As each dropped headfirst, being born again in Hell as
it were, a minor demon snatched his brown-coated body and bore
him down into the bottomless flame.

"Master!" Therion cried. "Here they are!" He smiled triumphantly. "Now reward me with this one for myself!" He hauled on
Amaranth's arm.

Brother Paul stared. So that was it! Therion, having finally conquered his horror of women, now wanted to possess Amaranth permanently and was making his deal for her. For this he had betrayed them all!

Satan glared down. Beams of brilliant light speared from his eyes to bathe the couple, even as Brother Paul's stunned awareness came.

"And does the bitch want *you?*" Satan inquired. His voice reverberated as though from a great distance. "Will she buy her freedom by going with you?"

"Sure she will!" Therion cried. "She likes getting screwed!" And Amaranth, terrified by the presence of Satan, did not protest.

Satan laughed. His two claws swept down and forward and snatched the two of them. "Here is your reward!" the Horned God bellowed as the serpents' jaws closed on Therion's penis and testicles and on Amaranth's pudenda. Twin screams of agony rent the air, sounding above even the background bedlam of Hell.

"But You *promised!*" Therion cried as blood dribbled from his crotch. "I served You faithfully—"

His plea was interrupted as Satan bit off his head, chewed up his quivering torso, and swallowed him in a single, noisy gulp. Immediately after that, Satan chomped down on Amaranth so that her severed legs fell into the flame on one side and her head and arms and part of one breast fell on the other. Satan smacked His lips. "Those who seek Evil and those who acquiesce to Evil—delicious."

Now the talons came for Brother Paul and Carolyn.

"No!" Brother Paul cried, and the child screamed. They clung to each other—but the terrible claws clasped each body, sliding on the mucus and diarrhea that coated Satan's nails, and wedged between Brother Paul and Carolyn. They were wrenched apart and lifted high in the steaming air. The two snakes slid down Satan's forearms, their venom-dripping jaws opening wide.

"Take me! Spare her!" Brother Paul screamed.

Satan hesitated. Both snakes halted, obedient to the whim of their Master. The hideous, huge face loomed close. "The price of her is two orbs," Satan said. And the python on Brother Paul's side lifted its tusk-like eyeteeth toward his eyes. Its skin was mottled, its other teeth irregular, and its breath stank of ammonia. "These—" The snake's head dropped toward Brother Paul's groin. "Or these. Choose."

His sight—or his manhood. To save his daughter. The choice was worse than Satan's decision might have been! How could he give up either one?

Yet—if either of his organs had sinned, it was surely not the eyes. Let him be more like Jesus Christ, innocent of sexual lust. He would have little use for it in Hell, surely.

Even as that decision formed in his mind, the serpent struck down. Its jaws closed about his scrotum, the teeth punching in like the spikes of an iron maiden. There was a flare of unbearable agony, and Brother Paul screamed. Not only with pain, but with loss.

As the blood dripped down from his bitten, empty crotch, Brother Paul saw the other claw return Carolyn to the pentagon. She was sobbing uncontrollably, having been witness to it all.

Lee strode forward, caught her hand, steadied her, and put his arm about her shoulders. The pentagon platform began to move back down the track, away from Satan, away from Hell.

Then Brother Paul was lifted the rest of the way to the Horned God's maw. Headfirst he plunged into the cavernous mouth and slid down the greasy gullet into the guts of the Devil. Now he was one with Satan.

21

REVELATION
(LIGHTNING-STRUCK TOWER)

According to one humorous legend of the Creation, God formed Adam and Eve by cutting them apart from a single original hermaphrodite. Their bellies were left open as the result of this separation, so He gave them each a cord of clay or whang string leather to use to sew their bodies up. Adam, in the fashion of the male, took great long stitches with the result that some of his cord was left over and dangled in front. Eve, in the fashion of the female, made tiny neat stitches with the result that she ran out of string and was left with a slit at the bottom of her belly. She begged Adam to sever his extra length and give it to her so that she could finish the job, but he was selfishly unwilling. And so it has been ever since, this contention between men and women over "That Little Piece of Whang," because the men refuse to give it to the women and will only lend it to them briefly.

Brother Paul landed—in a plush modern office. "Please be seated," a pretty secretary said. "The Prince of Darkness will be with you in a moment."

Nonplused, he looked around. Could this be the inside of Satan? What had happened? Every office artifact was in place from the electronic voicescriber to the soft classical music issuing from concealed speakers to the holographic photograph of a pleasant rustic scene mounted on the wall. Something was wrong!

Suddenly his bowels reacted with the letdown. He had not expended the content of his guts during the river crossing. "Please, Miss—is there a—a rest-room here?"

The shapely woman made an indication with one thumb. There was the sign: MEN. Had he looked about more carefully, he would have been able to spare himself the embarrassment of asking —though he could have sworn the sign had not been there a moment ago. With grudging gratefulness he pushed open the door and went through.

All was in order. Brother Paul positioned himself, took down his trousers (he was now informally garbed in civilian Earth-style clothing)—and discovered what he lacked. His penis was intact, but he had no scrotum and no testicles. The skin of that region was smooth and unscarred; it was as if he had never had anything there. There was no pain, no discomfort. He might as well have been an immature boy—with no prospect of ever maturing. He was a eunuch.

He sat on the aseptic sonic-flush toilet and relieved himself of the material portion of his concern. He reached for the toilet paper—and saw words printed on it. He held it up to read. It said: BROTHER PAUL CENJI.

Every piece of paper was printed with his name.

He smiled. Hell had surprises yet! He reached behind—and paused. Was he to wipe his ass with his own name?

Well, why not! It was only a joke like the toilet paper that said "Never put off till tomorrow what you can do today" or "Get a load off your mind" or "Film for your Brownie." A fiendishly minor joke. His pride had better things to feed on than this. He took the paper and completed his mission.

"The Horned God will see you now," the secretary announced as he emerged. She *had* to be Amaranth, this time in a minor part—but what about his seeing her body crunched into pieces and dropping down . . . ? He squelched that thought; she was indicating another door, and obviously all her appurtenances were intact. Rather than stare at them a second time with more than sexual curiosity, he walked on through.

Satan came forward to shake Brother Paul's hand heartily. The Horned God was human-sized, had human hands and feet, and wore a conservative, circa 1995 plastic business suit complete with Gordian-Knot tie. Only His small, neat horns betrayed His nature. "So good to meet a good man!" He said.

Brother Paul gave up trying to make sense of things. He was here, and this was surely another aspect of Hell. The Devil would have His way, regardless. "It has been an interesting experience, so far," Brother Paul said.

"It has not yet begun," Satan said pleasantly. Who played this part, Brother Paul wondered. There seemed to be only one reasonable prospect, yet that—well, who could make sense of Hell anyway! "Please make yourself comfortable. This may take some time."

"Eternity?"

Satan laughed with mellow empathy. "Not that long, I trust."

The question burst out before Brother Paul knew it was coming. "You just swallowed me! How is it that I'm here, in this office —and that You're here, in human size?

"I am everywhere," the Devil said easily. "I am in you, and you are in Me. Evil is ubiquitous; it has no limits."

"But—"

"If you feel more comfortable knowing the specific geography, I shall provide it. I swallowed you; you are now in My belly. You are being digested. My Stomach acids will dissolve away, layer by layer, all the protective mechanisms you have clothed yourself with, until the fundamental truth of your being is achieved. Then, and only then, may you be fairly judged."

"But you—"

"I am in Myself too. I am everywhere. At this moment, a myriad of other souls are being similarly interviewed in separate offices. I am with each—within My own belly. Only when a given soul is properly processed is it ejected for conveyance to its permanent station."

"Defecated out?"

Satan made a little gesture of unconcern. "Most souls are shit; they must be treated as shit. This is, after all, the region of just desserts."

"I think my soul is shit too," Brother Paul said. "I saw it once when I was in meditation. However, it was pointed out to me that shit is ideal compost, a necessary stage in the renewal of life—"

"Well, we shall find out for sure, now. Shall we proceed?"

Brother Paul smiled wanly. "Have I any choice?"

"Oh, yes! Choice is the worst torture of all. Indecision can be far worse than wrong decision. Would you rather postpone this interview?"

Where would he stay, during the postponement? In one of the several sub-Hells he had toured? "No. Let's get it over with."

"You are intelligent. Were there more like you, My own Redemption would arrive more quickly."

"*Your* Redemption?" Brother Paul asked, astonished.

Satan shrugged. "I am supposedly anti-life. It is my ironic torture to be associated with procreation, for with every act of procreation there is another soul, new life. I am the Lord of Evil, and as Evil triumphs in the world, a greater percentage of souls must come to Me. Thus My punishment is governed by yours and outweighs that of all human souls combined. I wish there would be fewer people born and that more of them would go to Heaven. When *no* souls come to Hell, I will at last be free—and I fear that will be a long, long time yet."

"I never thought of that," Brother Paul said musingly. "God assigned to you all the dirty work—"

"Precisely. Now if you will lie on that couch, please—"

"This is a psychoanalysis?"

"The ultimate. Not for nothing does that term contain the word *anal.* Sigmund Freud originated the couch posture so that his patients would not see the look of shock on his face as he heard the horrors in their case histories. I really do not suffer from that particular problem, but the couch does seem to work adequately for contemporary occidentals."

Brother Paul spread himself on the comfortable couch. "What now?" he asked. "Do I just talk, or—?"

There was a rustle of papers. "According to your dossier, there was a certain matter of—a clothespin."

The clothespin. Instantly Paul was a boy again back on Earth. It was his first time out in a new neighborhood, and he knew no one. He saw a group of children seated in a circle behind a building. They were little girls no older than he, playing some kind of game with many exclamations and titters.

"Can I play too?" Paul inquired.

They looked at him, the stranger, with merry incredulity. "You're a *boy!*"

Paul's lip pushed out in mild belligerence. "S'not s'pose to be sexcrimination. A boy can do anything a girl can do."

They responded with a spontaneous burst of laughter.

"Well I *can!*" he insisted.

"That's what *yoooou* think," one girl said, greatly elevating and extending the *you* so that it sounded almost like a train whistle.

"I can play your ol' game as well as you can!" It wasn't that he cared about their game; his fledgling pride was at stake.

"Pride," Satan said in the background. "One of the Seven Basics. Relates to the Suit of Pentacles. Misapplied Pride brings more souls to Me than any other thing except perhaps Greed —which ties in to the same Suit."

The girl studied Paul. She was elfin with curly reddish hair, quite cute. She reminded him of someone—but of course all little girls were played by the same actress. "Wanna bet?"

"Sure I'll bet!" But he was uneasy. These girls were too certain of themselves, too full of some secret. They knew something he didn't. Yet he had no way to retreat.

"Okay, let him play," the redhead decided. This was answered by another outbreak of mirth. Strangely, some of it seemed embarrassed; one child was blushing. "But you must promise never to tell."

"Okay, I promise," Paul said. "What's the game?"

"Clothespin," she said, and there was yet another general titter. *What was so funny?*

"Okay," he repeated. "How do you play it?"

"It's a contest," she said. She held up a clothespin—the old fashioned kind without a spring, just a cylinder of wood bifurcated at one end. The prongs normally slid over the clothes, pinning them to the clothesline so that the wind would not blow them away before the sun dried them out. This was a big clothespin, about fifteen centimeters long. There was a blob of grease on the solid end. "You push it in."

"In?" This made no sense to him.

"Like this," she said. She bent her knees and hiked up her dress, showing that she wore no panties. The space between her legs was cleft by a hairless crease quite unlike his own apparatus; he was both fascinated and alarmed. She was incomplete! She fitted the clothespin into the crevice and slowly slid it into her body, one centimeter, two, three, four. "Whoever gets it in deepest wins."

Paul was not entirely naive about sex. He had heard stories and seen suggestive things on TV and had been able to piece together a fair picture of the mechanics of human copulation. After his initial surprise at his first direct view of the secret region, he was able to integrate the mental picture with the physical geometry. He recognized this game of "Clothespin" as preliminary, surrogate fornication. But more immediate, and far more important, he realized that he had lost his bet. This was not a game a boy could play, for he had no *place* to insert the pin.

She withdrew the clothespin and held it up, glistening with the spread grease. "Now you try it. My mark is there." And she scratched the wood with her fingernail, indicating the level of deepest penetration.

All eyes turned to him expectantly, the laughter barely suppressed. Oh, they had shown him all right! He was stuck in an impossible position. Outwitted by a bunch of dumb girls!

Then he had an inspiration. Girls had more apertures than boys had—but he still did have a place. He took the clothespin, took down his pants while the girls went into a fury of guilty tittering, and jammed it in to the shocked amazement of his audience.

Paul won his bet—and the contest. But at a price. No one told on him, for the girls were well aware that they could not do so without incriminating themselves, and adults tended to take very dim views of children's private pleasures and explorations. So the matter never came to the attention of the parental authorities. But these girls attended the same school Paul did, as it turned out, and some of them were in his own class, and every time he met one of them she would giggle secretively and pass on without speaking to him. He lived in fear that an adult would catch on to the secret. He should have accepted defeat, rather than the victory.

For when the clothespin came out, there had adhered to it a blob of shit.

"So that was the root source of your vision of the Turd back in Triumph Seven, Cup Seven!" Satan exclaimed gleefully. "Oh, beautiful; this one will go into my special file!"

Brother Paul knew he was blushing furiously with the shame of that memory. Naturally Satan was delighted; this was Hell. No physical pitchfork could have given him equivalent agony. Yet it was a relief to know this consciously now.

"You chose to seal off the original episode," Satan continued. "The memory drug withdrawal must have also helped to bury it. But it remained in your subconscious, prejudicing both your self-respect and your relations with women. Shit was your nemesis —and now we know the truth."

But that was hardly the whole story.

"Hmm," Satan mused. "There remains opacity. We have peeled off only one layer of the onion." He leafed through His papers.

"Was it that episode with Therion? No, that was entrapment and too recent. It is necessary for you to realize that your control of these Animations is not complete. When you enter the area of special expertise of another person, his knowledge and thrust preempt the scene. This was especially true in the early stages before your discipline asserted itself. Thus you were only partially responsible for the act in the Castle of the Seven Cups and cannot be damned to Hell solely on that account. The detail—"

"I don't want to review the detail!" Brother Paul cried.

"You forget where you are," Satan reminded him. "It is necessary to appraise your total record; we do not do shoddy anal-ysis here. Therion has had an anal fixation since his childhood, much stronger than yours; yours was merely a reflection of each boy's normal progression through this stage on the way to maturity. But the resolution of that belongs to his analysis, not yours. In this case he indulged in passive sodomy, then attempted to eject the result onto the face of the girl: symbolic defiling of all women in the exact manner of his namesake. The final effort he placed in the Seventh Cup for you to find. Thus he sent you into an extraordinary sequence—"

"Therion—did all that?"

"He dictated the scene. You merely played the role he specified for you—as others played the roles you specified for them in other scenes. Your will normally dominates; this was an exception owing partly to your private feeling of guilt. You were not properly aware of the nature of the role and would have balked it had you known. So you are guilty of laxity, not intent. We shall have to look deeper to judge you properly."

"But I participated!" Brother Paul cried in anguish.

"So you believe that even in the absence of knowledge or intent, you were culpable because of the act?"

"Yes," Brother Paul said without full conviction. "I *should* have guessed or stayed off those drugs. I should have kept control so as to prevent it happening."

"Then you must answer for it," Satan said. "You must do penance, and the penance is this: provide a species-survival rationale for sodomy."

"You want *me* to justify human homosexuality?" Brother Paul demanded, shocked.

"I don't *want;* I *require,"* Satan said. "You seem to be having the damnedest trouble remembering your situation. Kindly confine yourself to the issue: sodomy is not identical to homosexuality. The former is an act; the latter is a preference."

"My situation," Brother Paul repeated. He could not at the moment imagine anything more hellish than this penance.

"No stalling," Satan said. Flames danced about Brother Paul's feet: hot-foot galore. The pain was intense.

"I'm answering!" he screamed, and the flames subsided. Rationale? What rationale could there possibly be? Sodomy was an abomination!

The flames began to rise again. And under that savage prodding, Brother Paul vomited out his answer, the connection between feet and mouth virtually bypassing brain. "Reproduction is essential to the species. Therefore, it is compulsory behavior, rather than voluntary. Animals have in-heat cycles, with the smell of the female coercing the male to copulation. But human beings are more intelligent; they take longer to mature and have much more to learn. So they need a family situation with a male staying close to help protect, feed, and educate the offspring—"

"I question the relevance of this line of exploration," Satan said. "It sounds like an argument for heterosexuality." The flames reappeared, flicking playfully at Brother Paul's toes. His feet now seemed to be bare.

"It's relevant!" Brother Paul cried. "I am not talking about homosexuality, as you pointed out. I'm talking about the rationale for an act that may occur in a normally heterosexual situation."

"Well, I'll allow it this time," Satan said. The flames subsided again.

"So in primates the heat cycle is abandoned," Brother Paul continued hurriedly. "Sexuality is perennial. The female can be receptive any time of the day or year, and in this way she holds her man. But sometimes the family is interrupted by circumstance, such as war or natural catastrophe. A function that goes too long unused is apt to be lost, such as man's former ability to manufacture ascorbic acid in his body. Vitamin C. So the sexual drive in men is continuous and insistent. When there are no women, it expresses itself in various alternate ways—and one of these is sodomy. If it were not so, the drive to indulge in the sexual act with another individual might atrophy at the peril of the species."

"Yes, that will do nicely," Satan said. "Is sodomy therefore a sin?"

"Well, considered that way, in special circumstances—"

"You see," Satan said decisively, "there is no such thing as objective sin. A person only sins when he does what he believes to be wrong. Your definition of sin does not, upon reflection, include involuntary sodomy. Case dismissed."

Maybe so. Brother Paul would have to sort it all out more carefully at another time. "Therion—he served you well, if selfishly. Why did you kill him?"

"I did not kill him. There is no death in Hell. That's the Hell of it! Death would represent escape from retribution. I merely tortured him a little. A well-deserved humiliation, preparing him for the penance he must do."

Again Brother Paul wondered who was playing the part of Satan. It had to be Therion—yet how could he talk about himself this way? Unless this whole Animation really was guided by some Godly power, and this role was part of Therion's penance. Was there any way to be sure? "But if he made a bargain with You to bring us all here—"

"The Horned God makes no bargains! All souls that are My due will come to Me in due course. Why should I bargain for what is already Mine?"

"But you accepted *my* bargain—to spare Carolyn."

"Not really. She is innocent—not even a clothespin mars her record. She is as yet unborn. I cannot take her. And you—were already in My power."

"Then why did You torture me by threatening her?"

"This is Hell," Satan said simply. And of course that was true. Brother Paul realized that he had taken too narrow a view of Hell. Torture came in many forms—and the worst of these were internal.

More rustling of papers. "Why don't you computerize your damned records?" Brother Paul inquired irritably. Satan merely chuckled, and Brother Paul realized: this, too, was Hell.

"Sexual and/or scatological repression is not after all the root," Satan said. "Let's try the racial motif. You are of mixed ancestry—"

"Let's leave my ancestors out of it," Brother Paul said, fearing what would come out. *"They* are not on trial—" But the review was upon him. One did not get to argue much in Hell.

It was 1925. She was a young black woman too intelligent to remain in the ghetto. She had come to the high-rise district seeking quality employment. She had not been successful. This was not entirely racism; the fact that she was female had a lot to do with it. Now she was walking back to the apartment which she shared with another aspiring woman, because her money was running low and she still had to eat. It was early evening.

"Well, now!" A white man stepped out in front of her.

Instantly she reversed, fleeing him—but another man was behind her. He caught hold of her. There was the gleam of a knife. "You jus' be quiet, Brown Sugar," he said. "We ain't goin' to hurt you none—if you know your place."

She knew her situation, if not her place. She did not struggle or cry out. And they were true to their word. They did not beat her; after both had raped her, they let her go with only a perfunctory admonition about keeping her mouth shut if she didn't want them to come back and squeeze the chocolate milk out of her tits. They were pleased; they had saved two dollars apiece for a cleaner lay than the local house would have provided.

She kept it quiet. There was nothing she could do about it, for she didn't know either man. And if she *had,* it was the word of one nigger gal against two white men: forget it. She was a realist. She bought herself a good knife as insurance against future episodes, continued on her quest, and got her job. It was a good one as maid to a wealthy white family; they treated her well.

Then she learned that she was pregnant.

Her livelihood was destroyed, but not her life. She went home to her family and birthed her bastard son, and his skin was much lighter than hers. She raised him well with pride, for that light color was a mark of distinction. He was handsome and smart, and he married an open-minded white girl. Their daughter was lighter still, and race was less of a barrier than it had been. She married a white man who claimed to have some Indian blood somewhere in his ancestry; he was a career diplomat. Their son was Paul. He was no darker than a pure Caucasian with a summer tan—but he was one-eighth black. They went to Africa, partly because it was a prestigious, well-paid position. There was a political flare-up, minor on the world scene but quite serious for Americans in that region. Paul was hastily shipped out at the age of four; his parents wanted to assure his safety, if not their own.

Paul's paternal uncle took him in. Man and wife were conservative with an image to maintain; that little bit of Indian blood in their ancestry was a secret blot. They never told Paul he was black though this was the age when black was beautiful. Paul went to a white private school and associated only with whites. There was, of course, token integration at that school, but the occasional presence of blacks made no difference to Paul. He was not of their number. He had "passed."

He started school—with the snickering girls—but before the year was out his foster parents moved out to the country in the north. Paul had trouble in school, not so much with the teachers but with other children who teased him with the special cruelty only children understood. When he came home with a black eye, his foster father acted: "That boy is going to learn self-defense. We'll put him in a karate class."

There was such a class at a community center in a neighboring town; Paul and his foster father walked in and saw the people practicing in their white pajama-like outfits, landing on mattresses. "How much?" the father asked the instructor who was a young man in his mid twenties, mild-mannered and not large —hardly the type one would fear in the street. The rates were cheap. The man paid the money, completed the necessary form, obtained a pajama uniform called a *gi* for Paul, and left him there. Paul was about to learn self-defense.

Paul was nine years old and small for his age. The *gi* hung on him hugely. But there were other children there his size, and the instructor gave him personal attention for the first classes. The instructor's name was Steve—he demanded a no more formal address—and after Paul saw what he could do, he understood why there was no disrespect.

This was a judo class, not karate; they had walked into the wrong room. But as it turned out, judo was far better suited to Paul's needs than karate would have been, for it enabled a person to defend himself without hurting his opponent, and Paul did not like to hurt people. Judo was the science of throws and holds and, after those had been mastered, strikes and strangles and assorted leverages of pain. With this science a charging giant could be hurled violently to the ground and held there until he yielded. Two or more attackers could be tumbled into each other. A man with a knife or club could be rapidly disarmed. Yet the salient features of judo were courtesy and self-improvement. Students gave to their instructor and each other the respect due to people capable of dealing death—and of refraining from it.

It started slowly. First Paul had to learn to take falls so that he could be thrown to the mat without being hurt. Then he worked on basic throws. To his surprise, his first partner was a black girl slightly smaller than he was. But she wore a yellow belt, one grade higher than his white one, and he quickly discovered that she could beat him in physical combat and hold him down so that he could not get up. He developed an instant respect for this martial art; for if a girl who weighed less than he could do that to him, what might he do to a larger boy—once he learned judo?

At the end of the first class Steve took him aside. "How did you get that black eye, Paul?" he asked as if it were not obvious. He had the girl, whose name was Karolyn, follow Paul's instructions and reenact the way the school bully had stepped forward and punched with his right fist into Paul's left eye. Steve nodded. "Here is what you do for that. First, try to get away from him; step aside and run if you have to. Don't let him get close to you."

"But then the other kids—"

Steve nodded. "When, for one reason or another, you can't escape, you must defend yourself. There are many ways, but for you I think this is best." He summoned another boy, larger than Paul. *"Nage no kata,* second throw, Uki," Steve told the boy. The boy closed his fist and shot a punch at the girl's head. She blocked it up with her left forearm, whirled, caught his arm with her right arm, and heaved. The boy flew over her back and landed with a resounding slap on the mat. "That throw is called *ippon seoi nage,* the one-armed shoulder throw," Steve told Paul. "You are going to learn it—now."

Paul was hurt many times after that—but seldom did he suffer at the hands of his schoolmates, and never again did anyone land a punch on his face. Judo, to a certain extent, became a way of life for him. He progressed from white belt to yellow belt to orange and green and finally brown. He entered judo tournaments, winning some matches and losing others, but he always put up a good fight and was as courteous in defeat as in victory. Never did he seek a quarrel outside of class—and seldom did anyone seek one with him.

But he always remembered that first class, and how a little girl had overcome him and held him down—and never teased him about it. Paul was somewhat wary of girls in general, but in his secret fashion he loved Karolyn. She left the class a few months after he started, and he never saw her again, but she had left her mark on him in the form of a fond memory.

When Paul was eighteen, his foster parents were divorced. But by that time he was scheduled for college, and an education trust fund that had been arranged long ago by his parents carried him through. After college he sought his family roots—and for the first time learned of his black heritage.

"No, no!" Satan said. "That's not it! That's way too late! You have no guilty race secret; you were not even aware that you were passing—and if you had been, you would have been culpable only for the lie, not the fact. The culpability of your society that discriminated covertly on the basis of race was in any event worse than your own."

"This is Satan talking?" Brother Paul marveled aloud. "The Father of Lies?"

"Satan never lies. It is the minions of God who lie, cheat, steal and deceive—until the fruits of these iniquities come at last to Me. I am Truth—and because the truth is often ugly, I am called evil." The papers rustled again, annoyingly. "I'm going to try a somewhat random shot based on intuition. I suspect the blocked-out secret of your life occurs in childhood somewhere in the foster-parent era. I think it involves a female, but perhaps not in the sexual or racist way. So I want—one day of your life, at age eight."

Paul had to urinate. He wanted to continue sleeping as it was cold out there in the outhouse and scary at night, for there might be a porcupine. One thing a dog never did twice was nose after a porky; that first hellish noseful of barbed quills invariably suf-ficed. Paul did not care to walk into a porcupine by accident. Better simply to piss in the snow just outside the back door. But—he had to go, and that was the place.

He got up groggily, finding the air oddly comfortable, not cold at all though it was winter. He walked down the hall—and it opened out on a pleasant, modern, tiled bathroom with a flush toilet—how could he have forgotten about this? He stood at the toilet and let go. The sensation was immensely gratifying; the liquid flowed and flowed, seeming to have no end, but rather gaining in force and conviction.

Then he felt something strange. A wetness about his middle, as if he were standing waist deep in a hot bath. Yet there was nothing visible. He fought off the sensation—but it would not be denied. With slow horror, the realization forced itself upon him: he *was* standing in brine. Lying in it. For he was still in bed; everything had been a dream. Except the urination.

As usual, he had wet his bed. He opened his eyes. It was dark. It was still night. Too early to get up. Well, he was comfortable where he was; the rubber sheet sealed the depression of the sagging bed so that his hot bath stayed with him. So long as he kept the blankets on top and dry, he was all right.

He remembered when it had started two years ago. They had put him in a hospital for observation, and in five days there he had been so tense he never wet the bed, though they "forgot" to bring him the bedpan for as long as 24 hours at a time. One morning there, he had awoken to spy half a dozen nurses clustered just outside his door, whispering with animation. Were they talking about him? "Don't tell him . . ." but the words trailed into unintelligibility. There was hushed laughter like that of the clothespin girls, only these were big girls. "The way *I* do it. . . ." Do *what?* "Just shove it *in.*" Surely not a clothespin! Suddenly he caught on: this was a hospital. They were planning surgery in secret. Don't tell the patient because he might climb out the window and escape. Just take the knife and shove it *in.*

Paul lay in the bed bathed in cold sweat that resembled the urine. They were going to cut him open. He had been assured that they were only going to *look* at him (which was bad enough) in the hospital—but that was what they had said the first time he went to the dentist too. Grownups thought it was all right to lie to children "for their own good," which usually meant something painful or extremely unpleasant. It meant that no adult could be trusted, ever.

But the nurses dispersed, leaving him alone with his thoughts. If not now, *when?* All day he cowered in his prison bed, waiting for them to come, for it to start. His appetite decreased. He lost interest in the games provided, in his reading book, in his drawings. What was the use of them in the face of this terrible threat?

At last he was released. The hospital's verdict: there was nothing physically wrong with him. Presumption: he could stop wetting his bed if he wanted to. So he was encouraged to want to. He had to wash his own sheets each day. The word "punishment" was never used, but the message was plain: *You do this awful thing, you clean it up yourself.* Somehow that treatment was not effective. Paul needed no extra motivation; he *wanted* to have a dry bed—and could not. Something always happened in the night, no matter how hard he tried to resist.

He was drifting back to sleep this morning, fortunately. Nightmares seldom came after his bladder was empty. The hospital memory was fading; it no longer really bothered him. So long as he never had to go back for that lurking surgery. Mornings were not so bad. His feet were cold, but he was used to that. He heard the faint, eerie hoot of some wild animal ranging the forest; he was glad he was not out there. He remembered the prior year at the boarding school, he being the smallest of the small, beaten up as a matter of course in the initiation, fleeing, terrified. Yet even this nightmare was not total. One morning one of the bullies, a boy a year or two older than Paul, came in before Paul was up. "Hey, I hear you piddle in bed!" the bully exclaimed. "Lessee." And he ripped off Paul's blanket.

Paul had wet the bed. He had kicked off his soaking pajamas, and they lay in a damp wad at his feet; he was naked from the waist down, steaming in urine. The bully looked for a long moment while Paul lay still, not afraid to move but simply having no option. He had long since lost his pride of person as far as his body went. Then the bully replaced the blanket and went away without comment. Later that day, the bully talked to Paul privately. "When I piss last thing at night, sometimes I just stand there at the pisser a while, and then a little more will come. Then some more. Maybe if you waited long enough, you could get it all out, and—" He shrugged. He was trying to be helpful.

That bully never bothered Paul again; his sympathy had been aroused. A few days later, in the presence of a group of boys, another bully came to Paul. "I won't hit you any more," he said, and they shook hands. "And if he *does,* we'll hit *him,*" one of the larger boys said. And after that no one picked on Paul. Yet, for him, the school remained a horror; he just wanted to get home.

Now he was home and satisfied. He knew when he was well off. Sometimes he imagined this was all a long, bad dream, and that he would wake up and be four years old again in Africa in his happy real life, but for two years the conviction had been growing that this would never happen. *This,* now, was his real life; the other was the dream.

His feet had stopped hurting with cold; instead they were flaming as though a fire blazed about them. That was nice. Paul fancied he could see the leaping flames, gold and yellow, sending sparks up toward the ceiling. He could lie here forever enjoying that bonfire. If Hell were the place of heat and flames, he had no fear of it; better to go there than out into the snow on a windy morning.

The clangor of the alarm jolted him awake. He hadn't realized he had made it back to sleep. No question about it; the thin cold light of dawn was seeping in. Mornings in winter were so *bleak!* He lingered for a moment more, then took a breath, held it, gritted his teeth, and threw off the blanket. Oh, it was cold! The floor was wood, but it was so cold his flame-tender feet could not tolerate it; he danced from toe to toe with the acute discomfort of it. He dashed naked downstairs to the bathroom; it had no toilet since there was no running water in this room, but there was a pitcher by the table. Once all houses had had oil heat and city-piped water everywhere, but the crises of energy and water and pollution had driven many families out into the wilderness where the air was still clean and it was possible to be largely self-sufficient. Water that was carried by hand was seldom wasted; that helped the declining water table.

He sloshed some water into the basin, soaked the washcloth in it, then gritted his teeth, closed his eyes, and stabbed the wadded cloth at his chest. The shock was like ice, for winter in an unheated house brought ice very close. Sometimes the kitchen pipes froze, so that water could not be pumped inside, and they had to break the ice and dip it out in a wooden bucket. But soon his chest warmed the cloth somewhat, and he rubbed it in a zig-zag pattern down and around, getting his stomach and thighs. Then another clothful for his backside. He moved rapidly, for his teeth were chattering, his skin blue. Still, this was no worse than swimming in the mountain pool in summer; the water rushed through a narrow channel from its origin somewhere high in the mountains and was so chill he dared not dive in, but had to walk in slowly, letting his feet grow numb, then his shins, and slowly up until at last his whole body was numb and he could swim. Some people *could* dive in, venting a scream of reaction as the chill struck them all at once—but they were better padded than he with subcutaneous fat. That was the secret of the walrus. Paul was skinny; the cold went right through to his bones, and when he got out those bones radiated it back into his flesh. It took him half an hour to get warm again. But he liked swimming. It lifted him free of the visible ground, making it seem as though he were flying. Flight represented a kind of escape, however transitory.

In less than a minute he was through washing. He dumped the

basin into the tub, whose drainpipe poked through a hole in the wall to empty into the weeds outside, and he charged back upstairs. Theoretically this expenditure of energy should warm his body, but the magnitude of cold was simply too great to be dented by such measures. He used no towel; the water dried as he moved. Now at last he could dress, and that was a comfort. The worst of the morning was done. Pants and shirt and sweater and socks. He knocked his boots together at the heels before trusting his feet to them; once he had donned them without doing that, and he felt something funny, and found a big black multilegged roach inside. That had been enough to condition him for some years yet. He was not bug shy, but he didn't like such things in his shoes. Some bugs liked to bite.

Down to the warm kitchen heated by the wood stove. These same power crises had made wood fashionable again, especially in the country where wood was free for the picking up and cutting. That stove was lit in the morning and kept going all day; sometimes when it was zero outside, it was a hundred in the kitchen in the old F degrees the backwoods people still used. In real degrees C, it was minus 18 out, plus 38 in.

Paul liked the stove; there was just room behind it next to the back wall where he could sit, enjoying a steady temperature around 40° C. He could never get too much heat; it reminded him of the old happy years in Africa when it had always been warm physically and emotionally. The two were strongly linked for him. But no time for that now; his cracked-wheat porridge was ready, and he had to hurry. He poured some white goat's milk on top to cool it enough for the first spoonful and started in. It was good, filling stuff, and there was always plenty of it; he never went hungry.

"I wonder if we're getting anywhere?" Satan murmured. "Well, we have plenty of time. On with it."

Then the rush to cram into galoshes, overcoat, mittens, and hood, tying it close about his face to protect his ears. It was a long walk to school, but not bad once the path had been beaten down. It was cold out, but the wind was down; an inch of snow (a scant two centimeters in real measure) had fallen in the night, but this hardly obscured the deep track that had been broken through the crust last week. Snow crusts were something; they formed when the sun melted the top layer of snow, and then the night froze it back tight like ice on a lake. Once he had slipped on a hard crust at the top of the hill, and been unable to regain his footing because only an axe could cut through it when it was strong, and had to slide helplessly a quarter kilometer to the bottom. No harm done; it had been fun in fact. Another time he had stamped his foot to break through a thin crust to find the solid ground some centimeters below. Suddenly he had sunk down another ten centimeters: that was not ground, but a second crust! The ground was deeper than he had remembered. Then that, too, had broken, and he came at last to the *real* ground, hidden beneath three crusts, a full meter down. Once a crust was covered by new snowfall, it never melted until spring. Like life in a way; once he settled into a new level, he could not go back to the old one. Sometimes he tunneled under a crust, hollowing out a snow cave, using the crust as a roof. Snow was cold, but it had its points.

He crested the ridge and started down through the forest on the other side. Here there was wind; it whistled through the bare trees. Beeches, sugar maples, scattered clumps of white birches, scattered patches of white pine—which, of course, was not white but green, even in winter. It was four kilometers to the school, but he was used to the walk and liked it. The animals were harmless; he saw their tracks crisscrossing in the fresh snow. Sometimes he would spy a deer bounding away. He had never seen a bear though they were present. But at times the snow itself was more interesting. One night there had been a freezing rain; it formed icicles on every twig of every tree, weighting them down. The forest had become a fairyland of glassy pendants, tinkling as his passage disturbed them. He had never before witnessed such absolute beauty! Maybe part of his attraction was its fragility, its crystalline evanescence. In one day the ice had been dirtied and broken, and in three days it was largely gone. Trees were beautiful too—but you could always see a tree. The ice forest had been a once-in-a-lifetime experience, treasured less for its nature than for its rarity.

He passed a large old oak tree leaning over the trail. "Far and wide as the eye can wander, heath and bog are everywhere," he sang aloud, picturing the snow as heath and bog. "Not a bird sings out to cheer us, oaks are standing gaunt and bare. We are the peat-bog soldiers, marching with our spades, to the bog." He liked folk songs and enjoyed singing and humming them, but he couldn't do it at home. His foster father objected, calling it noisemaking. "But for us there is no complaining, winter will in time be past. One day we shall cry rejoicing: homeland, dear, you're mine at last!" He felt the tears coming to his eyes and got choked up so he couldn't sing any more. Would winter ever pass for him?

Down the mountain two kilometers, then up the next slope. This was a wilderness route though there was a plowed-out road he could have used. The problem with the road was that it went by the house of Mrs. Kurry. That story went way back to last year. One day at school, Paul had washed his hands and noted how distinctive the surface of the bar of soap was: firm yet impressionable. His artistic sense was awakened. He put the bar against the tap and twisted. Sure enough, there was a neat circular indentation as if a spaceship had landed in this miniature planet, melting the very stone by the heat of its jet, then departed, leaving only this melt mark on the airless surface. But later that day there was an outcry: "This water tastes like soap!" Oh oh—it had not occurred to Paul that soap would attach to the tap; he had been contemplating the other end of it, the art. He confessed what he had done, accepted his ridicule, and cleaned it off the tap, and forgotten the matter. But others had not forgotten. To them, this was an injury due to be avenged.

Another day Paul had enjoyed himself in new, light, fluffy snow beside the road to school by lying on his back and waving his arms to make "Angels" and running around saplings, one hand on the trunks to guide him in a perfect circle, to leave donut-shaped paths. How easy it was to form geometric shapes in nature if you only knew how! It was merely idle play on the way to school, not taking long enough to make him late. It happened to be near Mrs. Kurry's house. She stormed out and delivered the worst verbal abuse of his life. She accused him of ruining her trees, cutting a hole in one of her tires, and being sassy—when he tried to explain that he had not harmed the trees, knew nothing of her tire, and did not possess a knife. "You did it!" she screamed. "Just like you broke that tap at school!" And she chased him off.

The matter had not ended there; there was a letter to the teacher, complaints to Paul's family, and a charge from her house whenever he passed by. But he had to go to school, and this was the only road. Finally this alternate trail through the forest was set up so that Paul would not have to pass her house. His life had been made harder, and he had been terrorized—because this neighbor had borne false witness against him.

"Ah, yes," Satan observed. "We have her here in Hell now.

Beelzebub's dominion; I must make sure the Lord of the Flies has her doing penance for false witness." The papers rustled as He made a note.

At school it was okay. The kids hardly teased him anymore about his hand twitches or compulsive counting of things, and he had a lively interest in many fields, so it wasn't so bad. He had a couple of stomach aches in the course of the day, but he was used to these. Only when a bad one struck, the kind that hung him up writhing in agony for half a day straight, did he really mind—and fortunately those powerful ones did not come often. Today was just a minor-pain day, no problem at all.

He finished his written work early and doodled on his paper, trying to draw a realistic dormer window—the kind that poked out of a slanting roof. A straight window was easy because it was all straight lines, but a dormer had all sorts of angles that were hard to visualize. It was difficult to draw it on a flat paper so that it looked real, and he wasn't quite sure it could be done at all. After all, *it* was three dimensional. But it was a challenge. Maybe if he angled a line *here*—

Uh-oh. The teacher had called on him, and he hadn't heard her at all. His classmates were laughing at him. They thought he was stupid, and he suspected they were right. Why couldn't he pay proper attention? Others were smart; *they* paid attention. And he had lost his inspiration for the dormer.

On the way home he heard the distant barking of a dog. The hair on his skin reacted, and he looked about nervously, hoping the animal didn't come this way. Once he had petted a strange dog, and it had jumped up and bared its teeth in his face with such a growl he had fled in tears. Other children had thought that very funny. Last year some lumbercamp dogs had charged him in a pack, barking, nosing up, scaring him. One had nipped him in the rear, but no one paid attention. They always said that a barking dog didn't bite though that was manifestly untrue. The thing was, a twenty kilogram dog seemed a lot bigger to a twenty-seven kilogram boy than it did to a seventy kilogram man. But today Paul was lucky; the distant dog went elsewhere.

Actually, the dogs were not nearly so bad as the Monster. At least he could *see* them. The Monster was quite another matter. It followed him home from school each day, huge and malignant, like a centipede the size of a dragon with deadly pincers in front and a ten meter long sting tail behind and little glowing eyes on the ends of its eye stalks that could twist about to see anything. Its myriad side legs stretched out to comb the brush: that was to prevent Paul from hiding in a bush in order to let it pass and get ahead of him. If that ever happened, Paul would have power over the Monster because then *he* would be following *it* and he would have *seen* it. But he dared not ambush it because of the extreme care it took with bushes. He had to see it from *behind*. That was the law of their encounter.

He looked back, feeling that prickle of apprehension up his back. Nothing was visible. That was also the way of it; the Monster could retreat in an instant. If Paul only had eyes in the back of his head . . . the thing was, it could only approach him from behind, from the direction he wasn't looking. When he turned around, the direct force of his vision made it back off, giving him more leeway. But if he should run without turning back to look, too long, it would overtake him and—

No! Paul stopped, nerved himself, turned, and strode back down the snow trail. He would show it he was not afraid of it though he trembled in his knees. He would spot its tracks, *proving* it had been following him. That would be a point for him. Once he got an advantage, however trivial, he would be able to use that leverage to drive the Monster back and back until finally it was gone. Then it would seek some other prey instead of him.

There were no tracks, of course; he should have anticipated this. Its hundred padded feet made little impression in the snow; each carried very little weight, and the Monster was very cunning about brushing away any telltale marks. Almost too clever for him. . . .

Paul turned about again. With a soundless gloat the Monster resumed the pursuit. Paul looked back, but it had dodged out of sight already. He could not defeat it this way. Now he had to re-retrace his path, enduring the hazard again. He had only complicated his journey.

Strange that the Monster never pursued him in the morning. Maybe that was because then he was fresh and vigorous—or because he was going toward the long chore that was school. Why should the Monster interfere when he was heading *in* to trouble? It preferred to go after him when he was on the verge of safety. But mostly, he thought, it was because the shadows were lengthening in the afternoon. The Monster was a devotee of shadows, a beast of darkness, whose strength increased as light decreased.

"You were a bit too smart for the Monster," Satan remarked

appreciatively. "I remember with what gnashing of tooth it complained about the way you kept backing it off, just when it thought it had you. We finally had to reassign it." Infernal humor!

Now, as Paul came near the crest, he saw the late sun shifting through the trees, making the forest brighter, prettier, as though there were a clearing. In the summer this effect was enhanced, shaping seeming glades where ferns and flowers grew lovely. In winter the entire forest was lighter, so the effect diminished. Still, in places it remained strong, and this was such a place. But Paul gave no glad start of discovery; instead he averted his eyes from the effect, breathing hard, and ran until he could no longer see it.

He made it home. Junie was nibbling the bark of a tree near the house; she made a little bleat of pleasure and plowed through the snow toward him. He liked Junie as he liked all goats; not only did she provide good milk, she was affectionate. He stroked her white-striped nose. She was a Toggenburg, the handsomest of goats. Too bad she couldn't come to school with him; if the Monster came, she would just butt it with her sawed-off horns. No one won a head-to-head collision with a goat!

But he had chores to do. First he had to split tomorrow's kindling for the stove, then wash out last night's sheets. The splitting was fun; he liked wood, and he liked the feel of its splitting. The first split was hard, halving the log; but doing the halves was easier, and rendering each quarter into fine kindling was easiest with such a rapid feeling of accomplishment. If only the problems of life could be divided and conquered similarly!

Laundering the big sheet was not fun. The water was cold, making his hands get pink and hurty, and it was hard to wring out. He twisted it, on and on, until it resembled a giant rope, a hawser like that used to anchor a ship, but there was always more water in it, waiting to drip, no matter how hard he squeezed. But it had to be done.

He looked at the drips descending from the sheet. He was suddenly thirsty—and he had forgotten to tank up on water. He was under a proscription. They had taken him to a doctor one day about the bedwetting, and the doctor had said: "No water after four in the afternoon." And that had been the word. It had had no effect on the bedwetting, but it made his evening life a torment of thirst. Now he put a corner of the wet sheet between his teeth, tasting the faint remainder of urine, helping to hold it while he wrung it out with both hands (he told himself), and sucked a few precious drops surreptitiously. It wasn't enough, but it helped some; even a single drop became gratifying.

In the evening his foster father read to him: stories of adventure, fantasy, history—all fascinating. Paul was in love with the past, the future, and the imaginary. Those other realms were always so interesting, partly because of their exotic nature and partly because they were not *here*.

But at last it was full night and time to sleep. Paul had a lamp, a dim night light, but it wasn't enough. For now the ultimate dread of his existence loomed, and the name of it was Fear. Yet it was admixed with wonder, too, that lured him back again and again to—

America! Perhaps only the foreign born could appreciate the full meaning of that word. He had come to find the glories of the new land spelled out by a single beautiful song. He did not know its title or all its words and could not fathom its allusions, but he did not need to. This song—it was not so much a reflection of the new world, it was the new world itself.

He could see the vast terrain, covered with fruited plains and waving with amber grain and studded with jewel-like alabaster cities that gleamed under the spacious skies. Magnificent purple mountains extended from the ordinary sea in the east, that he had crossed, to the wonderful shining sea in the far far west, almost beyond imagination. It all blended into a vague yet brilliant image somewhat resembling a single field where the great trees became smaller, dwindling to saplings and finally to brush and green fern and pretty flowers. A field of rapture whose brief image brought warmth to his being. America! America! He loved her through that song.

Yet America was the city too—a great metropolis whose architecture scraped the sky, the smoke of industry rising up toward God. Cars, trains, ships, aircraft, spacecraft, printing presses, atomic power plants, huge solar reflectors in orbit—the wonderful technology of civilization. Nature and Science: two images, each alluring.

The two fragmented into four, and these became framed and frozen. Four pictures seemingly innocent—yet taken together, they were nightmare.

1. A woman walking along a city street, a small boy at her side.
2. The woman in a vidphone booth, the child looking in through the glass.

3. A man standing in a clearing, a lion at his side. Nearby, a lightly but richly clad woman, lying on a pallet.

4. The man holding the lion in the air, chest high.

What was the secret of these still images that made them horrible? His mind proceeded inexorably to the interpretation though he dreaded it.

America! Yet somehow the rousing cadences echoed hollowly, for the city through which he walked with his foster mother was not exactly alabaster. Nevertheless, it had some of the luster and excitement characteristic of the new world. It was not lonely like the farm; there were people, and stores, and television, and things happening. A happy picture.

One of his earliest memories of Africa was not Africa at all, but the vision of Tomorrow. Tomorrow was a row of houses down the street, and he knew he was going down that street and that someday he would be there at those strange houses instead of here in the familiar. Suddenly Tomorrow came, and it was called America, and he was unprepared for it. He had thought his parents would be there with him. There were nice people in the new world, but all he really wanted was to go back home.

He realized that the city could be a trap. His foster mother went into the glassy doorway to play with the marvelous contraption called the vidphone: some mysterious adult business of the machine age. Then she put her hand to the door to come out again, but the door was stuck. She could not leave. Sudden alarm; the machines could not be trusted, the city would not let go. The promise of America had become a threat even to its own people.

Paul's foster father preferred the farm, while his foster mother preferred the city. The two seemed destined never quite to meet. Paul did not understand the laws of the conflict; he saw only the opposing forces: the city and the country. The woman was the creature of the city, the man of the country. They were married, yet could not unite. He could call neither one good or evil, right or wrong; both were good, both right—yet they warred.

The man stood in the country amid the trees, the symbol of strength, dominating the lion. The woman was now in his power, spirited from the vid-trap to the pallet, sedated. Surely the man would prevent the lion from doing her harm!

Paul wandered one day through the open fields so like the glorious spaces of the song. He had not chosen, *could* not choose between the rival forces; both city and country were parts of

America, the promised land, Tomorrow. At the foot of a grassy hillside he saw a skull. It was the vast white hollow-eyed bone of a cow. He realized that this dead thing had once been part of a living animal similar to the animals he knew like Junie. Now it was defunct, its warm flesh gone, its hooves nevermore to walk the green field. Had it mooed high, or had it mooed low? He could not know; it was gone. He looked upon the fact of death, the face of death, and began to realize the utter finality of it. *Nevermore!* How had it died? Maybe an African lion had killed it.

Now the man was holding the lion in the air, happy with the beast, smiling. Yet death was in that picture: not the specific act of killing, but the morbid knowledge that death had come and swept its scythe and left its mark, and nothing would ever take that mark away, for it was final. The lion had fed. The pallet was empty. The country had devoured the city. The man was holding up the lion to see how much weight it had gained.

Now the field that was America was intertwined with the stigmata of horror, terror, and death. The fear was real, the fear was ultimate; by day it could be largely avoided or blunted, but by night it became overwhelming. He was gifted, cursed, with a graphic imagination; when darkness cut off normal sight, his mind's eye filled the world with spectral images so real that he could see every detail. Light was the only defense; so long as his eyes remained open and seeing, the nightmare was held at bay, like the Monster of the forest.

It was the body that haunted him. The body that had not quite been in the four pictures, but that he knew was there, perhaps in the hidden fifth picture. The body with the flesh torn off where the lion had fed; the hollow, sightless eyes, the bleached white bones protruding from that which had once been—

Screams, screams in the night! It was a sight too mind shattering to face, yet too persistent to ignore. It impinged upon his consciousness, inescapable no matter how he fled. It loomed in fair fields, it cruised by like the engine of a locomotive, always lurking, a mass of horror driving him relentlessly toward insanity. It impinged upon his very soul, and almost, now, it had *become* his soul.

"Now I lay me down to sleep, I pray the Lord my soul to keep," he whispered. "If I should die before I wake, I pray the Lord my soul to take." He repeated it in singsong, in the tune he had learned for it, trying to blot out the horror, to shove it away so he

could sleep at last. But it would not be denied, and every flicker of
the lamp brought it closer until he fancied he could feel it touching
his cold toes, nudging them, where he could not quite see, and he
dared not look. How could he look at a feeling? How he wished
day would come to release him from his torture. But the somber
mass of the night loomed between him and day, forcing its torture
on him. Tomorrow—yet this *was* Tomorrow, and so there was no
escape. This night's Tomorrow would only start the cycle again; he
was bound to it with no relief possible. For the horror was what
was past, not what was to happen. With sudden inspiration, he
modified his prayer: "May I sleep—and never wake," he said, and
then he slept.

"And so you sealed it over," Satan said as Brother Paul lay
bathed in sweat steaming like urine, eyes staring, hands twitching.
"You had adapted to everything in your youth, except for that.
You could neither explain it nor accept it. You chose to block out
that entire segment of your life; that was the only course available
to you, given your then existing needs and capabilities. But of
course it did not leave you. It remained as subconscious motivation. The five great forces of your life—Fire, Water, Air, Earth
and Spirit—evoked piecemeal by the cards of the Tarot. The Fire
of the burning wood, granting temporary relief from the
encompassing cold; the Water of your wet bed, while yet you
suffered from thirst; the Air of the violence about you in the form
of Mrs. Kurry, the dogs and the invisible Monster, not to mention
the gas in your tummy that caused you small and great pains; the
Earth of your ruptured self-esteem, your neurotic twitchings, lack
of social status; and the Spirit that ruled over all of you supreme:
Fear."

"Fear," Brother Paul repeated weakly.

"Yet you had a lot of frustrated talent, for art is a thing of the
Spirit," Satan continued. "You might have been a sculptor, but
your soap carving on the tap scotched that. You could have gone
into music, but your parents stopped your singing in company at
the outset. You had fair artistic talent and could have been a
painter—but your teacher thought your drawings mere distractions. So your potential achievement of self-esteem and escape
from nothingness via the route of creative expression was denied,
and in the end you had to write it all off as a loss."

Brother Paul did not argue.

Satan shook his head. "This is a tough one! I had figured you for hidden sexual or racial sin, considering your background, but fear is not a sin by conventional definitions. Cowardice is another matter—but there is little to suggest you were ever a coward. You tried to fight back, but were overwhelmed by events."

"But the sealing off—I finally gave up on the problem," Brother Paul said, not caring that he was arguing against his own interest. "I couldn't face the fear, so I fled it. I—"

"You are honest; that's the most awkward thing about you," Satan said. "You were uprooted, removed from your home and family in Africa, and planted in new soil. But your foster parents had problems of their own. It was in part the city-country schism. Their lifestyles differed, and they could not agree, so they engaged in a decade-long tug-of-war that terminated in separation and divorce. Your fragile new roots were broken again as you shuttled from city to country, needing both, needing a unified family. You finally got the country—at the price of the family. You were too small to understand that it was not your fault; when your foster mother returned to the city, you thought *you* had driven her away: figuratively killed her. You were unable to stand on one foot, on half a family—not in your root-pruned condition. So it is scarcely surprising that you fell. Your bedwetting, twitching, and nightmare were merely symptoms; it was no longer possible for you to survive whole and sane in that situation. So—you stepped out of it when you had the opportunity—by orienting your life around the lifestyle of judo and sealing off your memories of home. I really hesitate to condemn you to eternal damnation for that."

"You have already done it," Brother Paul said. "You have opened out my secret. Now Hell is with me—in my memory where it once was shut out."

"But you are stronger now than you were then," Satan pointed out. "You have regrown your roots in the Holy Order of Vision. Your life in that capacity has been exemplary ever since you suffered your Vision of Conversion. And in fact you have not been dragged before Me kicking and screaming; you descended voluntarily to Hell itself. Your last free act before being consumed by Me was to plead for your innocent daughter, who does not even exist yet, named in honor of a girl you admired twenty years ago, and for her safety you sacrificed your manhood."

Satan paused thoughtfully, rustling His papers again. "Of course, that was governed by your fear of losing your sight, so that you would not be limited to the nightmares of perpetual darkness, the Monster and the Corpse. But overall, the nobility of the sacrifice outweighs the specific motive of choice of punishments. No, I'm very much afraid your case remains in doubt. You *do* have evil on your conscience, and you are humanly fallible, but there is no clear shifting of the scales."

Brother Paul was coming out of his lingering shock of memory. This might be an Animation, but those memories were real. Yet Satan was correct: he *was* stronger now than he had been as a child: he had a much broader perspective. He could appreciate how much beauty and good there had been in his sealed-over life; it had been a shame to obliterate that along with the unfaceable. Satan had made an accurate assessment. "Do with me what you will," Brother Paul said. He was discovering a genuine, fundamental, disconcerting respect for Satan.

"I shall put you to the torture of the Three Wishes," Satan decided. "Three because it took me three attempts to evoke your guiltiest secret. I am always fair."

"Three wishes?"

"That is correct. I will grant you three wishes—and upon the use you make of them, shall you be judged."

"But I could simply wish for Salvation!" Brother Paul protested.

Satan shook His horned head again. "So hard to deceive an honest man! Now I must confess the trap: you could wish for Salvation—and you would lose it because your wish was selfish. I would honor it by shipping you to Heaven—you alone, not your friends or your daughter—and the Pearly Gates would not open for your selfish soul. You cannot knowingly seek purely personal gain by demonic means."

"That rules out a lot of things," Brother Paul said. "But I don't see that it should be a torture even so. There are innocuous wishes I could make."

Satan smiled, and now the tusks showed. "You will surely find out."

"Do I have any time to think about it?"

"You have eternity. Right here."

"Oh. Very well. I wish for knowledge of the true origin and meaning of Tarot."

Satan nodded slowly. "You are a clever man. I perceive the likely nature of your following wishes."

No doubt. Brother Paul hoped that the responses to the first two wishes would enable him to phrase the third one in such a way as to obtain the answer to his quest here. If he finally discovered the way to learn whether there was a separate, objective God of Tarot—

"But knowledge itself is neither good nor evil," Satan continued. "It is how you acquire it and what you do with it that counts—as you shall discover. Therefore—on your way, Uncle!"

Suddenly Brother Paul dropped through a hole in the floor. He slid down a chute that twisted and looped like an intestine. *Oh, no!* he thought. *I'm to be shit out, colored brown, like the insult of the Dozens game!*

But as he reached the nadir, the passage closed in about him, squeezing him through a nether loop, then upward. Fluid surrounded him, moving him hydraulically on. The pressure became almost intolerable as the tube constricted yet more. Then there was an abrupt release as he was geysered up and out with climactic force. He had a vision of the Tarot Tower exploding. He sailed through the air, looking back, and realized: this was indeed the meaning of that card, the House of God or the House of the Devil. This was Revelation! *He had been ejaculated from Satan's monstrous erect phallus.* He was the Seed, proceeding to what fate he could not guess.

22

HOPE/FEAR
(STAR)

When the High Patriarch of the Christians in Constantinople made a motion, the priests would diligently collect it in squares of silk and dry it in the sun. Then they would mix it with musk, amber and benzoin, and, when it was quite dry, powder it and put it up in little gold boxes. These boxes were sent to all Christian kings and churches, and the powder was used as the holiest incense for the sanctification of Christians on all solemn occasions, to bless the bride, to fumigate the newly born, and to purify a priest on ordination. As the genuine excrements of the High Patriarch could hardly suffice for ten provinces, much less for all Christian lands, the priests used to forge the powder by mixing less holy matters with it, that is to say, the excrements of lesser patriarchs and even of the priests themselves. This imposture was not easy to detect. These Greek swine valued the powder for other virtues; they used it as a salve for sore eyes and as a medicine for the stomach and bowels. But only kings and queens and the very rich could obtain these cures, since, owing to the limited quantity of raw material, a dirham-weight of the powder used to be sold for a thousand dinars in gold.

—THE BOOK OF THE THOUSAND NIGHTS AND ONE NIGHT: translated from Arabic to French by Dr. J.C. Mardrus, and from French to English by Powys Mathers: Volume I, London, The Casanova Society, 1923.

The first thing Brother Paul saw was the star. It hovered just above the horizon, bright and beautiful and marvelously pure: the Star of Hope.

But immediately he felt fear: where was he? Was this another aspect of Hell? What menace lurked in this unknown region? He hardly dared move until he knew whether he stood on a plain—or the brink of a precipice.

Fortunately he had not long to wait. Light grew; it was breaking dawn, brighter in one portion of the firmament, giving him convenient orientation. He knew which way North was. Now if only he knew where in the universe *he* was. Not Planet Tarot, it seemed; the vegetation, air and gravity were too Earth-like to occur anywhere but on Planet Earth. But he needed to narrow it down more than that! It had to be the temperate zone, for now he saw that the trees were deciduous.

Perhaps he had seen the Morning Star, actually the Planet Venus, symbol of love. He hoped that was a good sign. But other stars could shine in the morning too, depending on the season, cloud cover, and mood of the viewer.

He stood on a pleasant hillside. It was evidently spring. Though the morning was cool, it was not unpleasant, and the odors of nature were wonderful. Flowers were opening, and they seemed to be of familiar types though he could not identify them precisely. If he had his life to do over again, he would pay more attention to flowers! Carolyn would have enjoyed this scene.

Carolyn—where was she now? Not until the recent review of his past had he realized consciously the rationale of her naming. Carolyn, one-sixteenth black, in honor of the all-black Karolyn who had shown him what judo could do and never snickered. Satan had said Carolyn did not yet exist—yet she *did* exist, for he knew her and loved her and she was his daughter. The colonist child was merely the actress, standing in lieu of the real Carolyn, who was—where? He could not believe she was a creature solely of his imagination; he was emotionally unable to accept that. Well, at least she had avoided Hell; probably Lee had taken her back out of the Vision. Thank God!

Or was it Satan that deserved the thanks?

Music interrupted his thoughts. Beautiful, flute-like—was the melody the "Song of the Morning"? Edvard Grieg, who composed it as part of the famous *Peer Gynt* suites, had lived in the late

19th century, and he was Swedish—no, Norwegian. Could that be where and when Brother Paul found himself—in historical Europe? Given the capacities of Animation, this was well within the range of possibility. How he would love to meet that marvelous musician, one of his favorites! But no, this melody was not that; one passage had merely seemed similar. So—forget Grieg, unfortunately. Satan would hardly have granted him that incidental pleasure.

But why guess at all? The tune issued from the vale to the west. Brother Paul walked toward it. He realized he was wearing a belted tunic and crude leather shoes made comfortable by use. But something itched him—ouch! He suspected it was lice. That put him back somewhere in the Middle Ages, probably Europe. Sanitation was not well regarded then. Not by the Christians. In fact it had been said that Christianity was the only great religion where dirtiness was next to Godliness. The Moslems in particular had ridiculed that attitude, perhaps angered by the impertinence of the Crusades. Only in relatively recent times had the Christian attitude changed.

The musician came into view. He was a young man, tall and slim and strong, garbed in garishly colored pantaloons and jacket and hat. One slipper was blue, the other red. His stockings were the reverse. There were small bells on his knees, and he wore a bright blue cape. The brim of the hat spread so widely it flopped down over his eyes. Yet this comic personage seemed in no way embarrassed. He rested on the ground under a densely leaved tree, and he was playing on a strange double flute, his right hand fingering the holes on one side, his left the other.

"Pan pipes!" Brother Paul exclaimed.

The man stopped. He looked up questioningly. "Ja?" he inquired.

Brother Paul did some quick readjusting. That sounded like German! He was not proficient in that language, but he might get by. "I—was admiring your music," he said haltingly in German.

"The shepherd's flute," the man agreed in the same language. His accent was strange, but not unintelligible. "It sets the mood for the day. Will you join me?"

"I would like to," Brother Paul said.

"Have some bread," the man said, tearing off the end of a long loaf and proffering it. This was hard black stuff, but it smelled good.

"Thank you," Brother Paul said. "I fear I have no favor to return. I am a stranger here, without substance."

The man smiled. "There are no strangers under the eye of God."

"None indeed!" Brother Paul agreed, encouraged. "I am Brother Paul of the Holy Order of Vision." He broke off, uncertain whether that would make any sense in this context.

"Would that have anything to do with the Apostle Paul's vision on the road to Damascus?"

"Yes," Brother Paul agreed, gratified. Here was a kindred soul! The actor was obviously Lee, but now the role itself was harmonious. "For both my Order and myself. We believe that the foundation of present-day Christianity was when the Pharisee Jew of Tarsus was converted to Christ. To a considerable extent, he made Christianity what it is. More correctly, he laid down the principles this great religion should follow although many bearing the title of Christians have strayed from those precepts. We of the Order of Vision try to restore, to the extent we are able, the Christianity of Saint Paul's vision. A faith open to all people, regardless of the name they choose to put upon their belief." He knew he was not speaking with the eloquence he wished, handicapped by the language, but it was getting easier as he progressed. Lee, of course, knew all this—but it was necessary to get it on record for this Animation, as it were anchoring the philosophical basis.

"Very well spoken, Brother! You are then a traveling friar?"

"No, not at all. I am here—well, by accident. I don't even know where this is. Or *when* this is. I am from America, circa 2000 A.D." How would *that* go over?

The man smiled again, shaking his head. "I regret I know of neither your Order nor your country, and I surely misunderstand your calendar. But I am ignorant of the fine points of religion; my folk always believed religion originated with fear. I have no knowledge whether this is true. But on geography I am more conversant: this is the land west of the Rhine, north of the Alps, and this is the year of Our Lord 1392, and I am a simple itinerant minstrel, entertainer, and magician. I go by many names, none of them significant; you may call me simply *Le Bateleur*, or the Juggler."

"The Juggler!" Brother Paul repeated, astonished. "Thirteen ninety-two!"

"You seem surprised, friend. Have I given offense?"

"No, no offense! It's just that—in my framework—which seems to be some six centuries after yours—your name is the title of a—what some call a fortune-telling card!"

The man waved a flute in a careless gesture. "This, too, I do, if there be an obolus in it." He flipped the flute in the air and caught it expertly. "Do you wish your fortune told?"

"I, uh—no thank you. If an obolus is a unit of money, I have none." Brother Paul seemed to remember a medieval coin worth a cent or so; this could be it. "In fact, I seem to be without resources and cannot repay you for your bread unless there is some service I can do."

The Juggler looked at him appraisingly. "I will accept payment with a mere song."

"A song?" Brother Paul found himself liking this unpretentious yet talented character, but this was confusing. "I do not claim to be an accomplished singer, though I do enjoy the form."

"I will give you the tune so that you may hum as I play." And the Juggler put his shepherd's flute to his lips and played an oddly sad melody.

"I like it," Brother Paul said. He began to hum, picking up the tune readily. He remembered how, as a child, he had been rebuked for humming. But now he was freed of that geas and could enjoy it.

As he mastered the song and hummed more forcefully, the Juggler changed his playing. Now it was the descant, complementing and counterpointing Brother Paul's voice. The pipes with their linked yet separate themes were lovely in themselves; but now, augmenting Brother Paul's voice, they lifted the song into a creation of such simple beauty that he found himself in a minor transport of rapture. Music soothed the savage breast indeed.

When it finished, the Juggler smiled. "Brother Paul, man of Vision, you were unduly modest. You have a voice second only to that of a castrato."

Brother Paul suffered a feeling of horror quite removed from the intended compliment. In medieval times young boys with good voices were castrated before puberty so that they could retain their sweet high ranges and continue singing in church choirs. The Bible forbade any man "injured in the stones" to enter a congregation of the Lord, but the Church ignored that when its convenience suited. What about himself: had he recovered his masculinity, or was Satan's excision permanent? The Juggler had spoken figuratively; Brother Paul's voice remained tenor since castration after the age of puberty had no immediate effect on range. Yet—

He could check readily enough. But not right now! "I thank you for the bread—and for the song. I must be on my way. Could you direct me to the nearest town or city?"

"Merely follow the river, friend! There are hamlets throughout, and eventually to the north you will come to the great city of Worms, the first Imperial Free City of the Empire."

"Worms! I remember the Diet of Worms, where Martin Luther —" He broke off. The Diet of Worms occurred in 1521—a hundred and thirty years after the year this was supposed to be. He remembered that date with special clarity because there had been a joke among his schoolmates about the "diet of worms" they would have to eat if they misremembered that date. One thousand, five hundred, and twenty one worms to be exact.

"You have friends in Worms then?" Of course the pronunciation was different with the *W* sounding more like a *V*, so the joke was no good for adults.

Brother Paul cut off his continuing, worm-like thought and answered. "Uh, not exactly. But perhaps I shall find what I seek there."

"May I inquire what you seek? It is not my business, but I have made many contacts in the course of my travels and perhaps can help direct you."

"I am looking for a deck of cards called the Tarot."

The Juggler's brow furrowed. "Ta-row? I think I have heard of some such pastime indulged in by the wealthy."

"They are special cards with pictured trumps and numerical suits. We use them as an aid to meditation, but they have a long and checkered history." But the Juggler's obvious perplexity made him pause. Apparently in this role he had no direct knowledge of Tarot. "This is the deck I mentioned where one card has your name: the Juggler or Magician."

The Juggler spread his hands. "I would be flattered, but this is surely a coincidence. There are many of my ilk, begging our bread and a night's lodging from village to village. Are there also cards for merchants and plowmen and friars?"

"Not specifically. The cards favor kings, queens, emperors, and popes," Brother Paul said with a smile. "As you suggested: an entertainment of the wealthy."

"Worms would be the place to seek then," the Juggler said. "It is the capital of the Bishop-Princes and a center of Empire intrigue. I wish you well."

"Thank you." Brother Paul rose and oriented northward.

"Move east until you spy the river," the Juggler advised. "The roads are better along its bank, and the villagers are accustomed to travelers."

Brother Paul nodded appreciatively and walked east.

By mid-afternoon he was hungry and footsore. He had found the river and a suitable trail north, but the villagers were not particularly hospitable to one who had no money. This idyllic historic land had its drawbacks. But he plodded on.

A party of ill-kempt soldiers rounded the turn, going south. Brother Paul knew that excellent armor and mail were available to those who could afford it in the fourteenth century, but these men were more like rabble. Instead of chain and gauntlets and swords they wore doublets with patches of leather sewn on for protection, their hands were bare and calloused, and they carried assorted knives and staffs evidently scrounged from what was most readily available.

They were upon Brother Paul before he realized their nature; because he was hot, grimy, and tired he had not been paying proper attention to his surroundings. "Out of the way, ruffian!" the leader said, striking forward with his staff.

Brother Paul reacted automatically. Adrenaline flooded his system, abolishing his fatigue. He stepped aside, reaching out with his left hand to catch hold of the moving staff. He turned to the left, his right hand coming down on the soldier's right hand, pinning it to the staff. Now he was beside the soldier, his two hands on the staff along with those of the other man. Brother Paul bent his knees, pushing the staff up and forward, causing the soldier to overbalance. He heaved—and the man flew over Brother Paul's right shoulder to land resoundingly in the dirt. The staff, by no coincidence, remained in Brother Paul's hands.

"Sorry," he said in his imperfect German. "I thought you meant to attack me." Better to put the most positive face on it!

But now the other soldiers ringed him, knives drawn. They looked ugly, in feature and attitude. "Who are you, churl?" one demanded.

"Just a traveler to Worms," Brother Paul said innocently.

"Who's your Lord?"

They thought him a servant. "I have no Lord. I'm just looking for the Tarot deck—"

The soldiers exchanged glances. "Sounds like a heretic to me," one said, and the others nodded agreement. "No protector, interfering with honest troops—let's teach him his place."

Uh oh. Brother Paul looked around, but there was no retreat. They had him, and they meant trouble. They had delayed their revenge only long enough to ascertain that there would be no likely retribution from some powerful noble who might have sent this stranger on some mission. If Brother Paul tried to escape, he would get stabbed by a dirty knife. If he fought—the same. Better to accept their chastisement—and be more careful next time.

"We'll flog him," the leader decided, dusting himself off. Brother Paul had not thrown him with damaging force, and the turf had broken the man's fall, so he had taken no injury worse than bruises. "Strip him!"

Rough hands ripped away Brother Paul's clothing while one of the men unwound a brutal-looking whip. This was not going to be pleasant at all!

They hauled off the last cloth—and paused. "He's gelded!" one exclaimed.

"Must be a slave, escaped from a galley—or a convict. We'd better kill him and cut off his ears; might be a reward."

"Cut off his ears *first*," one suggested. "I want to hear how a gelding screams."

Now Brother Paul knew he would have to fight. He had no choice. These were brute men to whom life was cheap, and they had no mercy. By beating and killing others, they sought to redeem their own sorry lot. The leader looked like Therion. Brother Paul braced, noting the position of each. If he caught one and threw him into two others—

"What's this?" a new voice demanded.

All turned, startled. It was a priest in black robe with a silver cross glinting at his throat. Even without his uniform, his demeanor would have cowed strangers. It was as if light glinted from his steely eyes.

"It's nothing, Father," the chief soldier said. "We caught this felon, and—"

"A heretic," another put in.

"Allow me to be judge of what is or is not significant, and who is or is not a heretic," the priest said sternly. His pale eyes glared down on Brother Paul as from a great height. He rubbed his nose with two fingers, squinting appraisingly. "Are you not the eunuch of the Apostle?" he demanded.

Startled, Brother Paul could not answer.

The priest gestured imperiously. "The Holy Office wants this miscreant. Garb him and bind him; I will convey him to Worms myself."

"Yes, Father," the soldier agreed, cowed. "But can you handle him alone? We could hamstring him for you. He's a rough—"

The priest peered down at the man. Something very like a sneer curled his aristocratic lip. "Your tongue wags rather freely, minion. Is it too long?"

"Father, I—"

"The Holy Office might arrange to have it cut shorter so that it will no longer interfere with your work."

With a visible gulp and tightly closed mouth, the soldier turned to get to work on Brother Paul, and the others jumped to help. They could easily have over-powered the priest, but this thought apparently was not in their repertoire. Quickly they replaced Brother Paul's tatters and tied his hands behind him with a length of cloth. It was evident that the mere mention of the Holy Office put a chill into the stoutest military heart.

"Good men," the priest said gruffly. He lifted two fingers in a careless benediction. "God be with you. Be about your business."

The soldiers bowed their heads. "Thank you, Father," one said and hastily retreated. In moments they were away and out of sight.

From the frying pan into the fire?

The priest considered Brother Paul again. He lifted the crucifix in one hand. "Miscreant, kiss the divine symbol of your Savior," he snapped imperiously.

The memory of a friend suffering and bleeding on that cross was too fresh. "Kiss my ass," Brother Paul muttered in English. He had read of the corrupt, venial medieval priests, and this one seemed typical of the breed. He spoke of tortures more readily than he spoke of the love of Jesus. Better the untender mercies of the soldiers; at least they were not such hypocrites. When Jesus Christ had gone out for his second crucifixion, men of this ilk had been awaiting him.

"I could have your ears sent to join your privates," the priest said warningly. Then he smiled. "Do you not know me, Brother Paul?"

Amazed, Brother Paul recognized him. "Juggler!"

"Stumble onward, friend; the ruffians may be suspicious. When it is safe, I will release you." And Juggler gave him a cuff on the neck that landed without force. What an actor he was!

Brother Paul stumbled forward, hunching his back as if cowed. "How—how did you—?"

"I followed you because my mind was in doubt about you. When it seemed you were authentic, I donned one of the disguises in which I am versed."

"Just in time, too! They were going to kill me! But why should you—?"

The Juggler shook his head ruefully. "My friend, I apologize. I took you for a spy of the Inquisition, but such a person would never have sung the heretical melody or have suffered himself to be humiliated as you were by those soldiers, and a eunuch could not have been admitted to the Holy Office. I realized I had misjudged you."

"The Inquisition? I?" Brother Paul laughed. "I abhor the repression for which the Inquisition stood!"

"So do I. If I were to fall into the power of the Holy Office—" The Juggler shook his head gravely.

"But why should they bother you? A mere minstrel and juggler, however talented—"

"Friend, I must confess that I juggle more than batons," Juggler said, untying Brother Paul's hands. "I am a *barba*. An Uncle."

"Uncle?" Brother Paul repeated blankly. He seemed to remember Satan using the term.

"A missionary of the Waldenses."

"The Waldenses!" Brother Paul had heard that name before. A historical sect, persecuted for their heretical beliefs.

"My partner fell victim to the Black Death. I would have saved him if I could—but it was in God's hands, not mine. Now I continue alone, for the believers must be served. But I fear lest my mission be incomplete."

Now the Juggler quickly removed and reversed his priestly robe. On the inside was his peasant-magician garb. The silver cross was shoved into a deep pocket with a contemptuous twitch of his lip. Now Brother Paul understood the necessity for the Juggler's dramatic abilities. The life expectancy of a suspected heretic was brief indeed. How much worse for a heretic missionary!

"Juggler—it may be presumptuous to ask—but do you think I might accompany you? I don't know my way around and have no money, but there might be some way I could help if you tell me what to do, and perhaps your route will take me where I am going. I bear no malice to your sect; in my framework there are many Christian and non-Christian religions, and tolerance is part of our custom and our law." Thanks to John Murray and others.

The Juggler turned to him seriously. "Brother Paul, I was hoping you would make the offer. I think I followed you in the hope that you would turn out to be a compatriot. You see, there are certain aids I need when performing my tricks—and I must perform or the Holy Office will be suspicious, and suspicion is nine-tenths of the law. I do not cheat anyone—my faith forbids that!—but I must put on a realistic show. Only in that manner can I justify my presence so that I can meet with those to whom I bring my message."

"And what is your message? I am a man of some religious scruple myself, and while I would not seek to interfere with your belief, I—"

"The Waldenses follow precepts similar to those of the Albigensians. The Albigensians were suppressed by the sword and cross two generations ago, so we profit by their misfortune and tread carefully. A number of their survivors have joined us. We rely on the authority of the Bible, rather than that of the Church. We emphasize the virtues of poverty, and so we cater chiefly to the poor. We insist on the direct relationship between man and God so that priests become irrelevant. We do not believe in confessions or prayers for the dead or the intercession of Saints. Men and women are equal. We do not venerate the cross, which is the torture implement on which Christ died. We missionaries are known as the *barbe* or Uncles to those we encounter of our faith and to those we convert. Because we spread a message that runs counter to that of the Church—indeed, we feel Christianity could dispense with the formal Church entirely and be the better for it!—we are deemed heretics and suffer the opprobrium thereof. Yet we see the temptations of Satan on every side while God remains aloof. We feel that if God recruited as actively as Satan does, this would be a better world. Therefore, we proselytize."

"There is little in your philosophy to which I take exception,"

Brother Paul said. "My sect honors the Bible, but also respects the texts of other religions, such as the Buddhists and the Moslems and the Confucians. We would not abolish any sect, but rather seek to coexist in peace with all faiths. Yet I can see that much of your philosophy of religion has come down to my own time and has been incorporated into the faiths of my world including my own Order of Vision. The Quakers honor the direct relation between man and God, calling it the 'Inner Light,' and the Jehovah's Witnesses attempt to combat Satan by active recruiting, and we take what amount to vows of poverty at the Holy Order of Vision—" He spread his hands. "There is too much to cover at the moment."

"I had hoped this would be the case. Your Order sounds like a sister school."

"It may be," Brother Paul agreed. "We do not seek converts, but we do lend support to those in need of faith." He paused. "You remind me of someone I knew—in my own time. He—" He broke off. He was getting so carried away with this play that he was forgetting who was playing what part! This *was* his friend Lee in a new guise. No need to disrupt the scene by remarking on it. "But of course that is irrelevant. I believe your message should be spread, for this age has need of it, and I will help you in what ever way I can."

"Then let me show you the lesson plan," the Juggler said. "Our devotees are mainly illiterate peasants. They are good people, but they could not read the Bible even if they were permitted to possess it. Even if it were translated to their language from the Latin. What point is there in an unreadable, unavailable Word of God! Yet we dare not carry the Bible with us or anything else that might betray our nature to the Holy Office. So—we use these little pictures whose real nature we carefully conceal from the minions of the Church."

And the Juggler produced a pack of thirty drawings. Brother Paul looked at them as he walked beside his friend, amazed—for these were very like the Major Arcana of the Tarot. Suddenly he realized that Satan was honoring his first wish: knowledge of the true origin and purpose of the Tarot. "This—this is what I seek!" he exclaimed.

"When you named the Tarot, I was sure you were attempting to trap me," the Juggler admitted. "Yet not *quite* sure—and I could not condemn you on the basis of mere suspicion because that is the way of the Holy Office we abhor." He shook his head sadly. "What a fine world it would be if one man trusted another and had that trust returned! Is this the case in your world?"

"No," Brother Paul said. "Not yet."

"We conceal our card lessons in the one place the Holy Office will never suspect: the pack of playing cards used by gamblers and wealthy degenerates," the Juggler said, passing the rest of the deck to Brother Paul. "These become the minor cards of the greater deck, the whole of which we call the Tarot, or Tzarot, the ruler of cards. We have not changed the minor cards, for that would betray our secret, but we have adapted them symbolically to our purpose. Each of the five suits represents—"

"*Five* suits?" Brother Paul asked, astonished.

"Some common decks have six, others four—in fact there seem to be many variations in number and symbols as each local printer or copyist innovates to suit himself. But we feel the appropriate number is five to represent the five fundamental elements as taught by the ancients."

"The Ancients!" Brother Paul repeated, thinking of something the alien Antares had said. A Galactic civilization that had existed three million years ago and disappeared.

"The Sumerians, the Egyptians, the Minoans, the Eblans, the Hittites, the Greeks, the Megalithic society—all the ancient peoples who knew so much more than history has credited them with," the Juggler said, and in that moment it was indeed Antares that looked out of his eyes, smiling sadly.

"Oh. Yes. Certainly." Animation though this might be, it seemed important not to introduce anachronism. But there was another matter. "*Five* elements? Fire, Water, Air, Earth, and—?"

"And Spirit," the Juggler said gently. "That which distinguishes man from animal. Man has conscience; man knows right from wrong. Man ate from the fruit of the Tree of Knowledge of Good and Evil and thereby separated himself from the ignorant beasts. Some call that a curse; we call it man's most important attribute."

"Spirit," Brother Paul repeated, appreciating it. It seemed that he had always known it. "What separates man from beast."

"The other suits may be interpreted on many levels," the Juggler continued. "As virtues or as classes of society or qualities of character. There is the Stave of Fortitude—or of the peasant. The Cup of Faith—or of the Church." He made a wry face. "Much good the peasant gets from the corrupt established

Church! Then there is the Sword of Justice—or of the military."
He smiled at Brother Paul's expression; there had not been any
direct association of justice and military in his own recent
experience! "The Coin of Charity—and of the merchant. And of
course the Lamp of the Spirit—and of our wandering souls,
seeking to bring that light to those ready to receive it."

"The Waldenses," Brother Paul said, nodding.

"Or *any* good people of whatever faith who follow their
conscience and seek love and truth," the Juggler amended. "As
the early Christians did before they were corrupted by power. We
Waldenses claim no special privilege or right; we merely do what
we can, hoping our seeds will find fertile soil."

And the most fertile soil came from compost, fed by fecal
matter. Satan had made Brother Paul into a seed and planted him
here. What meaning did that have?

"This picture, The Juggler, represents—me," the Juggler said
with a smile. It was, indeed, the Tarot Juggler or Magician—a
gaudily dressed man standing at a table upon which various items
of parlor magic rested. "The Juggler is of course the master of
disguises—as we Waldenses have to be. At times he may appear
very much the fool. But the sight of this image alerts the faithful,
and when I see the countersign, thus—" He made a gesture with
his forefinger like a figure eight turned sidewise. "That is the
double symbol of the sun and moon, two circles touching, the
eternal progress of day and night reflected in my hat." And he took
down his floppy hat to show how the rim formed a similar
lemniscate. "I know then to whom to address myself after the
show is over. Circumspectly. Usually the believer will find some
pretext to bring me to his home, and I will conduct the lesson
there. Thus is another segment of my mission accomplished under
the dangerously sensitive nose of the Holy Office."

"Beautiful," Brother Paul murmured. "In my day, these cards
have lost much of this meaning. You hide them under superficial
interpretations so that the Inquisition will not suspect, and those
superficial aspects have carried through so that most people do
not even suspect the primary purpose."

"That is exactly as it should be," the Juggler agreed, pleased. "It
means the Holy Office will not prevail in your land either." He
indicated the next card. "This is the Lady Pope. Do you know the
legend of the Popess?"

Brother Paul nodded affirmatively. "However, our researches

show that no such person existed historically."

"Perhaps not on that level. But symbolically she certainly exists! This is the way we see the Church, the Whore of Babylon who has taken upon herself the attributes of secular power and become as one with the kings of the flesh. This picture follows naturally on the first, as a false Pope follows a false Magician. A harlot disguised as a priest, treading in the footprints of a priest, disguised as a juggler. Those of true faith will perceive the reality behind these facades."

"Yes, I should hope so," Brother Paul agreed.

"Now here is a very special representation," the Juggler continued, showing another card. "Kindly admire the art."

"But it is blank!" Brother Paul protested.

"It is and it isn't," Juggler said. "Some say this is the Holy Ghost, the invisible Spirit of God. But we prefer to call it the Unknown—that ineffable force that governs the life of man."

"Fate!" Brother Paul said. He remembered this card now from his rapid tour of the gallery under the Pyramid.

"Perhaps. It is really up to each person to interpret it for himself. If he draws a card randomly from the deck and this one appears, it is a signal that he is proceeding on erroneous assumptions and should re-examine his situation."

"Interesting," Brother Paul said, more than interested. "Is there a particular reason it appears here in the deck, right after the Lady Pope, rather than at the beginning or end? I note it has no number."

"It is numberless and also infinite," the Juggler agreed. "Therefore, it has no assigned place in the deck. When the cards are arranged in order by number and suit, the Ghost is inserted randomly. We do try to keep it with the Triumphs because often we separate them from the suits in order to avoid suspicion, but if it falls among the suits and turns up in the course of a card trick—well, it is merely a blank card of no significance." He contemplated the empty card a moment. "Seldom does it manifest this early in the deck. There must be a reason for that but I confess I do not fathom it. Perhaps it relates to you." And Antares looked out at him again.

Brother Paul shrugged. "I do seem to be an unknown quantity in this world." The Ghost concept was growing on him. He had never, before he entered the Animations, suspected that a thing like this could be in the Tarot—but it seemed it was. Or once had been.

"Next come the Empress and Emperor, of equal rank according to our precepts, lawfully wedded. We believe in the married state and find the celibacy now fashionable in the Church to be hypocritical. God did not create man and woman that they should not know one another and not have the fulfillment of families! There are so many innocent bastards sired by priests! They breathe on young women during Confession and get them unknowingly excited, easy prey for lechery, and such women dare not expose their seducers lest the seducers charge them with heresy and destroy them without trial. Better those priests should marry and be openly fruitful as the Holy Book decrees."

"Yes . . ." Brother Paul murmured. But he, without testicles —what of him?

"And the Pope himself," the Juggler continued, showing the next. "So like the Emperor that one can hardly tell the difference, adorned with costly robes, coronets, scepter, on a throne yet! What would you take the meaning of this image to be?"

"That the Church has become overly materialistic," Brother Paul said promptly. Never before had it occurred to him that the close similarity between Emperor and Hierophant (Pope) was not coincidental!

"Very good, Brother Paul; you have a very quick perception! We feel that when the Church consented to be endowed by the Roman state, she became morally corrupt and lost the mandate of Christ. She has been led astray by worldly power, dominion, and wealth —as any religion *would* be, however pure its original tenets. We protest against all religious endowments and *any* temporal powers of clergy."

Brother Paul had to interrupt. "In fairness, I must say that this situation is much improved in my day, perhaps again because of your efforts. The Catholic Church stands as a bulwark against oppression, and its priests are persecuted by totalitarian regimes. In broad parts of Asia it has been almost entirely suppressed, and in Europe during recent political upheavals priests were tortured. In Latin America—" But he had to stop, prompted by the Juggler's look of perplexity. There *was* no "Latin" America at this period of history.

"Perhaps in your day the Church has recovered some basic

humility and purpose," the Juggler said. "But right now the Pope is weighted down with those odious instruments of torture called crosses and other ornaments never authorized by the Scriptures. Call it heresy if you will, but we insist on separation of State and Church, not this ludicrous and oppressive amalgam. Why, the Cardinals are so greedy for power they contest with each other for the papal throne."

"Ah," Brother Paul said, remembering. "The Great Schism! Three Popes—"

The Juggler smiled. "Not quite that bad, yet. Fourteen years ago, when Pope Gregory XI died—is he in your records? The one who ended the 'Babylonian Captivity' of the papacy by returning to Rome from Avignon, France—"

"Babylonian captivity for the Whore of Babylon!" Brother Paul interjected, laughing.

"Just so. When Gregory died, the Roman mob pressured the Cardinals to install a local boy. Rome is an unruly city, and non-Italian popes don't feel quite safe there, perhaps for good reason. The Cardinals responded by electing Urban VI. I do not claim Urban was a bad man as these things go; he was an uncompromising reformer who yielded to no man on matters of principle."

"Trouble, surely!" Brother Paul murmured.

"Correct. His harsh mode soon alienated the Cardinals, especially the French ones. They declared his election null and elected Robert of Geneva, who became Pope Clement VII and took up residence in Avignon. He had to; his life would have been hazardous in Rome! Three years ago Urban died, but that did not resolve the problem. The Italians replaced him with Pope Boniface IX."

The Juggler pinched a louse out of his hair with obvious satisfaction. "So now we have two popes," he continued. "Which is the real one and which is the Antipope no one can say for sure. In Italy it is best to say Boniface; in France say Clement." He made a gesture of good-natured helplessness. "How glad I am that we Waldenses do not recognize either of these clown priests! But make no mistake, either one would string me up by one foot if he caught me or any other *barba*. The *men* may be ludicrous, but the *office* remains powerful."

Brother Paul thought of some of the politics of his own period and had to agree. "If it is any comfort to you, this eventually got straightened out. In my time there is only one pope. But of course there are many Christian religions who do not follow the Catholic pope, so in that sense it is more confused than ever."

The Juggler continued on through the deck, picture by picture, while Brother Paul listened so raptly that he felt no further fatigue despite the distance they were walking. Here at last was True Tarot!

They followed the Rhine downstream, coming to a village in the Holy Roman Empire—a region that would be known in Brother Paul's day as Germany. The Juggler was exceedingly cautious in populated areas, fearing overt persecution; the Empire was not the safest place for Waldenses this year.

Much of the region was forested and beautifully unspoiled, but the fascination of the Tarot was such that Brother Paul hardly noticed where they were going or what was around them. The individual trees could have been twentieth century skyscrapers or completely alien life forms, and he would have passed them blithely by.

At the village the Juggler set up his table and performed his cardboard miracles, and he was a most proficient stage magician who obviously enjoyed amazing the credulous and making children laugh. The peasants threw small coins in appreciation: not many, for they were poor, but even an obolus went a long way here.

However, no secret signal was given, so there was no ministering to the Waldenses faithful. "I did not expect a contact here," Juggler confided. "Up nearer Worms there are more believers. I'll make arrangements to spend the night in a stable."

"The stable was good enough for our Savior's birth," Brother Paul murmured. He already had a load of lice in his clothing, so could not take on many more bugs from the environment. His feet were sore, his muscles stiffening, and his unfamiliar clothing was chafing the skin raw in places; *any*where was fine for a rest. When he slept, he would dream of Tarot—assuming he remained in this situation now that his wish had been fulfilled.

Next morning he remained in the fourteenth century, his body stiffer and rawer than ever with assorted welts from the bites of unseen insects. But fresh water and some more black bread made him feel better, and the resumed walk gradually worked out the kinks. He was not comfortable, but he could get by. But he wondered: why was he still here?

As they trekked north toward the great free city of Worms, the Juggler abruptly staggered. "Ah, the thirst!" he cried.

Thirst? Brother Paul caught his arm, steadying him. The man was hot! "Friend, you have a fever!" Brother Paul said. "You must rest; I will fetch water to cool you."

The Juggler slumped down against a tree. "I fear it will do no good," he gasped. "I felt it coming, but tried to persuade myself it was not." He vomited weakly, soiling his uniform.

Alarmed, Brother Paul hurried to fetch water from the river anyway. But when he reached the bank, he found he had no container for it. He had not thought, in his worried haste, to bring one of the Juggler's trick cups, and in any event that would have been too small. Maybe he could find something by the bank—

He ran along the riverside, searching desperately. There was nothing. But his friend was gravely ill!

He burst through a copse of trees. There was a girl dipping water from the river. She had an earthen pitcher in each hand and was evidently rinsing them out, swishing water in them and pouring it out again. Over her shoulder near the eastern horizon he saw the first star of dusk. Uncommonly bright, almost blindingly brilliant. He suffered the feeling of *déjà vu*.

But he had no time to figure it out. "Miss, oh Miss!" he called. "Fraülein—may I borrow a pitcher?"

The girl looked up, startled. She resembled—but of course Amaranth played this part; why did he keep being surprised by the new ways in which the basic cast appeared?

"I have a friend, sick," Brother Paul explained breathlessly. "He needs water."

She hesitated. "Sick?"

"A fever, vomiting, thirst—"

"The Black Death!" She got up so hastily she dropped a pitcher in the water and fled.

He had no time or reason to pursue her. What could he do with a woman anyway, had he the time and inclination? He was a eunuch. He sloshed into the water to recover the bobbing pitcher before it sank. At least he had that!

The Juggler was worse when he returned. Brother Paul splashed water on his friend's face and on his hot, dry skin. He offered a cup, and the Juggler gulped avidly.

Now Brother Paul saw it: black spots forming on the man's skin. "Uh oh."

"It is the Black Death," the Juggler said. "I buried my companion, may God accept his soul, and I hoped I had escaped—" He looked up, alarmed. "My friend, get away from me! You cannot save me; you can only infect yourself."

"No danger of that," Brother Paul assured him. "The plague was spread from rats to men by infected fleas."

"Fleas! But fleas are everywhere!"

He was right. Lice, nits, fleas—there was no escaping them here. Probably fleas had left the dying *barba* companion and hidden in the Juggler's clothes. Now, after the incubation period of several days, Juggler had come down with it. Rat fleas might spread it, but they didn't need rats once they infested human clothing.

"You saved my life from the soldiers," Brother Paul said. Actually, he might have fought off the soldiers successfully—but it had been no certain thing. "I will do what I can for you."

The Juggler retched again. "There is only one thing needing doing for me, friend—and that is more than any man can ask of another, were it even possible."

The man was extremely sick, and Brother Paul did not know how to care for him. Even with hospital care, the outlook would be doubtful, for the bubonic plague had killed about a third of the population of Europe in the latter part of the fourteenth century. Even had Brother Paul known where to get help, he would not dare to take the Juggler there. A heretic missionary in a time of persecution—no, he could not seek help! "What is this impossible thing?"

"My mission," the Juggler said. "There are good people who depend on the Uncles to uplift their faith. They should be told—that they must wait a few more months, until the persecution dies down, until the next *barba* comes. They must not give up hope!"

"I can tell them that," Brother Paul said.

"But they are hidden—and to seek them out is to risk discovery by the Holy Office—for you *and* them. You dare not—" the Juggler lapsed into silence for a time. He was fading rapidly.

When a killer disease took hold of the body of a medieval man, already weakened by fatigue and malnutrition, its ravages were swift!

The Juggler summoned strength. "Take the sacred pictures, friend. Guard them well. They must not fall into the hands of—" He had to stop, gasping.

"I will guard the Sacred Tarot with my life," Brother Paul said soberly. "The Inquisition shall not have it."

The Juggler could no longer speak. His fevered hand touched Brother Paul's in mute thanks. He shuddered, trying to vomit again, but nothing came. Then with what seemed a superhuman effort he managed a few more words. "Abra-Melim, the Mage of Egypt—Abraham the Jew in Worms—tell—" He choked—and before Brother Paul could help him, he collapsed.

Brother Paul tried to revive him with more water, to make him comfortable—but in a moment he realized that his friend was dead.

"Let him only change parts . . ." Brother Paul prayed, feeling an intensity of loss that threatened to overwhelm him. "Let the role die, not the player—" But he could not be sure that prayer would be answered, for this was an aspect of Hell.

23

DECEPTION
(MOON)

*There is no more immoral work than the "Old Testament." Its deity is
an ancient Hebrew of the worst type, who condones, permits or
commands every sin in the Decalogue to a Jewish patriarch, qua
patriarch. He orders Abraham to murder his son and allows Jacob to
swindle his brother; Moses to slaughter an Egyptian and the Jews to
plunder and spoil a whole people, after inflicting upon them a series of
plagues which would be the height of atrocity if the tale were true. The
nations of Canaan are then extirpated. Ehud, for treacherously disem-
bowelling King Eglon, is made judge over Israel. Jael is blessed above
women (Joshua v. 24) for vilely murdering a sleeping guest; the horrid
deeds of Judith and Esther are made examples to mankind; and David,
after an adultery and a homicide which deserved ignominious death, is
suffered to massacre a host of his enemies, cutting some in two with
saws and axes and putting others into brick-kilns. For obscenity and
impurity we have the tales of Onan and Tamar, Lot and his daughters,
Amnon and his fair sister (2 Sam. xiii.), Absalom and his father's
concubines, the "wife of whoredoms" of Hosea and, capping all, the
Song of Solomon. For the horrors forbidden to the Jews, who, therefore,
must have practiced them, see Levit. viii. 24; xi. 5; xvii. 7, xviii. 7, 9, 10,
12, 15, 17, 21, 23, and xx. 3. For mere filth what can be fouler than 1st
Kings xviii. 27; Tobias ii. 11; Esther xiv. 2; Eccl. xxii. 2; Isaiah xxxvi.
12; Jeremiah iv. 5, and (Ezekiel iv. 12-15), where the Lord changes*

*human ordure into "Cow-chips!" Ce qui excuse Dieu, said Henri Beyle,
c'est qu'il n'existe pas,—I add, as man has made him.*

—THE BOOK OF THE THOUSAND NIGHTS AND A NIGHT: Translated and
annotated by Richard F. Burton: Volume Ten, n.p., The Burton Club,
n.d.

Brother Paul collected the Juggler's things into a little pile, then
set about burying him. The actor, in this role, was not mutilated:
that was a minor relief. That circumcision of Jesus had been
uncomfortably convincing!

Brother Paul did not want to bury the man just anywhere, but
lacked the strength and will in his grief to be choosy. So he cut a
stick with the Juggler's magic-tricks knife and used it to excavate a
shallow grave. He was afraid this would be scant protection
against the ravages of scavenging animals, but it was the best he
could do.

He did not know what manner of ceremony the Waldenses used
at a burial, so he said a few words of his own choosing. "May the
mission on which this good man went be somehow fulfilled." Yet
he knew from history that, in the narrow sense, it had not been.
Juggler had died in vain. The Waldenses had never gained many
converts although their ideas had had broad influence.

Now he sorted through the Juggler's belongings. They were
routine: the reversible cloak, jacket and pants; the infinity-rimmed
floppy hat; the vials of powder for coloring fire and other special
effects; the trick wand that sagged limply when held one way, yet
was stiff when held another way (oh, the phallic symbolism
there!); the cup and knife and coin. The twinbodied flute. That
hurt most of all, for it was the instrument that had summoned
Brother Paul and brought the beauty of song into his fourteenth
century life. Such a pitiful remembrance! But these items were
overwhelmed by the significance of the Tarot deck, the true
original of an idea that had branched into many forms. This,
perhaps, was the true mission of the man—giving to the world the
truth in Tarot. In that sense, maybe the Juggler's mission had not
been futile.

The crescent moon had risen. Brother Paul went to the river to
wash and drink, then looked back toward the grave site. He was
horrified to see two wild curs approaching it, sniffing. "Hey! Get

away from there!" he cried. The dogs paused, hearing his voice, poised for flight. But then they spied the moon and lifted their muzzles to bay at it. Brother Paul knew that canines, being nose-oriented, had difficulty dealing with a thing they could see but not smell; one sense told them it was there, but another denied it. A man who heard a voice but found no person there was similarly perplexed, calling it a ghost. A dog merely howled.

Something attracted his attention almost at his feet. It seemed to be a crayfish trying to climb out, as though attracted also by the moon. Or attracted by the grave, Brother Paul amended his thought with a shudder. He looked again toward that grave and saw the silhouettes of the dogs sitting there with two giant trees rising to frame the moon like dark castles. A pretty nocturnal scene, in its way—but also as horrible as his own vision of the field with the lion. Death lurked beneath each: not the brief shock of violent destruction, but the lifelong grief of the loss of a loved one.

He strode toward the dogs, and they skulked away. The grave was undisturbed—but how long would it remain so? Yet he could not remain here indefinitely to guard it. The Juggler would simply have to take his chances in death as in life.

The night was warm. This must be the season of the "Dog Days"—hot. When the "Dog Star" Sirius was prominent . . . that must be the star he had seen in the morning or evening. He could survive the night's temperature without trouble.

Brother Paul found a suitable tree and climbed to its crotch, bracing himself and squirming around until reasonably comfortable. Before he knew it, he slept.

He woke hungry and with additional stiffness. There might be fruit trees in the forest—but he did not know where to look and did not want to steal. Obviously this Animation was not yet through with him, and he did not wish to become one of the failure statistics, i.e., dead. Satan had promised him information on the True Tarot; Satan had not promised he could take it with him from the fourteenth century. He would have to shift for himself until he could demonstrate his ability to survive here indefinitely.

Yet what legitimate way was there to obtain food? He did not want to get too close to villagers because he had to hide and preserve the invaluable Tarot deck. He was an obvious stranger, speaking awkwardly, not to be trusted by the clannish locals, and liable to suspicion by soldiers. If he even showed his face in a village, he might be mobbed. Unless—

He almost fell out of the tree. Well, why not? It had worked for the Juggler!

With nervous confidence, Brother Paul descended, stretched his cramped limbs, urinated against the roots of the tree, and donned the magical robe. He was about to do tricks for his dinner. His strangeness should only enhance the effect.

First he rehearsed the tricks. His own youthful experience stood him in good stead; he could do sleight of hand as well as was needed. He hated to have to use the Sacred Cards for parlor tricks, but they were his best tool—and indeed, he had used Tarot in this capacity before. He riffled through the crude cards, making sure he could handle them with sufficient dexterity. They were printed cards, but not uniform; probably some kind of wooden block print, itself hand carved, for it would be over half a century before the printing press was developed.

Then he put them away and turned over some rocks and was lucky enough to spot a small harmless snake. "Easy, fellow," he murmured, catching it and putting it in a tied handkerchief. "I will let you go in due course." Yes—he was ready.

He set out again, following the trail to the north, working the kinks from his body. He did not feel good, but he felt halfway confident. There had to be a village along this trail somewhere, and now he had no intention of avoiding it.

It turned out to be surprisingly easy. His bright Juggler costume identified him instantly, and within moments of his appearance at the next village there was a crowd around him. Without further fanfare he set up the table a villager brought and began his act. He made a small silver coin appear between his fingers, vanish, and reappear from the ear of the nearest urchin. He poured water from one cup into another, then showed the second cup to be empty. He waved his wand—and the little snake appeared on the table and slithered away. Finally he did tricks with the cards, making the Ace of Wands come up repeatedly, no matter how carefully it was shuffled into the deck.

Suddenly, in the midst of his act, he remembered what had somehow faded from his consciousness for the past day. *This deck had five suits.*

He continued almost mechanically, going through his limited

repertoire while his mind and eye reviewed the suits. Wands —Cups—Swords—Coins—and Lamps, just as the Juggler had told him. Ace through ten in each, plus Page, Knight, Queen, and King. Fifty numbered cards in all, plus twenty Court Cards and thirty Waldenses Triumphs—a deck of one hundred cards in all. A magical number in this age and his own!

How had the scholars of later centuries missed this obvious clue that their decks were incomplete? 100 was a number to conjure with while 78 was nothing. They must have looked at individual cards, instead of at the deck as a whole. Almost literally missing the forest for the trees.

Maybe this was another aspect of the Tarot he had yet to discover. He could not leave this framework until his *whole* wish had been granted—including the ramifications of it he had not known about.

He wrapped up his show and made his bow. A few small coins were set on his table. Success! Now he could buy some food, and no one would question his presence here. He could survive.

As the crowd dispersed, a young woman approached hesitantly. "Sir—your cards—is there a picture of the Juggler among them?"

The Juggler. He had not employed that card or any of the Triumphs in his act, both because they were too valuable to risk and because he feared they might arouse suspicion. He had promised to keep them out of the hands of the Inquisition, and this was best accomplished by keeping them out of sight. But how could he deny the card that stood for his dead benefactor? Slowly, he nodded.

She made a sidewise figure eight in the air with her forefinger. "*Barba,*" she whispered. "We have awaited your coming! Please, visit our hut tonight."

Brother Paul paused in chagrin. Here was Amaranth in a new part, delivering the signal of identification for the Waldenses. Of course these believers were on the lookout for traveling entertainers! Why hadn't he thought of that when he set out to imitate his friend? He should have answered no about that card so as not to arouse false hopes.

Yet he had promised to inform the believers of the delay before the next Uncle came so they would not lose hope. This was his opportunity. He had almost forgotten that commitment, but had no alternative now. "Miss, I regret to inform you that—"

"Oh, don't speak about it here!" she protested, glancing nervously over her shoulder. Sure enough, another villager was approaching, and Brother Paul had to break off.

"Then you will perform for us tonight," Amaranth said brightly. "We will give you supper and straw for the night."

"Uh, yes, that will be fine," Brother Paul agreed lamely. He smiled at the other villager. "I trust you enjoyed the show?"

"That snake—it was alive!"

"Of course," Brother Paul said with a smile. "I would not want to conjure a *dead* snake."

The man's eyes widened. "Then you are in league with Satan!"

Uh oh. These primitives believed in magic. He had made his show too good. He was, perhaps literally, in league with Satan, but that was not relevant to this issue. "No, it is merely a trick. I caught the snake in the forest this morning and hid it in my sleeve. Don't tell anyone!"

Disappointed, the man departed. There went a close call! He could not afford to be too convincing!

There was nothing resembling a supermarket here, but there was a local baker from whom Brother Paul obtained a loaf of black bread. His stomach did not like the stuff very well; it was too much like his childhood bread. But at least it was familiar.

In the afternoon he ranged the area and managed to catch several beetles and caterpillars: ammunition for the evening show. He spotted one rather pretty little stone and pocketed that too, although he wasn't sure he could use it in a magic trick. He chatted with people who were curious about news of the world —and fortunately the world was limited to a few square leagues in their awareness.

In the evening the young woman fetched him to her hut, which actually turned out to be a good sized cottage some ten meters by five with a thatched roof, and constructed of fairly sturdy hand-hewn beams. Inside, however, he discovered it did double duty as a shed for animals; straw was on the floor, and the ambient odor was strong. But what had he expected among peasants? The lowest classes of the medieval societies had never had a good life and always had to live pretty much from hand to mouth.

This house was crowded with people of all ages. *"Barba!"* an old woman cried. "I feared I would die before I had your blessing!"

And he had to tell them he was not the Waldenses missionary. This was going to hurt. Yet they deserved to know the brutal truth: that the true Juggler had died of the plague not half a day's walk

from here, trying to reach them. "I regret to explain that I am
not—"

"Oh, it's all right, Uncle," she said. "We are all of the faith here.
From all the villages around, we have come. Some will be
punished for failing to work for their Lords today, but they had far
to travel to get here on time. A young couple have delayed
marrying lo these many months so that you could do it, and we
have a child sick near to death, and we all stand in such desperate
need of your counsel, for our life is hard and some of us have
suffered in the persecution and we know not even how to pray
properly to God for relief. We have had no one in a year to preach
the True Faith to us, and now at last you have come, and what a
blessing it is! If I die tomorrow, I die happy, for I die with my faith
uplifted by your touch!" And she held out her withered hand to be
touched.

And what was he to say now? At such sacrifice had they gathered
to meet him, risking their very lives to have the blessing and
encouragement of the *barba*. How great was their simple faith in
the terrible shadow of the Inquisition! How could he tell them
now that the true missionary was dead?

Suddenly he appreciated with much greater clarity the situation
of the Universalist John Murray who was prevented by a lack of
wind from sailing away and going about his business until he
agreed to preach at the local church. Murray had not felt qualified,
yet—

Yet if he, Brother Paul, did not tell these good people the truth,
he would have to impersonate the Uncle they thought he was, the
representative of a religion to which he did not belong. Even if
that could be called ethical, he wasn't sure it was possible. And
how could he participate in such a terrible lie?

The old woman was waiting. He had to do something now!
Should he kill her with the truth or provide salvation with a lie?
Was this a test of his own mettle? If he lied, he was surely doomed
to Hell. Yet how many other people would the truth doom?

Brother Paul touched her hand. "It is your own great faith that
uplifts you, good woman," he said gently, knowing she would
misinterpret his words. *If this be the road to Hell, so let it be.* "I am
only a man."

"Yes, yes!" she breathed raptly.

"No man can stand between you and God. You have no need of
priest or *barba*, so long as your heart is open to Our Lord."

"Ah, but you make it so clear!" she exclaimed. "Oh, Uncle, my faith has wavered so often, but your words restore it stronger than before! Give me your blessing!"

"My blessing means no more than that of any other person," Brother Paul said, troubled. No matter how he tried to defuse the lie, it became stronger like her faith. "There is no special power in me; I am as nothing, unworthy. I have no avenue to God that is not as readily available to you. I could say the words, but that would not—"

"Say the words!" she cried raptly.

There was no way out. "May the blessing of Our Holy Father be upon you," he murmured.

It was as though she had been reprieved from Hell. Her wrinkled face was transformed by rapture.

Now the others crowded in, nudging the old woman aside, and she suffered herself to be moved, oblivious in her joy. "The *barba* blesses us all by his presence," a man said. "Come, Uncle—we must tend first to the child, lest she die unclean." He hustled Brother Paul to the corner where the child lay on a straw pallet amid flies.

Brother Paul looked at her again on the verge of protesting the confusion of identities. But as he looked, he recognized —Carolyn. This girl was about twelve years old, but so wasted and thin she could have been eight. Yet the face—obviously it was the same actress, and so, in the terms he dealt with, the same girl. She had not escaped Hell's aftermath after all. Satan had betrayed him. He should have guessed when Lee showed up in this sequence! Now—he had to save Carolyn again. If he could.

What was her illness? Should he ask? No, he could get no useful answer. Had it been anything routine, she would have recovered on her own. Malnutrition? Then why hadn't it affected other members of her family? It must be some individual, slow debilitation, not susceptible to the treatment available. Something like —cancer.

In which case, nobody could save her. The medical technology for abolishing cancer had not been developed until the 20th century. The *barba* had a hopeless task. Even the genuine Waldens Juggler could not have done what these people hoped.

But if she died, here in Animation, would she also die in real life? He was uncertain. Some people did die in Animation—and the odds seemed against his own survival. But some survived. If a person *thought* he died in Animation, would his life expire in his mundane existence? The witch-doctor power of Voodoo suggested this was a solid possibility. Suppose a person only played the part of a character who died and knew that—could he then survive?

What was the present state of Lee, his Good Companion? Infused by the aura of Antares, he had played the role of Jesus Christ and had not died. But historically, Jesus had risen again. Now Lee, as the Juggler, had died again, more convincingly, for he was no longer the Son of God but a mere mortal man. A played part or reality?

If the player died, surely his part died too, for a dead person could not animate a living one—not in this manner. Antares was a special case. If a part died, the player might live or die, depending. If a part lived, the player *had* to live. Therefore, the only way to be certain was to keep this part alive; then he would know that Carolyn lived in all forms. Even though the form he loved had not yet been born in his own time framework.

The logic might be suspect, but his feeling was not. He *had* to save her. Though Satan Himself dictated otherwise. To Hell with Satan!

"I will try," Brother Paul said, realizing that these words committed him with finality to this part within the play. He was impersonating the Juggler, the part that belonged to his friend. He was deceiving these good people. *The Moon,* he thought, experiencing the awful poignancy of it. *Planet of deceit.* He had thought his honor was his most important asset; now Satan had shown him it was not. For the sake of an unborn child, the mere part in a play, his honor was forfeit.

If this manifest failure in his character damned him to Hell, he thought again, so be it. These people might be illusory, and this play might be scripted by Satan, but Brother Paul was what he was in reality or imagination. He had to try to save this child.

He knelt beside her and put the fingers of his right hand to her forehead. The flies buzzed up angrily. Her body was not feverish. Was this a good sign? Maybe not; cancer would not necessarily cause a fever. His left hand took her thin right hand. How bony her fingers were!

"My dear," he said.

There was no perceptible response. Her breathing continued

with labored regularity. She was asleep, but not blithely so; he feared she was locked in some internal nightmare as bad as his own.

He concentrated, willing her to wake, to recover. Antares had told him he had an aura and that this might be used to heal; Jesus Christ had implied the same. If this were true, he might be able to help this child. "Wake, little one," he said, praying for it to happen.

But it did not happen. His prayer met a blank wall. Brother Paul was not Jesus Christ; he could not heal by mere touch and will. Not even when the subject was his daughter.

At last, defeated, he rose. "We cannot know the ways of God, except when He wills it," he said sadly. *What had he done wrong?* "I will see this child again." And he would. Again and again, for this was the one defeat he could not accept as final.

The old woman nodded soberly. Had she expected more from him?

Brother Paul returned to the center of the room. All eyes followed him expectantly. He had come prepared to put on a magic show, but this was obviously not what they had come for. They wanted a message from the Waldenses, an affirmation of faith.

He had in effect perjured himself when he ministered to the child. Should he aggravate it now? He looked at the faces of old and young, shining with hope, and knew that he had to complete his own damnation. He could not destroy their belief when he knew there was no alternative for them. Both true *barbe* for this route were dead, and it might be another year before another set came this way. Better a makeshift message than none at all. Even the actors of a play written in Hell deserved some consideration.

What of the Juggler? What would *he* have done in this situation? Brother Paul knew: he would have given a ringing presentation of his faith. Now Brother Paul had assumed the missionary's place; was there any more fitting way to repay the favors the Juggler had done him? What better epitaph than a declaration of the message the Juggler had sought to bring!

"Brothers and Sisters of the faith," Brother Paul began, experiencing sudden stage fright. "I—am a novice. The true *barba* who was instructing me, guiding me, to whom I was apprentice—that good man perished before he could reach you. I beg your indulgence, for I have not before presented the message of the Waldenses alone."

No one responded. They took his words as mere apology, the ritual modesty, missing the literal import. He was the uncle, the religious guide; experience made little difference. So his partial confession of his deceit was no confession at all. Satan made it very easy to sin!

Well, he would simply have to do it. He would give them the message of the Waldenses as well as he was able. It was not a bad message—not at all.

"The Waldenses follow precepts similar to those of the Albigensians," Brother Paul began. But immediately he saw that it wasn't going over. These people had no knowledge of foreign religious philosophies or the history of heretic sects; they simply believed in the word of the *barba*.

He tried again. "The Waldenses believe that people should return to the principles that Jesus Christ and the Apostle Paul established. Simplicity, humility, and disinterested love for all mankind." But this wasn't working either. It was a lecture. The Juggler had spoken clearly and rationally to Brother Paul, but that was one literate, educated scholar communicating with another. Peasants and serfs needed something more tangible. The Juggler, when doing his magic show, had appealed to the least sophisticated element of society with the same finesse he had shown Brother Paul. He had been a man for all levels.

It was not enough for the people to desire enlightenment; it had to come in palatable form. These people were what they were: uneducated. Philosophically they were like children: ready to learn, but with limited intellectual experience.

What he really needed was a programmed lesson, preferably illustrated. Pictures were great for illiterates.

Pictures—programmed text. Suddenly it burst upon him. *Of course!*

Brother Paul brought out the thirty Tarot Triumphs. He extracted the Fool and showed it before him. "Look at this buffoon!" he exclaimed. "He walks with his eyes to the sky while the town cur rips the pants off his bum!"

Now they responded with appreciative surprise. Now he had their attention. Now he could score!

"It is hard indeed for a rich man to approach God," Brother

Paul said. "'Or for the powerful noble, or the proud priest. What is wealth or power or pride to God? Better to leave all that behind, and seek God with a heart unfettered by worldly things. To be like the Fool, stepping boldly toward his goal, eyes fixed on the splendor of the rainbow, seeking God with pure, selfless love.'"

There was a murmur of agreement; the poor people were receptive to news that the poor could achieve salvation more readily than the rich. That the buffoon might be nearer to God than the Lord.

"Even if at times it hurts," he concluded, rubbing his own posterior as if it were sore. "For the dogs of Manor and Church have sharp teeth."

The peasants' faces burst into appreciative smiles. The arrogance of the civil and religious authorities was a chronic sore point with them, and they liked hearing them likened to dogs. No doubt about it: Brother Paul was uttering heresy by the definitions of this medieval society—and he was enjoying it.

"This picture is Everyman," he continued. "Every person who seeks truth and enlightenment. He does not have to wander the countryside; the way is prickly enough though he never depart his village. His companions may laugh—yet he presses on, his eyes fixed on that glory that awaits those who persevere despite ridicule and even torture. Call him a fool—but those who laugh are the real fools."

Some peasants started to laugh—then caught themselves. Others began to laugh at *them*—and suffered similar second thoughts. Most nodded knowingly. They were all fools in this room, suffering persecution for their particular faith in God. Brother Paul had scored again—thanks to the card. It was a good feeling.

"Yet is it better to have some direction," he continued with more confidence. "And so we have the Juggler—" he held up the appropriate card— "'who comes in many forms, but always with the same message. It is the message of Jesus Christ, the first great Magician, who sought to lead erring human souls to the majesty of God. Even with that divine example to follow, many of us can hardly find the way. It is as though the message is magic, appearing and disappearing, eluding us just as we seek to grasp it." And the wand appeared in his hand, waved, and vanished.

He paused. They were with him now, raptly studying the little picture. It spoke better than his words ever could—but it needed interpretation. Perhaps the picture messages could have been made more obvious—but then the Inquisition would have deciphered them too. They had to be clear—only when properly explained. Like locks, they had to open to the proper keys—and resist all other efforts. Indeed they did this; imposter philosophers had missed the point of Tarot for centuries! Alas, even the deck of the Holy Order of Vision was sadly flawed, distorted by a chain of errors of interpretation—yet he had never realized this until he came here to the late fourteenth century. Satan had granted him his wish in full, providing not only the authentic original deck, but also its proper meaning. Yet he had to work out much of that meaning for himself; there was no instant comprehension of a philosophy as complex as Tarot.

Brother Paul held up the Lady Pope. "Yet who tries to give us that divine message? The Whore of Babylon!" He was interrupted by a shout of savage laughter. Oh, yes, they were familiar with that story! "The Church has become a giant succubus, tempting us with the promise of Salvation but leading us into damnation."

He showed the Ghost card. "It is hard to know right from wrong. 'Tell us what to do!' we cry, yet the answer is a blank space. We are all creatures of ignorance. Only God knows all, the Infinite, the Holy Spirit, the Ghost! Our past, present and future are all clouded by the unknown. Who knows which of us will die tomorrow—" He paused, thinking of the sick girl.

Then he thought of himself. His whole participation here was another unknown. In fact, his mission to Planet Tarot in that distant, almost forgotten other reality—

He cut off that line of thought and followed through with the same presentation the Juggler had given him, through Empress, Emperor, and Pope. Already he felt like a true Waldens missionary.

Now he came to Love. Except that this was not Love, primarily, but Choice. Through the centuries, he now realized, this card had been interpreted according to its purposely misleading illustration, rather than its more fundamental meaning. Iconographical transformation. Interpreting from the superficial image, rather than comprehending the intent of the symbol. Similar confusion must have phased the Ghost entirely out of existence! It was blank, therefore it stood for nothing, therefore it did not exist. Lord, how many fools had tinkered with Tarot!

But back to Choice: "A person cannot serve both God and Mammon. Riches and worldliness may be very tempting, but their benefit is superficial. Evil often puts on a fair face—yet it remains evil." He himself had been deceived by that fair face in the form of a sparkling intellect when he selected Therion to be his guide in the First Animation. What a price he had paid for that error! Yet it had forced on him a profound humility without which he could not have progressed this far through the rest. After compost, everything smelled better. "Do not choose Love of Possessions over Love of God! Give your heart and soul to Jesus Christ. Dedicate yourselves to doing good—"

A small sigh interrupted him. It should not have been audible over the general rustle of the people in the crowded room, but it sounded like a clarion in his ear. The sick child!

He broke off the presentation and went to the child and took her limp little hand again. "Do not choose the wrong path," he murmured only for her. He became oblivious to the rest of the room. "Come to the light, for we love you."

A tremor passed through her body. Her eyelids flickered. But she did not wake.

Brother Paul felt a horrible premonition: if he did not rouse her now, he would never succeed because she would fade out of part and life together. Whether the strain of three Animations was bearing her down, or whether her physical condition was causing her part to fade with her, or a combination—she was going.

He could not *let* her go. He had never known her before the Animations, and what he did know was only a young colonist playing a part. But somehow he was sure that there was—or would be—a Carolyn, his daughter. Who would die—or might never exist—if he let her go now. Ludicrous as it might seem to take this premonition seriously, he believed it.

"Pretty child," he murmured, speaking to that most precious spirit he sought, oblivious to all else. "You can only exist if someone believes in you. *I* believe in you. Someone must love you. *I* love you. Someone must need you. *I* need you. If you pass on, I shall have to go with you wherever your spirit leads. You are my future. Without you, my love is wasted. My life is empty. You must wake for me." And he put both hands on the sides of her face, cupping it tenderly, smoothing down the straggly hair, and leaned over and kissed her forehead. There were tears in her eyes, and as he came near her they spilled out and fell on her pale cheek.

He felt a power stirring like the flux of a magnetic field as it might feel to the magnet. It was the aura. *Oh, God*, he prayed silently. *If there is healing power in me, let it heal her now.*

"So much care," the old woman murmured, "for a child he doesn't even know." She was speaking with awe, not with cynicism.

"The *barba* reflects the love he speaks of—the love of God," another said.

If only that were true! Brother Paul's affinities seemed to be much closer to Satan than to God. He had bargained with Satan to save Carolyn from Hell—but had not thought to save her from death. That was the fallacy in dealing with the Devil; no man could outwit that horrendous evil intelligence. Had Satan granted his wish for Tarot knowledge—at the expense of his friend Lee and his child Carolyn?

Somehow he didn't believe that. *Couldn't* believe that. He had to have faith that Satan, like God, kept His word. Satan could not accurately judge souls if He were corrupt Himself. So this had to be another trial, not a punishment. Maybe Brother Paul was being offered another chance to promote his own private welfare at the expense of hers. To renege on his deal with Satan. All he had to do was let her die and return with his knowledge of Tarot.

"Wake," he murmured desperately. "There is so much for you to live for! Remember the field of flowers, the pine trees, the pretty stones." He almost said "airplane" but caught himself in time.

Her eyelids flickered again. "Stones . . ." she breathed.

All little girls liked pretty stones! This was fair game. "At the edge of the river," he said urgently. "All colors, rounded, some with streaks of brown or red. Each one separate, each one precious—because it is yours, because you value it. Nothing else can take its place." With inspiration, he reached into a pocket, his fingers sifting through what was there. He found what he wanted, brought it out, pressed it into her hand, and closed her fingers about it. "A stone!" he said. "The most wonderful thing there is! A little chunk of God."

Her hand tightened, feeling the contours of the stone. "Yes. . . ."

"Most wonderful—except for a little girl," he amended. "The stone is nothing without you. It needs you! Take care of it."

A shock of realization went through her. Her eyes popped open.

She looked at him, her eyes suddenly great and blue, too large for her face, strikingly beautiful. Her lips trembled, then parted. "Uncle," she whispered.

"Glory!" the old woman exclaimed. "She wakes!" Tears of joy streamed down her face.

Brother Paul felt tears on his own face again. He squeezed the child's hand gently. "Rest, Precious, rest. God is with you." And this was no line in any play; he had never been more sincere.

"God . . ." she repeated weakly.

"Only have faith in Him; you are His child. No one stands between you and Him. Put your soul in His care; He will not betray you." He squeezed her hand again. "God loves you. This you must believe." Yet there was an underlying current, for when he said God he also meant "I". This was his child too, and he loved her. And had it really been God who had restored her—or Satan?

"I believe . . ." she said dutifully.

"I believe . . ." the old woman echoed.

"It is a miracle of healing," the man said.

The child's eyes closed. She was sleeping now, a small smile on her face, the stone tightly held. Brother Paul released her hand and stood up. "It shall be as God wills," he said. "I do not know whether God will take her today—or in twenty years. But she is a creature of God—as are we all."

"Yes, Uncle!" the woman agreed. "How wonderful is the faith you bring!"

"It is the love that Jesus Christ showed to man," Brother Paul said. And silently: *Thank you, Jesus!*

He thought of returning to his Tarot presentation—but decided against it. The recovery of the child was a better message than any other. If it were really recovery, and not some temporary remission. . . .

Next morning Brother Paul resumed his journey toward Worms. He already knew as much about the Tarot as he had ever hoped to learn—but it seemed this "wish" had not yet run its full course.

He hoped the sick child recovered fully. It was uncertain at this stage. He had wanted to make provision for news of her progress, but knew there was no safe way to handle this. Even a cryptic message: THE LAMP IS LIT or THE LAMP IS OUT could be hazardous to the health of the messenger—and perhaps the child too. What would the Inquisition do to the living evidence of heretic healing? And peasants could not travel far freely; they were fairly well bound to their lots by the ties of the feudal system. Any man who did not pay his required rents on time, or serve on his Lord's estate, or appear at the regular church services—that man was in trouble.

Brother Paul did not like impersonating the *barba,* but now there seemed to be no way to avoid it. Only soldiers, minstrels, and the aristocracy could travel freely without being challenged. Soldiers went in groups, and the Lords and priests had horses and retainers. Had the soldiers he had encountered before been quicker witted, they would have been suspicious of a preist afoot and alone; fortunately the Juggler's bold ruse had worked. Brother Paul did not care even to attempt impersonating a bishop!

He approached another hamlet. But before he could set up his show, a child hurried up. Children seemed to be ubiquitous messengers, perhaps because they were not yet locked into the labor system. "Juggler—the Lord of the Manor suspects—you must go!"

Brother Paul did not question the message. There could have been an informer at last night's meeting. A horseman could have ridden at night, carrying the news: a heretic missionary! He packed up his equipment immediately and departed the village. He was weary—but this was no place to stay.

He cleared the village, but now was not sure what to do. He had not eaten in several hours, though the pangs of hunger had not yet touched him. He was more tired than he really should be, and the thought of sleeping in another tree crotch did not appeal. Yet if the villages were not safe—

The path led up a hill—and there at the height, gruesome in the gloom of husk, was a gibbet. A man was working at it, taking down the rope. He spied Brother Paul. "Too late!" he called down cheerily. "You missed it. He's already been hanged, taken down, drawn and quartered."

Brother Paul paused. He was not feeling good, and this did not improve his outlook. Since he might be under suspicion himself, he could not openly express his revulsion. "Well, I had a long way to come."

"You should have hurried." The man's tongue ran around his mouth, tasting the memory. "It was something to see! He must've kicked his feet a full minute! Still, it was too good for him. I'd have had him quartered live! Stealing the Lord's best horse, running it half to death—we're well rid of him!"

So a poor peasant had been executed publicly for stealing a horse. Well, that was justice in the medieval age; horses were valuable.

"But stay around," the man said. "Almost every week we have a new show. Mostly foot hangings, but some of them aren't bad. They—"

"Foot hangings?" Something piqued Brother Paul's curiosity, morbidly.

"Right. For minor stuff like killing a peasant or fucking a witch." The gibbetsman laughed coursely, but Brother Paul was not certain this was humor. "String him up by one foot, let him swing a day. Some are tough; they don't seem to notice it. But some scream like all hell, and some die without a mark on them."

Hanging by one foot. Now Brother Paul recognized what had jogged his curiosity. One of the Triumphs of the Tarot was titled the Hanged Man, and that man was suspended by one foot. He had put another interpretation on that card before, but naturally it related to this crude medieval torture. The Tarot reflected the life of its times. How much misinterpretation there had been in subsequent centuries of *that* card!

Brother Paul shook his head and moved on, feeling worse. But he had hardly put the gibbet out of sight when he heard something. A horse!

He hurried off the path. Maybe what he heard was innocent —but he could not take the risk. Even though he had merely impersonated the *barba,* he had spoken heresy, which was against what this medieval culture called the word of God, and that was a serious matter. The Inquisition—

The horseman passed. Brother Paul heaved a sigh of relief and returned to the path. He would go as far as he could while light remained, watching for a good place to spend the night.

His groin hurt. He paused to explore it, for a moment harboring the wild hope that his genitals were somehow growing back. This was not the case; there was merely some sort of swelling there, perhaps of the lymph nodes. It made walking awkward. As if he didn't have problems enough, without food or lodging or water—

Water! Suddenly he was ravenously thirsty. Was there a spring near here? The path had strayed away from the great river, rising into the hills; he needed water *here*, not a league away.

He staggered, feeling dizzy. He was hot, burning up; he knew it though he had no objective way to check his temperature. His skin itched.

Slowly the realization dawned. He had observed these symptoms before. In the Juggler—just before he died.

He had the dread plague.

Brother Paul fell headlong in the path, striking heavily and rolling part way over. He saw the moon hanging in the gloomy dusk sky. Isis, Goddess of Luna, the principle of female deception, stared obscurely down at him from her filling crescent: the face of the womb. Somewhere a sad hound bayed.

It was no time at all—but also an eternity of fading in and out, retching, burning thirst, pain. Discovery; exclamations. "Get it off the road!" But he remained because no one would touch him for fear of contamination. Then one came who was willing, and Brother Paul was dumped unceremoniously into a wagon. He bumped along, being taken—where? Obviously to the burial dump for plague victims.

He tried to say something, but his mouth would not work properly, and the noise of the wheels was loud. And what difference did it make? He would soon be dead anyway. Satan had granted his wish. He had not wished for life. Not his *own* life.

Lights shone: lamps in the night. Buildings loomed. He was coming into metropolitan Hell. The demon driving the wagon stopped to converse with a devil guarding the gate to some torture station. Money changed hands. Money—the love of which was the root of all evil. How fitting that it dominate the rituals of Hell! Then the two of them came back to Brother Paul and hauled him out of the wagon and walked him through the narrow portal of the building. They dragged him stumbling upstairs and finally laid him out on a pallet. Maybe some vivisection to lead off the festivities. . . .

Troubled unconsciousness. Something at his face: he felt wetness. The water torture! But he was so parched he had to gulp it down. Then other tortures; bitter herbs to eat, cold washing of body, sleep.

Now he woke in a clean bed. A man about his own age stood over him. He had a full black beard, above which dark, seemingly hooded eyes looked out. "I think you have passed the nadir, stranger." The voice was familiar.

"I have the Black Death," Brother Paul said. "My companion died of it."

"Many do. You came close. But I have a certain finesse with herbs, and your constitution is strong." He drew up a wooden chair and seated himself beside the bed. "The question is, why did a castrate Waldens *barba* stricken by plague call my name?"

Brother Paul focused on him, confused. "Your name?"

"I am Abraham the Jew."

Oh. "My companion gave me two names before he died. One was yours. I did not realize I spoke it aloud."

"Fortunate for you that you did. I am interested in strange things—in magic and sorcery and odd faiths. So when the burial detail heard you name me, they brought you here. I saw at once that you were of a heretical sect—but what is Christian heresy to a Jew? I neither gave away your secret nor let them dump you to die. Intrigued by curiosity, I paid their fee and gave you drink and medication. Now I seek my reward: complete information on you and your magic."

Could he trust this man? Did it matter? Evidently this was not formal Hell, after all, but a continuation of the medieval vision. Brother Paul decided to tell the truth or as much of it as made sense. "I am no *barba*. I am a stranger to this realm, who was befriended by a Waldens missionary who had lost his companion. Then he died, and I took his place."

"A risky impersonation. Are you not aware what they do to heretics?"

"I was fleeing the Holy Office when I fell ill," Brother Paul admitted.

"You say the *barba* named me. Where did he get my name? I have not before had dealings with the Waldenses. In fact, I had not realized they were into sorcery."

"Only the magic of God's great love," Brother Paul said. "The rest is stage trickery to entertain the masses and allay suspicion. I suppose the Waldenses keep track of those who might help them in emergency, and you were the one for the city of Worms."

"That seems reasonable," Abraham agreed. "For as it developed, I *have* helped you. Yet surely they were aware that all Jews are grasping usurers and that I would not help one of their number unless they made it amply worth my while." He smiled briefly. "I am sorry you are not the real Uncle; I am most curious what payment they proposed to proffer. What was the other name the dead man uttered?"

Brother Paul concentrated, and it came back. "Abra-Melim, the Mage of Egypt."

The Jew shook his head. "That name means nothing to me. And Egypt is far away from Worms."

"True." Brother Paul felt tired already. He dropped off to sleep, and Abraham let him be.

He woke later—perhaps it was another day—feeling stronger. The Jew's herbs must have been potent! Some sound had disturbed him. Maybe it had been the Jew delivering food; at any rate, there was a sweet roll and an ewer of milk beside his bed, though he was alone.

Brother Paul began to eat and drink, glad for his hunger; he was definitely on the mend. He had thought he was finished when he came down with the bubonic plague, but of course it was not a hundred per cent fatal. Good care had been all that he needed. How fortunate that he had cried out Abraham's name in his delirium!

Abraham the Jew—there was a nagging familiarity about him. Shave off that beard and—of course! He was Therion in this new role.

What did that mean? The Good Companion had died; now he was again in the power of the Evil Companion. Lee had been the Wand of Fire; Therion was the Sword of Air. What did this devious servant of Satan have in mind for him this time?

Now he heard voices and realized that this was what had awakened him. One was Abraham; the other—no, it could not be the Juggler, for he was dead in this sequence. A stranger, then.

What stranger would seek him out? Had the Jew, angry because he could not repay his board, betrayed him for a price to the Inquisition? If so, how could he escape? He was feeling better, but not that much better. This was the first food he had eaten in perhaps two days: good, but hardly enough.

". . . minstrel, ill with the Black Death," Abraham's voice came more clearly. "No harm in him."

"I shall be the judge of that," the other responded firmly. "There is news of a shameless heretic in this region."

"Heresy!" Abraham snorted derisively. "Your entire Church is a heresy by our definition!"

"Jew, you have had an easy life in this fair city," the other retorted grimly. "It could become more difficult." There was cold menace in the too-familiar voice. It sounded so very much like the Juggler in his guise as a priest.

"I merely expressed a viewpoint." Abraham's voice had turned conciliatory; the threat had had its effect. "To us, there is not a great difference between Christians and the Moors. Both of their founders were prophets subscribing to our principles; both cults are comparatively young."

They had evidently halted on the landing near Brother Paul's door, engrossed in their unamiable dialogue. "Jew, you do not draw on an inexhaustible supply of tolerance," the other said warningly. "I will interview this man."

"I do not know whether he is in fit condition to be interviewed," Abraham protested. He spoke loudly and clearly —obviously intending Brother Paul to overhear. That did not seem like betrayal—yet the ways of the Evil Companion were invariably devious. "He is merely a stage magician who fooled me into supposing he might possess real magic; a charlatan. Of no interest to your Order."

"Jew—" The freighting of that single word was eloquent.

"Well, we shall see." Abraham opened the door.

Brother Paul refused to play a game of deception by feigning sleep. He had had enough of deception! "Greetings," he said as they entered. He continued munching his bread.

The visitor wore a white habit with a black mantle: the classical garb of a Dominican monk. His beard was neat, his eyes piercing, and he had an air of grim concentration. "I am Brother Thomas, a Black Friar," he said.

It was! It was Lee in a new part! He *had* survived the death of his prior part! "How glad I am to see you, friend!" Brother Paul exclaimed.

The Friar looked at him sternly. "Have we met before?"

Of course Lee would play the part properly, inflexibly; that was his way. And what a part he had now! He had become his former enemy, the Inquisition.

Lee had also, in life, been something of a racist. Now he was a "Black" Friar. It was only a name, of course—but in these Animations names were often a vital part of the symbolism. Lee was really making up for past indiscretions! Of course, since this was an aspect of Hell, Satan might have required—

"Perhaps he performed a show at your house, one time," Abraham said. And what of Therion: he had ridiculed the Bible, and now was a Jew. Satan had given him a hellish assignment too!

"Let him speak for himself." The Friar's penetrating gaze swung to bear on Brother Paul again. "Juggler, why did you address me as 'friend'?"

Brother Paul had allowed his racing thoughts to distract him from his present situation. Now he had to play his own part. "I thought I recognized you, but I may have been mistaken."

Brother Thomas's glance was too keen. This man would make a devastating enemy! "Surely we have not encountered each other before; I have no connection with stage magicians or others of that ilk. Yet there is no doubting the flash of recognition that illuminated your features just now."

This was awkward. Surely Lee-the-player recognized and remembered Brother-Paul-the-player. But this part of "Brother Thomas" had not met him. So the Dominican would have to verify by some legitimate means what the player Lee already knew to be the case: that Brother Paul was playing the part of a heretic missionary. Probably, by the standards of historical Dominicans, Brother Paul's own Holy Order of Vision was heretical. So he was in trouble, regardless.

Or *was* he? Lee would play the part of Brother Thomas straight, inflexibly accurate—but the player was limited in his interpretation of the part by his own background. Brother Paul would not be able to best a true Dominican in theological debate; after all, Saint Thomas Aquinas, from whose name this part had probably been drawn, had been a Dominican—perhaps the most redoubtable Catholic theologian of all time. But Lee was no Dominican, in life, and no Catholic. He was at a disadvantage. So was Therion, whose Horned God was the antithesis of the Jewish Jehovah. Brother Paul found he rather enjoyed the irony.

"You do not answer?" the Friar demanded. "This is suspicious."

And suspicion was tantamont to conviction with the Inquisition! He had to get talking! "I am not a common juggler," Brother Paul said. What was the best line to take, knowing that part of this man knew the truth, and so could not be deceived? How close to that truth could he come without, by the rules of this grim game, giving away the Waldenses and thus betraying his promise to this same player in another guise? Yet Brother Paul's own religious and ethical scruples prevented him from lying. The *barba* impersonation was a very special case. Never, since he joined the Holy Order of Vision, had Brother Paul failed to honor the truth as he understood it. He had once concealed his childhood fears even from himself, and his one-time addiction to the memory drug had caused other obscurities in his life. That was over; he did not intend to practice concealment again, no matter what pressure Satan applied.

"And what would be behind that innocent facade?" Brother Thomas inquired. He was intent, expectant, closing in on the heresy his memory from his previous role knew was there, if only he could prove it *here*. Yet Brother Paul perceived a misgiving in him, the suppressed regret of a man who did what was required though it was personally painful. Lee wanted to lose this fish—but as the Black Friar he was bound to do his utmost to reel it in. And his chances of failure were diminishingly small.

Oh, Satan, you have crafted the most artistic fiendishness yet! You have forced us to destroy ourselves, knowingly. For even Therion, in the role of a man who had harbored a heretic, would be doomed.

Well, why *not* the truth? Extraordinary measures would be required to extricate themselves from this maelstrom. Brother Paul had told it before. The other players had assigned parts, but Brother Paul played himself, even when he assumed another role as now. He was himself pretending to be the Juggler, not himself cast in the role of the Juggler. A difficult but key distinction. He was under no obligation that he knew of to make pretenses. "I am a visitor from another—"

But his own self-protective censor cut him off. There were different levels of truth here in Animation. He had experienced how directly these visions could affect the people within them. If he said something here that convinced the Friar that he was a lunatic or a heretic, he could lose his part. And for him, unlike the others, his part *was* his life. This was not worth the risk. "Land," he finished lamely. Then, before the Friar could follow that up, he added: "I am a Brother of a Christian Order there."

"Would that land be Italy?" Brother Thomas asked.

Italy—the home of the Pope (one of them, anyway) and of the Waldens heresy. Loaded question! "No. It is across the ocean, perhaps unknown to you. But we have Dominican monks, and I thought you were one I knew until I saw that you were merely another of that excellent Order." Which disposed of the recognition problem—he hoped. "We believe in the original message of Jesus Christ and the Apostle Paul." Brother Paul was not about to be caught up in any great ignorance concerning Jesus or his namesake Paul; he was on secure footing here.

"Those are apt beliefs," the Dominican observed wryly.

"The Holy Bible is an apt tutor."

"Now that I can agree with," Abraham put in. "Certainly the Hebrew Text which you refer to as the Old Testament. To us, Jesus was merely a man—a good man, perhaps, and a prophet, but nevertheless a man. Jesus was a Jew; he followed the Scriptures we originated and codified." In this role, Therion could not challenge the origin of the Old Testament, whatever private doubts he had.

"Yet you slew Him!" Brother Thomas snapped. "For that you are forever accursed!"

Abraham spread his hands disingenuously. "An unfortunate complication. Your Saint Paul was also a Christian killer, you know. Remember how he had Stephen stoned?"

Oh, Therion was enjoying this now!

"Saint Paul repented!" the Friar said hotly. "He himself suffered stoning for his Christian faith!"

"And now you Christians are eager to stone your own kind, calling them heretics when they protest the manifest corruption in your ranks."

"The Holy Office does not stone Christians," Brother Thomas said stiffly.

"No. The Holy Office merely strings dissenters up by the thumbs like so many carcasses of venison with a scribe meticulously recording every scream. How your Jesus must appreciate those screams!"

This was getting dirty. The Dominican blanched. Brother Paul knew Lee was remembering his role of Jesus in the other Animation and his own objection to the very evil Therion now pointed out. Oh, telling thrust!

This also suggested why a Jew might help a Christian heretic. The Jews had known centuries of persecution at the hands of righteous Christians, many of whom were hypocrites with little inkling of the original precepts of their religion. Now the Waldenses, like other sects before them, were advocating a return to those original precepts—and were suffering similar persecution. Therion, as a member of another persecuted sect, could play this role with gusto. For who had been more vilified by Christianity than the Horned God?

Brother Thomas had recovered somewhat. Lee, as a Mormon, also knew the meaning of persecution. The Mormons had had to migrate more than once from hostile country to preserve their freedom of worship only to have that country, in the form of the expanding United States of America, annex their new territory and outlaw their style of marriage. Yet he had a role to play here, and he would play it well. "The Holy Office takes no joy in suffering. But it is not always easy to salvage the immortal soul of a hardened heretic. Surely the momentary discomfort he may feel during interrogation is an infinitesimal price to pay for his release from the eternal fires of Hell. The boil must be lanced, though it hurt for an instant, lest it poison the whole."

That was a good statement, Brother Paul thought. Lee was coming through well in this very difficult role.

But the Jew was pressing for the kill. It was The Dozens, again. "I think Hell might well be a better place to spend eternity than among hypocrites."

"No, the hypocrites are relegated to the infernal regions," Brother Thomas said evenly. "There they suffer the eternal torment they so richly deserve."

Abraham affected surprise. "With no reprieve?"

"With no reprieve. They had their chance in life."

"No rehabilitation?"

"No rehabilitation after death."

"Not even if the hypocrite sincerely repents his hypocrisy?"

"No, once he is damned, he is damned forever."

"Is this what your Jesus Christ said? That there be no forgiveness when the prodigal son returned?"

"Forgiveness in *life*," the Dominican said grimly. "There must be a point of no return," and that point is at the terminus of life. At death the decision is final. This is the reason we labor so diligently to save a person's soul in time by whatever means we possess. We do not wish *any* immortal soul to suffer indefinitely." He glanced piercingly at Abraham. "There may still be time even for you, Jew."

Abraham laughed. "I do not fear Satan! I'd prefer to live as Jacob did, money-grubbing and lusty, cheating and being cheated —and human throughout. When the time comes, I will wrestle with God as he did, and we shall see what we shall see. Yahveh will understand."

This was Therion's interpretation, Brother Paul thought. He doubted a genuine Jew would have put it that way. Therion, like Lee, was limited by his own religious background. Thus God was cast in a Satanic mold.

But strait-laced Lee could not accept such a statement and neither could the Dominican Friar. "God accepts no money-grubbers, no cheaters, no lust! You blaspheme!"

"God seems to accept the Holy Office," Abraham remarked.

But Brother Thomas was too worked up to grasp the full nature of that insult. "*No* culture could justify such things. They are abominations before God!" This too matched what Brother Paul knew of Mormon tenets; the forbidden fruit of the Garden of Eden was sexual intercourse. But because God had commanded man to be fruitful and multiply, Adam and Eve had chosen the lesser of evils and indulged in the fruit of sex. This really was not too different from medieval Church doctrine to Brother Paul's mind.

The problem was that Lee was far better versed in *The Book of Mormon* than in the Bible. A number of names overlapped, but they stood for different people. The Jacob of the Mormons was not the Jacob of the Jews.

"Your God accepted a man who sent his own firstborn son out into the wilderness with his mother!" Abraham said. "Abraham's firstborn was Ishmael—and he cast him out in favor of his second son Isaac. From Isaac and his cheating second-born son Jacob are the Jews descended, and from them came the Jew called Jesus, whom you—"

He broke off, for Brother Thomas was staring at him. Oops —the Baal-worshiper Therion had allowed his personal feelings to carry him away, forgetting that in this part he was the Jew. As Therion, it was natural that he resent the exclusion of his philosophic ancestor Ishmael—but as the Jew, he had fluffed his part.

That fluff could give the advantage to the Dominican—and undermine Brother Paul's own position. His own role was at stake; Abraham knew his Waldens association and Brother Thomas suspected it. Discovery or betrayal would probably finish him. Would Therion sell him out to protect himself? Therion certainly would! He had to step in.

"There may be misunderstanding," Brother Paul said carefully. "Abraham was the father, according to the Bible, of Ishmael by his wife's maid Hagar. Abraham's wife Sarah was barren, so she gave him her Egyptian maid for the purpose of siring an heir. This was standard practice in those days, for to the nomads children were vitally important. The custom seems to derive from the Hurrians. Plural marriages were permitted, and no blame attaches to Abraham for this. He would have been remiss had he not taken steps to provide offspring, to continue the tribe."

The Friar might have objected—but the player Lee, sensitive about the furor over the former Mormon practice of polygamy, could not bring himself to do it. The Jew was happy to have his namesake Abraham defended, and the player Abraham eager to have his fluff covered. So Brother Paul had the floor—for now.

"The problem came because, though Ishmael was the first son, Isaac was the legitimate son. God made Sarah fertile at the age of ninety, and Abraham was a hundred when Isaac was born. So it was a remarkable circumstance, unanticipated. There was fierce rivalry between the two women, and in the end the only way Abraham could settle it was by sending away Hagar and Ishmael. But Yahveh looked after them, and their descendents became the Arabs—actually more numerous and prosperous than the descendents of Isaac, the Jews. So it was a difficult situation, and an unkind compromise had to be made, but I don't think blame should attach to either the Arabs or the Jews for that."

"Attach the blame to the Hurrians," Abraham said, relieved.

Brother Thomas was not so eager to let it go. "Yet I believe the Jew said something about Jacob, cheating and lusting and fighting with God? This sounds heretical to me."

Meaning that if Brother Paul tried to defend such actions by Jacob, instead of denying them, he might be accused of heresy himself—the very thing he was trying to avoid. Once the Inquisition put him to the torture on this pretext, the torturers would quickly extract from him the rest of his information. Therion, obviously unsympathetic to the children of Isaac despite his present role, was ill-equipped to reverse himself there. So it was Brother Paul's problem again. Had this been engineered by Satan? Regardless, it was hellish.

"Those were hard times," Brother Paul said carefully. He felt as if he were treading a thin sheet of ice covering the rumbling maw of a volcano. One misstep, a single mischance—doom. Satan charged a high price for the wish He granted! "Abraham had many problems and very difficult decisions. His son Isaac had his own problems; it was all he could do to protect his pretty wife Rebekah from the attentions of other tribesmen. Isaac's twin sons Esau and Jacob were rivals for his favor; Isaac tended to favor the strong hunter Esau, while Rebekah liked the more moderate Jacob. So there was a very human dissension in that family too. It might be taken as an analogy to the contrasting pulls of the rugged country life of the nomads, and the more comfortable, settled life of city peoples." And there was his own crisis: country vs. city! "In which direction would this tribe go? Thus the strife was subtle but intense. Jacob, as boys will, made a deal with Esau to obtain his brother's birthright and followed it up by tricking their father Isaac into granting his blessing to Jacob. This was a form of cheating. But the point is, the men of Biblical times were human with human stresses and failings, and they did make errors of judgment and passion. They were a great trial to Yahveh."

"Yes," Abraham agreed, and Brother Thomas nodded. So far, so good. But he wasn't out of trouble yet.

"Jacob was cheated in his turn, perhaps in retribution," Brother Paul continued. His hands were sweating; surreptitiously he wiped them on the blanket. "When he worked for seven years to marry the fair Rachel, he discovered after the consummation that her father had substituted her older sister Leah. Now he had to work another seven years for Rachel. He was actually allowed to marry Rachel within a week, however, so he did not have to wait; he had two wives while he worked off the debt. And perhaps the hand of God was in this too, for as it turned out, Rachel was barren. So it was Leah who provided him with a number of fine sons. Then Rachel, to preserve her status, gave him her maid for procreative purposes in order to have at least a surrogate son. So Leah gave him *her* pretty maid for another son, and—well, you could call this lust, but I don't think that's quite fair. All of it was for the purpose of increasing the size of the tribe, and since underpopulation was the main problem of that day—"

Brother Thomas the Dominican Friar spread his hands. "Brother, I thought you were practicing deceit, but you evidently have a fine knowledge of the Bible."

"It was Jacob who practiced deceit," Brother Paul agreed, weak with relief. "And his father-in-law. Each had his motives—"

"In fact, your knowledge of the Bible is so specific that I suspect you must have been reading it yourself."

Oh, no! Now Brother Paul remembered: in medieval times the Church frowned on common reading of the Bible. It was deemed too important to be left to the run-of-the-mill believer, and instead had to be read and interpreted by the hierarchy. He had marched into another trap.

"In my country, the study of the Bible reaches further toward the layman than it does here," he said. Understatement of the mission! "And as a traveling minstrel I am accustomed to remembering stories. It is easy to remember the greatest story ever told." Would that pass?

"I must accept your credits as a Christian scholar," Brother Thomas continued. "I apologize for questioning you during your infirmity."

Victory! Brother Paul had so phrased his commentary as to defend the Mormons along with the Biblical Jews, and this had paid off. Multiple wives, for a good cause. . . .

"Ah, but this matter of wrestling with God—" Abraham said, unable to resist the gibe.

Brother Paul saw disaster looming again. If Brother Thomas resumed the fray—

"We all wrestle with God at times," the Dominican said. "We call it conscience. The human flesh is weak, while God is strong; we must listen to God always."

"Yes," Brother Paul agreed, relaxing again. So the dogs really had been called off!

Brother Thomas faced the door. "I apologize again for the intrusion. Farewell." He crossed himself.

"Farewell," Brother Paul echoed, making the sign of the cross with his own hand. A true *barba* would never have done that.

It was a mistake. His hand knocked the table at his bedside, and the Tarot deck fell to the floor. It landed face up with a sound like thunder, the cards splaying apart.

Brother Thomas whirled and stepped back in and stopped wtih dismaying alacrity. "What is this?" he inquired, picking up the cards.

"A tool of the Juggler's trade," Abraham said quickly. "He performs magic tricks with them for the entertainment of peasants."

"Magic is heresy," the Dominican said with an abrupt return of grimness.

"Stage magic," Brother Paul said. Why had this had to happen now? The worst possible break! Satan's work, of course. "Sleight of hand. I can demonstrate."

But the Friar was looking through the cards. "Many of these seem to be conventional images such as are used by riff-raff for gaming. But some are more complicated representations." He held up the card for Deception with its sinister Lunar theme. "What is the meaning of this?"

"That seems to be an astrological motif," Abraham said quickly. "I have made some considerable study of astrology and other types of magic—" He smiled at the Dominican's expression. "Do not look so shocked, Friar! Magic is not forbidden to us Jews! In fact, we often have need of it to hold our own in this Christian country."

Brother Paul knew what he meant. The Jews had some of the most authoritative magic in the form of the Qabala, Cabala, Kabbalah or however it was transcribed. They had guarded that knowledge so well that it was unknown to the Christians of this period. Thus the Qabala had no connection with the Tarot although later "experts" had done their best to merge the two.

"This is astrology?" Brother Thomas inquired dubiously. Astrology, if Brother Paul remembered correctly, was regarded as more of a science than magic in medieval times. Thus it was not heretical by Church definitions; indeed, some Church scholars were astrologers. "Where is the horoscope?"

"The entire deck would be the horoscope," Abraham explained glibly. "The symbols would not be arranged on charts, but on individual cards, and the fall of the cards must determine the reading. This is obviously the planet of the Moon."

Again, the Dominican's piercing glance stabbed Brother Paul. "Brother, do you practice divination for your audience?"

"No," Brother Paul answered honestly. "What these pictures evoke is in the mind of the beholders. If you see an astrological symbol in an ordinary Lunar landscape, and wish to pay me a coin for that encouragement, you are a fool and I am richer by that coin."

Brother Thomas hesitated, then smiled. "There are many fools in this world," he said. He turned again, setting down the cards. "Methinks you are not above preying on foolishness on occasion,

Brother, when you are hungry. And the biggest fool of all is the Jew who believes in magic." He crossed himself again and marched out.

"The hypocrite!" Abraham muttered. "His whole Church is built on magic! The reason they burn heretics is that those people practice magic that is outside Church control. They can't tolerate competition! Jesus Christ was a magician; he made water into wine, and a few crumbs of bread sufficient to feed a multitude. *I* seek magic openly—and someday I shall find it!"

Brother Paul found he agreed with him. "There is a lot of hypocrisy in religion. But why have you helped me, knowing that I practice no genuine magic?"

"Well, I didn't *know* that," Abraham said candidly. "I was sure that most of your tricks were innocuous. But I have heard of the Waldenses and their cards, and I suspected there could be magic in it. So—" He broke off, his face twisting into alarm. "The Friar crossed himself. Twice."

"Friars do," Brother Paul agreed.

"When there is a challenge or a threat, they do. But Brother Thomas was departing. Why should he cross himself before leaving the presence of a Jew?"

Brother Paul was getting tired and wanted to sleep again. "Maybe he was warding off heresy."

Abraham shook his head in grim affirmation. "He crossed himself because he believed he had confirmation of the presence of evil. By his twisted definition, I am a known evil, but you—"

"If he really suspects me, why didn't he just take me in when he had the chance? I am weak from my illness; I could not have offered much resistance."

Abraham paced the floor nervously. "That is what *I* would like to know. I would not have dared to interfere, had he declared you heretic; any little pretext will do for a new pogrom! Soft-heartedness can only go so far! I would have had to renounce you, and he knew it. So why should he practice such deception? He surely has great mischief in mind."

The more Brother Paul considered that, the more concerned he became. Suppose the Dominican had decided he had a live heretic on the line—and thought he might reel in more heretics with a little cunning patience? He might indeed pretend to be satisfied so as to reassure the quarry—then watch that suspect. "I fear I must be on my way," Brother Paul said regretfully. Rest seemed wonderful, but not if a conspiracy was building against him and the Waldenses. He had to lose himself quickly.

"I think our minds are moving in similar channels," Abraham said. "The Dominican is unconvinced—rather, he *is* convinced! He smells heresy! I saw his eyes glint when he saw your Tarot. He has seen such cards before, I'll warrant, or heard them described! I believe he has returned to consult the other demons of his Order, and if they don't arrest you they will spy on you, trying to discover your contacts and methods of identification so that they can burn many heretics instead of one. I believe you should escape this city in haste. I shall have to denounce you as soon as you are gone to save my own skin. Are you able to travel?"

"I'm not sure," Brother Paul said. "Your attentions have helped, but the black plague is nothing to fool with; I remain weak."

"No doubt the Friar is certain you can not move about today, therefore is not casting his net quite yet. But tomorrow—" He paused, grimacing. "It will have to be risked," he decided. "I am a Jew; my situation is precarious. I have money, so they deal with me carefully, but it is not wise to push them too far. I will give you directions how to escape, but I cannot provide any material assistance. It must seem that you fled while I was preparing to turn you in."

Brother Paul agreed. He had to move on today, now—for the Jew's sake, his own, and the Waldenses'.

"What was that other name the missionary gave you?" Abraham asked suddenly.

"Name? Oh—Abra-Melim, the Mage of Egypt."

"Abra-Melim, the Mage of Egypt," the Jew repeated, memorizing it. "They have outstanding lore in Egypt. This may be the magician I am looking for. Surely the Waldenses believe the Mage has what I seek."

Brother Paul shrugged as he dressed. "I wouldn't know. It is only a name to me."

"Maybe I should go to Egypt," Abraham mused. "If you slip their noose, it may not be safe for me in Worms for a time." But then he smiled. "But I shall be glad to take the risk if only to aggravate that sanctimonious cleric. Come, we shall effect your escape."

24

TRIUMPH
(SUN)

The Bible, according to Fred Gladstone Bratton in A History of the
Bible, *is not a textbook in science. Its cosmology is primitive. It sees
the earth as flat, the sky as a vault, and the sun, moon and stars
contained within this vault. Beneath it is the realm of the dead. The
whole was created in six days. Sickness was caused by demons, destiny
determined by the stars, angels healed the sick and miracles abounded.
To take it literally seems foolish. But its value for moral principles and
spiritual guidance remains, untouched by the changes in our geograph-
ical and scientific perspective. Faith, hope and love are universally valid
today, as they were when the Bible was written.*

Two days later just as hope was rising, Brother Paul felt renewed
fatigue and fever. A deep cough developed. It was not a return of
the plague, but something else whose symptoms he recognized:
pneumonia. He had driven himself too hard, too soon after his
prior illness. Now he *had* to rest—or return to Hell permanently.
He had not consciously felt threatened by the plague, awful as it
was; it was not a disease to which a twentieth or twenty-first
century man was attuned. But pneumonia—*that* he respected.

Where could he go? He had headed west from Worms, disguised
as a beggar, avoiding any possible contact with likely Waldenses.

He had trekked toward France, hoping the minions of the Holy Office would not pursue him beyond the boundaries of the Holy Roman Empire, assuming they picked up his trail. He could not afford any friends, of course; anyone who helped him might suffer at the hands of the Inquisition.

Abraham, despite his protestations, had given him some money and general advice. He might obtain lodging at some isolated farm for a pittance, and no one would know he was there until days after he was gone.

Odd how the roles had reversed. Therion had helped him (apologizing for it by muttering about possible reward and aggravation of the status quo), while Lee was out to destroy him. Satan certainly knew how to turn the knife in the wound!

Brother Paul heard horses on the path. Should he hide—or try to bluff it out? The odds were they weren't after him. What was one suspected heretic in the whole medieval society? Maybe they had never been after him; the Jew had wanted him out, so had concocted the notion of this plot. . . .

No, he couldn't convince himself. This was not the medieval society; it was an Animation set in it. Historical fiction, and he was the central character. All conspiracies would revolve around him.

"Brother, you're paranoid," he told himself. He hunched his shoulders within the cloak and trod on. The sounds of the horse became distinguishable: two horses and the creak of wheels. A fast-traveling coach or wagon. He moved over so as to give it room to pass; a coach probably meant a noble and they tended to be arrogant. The horses could run him down and trample him if he got in the way. Beggars weren't worth much.

The horses came abreast of him, snorting. He glanced sidelong, without turning his head. It was a two-wheeled wagon, canopied, reminding him of a chariot. The chariot of the Tarot of course —power on the move, symbolic of man's journey along the road to salvation.

He kept on walking, letting it pass, still sneaking looks at the horses. The chariot seemed to have slowed, pacing him rather than passing.

"Juggler!" a too-familiar voice called.

Oh, no! It was Brother Thomas, the Dominican Friar.

"Juggler—no need to walk when you can ride," the enemy said

cheerily. "How fortunate I am traveling your way!"

Brother Paul considered running. But he could not outdistance the chariot on the road; he would have to go cross country. He knew he could not get far; he was sick and weak and had to rest, while the Dominican was well and strong.

Dispiritedly, Brother Paul climbed up into the chariot beside the Friar. There was a seat there, and he sank down on it with physical relief. What else could he do?

The chariot halted. Brother Thomas steadied him with a firm hand. "We have a barber who can help you," he said. Was there menace there? A barber—surely not a mere cutter of hair. A medieval doctor. Letting out the bad blood, so the patient could improve. A treatment that could be fatal. "No . . ." Brother Paul protested weakly.

"Have no fear," the Dominican said reassuringly. "Our barber employs only the very best leeches, culled weekly from the Seine."

Bloodsucking worms from the river. Brother Paul thought about vomiting, but lacked the energy. Then something else nagged him. "The Seine?"

"We are a long way from Worms, friend," Brother Thomas informed him. "You slept like the dead—and indeed, I feared that might not be much exaggeration. This is the heart of France, our chief monastery. Is it not beautiful?"

Brother Paul roused himself enough to look. The gate was barred. The windows were small and high. The walls were thick. This was a veritable fortress. "Beautiful," he echoed dismally.

The gate closed behind him. He was trapped—and he had not been able to dispose of the cards. He must have maintained a death grip on them to protect them from the Friar's curiosity. Or maybe the Animation had skipped over this dull passage so that nothing at all had happened between scenes. Animation was real, but on its own terms.

They came to a central room where a great fire blazed in a fireplace. Brother Paul, shivering with a chill, moved toward it gladly. Several hooded monks appeared, closing in about him. "You must rest," Brother Thomas said. "A room has been prepared. We shall take your soiled clothes and provide you with fresh apparel."

Should he try to resist? It was hopeless; he was sick and weak, and they were many and strong. He could gain nothing—and there was always the chance that they did mean well, that the Jew had deceived him about the motives of the Dominicans.

Except for the Tarot. Brother Thomas had seen that deck, and player Lee would have known its nature from his previous part. So Lee knew what he was looking for, and with that deck in his possession he could investigate legitimately and zero in on the secret. Brother Paul's decision to avoid the Waldenses must have nullified the spying strategy, so the Animation had shunted right across to the next contest of wills. The cards were now the key; if Brother Thomas and the Inquisition gained possession of the cards, exposure of the Waldenses was a virtual certainty. The Dominicans would reproduce the cards, put on jugglers' suits, give sermons based on the cards—and take whole audiences into custody, cleaning out entire cities with single sweeps. It would work because the people would believe in the authenticity of anyone who carried such cards—as they had believed in Brother Paul.

Without those cards, Brother Thomas the Dominican would have no certain evidence that Brother Paul was a heretic and no lever to use against the Waldenses. He would be unable to proceed with the persecution. Not according to the rules of this play, no matter how much he knew privately. And Lee would follow the rules, absolutely.

The monks pressed close. This was an Animation; were they real? Maybe he could walk right through them and on through the cloister walls. Yet this too would be misplaying the part, cheating. Satan had sent him here at his own request, as it were; he should not have been surprised to discover Satanic elements of the sequence. Perhaps he played the part of a genuinely historical character, and significant revelations remained. He had to play the animation game or forfeit all that Animation held for him. Which meant that he had to submit now to the power of the monks.

Except for the Tarot deck. If he believed in the play, he had also to believe in the Waldenses who would be routed by his betrayal of the Juggler's trust. They would be put on trial for heresy, perhaps tortured, perhaps burned at the stake. As Joan of Arc had been burned—*would be* burned—in this area a generation hence. Brother Paul could not allow himself to be the instrument of these good people's doom.

He could afford neither to invoke the power of his disbelief in the reality of this Animation nor to go along with it completely.

He had to do the right thing despite increasing pressure. Yet what *was* right in this hell of indecision?

Brother Paul reached inside his robe into the secret pocket. His fingers closed about the deck. He lifted it out, holding it for a moment, gazing on this most precious object he had ever possessed: the True Tarot. He had suffered a tour of Hell itself and the black plague to obtain this cardboard Grail.

He nerved himself. Then, quickly, he hurled the Tarot into the open fire, spreading the cards with a twist of his wrist so that they would burn rapidly.

Brother Thomas screamed as though his own body were afire. He dived at the hearth, reaching in with his bare hands, trying to recover the blazing cards. The other monks rushed to restrain him, thinking him mad—as indeed he was at that moment!—and Brother Thomas had to allow them to haul him away from the searing heat.

Brother Paul knew the agony the Friar suffered; he was experiencing it himself. He watched the cards curl and writhe in the flame as though struggling to escape. Colored tongues danced above the pigments. The heat of the sun, the flames of Hell, the conflagration of the spirit—in microcosm!

The blaze died down. Dismal ashes settled out. It was done; the treasure had been destroyed. The tainted Gift had been rejected. Brother Paul had played the game by the rules and won. At the cost of his Grail. Now at last the Animation could end, releasing him from the torture of his first wish.

They waited, as it were in tableau. Nothing happened. The issue had been decided—yet the scene continued. Evidently Satan had not finished the sequence.

Back into their roles! "You may have destroyed the demon deck, the physical evidence against you," Brother Thomas said. "But it remains in your mind. Heresy is an affliction not of matter, but of the spirit. It is this we must cleanse—for the good of your soul, and the souls of the other people led astray by heretic teachings."

So there was after all no way to avoid this thing. The medieval Church was partial to physical means to achieve its spiritual ends. The ultimate deprogramming: torture.

"We must take him to the interrogation center," Brother Thomas decided. "This matter must be competently handled."

Brother Paul coughed. This was no polite objection; he felt his fever peaking, and his lungs were rattling. The pneumonia was taking firm hold. He was not in condition to be tortured; he might expire before they got any information from him.

No such luck. Brother Thomas arranged for the best herbal remedies, wholesome milk and bread, a comfortable bed in a quiet room, and summoned no barber. He took very good care of Brother Paul, doing everything medievally possible to promote his health. Was this merely because the role required it—or because of the friendship that had once existed between them in other roles?

He slept and dreamed of Paris: the city he had never seen either in life or in Animation. He woke in his comfortable chamber. He had had no idea that monks lived so well! This was no dark ascetic cell, but a pleasant residence. Yet of course this was the sort of thing the cards of the Waldenses protested: a priestess living like an empress, a priest like an emperor. While the common people lived like the serfs they were.

However, Brother Paul would be glad to trade this fine accommodation for the poor but kindly hospitality of the peasants. It was torture he faced here; he had no doubt of it. At any moment that door would open and he would be taken to—

The door opened. Brother Paul closed his eyes, steeling himself. He was sure that torture in Animation would be just as terrible as—

The scent of perfume touched him. "Am I then so ugly as all that?" a soft voice inquired.

Brother Paul's eyes popped open. A most comely young woman stood beside his bed. Hastily he drew the covers about him. "Who—?" he asked, amazed.

"I am the Lady Yvette," she said, making a kind of curtsy.

She was a beauty, wearing a long tunic under a sideless surcoat, closely fitted so as to make the femininity of her figure quite evident, though her natural endowments hardly required this service. She had a buttoned hood, but wore it unbuttoned under the chin so that a suggestive amount of bosom was displayed. Amaranth, of course.

Brother Paul was not so weak as to be unmoved by her appearance. Yet he was guarded, knowing Satan had placed her in this scene. "What can I do for you, Yvette?"

"I understand you have knowledge of a beautiful set of playing cards," she said.

As expected. Another ploy for betrayal. "I had such a deck, but it was unfortunately lost in a fire."

"Yes, but you could recreate it," she said hopefully.

He smiled. "I am no painter!" Yet he might have aspired to be, once. . . . "The artwork is well beyond my talents."

She looked at him intently. What was behind that lovely facade this time? He had seen her more or less raped in the Black Mass, then reconstituted as Satan's secretary, then as assorted bit parts in this wish-vision. What did Amaranth really feel for him? Once he had thought he loved her, but recent events had chilled that somewhat. "We could employ a good artist. You could describe the pictures to him, and he would paint at your direction. It might take some time, but—"

"I may not have time," he said. "I am to be interrogated by the Holy Order as a suspected heretic."

She raised a finger knowingly. "This set of cards—it would be for the King who is a great lover—"

"Oho!" His own bitterness burst out, surprising him. "You are his mistress!"

She colored. "A great lover of culture," she continued. "Fine sculpture, fine paintings—these things Charles takes great pleasure in. More than in the government of the realm. If we suggested to him that the culture of the court would be enhanced by a really fine set of cards with mystical elements, I'm sure he would be most intrigued and would commission the very best artist. Especially for cards with magical properties."

"Magical properties? Why should the King care about such nonsense?"

She shook her head so vigorously her bosom bounced. "No, no—magic is not nonsense! And Charles VI is—" She faltered. "His Majesty has a certain peculiar interest in the occult." She leaned forward to whisper. There was no way she could be unaware of what this did to her cleavage. "Some say he is mad, at least at times. So such a device—cards he could use to summon spirits—"

It was coming clear. A king of dubious sanity, interested in art and magic. Maybe they hoped the cards would distract him, while others ran the kingdom. Well, that was not much of Brother Paul's concern. However, if he recreated the Tarot of the Waldenses —that would be a certain route to betrayal. "I am sorry," he said.

She leaned closer, as though concluding that if a study of her globes from a meter's distance wasn't sufficient argument, half a meter's distance might do better. "You don't understand, sir," she said urgently. "If you do this thing for Charles—if you make him happy—the Holy Office can have no power over you. Charles is the King!"

Oho! Her offer had real substance like her bosom. Play along with the palace politics and avoid torture. The notion had an insidious appeal. Still, how could he imperil all the faithful followers of the *barba,* the missionary Uncles? The Inquisition would surely use those cards to trap unwary believers into admissions of heresy. "No," he said regretfully.

"I would be most grateful," she murmured, touching her bodice with the delicate fingers of one hand. "The set would take many weeks to paint, and I would be with you always—"

And there was the final facet of the offer. The love of a beautiful woman.

She did not know he was castrate. She had been treated much the same way as he had, by Satan's pythons, but apparently that mutilation had not carried over into this sequence. After all, she had her limbs and head back: she had been crunched into pieces by Satan's jaws and restored. Naturally she assumed he had been rendered whole again too.

Her appearance and manner might excite him, but any attempt on his part to follow through would be futile. "Get out of here!" he said savagely.

Surprised, she withdrew. And now he wondered: would he have been able to resist such an offer had he retained his testicles?

In due course Brother Thomas conducted a friendly little tour of the local facilities. Down in the cellar of the building was a dank, old, but serviceable torture chamber.

"Today we merely show you the instruments," Brother Thomas explained with an enigmatic glance. What were his private Mormon reactions to this role? "I must apologize for the gloom. Since Charles VI came to power in France there has not been as rigorous a campaign against doctrinal error as we of the Church deem proper. Thus our facilities suffer somewhat from disuse."

"Unfortunate," Brother Paul said grimly. Inside his stomach knotted.

"However, the situation will surely improve in due course; the sun can not forever remain behind a cloud," Brother Thomas continued. "And it does mean that you will not be subjected to the annoyance of delay."

"Nice." No question about it: Brother Paul was desperately afraid. He had never been tortured in this fashion and knew the Inquisition was expert at this type of thing. This might be a kind of play, but he knew the torture would feel real and perhaps *be* real. Had any of the prior Animation fatalities occurred by torture? It was all too possible.

Brother Thomas drew open a great oaken door and showed the way into the darkest chamber yet. He picked a torch out of its socket, lighted it with his own, and replaced it. Now the room could be seen in all its awful splendor, the details imperfect but still far too suggestive for Brother Paul's taste. It was filled with metal and wooden structures. The purpose or function of some were obscure, while others evinced their nature all too brutally. There was a large fireplace with assorted kettles placed about, filled with water, oil or other fluid. There were knives and irons and axes. Ropes descended from rafters. Chains and manacles were at the walls. Ladders and large spoked wheels abounded.

"You see, the practice of magic by laymen is witchcraft," Brother Thomas said, as though this were a matter of merely academic interest. "And witchcraft is heresy. France has led the world in the definition and clarification of this threat. Our theologians are well on the way to formulating a comprehensive system of procedure that will rid the world of this evil. Archbishop Guillaume d' Auvergne of Paris showed the way more than a century ago, and Thomas Aquinas did much to develop it further. We Dominicans were assigned by Pope Gregory to perform this holy office, subject only to the Pope. We do our best."

"No doubt," Brother Paul agreed.

"Yet we would not willingly cause distress to any person. It is our desire only to abolish willful religious error and establish the truth as it has been declared by the Church. For the good of the souls of all the people. Therefore, we use every device to encourage voluntary renunciation of heresy."

"Such as torture," Brother Paul agreed.

"We prefer to call it interrogation," Brother Thomas said with a wry expression. His eyes met Brother Paul's momentarily, and now there was no doubt about the agony of conscience behind the discipline of the role. "I sincerely hope you will be persuaded to

cooperate voluntarily, making recourse to coercive methods unnecessary."

The Vice Squad at college had entertained similar hopes back in
Brother Paul's youth. But seldom was human dignity and freedom
suppressed voluntarily. People always fought back, some in token
degree, others completely. Brother Paul knew he was fated to be
the latter type.

Yet he knew that Lee did not want to torture him. So though the
lines of the play were intended to be hypocritical, in this case they
were sincere. "I believe you," Brother Paul said. "Yet, merely as
supposition, what would become of the soul of a man who
betrayed those who had placed their trust in him? If he saved
himself from discomfort by yielding them up to the burning
stake?"

"Heretics?" Brother Thomas snorted. Yet, again he showed the
stigmata of stress. There was a tremor in the muscle of one cheek,
and his eyes were narrow. He abated these symptoms somewhat
by proceeding to the first implement of torture.

"These are thumbscrews," Brother Thomas said, lifting small
metal contraptions and holding them in the light of the torch.
"The vise is applied to the tips of the thumb or finger, no higher
than the base of the nail, and tightened until the blood flows or the
bone splinters. It is amazing how well this promotes confession;
often the very first finger suffices. In recalcitrant cases, however,
the screws may become stuck, so that they can not be removed
except by cutting off the finger. We hope to develop better
instruments so as to avoid this messiness."

Brother Paul forced himself to examine the thumbscrews. They
were crude things, not screws at all but merely bands of metal,
tightened by twisted wires. This was, after all, early in the
Inquisition; in the next three centuries the torture instruments
would develop greater sophistication—as Brother Thomas had
anticipated. In the early days it was possible for subjects to die
before they confessed and recanted; in the later days this seldom
happened. Should he consider himself lucky—or unlucky?

"Here are the whips," Brother Thomas continued, showing the
next niche. "We generally strip the suspect, bind him tightly, and
whip him about the back and buttocks. This is the first degree of
interrogation. If this is not effective, we stretch him on the
ladder—" He indicated an ordinary wooden ladder. "And pour
boiling fat over his body. Normally he will confess at this time."

"How convenient." This stuff was crude, yet surely sufficient. Brother Paul was sure that he himself could not withstand such tortures. Yet, knowing that many Waldenses, whose only crime was their belief in the original precepts of Jesus Christ and the sanctity of the Holy Bible, would be routed out and similarly tortured if he yielded—how *could* he yield? He thought of the thankful old woman, racked on the ladder, and of the sick little girl with thumbscrews on her thin little fingers. Something very like Satanic rage clouded his vision.

"Suppose the suspect is innocent?" Brother Paul inquired, surprised to find no quaver in his voice. "What would your torture avail when a man has nothing to confess?"

"There *are* no innocent suspects," Brother Thomas said with chilling conviction. "There are only taciturn heretics. Those who resist the preparatory interrogation are then subject to the second degree, called ordinary torture." He indicated a rope strung over a beam. "This is for the strappado. The suspect's arms are tied behind his back. He is then hoisted into the air and weights are attached to his feet in order to wrench his shoulders from their sockets without shedding his blood or marking him."

Dislocation of limbs. That meant that even if the hapless prisoner were released thereafter, he would probably never regain his former health. But of course he would not be released; his agony would end only in death. The prospect sickened Brother Paul, yet morbid curiosity forced him to inquire further: "And if his taciturnity persists?"

"Then we must regretfully apply the third degree, called extraordinary torture. This is squassation. This resembles strappado, except that he is hoisted higher, then suddenly dropped to within a few inches of the floor. Because stones weighing as much as a hundred kilograms are attached to his feet, his arms are instantly disjointed and his whole body stretched cruelly. Three applications are deemed sufficient to cause death."

Had they used the kilogram as a unit of measure of weight in medieval France? Regardless, that was more than the weight of a man. By any measure, the business was grim enough! "And if even this does not bring confession?"

"The surviving subject may then be interrogated by special means." The Dominican showed a crude pair of pincers. "These are heated in the fire, and when red-hot are used to tear the flesh. Or he may be seated in a metal chair placed over the fire itself so that his posterior slowly cooks. His hands or feet may be cut off. Or—"

"I think that suffices," Brother Paul said. Was there a place he could safely vomit?

"I am glad to hear that." The look Brother Thomas turned on him was compounded of victory, relief, and barely suppressed horror. *How can we know the dancer from the dance?* Brother Paul thought, appreciating the deepest meaning of the line from W. B. Yeats' poem with sudden intensity. What nostalgia for that 500-year future he felt! How could the Friar live with the conscience of the Juggler within him? Satan was surely testing him as severely as he was testing Brother Paul. "Come upstairs, where our scribe will record your statement."

"You misunderstand," Brother Paul said. "I have no confession to make—except for my belief in the timeless and measureless beneficence of God."

Disappointment—and muted hope. "You renounce your heretical belief, and take sanctuary in the bosom of the Holy Mother Church?" Which would mean capitulating and yielding up the information and producing the complete Waldens' Tarot deck from memory, as well as betraying all the Waldenses he already had encountered. Lee did not want to participate in the torture of his friend as surely as Brother Paul had not wanted to hammer a nail through the wrist of his friend on the cross. But Lee also did not want to see the Waldenses persecuted. But he had to play his part faithfully, seeing no way out. "I warn you, you can not escape from our power; no ruse, no false recantation will avail." For him, it would be best if Brother Paul escaped so that neither torture nor betrayal occurred. Thus, this covert suggestion: *at least TRY to escape our power.* Brother Paul might be able to kill himself in the attempt, and that would be better than the Churchly alternatives.

"I mean that I have more than sufficient understanding of the specific instruments of the Church's beneficence," Brother Paul said, gesturing at the assembled torture devices. "Now I must retire to consider my decision."

"Of course." Brother Thomas guided him out, locking the dread chamber behind them. It wouldn't do to have anyone sneaking in here and playing with the instruments! "You may consider as long as you wish—but I regret you must do so without the benefit of water."

Thirst—a most effective inducement! The longer Brother Paul

delayed, the worse it would get. Had Lee known of his sensitivity to thirst, dating from his childhood misery, or had it merely been a lucky guess? His torture had already begun!

Back in his chamber, Brother Paul re-examined the barred window. No hope there; it was completely solid, and it opened to an inner court. He would have to depart by the regular passages and doors—which would surely be guarded. Of course he had special physical skills; he could overcome the monks, rendering them safely unconscious by careful judo strangles during the night—

No. First, he was ill; his pneumonia had abated during this rest, but he could still feel its variable fever and the catch in his breath, signaling the involvement of his lungs. Violence and flight would quickly throw him into a potentially fatal relapse—but not so rapidly as to prevent them from nursing him back to health for the torture. Second, he knew that these monks were merely actors to the extent they had any tangible existence at all; he had no moral right to practice violence on them.

Yet the alternative to escape was torture—or betrayal. If he were tortured, he might confess anyway—but possibly the others would be restrained by the same considerations that restrained him—reason, friendship, and ethics—and ease off after token punishment. Then he might be able to get through. Yet if Lee played his role with complete integrity that torture would *hurt*. So the impasse remained.

There was a delicate knock on his door. "I'm here," he called sourly. As if there were any question!

The door opened. Yvette stood there. She had changed her attire; now she was more Italian in style, her hair braided and bound circularly about her head like a coronet. Her dress was closely contoured about her upper body with sleeves closing in firmly about her wrists and the front molded exactly to the shape of her full bosom. The neckline was almost straight from the curves of her shoulders across the uppermost swell of her breasts. In back it became a cape, whose excess material had to be held out of the way by hand. In all, it was strikingly like the costuming in the earliest Tarot cards and most attractive to the male eye. But of course that was the way of Amaranth; in whatever role she played, she had strong sex appeal. The question was, did she have anything else?

"Come," she murmured conspiratorially. "The King has granted you audience."

"What?" He had been distracted by the costume.

"King Charles VI," she said, winking. "I told him of your magic cards, and he is interested. This is our chance!" She took him by the arm and drew him on.

Well, at best it was a chance to make a break. Brother Paul suffered himself to be guided through the silent halls and out into a chariot whose canopy descended to close off the outside view entirely. The ride was rough, but quite private, jammed in with Yvette.

She turned to him, enjoying it. Apparently his prior rebuff had fazed her only temporarily; like a healthy young animal, she had bounced back for another try. And bounce she did; her breasts threatened to detach themselves entirely from the dress. She might as well have been naked above the waist. Yet what use was this to him? Eunuch that he was, the stimulation was all in his mind.

"I do so admire a man with discipline," she said. "If only ycu perform this service for the King—"

Brother Paul merely shrugged. He was sorry he could not see the great city of Paris. Even in the fourteenth century, it must be something! Obviously Yvette was working with Brother Thomas, carrot and stick under the Devil's direction, trying to lure him into the betrayal he resisted. So both of them took care that he should not pick up any notion of the local geography that might facilitate his escape.

Of course he could simply jump out of the chariot and run —but he was sure guards on horseback were following. No chance there! He had to bide his time, waiting his opportunity—if it ever came.

The palace was impressive both in scale and primitiveness. They entered a huge central hall from which doors led to the kitchen; he knew this by the constantly trooping servants carrying loaded platters of fish, venison, boiled meat, fritters, and pastries.

Suddenly Brother Paul was hungry. This entrance must have been carefully timed to expose him to the main meal of the day. He had been so concerned with thirst he had not realized he had not yet eaten today. He certainly knew it now!

"The King doesn't seem to have arrived yet," Yvette observed.

Brother Paul was uncertain how she could tell since this room was filled with people lustily feasting at the long tables. Many of them were well dressed in furlined robes and capes; since the air was chill, Brother Paul wished for heavier clothing himself.

She noticed. "Oh, are you cold? Come over here by the fire." And indeed, there was a raised hearth in the center of the hall with a great fire blazing. But there was no flue. The smoke rose and spread voluminously until it found egress through an aperture high in the ceiling. Well, at least this bonfire was warm! No wonder they needed a large dining hall; otherwise the smoke would stifle everything.

"Let me fetch you some food and wine," Yvette offered solicitously.

Temptation indeed! "Is that permitted?"

"Of course. You are here for audience with the King; he would not let it be bruited about that you were not treated properly. You will always eat well here."

That was not precisely what he had meant. Well, he would experiment. "If I could just have something to drink—"

"If the King enters, there'll be a fanfare and silence. You must face the royal entourage and bow. Otherwise, just stay here and keep warm." She traipsed off, hips swinging beautifully in the gown as she marched toward the nearest table. Now came the test: did this role allow her to abate his thirst, undermining the Friar's coercion?

Brother Paul glanced about. What would stop him from walking out right now while he was unattended? Apart from hunger and thirst. His eye caught that of a guard standing near the wind baffle at an exit. Unattended? Ha!

He refocused his attention on something more positive: the groaning tables of food. Multiple dishes had been set out simultaneously, and with a little analysis he was able to identify a number of them with fair certainty. Beef marrow fritters, a popular medieval dish; large cuts of roast meat, origin dubious; saltwater and freshwater fish; broth with bacon; blancmange, which was shredded chicken blended with rice, boiled in almond milk, seasoned with sugar, and cooked until thick. Surprising how much he remembered once he put his hunger-sharpened mind to it! He hoped Yvette brought him some of that!

But first he hoped she brought him something to drink. She had not answered his plea directly; until he had that drink, he could not be certain this was not merely a refinement of the torture. Maybe he would be allowed all he wanted of thirst-producing food, without liquid.

Dogs chewed on the bones and scraps under the table. No problem with waste disposal here! The diners tore fragments of meat from the main roasts with their hands, openly licking off their fingers before grabbing again. One noble evidently had a cold; he blew his nose noisily with his bare finger and thumb, wiped the digits off on his robe, and fished with them in another stew for a succulent chunk. There were no napkins or eating utensils.

There was a sound like that of a horn, followed by a brief, astonished silence. The fanfare announcing the King? No, a false alarm; someone had broken wind so vociferously as to be audible above the tremendous clatter of the meal. People in that vicinity edged this way and that, making exaggerated faces and snufflings, but it was impossible to tell who was the culprit. Obviously a meal like this was bound to produce considerable flatulence, but the proscription against audible venting was strong. Brother Paul was reminded of Mark Twain's commentary on the subject, titled *1601*—supposedly a conversation between Queen Elizabeth of England and her courtiers, including William Shakespeare. "The pit itself hath furnished forth the stink," Brother Paul murmured, quoting the famous playwright's response when accused of authoring the stench. "And heaven's artillery hath shook the globe in admiration of it." A fitting comment for this sequence spawned by the Devil, the Lord of Air. And how did the Biblical "Wind of God" relate? Could the Suit of Swords of the Tarot actually embrace flatulence?

But now Yvette was back. She had assembled a splendid platter for him: brewet—pieces of meat in thin cinnamon sauce; eels in a thick spicy puree; frumenty, which was a thick pudding of whole wheat grains and almond milk enriched with egg yokes and colored with saffron; venison; and several obscure blobs he hoped were edible by his modern definitions. And—bless her!—the spiced wine he had requested. The abatement of thirst!

What a contrast this plate was to the poor fare of the peasants! But no eating utensils. He could of course employ his fingers, but didn't want to emulate the slobbish manners he had observed here.

"Use the trencher," Yvette suggested delicately. That was

Amaranth speaking, misinterpreting her part; the true medieval lady would not have realized his problem.

Oh, yes—the trencher. A thick slice of stale bread about fifteen centimeters long: the all-purpose pusher, sop, spoon, and plate. Essential in a situation like this.

Brother Paul scooped up some frumenty and washed it down with a gulp of wine. Hoo! That stuff was strong! They had to spice it to cover its rabid bite! Yet if his memory of conditions in the medieval cities was true, this stuff was a good deal safer than water to drink; the alcohol cleaned out the other contaminants. The water of the upper reaches of the Rhine might be sanitary, but Paris was far from that wilderness.

He was allowed to eat undisturbed, standing by the fire, and to drink several tumblers of wine. His head began to feel light; he would have preferred something nonalcoholic, but his thirst overrode that consideration. Apparently it was true: the Inquisition had no power in the palace of the King. If he wanted to avoid torture. . . .

Yvette peered past the pillars that supported the roof. "King Charles has not come," she remarked. "I shall have to take you to his bedroom."

"Is that proper?" Brother Paul inquired.

"Oh, yes—I have been there often," she said, leading the way. Well, he had asked.

But the bedroom, set on a higher level than the main hall, was more than a sleeping place. There was a fireplace set against the wall, and it had a genuine flue so that the smoke was not intrusive. Courtiers abounded; this was evidently a semi-public receiving hall.

The King reclined on his great square canopied bed. The thing was like a chariot, and he the charioteer. He wore a turban-like headdress instead of a crown, but his ornate embroidered robe showed his rank. Regardless, Brother Paul knew him—for he was Therion. As Lee had progressed from heretic to Dominican, Therion had gone from Jew to Monarch. Was Satan taking care of his own?

King Charles VI of France looked up and spied them. "Hey, my pretty!" he exclaimed. "Come up for a kiss!"

Yvette went to him—and suddenly Brother Paul, remembering the conclusion of the Black Mass, could stand it no more. He turned and stalked out of the room.

And Brother Thomas was there before him, present at a suspiciously opportune occasion. "Now you comprehend the alternative. Would it not be better to return to the bosom of the Church?"

The alternative: reprieve through the intercession of the mistress of the Mad King. And Amaranth would play that part faithfully, as the minionette of the Monarch, to spare Brother Paul from torture. The cards were only a pretext. It was not intellectual gratification Charles most craved.

Brother Paul's real choice was between torture—and betrayal of his relation with Amaranth. Whatever that relation might be.

He suffered an indefinable terror. There seemed to be a heavy weight on his chest, interfering with his breathing, yet nothing was visible. He felt completely helpless in the face of this unknown menace—yet there was an ironically voluptuous element. Was he a masochist—one who derived erotic pleasure from pain?

Then an extremely shapely young woman entered the room, whose very presence seemed to illuminate the air. It was Yvette, nude, glowing. He knew he must avoid her, and as she approached he struck at her with his fist; but he felt nothing, only air. She was an illusion.

Then she touched him, drawing off the covers and removing his night clothes, laying him bare before her. Though he resisted with all his strength he could do nothing, for his hands passed through her while hers handled him with substance. He was invisibly bound, and could not move from the bed or change his supine position. He had to lie there in stasis, except for his uselessly flailing arms.

She leaned down over him, her fine breasts dangling ponderously, and kissed him on the mouth, and her lips were solid. He could not turn his head away or even close his eyes. He remembered that one of the Saints had bitten off his own tongue to prevent contamination in a similar situation, but his jaws were immobile.

Her deep kiss stirred him immeasurably despite his reluctance. He concentrated on diversionary thoughts, on icy-cold showers, on trigonometric functions, and his body relaxed.

But the nymph had only begun to fight. More correctly, to love. Small difference! She moved down and leaned over his hips, lifting up his member and placing it between her smooth breasts. She pressed them together with her hands, his member sandwiched between their protean fullness. The flesh flowed warmly around it, enclosing it with gentle hydraulic pressure. She kneaded her own breasts, and the motions were transmitted to him muted yet quintessentially potent. Under that firm yet fluid incentive, his member swelled until it seemed ready to burst, becoming simultaneously as rigid as cast iron.

But I'm castrate! he cried in his mind. *This can't be happening! I can't react sexually!*

Obviously he *could* react! She had seen his empty scrotum —empty? It didn't exist at all!—and knew his handicap. What did she know that he didn't?

Satisfied with her priming operation, the nymph let go her breasts and lifted them away with a flex of her upper torso. Now his member angled up stiffly. She climbed upon him, moving carefully to slant her posterior and take him neatly into her hot, moist orifice. Once more he struck at her with his fist—and once more her visible body was no more than smoke. Yet her vulva moved down, melting about him, and he felt himself penetrating her, being enveloped. At last the connection was complete, full depth.

Now she brought her lips to his again, and as she kissed him she slid her body slowly up and down, drawing it slickly along his torso and causing his penetration to diminish, then increase again. Her tongue slid between his lips and played with his own in counterpoint. It was the rhythm of coitus, and he had no defense.

It continued for seconds, then minutes; then it seemed an hour. The weight on his body was the same; before it had been nameless, but now it was female. His terror had been replaced by disgust: a mere transmutation of the same emotion. This was merely torture in a different form.

And he realized: his masculinity was like that of a boy before puberty. He could be stimulated to the point of urgency—but could never climax. This could go on until his penis blistered. . . .

The door crashed open. Brother Thomas stood there, glowering. Yvette evanesced: she faded gently away, leaving Brother Paul lying naked with erection.

"So you have lain with a succubus!" Brother Thomas thundered. "Pollution of Satan! You are an unrecalcitrant heretic!"

Brother Paul could not deny it.

Now he was in the torture chamber. Brother Thomas sprinkled Holy Water on the instruments. "Bless these holy mechanisms,

God's tools on Earth," he intoned. "Thy will be done."

He put both Brother Paul's hands together in the vise and screwed it inexorably closed. Brother Paul screamed, but the pressure did not abate. The agony quickly became intolerable. The fingernails cracked; blood spurted forth like a series of ejaculations, one from each digit. Flesh and bone were pulped together. He knew he would never be able to use his hands again.

And was that not fitting? His hands—during his stasis, they alone had been free. They had not touched the succubus because she did not exist; she was a phantasm. Yet hands had touched *him*—and what hands could these have been except his own? He had touched his own lips, poked his finger in his own mouth, and stroked his own body under the guise of flailing at the apparition. He had manipulated and stimulated his own member in a desperate effort to refute his demoniac castration. His own hands were the instruments of his attempted pollution; they had now paid the Churchly penalty.

The scribe-witness held his quill ready. "We will record your recantation now," Brother Thomas said.

Brother Paul suffered a lucid moment. "Shove it up your ass," he said delicately.

"The mouth must pay the penalty for blasphemy," Brother Thomas said sadly. Now he inserted the metal choking-pear into Brother Paul's mouth, and rotated the handle so that the two halves of it pressed pitilessly apart, forcing open the mouth until the hinge of the jaw broke. The temperomandibular joint. He could no longer even scream effectively—

Yet out of his mouth he had spoken heresy, supporting the gross impertinence of the Waldenses. He had uttered the sacrilegious interpretations of the Tarot and demeaned the Holy imperatives of the loving Mother Church. Thus the mouth that had so gravely transgressed was indeed punished: an eye for an eye, a tooth for a tooth—

No! he cried internally. *I may be a sinner, but the Waldenses are good people and the Tarot is valid. I cannot betray them!*

Brother Paul woke in sweat. It had been a nightmare—a demon of sleep. His hands were whole, his jaw hinged.

As he lay there and let his sweat dissipate, he realized that the signs of nightmare had been evident all along. The succubus had looked like Yvette—like Amaranth. That meant she was a creation from his memory, rather than an external character of the

Animation. Real women did not act like that, which was why men had to make do with the guilty dreams. And the torture instruments—the hand-press and choking-pear—these had been levered by threaded metal screws. They were more sophisticated devices, more technologically progressed; they existed in the later centuries of the Inquisition, not here in the 14th century.

The whole thing had been a Freudian dream-within-a-dream, a mechanism of double censorship showing him the lusts and fears his own mind balked at admitting. Now he had reverted to the more general dream, which was this Animation—itself a vision sponsored by Satan in the original Animation. Now that he had seen what was buried within the triple prison—

Well, what about it? So he had lusts! So he feared pain! Weren't these natural feelings? The dream had only shown up the foolishness of his secrets!

Still, the local tortures were fully sufficient to the need. If he were tortured at *this* level of reality, he would surely yield up his information and betray his friends. Only in the exaggerated dream state was he bold enough to tell the Inquisition to shove anything, anywhere. No one could withstand such savage physical coercion indefinitely! Thus he could only hurt himself by holding out.

Yvette opened the door and stood there a moment, a lamp in her hand, like the succubus she had seemed to be. She glided in. "Juggler—I came in haste before dawn, lest we both suffer. You acted precipitously by walking out on the King. But I convinced him you had a sudden call of nature and fled lest you disgrace yourself in his presence like old Blowhard in the dining room. Charles is so fascinated by the notion of the magic cards he is willing to forgive your indiscretion if you return to him immediately." She stood over him, an ethereal female spirit, breathtakingly lovely. If he were to draw her down now, remove her dress, would she perform, after all, like the succubus? He suffered abrupt, savage temptation, yet did not act. "I beg of you, friend," she continued. "Come with me before the Holy Office takes you below. Once the torture starts even the King will not intercede, lest he suffer excommunication by Pope Clement."

Excommunication by the Pope! The Church knew no limits to its abuses! On top of that, Clement was known historically as an antipope, though his election had been no more political than that of a number of authorized popes. Perhaps his major crime was that he did not reside in Rome. The Church forced complete compliance with its dictates, yet could not even agree on its Pope, or that the Office was more important than the residence. Suddenly Brother Paul decided. "I will come with you."

"You will?" she asked, amazed.

Her surprise made him pause. *What was he doing?* He knew that giving the cards to the King would be the same as confessing to Brother Thomas. In either case the Waldenses in France, the Holy Roman Empire, and perhaps even in Italy itself would be routed out by the Inquisition. They would be tortured and perhaps exterminated, as the Albigensians had been.

Yet there was no way he could hold out against the tender persuasions of the Church. It was not a choice between right and wrong, but between obvious wrong and subtle wrong. The only question was whether he would yield up the information before or after suffering dislocation of his arms or destruction of his fingers. Since he was bound to capitulate, he might as well do it comfortably, feasting at the King's table and dallying with the King's mistress.

Shame! Yet what better course was there? His sense of personal dignity, the last of the qualities in himself he valued, had been beaten down. He had been degraded by this Hell stage by stage, until he could not maintain his pride intact any longer. So he would do what he had to do—if only he knew what that was.

Well, he could run away. They could not watch him *all* the time, and in time his health should improve, and if he started out describing unimportant cards of the deck he might get a chance to make his break before the key cards came up. By accepting King Charles' offer, he was buying time and leeway—

No! He would not bargain in bad faith. If he gave his word to produce the cards for the Mad King, he would have to do the job. His pride had not yet descended below that level.

Though the originators of the Tarot suffered their special genocide in consequence? What kind of pride was that?

Yvette was leading him on, in more senses than one, out of the silent monastery into the hooded chariot away from the place of torture. The eastern horizon was brightening. He wished he could see the sunrise!

She paused to kiss him. "I'm so glad you have come to your senses! Everything is ready. I shall introduce you to the artist immediately."

"Artist?"

"The one who will paint the cards as you direct. His name is Jacquemin Gringonneur. It is imperative that the work proceed quickly, for the King is impatient and already just a bit wroth with you. He is a young man, not yet twenty-five years of age, but let that not deceive you. He is capable of truly mad acts."

"I'm sure he is," Brother Paul agreed, thinking of the historical Charles VI who assumed the throne as a boy of twelve and became insane at age twenty-four—and of Therion now playing that part. But he was more concerned with his own problem. It seemed the only practical and honorable way remaining to him to save himself from torture and to save the Waldenses from destruction —was suicide. That must have been hovering somewhere in his secret mind when he agreed to come to the palace. So long as the Juggler lived, in any form, the Waldenses were not safe, and the Tarot itself was in danger of obliteration. That last was especially ironic: the rendering of the Tarot in a beautiful court edition, publicizing it—would destroy it because of the extermination of its originators. It would cease to have meaning and become—just another pack of cards.

Did he have the courage to sacrifice himself? Was this the pass that prior investigators of the Animation phenomenon had come to? Very soon he would find out!

The chariot stopped. Yvette led him this time to a garden within the palace estate concealed from outside by a stone wall. "Wait here," she said. "I will fetch the artist."

As she spoke, the dawn sun emerged from behind clouds to shine brilliantly over the wall into the garden. Its first beam struck a sundial set on a pedestal. Tall flowers waved in the morning breeze; were they sunflowers so early in the season? Yet he could not know precisely what season it was; he had assumed spring, but it might be fall. The sun was so brilliant the beams of it speared out in sixteen directions, quartering the quarter circles, illuminating all the world.

Brother Paul stood there, holding Yvette's hand, loath to let her go despite his judgment of her nature. After all, she was doing it for him; she could have seduced King Charles without bothering with any Tarot deck. By her morality, she was doing right. It was wrong to condemn her merely because her values differed somewhat from his own. And somehow it was easier to forgive a lovely woman.

Suddenly, in an incandescence rivaling that of the sun, he had his revelation. *He had another alternative*—one that would satisfy all parties, hurting none—except perhaps the Inquisition itself.

"Let me tell you of the first card I shall describe to the court artist," he said to her. "This one is dedicated to you, my pretty minionette."

"For me?" She smiled, flattered.

"For you, child of the garden. It is a scene of this very place at dawn with the wall and the flowers—and two young people, virtually children before the glories of creation, naked as it were like Adam and Eve—"

"Sir?" she inquired archly.

"Clothed, then," he said with a smile. He had visualized the card of the Holy Order of Vision Tarot, but of course that was anachronistic. "Bathed in the brilliant light of the golden disk. And the name of this picture is—The Sun."

"The Sun!" she repeated, pleased.

Her pleasure was no less than his own. For now he knew his course. He would create a Tarot for the King—but not precisely the Tarot of the Waldenses. He would truncate it, eliminating certain cards of the Triumphs so that the Inquisition would never be able to divine the full meaning of the deck. Some cards the Dominicans already knew about, so these Brother Paul had to retain, though he would delete key symbols so as to render the meanings obscure. Since the pictures were already designed to be interpreted on two levels, the genuine and the superficial, this part was easy; he would never betray the true nature of any picture. And if he could eliminate entirely as many as eight Triumphs and abolish in one bold stroke the whole of the key suit of Spirit—

He smiled again, still holding her hand as they stood before the wall. Mad King Charles VI would never know the difference; he cared only for the beauty of the cards (or the beauty of the lady who sold him on the project) and their supposedly magic properties. Brother Thomas would not realize that the deck was incomplete for some time because he had not had an opportunity to count the cards of the full deck, and Brother Paul would present the cards in mixed order. He would retain the first half-dozen of the Waldens' order intact just in case. Given the time it would take the artist to complete each one, especially if Brother Paul arranged to be picky about details—so that the King might have the very *best* deck of course—it could be months before the deck was done. By then, who could say for sure whether it was complete or which items might be missing? Lee would know, but as Brother Thomas he would not be able to prove it—not by the rules of this game.

Brother Paul would in fact create a new Tarot, consisting of a score or so of Triumphs, and four suits of thirteen cards each —well, maybe fourteen, no harm in that. A full deck of around 75 to 80 cards, each with its superficial title and interpretation concealing the real message. The Inquisition could play with copies of this deck as long as it chose; it would only waste its effort. The Waldenses would not long be fooled by a "Juggler" who never spoke of the Ghost, or Nature, or Vision, or the Lady of Expression, or the Two of Aura. Or who, for that matter, failed to discuss the underlying meaning of the Triumph known popularly as The Sun.

For the Waldenses interpretation of that last card was— Triumph.

25

REASON
(THOUGHT)

The slime rose up to criticize the work of art. "There you sit," it said, "serene and content in your ebony gloss—yet utterly useless. You think you are beautiful, but you are only a molded husk. You are glazed, but you are brittle and shallow. Where is there any softness in you? Where is that fine slippery resiliency that is the heritage of the commonest blob of grease? Where is the rippling undulation of fluid motion, the flexibility and warmth of dishwater? You lack the variety of size and shape and color that glorifies the contents of every garbage can. You cannot take flight in the soft air in the free manner known to every particle of dust swept from the floor. You cannot appreciate the refractive art of the dirty window pane in the sunlight. You can never immortalize your substance by leaving a pretty stain on the wall. And never, never will you bring that worthy satisfaction of a job well done that every human being obtains from cleaning up rubbish like me."

"You are not beautiful—you are a monstrosity."

The work of art listened and was ashamed. It fell off the antique table and shattered on the floor. The slime looked on as the housewife swept up the myriad fragments, all shapes and colors and sizes, and dumped them sadly into the wastebasket.

"Now you are beautiful," said the slime, and it vanished down the drain.

"Well," Satan said, "are you satisfied about the origin and nature of Tarot?"

"Yes," Brother Paul agreed. "It was some lesson. But how did I acquit myself in the matter of the wish?"

"You passed," Satan said frankly. "I thought I had you there for a while, caught between sin and torture, but you threaded the needle. Of course you compromised yourself somewhat by consciously misleading the Inquisition—but the point of the dilemma was that you were left not with a choice between good and evil—"

"But with a choice between evils," Brother Paul filled in. "That was the Hell of it."

"Precisely. Anyone can tell good from evil if he wants to in a limited situation; not everyone can comprehend evil well enough to deal with it sensibly. You did an excellent job, and I fear you are not destined to reside in Hell—but there remain two wishes. Often a person who surmounts the most devastating challenge succumbs to the minor one. Shall we proceed?"

What use was there in waiting? Brother Paul wanted to be through with this awful examination! "Proceed," he said, buoyed by his triumph. What could be worse than the medieval Hell he had just been through?

"Name your second wish."

"I wish to know the evolution and future of Tarot."

Satan flicked his tail with a snap like that of a whip. "So shall it be—"

"but not in physical incorporation!" Brother Paul cried. "I just want to *perceive* it, not *live* it!" Would Satan accept the modification? One physical experience of history had been more than enough!

"Very well. Bye-bye," Satan said, making a little wave with four fingers. That gesture, by any other entity, would have seemed effeminate.

Brother Paul felt himself rising. He looked down—and there was his body, standing in Satan's office. Satan and the furniture remained in place. As Brother Paul continued to rise, he saw the secretary's office too—she was cleaning her nails in the timeless manner of the type—and the surrounding rooms. He could see through the walls, focusing on any portion he wished, seeing that portion clearly: a variable X-ray vision.

So this was what soul travel was like! His aura had detached from the host body and was now traveling and perceiving by itself. He had, as it were, become one with the fifth suit of Tarot.

There were scores of offices—hundreds—thousands—too many to count. Each was a mere cell in the total, connected to its neighbors by vessels, forming cohesive larger organs. "And each in the cell of himself is almost convinced of his freedom," he thought, remembering the words of the poet Auden. The whole mass formed into a monstrous building thousands of stories tall, irregular in outline, supported by two massive round columns —the shape of Satan Himself.

Then on up, out, he viewed the environs of Hell with its own myriad cells, each with its special tortures. And finally he burst into the bright day of the world. He was out of Hell at last—but only by the spirit.

Now he coasted to the continent of medieval Europe, aware of the date without knowing how, and to the city of Paris. Still he had no chance to look at it, for he phased in to the bedroom of the King. Charles VI was abating his melancholy by playing with his Gringonneur Tarot. The deck was pretty much as Brother Paul had edited it: twenty-two Triumphs, four suits, seventy-eight cards in all. The mere shadow of True Tarot, but a private victory for Brother Paul!

Because Charles liked companions for his gaming, he impressed his courtiers into Tarot playing sessions. It was fun for them; they became adept at inventing new interpretations for given cards and given spreads that catered to the King's ego. Soon more decks were made, and it became fashionable to play Tarocchi all over France, and Europe, wherever they could be afforded. Tarot became a status symbol. Quickly variations appeared, associated with special locales or interests. Some decks had as many as forty-one Triumphs—the word soon simplified to Trumps —consisting of the "basics" Brother Paul had retained plus twelve signs of the astrological zodiac, plus the four "elements" (he really had succeeded in eliminating the fifth one!), and certain Virtues. Some decks had eight suits. But none restored the particular cards Brother Paul had hidden: eight Triumphs and the entire suit of Aura.

The Waldenses, of course, knew the truth—but they never made it public. And so they survived despite persecutions and plagues, eventually surfacing as a legitimate Christian sect with branches all over the world, even in America. In later centuries, when heresy became respectable under the name of Protestantism, the secret could have been safely told—but by then it was no longer important enough to recall. Persecution had made the original Tarot what it was; in the absence of persecution, it faded. The truncated Tarot became a virtual property of the Gypsies and other fringe elements of society who used it primarily for fortune telling. And so the secret remained, forgotten at last even by the Waldenses themselves.

The development of printing at the end of the fifteenth century brought playing cards to the masses. But many people found the full deck too cumbersome. As the cards sifted down from the nobles and the rich to the poor, full pictures were too expensive. More cards were dropped until the deck returned almost to the original form that the Waldenses had hidden their illustrated lecture in. Of all the Trumps only the Fool remained, now called the Joker. Sometimes a blank replacement card was also provided, the manufacturer's unwitting ghost of the Ghost. The Knights were banished, reducing each suit to thirteen cards. Thus the peasant deck came to rest at fifty-three cards—the number of weeks in the year plus one for the fraction left over. The symbols of the suits metamorphosed to the peasant level too: Swords converted to Bells, Pomegranates, or Parakeets, and then to Spades (Tarot really did beat its swords into plowshares!), Cups to Roses and to Hearts, Wands to Acorns to Clovers later called Clubs, and Coins to Leaves and to Diamonds. German cards of 1437 depicted hunting scenes, with suits of Ducks, Falcons, Stags, and Dogs. A later deck had sixteen suit signs: Suns, Moons, Stars, Shields, Crowns, Fish, Scorpions, Cats, Birds, Serpents, and others. People played games called Trappola, Hazard, Bassett, and Flush; and they gambled avidly. The cards had come of age—at the lowest common denominator.

But the "complete" Tarot continued as a subgenre with a strong appeal to persons interested in the occult. In Italy, Philippo Maria Visconti, Duke of Milan, loved cards and commissioned for a small fortune several expensive sets, including an elegant heraldic deck to commemorate the union of his daughter with the scion of Sforza in 1441. "Ah yes, the most beautiful of the classic decks," Brother Paul murmured soundlessly as he hovered, contemplating the cards in their original splendor. There was the Cardinal Virtue Justice pictured by a lady robed in a dress of spun silver, holding sword and scales, and in the background a knight galloping his charger. There was the Moon held by a lady's right hand while her left tugged at the cord securing her skirt: if the lunar symbol was too obscure for the viewer, the left hand made the female mystique somewhat more evident. Ah, woman: where would she be without her hinted secrets? And the card of the World, showing a walled city suspended between sky and sea. Cardinal Virtue Fortitude, showing a burly Hercules beating a lion with a club. Skeletal Death with his giant longbow. And Time with a bright blue cloak over a yellow tunic, hourglass in hand.

But Brother Paul could not stay. He had to move on, tracing the Tarot wherever it might lead. He saw a simplified, almost cartoon-figure Tarot emerge in Italy; this was easier for the peasants to understand, and it became very popular among the lowest classes. It was soon copied in France and called the Marseilles Tarot. Further variants developed over the decades, culminating in the famous Swiss Tarot classic of the eighteenth century. Unfortunately, the symbolism had suffered further degregation over the centuries, much of it by "iconographic transformation"—the misreading of the pictures and revised interpretation based on those misreadings. Time lost his hourglass and became the Hermit with a lamp, and the Hercules of Fortitude became a lady gently controlling the lion, the card labeled Strength.

Experts came along, vowing to restore the Tarot to its pristine state—but though the Inquisition had passed, they did not discover the missing cards. Count de Gebelin decided the Tarot was of ancient Egyptian origin, based on sevens: twice seven cards in each suit, three times seven Trumps (plus the numberless Fool; eleven times seven total (plus Fool). The name itself, he said, derived from the Egyptian *tar,* meaning "road," and *ro,* meaning "royal." Therefore, Tarot translated as the "Royal Road of Life."

Brother Paul shook his head invisibly and moved on. He encountered a disciple of Gebelin called Aliette, a wigmaker by profession, who decided that the origin of Tarot dated back almost four thousand years to the general time of the Deluge. He reversed his name and used it to entitle his deck, adding a modest description of its worth: the Grand Etteila. Here the Lady Pope became the Lady Consultant, a lovely nude woman standing within a whirlwind; that card also bore his name, Etteila. The Kings and Queens became professional men and social ladies, and the Fool was Folly or Madness. The deck was well illustrated and very pretty—but Brother Paul was not inclined to linger.

Next he found Alphonse Louis Constant, who under the *nom de plume* Eliphas Levi traced Tarot back further yet to Enoch, the Biblical son of Cain. He tied it in with the Jewish Qabalah, aligning the Trumps to correspond to paths along the Qabalistic Tree of Life. Then Brother Paul saw Gerhard Encausse, who under the name of Papus aligned the Trumps to the twenty-two letters of the Hebrew alphabet. "Abraham the Jew would have loved that!" Brother Paul commented and moved on.

At last he approached the twentieth century. There was the Order of the Golden Dawn, and there was Arthur Edward Waite, designing yet another "corrected" Tarot. Waite made the Fool into a saintly figure with the dog a prancing pet instead of a seat-biting menace, and the notorious Lady Pope became a virginal High Priestess. He converted one of the Devil's imps into a full-breasted nude woman suggestive of Eve, and he dabbled generally with the symbolism like an editor blue penciling a manuscript he did not understand. And of course he failed to restore the Hermit to Time. Paul Foster Case, another *Dawn* member, refined the images, retaining all Waite's errors for his B.O.T.A. (Builders of the Adytum) deck, and Brother Paul's own Holy Order of Vision further refined the Case variant for its private Tarot.

But Brother Paul now discovered he could no longer accept the Vision Tarot. It had only partial relation to the truth as he now saw it. "Oh, Satan—you have divested me of something I valued," he said. "I was satisfied with the Vision Tarot, believing it to be the most refined and authentic deck available—until I went to Hell."

Nevertheless, he moved on. Aleister Crowley was another *Dawn* member who had to dabble. He converted Fortitude to Lust with the nude woman voluptuously bestriding the multi-headed beast, one of her hands resting on the animal's penis while the other supported a cup like a filling womb against a background of sperm and egg cells. His Devil most resembled a monstrous phallus with a buck goat superimposed. Justice became Adjustment, Temperance became Art, Judgment became Aeon, the Hanged Man was castrate (Brother Paul suffered a sudden shock of empathy), and the Hermit—remained the Hermit. Brother Paul threw up his invisible hands and moved on. Now he knew the theoretical indentity of his Bad Companion and wasn't sure he cared to know more.

Yet the Tarot variations multiplied. One group used mediums

and a ouija board to derive a "New" Tarot quite different from all prior decks. There was also a military Tarot, and an animal Tarot, and a nude-woman Tarot and a Star Maiden Cosmic Tarot and even a Devil's Tarot—

"Enough, Satan!" Brother Paul cried soundlessly. "They are all variants of the meaningless deck I foisted on the world, interpreted to destruction by idiots! Let me center on something meaningful, not this interminable proliferation! And let me interact at least a *little*!" If this was the life of a ghost or traveling soul, it was frustrating enough to be another version of Hell. In assimilating the world's knowledge, the ghost also assimilated its follies—and could do nothing to abate them.

"So shall it be," Satan agreed. The cards flew up, exploding from their packs to fill the scene with multiple pictures like the conclusion to the story *Alice in Wonderland,* spinning about him with increasing rapidity until their images blurred and he was in a wash of confusion.

Help!

Was it his own cry? No, he knew he was in the power of Satan and needed no other assistance; the cry had come from elsewhere, perhaps telepathically. In his aural state he might be receptive to such a message.

Brother Paul tried to orient on the soundless plea, but he remained in chaos. Colors swirled about him, yielding no fixed forms. It was as though he floated through a waterless ocean, unbreathing, for his traveling aura had no lungs. Disembodied yet sentient, he was unable to control his whereabouts without Satan's imperative.

My soul drifts free, he thought.

But not without purpose. Someone had called for help, and Brother Paul had received that plea and was drawn by that need.

Am I dead?

It was a flashing of light, the meaning in the flow. A spirit newly freed of its mortality, a soul rising toward Nirvana or sinking toward Hell. If he could only reach it, help guide it—

I am a fool! it flashed.

Brother Paul began to learn how to navigate in this chaotic state. He oriented on the flashing voice. Of course this person was a fool—the Fool of Tarot. *Every* person was. Brother Paul moved along a corridor that opened ahead, not a special avenue exactly but a—

The person screamed. The Fool must have stepped off the precipice! That was the nature of Fools. So noble, idealistic, well intentioned—the epitome of the finest expectations of civilization. Yet also supremely impractical. Fools tended to get bitten in the posterior by unruly canines: anal sadism to gratify the spectators. Especially when practiced on an individual of lofty aspirations.

The journey was amazingly far, though not precisely long. He moved at impossible velocity through a veil he could not quite define. At last he saw the person who had summoned him. Flashing for help, it was no human being at all, yet not a creature like Antares either. This was a hideous animate disk harrow. A savagely ringed worm with laser lenses.

I need a guide! it flashed.

Brother Paul was taken aback. He had somehow anticipated a human being, not this flashing slash thing. Yet it seemed this *was* a creature in need. How could he refuse? "I will be your guide," he said almost before the thought was complete. Yet how could he guide when he was lost himself?

As he spoke, his setting filled in about him: the Station of the Holy Order of Vision with its important windmill turning behind him. His last conscious contact with the elements of nature and Tarot before he had been summoned to this unique quest, what seemed thousands of years ago. It was good to feel firm ground beneath his feet again; chaos really did not appeal.

Could he simply walk back into his former life at the Station, leaving all Hell behind him now? He was tempted to try! But first he had to help this entity who was in need, if he could.

What mode of thing are you? the creature demanded, just as though it were the normal entity and he the weird monster. Well, its viewpoint was no doubt valid for it—and after what Brother Paul had learned about himself, he could well understand how monstrous he might seem to another sapience.

He suddenly realized that this was no part of his own framework, but that of the summoning creature. His setting of the Order Station was merely a bit of mocked-up background to make him seem more natural, much as a specimen in a modern zoo might be placed in a cage painted to resemble its home milieu. This was in fact—the future! He had traveled forward through time to a period far beyond his own mortal termination.

"No thing am I, though once a thing I was," Brother Paul said with a smile. He, like the Roman poet Vergil, author of the *Aeneid*, had been brought forward in time to assist one who knew of him. No wonder he had been so conscious of the Triumph of Time in the Tarot! "I lived on Planet Earth, circa 2000, in the time of the Fool emigration program that depleted our planet." He explained his origin in more detail, knowing it would be difficult for this entity to credit.

Sibling Paul of Tarot! the creature interrupted him. *The Patriarch of the Temple!*

Well, these confusions had to be expected. "No, I am merely Brother Paul, a humble human creature. No patriarch, no temple —the Holy Order of Vision is not that type. But I will help you all I can since you seem to be in need and have called, and I have heard, and this is my purpose in life—and it seems in death also. But I shall be able to help you better once I am oriented. Of what species, region, and time are you that you thus invoke me?"

To you, your repute may seem minor, the thing flashed. *But to me, a Slash of Andromeda 2,500 years of Sol after your time, there is no greater name than Sib—than Brother Paul. You are the creator of the Cluster Tarot, one of the great forces in the shaping of the contemporary scene.*

Cluster Tarot? Brother Paul did not place that one. Surely some misunderstanding there. For the moment, another matter was more pressing: the time span. Two thousand five hundred years after his time? That would be about the year 4,500! And this was a sapient creature of another galaxy, Andromeda! What a jump he had taken! "But who are you, friend? I can't just call you Slash, can I?"

I am Herald the Healer—though I am in sore need of healing myself!

"Ah, heraldry," Brother Paul said. "I have often admired the herald's art, though I supposed that would be forgotten in your century, if indeed it can really be known in Andromeda."

It survives, it flourishes, Herald flashed. *Especially in your Cluster Tarot.*

Brother Paul shook off the misplaced reference again. "No matter. Come, creature of the future: let us explore together. Where are we, and what is our purpose?"

And the Andromedan explained: he had been injured during a visit to the Planet Mars of System Sol in Segment Etamin in Galaxy Milky Way of the Cluster—injured by a laser strike from an enemy spaceship. He had been dug out of the rubble and taken to something called a Tarot Temple where they practiced Animation Therapy to reconstitute minds. Herald had conjured Brother Paul from the distant past to aid in this reorientation.

Did that mean that Herald of Andromeda was the real person while Brother Paul himself was a figment of the imagination of an entity 2,500 years yet uncreated? That was a difficult concept to accept completely! "I suffer from some confusion," Brother Paul said, feeling dizzy.

The Andromedan flashed a laser beam on him, and Brother Paul abruptly felt more secure. Apparently he could exist in this framework so long as his companion believed in him. After all, he had visited the human colony in the Hyades, in Sphere Nath, three hundred years after his time; this was merely a greater extension of that mechanism. *What do you wish to know, Sibling Patriarch?*

"Just call me Brother, if you don't mind." Brother Paul cast about for a suitable starting point to enable him to relate to this alien properly. "Let's start with this: why did you conjure a human being instead of a creature of your own type?" What did he really wish to know? *Everything*—but it was obviously not his purpose here to aggrandize his personal curiosity. Not directly at any rate. He had been on a quest for the future of Tarot, but that had to wait; his human conscience would not allow him to neglect an entity in need.

I loved a female of your species, the creature confessed.

This absolute alien loved a human girl? How was this possible? But Brother Paul concealed his confusion. "So did I, so did I! There is nothing like a sweet, pretty girl, is there!"

Nothing in the Cluster! Herald agreed. *I was in Solarian host, and she—*

Solarian—that would be a creature associated with the star Sol—or a human being. And host—but better not to make assumptions. The way of Antares might not be that of Andromeda. "Let's start just a little further back," Brother Paul said. "This matter of—Solarian hosts?"

After your time, Herald said. *Naturally you have not encountered it. Today we shift from body to body, since our identities are incarnate in our auras. Transfer the aura—perhaps you call it soul—and—*

Confirmation! "The soul! You *can* move souls from body to body?"

We can. We do, Brother. Though I am a Slash of Andromeda, I can inhabit the body of one of your kind. In that form, I naturally react in the manner of—

"Ah, yes. As a human being, you could take an interest in a human girl. Sorry I was slow to grasp your meaning. No doubt if I were to occupy a Slash body, I would pay similar respects to Slash females." That seemed impossible; he could not at the moment imagine an animate light-emitting disk harrow with sex appeal. But intellectually he could concede the validity of the concept. "Yet you *are* of completely different species, so no lasting emotion exists—"

On the contrary! Aural love is absolute.

"Love is the Law—Love under Will," Brother Paul agreed —then paused, realizing that that was what Therion liked to say. Was Herald the Slash another manifestation of Therion ready to lead him into yet another aspect of Hell? Alien miscegenation, Slash breeding with Human?

No, it did not matter. Brother Paul had survived this much of Hell and perhaps been somewhat cleansed. He was not about to be led into further compromise. He would do what was right *because* it was right. If Herald were an aspect of Therion—well, who needed help more than Therion did? In fact, with the retrospect of several thousand years, he could not even call Therion evil; in the fourteenth century roles had been reversed with Lee playing the persecutor and Therion the persecutee. How did that little saying go? "There's so much good in the worst of us, and bad in the best of us, it ill behooves the most of us to talk about the rest of us." Whoever had said that had really understood human nature. Therion had a lot of good in him, many admirable qualities despite some appalling lapses. And surely Satan was cauterizing out those lapses by forcing him to play the role of an insane king. . . .

With that reconciliation of attitude, Brother Paul felt an exhilaration akin to Redemption. He *had* learned something by his experience in Hell. He had learned caution in judging, lest he be judged himself. Maybe in time he would master the art of forgiveness that he preached.

Love is the Law—Love under Will, Herald echoed in pretty

flashes. *I do not know whether that is a universal truth, but it is true for me. I suffer grievously the loss of my Solarian bride. Life means little to me without her.*

"Tell me more about this," Brother Paul urged. "I do not know how I can help, but I will do what I can."

I cannot face it directly, yet.

"Approach it obliquely," Brother Paul said. "You summoned me—"

Yes. I was flashing through the Cluster Tarot Triumphs in order, in the standard reorientation program, and—

There it was again. Maybe he *was* here to learn the future of Tarot. If his own quest related to Herald's problem, he should check it out. "I am familiar with a number of versions of the Tarot deck, but not this 'Cluster' you mention. Does it most nearly relate to the Waite, or Thoth, or Light, or—?"

I know nothing of these names. It is the one you created on Planet Tarot. Don't you remember?

Brother Paul shook his head. "I have created no deck, except in the sense that I may have expurgated the original Waldens' deck to protect—"

Perhaps you called it by another name. It may be that it was termed Cluster after your death.

Brother Paul thought about that. He had not yet finished his life; he could not speak for what he might do in later years if he survived the Animation sequence. He *was* dissatisfied with conventional Tarot decks, including that of the Holy Order of Vision. Only the original Waldens' deck suited him now, and that one had been lost to the world since 1392, though there was no longer any reason for it to be hidden.

It burst upon him like the Vision of Saint Paul: *he* could restore the Waldens deck and give it back to the world! He could undo the damage he had done, now that the world was safe for genuine Tarot. "That so-called Cluster deck—does it have five suits?"

Certainly.

"And thirty Triumphs? One hundred cards in all?"

You remember it now! That is the one. And the Ghost has fifteen alternate faces, for those who require forty-four Triumphs or an extra suit.

Fifteen faces for the Ghost card? *That* did not match the Waldens' deck! Still, the puzzle seemed to have been partly solved. "I believe what happened was that I restored the original Tarot, and later generations elaborated and retitled it. I deserve no credit for creating it; that belongs to the anonymous people six hundred years before my time. And I have nothing to do with any temple."

My knowledge of ancient history in alien Spheres is inexact, Herald said diplomatically. *But I am certain you are the Founder.*

And who could say what might be attributed to him after his death when he could not protest? Pointless to discuss it further. "I came here to assist in your problem, not mine. What is most meaningful to you?"

There was some confusion, but in due course the Andromedan nerved himself to respond. *You ask what is meaningful to me? It is my Solarian child bride, burned for possession, though innocent—*

"Possession? Of what? A proscribed drug?"

Of alien aura.

"Oh. You said it was possible to transfer the soul from one body to another." This would have made very little sense if he hadn't interviewed Antares! "And some souls—some auras are not permitted in some bodies—some hosts? So they punish—"

Abruptly Herald projected the image of a castle: a medieval edifice of Earth complete with turrets and a moat as big as a lake. It was very like the structure Brother Paul had sought in the first Animation. This one was under siege with strange wheeled creatures driving along a gravel ramp or fill extending from one shore across the water toward the outer wall.

"The Tower of Truth!" Brother Paul breathed. "Or is it the Dungeon of Wrong?"

The Slash did not respond directly. The view expanded. The effect was of flying across the lake and into the forbidding island fortress. More soul travel!

In the central courtyard was a great bonfire—and in that fire, suspended from a bar, was a lovely nude young girl. The flames were leaping up around her legs which she vainly tried to lift out of the heat.

Her skin was an alien tint of green or blue, but her features were immediately familiar. "Carolyn!" Brother Paul gasped in sudden anguish. His daughter!

Herald flashed at him questioningly, and Brother Paul realized that the Slash did not perceive the same identity. The girl was not, could not be, the original Carolyn; she would have lived and died in the twenty-first century. Yet this was her surrogate, perhaps her far future descendent, his Daughter-image, the innocent child.

Here she had grown to early nubility—as well she might in twenty-five centuries!—and she was beautiful. If her character matched what Brother Paul had known, it was no wonder Herald had loved her. To know her was to love her, whatever the situation! Brother Paul himself loved her—but that was not competitive with Herald's love; it was the natural complement.

But such conjecture was a waste of thought in the present crisis. "This was real?" Brother Paul demanded, appalled by the flames, the obvious and horrible torture. *Carolyn—in the flames of Hell!* Had Satan lied to him, sparing her from the sacrificial knife at the Black Mass only to claim her in this far worse fashion? "In this far future, this age of intergalactic empire and the concourse of myriad sapient species via the miracle of the transfer of auras, this happens?" Yet obviously it did.

Oh, help me, Patriarch! She is my beloved!

The image disappeared, perhaps abolished by Brother Paul's own revulsion. Patriarch? If he were sure that any descendant of his would perish barbarically, chained in flames, he would never beget the line! "In the face of such a loss, there is little I can offer except my own grief." But that would not solve anything! He tried to continue: "Though I hope there is some feasible way for you to find relief." How utterly, inanely callous he sounded—yet if he had spoken the way he felt, it would have been a cry of simple pain and horror: *oh, Satan, you saved your worst torture until last!*

Then show it me! the creature flashed. *This Healer needs healing!*

Show him—yet what *was* there? How could death itself be negated? Especially when Brother Paul was only visiting this time as an incorporeal aura. "Perhaps a Tarot reading would help."

This is the Temple of Tarot. But no mere Animation can satisfy me long. I need reality, not illusion.

An interesting comment in this situation. Brother Paul had traversed so many levels of illusion he was not sure whether he would ever recover reality. Still, he had to believe that some things were constant, and the Andromedan had a good, solid orientation. "The Tarot reveals reality. Shall we try a spread?"

The Cluster Satellite Spread is best.

"I haven't heard of that one. Suppose you describe it, and I'll lay it out." Brother Paul found a deck of cards in his hand. He shuffled them, resisting the temptation to look at their faces. What was important was that they related to Herald's need, and he was sure they did.

Deal them into five piles, the Slash flashed. *The piles signify DO, THINK, FEEL, HAVE and BE.*

Brother Paul dealt them out face down. What an interesting set of representations! Surely they matched the five suits, which in the Waldens deck stood for WORK, TROUBLE, LOVE, MONEY, and SPIRIT. In the popularized version, anyway, that matched the superficial titles. The fundamental meanings were much closer to those Herald had listed. He had seen how they also equated to the medieval elements of society: Peasant, Soldier, Priest, Merchant, and the whole class of rootless people like entertainers, gypsies (who had not actually come on the European scene by 1392), and criminals. It was an intellectual challenge to line things up by fives. The Rhine experiments had used five symbols; did these also match the Tarot suits? Square, circle, cross, star, and wavy lines. The wavy lines obviously stood for water or the suit of Cups; the circle was a disk or Coin; the cross would be a Sword. But the square, now—well, four sticks, clubs, or scepters could form a square, so that might be the suit of Wands. And the star, like the Star of Bethlehem, signaling the location of the holy spirit of Jesus—that would be Aura. Somewhat forced, maybe, but still—

He had come to the end of the cards. Now they were in five piles, twenty cards to a pile. The mode of this new layout came to him. "Your Significator, the card that most nearly represents you—that should be the King of Aura." For he was abruptly aware that Herald the Healer had a phenomenal aura; he could feel it impinging on his own. Not since Jesus Christ had he experienced its like. Perhaps that was what had really reached out across the millennia to summon him. "We must locate that card."

You are of equivalent aura yourself—as of course you would be, the Andromedan flashed.

Antares had said the same. Extremely high aura—that notion jogged something. Something highly significant. There must be a fundamental connection between aura and Animation—

Then the card came up, breaking the chain of thought. "Here it is in Pile Two: THINK. In my terms, TROUBLE or MAGIC, that I'm sure has metamorphosed in your day to SCIENCE."

But my problem is FEEL, Herald protested.

"Perhaps the Tarot is telling you that the solution lies in your thinking rather than in your emotion. We can at least explore the possibilities." But privately he doubted. What mode of thinking could justify the burning of an innocent young woman? "Now how does this 'Cluster' spread go?"

Following Herald's directions, Brother Paul formed the layout. He started with the Significator, crossed it with Definition, and followed with cards to the South, West, North, and East, forming a cross. "Past, Present, Future, and Destiny," Brother Paul murmured, appreciating the simplicity of it. "Modified Celtic layout."

Celtic? the Andromedan flashed, perplexed.

"A spread of my day, having little if anything to do with the historical Celts. This spread of yours seems to be oriented on fives, and it rather appeals to me. The spreads of my day may have been less precise." But again he was dubious; how could five cards define a problem as aptly as ten or twenty cards?

Brother Paul considered the cards he had dealt. The Significator was crossed by the Three of Aura, labeled Perspective or Experience. Because it was sidewise, he could not tell which aspect dominated; probably both applied. Regardless, it was relevant. The card in the PAST location was—

Because Paul paused, amazed and gratified. "Ah, the vanity of the flesh!" For the card was Vision, eighteenth Triumph in the Waldens' deck, and it was illustrated by the scene he had visited from *The Vision of Piers Plowman.* He must have had a hand in this, for though that classic was contemporary with the Waldenses in the fourteenth century, the Waldens' Tarot had not used this particular illustration. He could not remember now what they *had* used, but not this. He must have successfully re-created the deck, drawing at least to some extent on his own experiences.

Half bemused by his growing awareness of his own complicity in the shaping of this deck, Brother Paul moved on through the Cluster Satellite Spread, tracing Herald's problem. Yet revealing as the messages of the cards might be to the Andromedan, they spoke with perhaps even greater eloquence to Brother Paul himself. For these cards were not as a rule illustrated by medieval scenes; the court cards were alien creatures and the Triumphs—

He was unable to grasp or retain the whole of the illustrations for the Triumphs. Many related to concepts that seemed not to exist in his own framework, though they obviously derived from the basic notions of the Waldenses. Here in Animation the cards became mind-stretching aspects of the future universe, and all he could do was absorb as much of it as possible without critical examination. His assimilation came in diverse gouts, but the overall picture was roughly this:

After the Fool period of mankind's history the expansion of Sphere Sol slowed, stabilizing at a radius of about a hundred light years. The farthest human settlement was Planet Outworld whose people were green; the King of Swords had a picture of Flint of Outworld, a high-aura native of this facet. But the Tarot in its multiple variations continued to expand explosively, knowing no Spherical or species boundaries. The Animation effect of Planet Tarot was exported to other planets, though it was proscribed by Sphere Sol. The Tarot symbols took on four dimensional attributes that multiplied the effectiveness of divinatory readings. Alien missionaries carried Animation Tarot across the Milky Way Galaxy. Most Spheres adopted variations of the 100 card Cluster deck, but some used the 78 card decks or other sizes. Temples of Tarot were established among the wheeled Polarians (78 cards), and the swimming Spicans (100 cards), and the musical Mintakans (114 cards, counting the variations of the Ghost). In just a few short centuries Tarot ranged thousands of light years, coming to dominate the culture of the great conglomeration of species that formed the mighty interstellar empire called Segment Qaval, whose dominant sapients resembled nothing so much as vertical crocodiles. Then Tarot leaped a million light years to Galaxy Andromeda and Galaxy Pinwheel. Sophisticated interstellar organizations drew on Tarot for symbols, such as the Society of Hosts whose card was Temperance: the soul or aura being transferred from the living vessel of one host to another. Indeed, the proper designation for that card was Transfer. In a devious but compelling sense, Tarot helped organize the entire local Cluster of galaxies.

Brother Paul saw a fleet of huge spaceships, each one to two kilometers in diameter, each one shaped like the symbol for one of the Tarot suits. Ships like Swords battled with ships like Scepters and Cups and Disks and Atoms. It seemed the suit of Aura was variously known as Lamps, Plasma, and Atoms; in fact the variations of Tarot among alien creatures dwarfed in number and imagination those Brother Paul had surveyed on Earth. This did not mean the medieval Tarot decks of Earth were forgotten; quite the opposite. The aliens gleefully adapted *all* the old cards to new purposes, filling out each deck to a hundred cards and overflowing into the Ghost. Every Tarot deck that had ever existed anywhere was, by the definition of the Temple of Tarot, valid.

Concurrently, every deity that had ever related to Tarot was also considered valid. Thus the God of Tarot was a composite of every conceived and conceivable deity in all time and space. "All Gods are valid," became a common saying.

The shortage of energy caused galaxy to war against galaxy. Only the phenomenal efforts of Tarot-inspired heroes prevented horrendous destruction. The Solarian Flint of Outworld, spying his enemy by a Tarot reading and neutralizing her; Melody of Mintaka, herself an expert Tarotist; and Herald the Healer, laboring to save the entire Cluster from the threat of alien conquest and destruction—

And *this* was the Tarot spread that might motivate Herald to achieve his vital mission. And Brother Paul was the guide. He shook his head, bemused again. "I have come from Hell to help you," he murmured.

I do not comprehend.

"It is not comprehendable. Perhaps the whole of my life and death has been for no other purpose than to facilitate your mission. On the other hand, this could be an incredible delusion of grandeur. Regardless, I shall do what I can." Brother Paul looked at the final card of the reading. "Here is Destiny—but it is the Ghost, the great Unknown. The reading cannot end here!"

The spread can be augmented, Herald flashed. Actually, this exchange occurred somewhere during Brother Paul's series of revelations about the future history of Tarot; everything was mixed hopelessly together, but it did not matter.

Lo, they dealt a satellite spread, modifying and clarifying the main layout. Somewhere here or elsewhere the cards augmented his knowledge of the Ancients, those creatures whose civilization had spanned the entire Cluster, three million years ago. Their technology had been well beyond anything known even in the modern, Solarian-year-4500 Cluster. Yet they had vanished completely. Now an alien invader known only as the Amoeba was attacking with technology that seemed to approach the Ancient level. The only hope of repelling the Amoeba was to discover Ancient technology—in a hurry.

How was a Tarot reading guided by a man two and a half

millennia out of date to accomplish such a thing? Tarot could evoke only what was already in the mind of the querent—and Animation was much the same. Yet what could he do but go on?

Still, something nagged at his awareness. Ancients—Animation—Amoeba . . . there was some critical connection of such overwhelming importance that . . . but he could not quite get his thought around it, and the revelation escaped.

They formed a second satellite spread. This one animated—the Daughter figure again. She was in the fire as before, writhing in silent but devastatingly evocative agony, trying to draw her slender legs out of it, then resigning herself to her doom. As Jesus resigned himself to his doom on the cross—

"No—I forbid this!" Brother Paul cried. "There is no way this torture can promote the welfare of your culture! I have felt the fires of Hell myself; do not do this to her again!"

She is my wife, the Page of Swords! Herald flashed, and his agony was a terrible thing in its brilliance. His love was in the flame, and his sanity was breaking. *Suffer as I suffer! She burns, she burns!*

It was Herald's vision, not Brother Paul's. But it was the Page of Disks he saw more than the Page of Swords. Carolyn. His child. Or the child of his child, a hundred generations removed. One card of the Tarot for each generation. But the connection —absolute. There was no way he could tolerate the infliction of such horror on her.

Brother Paul aspired to be a peaceful man, but now he had to fight. "I sub-define!" he cried, slapping down another satellite card. "The Eight of Aura—Conscience!" Maybe in this distant future the card no longer represented this concept, but he willed it so regardless.

Carolyn did not fade. Her anguished mouth opened, and she cried: "Herald forgive them—they know not what they do!"

As Jesus had cried. Now Brother Paul's own descendant begged the same reprieve for her tormentors. In this moment her aura was like that of Christ; he could feel the gentle power of it like none other in the universe. Yet Christ's sacrifice had not purified the erring populace, had not expunged evil from the world. Instead evil had infiltrated Christ's own Church and prospered as never before. The tears of Jesus—

Now another innocent was being sacrificed, as it were, progressing from the incarceration of a sealed-in chamber in a wall to the dancing flames. Her lovely hair puffed into a blaze, shriveling with horrible speed into a black mass.

Herald charged the fire, but this was useless; even in the Andromedan's own framework, this was only a memory vision. Brother Paul slammed down another card, not knowing what it was, only praying that somehow this recurring wrong could be righted.

Time froze. This card was blank, for he had not selected any, and in this Animation there was no random manifestation. He had to choose, consciously or subconsciously. What *did* he want?

"Oh, God, I want her safe, unburned," Brother Paul whispered.

God did not answer. And why should He? It was not God's way to interfere directly in the affairs of living species. That was Satan's business.

"Then what do You offer, Satan?" Brother Paul asked.

The response was instant: *Vengeance.*

God was distant, aloof; Satan was near and relevant. Suddenly it was easy to appreciate why a man like Therion would prefer to worship the Horned God. The promises of God were nebulous and often postponed until their completion became pointless; justice delayed, justice denied. Satan operated on a much more direct, responsive basis. Satan was a businessman; He set a price on what He offered—but He damn well delivered. He never cheated, not directly; He used any conceivable loophole to make His gifts more costly than any person would voluntarily pay, but He abided by His infernal rules. He had shown Brother Paul the origin and purpose of Tarot and also the evolution and future of Tarot; now He was angling for that fateful third wish.

To make that bargain would be in effect to worship Satan. Yet there was much that was worthy in Satan. Perhaps Brother Paul had spent his life seeking the wrong deity.

But he could not make this bargain. Not quite. "No! I want her alive!"

"Vengeance—and life," Satan replied, right on top of the situation. To bargain with God was an exercise in futility; Satan was the one in control.

Brother Paul looked again at the awful flame. "I'll take it!" Carolyn had prayed for forgiveness of her persecutors. Instead Brother Paul was bringing vengeance. Surely Jesus' tears were flowing yet!

The card he had chosen manifested as the Tower—the House of God—and of the Devil. It was the Tower of Truth, and the

Dungeon of Wrong, and this very castle. From the sky a bolt of energy came—and everything was a blinding brilliance.

Revelation! The vision retreated, and he saw the roiling fireball of an atomic explosion. This was the vengeance sponsored by Satan; fiery destruction of the entire castle. All those who had perpetrated the atrocity of burning Carolyn had been hoist by their own petard. All had died in fire.

Now Satan guided him on a kaleidoscopic tour of the Cluster, showing him the war with the alien Amoeba. This was the Age of Aura; the soul of Carolyn, known to Herald as Psyche, was captive in the Transfer network of the Ancients. As this network was restored, that soul was freed.

Carolyn/Psyche had lost her lovely human host, but she lived eternally in other hosts. She and Herald were happy. She was no longer Brother Paul's little girl in either body or spirit. She had found her own life. And that was the way it had to be.

Satan had granted the third wish—and Brother Paul knew he had expended it in a selfish manner. When the final test of his conscience had come, he had sacrificed his personal honor for this. It was the measure of his nature that he was not sorry.

And do you know the verdict on your soul? Satan inquired from the swirling chaos of the void.

"In the final crisis, I yielded to my baser instincts," Brother Paul said. "I am, after all, a worshipper of the Horned God."

What fate awaits you now?

"I am doomed to Hell," Brother Paul answered, knowing that his unworthiness only reflected that of mankind. Man was not yet ready to meet God—not in Brother Paul's time, not in the forty-fifth century, perhaps never. Satan had brought him at last to reason. "I am ready."

So shall it be!

Abruptly chaos vanished. Brother Paul found himself standing on the green turf of Planet Tarot. Scattered about within a half-kilometer radius were Lee, Therion, Amaranth, and Carolyn.

Brother Paul looked about, realizing that the third and final Animation was over. All five of them had survived it. He himself stood restored in health and sanity, uncastrate.

With increasing amazement and horror he grasped the reason.

26

DECISION
(JUDGMENT)

We may have misunderstood the nature of the Devil, according to Paul Carus in The History of the Devil and the Idea of Evil. *The Devil is the spirit that causes us to try new paths, to venture into unknown seas, to be original in thought and deed. He makes us hope for wealth and dream of happiness. The discontent that he engenders causes us to achieve better ways. Thus the Devil is actually God's way of stimulating us to our noblest efforts. God is neither good nor evil, but he is in both. He is in both growth and decay, in both storm and calm, in life and in death. He is in the guilty conscience and in the curse of sin, for these are excellent teachers. So Satan is the loyal helpmate to God, and to speak of the existence of the Devil is to be filled with the presence of God.*

"**I can** see you have the answer at last," the Reverend Siltz said.

"No, no answer. I fear it was an impossible mission," Brother Paul said, chewing on the good bread his host provided. It was not as interesting as the dishes of Charles VI's palace, but it was satisfying. "I went to Hell—but I learned about Tarot, not God."

"Tomorrow we shall see," Siltz said confidently. "I observed your face as you emerged from Animation and the faces of the others. It was as if you were of a single family, transfigured. We shall have the truth from you."

"The truth is hardly relevant," Brother Paul said. "I learned of the original Tarot, which has thirty Triumphs, each with a pseudo-meaning and a genuine meaning. Together, these Triumphs represent the life of Jesus which is also the life of Everyman, beginning in nothingness, developing through childhood and adolescence to maturity, then undergoing the vicissitudes of chance, error, trial, punishment, and transformation to another status where his real education begins. In the end he is subject to the final judgment and perhaps salvation. The minor cards offer spot guidance along the way—five suits, each covering a fundamental aspect of life, each card with two versions of the basic message. A most sophisticated deck of cards—yet so much more than that. All religious history is reflected in the Tarot!"

"So it would seem," Siltz agreed. "Perhaps you should record this special deck before it fades from your memory."

Brother Paul nodded. "Yes—I destroyed it; I must restore it. Humanity deserves the true Tarot! And I must give the world the Cluster Satellite Spread too—or would that be stealing from the future?"

"That must certainly have been a remarkable Animation," Siltz observed. "I become most curious. What were the meanings of the cards of this extra suit?"

"That would be the suit of Aura. The ace is titled BE, and the symbol is an oil lamp in the shape of a cosmic lemniscate." He made a figure with his finger in the air: ∞. "In the future they will render it as a broken atom, a proton-neutron nucleus surrounded by a spiral electron shell. He made another figure: ∞ "It also resembles a galaxy, by no coincidence." He smiled. "Iconographic transformation. The cultures of the Cluster draw from any variants that please them, just as they do with measurements. In Etamin they use miles instead of kilometers—" He caught himself. "I'm drifting! The deuce is illustrated by an outline of the human aura, and its interpretations are SOUL or SELF, depending on the way it falls. The trey covers PERSPECTIVE or EXPERIENCE—"

"Here, write it down, write it down!" Siltz said. "I am most intrigued by your dream deck! A symbol for each small card?"

"Yes. All symbols in a suit relate to the suit theme, and of course each suit is color coded. This is the suit of Art, coded violet—"

"I thought you termed it the suit of Aura."

"Merely alternate aspects. Aura, Art, Spirit, Plasma, Atoms—"

"All one suit?" Siltz inquired, frowning.

"Yes. Each suit has many interpretations, depending on the frame of reference. It is like the function key on a calculator. The cards look the same, but a shift of function makes them perform in a different manner. That way the usefulness of a single deck is multiplied. Instead of one hundred or two hundred aspects, there are a thousand or more, each fairly specific. When the reference is the classical elements, we call the suits FIRE, AIR, WATER, EARTH, and AURA. When it is the endeavors of man, we call them NATURE, SCIENCE, FAITH, TRADE, and ART. In medieval times that second suit was MAGIC rather than a SCIENCE, but the meaning hasn't changed."

Siltz laughed. "I dare say it has not!"

"When the reference is popularized divination, the suits are WORK, TROUBLE, LOVE, MONEY, and SPIRIT. When it is the states of matter they are ENERGY, GAS, LIQUID, SOLID, and PLASMA. When—"

"Plasma?"

"In physics that is the compressed state that occurs in the hearts of superdense stars where the pressure is so great that the normal nucleus-electron structure breaks down—"

"Oh, I comprehend. The broken atom! The squashed galaxy. Write it down, write it down! You do not want to have to go into Animation for what you forget. Make a table for your titles and numbers and symbols." He drew lines on the paper, making boxes. "Now your five aces stand for—"

"DO, THINK, FEEL, HAVE, and BE," Brother Paul said, filling them in. "With symbols of Scepter, Sword, Cup, Coin, and—"

A knock on the door interrupted him. "Come in, girl," Siltz called without removing his eyes from the developing chart. Privately to Brother Paul, he muttered: "I thought she'd never relent! It has been several days and not a night at my house!"

Jeanette entered. She was almost beautiful in a surprisingly feminine dress, her hair set just so, her legs well exposed and well formed. "You—how did you know—?"

"Brother Paul's hundred-proof Animation Tarot informed me that mischief was afoot. Your business has to do with work, trouble, love, money, and spirit."

"Not with money!" she snapped. Then, abruptly shy, she

dropped to one knee before him. "Reverend Siltz of the Church of Communism, I beg permission to marry your son."

Siltz pointed his finger at her pert nose. "Two grandchildren!"

"The first two children shall be raised in your faith," she said grimly. "*Only* the first two!"

Siltz smiled with crocodilian victory. "I am a reasonable man, though at times it pains me. I grant permission."

Jeanette's reserve crumbled. "Oh, Reverend, I thank you!" she exclaimed, jumping up and flinging her arms about him.

"Please, daughter—you will scatter Brother Paul's valuable cards, flaunting your pretty skirt about like that."

"Never mind my cards," Brother Paul said quickly. "I'm sure you two have details to negotiate about the wedding and such. I'll take a walk." He moved to the door.

Neither of them seemed to hear him. "You called me 'daughter'!" Jeanette exclaimed. "How sweet!"

"Just you take good care of my son," Siltz grumbled. "He is not used to marriage. He will not know what to do."

"He has a fair idea how to start," she said, flushing passingly.

Brother Paul emerged from the house. He was touched by the reconciliation, but it reminded him strongly of his own problems. He, too, wanted a daughter—but the daughter he had in mind belonged to another man, and he had no wife. In any event he would soon be mattermitting back to Earth—and the others could not go. Above all, he did not have the answer he had come to find. Not any answer he was prepared to present to the colonists! How could he stand before the community tomorrow and disappoint them?

It was dark. Light spilled from the cabin windows, helping him make his way, but beyond the village he had to depend on starlight. He wondered whether any of the stars of the entities he had learned about were visible now: Etamin, Mintaka, Spika, Polaris, or the galaxy Andromeda. And where would the galaxy called Pinwheel be? He had never heard of that one! Here in the night, those alien civilized Spheres seemed both very close and painfully distant in time and space. He wished—but that was futile. He had used up his three wishes, and now he was in Hell where he belonged.

He proceeded toward Northole, aware that he was taking a foolish risk by departing the village stockade alone and unarmed, but he did not care. He had seen and lost the universe; what did he have to lose now? What beast of prey could be worse than what he had already faced in Hell?

Ahead he spied the flashes of the nova-bugs. There was the place to walk! But one foot snagged on something. He dragged it violently forward, recovering his balance. There was a series of faint pops. Tarot bubbles—he had walked through a cluster of them nestled in a hollow of the ground. A nova-bug flashed brightly right before him, illuminating the shriveling Bubble remains.

Triggered by that, something illuminated in Brother Paul's mind. "Animation!" he exclaimed aloud. "The source of Animation! Now at last I understand!"

He concentrated. Light flared—no nova-bug this time, but illumination Brother Paul had willed. Yet he was not yet in the Animation area. "I control it," he said. "I have solved the problem of Animation!" Then, more slowly, "But I have not solved the problem of God."

He stood for some time in thought, working out the presentation he would make to the colonists. "Animation," he said. "The Ancients. Aura. It all ties together as I almost discovered two thousand five hundred years hence in Herald the Healer's vision." Then he set about gathering Tarot Bubbles with which to decorate tomorrow's stage.

Brother Paul stood at the apex of the wood pile. "I came here to identify the God of Tarot," he said. "The question was whether God is behind the Animation effect, and if so, what God he is. I now have an answer—but it is not one that pleases me or will please you. I could tell you that Animation tells me that *all* Gods are valid—" But as he had guessed, they were shaking their heads. They could not accept that answer. They wanted a single, dominant God, not a compromise philosophy.

He paused, trying to phrase his decision in a manner that would not be as painful for this group as he feared it would be. Yet what point was there in balking, after he had passed through Hell? But he found that he could not state his conclusion baldly; he had to lead up to it. "Much of the data on which I base my opinion is suspect because it derives from Animation which is the thing being studied. Animation is a tangible composite of the imaginations of the participants. A shared dream, if you will. It seems that

the dream was principally mine, and I am an imperfect vessel—
how imperfect I never properly appreciated until I had this
experience! So you may reject my conclusion if you will."

All were watching him in silence. Deacon Brown of the Church
of Lemuria, eyes downcast, yet watching: an eerie effect! Minister
Malcolm of the Nation of Islam. Mrs. Ellend of the Church of
Christ: Scientist, perhaps the oldest member of this audience.
Pastor Runford, the Jehovah's Witness. Jeanette, sitting closely
beside the Reverend Siltz: Scientology and Communist united at
last. But not the Swami, who remained unconscious.

"Three million years ago there existed a species of creature we
know only as 'The Ancients.' They were not human; rather they
were part of an alien culture embracing the several galaxies of this
Cluster: Milky Way, Andromeda, Pinwheel, and assorted lesser
structures. They were highly sophisticated creatures whose tech-
nology.has never been matched elsewhere. One of their many
avenues of exploration related to the expression of Art as controlled by sapient consciousness. They were much concerned with
the mechanisms of imagination and sought ways to make Art
more direct. Why go through the tedium of painting a picture or
molding a sculpture if the mind can create the images direct
without the intercession of material things? Not only would such
dream art be more convenient, occurring virtually instantaneous-
ly, but it would be far more versatile than any prior medium. Thus
the Ancients created Animation."

Brother Paul paused. He was oversimplifying, for he knew that
much of the joy in art lay in the doing of it. But he had a problem
of timing. The sun was beating down warmly now. Most of the
pretty Tarot Bubbles had popped. It was time.

"This," Brother Paul said, lifting and spreading his arms, "is
Animation."

Abruptly the world turned purple. The wood, the ground, the
people—all were shades of purple. They looked about and stared
at each other, amazed.

Then they turned green. And black. Stygian darkness closed
about them—until nova-bugs flashed, restoring intermittent light.

The effects faded. All was as before. "The nova-bugs make their
light by Animation," Brother Paul said. "That is why their
physical light-making apparatus has baffled science. The mechanism is not physical at all. It is imaginative—literally. I dare say
many other unusual features of this planet's life will become

explicable by the application of this insight."

Reverend Siltz, as baffled as the rest, faced Brother Paul. "How—?"

"I am coming to that, Reverend Communist," Brother Paul said. "Let's relax with something pretty while I cover the dreary details." The village houses vanished, replaced by lovely flowering trees. A sparkling stream coursed in a meandering path between people, arriving at a central conic fountain. Brother Paul stood at the apex of the fountain. "As you see, Animation can make images appear where there is nothing or conceal what is actually present. It can also produce sounds to a lesser extent; but most meaningful speech has to be spoken by a living person. It affects touch, but usually only to the extent of modifying existing surfaces. In short, there is normally a physical basis for a structure of Animation —but the basis and the appearance need not correspond very closely. Animation can produce the sensations of water—" and here the fountain spread out to become a rising lake surrounding the colonists, wetting them—"but it can not actually drown you unless you fall into *real* water. You might suffocate because you believe you are underwater, but that would not be the direct result of Animation." The water was above waist level, swirling ever higher as the colonists stood, causing considerable alarm. "But I do not mean to torture you, only to show you how it is possible to die in Animation without actually being killed by it." The water dropped, forming back into the fountain.

"Note that this is not mass hypnosis," Brother Paul continued. "I have shown you rather than told you of these effects. All living creatures have an intangible force about them we call Aura. An aspect of it has been photographed by the Kirlian process—but this appears to be only a refraction caused by water vapor associated with our type of life. The original aura can be detected only by extremely sophisticated equipment which our human species will not develop for several centuries yet. Some would call it the Soul—the ultimate essence of individuality, independent of body. In fact, some alien cultures can transfer that soul to other bodies, in effect giving their people the chance to travel on other worlds in other hosts.

"As will be discovered, the auras of individual entities vary widely in type and intensity; most are near 'Sapient Norm' which is coded by the numeral 1; some are more intense, coded by higher numbers. *Every* aura is unique and wonderful—but the extremely intense auras are spectacular in special ways." He paused, and the fountain turned bright yellow and developed a ring of green eyes at the base.

"Still no verbal suggestion," Brother Paul said with a smile. "Yet obviously my will is being communicated to you! Have no concern for your sanity; each of you perceives the same impossibility. I possess one of the most intense auras found among our species. I do not claim this makes me a superior man; far from it! I am an imperfect vessel with extremely human failings. Chance bestowed this gift on me. Until I came to this planet I was not even aware of it, and until last night I did not appreciate it. But it turns out that aura controls the Animations—and so this is my power." The yellow water solidified into a yellow monster that quivered and roared, supporting Brother Paul on its tongue.

"When we went into Animation, my aura extended out, interacting with the weaker auras of the others, informing them of my will. And so they saw what I saw and spoke as I would have them speak, in a general way. It resembles telepathy, but it is not direct mind-to-mind rapport. Since Animation does not affect the mind directly, only the perceptions, they actually interpreted their parts rather freely—but the play was always mine."

"But what makes it happen?" Reverend Siltz cried, staring at the monster. "Why does Animation only happen here on Planet Tarot? Surely other people on Earth have auras."

The monster dissolved into a pile of yellow rubble with a ring of green jewels. "The Ancients used their sophisticated science to create a special life form whose purpose was to facilitate the communication of auras," Brother Paul said. "This unique creature generates a—I suppose you'd call it a kind of gas that somehow enhances the overlapping of auras so that much improved contact occurs. A catalyst. Ordinarily auras are discrete, maintaining their separateness even when these auras overlap. Some creatures like to associate in close physical proximity so that their auras form something like a common pool, while others prefer to stay apart. This substance nullifies that separateness of aura to a certain extent, making the auras permeable, merging them. In a rather fundamental respect, groups of people in the vicinity of this gas join together, sharing themselves. Animation may be the ultimate tool for unity."

"But some Animations are nightmares!" Pastor Runford cried.

"Yes, indeed!" Brother Paul agreed. "Because the average

person is not ready for unity. He has enough trouble with his own nightmares, which Animation makes starkly tangible, without sharing those of others. Those of us who participated in this experiment suffered horrors that only we could imagine. Others before us have actually died. It is dangerous to loose the untamed horrors of the mind, especially when they have been so long suppressed. The Swami Kundalini tried to warn me of this." He paused, reflecting. "Fortunately we were a fairly balanced group with our horrors canceling each other out as much as they augmented each other. We experienced a kind of composite that became largely independent of the will of any one of us, including myself. The application of Tarot images helped, for the Tarot is a refined body of imagery and philosophy with roots deep in human experience and symbolism. Without that to lean on, to structure our creations, we could have been in very bad trouble. In the future, the Temple of Tarot will integrate Tarot with Animation with potent but precisely controlled effect, spreading its system safely across the Galactic Cluster." He smiled. "Everywhere but in Sphere Sol. The human government will ban such use of Animation, and thereby fall behind other Spheres in this respect, ironically."

Jeanette's brow had furrowed during this speech. Now she jogged Siltz's arm and leaned closer to whisper in his ear. How rapidly she had assumed proprietary rights, advertising them to the entire community! She could have spoken for herself, but now preferred to have the Reverend speak for her. She showed her power not so much by marrying young Ivan—who it seemed was not even attending this meeting—but by her proximity to Ivan's father, the head of the family. She had become one of the family, and in her public deferral she claimed her victory.

Siltz listened gravely, as a man listens to his daughter, then spoke aloud. "You have not answered, Brother Paul. Where *are* these Animation creatures? Can you show us one?"

Ah, yes; he had drifted from the subject, as was his wont. "Everywhere. They are the Tarot Bubbles."

"The Bubbles!" several others exclaimed.

"Correct. These innocuous fragments of froth that generate in the night and pop by day. They are a form of life—whether plant or animal or fungus or germ or some alien type I can't say. But I suspect the last, as things seem to fall naturally into divisions of five here, like the Tarot suits. They multiply and grow and feed and seek to survive—"

"But they just sit there or float about!"

"They sit there in the shade," Brother Paul explained. "When they pop, they release their hallucinogenic agent and some spores so that new ones can grow when favorable conditions return."

"But why bother with the Animation effect, then? *They* don't need it!"

"They did not evolve naturally. They were created or modified by the science of a culture whose motives and abilities were incredibly sophisticated. But Animation may be a survival mechanism after all. It may protect the Bubbles from molestation by evoking distractions culled from the minds of the marauders. And the desire that most sapient species seem to have for hallucinogenic experience may cause them to spread the Bubbles all across the Cluster, much as they spread fruit-producing plants or sweets-producing insects or useful animals. I also suspect controlled Animation can serve as a natural painkiller and as an excellent teaching tool. Thus specialists of various types will find uses for it. To control Animation they need the Bubbles. I believe the survival of the species is assured." Brother Paul frowned. "However, I am less sanguine about the prospects for our own human species, whose madness may be aggravated. Many quite beneficial drugs have been sorely abused in the past such as morphine and mnem. What will happen to Earth when Animation arrives there? Obviously the repercussions will be sufficient to cause Animation to be banned."

The yellow monster faded out. Brother Paul was back on the pile of wood in the center of the village. "The gas seems to have dissipated," he said. "When the threshold of Animation passes, the effect disappears rapidly like a candle going out. I brought a number of ripe Bubbles here last night, but they were not enough to maintain the effect for long. In the depression of Northole, where conditions are better for them, Animation is much more persistent, except when storms move the gas elsewhere. But I trust I have made my point."

"You have made your point," Reverend Siltz said. "But what is your answer? Who is the God of Tarot?"

"That is the difficult answer since you declined to accept the one I proffered," Brother Paul said slowly. This was the part he hated!

"All the manifestations of Animation turn out to have a physical explanation. The variables of the Bubbles and individual auras made that explanation difficult to come by, but I believe independent investigation will corroborate my conjectures. Thus we do not need to assume the direct participation of a deity."

There was a moment of silence. "There is no God?" Siltz asked slowly. He seemed to have become the spokesman for the community. Brother Paul was not sure from the way the man spoke whether this, to him, represented defeat or victory. Many humanists believed in the spirit of Man, not God; what was the stand of the Church of Communism?

"I—can not say that," Brother Paul said. "I can only say that God did not make Himself manifest to me through Animation. Therefore, I can not identify the God of Tarot—because I have no concrete evidence there *is* a God of Tarot."

"Yet there *is* a God," Siltz persisted. "And that God is found within the human heart. And Animation makes manifest what is in the human heart. You were questing for that truth. Surely you found *something.*"

"No," Brother Paul said heavily. "I am no longer sure there is a God. I looked for Him as hard as I could, yet was invariably turned aside, and found only the debunking of my most cherished beliefs. The closest I came to God's presence was, through the irony of precession, when I was questing in quite another direction."

There was no cry of outrage. The assembled villagers of diverse faiths looked at him with regret and compassion. "Surely you retain your faith in your prophet, Jesus Christ," Reverend Siltz said. "We asked you to choose among our Gods, not to renounce your own."

"I am not sure I do retain that faith," Brother Paul said. "What Jesus did can be accounted for by the presence of aura. He could have been an ordinary man, even a—a mutilated one, with an extremely intense aura. Aura can sponsor visions; aura can heal. In the future there will be entities who make a business of healing through aura, attributing no religious significance to it." *Herald the Healer, where are you now?* "God—I find it difficult to discover an objective rationale for the existence of a Supreme Being in the face of what I now know of Animation and aura."

"But this is not negation!" Siltz insisted. "These things may prove only that God operates through such tools as Ancients and aura. There are unknowns we can not explain; there are rights and wrongs. There must be Divine inspiration, a Guiding Force—and you must have had some hint as to the identity of that Force."

"Perhaps," Brother Paul agreed reluctantly. He knew what Siltz was trying to do: rescue Planet Tarot from the depression and chaos that a negative decision could mean. Better a foreign God than anarchy. This colony needed to unite, at least politically, about a single diety—*any* deity. "Yet I am not certain, now, what is right and what is wrong or whether there is in fact any distinction between them. One concept is meaningless without the other, much as the black markings we call writing are meaningless without the white background of the paper. Black and white must work together to form meaning; it is foolish to call either color God. Right and wrong exist only as companions, as extremes of perspective; God may be in both or in neither, but God can not be taken *as* one or the other. Yet I would not presume on the basis of such subjective evidence—"

"It is not presumption! Five of you participated in the Animations; all contributed to the visions. In that group effort, some consensus must have developed or you would have destroyed each other. You emerged unified—it shows in each one of you, even the child. As a group you have agreed, even if you have not consciously understood the rationale of that agreement. If as diverse a group as you five can unify, so can our colony—about the same deity. As a group, *you have identified God!"*

Brother Paul looked at Lee, and at Therion, and Amaranth and Carolyn, all sitting on the wood behind him. Slowly, each nodded. Yet he resisted. "What we experienced," Brother Paul said, "this was a special situation probably not applicable to the outside world. You would not be able to accept—"

"Must we direct the question to the Watchers?" Siltz inquired.

Brother Paul did not reply.

"We require an answer," Siltz insisted. "Mormon—your credibility is unblemished. We know you will not mislead us, though your own faith be forfeit. Who is the God of Tarot?" But Lee shook his head in negation, refusing to answer.

Siltz turned on Amaranth. "Abraxis? You were not scheduled to be a Watcher, but by your survival of three Animations you have proven yourself. Who?" But Amaranth also declined.

The Reverend's gaze now fixed on Carolyn. "Child, the Nine Unknown Men will not be pleased if you do not reveal what you agreed to Watch. Who is God?"

The girl tried to resist, but under the group's uncompromising cynosure she wilted and broke. "S-sa'n," she whispered.

"I did not hear," Siltz said sternly. "Speak clearly!"

Carolyn tried again. "Sa—Satan is the God of Tarot."

Now Therion, who had held himself impassive, smiled. "Otherwise known as the Horned God," he said. "Returned after thousands of years to claim His own. From me you would not have believed it, but from these others you *must* believe it." He turned to address the other Watchers and Brother Paul. "Who here denies it?"

No one denied it. Brother Paul felt a special agony of faith. What had he done, when he yielded to his baser nature in making his third wish? He had been relegated to Hell—and this was now Hell. Satan was the God of Hell.

"Humanity belongs to the Devil," Therion said triumphantly. "And the world of the living is but an aspect of Hell. We failed to find grace in Animation—yea, even the Mormon, even the child, even Brother Paul of Vision!—and so Satan returned us to His realm. We have the truth at last."

And the congregation was silent.

27

WISDOM
(SAVANT)

Man's population is increasing, and he is polluting land, sea and air at a rate that cannot continue much longer. Ironically, he could feed himself for many centuries to come if he reprocessed human wastes instead of pouring them into the environment. Instead he makes it worse by overusing poisons (insecticides) and fertilizers, and energy that leads to further pollution, as with nuclear reactors. The irony, as G. Legman points out in Rationale of the Dirty Joke, *is that "It is shit that is clean, and the 'pure white powders' that pollute!" But it seems that the rational course will not be followed, and that careless exploitation will continue until our food supply is doomed.*

Therion was leading several villagers in solemn prayer:
Our Father, Who art in Hell, Damned by Thy Name
Thy Kingdom come, Thy Will be done, on Earth as
it is in Hell.

"This *is* Hell," Brother Paul muttered. And thought with sudden hope: had his failure in the trial of the third wish really brought the entire planet to this, doomed by himself as imperfect Everyman? Or was this merely another Animation masquerading as reality, as the airport scene had been? It was difficult to be certain anymore. So maybe—

No. If this were *not* reality, then he could never in his life be sure of the distinction between reality and Animation. Assuming it was what it seemed to be, it was still Hellish. How would Satan answer the prayers of his new constituents? Surely only in such a fashion as to make them regret it!

"Oh, Swami," he murmured. "You were so right in your warning! I unlocked the secret of Animation—and loosed Satan upon us all!"

Yet Satan had honored His bargains with Brother Paul. Satan had answered when God stood aloof. Satan was honest and responsive. Perhaps Satan was indeed more worthy of worship.

"Sad, isn't it," a man said beside him. Brother Paul turned. It was Deacon Brown, the Lemurian.

"Not for me, really," Brother Paul said insincerely. "I'm leaving soon."

"For *him,*" the Deacon said, indicating Therion. "He has been granted what he thought he wanted—and that's Hell."

"But he's happy, isn't he?"

"Not at all. Listen to him."

Brother Paul listened. Therion, it seemed, was now telling a dirty joke, ". . . so he went on down to Hell. 'I was bored up there,' he said to Satan. 'No liquor, no women, no parties.' Satan waved his hoof, and there was a roomful of drunken, naked, eager, beautiful women. So Prufrock dived in amongst them. But in a moment he cried, 'Hey, these gals have no holes!' 'That's right,' Satan replied. 'This is Hell.'"

The reaction of the congregation was less than enthusiastic. "You see, now he has responsibility," the Deacon said. "He has to guide them and entertain them, and their values don't coincide with his. He's trying to get through to them, to shrive himself by making them react with laughter or horror or anger, and they aren't reacting. That leaves him the obvious butt—and that's Hell for him. His own refuse is bouncing back in his face."

"Yes . . ." Brother Paul said, seeing it. "But surely he should have anticipated this sort of thing when he took the Horned God as his deity."

"He did not choose the Horned God; that was thrust upon him. Back on Earth he married the most beautiful and intellectual woman he found—then she turned out to be a lesbian, using him only as a cover."

"She had no hole!" Brother Paul exclaimed, catching on.

"None he could use. She two-timed him with a female lover. That sort of thing is Hell-on-Earth for a normal man—and perhaps worse for an abnormal one, strongly sexed but afraid of the opposite sex."

"The Gorgon," Brother Paul said. "The castration complex. He has it with a vengeance! In the Animations—" But he decided he didn't want to talk about his own castration; he now saw that it was no more a product of his own desire than the soul-as-excrement concept had been. "She put horns on him—without another man, really complicating his complexes. So he adopted the Horned God!"

"That's why he distrusts all women now and seeks to defile them," the Deacon agreed. "He's afraid anyone he loves will betray him."

"Seeks to defile women . . ." Brother Paul repeated, again reminded of his disaster of the Seven Cups, and Satan's clarification of it. Excrement in the face of the female! The Black Mass too—the attempt to have a young female killed on the body of a mature one. Much was coming clear now. "Yet if he found one that *wasn't* lesbian—how would he know? By rejecting *all* women, he makes his own Hell."

"Precisely," the Deacon agreed. "And what woman would attempt to break through his defense and abate that Hell? A thankless task!"

Brother Paul shook his head. "He is a man of many qualities. I believe his attitudes suffered fundamental changes in Animation, and he is ready to accept normal heterosexual relations. Perhaps one day some hardy woman will perceive those qualities and make the effort."

Meanwhile, Therion was still trying, almost pitiful in the new perspective. "Now let me tell you about the Sleeve Job. This man had tried every conceivable kind of sexual experience and wanted something really different. So. . . ."

Brother Paul walked away, leaving Therion, leaving Deacon Brown. His mission here was over. Now he was only waiting for the return of his capsule to Earth. This had been pre-scheduled when this mission had first been instituted; the capsule would return at its appointed time with or without him. Certain Planet Tarot artifacts would be shipped back, including a sealed terrarium containing Tarot Bubble spores, as a supplement to his report. All Brother Paul had to do was wrap up his personal affairs. No easy task!

First he had to settle with Amaranth. She had expressed serious interest in him between Animations as well as during them, but despite temptation he had found his own emotion falling short. She had a marvelous body and a willing nature—but somehow he could not envision himself married to a perpetual temptress, a Lilith figure. There were other things in his life besides sex. So even if it had been possible for him to take her back to Earth with him, he would not have done so. The roles the two of them played in life were too different. Had she been more like Sister Beth and less like a minionette of Satan—

The problem was, how could he tell her that? She had, by her definitions, done everything right. She had undressed herself frequently and to advantage and had not bothered him with intellectual discussion. Her notion of the ideal woman. He knew from her prior discussion about nature and the Breaker that she had more depth than that; the shallowness was merely a role she played. She would make a good wife—for the right man. It just happened that he was not that man.

He found that he could not tell her that. Not directly. So he retired to Reverend Siltz's house and pondered his Tarot chart —and it came to him. Therion's demon Thoth Tarot was adaptable to this purpose!

In the end he found he had written a poem titled "Four Swords"—in the Thoth Tarot, the Four of Swords signified Truce. He would give her this Tarot poem message, explaining about the problem of roles, and perhaps she would understand. This was also his farewell to the Thoth Tarot, and to all other four-suit Tarot decks; henceforth, he would devote his energies to restoring and perfecting the five suit Tarot of the Waldenses. Satan had given him this, and he could not let it go. Perhaps he was, after all, a worshiper of—

There was a knock on the door. Brother Paul went to open it—and there stood Amaranth.

"I'm sorry," she said. "I can't go with you, Brother Paul. I thought you were the one for me, I really did, but those Animations showed me things—I really got to know myself better, playing those roles, and I saw how dumb some of them were. That's not what I really want to be."

"I understand," Brother Paul said. How well he did!

"I—have a greater affinity for another man," she continued. "One I wouldn't have looked at before Animation. I prayed to Satan to solve my dilemma, and He sent me—"

"Therion!" Brother Paul exclaimed.

"Yes. He—he's really more my type. He likes my body, and I like his mind. In the Animations—it worked out pretty well. Actually. When he was King Charles. He does with gusto what you resist, and I—I need to be gustoed."

"Yes," Brother Paul agreed.

"He's not really bisexual or whatever. He just never got close to a female woman before, despite all his talk. He has very broad horizons. Broader than mine. So he can show me new avenues, and I *need* those avenues because I can't stand dullness. It never would have worked out between you and me, Paul. I was never Sister Beth, or the Virgin Mary, or any of those lovely pure women that turn you on. I'm a creature of indulgence, uninhibited. I want a man foaming at the lips to get at my secrets, tearing the clothes off me—"

She broke off. "But I know it bothers you, my just telling you this. You never tore clothing off anybody. Even in the middle of the act, you just lay there without responding."

In the middle of the act? She was referring to his dream within a dream, being ravished by a succubus, unable to respond because he was paralyzed and castrate. That really had been her playing that part!

"So—farewell." She turned and walked away.

Brother Paul looked down at the paper in his hand. He had never even given her the poem. He *had* been unresponsive!

Should he destroy the poem? It had had only one purpose, and that was now passed. No—he did not believe in book burning or anything that smacked of it. He would file it away; maybe future scholars of the Temple of Tarot would find it in his papers and wonder what it meant. It was about as anonymous as a poem could be; he didn't even know the proper name of its addressee. With luck, he would never know.

Yet, now that it was over, he felt a letdown. It might have been fun Amaranth's way. Tearing the clothes off her. She was the creature for which man's lust had been designed, and he was after all a man. Too bad the fourteenth century Animation had cut off before they had gotten into the Palace affair; she might have discovered that he was not always paralyzed.

He shook his head. Therion's Satan, perhaps in His jealousy, had made sure Brother Paul could not climax anything with Amaranth in that sequence. And there *were* other matters.

Now he had to settle with Carolyn. His love for her was stronger than anything he had felt for Amaranth, if of a different nature. He would have to explain to her that even if he could take another person home with him (which he could not), he could not take a child away from her natural father. What had been in Animation —could not be in life.

This was Hell all right.

He walked slowly to the Swami's house. Reverend Siltz had mentioned that the Swami had finally recovered consciousness, perhaps in response to Mrs. Ellend's ministrations, so Carolyn was moving back in with him. Most of the villagers were out about their work in field and forest; the rigorous climate of this planet did not permit much time off from chores. There was the sound of hammering, momentarily sending a chill through him until he realized it was from the shop of the stove-smith. The man was laboring to convert the first units to body heating rather than space heating. Several fisherpeople were trawling a net through Eastlake, harvesting waterlife for drying and salting for winter. What would happen if Lee passed by in his Christ-visage and said "Rise, follow me, and I will make you fishers of men"? Probably nothing, for Satan ruled here. One man was working on his roof, thatching an annex with freshly cured broadleaves. The main section remained turf, but evidently in summer other roofing could make do. Everywhere were reminders that this was but the summer interstice; the rest of the year was—Hell.

Therion was concluding his service: "Satan is my Shepherd; I shall not be satisfied. . . ." Brother Paul hurried on. He had brought this answer to this colony, but he could not accept it. Satan might have commendable qualities, but surely. . . .

The Swami's house was empty. Then where was Carolyn? She was not yet required to work, and the village school was not in session this day because the community had not yet agreed on the necessary revisions of texts to reflect the revealed reality of the God of Tarot. She must be taking a walk in the countryside, sorting out her own feelings. She knew she had to make a life of her own here, even if she could not accept it. He would find her.

She was not in the village. That meant she was out in the

country. That bothered him; the wilderness was unsafe at best for any lone person and worse for a troubled child. Why had she risked herself so foolishly?

Why, indeed! Her whole life was in crisis; what did one extra hazard matter? Somehow he had to convince her that life was worthwhile . . . even life in Hell. Sure.

He found her in the afternoon on the steep eastern slope of Southmount, as the wind was stirring. He saw her small body on a ledge, the feet dangling over and swinging idly in little girl fashion. Suicide? No, she was not the type; she was merely comfortable there. But clouds were boiling up in the north, presaging another storm. These tempests seemed to be an almost daily occurrence, and they moved and spread rapidly—and brought unwanted Animation. Carolyn had to get off that mountain in the next few minutes!

Brother Paul ran to the foot of the nearer cone, getting pleasantly winded. He had neglected his exercises here on Planet Tarot!

The storm, racing him, loomed horrendously. Brother Paul could see the thunderhead of it shoving high into the sky, challengingly, a great black knob like the head of Satan, rotating its eyeless visage to bear upon this newly liberated settlement. Below, the shifting vapors showed the turbulence folding in on itself in living layers. This was a bad one!

"Get down from there!" he cried, doubting she could hear him from this distance over the swish of the fringe wind. But Carolyn looked down, her eyes bearing on him as the air tugged at her dress. Now she was aware of the threat. She scrambled onto the flat of the ledge, then started down, running fleetly along its broken slopes, hurdling the crevices with an agility that seemed foolhardy.

The wind stiffened. The first splats of rain struck the slope. This storm was straight from Northole; it would be carrying a full charge of Animation. Carolyn had to make it down before the effect distorted her perceptions. She could take a fatal fall!

Abruptly she stopped on a ledge about ten meters above Brother Paul's level. She screamed.

"Don't be frightened!" Brother Paul called. "Come down carefully, and we'll talk. Watch out for slippery rock where it's wet. I can control the visions—"

But she was pointing over his head. Alarmed, Brother Paul turned.

There was Bigfoot as huge and hairy as before.

"Stay up there!" Brother Paul cried to Carolyn. "I'll stop it from climbing." For there was no question of the monster's objective; it was heading not for Brother Paul, but for the nearest ramp ledge leading from the base toward Carolyn's perch. It was after her!

Brother Paul charged. He had no illusions after his prior encounter with this creature about his ability to beat it in physical combat. He had bested the Breaker, and the Breaker had balked Bigfoot—but it was also possible that Bigfoot had finally realized that Amaranth was not the woman it sought to kill, so had given up the attack. At any rate, Bigfoot's terrible mass and power would tell; judo could go far to equalize the imbalance, but at best the match was chancy. Brother Paul, in challenging this thing, was undertaking the fight of his life.

But he had to do it. Bigfoot had reached the foot of the cone and was starting up the ledge. Carolyn's frightened face poked over the edge, staring down. Bigfoot saw her and made that soul-chilling scream, and her face disappeared. All children of the human species had imaginary monsters that terrified them in the dark; Carolyn had a *real* one.

The wind intensified, buffeting the rock; Brother Paul hoped the child was bracing herself securely in some alcove so that she could not be dislodged. Bigfoot was not the only threat here!

He reached the ledge and ran up it. Bigfoot, quite agile, was negotiating the first bend. Brother Paul caught up, reaching for the creature's massive arm.

Bigfoot turned to face him, making that terrible swipe. But Brother Paul had anticipated this. He ducked under, caught that arm with both his own, and tried to heave the monster over his shoulder and off the face of the mountain.

Tried. For heave as he might, he could not budge Bigfoot. Despite the slick-smooth surface of the rock, the creature seemed to be rooted. What weight the thing must have to balk a throw of this power!

But if he didn't throw it now, he would be in Bigfoot's power, for he could not match its strength. Brother Paul threw his weight forward, his right arm extended in the *uchi makikomi* or inside wraparound throw. His own weight was leaning over the ledge, over a drop of about two meters, hauling Bigfoot's weight behind. This was one of the most powerful techniques in judo; the fall could knock the victim unconscious. Yet still Bigfoot resisted.

Brother Paul made his final effort. He twisted violently to the left, balanced on his left foot, and swept his right foot back against Bigfoot's leg in a *hane* motion. This should have lifted the creature right off the ledge and hurled the two of them to the ground below—but it didn't.

Now Bigfoot's hairy arms closed about him, squeezing. Brother Paul was lifted into the air, his feet dangling.

He jammed one elbow back, hard. It bounced off solid hide. He bent one knee and stomped backwards with his heel. The strike should have crushed tender anatomy—but it too bounced off harmlessly. He clutched at one of the hairy hands that pressed against his chest, seeking to hook one finger and bend it backwards until pain made the creature go—but the fingers were each like iron rods, immovable. He tried to shove his own two arms up and forward, forcing the enclosing arms apart so that he could drop free, but he could not get purchase. Bigfoot seemed invulnerable!

Now Brother Paul felt the breath of the monster on his neck. The thing was going to bite him!

Suddenly he had the inspiration of desperation. He could not overcome this thing physically—but maybe he could use Animation!

Brother Paul concentrated. He made himself resemble the Breaker.

Bigfoot reacted immediately, hurling away this dread infighter. Brother Paul sailed out over the ledge, oriented himself, and landed fairly neatly on his feet. It was a bone-shaking impact, but not a destructive one. Brother Paul absorbed the shock in his legs, fell forward, and took a rolling break-fall. This was not comfortable on this hard terrain—but a lot better than what Bigfoot had had in mind for him. As his back struck with a rolling impact it was cushioned by a cluster of Tarot Bubbles that skidded by; they popped all about him, releasing their gas.

He lurched back to his feet and looked for Bigfoot. The creature had resumed its climb, hugging the face of the rock so as to keep out of the buffeting wind. The rain remained light. Soon Bigfoot would reach Carolyn's ledge; then—

Brother Paul concentrated. The path in front of the monster became a void, dropping into an immeasurably deep chasm. Bigfoot halted, as well it might.

Now was the test: was this a stupid beast or a smart one? If the former, Brother Paul had it beaten—so long as the Animation effect lasted. He could show it a ledge that would drop it off the mountain. If the latter, Bigfoot would soon see through the ruse. That would mean real trouble.

The monster put one foot forward cautiously, one paw sliding along the cliff wall. The continuing ledge might be invisible to it, even unfeelable to it, but the substance was there and so there was no fall. So—Bigfoot was too smart to be fooled by illusion more than momentarily. That was bad. Still, its progress had been greatly impeded.

Could he conjure a sword and hurl it at the monster? The conjurations of the men at the mess hall, back at the outset, had been solid. But Brother Paul realized now that those would have been converted objects of the table, wooden bowls and such, rather than constructs of air. Anything solid in Animation had to have some solid basis; otherwise it was no more than an illusion that would have no substance when touched. Illusory knives would not faze Bigfoot much longer than the illusory void had.

Still, it was necessary to try. Brother Paul conjured a huge black winged hawk. The bird of prey dived on Bigfoot. But the monster ignored it. Such hawks were not native to this planet, so were obviously fabrications. No luck there; the monster had human cunning.

How was he to stop Bigfoot? The thing was now halfway up the slope toward Carolyn, and once it got its paws on her, no illusion would help her. The Animations were losing their effect, and Brother Paul could not handle the creature physically. There were no convenient rocks here to throw, no suitable weapons. Nothing to adapt! Yet he could not let the thing get at Carolyn!

Only one thing seemed to offer a chance: Brother Paul had to fight it again—masking his location and intent by means of Animation. If Bigfoot could navigate a treacherous slope in a storm while under attack by an invisible enemy, then nothing could stop it.

One other notion. Brother Paul conjured an airplane towing a sky sign: HELP—SOUTHMOUNT. He sent it flying toward the village. If that Animation lasted, if the effect extended to the village, someone would see it, and then an armed party would have to investigate. They probably would not arrive in time, but at least it was a chance.

Now he conjured a group of Breakers. One by one they

closed—and had no physical effect. Bigfoot had been fooled the first time; now it ignored Breakers. But one among that charging line was no phantom; it was Brother Paul in disguise. If he could get between the monster and the wall and shove outward, striking suddenly and by surprise—

Bigfoot was almost to Carolyn's ledge when Brother Paul caught up. The girl was cowering at the far edge of a level area; from there it was necessary either to climb up a meter—or down ten meters. The rock faces were slick with rain, and the wind was still gusting powerfully; it would be suicidal for her to attempt that route.

Before, she had foiled Bigfoot herself by making an Animation river the monster couldn't cross. This time she was too frightened to think of that—and the monster was not about to be fooled that way again anyway. It knew she was trapped.

The moment Brother Paul touched Bigfoot physically, the monster would recognize him—and that would be the end. Bigfoot was just too strong for him! Yet the thing's progress was inexorable—and now its eyes were fixed on the girl. No mock gulf or barrier would stop it, and she couldn't run. What to do?

Brother Paul concentrated. A wall of dancing yellow flames sprang up between monster and child. Bigfoot hesitated, then pushed through. Beyond—was nothing. The girl was gone.

Bigfoot paused, momentarily baffled—then made a human-sounding chuckle. It had caught on; Carolyn was there—but now she was invisible. Brother Paul had blotted her out via Animation. The monster cocked its head, listening.

Behind it, Brother Paul breathed hard, trying to drown out the sound of Carolyn's respiration. He hadn't learned how to control sounds yet. But that gave *him* away; now Bigfoot knew there was another person on the ledge. Brother Paul in his haste was making errors as fast as good moves. And time was running out.

There was a cry from below. It was Lee from the village. "What's going on up there? There's a storm breaking!"

"Bigfoot's after Carolyn!" Brother Paul cried. "I can't stop it!"

"I'm coming up there!" Lee cried.

"No! There isn't time! Find a weapon, rocks, anything!" But in his agony of indecision, Brother Paul had let his Animation fade. Carolyn reappeared.

Bigfoot uttered a harsh scream of victory. It charged.

Brother Paul charged after it, concentrating again. A second Carolyn appeared beside the first, then a third. "Move about!" he cried to her. "So it can't tell which one is you." But she was frozen by terror.

Bigfoot closed on the real one. One hairy arm went out, catching the girl, lifting her up. "Daddy!" she screamed despairingly.

Brother Paul struck. Headfirst, he butted Bigfoot in the belly. All his weight was behind it; the monster was shoved backward one step, two. Brother Paul assumed a new form as he straightened up within the grasp of Bigfoot, reaching for the child.

Bigfoot stared in almost human dismay. Then its rear foot, seeking the ledge, came down on nothing.

Brother Paul wrenched Carolyn from the monster's grasp as it fell. Bigfoot windmilled its arms but could not recover balance. It fell—ten meters to the base of the cliff.

Lee arrived on the ledge. He came to look down on the still monster. "My God!" he exclaimed. "It's the Swami!"

Brother Paul stared. It *was* the Swami—and he looked dead.

Carolyn had cried "Daddy!" Brother Paul had misunderstood the reference. She had recognized her natural father at the last moment. And so had Brother Paul, unconsciously; only the Swami's power of *ki* or *kundalini* could account for the strength Bigfoot had. The last form Brother Paul had assumed had been that of the Swami himself. Bigfoot, seeing its alter ego, had been amazed—and had made that one careless misstep that had doomed it.

Brother Paul had killed Carolyn's real father.

"Come away from here, dear," Lee murmured, putting his arm around Carolyn. Her face a dry-eyed mask, she yielded. Dully, Brother Paul watched them go, experiencing *déjà vu*. This had happened before, this departure of man and girl from horror—at the gate of Hell.

And this was Hell too—and this was real.

Brother Paul paced alone in Reverend Siltz's cabin, waiting for his honor guard to accompany him to the mattermission capsule station. His mission here was over, his personal entanglements abated—but his depression had not lifted. If only he had achieved the wisdom of experience sooner, before he killed his daughter's true father! The signals had been there had he had the wit to interpret them correctly. The Swami, a serious man, intolerant of other religions, possessing strong psychic power, was unable to accept his wife's refusal to convert to his own faith. At the Animation fringe his savage and bestial rage had assumed physical shape—perhaps the result of intensive positive feedback. Anger, guilt, madness: Animation could be a destructive drug like heroine, cocaine, LSD, or mnem, abolishing the human mind's natural curbs and loosing monsters. How right the Swami had been in his initial warning: there was special danger in Animation. The Swami had known whereof he spoke first hand.

Yet Brother Paul could not believe the man had been evil. The Swami had evidently taken good care of Carolyn during his human phase; had his transformation into Bigfoot been conscious? Probably not. Had the Swami been a criminal, he would not have needed the assistance of Animation to kill his wife and daughter. Animation might seem to lend a special ability, as with Therion and his judo skill when he played the monster Apollyon, but that had really been Brother Paul's doing; he had credited Therion with a talent the man actually lacked, and played along governed by the role. The skill that the Swami had had, in contrast, had been genuine. Bigfoot's enormous size and mass were of course Animation enhanced, but the *ki* that had balked Brother Paul's attacks was inherent. Had the Swami's psychic power been directed in the area of aura, as Brother Paul's was, the Swami could have been a similar magician in Animation. But he had focused on one thing only: Bigfoot. This had been the man's private war between the conscious and unconscious minds, Dr. Jekyll and Mr. Hyde, two irreconcilable attitudes. Schizophrenia. Satan only knew how deep religious currents ran in some individuals! Brother Paul knew he would never understand the full nature of the Swami's motivation. To seek to kill one's own offspring—!

Now the child was doubly orphaned. Her mother had been killed, her natural father had become a monster, and her Animation adopted father a murderer. Justifiable homicide, legally, or self defense; Lee had been witness to Brother Paul's good intent. But in the eyes of Carolyn—

There was a measured knock on the door. Time to go. Brother Paul opened it—and there stood Lee. "Oh—I thought it would be—"

"Soon, not yet," Lee replied gravely. "I regret bracing you with a personal concern at this time, but I have no choice."

"Come in, sit down!" Brother Paul said heartily. "I am in the depths of a depression and need distraction though I may not deserve it. I failed my mission, wreaked religious havoc on this colony, and orphaned an innocent child. Planet Tarot deserved better!"

Lee faced him squarely. He was a handsome man whose strong character showed in his manner. He did indeed seem Christlike. "Who in Hell do you think you're fooling?" he asked evenly.

Brother Paul almost laughed at the incongruity. Yet in the context of the Animations, Christ and Hell were compatible. "I hope to fool nobody. I will make an honest report, buttressed by the holographic recording I was required to make, and then return to my Order of Vision station to seek what respite I am able from my conscience. I would apologize to you and the others of this Planet, if that were not ludicrously insufficient."

Lee shook his head. "I sent myself to Hell, and I deserved to go. You brought me out by showing me the error of my thinking, acquainting me with my true sin and exorcising it. Now it seems you have sent yourself to Hell—and it falls on me to return the favor. Paul, you succeeded in your mission, brought this colony the answer it demanded and deserved, and released a wonderful girl from certain death. I saw you in Hell and came to know you as well as a stranger can. You are determined and true, a great and good man, the closest approach to a living saint I know."

This time Brother Paul did laugh. "Hyperbole will get you nowhere! I daresay the truth is somewhere between the extremes we two have described. I once heard it said that truth is a shade of gray."

Lee smiled. "Or of brown. I will never forget what you did for me. You broadened my perspective and restored my faith when I doubted it sorely. Because of you, I questioned tenets of my religion I had never thought to question before and learned that Jesus would not have acted as I had. In fact, through you I came to understand Jesus Christ in a deep and personal manner. He will always be with me, henceforth; I bear the stigmata of his presence. I know now that a man's soul cannot be judged by his race—and I will exercise such powers as I can muster to have that doctrine of my Church revised. Yea, I will preach even the Parable of the Good Nigger—for you are that man."

"Thank you," Brother Paul said, uncertain whether to smile or frown. Just as the derogatory term "black" had come in the mid-twentieth century to be a mark of pride for those affected, so had the term "nigger" by the turn of the century. The same thing had happened earlier with the "Quakers" and no doubt would happen in future centuries too. Perhaps one day "Hell" would be an analogy for spiritual enlightenment. Perhaps that had already happened.

"And that brings me to my immediate business with you," Lee continued. "Your daughter necessarily also has black ancestry—"

"Carolyn? She is not my daughter; in reality she has *red* ancestry. The Swami was Amerind, not Asiaind."

"Oh?" Lee said, surprised. "The Mormons have compassion for Amerinds, who are the descendants of the early Israelite colonies of America. But this is irrelevant. I do this neither to show my freedom from the racial bias I carried into Hell nor to test it; I mention it only to clarify that without your intercession I would have been unable to consider it."

"Consider what?" Brother Paul asked, confused.

"The merging of the races of man."

"I must be of slow wit this morning. I don't follow—"

"She has no father now but you, and so it is to you I must, according to the custom of this Planet, make petition for—"

"Please stop!" Brother Paul said, pained. "I have no authority of any kind over Carolyn! Even her name is a construct of my ignorance; she must assume her own name. I am about to leave this planet."

"Yes. That is why I had to ask you now, for she is as yet underage and of a foreign faith. I would not change that faith, but will compromise in the manner shown by Reverend Siltz and—"

Brother Paul's brows furrowed. "Underage for *what?*"

"Sir," Lee said formally. "I humbly request permission to take your daughter's hand in matrimony."

Stunned, Brother Paul could only stutter. "You—you—"

"I was, among other roles, Herald the Healer of the far future. She was Psyche. Suddenly I knew that I loved her, and that love had been growing from the time of her act of courage in becoming a Watcher of the Animations, and that I had to have her though Hell itself bar the union. When I saw Bigfoot about to kill her—"

Still overwhelmed by the chaos of his emotions, Brother Paul lurched to his feet and stumbled outside.

Carolyn stood there, as he had somehow expected. She wore a sleek white dress, and her hair was elegantly braided and looped like a diadem. She resembled a fairy princess—no longer a child. For an instant Brother Paul saw Psyche, writhing in the terrible flame, the sacrificial child bride: a soul-searing image, yet indicative of the new reality. Little girls did grow up, and the jump from age twelve to age thirteen could be a giant one.

"Daddy!" she cried and flung herself into his arms in much the way Jeanette had gone to the Reverend Siltz. Child yesterday —woman tomorrow.

"Yes!" he cried, hugging her close, joy bursting upon him like the light of a nova. "Yes, Carolyn, yes—marry him! There is not a finer man on the planet! You will never burn, you will never suffer fear again, you will never be alone! You will make your own family, needing no other!"

She kissed him gently and disengaged. Through the blur of his tears Brother Paul saw Lee standing beside them. He caught Lee's hand—and saw the spot, the mark of the puncture of the nail. The stigmata of Christ. Only a scar, yet—

He set Carolyn's hand in Lee's, aware of his own intense relief. Now he knew she would be well cared for! "With my blessing," he said, squeezing their hands together.

There was a smattering of applause. Brother Paul blinked—and saw Reverend Siltz and his wife, and beside them Jeanette and a young man who favored Siltz in a meek way, and Therion and Amaranth and the rest of the villagers.

"It is time to march to the mattermitter," Siltz said.

"Bless you all," Brother Paul said, his depression abating.

Alone in the mattermission capsule, Brother Paul laid down his mock-up Animation Tarot cards on the crate of Bubbles in a game of Accordion. Each card had only its Triumph or suit and number designation notes; there were no illustrations. This makeshift deck was not pretty, but it satisfied his present purpose. In his mind's eye he saw the symbols as they had been in the Waldens' deck, and as they would be in the Cluster deck.

He was playing this game because otherwise the sudden loneliness would overwhelm him. What he had experienced here, in person and in Animation—forever finished.

The Ghost Triumph came up. From its blank surface a film spread out and up, solidifying in air. It swelled, extending a pseudopod to touch the floor. Soon a substantial mass of protoplasm rested there. "Salutation, human friend," it signaled.

"Hello, Antares," Brother Paul said. "Good to meet you again."

"It was an intriguing adventure, much relief of tedium,"

Antares said. "This is a marvelous deck of concepts you are living."

"The Animation Tarot? Did you really participate?"

"In Animation, yes. Your aura made this possible. And your imagination. Perhaps there was an affinity of effects because both aura enhancement and Animation derive ultimately from the science of the Ancients. But you were the one who reunified them. Do you realize that this experience relates most closely to your deck of concepts?"

"My experience?"

"Your world sets the stage with its folly of mattermission. The other cards follow in sequence, right until this present aspect of your wisdom. You have become a savant, more experienced in this unique area than others of your kind. Now you go forward toward Completion."

"You mean I did not discover the Original Tarot?" Brother Paul asked, troubled. "I merely translated my own life into the cards?"

"Not at all. Your life *reflects* the original Tarot, as all lives do. But for you it has been more dramatic than usual and more artistic. Even the five suits have direct force as segments of your adventure. This Tarot of yours will spread across the Cluster, affecting many alien civilizations and finally saving the Cluster itself from disaster."

Brother Paul smiled. "So the Animation suggested. But we have no way of knowing such a thing, alien friend. It was merely our imaginations functioning."

"I confess that much of the futuristic detail was my doing," Antares replied. "The culture of Sphere Nath, for example. But not all of it. There was an element that cannot be accounted for by rational means."

"Meaning this was all one big fantasy," Brother Paul said. "Yet I would never trade the experience for another. My life has been marked by what passed on Planet Tarot." Lee wore his stigmata on his body; Brother Paul wore his on his soul.

"I'm sure it has. But I do not believe it was fantasy. I prefer to call that unknown element the handiwork of God in whatever manner He may choose to manifest. In fact I am inclined to agree with the thesis of the Tarot Temple that *all* forms of God and all faiths are valid."

"The Tarot Temple . . ." Brother Paul repeated. Could he really be about to found anything like that? Surely not!

"When I was Herald the Healer, sharing the role with your son-in-law, I learned the history record of your life. You were quite famous as an ancient figure, in the forty-fifth century of the birth of your Jesus of Christ. You popularized the Cluster Tarot and the notion that true belief, rather than its particular form, was the essence of faith and that no religion should question the mode or precepts of any other. The Temple of Tarot was formed in your name, perhaps after your death, and every novice had to experience the Animation record of your adventure on Planet Tarot. You were called the Patriarch of Tarot."

"Over my dead body," Brother Paul said tolerantly. "Does your imaginative memory of my future also tell you what happened to my little girl in the airline terminal?"

Antares considered. "No, that detail was lost to history. But I am certain no bad thing happened to her, for she grew up to illustrate the Animation cards most prettily. I conjecture that the normal prediction of that vision was interrupted by the role player's imposition of her own concerns so that the sequence became invalid at that point. Probably the *real* Carolyn remained with you throughout, and the two of you returned to your wife, her mother, without further event."

What wife? "That is a comfort to know," Brother Paul said. "Tell me, friend—since you manifest only in Animation or mattermission, will I ever meet you again? I don't expect to make any more such trips."

"This is unknown," Antares responded. "But since you are conveying a sample of the Animation Bubbles to Earth, you may experience the effect again, and if you think of me at that time I shall be with you."

"But how will I know it is *you*, and not just a wish fulfillment?"

There was no answer. Brother Paul found himself looking at his Ghost card—the symbol of the unknown. The trip was over.

Yet the significance remained, which the colonists had rejected but, it seemed, future civilization accepted: *All faiths were valid.* If that were so, why not his faith in his friend, the alien Antares?

28

COMPLETION
(UNIVERSE)

James Drought was a fascinating character. Unable to sell his books to regular publishers, he set up to publish perhaps half a dozen of them himself, under the imprint Skylight Press—and then resold The Secret *to a major paperback house, Avon, for a five-figure advance. His prose was alive and fervent and highly opinionated: in short, a thing to be envied and admired by other struggling writers. He urged that we not give in passively to God's demand for our lives; that we "smash God in the face" and slip away so as to avoid that sacrificial knife, dodging so that God could not catch us, holding out as long as we possibly could, so that when God finally did catch us, he would know we made a good fight of it. That appears to have been the essence of his "Secret". But when we sought James Drought for permission to quote his words, he could not be found, and later there was a note about his death at age fifty-two. Was he true to his own words? We cannot know, but it would be nice to believe that he did elude God, as he eluded us, until the last possible moment, and that he thus earned God's respect.*

Brother Paul expected complications of debriefing, but these were few. Bored clerks took his recording equipment, and a physician checked his vital signs. "You have suffered some physical regression, Father, but it is not serious. Get a few good nights sleep, exercise a little, eat well and you'll be back to norm quickly enough."

He was dressed and on his way to the next office before it registered. *Father?* He must have misheard.

"We are through with you," the clerk said. "The computer is analyzing your holographic record now; we will be in touch if any clarification is required." Obviously neither clerk nor computer had any notion what was in that record; to them, this was mere routine. Brother Paul wanted to get out of here and into the hinterland before anyone was disabused! "Where will we be able to reach you?"

"I will report first to my superior, the Right Reverend Father Crowder of the Holy Order of Vision," Brother Paul said. "His address is in your records. Then I expect to return to my own Station and start catching up on backlogged chores. They must be just about out of wood by now." But the clerk did not smile; he was hardly paying attention. He was making his notes on a slip of paper. Brother Paul was reminded of the old definition of lecturing: a system whereby the material passed from the notes of the instructor to the notes of the student without going through the mind of either. "You will be able to reach me through the Right Reverend."

"Good enough," the clerk agreed, marking "RR" on his slip. He smiled. "Good luck, Father."

Was he back in Animation? Brother Paul shook his head, accepted the travel voucher, caught the electric bus, and in four hours was met by the Right Reverend himself. "Welcome back to Earth, Father Paul. I trust you are well?"

"I seem to be having some difficulty readjusting to reality. By what title did you address me, Reverend?"

"I shall clarify the situation succinctly," Rt. Rev. Crowder said briskly. "The Holy Order of Vision is expanding rapidly. It seems that the accelerating deceleration of our culture resulting from the colonization program creates an insatiable need for our type of ministry. No doubt the tide of social history will turn in due course, and we shall have to contract again, but at the moment we are desperately in need of competent organizers for new Stations. We must provide service where service is needed; that has always been our mission. In certain cases we have been forced to waive normal requirements. You have excellent recommendations, and your performance on this extraterrestrial mission did not diminish your prospects. You have suffered promotion, Father Paul."

"My performance!" Father (what a strange ring to that word; he was not sure he liked it) Paul exclaimed. "How would you know of that?"

"Mere survival would have been sufficient; the promotion was in the works before you departed this planet. But since we are the parent institution for this project, we received an immediate computer statement, unedited," Rt. Rev. Crowder explained. "In only four hours I could not of course do more than skim it—but that sampling was enough to convince me that you are a remarkable man. You have, it appears, identified God."

"No!" Father Paul cried. "I cannot accept that!"

"Oh, the holographs are quite specific, and so are the supplementary data. You might be interested to know that the technicians ran a check on the mattermission circuitry and discovered an imbalance corresponding to the postulated 'aura' of the alien visitor who brought to Earth the secret of mattermission. And the Extraterrestrial Chemistry Laboratory has been locked into absolute security by your sample of 'Tarot Bubbles.' Thus, to the extent we can verify it, your experience has objective bases. I am convinced that you did encounter Satan."

Father Paul was afraid to ask how much of that holographic record would be made available to outsiders. He opposed censorship, but in this case he was tempted. "But I went in search of God, not Satan!"

"There is no question Satan answered the prayers of the colonists," the Rt. Rev. Crowder continued. "They wanted relief from the rigors of the planetary climate. They shall have it now. Planet Tarot is about to be declared proscribed; the Colonization Computer has declared Animation to be too dangerous for human use. All people there are to be resettled on other planets. The bureaucracy can move rapidly when it has to."

"They're destroying the colony?" Brother Paul asked, aghast. "All the people in all the villages of the planet?"

"Satan does not pussyfoot, as you well know."

"But this was not necessary to—"

"Do not be so shocked, Paul. There is no sacrilege here. Satan is but the nether face of God."

"Th nether face of God!" Father Paul exclaimed.

"There is and can be only one God—but He has many aspects. For those people who are unready to face Him in His Heavenly phase, He makes available one for their level. There need be no mystery about this. In fact, Christianity draws its dualism from the Gnostics: the belief that all things are dual. Black versus white, good versus bad, God versus Satan. Just as two sexes facilitate the evolution of species, it seems that two facets of deity facilitate the evolution of conscience. Through this constant interaction we are tested and improved until we are more than we might have been. Just as women complement men, to their confusion and advantage, Satan complements God."

"But everything had a rational explanation! There was nothing to show that the intercession of any Higher Power was necessary or that there was really any distinction between good and evil. In the framework of the intergalactic civilization of the Ancients—"

The Rt. Reverend looked at him shrewdly. "You do not regard these factors as products of your imagination?"

"I—" Father Paul hesitated, trying to marshal his mixture of thought and emotion. "You said yourself there is objective evidence for the existence of Antares in the—"

"I did indeed. I believe in the authenticity of your vision, Paul. I merely am verifying whether you believe in it yourself."

Again Father Paul hesitated. "I do believe—though it led me to Satan or to the renunciation of any concept of deity. I realize that makes me unfit for the promotion you have proffered or for any place in the Holy Order of Vision, and I regret intensely failing you in this way. But I must act on what I believe."

"And can you inform me what science or technology makes possible a divinatory look into the future?" the Rt. Reverend inquired.

"I—"

"And when you met Satan and were physically picked up by Him and consumed—what planetary reality accounted for that?"

"I cannot explain these things," Father Paul admitted. "I can only affirm that I believe in them."

"And so does your holograph—and the Colonization Computer, and a growing army of technicians," the Rt. Reverend said. "I believe them too. How would you explain the fantastic coincidence of the single man with the most potent aura among this species—being the one assigned to the planet where aura controls Animation?"

"I—" Father Paul began, baffled.

"I submit to you that there is only one agency that can reasonably account for the totality of your experience. What name would you put on that Great Unknown?"

"Why, that could only be—" The concept dwarfed his ability to express it. "I—saw God?" Father Paul asked numbly. Suddenly things were falling into place. Could all that precession have guided him accurately after all? "But God would not destroy the entire colony!"

"I offer a rationale," the Rt. Rev. Crowder said. "Let us surmise that, for the benefit of the Universe or at least the Galactic Cluster, it is necessary to educate a series of sapient entities in a very special way. High-Kirlian-Aura creatures to be suitable tools, perhaps fashioned from imperfect clay, yet tailored to the need. Call them Herald the Healer, or Melody of Mintaka, or Flint of Outworld—or Paul of Tarot. Perhaps even Jesus of Christ. Assume that these entities, properly prepared, will set in motion currents that will in the course of several millennia preserve the entire Cluster from needless and ironic destruction. As by devising or reconstituting a deck of cards whose images evoke key understandings on critical occasions—"

"Ridiculous!" Father Paul snapped.

The Rt. Reverend smiled. "No doubt. I certainly will not repeat such fancies to others. But were such a thing conceivably the case—would not the viability of a single colony planet be a trifling price to pay? We question God's purposes at our peril."

Father Paul put his hand to the pocket where he carried his mocked-up Animation Tarot deck. Could such a thing be true? "In that case," he said, awed, "God does exist—and this is His will."

"Is it not better to believe that—than to renounce your prior faith in Him?"

"Yes!" Father Paul exclaimed, as his balked belief was undammed. Undamned. Suddenly he felt whole again.

The Rt. Rev. Father smiled again. "Rest assured that neither this discussion nor the holographic record will be put into general circulation. The Colonization Computer, I am sure, is even now classifying the whole matter Absolute Satanic Secret, and I expect my copy of the holograph to be confiscated shortly. I only want you to know that I believe it was God's will that you be subjected to this experience, this tempering of your spirit in Hell, and that you surely acquitted yourself in a manner satisfactory to Him. It is easy to be noble and chaste when one is not subjected to stress and temptation and alteration of consciousness. You were Everyman; you were flawed, yet survived. Thereby, you justify the species and perhaps the form that life has taken in this segment of the Universe. Life with aura."

"Thank you," Father Paul murmured, not feeling noble or chaste.

Rt. Rev. Crowder made a gesture of subject dismissal. "There is another matter. The Holy Order of Vision is, as I mentioned, expanding. This is not from any missionary zeal on our part, but because we appear to answer a need of the contemporary society in crisis. But I repeat myself, I fear. My point is that it is important for attrition of our competent officers to be minimized."

"Of course," Father Paul agreed, uncertain where this was leading.

"I trust you will agree that the Reverend Mother Mary is competent."

The relevance became uncomfortably clear. "Yes! She helped lead me out of the darkness of my prior ignorance. But she would never leave—"

Rt. Rev. Crowder shook his head. "She has given notice."

Father Paul was shocked. "Her faith in God is absolute, not subject to vacillation like mine! She—"

"She wishes to leave the Holy Order of Vision. She is carrying on only until we arrange a replacement for her Station. It occurred to me that you might have some insight into her problem."

"I? No, I—" Father Paul broke off, dismayed. "You didn't promote *me* to take her job!"

"No, no, of course not! Not directly at any rate. She was due for rotation to a new Station anyway, so your assumption of the office at the familiar Station is appropriate for your first assignment. But since you know her better than I do, I thought it would be appropriate if you spoke to her before she left. I hardly need to stress the importance of persuading her to remain with us. She has been one of the very finest of our young officers, but I am thinking not merely of the welfare of the Order, but of Mary herself. I do not believe she would be happy in another occupation."

"No, she would not," Father Paul agreed. "The Order is her whole life. This—this is not like her!" He shook his head, troubled. "I had looked forward to working with her again. Do you have any hint why she—?"

The Rt. Rev. Crowder frowned. "Her personal file is available to me, of course, as is yours. I am aware of the manner you came to the Holy Order of Vision. I know you were converted by Sister Beth before she—"

"I killed her," Father Paul said. "You know this, yet you promote me—"

"You, like her, were a victim of circumstance. All of us have enough sin on our consciences without exaggerating the significance of events beyond our control. My point is this: we of the Holy Order of Vision know our members rather well, particularly those in whom we see special promise. Most of our people are rather literally from the gutter. *I* am. I have blood on my hands, and a micro-lobotomy scar on my brain. Like you, I failed my final test; but it was society, not Satan, that brought me to justice. It is a cruel world we live in. Hell, in fact. But it is Hell, not Heaven, that most needs social workers. Therefore, your own past history does not surprise or shock me. What matters is your *present* state —which I believe is the point you made to the Mormon. Mary was a similar convert."

"This I can not believe!"

"Your naivete becomes you, Paul. You have spent all your life in Hell and have hardly seen it. I shall not betray the details of Mary's prior existence or how she came to us. You have seen what a jewel she became. I only want to clarify that had she been allowed to undertake the Planet Tarot mission, the Animations would have been no more comfortable for her than they were for you."

"Allowed? You mean she—"

"Mary volunteered for the mission, yes. We forbade it because we felt she lacked the physical stamina necessary. And so we subjected her to the double indignity of assigning you instead."

"She—she suspected what it would be like?"

"Yes. And I rather think she suffers from guilt for sending you—much as you suffered guilt for releasing Sister Beth to the police. Fortunately you survived, vindicating my judgment—and I think if you were to talk to Mary—"

"Yes! Yes, of course," Father Paul agreed. "She need feel no guilt on my account!"

"I was sure you would understand," the Right Reverend Father Crowder said. But his smile was enigmatic.

Brother Paul's route home differed from his one to the matter-mitter so long ago in experience. This too was Order policy: to seek new territory even when only passing through, rather than retrace steps. Thus he found himself one night at the Tribe of the Picts. Whether they really resembled the original Gaelics or Celts of Europe was questionable, but he was too diplomatic to evince skepticism.

Their Chief was naked, his torso stained blue and green and horrendously tattooed: obviously a matter of great pride. "Seldom have I encountered such handsome art," Father Paul said tactfully.

"Welcome to our hospitality," the naked artist said appreciatively. "But Father, if you would—my child is sick—"

"I am not a doctor—" Father Paul said cautiously.

"We have doctors; they have been unable to help. They say she needs a hospital, X-rays, blood transfusion, diagnostics, drugs—" He faced Father Paul. "It is a long ride to civilization. She will die before we can get her to such help!"

"I will look at her," Father Paul said. One problem with this retreating technology was the return of ancient killers, increasing child mortality. Diseases of inattention and malsanitation and ignorance. The Picts *were* far from civilization—in a number of ways.

The child lay on a cot in a dark hut. As he came to her, Father Paul had another siege of *déjà vu*. Had he been here before? Not in this century surely!

She was certainly sick. She was about ten, her face wizened by pain, the rind of old vomit at the corners of her mouth. Malnutrition was probably a complicating factor, as it had been in medieval times. He reminded himself again that this was not intentional child neglect; primitives simply didn't *know* what good diet was or what a healthy environment was. Probably the doctors had tried to tell the Chief—but there was only so much any person could say in such a situation if he wished to keep his own health. Father Paul would make a prescription that might balance her intake somewhat if he were able to help her through this crisis; *if* he helped her, her father might pay attention.

Her skin was pale, almost translucent. She needed light and

attention—and love. Where was her mother? Someone to hold her and tell her stories and listen to her little joys and tribulations. True primitives centered their lives around their children, but these modern regressed people hadn't put it all together yet. Their families were likely to be destroyed along with their prior livelihoods. Different people regressed at different rates in different ways. It was Hell on marriages. He would have to make a prescription in that area too.

Yet it would all be academic if she were too far gone. First he had to catch his rabbit.

He sat beside her, taking one burning little hand. "Pretty child, I love you. Your father loves you. God loves you. Wake and be well." He put his other hand on her forehead and prayed silently: *God, help this child. Bring her out of Hell.*

His aura flowed through her body—that aura others said was one of the strongest known. This was not Animation of external appearances, but attempted animation of something more important: the will to live. He had to form a new self-image within her to make her believe that her illness was an illusion to be banished, that she, like the Christian Scientists, could conquer—if she had faith.

And—she healed. Her fever dropped, her tension eased, and she woke. He felt her consciousness rising through her modest aura, drawing strength from his strength, his love. Her eyes opened, bright blue. She smiled.

"From this day forward," the Chief said from behind Father Paul, his voice trembling with emotion, "this Tribe worships your God."

"My God is Love," Father Paul said.

Then the reaction struck him. *He had healed her!* He had touched her, willed her to live, called on God, and used his aura in a new way to make this child well—just as Herald the Healer had done in the far future and Jesus Christ in the near past.

The ability he had realized in Animation—remained with him in life. He was now a Healer.

The Station was poignantly familiar with its windmill and conservative buildings. Father Paul had to remind himself that he had been away only a fortnight or so, though he had roamed back and forth through some five thousand years in that interim. From the Buddha to the Amoeba!

Brother Peter emerged from the kitchen as he passed. "Congratulations, Father!" he exclaimed. "Go right on to the Reverend's office; she's expecting you."

Father Paul lingered a moment over the handshake. "Brother —how is she? I have heard she is not well."

Brother Peter glanced down at their merged hands. "There is something about you—some power—"

"The power of a renewed faith in God," Father Paul said. He did not care to explain about the aura at this time. "But about the Reverend—"

"Father, I'm sure you can handle it." And that was all Brother Peter would say.

Father Paul went to the office, though he was somewhat grimy from the trek. This was where his mission had started a world and time ago; it was appropriate that it also terminate here. He paused at the door, nervously rehearsing his arguments: how she could do so much more good within the Order than without it; how she had done him no disfavor by sending him to Planet Tarot, but instead had greatly facilitated his self-discovery; how the Right Reverend Father had spoken well of her performance in office; and how the Order needed her services now more than ever in this crisis of its expansion. He would not mention what he had learned of her pre-Order past of course; that would not be diplomatic, though it provided her with a human dimension in his mind that she had lacked before. Instead of an angel, she was an angelic woman: a significant distinction. But he would try his best to persuade her to remain. Yes.

He opened the door and stepped into the small office as he had before. She was standing by her desk, facing away from him, a stunningly forlorn figure. *What had happened to her?*

"Mary," he said, experiencing a rush of strange emotion. That had not been what he meant to say!

"Paul, I know what case you mean to make," she said, her voice partly muffled. "But my decision has been made. I only want to explain the mechanisms of the office and to congratulate you on—"

Something about her—the Animation scene of Dante's *Paradiso,* where—"Mary, face me," he said gently.

Slowly she turned about, not bothering to dab the tears from her cheeks. "You are safe. God bless you."

God bless you. Father Paul studied her face, recognizing only now what he had been unable to see before. *She* was the angel he had been questing for all through the Animations! No wonder he had never really acquiesced to Amaranth's advances. Amaranth had been at best a surrogate figure, standing in lieu of the woman he really loved. During his whole adventure in Animation he had been searching for—what he had left behind. The girl next door. Yet he had not dared, even in imagination, to hope that this ideal woman could ever be his.

And what made him suppose anything had changed? She had never given any hint of romantic interest in him; she had always been completely proper as befitted her position. It was difficult to believe that her pre-Order history could have been as checkered as his; she had to be of a higher plane. Now, upset at what she thought had been a bad decision on her part, did she propose to return to that lesser prior life?

He wanted to cry out his suddenly discovered love, but could not. What a fool he would be to suppose that this angel would ever consider his suit! To speak it would be to invite a polite, gentle, half-apologetic demurral: her attempt to set him straight without hurting his feelings. Despite her own pressing problem, she would make this effort out of the decency in her heart. To touch her would be to destroy her as he had destroyed Sister Beth—even if he only touched her with a word. He had no right!

Yet—why was she crying? He had never seen her in such open distress, such loss of equilibrium; he had never known there were tears in her. If it had been concern for him while on the dangerous mission she had been denied, she was now absolved. He had survived, he had grown, he had returned! If it was her sadness at resigning the Order, why was she *doing* it? There had to be something else.

"Mary, will you tell me what grieves you?" he asked. "If it is the loss of your Station here, I will gladly renounce the office. I know I can not measure up to the standard you have maintained. I will go away from here—"

Her voice was now normal, controlled, in contrast to her eyes. "Do not do that, Paul. I am glad for your success. I apologize for losing control; it ill becomes the occasion." She paused. Then: "You have seen God."

And she had not? She was not the type to envy him that! Still there was something unclear here, yet vital.

He thought of his new Tarot. Could it help him? No, he had to work this out alone. He had made the wrong decision with Sister Beth, a girl he hardly knew. How much more critical was *this* decision! Should he risk all by professing his love for Mary openly—or by concealing it? He could not bear to see her this way, so inexplicably tearful—yet he could not afford to aggravate the situation by making another error.

There was only one thing to do. Father Paul dropped to his knees to pray to God for the answer.

Opposite him, the Reverend Mother Mary did the same.

God of Tarot, God of Earth, God of my experience—show me the way! he prayed in silence.

God did not speak to him. God never had—not this way. Should he pray instead to Satan? The Devil was always responsive!

No! God and Satan might be one, and there might be no such thing as Evil—but he had to orient on the aspect he believed in. The God of Good, of Right, of Love. *Thy Will be done.*

Mary spoke. "I see you are troubled, Paul. It is not right to conceal my concern from you; God tells me that. I will tell it simply. I—had visions relating to you during your absence. It was at times as though I was a—a siren, a harlot, a temptress, as once I was before I found God. An evil creature, luring you into error in thought and action. Your heart and eye were fixed on God, but I was the agent of Satan, leading you to Hell itself, balking at nothing, using strange Tarot cards—" She hesitated, weeping. "I never suspected such depths of depravity remained in me. I must get out of your life forever. May God forgive me my sin against you!"

Father Paul opened his eyes and stared across the gulf that separated him from Mary. Her eyes remained closed, and her face was now in repose, hauntingly familiar in a new way. She had made her confession—without comprehending its true nature. *She had suffered a psychic linkage with him during his Animations!* She thought Amaranth's mischief and Therion's stemmed from her own imagination and will. She could not know that what was false to her was, paradoxically, true to him. She had seen Satan—and he recognized it as God.

What quirk could have linked their minds across the light years? No known force could explain it, other than God's will —expressed through the force of love.

She loved him!

He studied her face with new understanding. Mary had shared his experience. He would need to keep no secrets from her, hide no shame. She had seen him at his worst—and tried to absorb the evil to herself.

"And did you also stand before the Cross as Jesus was crucified?" he inquired gently. "And in the Tenth Heaven of Paradiso?"

"That too," she agreed, not comprehending. How blessed was her innocence!

In this calm pose she reminded him strangely of—

Like another nova burst, it came to him. *Of Carolyn!* His daughter of Animation! Not to the child actress, now bound with her fiancee for some distant colony planet where religion would not be so bad a problem and Animation would be no problem at all. Rather, to the one he had accompanied on the airplane, revisiting his old college, ten years hence. To the one he had struggled to save from death in the fourteenth century. His *real* daughter—or daughter-to-be.

This was the mother of that child.

Father Paul reached across and took Mary's hand, letting his aura heal her.

The God of Tarot had answered.

Appendix

ANIMATION TAROT

The Animation Tarot deck of concepts as recreated by Brother Paul of the Holy Order of Vision consists of thirty Triumphs roughly equivalent to the twenty-two Trumps of contemporary conventional Tarot decks, together with five variously titled suits roughly equivalent to the four conventional suits plus Aura. Each suit is numbered from one through ten, with the addition of four "Court" cards. The thirty Triumphs are represented by the table of contents of this novel, and keys to their complex meanings and derivations are to be found within the applicable chapters. For convenience the Triumphs are represented below, followed by a tabular representation of the suits, with their meanings or sets of meanings (for upright and reversed fall of the cards); the symbols are described by the italicized words. Since the suits are more than mere collections of concepts, five essays relating to their fundamental nature follow the chart.

No Animation Tarot deck exists in published form at present. Brother Paul used a pack of three-by-five-inch file cards to represent the one hundred concepts, simply writing the meanings on each card and sketching the symbols himself, together with any other notes he found pertinent. These were not as pretty or convenient as published cards, but were satisfactory for divination, study, entertainment, business and meditation as required.

A full discussion of each card and the special conventions relating to the Animation deck would be too complicated to cover here, but those who wish to make up their own decks and use them should discover revelations of their own. According to Brother Paul's vision of the future, this deck will eventually be published, perhaps in both archaic (Waldens) and future (Cluster) forms, utilizing in the first case medieval images and in the second case images drawn from the myriad cultures of the Galactic Cluster, circa 4500 A.D. It hardly seems worthwhile for interested persons to wait for that.

TRIUMPHS

0 Folly (Fool)
1 Skill (Magician)
2 Memory (High Priestess)
∞ Unknown (Ghost)
3 Action (Empress)
4 Power (Emperor)
5 Intuition (Hierophant)
6 Choice (Lovers)
7 Precession (Chariot)
8 Emotion (Desire)
9 Discipline (Strength)
10 Nature (Family)
11 Chance (Wheel of Fortune)
12 Time (Sphinx)
13 Reflection (Past)
14 Will (Future)
15 Honor (Justice)
16 Sacrifice (Hanged Man)
17 Change (Death)
18 Vision (Imagination)
19 Transfer (Temperance)
20 Violence (Devil)
21 Revelation (Lightning-Struck Tower)
22 Hope/Fear (Star)
23 Deception (Moon)
24 Triumph (Sun)
25 Reason (Thought)
26 Decision (Judgment)
27 Wisdom (Savant)
28 Completion (Universe)

SUIT CARDS

	NATURE	SCIENCE	FAITH	TRADE	ART
1	Do *Scepter*	Think *Sword*	Feel *Cup*	Have *Coin*	Be *Lemniscate*
2	Ambition Drive *Torch*	Health Sickness *Scalpel*	Quest Dream *Grail*	Inclusion Exclusion *Ring*	Soul Self *Aura*
3	Grow Shrink *Tree*	Intelligence Curiosity *Maze*	Bounty Windfall *Cornucopia*	Gain Loss *Wheel*	Perspective Experience *Holograph*
4	Leverage Travel *Lever*	Decision Commitment *Pen*	Joy Sorrow *Pandora's Box*	Investment Inheritance *Gears*	Information Literacy *Book*
5	Innovation Suspicion *Hand of Glory*	Equilibrium Stasis *Kite*	Security Confinement *Lock*	Permanence Evanescence *Pentacle*	Balance Bias *Scales*
6	Advance Retreat *Bridge*	Freedom Restraint *Balloon*	Temptation Guilt *Bottle*	Gift Theft *Package*	Change Stagnation *Möbius Strip*
7	Effort Error *Ladder*	Peace War *Plow*	Promise Threat *Ship*	Defense Vulnerability *Shield*	Beauty Ugliness *Face*
8	Potency Impotence *Rocket*	Victory Defeat *Flag*	Satisfaction Disappointment *Mirror*	Success Failure *Crown*	Conscience Ruthlessness *Yin-Yang*
9	Accomplishment Conservation *Trophy*	Truth Error *Key*	Love Hate *Klein Bottle*	Wealth Poverty *Money*	Light Dark *Lamp*
10	Hunger *Phallus*	Survival *Seed*	Reproduction *Womb*	Dignity *Egg*	Image *Compost*

COURT CARDS

	NATURE	SCIENCE	FAITH	TRADE	ART
PAGE	Child of Fire	Child of Air	Child of Water	Child of Earth	Child of Aura
KNIGHT	Youth of Work	Youth of Trouble	Youth of Love	Youth of Money	Youth of Spirit
QUEEN	Lady of Activity	Lady of Conflict	Lady of Emotion	Lady of Status	Lady of Expression
KING	Man of Nature	Man of Science	Man of Faith	Man of Trade	Man of Art
	ENERGY	GAS	LIQUID	SOLID	PLASMA

NATURE

The Goddess of Fertility was popular in spring. Primitive peoples believed in sympathetic magic: that the examples of men affect the processes of nature—that human sexuality makes the plants more fruitful. To make sure nature got the message, they set up the Tree of Life, which was a giant phallus, twice the height of a man, pointing stiffly into the sky. Nubile young women capered about it, singing and wrapping it with bright ribbons. This celebration settled on the first day of May, and so was called May Day, and the phallus was called the Maypole. The modern promotion of May Day by Communist countries has led to its decline in the Western world, but its underlying principle remains strong. The Maypole is the same Tree of Life found in the Garden of Eden, and is represented in the Tarot deck of cards as the symbol for the Suit of Nature: an upright rod formed of living, often sprouting wood. This suit is variously titled Wands, Staffs, Scepters, Batons, or, in conventional cards, Clubs. Life permeates it; it is the male principle, always ready to grow and plant its seed. It also relates to the classic "element" of Fire, and associates with all manner of firearms, rockets, and explosives. In religion, this rod becomes the scepter or crozier, and it can also be considered the measuring rod of faith, the "canon."

FAITH

The true source of the multiple legends of the Grail is unknown. Perhaps this famous chalice was originally a female symbol used in pagan fertility rites, a counterpart to the phallic Maypole. But it is best known in Christian mythology as the goblet formed from a single large emerald, from which Jesus Christ drank at the Last Supper. It was stolen by a servant of Pontius Pilate, who washed his hands from it when the case of the presumptuous King of the Jews came before him. When Christ was crucified, a rich Jew, who had been afraid before to confess his belief, used this cup to catch some of the blood that flowed from Jesus's wounds. This man Joseph deposited Jesus's body in his own tomb, from which Jesus was resurrected a few days later. But Joseph himself was punished; he was imprisoned for years without proper care. He received food, drink and spiritual sustenance from the Grail, which he retained, so that he survived. When he was released, he took the Grail to England, where he settled in 63 A.D. He began the conversion of that region to Christianity. The Grail was handed to his successors from generation to generation until it came at last to Sir Galahad of King Arthur's Round Table. Only the chaste were able even to perceive it. The Grail may also relate to the Cornucopia, or Horn of Plenty, the ancient symbol of the bounty of growing things. It is the cup of love and faith and fruitfulness, the container of the classic "element" of water, and the symbol of the essential female nature (i.e., the womb) represented in the Suit of Cups of the Tarot.

TRADE

It is intriguing to conjecture which of the human instincts is strongest. Many people assume it is sex, the reproductive urge —but an interesting experiment seems to refute that. A group of volunteers including several married couples was systematically starved. As hunger intensified, the pin-up pictures of girls were replaced by pictures of food. The sex impulse decreased, and some couples broke up. Food dominated the conversation. This suggests that hunger is stronger than sex. Similarly, survival—the instinct of self-preservation—seems stronger than hunger, for a starving person will not eat food he knows is poisoned, or drink salt water when dehydrating on a raft in the ocean. This hierarchy of instincts seems reasonable, for any species must secure its survival before it can successfully reproduce its kind. Yet there may be an even more fundamental instinct than these. When the Jews were confined brutally in Nazi concentration death-camps, they co-operated with each other as well as they could, sharing their belongings and scraps of food in a civilized manner. There, the last thing to go was personal dignity. The Nazis did their utmost to destroy the dignity of the captives, for people who retained their pride had not been truly conquered. Thus dignity, or status, or the perception of self-worth, may be the strongest human instinct. It is represented in the Tarot as the Suit of Disks, or Pentacles, or Coins, and associates with the "element" Earth, and with money (the ignorant person's status), and business or trade. Probably the original symbol was the blank disk of the Sun (gold) or Moon (silver).

MAGIC

In the Garden of Eden, Adam and Eve were tempted by the Serpent to eat of the fruit of the Tree of Knowledge of Good and Evil. The fruit is unidentified; popularly it is said to be the apple (i.e., breast), but was more probably the banana (i.e., phallus). Obviously the forbidden knowledge was sexual. There was a second special Tree in the Garden: the Tree of Life, which seems to have been related. Since the human couple's acquisition of sexual knowledge and shame caused them to be expelled from Eden and subject to the mortality of Earthly existence, they had to be provided an alternate means to preserve their kind. This was pro-creation—linked punitively to their sexual transgression. Thus the fruit of "knowledge" led to the fruit of "life," forever tainted by the Original Sin.

Naturally the couple would have escaped this fate if they could, by sneaking back into Eden. To prevent re-entry to the Garden, God set a flaming sword in the way. This was perhaps the origin of the symbol of the Suit of Swords of the Tarot, representing the "element" of air. The Sword associates with violence (war), and with science (scalpel) and intellect (intangible): God's manifest masculinity. Yet this vengeful if versatile weapon was transformed in Christian tradition into the symbol of Salvation: the Crucifix, in turn transformed by the bending of its extremities into the Nazi Swastika. And so as man proceeds from the ancient faith of Magic to the modern speculation of Science, the Sword proceeds inevitably from the Garden of Eden . . . to Hell.

ART

Man is frightened and fascinated by the unknown. He seeks in diverse ways to fathom what he does not comprehend, and when it is beyond his power to do this, he invents some rationale to serve in lieu of the truth. Perhaps the religious urge can be accounted for in this way, and also man's progress into civilization: man's insatiable curiosity driving him to the ultimate reaches of experience. Yet there remain secrets: the origin of the universe, the smallest unit of matter, the nature of God, and a number of odd phenomena. Do psychics really commune with the dead? How does water dowsing work? Is telepathy possible? What about faith healing? Casting out demons? Love at first contact? Divination? Ghosts?

Many of these inexplicable phenomena become explicable through the concept of aura. If the spirit or soul of man is a patterned force permeating the body and extending out from it with diminishing intensity, the proximity of two or more people would cause their surrounding auras to interpenetrate. They could thus become aware of each other on more than a physical basis. They might pick up each other's thoughts or feelings, much as an electronic receiver picks up broadcasts or the coil of a magnetic transformer picks up power. A dowser might feel his aura interacting with water deep in the ground, and so know the water's location. A person with a strong aura might touch one who was ill, and the strong aura could recharge the weak one and help the ill person recover the will to live. A man and a woman might find they had highly compatible auras, and be strongly attracted to each other. An evil aura might impinge on a person, and have to be exorcised. And after the physical death of the body, or host, an aura might float free, a spirit or ghost, able to communicate only with specially receptive individuals, or mediums.

In short, the concept of aura or spirit can make much of the supernatural become natural. It is represented in the Animation Tarot deck as the Suit of Aura, symbolized in medieval times by a lamp and in modern times by a lemniscate (infinity symbol: ∞), and embracing a fifth major human instinct or drive: art, or expression. Only man, of all the living creatures on Earth, cares about the esthetic nature of things. Only man appreciates painting, and sculpture, and music, and dancing, and literature, and mathematical harmonies, and ethical proprieties, and all the other forms and variants of artistic expression. Where man exists, these things exist—and when man passes on, these things remain as evidence of his unique nature. Man's soul, symbolized as art, distinguishes him from the animals.